Miljenko Jergović

KIN

Translated from the Croatian by Russell Scott Valentino

archipelago books

First Archipelago Books Edition, 2021

Library of Congress Cataloging-in-Publication Data
available upon request.

Archipelago Books
232 3rd Street #A111
Brooklyn, NY 11215
www.archipelagobooks.org
www.elsewhereeditions.org

Distributed by Penguin Random House
www.penguinrandomhouse.com

Cover art: Hieronymus Bosch

This publication was made possible with support from the National
Endowment for the Arts, Lannan Foundation, the Carl Lesnor Family
Foundation, the Nimick Forbesway Foundation, the New York State Council on
the Arts, a state agency, and the New York City Department of Cultural Affairs.

PRINTED IN CANADA

Contents

Kin

Where Other People Live:
A Presentation

My father and two uncles went to the same high school in Sarajevo that I did. Despite the nearly fifty years that had passed since my elder uncle was enrolled in the school – back in 1934 – the interior had remained the same. The person who noticed this was my grandmother, who came to the parent-teacher conferences for both him and me. My father and younger uncle were taught by the same art history professor, whom I would eventually have as well. When the old professor died at the beginning of my second year, all three of us attended his funeral.

From its founding in the 1880s it had been an elite school for the bourgeoisie. The Bosnian author and Nobel laureate Ivo Andrić graduated from it, after considerable torment, about which he would later speak with horror and disgust. This is probably why his name was never mentioned at school functions, when the director would enumerate all the distinguished personages and celebrities who had attended the school. In my own days communist revolutionaries were considered the most noteworthy graduates, in addition to the assassins of Franz Ferdinand, the heir to the Austro-Hungarian throne. Gavrilo Princip himself, who fired the shots that struck Ferdinand and his pregnant wife, did not graduate from the school, because he had moved to Belgrade by then, but several of his close associates did.

Our professors often told us that we must model ourselves after these figures – we lived in a socialist society, after all, which held especially fast to its bright and shining examples. Among them our parents and uncles were often held up to us as paragons of sacrifice and heroism.

Around the subject of my elder uncle there was silence. He never received any grade lower than the very highest. He had pen pals in other countries with whom he corresponded in Latin, he solved unsolvable math problems, he played the guitar, and he wrote an essay on Paul Valéry. In photographs, tall and fragile, with his blond hair and blue eyes, he looks like a young aristocrat in a Thomas Mann novel, someone who will die by the end of the book, from meningitis or gaping caverns in his lungs, but his will not be an ordinary, quotidian death for in it will be gathered the destiny of a family or even that of an entire generation. I should say that while this is how my elder uncle looked, nothing else about him was like in Mann, except that I'd have been happy to reproduce on his gravestone the words with which the doctor of philosophy Serenus Zeitblom takes leave of his own friend, the composer Adrian Leverkühn: "May God have pity on your poor soul, my friend, my homeland."

But I'm not at all certain what my uncle's homeland would have been. What's clearer, at any rate, is that I don't have one, which means in the end that I wouldn't really know what such an epitaph on his hypothetical grave would even mean.

He was born in Usora, a small town in central Bosnia, where his father, my grandfather, was employed as a railroad stationmaster. He grew up along the tracks built by the Austro-Hungarians, changing homes and friends often. From his father he learned Slovenian, while his mother tongue was Croatian, but his first language was German. This he learned from his grandfather, my great-grandfather, a high-ranking railroad official, a Swabian German from the Banat, who was born in a town that's now in Romania and went to schools in Vršac, Budapest, and Vienna. He too spent all his working life along the tracks of Bosnia.

You must understand, then, that my elder uncle – let's call him Mladen because things will get too confused if we keep this up without names – lived in complex surroundings and a complicated linguistic web. It is possible for language to determine a person's destiny. Mladen's grandfather Karlo was a nationally minded German, and he spoke only German to all four of his children until he died. Not once did he ever speak to them even a single Croatian word. With his daughters' husbands – two Croats and a Slovene – he spoke Croatian, despite the fact that all three of them spoke perfect German. With his grandchildren he spoke both languages, but only after he had been addressed in German. If anyone greeted him in Croatian, Opapa pretended not to hear.

They say the weekly meals at which the whole family would gather were quite something. There was a strict language protocol of the sort that today probably only exists at the headquarters of the European Union, though no one seems to have wondered why it had to be that way. Karlo's Germanness was especially important to him; everyone else around him would have to adapt. In return, no one, least of all he, prevented them from being something other than who they were or from speaking whatever languages they pleased. My great grandfather loved his sons-in-law, and it didn't bother him that they weren't German; rather, he was proud, I should note, of their civic calling. Belonging to the railroad workers' trade was for him something like being in a secret society, a Masonic lodge of sorts, whose members differed from other people by their understanding of the world and their own role within it. A German rail man and a Croatian rail man enjoy a brotherhood that allowed them greater mutual understanding than any members of a single nation among themselves. Opapa was a leftist, and in the early 1920s he ended up in prison and later lost his job for backing a rail men's strike. It wouldn't have been a scandal if he had not been a stationmaster and a German among the barbarous Slavs. He was harshly punished by the royal government for the betrayal of his caste and his nation.

But at home we were raised with the belief that all people have the same rights, regardless of their faith or economic status. The poor little country of Bosnia, where nearly 90 percent of the people in the 1920s and '30s were illiterate, where epidemics of typhus and cholera would take over with alarming frequency, and where an endemic syphilis ravaged generation upon generation without respite, like some kind of evil tradition, this Bosnia was – for Opapa Karlo and his ideas – the ideal place to be living. He never had any notion of returning to the Banat or of moving to Vienna or Germany. Those were foreign countries to him. When asked about it, he would quietly answer that he wouldn't ever be able to live in those places because that was "where other people lived." As far as I'm concerned, there's never been a more precise definition for the opposite of one's homeland.

Uncle Mladen was more like his grandfather than the other grandchildren were, even though one wouldn't have said he resembled him physically. The elderly Karlo had dark hair and a long gray beard; judging by his photographs, he looked more like a Romanian rabbi, or at least a learned Jewish man, than a German. But Mladen, with his Nordic blue eyes and his bearing, took after the Slovene peasants of his father's side. When I look at the two of them in the faded black-and-white photos, I wonder what their lives might have been like if German had not come so easily to Mladen, if he hadn't so willingly listened to his grandfather play the violin, if he had been seated farther from the old man during the Sunday meals. I wonder what might have been if the old man had hated the Slav in his grandson even a little bit.

In the courtyard of the building where my people had lived since the 1930s stood the Temple. There prayed those people who had – like Opapa Karlo and my other great-grandfather, the Slovene – by the will of Franz Joseph, brought their business affairs to Sarajevo, where they would long remain. Earlier, during the time of Turkish rule, there were no Ashkenazim in our town, only Sephardim, Spanish Jews. They were impoverished for the most part, distrustful of the new occupying power, and unwilling to allow the new arrivals to enter their shrine. In a certain sense, they did not even quite believe that these others were Jews, and so they called them, like their imperial and royal patrons, Swabians.

Right at the beginning of the war, the moment the Germans had entered town, a few days before the Ustaše would take power, a mob broke into the Temple and destroyed everything. These people wore no uniform and were what you might call regular, everyday folks. Among those who ransacked the Temple were the town's layabouts and thugs, petty thieves and gentlemen, but there were also Roma, who, together with Jews from Sarajevo, would in a few days' time find themselves in transports bound for concentration camps.

My Slovene grandfather, whose name was Franjo, watched his people destroy the Temple from his window. Nona Olga kept pulling him inside lest someone see him, but he stayed at the window despite the fear. It was a measure of his courage. He watched the people among whom he lived in the very moment of their transformation. First they would become outlaws, then murderers, and in the end martyrs, casualties of war.

At the time the Temple was destroyed, Franjo and Olga's son Mladen was starting the seventh grade. They taught him that what was happening was not right. They told him that Pavelić was a savage, that Hitler was insane and he would surely lose the war in the end. The two of them explained to him, as did Opapa Karlo, everything that from our perspective today seems necessary. Of course they also told him not to say anything anywhere, if he valued his life, about what he thought of Hitler or Pavelić. And he should steer clear of those who revolted against the new Ustaše government. My grandfather and grandmother, just as their parents and our entire family in the broadest sense of the word, were in principle opposed to any resistance to the authorities. Nothing could be done. It was not up to us to change the government. You would get yourself thrown in prison, nothing more.

When he graduated a year later, Mladen was preparing to study in Zagreb or Vienna. He wanted to study forestry: Opapa used to tell him that it was crazy to live in Bosnia and not live with the forests.

But then, in the summer of 1942, the conscription letter came, written in two languages (respecting the conventions of a "united Europe"). The unit in which Mladen was being called to serve was part of Hitler's army, not the Croatian armed forces, and the call included the best and brightest of Sarajevo's young men of German or Austrian descent.

There were two possibilities at that moment: either Mladen would report for military duty and go off to war, or he could escape to the Partisans. His parents, my grandfather Franjo and grandmother Olga, didn't doubt for an instant that Hitler would lose the war and Pavelić would end up on the gallows. Not for a single day, not for a single hour in his life did Franjo believe that those who had destroyed the Temple, those who had led away our Jewish neighbors, could be victorious. Although he was not a believer, it was out of the question that evil could win out in the end.

But instead of sending their son to the Partisans, they sent him to the Germans. They thought he would have a better chance of survival. There would be several months of basic training, but by then Hitler would have already lost the war. It was a mistaken calculation, and fourteen months later my eldest uncle was killed in battle against the Partisans. It was the first battle for his unit, and he was the first and last person to be killed. Several days later the entire unit together with its commander joined the Partisans. After the war, in the summer of 1945, four of Mladen's war buddies sought out his parents. They were now members of a liberating army, and Franjo and Olga were the parents of an enemy combatant. After the death of her son, my grandmother never again went to mass, never again crossed herself, and she stopped celebrating Christmas and Easter. When at five years old I asked if God existed, she answered, "For some he does, for others he doesn't."

"Does he for you?"

"No."

"Does he for me?"

"You'll have find that out for yourself."

While his grandson was fighting as a German soldier, Karlo lived in his house in the southern Sarajevo suburb of Ilidža, which at night was often raided by soldiers of various kinds, mostly drunk. When the Ustaše would set off on their nightly rounds to kill and loot in the Serbian homes, he would take in his neighbors – it wasn't unusual for there to be as many as fifty taken in at time. And when the Ustaše arrived at his gate to conduct a search, he'd wait for them on the shadowy threshold and call out to them in Croatian:

"This is a German house. You can't come in!"

And no matter how drunk they were, they would turn back and go away without a word. He stared at them with hatred and a look that altered his features so completely that he seemed a different person. A terrifying person. Someone once said that I inherited that look of his.

Sarajevo was liberated in April 1945. A month or two later they came for Opapa to take him to a camp, from which he, like all his compatriots, would later be deported to Germany. He walked the kilometer and a half to the train station in Ilidža, flanked by two Partisans while a third nudged him forward constantly with a rifle barrel. That man had known him from before the war, and he understood very well who and what Opapa Karlo was, but it made him feel good to mess with him a little. That's the way it goes. You never know who will get led off to a concentration camp, or why – only that people rarely think it could be them.

But when they got to the station, in front of the stock cars that the Partisans used to transport their victims to the camps, Opapa's Serbian neighbors had gathered. They said that for four years he had saved them from the Ustaše and even if he was a German a hundred times over they would not give up comrade Karlo, they would go where he was going. The Partisans tried to disperse them, they flared their rifle butts, some got their heads bashed in, but the more they were struck the more resilient the people grew.

They returned Karlo to his home that day, and no one ever came for him again. Who knows whether he would have made it there alive, so it's entirely possible his life was saved by the same people whose lives he had saved. One good deed repaid with another, as in a children's fable. Opapa died several years later, before I was born.

My father and my younger uncle, Dragan, were mobilized by the Partisans after the liberation of Sarajevo and fought in one of the bloodiest theaters at the end of the war, near Karlovac. They went into the war as high school students, and they graduated as demobilized Partisans. After that my uncle studied metallurgy and my father medicine. Both were successful in their specializations and became respected members of society. And both carried in their hearts and heads family stigmas, which went into their police files. My uncle's stigma was his kid brother, who had died as a German soldier; my father's was his mother, who along with her two sisters, was active with the Ustaše Youth in Sarajevo – after the war she was sentenced to prison, while her sisters emigrated to Argentina.

The two men both became members of the Communist League and remained loyal to the membership right up until the fall of Yugoslavia. So did my mother, who at the time of her brother's death was just a year old. She too would be reminded, on occasion, that Mladen had been on the wrong side during the war. She felt a little guilty about it. So did Dragan. Just as her future husband, my father, felt guilty about his mother and aunts. This guilt marked their lives and remained an important part of their identities.

When, in the summer of 1993, I was leaving Sarajevo, which was under siege by the tanks and artillery of the war criminals Mladić and Karadžić (I was on an American military transport on loan to the UN that had flown in humanitarian aid and journalists from Split). I thought that this could be goodbye forever. I was saving my own skin, that was all. My mother and father were both staying in the city. It occurred to me I might never see them again. All the same, after seventeen months of war and siege, I was saving myself. I was doing what my elder uncle had been unable to do. I was escaping from my war.

I knew I was going to Zagreb, to Croatia. But even though it is the land of my language, even though I am a Croat, I was leaving as Opapa Karlo would have left for Germany – I didn't know that then. In saving my neck I didn't consider that "other people" lived in Croatia, and I would be a foreigner, as Opapa had been. His Germanness was defined by his daily encounters, by the bizarre ceremonies of the weekly family meals, by his arrogant attitude toward the Croatian fascists when they wanted to search his house. My Croatianness was Bosnian, and more than that it was *kuferaš* Bosnian. This was what they had called the people who moved to Bosnia from various parts of the empire under Franz Joseph. With their cultures and languages in tow, they had created their own extra-national identity whose cultural bedrock was stronger than their ethnic affiliation. In my case, or rather, in the case of my family, this meant we were Bosnian Croats whose identities were marked by the Slovene, German, Italian, and rare other nations of the former monarchy. If there had been no Austro-Hungarian empire,

I would never have been born, the parents of my grandparents would have never met . . . In this sense my birth was, from before the beginning, a political project.

Finding myself in Croatia, in the land of "other people," I understood that I could live my entire life there, that I could be happy, but I would never be one of them. When I pronounced the word *we*, it would usually be a false *we*, the sort of *we* a person might feel a little ashamed of. And so I would more often use the pronouns *I* and *they*. I would mostly say things about myself that people didn't want to hear, or that they themselves would never say, lest they stand out. The moment you begin to separate yourself from the crowd, difference gives rise to antipathy.

When I arrived in Croatia, it was a very ethnically homogeneous country, where 90 percent of the people were ethnic Croats and Catholic, the majority of whom were uncommonly hostile to those who belonged to any sort of minority. This hostility was at the basis of the state's ideology, but it was also defined by the fact that the country was experiencing a prolonged war and a third of its territory was occupied. The former Yugoslav National Army played the role of occupier, while that of the domestic traitors was played by the country's Serb minority. At the same time, the small number of Croatian Muslims had also ended up as enemies, and it was then, in the summer of 1993, that Croatian forces launched their attack on Muslim territories in Bosnia and Herzegovina. Beyond national affiliations, atheists were also considered enemies of society, because they reminded the citizens of the preceding forty years of communist rule and probably of their own hypocrisy when it came to faith in God. When it was considered the social norm, the vast majority of people didn't believe, but now that times had changed the same majority was all of a sudden flocking to church.

In fact, it seemed people took pleasure in all these animosities and antagonisms. This too was nothing new: there is no sensation as overwhelming and fulfilling as hatred, and nothing other than hatred can go so quickly from being a private to a public emotion, one shared across a society. In the 1990s, during the presidency of Franjo Tuđman, Croatia truly became a land of hatred. This hatred was for the most part directed inward, toward aspects of the country's own society and, in turn, its own culture, history, identities, languages . . . In

Croatia even words were hated if they did not sound Croatian enough. But sound could sometimes be deceptive, and objects of hatred could fall into short supply, so people also took pleasure in directing hate toward things that had nothing to do with minorities.

A person can find countless excuses at such moments to be a part of the crowd. Especially if he's just come from a besieged city, on his own, without material assistance, as a boarder, an intellectual proletarian. Sarajevo was after all under siege by the very people who were then most vehemently hated in Croatia. So what was there to prevent a person from taking part in this hatred, from becoming socialized and moving from refugee to accepted member of the community? If we forget that hatred presupposes considerable intellectual and spiritual effort, then it becomes very hard to find a reason why someone arriving from Sarajevo in 1993 would oppose the prevailing mood of the city he had just stepped into.

My great-grandfather, as a Swabian German from the Banat residing in Sarajevo, spoke a variety of Croatian filled with words derived from Turkish, which was characteristic of the speech of Bosnian Muslims. He concealed his Serbian neighbors from the Ustaše not primarily because he was a good and unselfish man, but because they were an important part of his own world. He probably didn't even understand what it would have meant to be a German in a place where there weren't any Serbs, or Croats, Bosnians, Muslims, Jews . . . From his perspective, and mine, in multi-ethnic countries every form of hatred is just another form of hatred. This was why my Croatianness was so substantially different from that of the people I found myself surrounded by upon my arrival in Zagreb, and even from that of my friends and acquaintances. For while those people rejected hatred for intellectual and moral reasons, or simply as a fact of good breeding, I rejected it because it was a threat to who I was. Though I was a Croat, it threatened the Serb and the Bosniak inside me.

My younger uncle, Dragan, the one who'd later become a famous metallurgist and Bosnia's heavy industry representative in the USSR, was born in Kakanj, another of the towns where my grandfather Franjo had served as a stationmaster. Kakanj was inhabited by a majority Muslim population, and when Dragan started school he was the only Christian in his class. Religious instruction was mandatory in all schools of the Kingdom of Yugoslavia in the 1930s, and so my uncle too, from his first steps and in unusual circumstances, was required to study faith in God. During the early class period all the other children would receive instruction in Islam at a nearby mosque, but Dragan stayed in the classroom by himself because there was no one there to instruct him on the tenets of Catholicism, and the local parish priest, who should have stepped in to replace the absent instructor, did not know that a solitary christened lamb was waiting for him alone in the school. So there within the four white walls, beneath the blackboards and the photographs of King Alexander Karađorđević, my uncle felt that confusing, pernicious loneliness from which grown-ups flee, moving from towns and lands where they are a minority to towns and lands where they will be the majority.

But instead of moving his entire family, or consenting to have the parish priest teach his son about faith in God while all the boy's classmates were instructed by the local mullah, my grandfather Franjo told the teacher that he didn't want his child separated from the other children, and that the boy should go together with his friends for instruction in Islam. It was an unusual parental request but it wasn't against the law, nor did anyone protest. Thus did Dragan complete all four years of the *maktab*, the Muslim primary school, and though he was christened in the Catholic faith, he came to know the rules of Muslim prayer.

The important distinction is not in the difference between a multiethnic society and an ethnically homogeneous society but in the very orientation to multiplicity itself. We can take pleasure in hatred and build our identities upon it, or we can live in a different way. When we do not hate, we see ourselves reflected in others. Opapa Karlo knew this when he chose not to go to Germany. How would he even begin to communicate or come to an understanding with them? How would a German like him – except through resistance and conflict – be able to live in Germany?

I have written, in my novels and stories, about my great-grandfather, the Swabian German from the Banat, and his family, about the uncle who suffered as an enemy combatant, about the grandparents who sent their son into the enemy's army, and about the other major and minor characters whose destinies shaped my own. Mixing reality with fiction, I've resurrected these people and extended their lives. I cannot detach myself from their stories, nor can I allow my uncle, whose grave long ago disappeared among the uncut grass of a village cemetery somewhere in Slavonia, to lie alongside millions of Hitler's soldiers. He's part of my identity, of a remorse that passes from generation to generation, that which we carry. This is who I am, the Croat I am, the person.

I had assumed that after Franjo Tuđman's death and the dismantling of the nationalist oligarchy in Croatia, the differences between us would fade and my ill repute among the ethnic elite would sink into the past and become diluted along with all the other forms of hatred that had died away once the war had ended. Ultimately, this turned out to be the moment when Croatia began allowing the dissidents of the 1990s back to its maternal bosom, decorating them with ribbons of ethnic belonging and confirmations of exemplary patriotic conduct. The ethos of nationalism thus turned into an ethos of collective Europeanization, which, while perhaps equally irritating, is at least easier to live with. Now beside the flag of Croatia flies that of the European Union. This may indicate something of a colonial allegiance, a fragmented and schizophrenic identity, or perhaps simply the fact that in front of each public institution there are three poles, and it would be silly to fly just one flag.

It's not flags, however, that determine our lives. What yesterday was a banner of hatred can today fly as a flag of freedom, and vice versa. Simply look at how Bush's rule so thoroughly changed the significance of the American flag. My elder uncle once wrote on a postcard to his aunt in Sarajevo, "It's Sunday. This is a free day. The encampment is deserted. The German flag is flying. We have sold ours." While it's not completely coherent, this was perhaps his only political pronouncement. The surviving members of his family could console themselves with such words, however little they amounted to at heart. We're people who don't even know which flag to call our own. Those who do know also know that hatred tastes sweetest beneath a banner. Why else would flags be so prominently displayed during soccer championships and the Olympics? Our flags are there more to humiliate the losers than to celebrate the victors. Everyone knows this is the way it works. The best-known fan song in Croatia goes, "Let them suffer those it bothers, Croatia's champion of the world!" Why would someone else suffer because Croatia is champion? The sort of person who would ask himself such a question is probably not a Croat through and through.

A year after the fall of the nationalist government during the formation of the coalition led by the Social Democrats under Ivica Račan, I was at a film festival in Istria. It was held in an ancient walled city at the top of a hill that was once inhabited exclusively by Italians, who, after Istria became part of Yugoslavia, were given the opportunity to vote by the communists either to leave as Italians or to stay behind as Yugoslavs – and these people chose to set off on their way, bags in hand, to spend years in Italian refugee camps, leaving their Istrian homes behind forever. Of course the new minister of culture showed up, whose supporters and adjutants had taken to calling the "Croatian Malraux," an appellation he was prepared to accept, since in the Balkans it is common practice to name leaders and dignitaries after magnificent foreigners, Franz Beckenbauer, Emperor Selassie, Shakespeare – in short, who cares. Anyway, this minister of ours, this Croatian Malraux, was previously a lexicographer, which meant he mostly took it easy or had intellectual debates at the pub after inspecting the two or three lexical items that had turned up on his desk that day. I was not fond of the way he ran the ministry and wrote an article about it in the newspaper, though I was far gentler than I'd been in similar critiques against Tuđman's nationalists.

I wasn't thinking of my article that afternoon as I approached a café table around which, in the shade of an immense Slavic tree sat a group of directors, producers, and intellectuals, with Minister Malraux at the head. I knew these people, the minister too, and I merely wanted to convey an everyday hello in passing.

"Beat it, you Bosnian piece of shit! Go back where you came from so we don't have to send you ourselves!" shouted Malraux. I didn't get too upset, since I knew that the previous night had been filled with such hard work that the ministerial hangover could well have extended into the afternoon. But still I stopped long enough to look carefully at a director who'd been blacklisted during the Tuđman years and whose films had been banned from television. He was a tough dissident, as tough as Kundera if not tougher. He looked down and did not say anything. He needed to be watchful of this ministerial hangover because he wanted to make movies again, and that does not happen without government money. A promising young producer, an apologist for interethnic affection and fighter against nationalism in every form, also looked down, and everyone else one after another looked down, dissidents one and all from the time of Tuđman, until, eventually, I turned and made my way down that Istrian knoll, the Croatian Malraux shouting behind me.

I left and am still going, a happy man, because unlike Opapa Karlo I'm not being led away by two men with a third prodding me in the kidneys with a rifle. This is an important nuance of our identities – why we live where we don't belong to a majority. Happiness keeps us in this place, and happiness – I really believe this – has often cost us our lives. Reconciled to being who we are, while carrying inside us the idea of who we are not, we represent identities that cannot be defined by a single word, passport, identity card, entry pass. The masses know who they are from a coat of arms, a flag, a name, and then they chant it out, but we are left with winding, uncertain explanations, novels and films, true stories and invented ones; left with the need to visit a village in the Romanian Banat where – although now without Germans – the horizon is the same as when Opapa Karlo was a boy; left with empty villages in Bulgaria, Ukraine, Poland – where people went away in a puff of smoke – and with vague memories, the feeling that today we are one thing, tomorrow another, that our hymns and state borders constantly elude us. We feel remorse because perhaps a relative of ours lived and died as an enemy, because we ourselves are something of an enemy, and we are left with the faith in what we bury beneath our tongue, the truth that our homeland is no more, maybe never was, because for us every step and stretch of the world is foreign country.

The Stublers

A Family Novel

Have You Seen Regina Dragnev?

There in Bosowicz, in the Romanian Banat, on his departure for Bosnia, my great-grandfather Karlo Stubler left behind an elder brother. His name has been lost to family memory, but his daughter's survives. Karlo too would give the name Regina to one of his daughters. This is what his great-granddaughter would also be called. In the end, my mother too would come to carry the name when, on her birth in May 1942, they refused to inscribe her as Javorka in either the civic birth registry or the church registry. Thus she became Regina Javorka, and she would continue to be called by these two first names until, twenty years later, in the very same registry office, she was forced to choose between them, due to the fact that in our socialist society nothing could have two meanings or two names, and so neither could she. She decided on the second of her names superstitiously to avoid exchanging fates with any of the numerous other Reginas in the family.

The fate of the first Regina was by then well known. She was the mother of Opapa Karlo. And while we don't know precisely what made her great or important, our ignorance, along with familial and historical oblivion, have probably in some way served to make her greater.

My great-grandfather's niece was older than all her Bosnian cousins. In a certain sense she served them as a distant paragon because they never met her, though her name would come to leave its trace. Though from a peasant's home, albeit a Swabian and well-off one, Regina regularly attended high school in Timisoara, and then during the Balkan wars – while the burgeoning Yugoslavism was spilling its Serbian blood and dying of beauty in its Croatian schemes and tubercular fevers – she went to Sofia to study medicine. It was not terribly common then at the beginning of the twentieth century, not even among the Swabians of the Banat, or in Romania, which at the time was called the France of the Balkans, for a village girl to travel to a distant town to study medicine.

But perhaps Sofia was not all that far from Bosowicz back then. In Bulgaria there were lots of Germans, and maybe the Stublers had relatives or friends in the capital who would have been able to look after Regina.

She became a doctor by the end of the First World War.

She found work and married a Bulgarian about whom we know almost nothing, except his family name: Dragnev.

My great-grandfather, together with his family, was expelled in 1920 from Dubrovnik, where he had taken part in a strike as a high-ranking railroad official. He lost his job and ended up in his "place of domicile," Sarajevo, along with his wife and three of his four children. In the years after, his livelihood was mostly taken care of by the labor union. Two or three union members, who worked for the railroad as stokers or engineers, used their paychecks to help Karlo and his family, and this was how Karlo's children were able to finish their schooling. Karlo's daughter Regina fell in love and later married Vilko Novak, a son of one of the railroad union leaders.

Before the First World War, as a young and spirited railway man, Karlo Stubler would visit his brother in Bosowicz. But during the long years after the Second World War, he would never again return to his native land. All communication with his brother and remaining family took place through letters, and these would on some occasions be quite lively, dynamic, and, in a certain sense, fruitful. Just as Jewish immigrants sent pictures from America, along with trinkets of memorabilia and even packages to their families in the tiny, now nameless shtetlach of Galicia, so did Karlo and his compatriots operate with their relatives in the Banat. The correspondence flowed back and forth for decades between

Ilidža and Bosowicz, and while it was not clear which was America and which Galicia, or who would set out for where, their letters prepared for a meeting that would never arrive. Composed in German, these letters were exchanged at regular two-month intervals, with special postcards at Christmas and Easter, and the correspondence was maintained through the twenties, thirties, and the start of the forties, before the horrors of war dissipated the epistles.

Somewhere among the remains of the family archives, on Kasindol Street in Ilidža, in the home of the Novaks and Cezners, where most of what once belonged to the Stublers remains, there used to be, or still are photographs of Regina Dragnev. The doctor living in Sofia looks out at us from them: tall and beautiful, smiling as one does when posing for a photo for the sake of one's relatives.

What held our family together, what we were and what made up our very identity, was based – like any joining of culture and kin beneath a family roof – on an illusion. Part of this illusion was that one day we would see our cousin who lived in Sofia. We never even shook hands, let alone embraced.

No one except for Karlo Stubler ever touched Regina Dragnev. He had played with her as a little girl when he was a young rail worker. He would fold his right leg over his left, she would sit on his shin, and he would rock her. His leg was a horse that Regina would ride out into the distance.

After the war, near the close of 1945, when the mournful cry of the people for themselves and their illusions took hold, Rudolf Stubler initiated a search through the Red Cross for his relative, our cousin, Regina Dragnev, née Stubler, a doctor who'd lived in Sofia.

He would look for her for the next twenty years, through various organizations, for as long as there were people to search for someone, until the broadcasts on the radio changed, in some strange transformation of genre, from searches for the missing to transmissions of birthday wishes on listener request lines, or greetings from home to sailors at sea, but she would not be found, nor would anything at all about her fate be known. Regina Dragnev had slipped into the earth, transformed into smoke, or perhaps nothing happened at all.

At least three authors have written about such searches: Amos Oz, David

Grossman, and Ivan Lovrenović. Oz and Grossman have written about the quest for relatives whose fates were darkened in the Holocaust, Lovrenović about the fathers and uncles who, as soldiers of the defeated or enemy armies, flitted into nothingness during the victory celebration and great reprisal. But they have something in common, all the missing in Oz and Grossman and Lovrenović: it was possible for the searchers to say who and what the missing ones were, victims or aggressors.

Her cousin Rudi, my beloved Nano, would search for Regina Dragnev with two kinds of dread. The first he shared with millions of Europeans: was she alive and if so, where? And if not, did anyone know where she lay buried? The second kind of dread would be his and ours alone, a family form of it: who exactly was our relation Regina Dragnev from the standpoint of the war's victors, of justice, of antifascism? I mean, however many times in those two decades they wrote, neither Rudi nor the Regina in Ilidža ever knew anything of her political affinities. She had a husband and two children, she worked in a hospital, she cared about her patients – about whom she would sometimes write to her far-off relatives – she went to the theater from time to time, read the same books as they did, mentioned things she remembered about Bosowicz, asked about living and dead relatives, but never did she write a word, nor was a word written to her, about Hitler and the German eastward expansion, about communism or fascism, or about any of the other things that are so important now, but which one wouldn't think to elaborate on in letters to a distant relative.

Who was Regina Dragnev in 1941 and 1945, this cousin of ours, the German girl from the Banat who had married a Bulgarian? Had she collaborated with the enemy? This question made my Nano uncomfortable, but still he didn't give up. He was not a courageous person and was afraid one day they might burst in through the gate and start asking him why he was looking for this woman and was he perhaps planning some kind of counterrevolutionary action with her, but what else could he do when this search had become such an important part of his identity, of the identity of our family? For him the important thing was tracking down his relative – while for us today it is knowing who she was. This eternal ignorance would follow us for as long as we lived, its reverberations, like those of the Second World War, refused to cease.

My great-grandfather did not make inquiries about his brother. Karlo was taken from Bosowicz in 1945 and never brought back. His good Serb neighbors saved him in Ilidža, just as he had saved them from the Ustaše – he had sealed them up in his house and stood at the threshold; the cowardly Ustaše didn't dare strike a German, even one as feeble as he was.

There were no inquiries after the relatives in Bosowicz. No one was left: they had flitted off in 1945, turned to dust, an empty concept, something that would not be spoken of during Karlo's lifetime. In contrast to the fates of the Jews, those of the Germans cannot be spoken about. This is simply the case, and so it had to be for my great-grandfather. In his home they spoke German, but he was silent about the Germans. And out of the silence grew a memorial, a small Tower of Babel.

His son Rudolf Stubler often traveled in Europe, but he never went to Bosowicz. Wherever he went, in whatever city he found himself, he would go to a phone booth and look through the fat directory chained inside. They said Nano did this for fun. Stubler is not a common last name, which was why he had been looking for Stublers for so long. That's what they said.

To me it seemed that in the directories of Vienna, Paris, Berlin, Rome, Leningrad and Moscow, Budapest, Prague, Amsterdam, and Madrid, he had only ever looked for Regina Dragnev. But such a thing was no longer possible to say, for there was no one who could hear it and grasp the sense of such a long search.

This is What We Looked Like
on the First Day of the War

When Karlo Stubler was driven out of Dubrovnik in 1920, his eldest daughter did not want to accompany the family into exile. She had already graduated from the trade institute in Dubrovnik and wasn't the one who had been forced to go off to Bosnia, so she stayed, determined to be independent and live her life away from the railroads and their unions. While it wasn't common for daughters to disobey their fathers' will, Karlo had no choice but to walk away from Karla. Even as a child she refused to go by a name she considered masculine and paternal and started introducing herself as Lukretia, and this was the name she kept for her whole life.

When her people left for Sarajevo, she found herself alone in the city without family or friends, a *kuferaš*'s daughter, maladjusted, with a mind of her own, in eternal war with her surroundings. She made her way and was able to enchant a well-off financial officer – eighteen years her elder – from the island of Pelješac named Andrija Ćurlin. Our uncle Andrija was one of those men who measured fate for too long, considering all the marriageable girls, constantly changing their minds, until the time was suddenly up. Then, for fear of being left an old bachelor, they would make a hasty choice, as a rule mistaken, and marry someone who, like our great-aunt Lola, had been left behind after some sort of banishment, political upheaval, or natural catastrophe.

It would be crude to say that Lola married out of calculation. She married because she needed a strong footing, someone she could rely on, certain as she was at that moment that it would be easier for her if he made all the decisions, so that one day, reversing course, she would be the one making all the decisions, and she would be the one to drive him, Uncle Andrija, away, just as she had driven away old Karlo Stubler. The poor man could not have known anything about this, because among the well-bred daughters in his hometown of Kuna Pelješka, just as in Grad, there were no women like Karla, Lukretia, Lukre.

She didn't love him. Was it because one does not learn to love by force of habit, because she dreamed of a different sort of man, or because Aunt Lola could never really love anyone else, for what was great and strong and pure in her was her love for herself? I suppose this last idea was closest to the truth.

She gave birth to Željko and, five or six years later, to Branka.

This didn't change her either. A person either is or is not a mother. This is possible to know in advance, before any children are born. People often make the mistake of thinking that giving birth changes a willful woman's character and that because of it a clenched-up or closed-off heart will be touched by some great transformation. Aunt Lola did not change, she was no mother, and almost nothing inside her was altered.

Whenever she got fed up with her life, or rather whenever she got fed up with her Andrija, she would leave him with the children, and without saying much, be on her way. Ten or fifteen days later she'd come back, announcing angrily as she came in, "So here I am then!"

And that was that. Not a word more, and he would never ask. No one ever knew where Aunt Lola went during her seasonal tours. Dubrovnik was a small town back then, it would speak behind anyone's back in time, so there could not have been any secrets, except maybe little lies and small, unfair slanders, but still nothing leaked out, no one uttered a word about where Lukre Ćurlin went off to. Not among the family either, among her sisters, nieces, and nephews, did anyone ever learn anything, and no one, to her dying day, ever dared to ask. The only thing they knew, and everyone would recount it, some as a joke and others in fear that someone like her might one day appear in their own lives, was that phrase of hers: So here I am then!

Branka was still little at the time, but Željko must have been badly shaken by his mother's absences. He did everything he could to grow up as fast as possible and get out of the house. After middle school he went to the war, to aviators' school, and became a pilot in the famous Niš Air Corps, which would be dismantled and split up in 1941 along the lines of family and national affiliations, as well as predictions and prognostications regarding what would happen in the course of the war. Željko Ćurlin completed his pilot training in the Independent State of Croatia, under Franjo Džal, but then quickly escaped to the English and flew until the war's end as a pilot of the RAF.

Aunt Lola and Uncle Andrija meanwhile continued to live their empty and displaced marital life. Branka grew up, Andrija worked very hard, and Lola, by then in her forties, continued to enjoy herself like a young girl, actually living the kind of life that would become common for the majority of women at the end of the twentieth century. Aunt Lola, you might say, was the avant-garde of a future, dissolute, touristy Dubrovnik. And she was not overly concerned that somewhere high above Željko was flying, or about the fact that, up there in the air, among warring armies, he was changing one uniform for another. She was a staunch atheist and never believed in any sort of God, or expected anything from him. Death was always the definitive end.

On the first day of the war, Sunday, April 6, 1941, with her usual euphoria for leaving the house, Aunt Lola set out with a girlfriend on a walk through town. Dubrovnik at the time was patrolled, just as it would be decades later, by wandering photographers. They would take pictures of the men and women who seemed likely to pay, mostly foreigners, and then would offer them the photos for sale. If they accepted, the picture was purchased on the spot, and developed photos would be delivered later. The practice remained in place until the beginning of the eighties, when the photographers lost their jobs – by then all the tourists and travelers had their own cameras and considered themselves expert enough to take their own pictures of the world around them.

And so on that first day of the war, a Dubrovnik photographer (Studio Berner) snapped a photo of Aunt Lola and a friend of hers. We cannot know for certain, but maybe that was the only work he could get that day, when all of Dubrovnik was gathered around the radios listening to the news of the bombing of Belgrade and the public calls for mass military mobilization. Lukre acted her part meanwhile, defying through her nature the implacable logic of historical time – that day, yet again, she refused to go into exile.

She liked the photograph so much that she sent it to her sisters in Sarajevo, with a short note on the back: "This is how we looked on the first day of the war, so even the photographer thought it worth taking our picture." Her sisters at that point found Lola's folly comforting. As if her nonsense might protect them from all the miseries that sense could foresee and claim, miseries that would dictate the future trajectory of their lives.

Life in the Ćurlin home was secure and quiet, and they lacked for nothing even throughout the war years. Andrija Ćurlin, a respected gentleman who kept himself apart, had only ever messed with the authorities to the extent that it was necessary, meaning very little or not at all, and had remained useful to everyone because of his expertise in the business of trade and finance. In the Dubrovnik of that time his was one of the rare homes to have a telephone in it. We even find his name in the telephone directory of the Independent State of Croatia for the year 1942. Listed on page 396, his is one of the six subscriber names from Dubrovnik that begin with the letter Č/Ć. It notes that he is a "Secretary of the Commission for Trade" and that he resides at no. 1 Bunićeva poljana. Until Aunt Lola's death this address would remain one of the rare, unchanging details in the history of the Stubler family. Everything else would be altered many times over, lost, vanished, or even wiped away. The phone number where it was possible to reach Uncle Andrija Ćurlin was 640.

It's this number that we would call in the autumn of 1943 to say that, in a battle against the Partisans, Mladen had perished, the son of Lola's younger sister Olga, my Nona.

For Lola too this would be a terrible event. She would sense that it was not the end but the beginning of something that even today, after all their deaths, remains unresolved. The last of the Stublers had just been born, and all that was needed now was to see how each of them would die and on whom the heavy conscience for that death would fall.

When the three sisters and their brother met each other in the post-war peace, it would be the first time they clearly heard the differences in their speech, their accents and intonations. Lukre spoke like someone from Dubrovnik, and her siblings sounded to her like Bosnians. Only their German remained unchanged.

When it was clear the war was over, the family ace pilot Željko changed his uniform once again: from a flyer for the British Crown he would become a pilot in Tito's young army. One day he would drink himself into a stupor, take off from Zagreb's Borongaj barracks, and plunge to his death. How could such a thing happen? Had Željko killed himself?

After the war, the two Stubler sisters and their husbands would be separated by their dead sons.

It is not possible to express fully such long-suffering remorse, such all-consuming, silent, and unspeakable mutual blame. My Nono Franjo and Uncle Andrija did not send their sons off to die, nor did they expect any kind of heroism from them. My Nona Olga and Aunt Lola didn't do what the two men expected of them, which ultimately would have kept both Željko and Mladen alive. This passivity was palpable for years after, even up until Olga and Lola's deaths. To their own misery and that of their sons, the mothers had been stronger and more influential than the fathers. They'd made decisions for the boys, put pressure on them, sometimes for the boys' good, sometimes for their own, gratifying their own whims and dispositions, so that their sons might fill the shoes of husbands they'd never fully accepted or loved. Yet their sons had still fallen.

Aunt Lola was shaken by Željko's death more than any mother could be. She would wander around her apartment and through the streets of Dubrovnik, just as she continues to wander today through the family letters and reminiscences passed on thirdhand, by people who don't even remember her.

Up to that moment she had lived alone and free, but now it was her lot to live with Željko's shadow. She tried many different ways to manage: She forced Uncle Andrija to move to Peru but immediately wanted to return to Dubrovnik; she said that the altitude of Lima was too much for her. Then they adopted a child. His name was Šiško. Šiško was supposed to serve her as a way of forgetting Željko. He was her new son. But it didn't work, he was different. He seemed weaker than Željko, whose intellect and goodness had in the meantime taken on heroic proportions.

When Šiško grew up, he ran off to be a sailor. He'd come home to Dubrovnik once a year. I met him when I was three. Uncle Andrija had died long before, and we would visit Aunt Lola in her beautiful, spacious apartment above the city's main square. Šiško took me down to the harbor to show me the boats. He took my picture on an enormous metal bollard. I was terrified that I would fall into the sea.

That summer he quarreled with his adoptive mother. We don't know what it was about or what she might have said to him, but we never saw him again after that. Šiško disappeared forever, from Dubrovnik and from our lives. He had never got completely used to our family, just like Aunt Lola in fact, but he had been part of it. We don't know if he's still alive, but if he is, maybe he visits Dubrovnik occasionally. None of us are there anymore, none of us are anywhere anymore because, in turn and out of it, we have all disappeared. And now, if he's alive, Šiško lives in God's peace, alone.

My aunt Branka was a striking, upright woman. She completed medical school and became an anesthesiologist. From her father she inherited a gentle, clear disposition; from her mother, an inclination toward a life of beauty and freedom. She worked in the Vinograd Hospital in Zagreb and married the actor Jovan Ličina. When they divorced, she remarried in Germany in her late forties and gave birth to a daughter, Katarina, and then promptly died in her sleep. An aneurysm, they said. She'd lived five years longer than Aunt Lola.

Karla, Lukretia, Lukre, Lola Ćurlin, née Stubler, rests in the Boninovo

Cemetery, beside Uncle Andrija, Željko, and Branka. Their family vault is over-crowded. When Branka died, or rather, when it was time to bury her, it seemed that there wouldn't be enough space. But then one of the gravediggers banged his shovel into the coffin where Aunt Lola was lying and it burst into tiny pieces. Bad wood, they said, chipboard. Don't make them like they used to. So, freeing us from the burden of finding a new grave, they swept to one side what little remained of Lola's bones. Branka's coffin, which they'd brought from Germany, now had a place to rest.

If they hadn't done that, who knows what we would have done with the deceased. It was good that way. Excellent in fact. There was no one left in Dubrovnik besides those in that brimming vault, which we didn't visit, and which we wouldn't even recognize anymore among the innumerable graves.

May Josip Sigmund Be Upon Your Soul

It's a shame our Nano had no children. And it was for quite sentimental reasons that he didn't marry. While it might have long seemed, when looked at from outside, that Rudolf Stubler was a scatterbrained layabout – until well into his forties he still didn't have a single day of regular employment – Rudi was a man with a broken heart.

He had excelled in everything from an early age, had neat, elaborate hand-writing, was well-read and talented in all the fine arts, was a gifted mathematician – scholars from all parts of Bosnia and Dalmatia would come to Dubrovnik to watch and wonder as seven-year-old Rudi solved the most complex problems of arithmetic and geometry. No one questioned whether Rudi wanted to continue his education, it was assumed he would go to Vienna. The only question was which branch of learning he would choose and in which of the sciences he would distinguish himself.

The Great War had just been concluded, Germany's teeth had been smashed in, and forever, or so it was believed at the time, its imperial aspirations had been quashed. In the east the fiery dawn of communism was gobbling up Russia, and there was nothing left of the Habsburg monarchy beyond an oversized Vienna where minor geniuses from the peripheries of the vanished empire arrived, predestined to distinguish the great century of Europe. Mostly Germans and Jews, an occasional Serb, Croat, Slovene, or Czech, a gifted young painter or violinist would come to the great academies, impelled by ambition and sometimes fear, both dark and painful, an eccentric spirit that meant ruin for all those unable to conceal themselves in large cities.

Rudolf Stubler was a child of this future century. Or he should have been. But Rudi was free of any ambition or fear. And that is why he became a layabout.

He studied at polytechnic institutes in Vienna and Graz. He regularly wrote long, beautiful letters home in which he described life in the metropolises, gatherings with our Viennese relatives, theater productions, operas, and concerts. Rudi wrote about everything like a skilled newspaper reporter, but regarding his studies he noted only that he was spending days on end in the college lecture halls without seeing the sun for all his learning. Usually this was tucked into one or two sentences, a formality to pacify old Karlo.

It took him a long time to grasp what it was Rudi was actually doing in these studies of his. Or perhaps he understood immediately but hoped that something would change with time, that after a year or two of nights and days out in the Vienna cafés and vaudevilles, Rudi would finally grow diligent and would apply himself to real scientific learning.

But that did not happen.

Our Nano never finished his studies. His father tolerated the boy's being in Vienna and Graz, sent him pocket money from his meager means and from the help provided by the unions, until the day when news of the great scandal reached Sarajevo and Ilidža from far away – in Vienna Rudi had fallen in love, and with none other than Dora Dussel, our close cousin.

This loose and cheery incestuous adventure exceeded even his father's tolerance. In a terse, sharp letter, Karlo Stubler told his son to return home immediately. Rudi obeyed because he had no other choice but to do so. Such were the times, or such was the strength of the old Stubler's authority. On the whole, it didn't even enter his son's head not to return home. He'd left Dora behind unreservedly, and she remained until the end, until her own death and after, our dear Viennese relation. She would visit Sarajevo. In the fifties we took her to

Vrelo Bosne, the wellspring of the Bosna River, where great family dinners were organized, even during the leanest period of socialism.

They would sit next to each other at the overflowing table in Ilidža, talking about everything that relatives who have not seen each other in a long time talk about. It was a time when everyone lived with their own secrets. Only these secrets were of the sort that other people also knew about. And conversations went on as if there were no secrets at all.

On returning to Sarajevo, Rudi continued to live his own kind of life. As there were no Viennese cafés and vaudevilles, he solved math problems, played preferans, and frequented the theater. For years he played violin in the Sarajevo movie theaters, both before and during the films. Fortunately, the fashion of sound cinema developed slowly and with difficulty in Sarajevo, so he always had work. The theater owners were actually grateful to him, because as soon as Rudi had come back from Vienna they didn't need to keep a piano around anymore. They said that Rudi's violin conjured up whatever was happening on the screen better than any keyboard. Karlo Stubler never went to a movie. He wasn't angry at his son. It was his life. If he had decided to fritter away all his talents, so be it. But it made him sad all the same.

After the eccentric and half-baked love affair with Dora, our Nano fell in love only once more. Several years after he returned from Vienna, he took a shine to a girl in Mostar whose name we don't remember. All that is known is that she was a Muslim. Their romance was short and stormy. Her family rose up against this young Sarajevo native, prepared to perish in defense of honor and faith, and the virtue of the young woman. The vehemence of the attack astonished us and struck fear into our hearts.

"Why do they hate us so much?" asked the bewildered old Karlo, and this question, so naïve, would remain among the family lore, carried forward like a counterpoint to circumstances in the state, wars, neighborly quarrels, and even massacres. This memory, perhaps, appealed to a different time.

Why do they hate us so much? Opapa Karlo asked himself, not the family members around him. He asked out of fear, but also out of arrogance. There was arrogance because he felt a certain sense of superiority for not hating anyone.

But of greatest interest was, again, his fear. He was afraid, this Swabian from Bosowicz, of what he represented for them, as a foreigner in Bosnia, an eternal foreigner, an Ahasuerus, into whose family they would not allow their daughter to marry, even should the world come crashing down upon their heads.

Karlo Stubler didn't believe in God, and never had second thoughts about this – God had been permanently absent from his life. Everything that happened today was what had always happened. This didn't mean, however, that he was unable to distinguish the differences between himself and Muslims. However absent Jesus Christ was, along with Jehovah, the Father, the Son, and the Holy Spirit, they were his in their nonexistence, while Allah, their God, was something else. It wasn't his place to think about Allah's existence or lack thereof.

Our Nano, so the family story goes, was prepared to do anything to hold onto his bride-to-be. If necessary, he would turn apostate, run away with her, do all that her family might require of him. Nano was willing to humble himself, if only they would allow her to become his wife.

But it was all in vain: this unhappy love was the last of his life. He would travel to Mostar no more. He'd look at the town from the windows of his train car. This for the next thirty years until the memory faded.

For a while Rudi's sisters did their serious best to get him married. They'd bring home acquaintances from work, pretty, unmarried girls, a French teacher or hotel decorator, and he would excuse himself to the bathroom, then run off through the back garden and across the neighbor's courtyard, returning in the evening when the coast was clear. These incidents would then be talked about, and thus did new family legends arise in whose recitation he too would come to take part, until everything turned into a big joke.

There were such sons in those days, mostly among the *kuferaš* families, those who didn't have deep roots in Bosnia and in Sarajevo but rather, since the time of the Austrian annexation, had lived in an atmosphere of temporariness, as if preparing for an impending move, and the fathers often would not even notice that their sons were layabouts and were growing old. Anyway, they would think, somewhat presciently, the enemy would take all this away one day soon, drive us all off somewhere, leaving the land desolate and empty.

It didn't take much for Rudolf Stubler to be mobilized.

He was the ideal recruit. Unemployed, well educated, and an ethnic German to boot. They made him a first lieutenant, even though he had not served in the military before, and sent him to Bijeljina. He was paralyzed with fear and lived with it every day for months – because he was by nature something of a coward, a lone boy among sisters, and because heroism didn't come naturally, or in any other way, to the Stublers, and because Rudi found himself among people with whom he had little in common. He followed the rules, was a respectable citizen, a top student, and would not have revolted against the authority of the state in any way, no matter whose state or what kind of state it was, nor would he have gone to war, or spilled a drop of his own or another's blood in the name of the state, whatever state it might be.

After the fall of Stalingrad and a winter of starvation, followed by a series of failed German-Ustaše offensives, the Partisans attacked suddenly and from behind, often striking quiet, unassuming defense garrisons far in the rear. And so, at a certain point, they set upon the region of Semberija, reached Bijeljina, and along the way destroyed the unit in which Rudi was serving. In the battle where he managed to save his neck at a certain hopeless instant by lying under shallow cover with only his buttocks protruding, his head covered with his hands while he waited for the roaring to subside, the spectacle of him – as he himself recounted the story later – softened even the battle-tested Partisan machine gunners, and in the end he escaped at a run through the corn fields and was not even taken prisoner. When he realized that no one was chasing him, he ripped the officer's markings from his uniform with the intention of making his way by foot to Sarajevo. He had a friend with him, someone of similar character evidently, and together they struggled for days through the fields and woods, feeding themselves on the rare fruits of the forest that city kids like them could recognize, and they would have soon died of hunger had a Partisan patrol not taken them prisoner near Kladanj.

They brought him before the Partisan commissar, a kind, refined man. He offered Rudi a seat, spoke with him, and correctly concluded that he was in no sense a real enemy.

"Would you like to stay with us, Mr. Stubler? You won't be worse off, and we need interpreters. And you'll be fighting for the right cause."

"Must I stay?"

"The struggle for freedom is a voluntary affair," said the commissar with a frown. "Freedom cannot be forced on anyone."

"In that case, I think I'd rather go home," said Rudi sheepishly.

"Alright then, if that's what you've decided. But remember: Josip Sigmund was a German like you, and he laid down his life for this people. You will surely live to see freedom, people like you always survive, but may Josip Sigmund haunt you and your soul, if you have a soul." Saying this, he gave him a signed transit pass with which Rudi could travel to Sarajevo across Partisan-controlled territory.

When he arrived at the door to our apartment, we didn't recognize him. Rudi's sister Olga didn't even recognize him.

"What do you want?" she said, trying to sound angry, as she looked at the ragged man holding a shoe box in his hands, with crazed eyes, a face contorted into a spasm of weeping, stinking to high heaven.

"But it's me," he whispered, shuffling back.

If Olga had slammed the door then, if she hadn't taken another look and instantly recognized him, who knows what might have happened to our Nano.

First she gave him a careful examination to make sure he didn't have lice or fleas, while he was still clinging to the shoebox.

"What's this?" she asked, grabbing the box.

It was empty, not a thing was inside. Later we would ask him why he had carried an empty shoe box around with him, and Nano replied, "That's what happens when you've lost your mind."

I never believed this.

I've thought about it often during the forty years since I first was told the story of the box. I grew up, watched films, read books about wars and bouts of madness, I lived through one war and became a sort of *kuferaš* myself, finding my deepest foreignness in Zagreb and in Croatia, but I've never been able to fathom what First Lieutenant Rudolf Stubler carried inside the empty shoe box.

Whatever it was, it must have been important. It's hard for a person to walk empty handed, especially if he's ragged and hungry.

"I've had enough of your brother and his lying around. These are serious times!" said my Nono, intent on finding work for Rudi so he wouldn't be sent back to war.

This was the greatest, actually the only, instance of favoritism in the history of the Stublers.

Nono found him a job in a railroad stokehold. Rudi was then forty-three years old. In the stokehold he would continue to be a diligent and valued worker even after the war, someone who never took sick leave or was late for work, not even by five minutes. A true Swabian, they would say, while he also worked on the accounting and bookkeeping, despite the rules. As a single man, however, he was not able to get his own apartment. To the end of his life he lived with his relatives in Ilidža, in a basement room.

Near the entrance to the building where Rudolf Stubler worked until his retirement hung a commemorative plaque dedicated to Josip Sigmund Pepi, a skier, mountain climber, prewar communist, and locksmith in the railroad stokehold, who had worked in the Partisan underground, that is until the Ustaše criminals discovered him.

A Pine Floor Shining
Like the Sun Beneath Your Feet

Karlo's youngest child, my Nona Olga, was born in 1905 in Konjic, where her father served briefly as the stationmaster. She grew up in Dubrovnik, finished elementary school and then started at the Italian high school. Olga was the most intelligent of Karlo's children and the most interested in literature and art. By the time the century reached its end, we'd also need to add, the most unfortunate child too.

Olga fell in love the moment she arrived in Bosnia. Handsome like a tall cypress, he was a young railway worker who had just returned from Italian captivity where he had spent nearly four years, my future grandfather Franjo Rejc.

Whether Franjo defiled her in haste or Olga, who was barely seventeen, committed a wayward sin and got herself pregnant, or whether it was all a stormy but pure love in which they were both consumed for the rest of their lives, we no longer know because some of the important dates have since been lost (perhaps on purpose), so we aren't sure how many months passed between Olga and Franjo's wedding and the birth of their first son, my uncle Mladen.

All we know is that Olga's announcement to her father was quite ceremonious and that all were anxious about what would happen and in what state she would come out of Karlo's room, where she had gone to say that she'd fallen in love and would like to marry a young railway worker, a Slovene. My retroactive anxiety is perhaps deepest of all, for on this conversation my very birth depended.

Anything in all this could have put Karlo out. Olga had not finished her third year of the classical high school – she was a minor, the age Gypsy girls marry, the time of year young bitches first go into heat, by all accounts an absolutely inappropriate time for a Stubler daughter to marry. Besides, one of his daughters – Karla – had stayed behind in Dubrovnik, having refused to go with him to Bosnia, while now the other would come to be married several months later in the east. The old man surely had a feeling that she was promiscuous – his dearest, most gifted child. So beautifully did she play the zither, that mournful, solitary instrument he had carried with them all the way from Bosowicz . . .

He didn't say anything for a long time. He just looked at her silently, then finally pronounced what sounds today more like a prison sentence than a father's blessing:

"Fine. If this is what you have decided. But just remember, there's no coming back!"

They lived together in a house rented from strangers. Karlo supported them with money provided by the union, collected from people who were poorer than he was. He was humiliated, and it didn't look as if anything would ever change. But then suddenly someone took pity on him, or they mislaid his police file, because he landed a job in the largest railway junction in Bosnia, and for a while he moved to the town of Doboj.

What else could he have done but let Olga marry the first man she had taken a shine to? If he'd refused, Olga would have simply run off with Franjo. Or she would have drunk from the goblet, jumped from the tower, killed herself. But one thing is certain: in those days she would not have given birth to an illegitimate child.

Had Karlo not allowed his youngest daughter to decide for herself, perhaps quite a few future misfortunes might have been avoided, though that iteration of the Stublers, if someone were to tell it, would be an utter fiction. If my Nona had killed herself, I would not be telling this story.

My elder uncle Mladen was born in 1923, in Usora, a small railroad station near Doboj, where Franjo Rejc had become the stationmaster. Olga gave birth to him at home, far from the hospital, in the blood and sweat of her brow, in the middle of Bosnia, green, dense, misty, poor, disconsolate, and, in absolute truth, plain ugly Bosnia – at least when seen through the eyes of a certain Swabian daughter, a native of Dubrovnik, who once in happier times long ago shocked the solicitous citizenry with her head-first dives from Porporela.

Mladen was a child born of love.

But that did not stop Olga from falling in love with a certain Usora teacher, a man whose name we were never able to learn but about whom we fantasized for a good twenty years. Could he have been a Czech, a Pole, an Austrian, a Croat, or – please, God, let it be – some charming Serb with the hairline mustache of a lover from a silent Hollywood melodrama who was sent to Catholic Usora to reform and convert members of that mistrustful Yugoslav tribe prone to Roman schisms? Some imagined that lover of Olga's, the first after her husband, through the despair and anger of a betrayed and abandoned child, but I thought of him with pleasure and sweetness because my Nona, even as a young mother, fell in love with him and, good God, gave herself to him for all of us future children, born and yet to be born, who would not have the heart for such loves.

Franjo was traveling a lot at the time. He'd be away on business. He'd visit his relatives in Tolmino. Or he'd go to the railway headquarters in Sarajevo. He studied foreign languages, collected books on beekeeping, read patriotic Slovene newspapers, the works of Anton Aškerc and France Prešeren, and kept up a correspondence with his relatives, but whether he learned about the teacher we don't know. Either news never reached him of what everyone else knew, or he pretended not to know. Both are possible. It's also possible that he too had fallen in love with a beautiful teacher. Or with a nun at the Zenica hospital who rebandaged the painful abscess at the base of his spine, a wound that would occasionally reappear to torment him until the end of his days.

Three years after Mladen, Dragan was born. This was in Kakanj, where Franjo Rejc had received a transfer and was again stationmaster. Kakanj was the last station on his slow advancement toward Sarajevo. They stayed there until the midthirties, when Franjo was transferred to headquarters, where he would soon obtain his highest position: head of railway timetables.

The years in Kakanj would be remembered as the happiest in Olga and Franjo's fifty-year marriage. In this small industrial mining town, built during Austro-Hungarian times, which barely had even the smallest of Oriental bazaars, Muslims were the majority, mixed with a Catholic minority composed of indigenous people from the neighboring villages – actually from the oldest, most ancient, royal Bosnia – along with *kuferaši* from all the regions of the then monarchy of Franz Joseph. Engineers, master blacksmiths, toolmakers and locksmiths, railroad and postal officials, the odd botanist, stray piano instructor, geologist, and surveyor, lived together in Kakanj, taking on with a certain unexpected lightness the rhythms of life, as well as the customs, of the local Muslim population. These people of a different faith were, in a wondrous way, closer to them than the Catholics of the surrounding highlands. By nature the Muslims were closer to the city and to an urban way of life, they were often better off in terms of property, and their social and cultural interests were somehow broader, more diverse.

No one knows whether Olga fell in love in Kakanj too. Probably not, since she had two children on her hands and the social life was busier than in Usora, so there was not enough time for such excesses or for those excuses she'd once used as a means to slip away. They went on excursions to the surrounding hills or to the Bosna River, making the rounds to the Rejc relatives – there were so many of them, around Kakanj and Zenica in the early 1930s. It gave us the illusion, perhaps for the last time, of being a great and extensive family, whose closeness and sheer size would protect it from all evil.

In Kakanj Olga made one of the best friends of her life. In contrast to all her other girlfriends, from Dubrovnik and Sarajevo, whose names were long ago forgotten, though we look at their beautiful, young faces in photo albums, knowing nothing of these nameless faces except that they were Nona's friends – in contrast to all of them stood Zehra, a simple, illiterate woman.

In fact, she wasn't the least bit simple, but then how does one explain this to someone so they might believe you? Her husband, like most Kakanj men, was a miner. They lived in a humble house that nevertheless had one completely unexpected sign of comfort: in place of a floor of packed earth of the kind seen in the homes of most of the miners and iron workers, Zehra had a floor made of pine planks. Always irreproachably clean, it glowed and glistened like a ray of sun. When both Zehra and Kakanj had disappeared into the distant past, and nothing was left in her life but to die, my Nona would talk about never having seen anything cleaner or shinier under her feet than that floor of Zehra's. If a paradise exists, and if she had not been, like the rest of the Stublers, punished by God for her atheism, Nona's paradise would surely be covered with that floor of luminescent yellow pine.

Zehra, however, believed in God. In her world the question of God's existence would've been impossible to ask, meaningless, for there was no way that there could not be a God. What could there be without Him? She fasted, prayed, and did all that was expected of an old-fashioned Muslim woman. Nothing in her life resembled the way Olga lived. But Zehra somehow understood everything, and if there was ever anyone to whom Olga spelled out the pain of her life, to whom she explained why she had married Franjo Rejc, it was Zehra. Their friendship would be deep and lifelong, but its content would remain a secret. We can only guess what she saw in Zehra, and why she would remember her sunny yellow floor and talk about it with such wistfulness up to her dying day – but why Olga was so important to Zehra, why this city girl, in many ways a foreigner, should remain Zehra's dearest friend in life, we are still in no position to even imagine. Let alone the question of how she spoke about Olga to God. Of one thing I am certain: in Olga's whole life there was no one who spoke to God about her – surrounded as she was by nonbelievers – as Zehra did.

From Bosowicz, as a family gift and signifier, Karlo Stubler brought along something that would last longer for us than any memory and that would be transmitted forward to a time when we no longer even knew his German language anymore – migraines. Most of his children and his children's children would suffer from occasional intense headaches accompanied by visual and olfactory irritability, and the Stubler migraine, though less intense and growing rarer with age, would come to be my inheritance as well.

When Franjo would head off to work and Olga was left alone with her migraine and her two sons, who she found impossible to care for at times, she would lock herself in a darkened room and let them do as they pleased as long as they let her be.

"They can break the dishes for all I care, I won't say a word!"

This was known to go on for days. She would lie in the dark, moaning, not suspecting, fortunately, that these migraine-filled days, weeks, and months, would be the best of her life.

Through the closed door the boys could be heard fighting.

"You Kakanjan, Kakanjan!" Mladen would say to Dragan.

"Oh, yeah, you Usorian. Usorian . . ."

Nona would listen and laugh, which would only make her migraine worse.

Ivo Baškarad and Mujo the Eternal

Both Christmas and Easter decorations were on display in the Stubler household, despite Opapa Karlo's hardened atheism. He was areligious in the same way that some people are tone-deaf. Rationally he knew what God was supposed to be, and he didn't object to either profound or superficial religiosity in his house, nor did he have anything against the Church or priests. In his soul he was and would remain a union man, committed to justice and equality for all, and in this was very well read, such that neither Marx nor Engels had escaped his attention, but his godlessness had no connection whatsoever to their writings. For Karlo Stubler religion was not the "opiate of the masses" but a plaything and waste of time, a folkloric celebration for the entertainment and consolation of a simple-minded people that he had nothing inherently against. In truth, it wasn't just that Karlo didn't believe in God, he didn't believe that in today's world, in which the provenance of lightning and thunder had been explained, in which it was known that the earth is round and orbits the sun, that the tides rise and fall in connection with the moon's gravitation, that there really could exist people who still believed in God. From his perspective, the civilization of the West had been created by individuals, tribes, and peoples for whom it was important to act as though they believed in God. He had nothing against this, nor would he have fought in any sort of revolution against the Church, against faith or superstition. To him this battle simply did not seem serious, and perhaps that is why Karlo Stubler, despite his convictions and thorough reading, never became a communist.

Years after he'd retired, after the Second World War, he would sometimes briefly lose consciousness. During the afternoon siesta, he'd be sitting beneath the thick crown of a walnut tree, watching the people pass by along Kasindol Street, or he'd be in the midst of a lively conversation, after spending a long time sorting small pieces of wood to make a medicine chest, when he would suddenly stop, go silent, tune out – and everyone around him would hold up and wait.

"There was an accident, two trains collided . . ."

Or:

"A train flew down into the Neretva River . . ."

Or:

"A train jumped the tracks . . ."

All we had to do was turn on the wireless radio, wait for its green eye to light up, and we would hear the details of the accident. Opapa was never wrong. In the thirty years he lived in Bosnia after being exiled from Dubrovnik, he grew quiet like this five or six times, zoned out, disappeared, as if some gentle epilepsy had carried him off for a moment, and he would always come back with a frightening report, and each time it would be confirmed on the news. Karlo Stubler witnessed train wrecks that took place hundreds of kilometers away. This made him uncomfortable on every occasion, because he didn't believe in superstition or in prophecy.

Gypsies will examine your palm for spare change, women after their morning coffee will turn over their demitasses to read each other's fortune in the patterns of the grounds, old crones, before wars and after they were over, once tossed beans across rough-trimmed wooden tables to discover whether brothers and sons who'd disappeared would come back, and a certain Russian who was rumored to have been lady-in-waiting at the court from the house of Romanov – half of Ilidža thought that women of the court were actually upscale tsarist whores, while the other half, better educated and more cultured, said with a certain disdain for the former that women of the court were in fact countesses

– flawlessly read the past and future of Ilidža's pluckier inhabitants from her cards, which resembled those used for rummy and schnapsen except instead of gendarmes and kings printed on them there were people being hanged, court jesters, and Death with a rusty Turkish scythe. To anyone who had the courage to pay her, Liudmila would say when and from what illness death would come. It was said that just after the war Ivo Baškarad dutifully paid to have her tell him just one thing – where he was destined to die. In Ilidža, prophesied the Russian. Really? Ilidža? Yes, really. Ilidža.

The very same day Ivo Baškarad picked up the things he most needed from home, said goodbye to his family, and left for Sarajevo, never to return to Ilidža. When or how Ivo Baškarad died is no longer remembered.

Karlo Stubler smiled at all this good-naturedly. He transcended it all peacefully, not believing either the Gypsy women, or Liudmila, or the grounds in overturned demitasses, and we attributed his lack of belief to the fact that great-grandpa was a Swabian. And Swabians were, it appeared, rational people who didn't even believe in themselves without solid proof, who dealt with facts rather than wasting their time. True enough, and through him we too were German, but something of Bosnia and Ilidža had caught hold of us, clung to us and started to accumulate inside us, so we believed in everything others believed in. We would become Swabians only when others wanted to make it known we weren't the same as them.

So how then did Karlo Stubler reconcile his godlessness and firm disbelief in any form of superstition with the fact that he would every once in a while lose consciousness and see a train wreck happening? Was it perhaps from low blood pressure? Or had he never got over the fact of having been dismissed from the railroad, which had been everything to him in his life, so that to that very day he would see a collision of trains with the same eyes as a train dispatcher whose negligence had led to an accident? We would support his theory, and he'd calm down, believing, together with all of us, that those born and yet to be born, that everything before us, had arisen from tiny, almost meaningless, physiological disturbances.

Fathers wake up at night in fear. They check to be sure their sons and daughters haven't stopped breathing. But train dispatchers dream their whole life of the collisions caused by their mistake, two trains finding themselves on the same track. Karlo of course never was a dispatcher, he was a stationmaster.

Opapa was second sighted. And his second sight touched only upon trains and the railroad. He had no insight into our future lives. He did not see the time, not very far off, when there would no longer be any Stublers or Stubler descendants in Sarajevo or Bosnia. What little that remained of his lineage would be hidden within other family names, spread across the earth, drowning and disappearing amid the fates of strangers and foreign identities.

Likewise, Opapa was unable to foresee the destinies of his Banat relations, the brother who disappeared and the entire extinct world in which, long ago, the Stublers had been born. He was silent about them, and this silence was their only known grave – he did not see them while they were disappearing, neither in his dreams nor in reality. And he was quite convinced that a person could not see what was not present before him, or indicate the past or future with his eyes closed. Nevertheless, he saw railway wrecks more clearly than Liudmila the Russian saw the time and place of Ivo Baškarad's death. It seemed that of all the things he might have been in his long life, Karlo Stubler was in the end a rail man above all. Composite trains, engines, carriages, and car designs had inscribed themselves in him more deeply and for a longer period of time than Karla, Rudi, Regina, and Olga – more than his God-fearing spouse, our great-grandmother, about whose lifelong heart defect we've yet to tell. Although it seems that Karlo Stubler's life path was defined by his eternally German and *kuferaš* nature, there was another factor that was even stronger and more lasting.

In accordance with the customs of his day, for a man with his social status and heritage, Karlo Stubler wore a beard. Every few years he would shave it off, but he would leave the mustache. In photographs with the mustache he looks most like a German. But this was not him. The real great-grandfather wore a beard. He probably knew this, because it was just once in a while that he shaved it. Then he'd let it grow again. The beard would fill out and everything would be in its place. In reminiscences, photos, family mythology, and the stories of neighbors on Kasindol Street, Karlo Stubler wore a beard until he was completely forgotten. None of his descendants would wear one again.

When, at the beginning of the fifties, with everyone dirt poor, the stores empty, and people washing their faces with garment soaps made from tallow and ash, buck wash or lye, Karlo Stubler contracted some sort of disgusting skin infection that engulfed the roots of the hair on his face. He went to the doctor, who said that there was no remedy for his illness other than to pull out each hair from his face and beard by its roots with a pair of tweezers.

Every morning, for days and weeks, my great-grandfather would stand before a mirror, yanking out the hair from his beard. It hurt so badly that tears spurted out of his eyes. No one had ever seen him cry, it would not have befit him, but when he pulled the tough, fat hairs from the soft skin of his face, his eyes wept of their own accord.

When the household began to stir, he would cut short his beard-pulling session for the morning. Damn those idle young people, they just sleep and do nothing! Who knows if he'd ever considered he might have woken us with all his groans. Or if some of those hairs yanked out by the thousands might have perhaps shaken Karlo Stubler out of his godlessness, or if perhaps God was so merciless to Opapa that he refused to show himself in even a single tearfully plucked whisker.

Omama Johanna's Heart Defect

After she had given birth to her fourth child, Omama was diagnosed with a fatal heart defect. First the doctors in Dubrovnik and later the ones in Sarajevo said the same: nothing could save the young woman. It was a miracle that she'd survived as long as she had. Each of her births was its own inexplicable *casus* for medical science, but if you are a believer, one Sarajevo doctor said to Karlo Stubler, then surely you have some explanation. A sort of cosmic unease fell upon Karlo's shoulders. And yet at the time he needed to pretend that he was a believer and that a *casus* was something he completely understood.

Johanna Skedel, who acquired the married name Stubler, was born in the village of Lokve, near Škofja Loka, in Slovenia. This is the only piece of reliable information connected with her ancestry we have. Which means perhaps Omama's name was actually not Johanna Skedel but Ivana Škedelj. These two identities alternate with a certain monotonous regularity in her identification documents and family papers over the course of her life. On her report cards they used one, in the marriage registry the other; on her identity card she was called one, in her travel documents the other. In the places where she was called Johanna, she was a German, but where she was Ivana, she was considered a Slovene, and later a Croat. Everything had a certain order that might seem absurd to us now, but in the days when Omama was growing up, it was possible to live according to that order. Not everyone lived this way, there were those who perished, fomented revolution, and served time in prison because of a name in a birth registry and for the right to be called by one name rather than another. But to Omama it was all one, and therefore, according to the customs of the time and the rules of propriety under the Stubler roof, it was all one to us too. This is how it was among the Stublers in 1910, when the Southern Slavs began fooling around with unification, prepared to rise up against our good old tsar and king, and again in 1918, when by some miracle they managed to unite, and in 1920, when Karlo Stubler was exiled from Dubrovnik, and in 1933, and 1941, and 1945. Omama was called Ivana Škedelj in some papers, Johanna Skedel in others, and there was no one to ask her whether she was a Slovene or a German.

Omama had two sisters. The eldest got married in Vienna and the middle one in Loznica, Serbia. Johanna was the youngest. She moved with her parents to Slavonski Brod. There her carpenter father, Martin Skedel, had got work on the railroad. Karlo Stubler worked on the other side of the Sava River, in Bosanski Brod. This was how they met, fell in love, and were married in one of the final years of the nineteenth century. Johanna's father didn't live long, but her mother Josefina Skedel, née Patat, continued to live with her daughter and son-in-law, moving with them from station to station along the Bosnian rails, coming to know that dark, distant country that seemed so far away from their homeland, as far as Bangladesh seems to me today.

My great-great-grandmother Josefina Patat, whose married name was Skedel, the mother of my great-grandmother Johanna Skedel, who gave birth to my grandmother Olga Stubler, whose married name was Rejc, was born in Udine and was actually Italian.

So this too was known: Omama was Italian on her mother's side. But on her father's was she Slovene or German? The answer, which would forever remain secret, would not have changed anything in the story of the Stublers, in the long history of their fading away, nor would it have been important in my life that a few drops more of German or Slovene blood flowed through my veins, but in the time of the Stublers, Omama's national ambivalence – or more correctly, her national indifference – was important.

Were we to judge by the spirit and logic of the language – which is always fatally incorrect when the judgments are about last names – then it is more probable that Omama was Ivana Škedelj than Johanna Skedel. Skedel is a Germanized version of the Slovene Škedelj, but many Germans and Austrians had Slovene last names, just as Slovenes had German ones.

A possible elucidation of this doubt, or just a way of multiplying it still further, would arise in Doboj in 1922, when the youngest daughter, Olga, brought to the house the handsome young rail worker and future Stubler son-in-law Franjo, who was by nationality, but more importantly by his sense of cultural belonging, a Slovene. Knowing that his mother-in-law was from Škofja Loka and wanting to please her, he began speaking in Slovenian.

And this was when we learned that Omama didn't know Slovenian.

She spoke German, and Serbo-Croatian, with the consistent old-fashioned accent and intonations of central Bosnia, and even a little Italian, but Slovenian she did not know. Not a single word. Nor was she pretending – why would she? She really didn't speak Slovenian. In those days this still did not mean out of hand that she could not be a Slovene. Maybe the carpenter Martin Škedelj thought his daughters would be happier and find better marriages if they spoke German in the house, if they were Germans. The nineteenth century was a time when people could choose from among everything on offer, both what ethnicity to be and what language with which to pray to God. At the time they arrived in Bosnia, they could still have chosen even the faith they'd belong to, but we, unfortunately, did not take advantage of that opportunity. We remained Catholics and, maybe for that very reason, without faith. God was tired of us.

In contrast to Opapa, Omama was religious. She went to church on Sundays, prayed before going to sleep, and lived according to the catechism of her time. She was not, by the way, one of those God-fearing family missionary ladies who fuss about their grandchildren regularly taking the sacrament and going to church for religious instruction. She kept to her faith, which would be the one thing that helped her after the Dubrovnik and Sarajevo doctors said her heart would soon stop. It was the weakest still-beating heart they had ever heard. Omama did not feel her illness, no matter how aware she was of its presence. Diseases of the heart are often pure metaphysics and don't resemble other diseases in the least.

Karlo's employment in Doboj was awaited like a miracle. Until the last minute, during our move, carrying the bed linen, dishes, and what little furniture we brought with us from Dubrovnik, as we set out on the train from Sarajevo's Alipašin Bridge to Kakanj, Zenica, and onward, we weren't sure someone wasn't playing a cruel joke on both Opapa and us. We could not know whether anyone might, at the last minute, take a peek into the police documentation and be horrified by his official record.

And we could not know then, in our first-class compartment, with our complimentary company tickets, that a fateful event was indeed in the making, the prerequisite for the line of our future births: if Karlo Stubler had not been driven from Dubrovnik to Bosnia, if two years later he had not miraculously been given work in Doboj, precisely where the young rail man Franjo Rejc was employed, if Olga had not met Franjo, if she had not liked him, and maybe if Franjo had not been – as she would complain twenty years later to her friends – an "empty prick," there would have been nothing for me to be born from.

For Omama it was God's will. If so, God certainly had a sense of humor.

After getting back to work, Karlo Stubler decided to make every effort to find a cure for Johanna, or, at least, to keep her alive longer. Perhaps the reason he eventually lived in his children's homes might have been that for years he'd spent a large part of his salary sending Johanna to thermal spas. After he had sent Rudi money in Graz or Vienna, hoping his son would bring his studies to a happy conclusion, and after he'd sent Johanna off to some German bath or other, there was still enough money left for normal city life. (Otherwise, at the time, the twenties and thirties, we were in good shape with regard to paychecks and monthly income: engineers, stationmasters, and dispatchers made about as much as pilots and air traffic controllers do today.)

Twice a year, in the fall and spring, we saw Omama off to Germany for treatment, not knowing whether she would come back to us. We laid her to rest each time in that last platform glance at her delicate face looking out from the compartment window and at her hand waving goodbye, and each time she came home we saw it as a miracle. Omama would return to us from the dead after a month at the hot springs. And there were a countless number of baths in Germany, so it seemed to us. She would come back from them, as from a Grimm fairy tale, hale of heart and strong like the giant Rübezahl.

Johanna Stubler would continue her spa therapy throughout the 1920s and a good part of the 1930s. How she found Germany, whether she met anyone there and made friends, whether she noticed that the world around her was changing, that Germany was changing ominously, what her thoughts were as the Weimar Republic was transformed into the Third Reich, whether this change could be felt in the atmosphere of the hot springs, what the heart patients and arthritics were saying about Hitler, or Marshal Hindenburg – about all of this we knew almost nothing.

In the Stubler nature, and perhaps in that of the majority of *kuferaši*, there was a tendency to look away from the miseries of the century. Temporary residents foreign to this homeland, similar to the Jews, the Stublers concealed bad news from one another.

At any rate, good news was so fantastic that we didn't even have time for the bad. Thanks to the German waters, or so we believed, while Adolf Hitler was becoming chancellor, Omama had outlived all the medical prognoses. Her heart was and would continue to be weak. It almost wasn't even a heart but a barely perceptible whisper at the bottom of a deep, dark cave. Johanna Stubler woke up every morning resigned to the fact that she would not live to the evening. All her life's accounts forever needed to be reconciled, she could not afford to have any unpaid debts to those who were close to her or unresolved arguments with her neighbors, for death would soon be arriving at her door like a welcome, long-awaited guest.

If there were peace, and if I could quiet my life as she did, I would write a novel about all this. About life in the German baths of the twenties and thirties, about the sendoffs from the station at Alipašin Bridge, and about death that had so often passed idly through the Stubler house that Omama no longer feared it.

She was the only one in our home who was not afraid – this was not because she was a believer, for she did not talk about dying with God, but with the German doctors.

When she wasn't at the springs, Omama read books (novels in German and Croatian, adventure stories, both serious and non-serious literature), listened to the radio, or had quiet conversations with her children. She did not cook dinner, clean the house, or take care of guests. Omama never lifted anything heavier than a spoon.

She was a good and cheerful woman. She didn't unload her own suffering onto others. She laughed easily and often but in laughing would clutch at her chest. She would not have regretted dying in that way, while laughing. We kept all other forms of stress from her, but never laughter. It might have seemed occasionally that we were trying kill her off by getting her to laugh, but who would have believed that her children, grandchildren, great-grandchildren, and great-great-grandchildren had killed Johanna Stubler through laughter, to spare old Karlo the expense, all in the hope of his building a home and providing us with deeper roots?

In old age she would get anxious. It would seem that a form of Parkinson's disease seized her in those moments. But then she would again start to smile. Or a laugh would rumble up through her body.

Omama outlived Opapa. She died just before her ninetieth birthday, quietly, without great upheaval, the way heart patients depart.

The year before she died, with a resigned air, she'd asked one of her grown granddaughters, who had just become a bonafide member of the Yugoslav Communist Party: "Do you ever cross yourself, my child?"

Eat – It Won't Get Stuck in Your Seat

The weekly dinner in the Stubler home in Ilidža. Beef soup, boiled meat with sautéed potatoes and horseradish, and at the end – *buhtle*. Such a meal is a child's torment: we would need to grow up, maybe get a lot older, in order to start liking that heavy Swabian soup with the homemade yellow noodles and archipelagos of fat floating in the dead calm of the weekly family peace and harmony; and after the soup, that meat, full of tendons and gristle, and the bones from which Opapa and Nano loudly sucked the marrow – they said that was the very best part and the reason we made beef soup each and every Sunday. Great suffering and affliction fell upon us at the children's table because, according to an old family rule, we had to eat everthing on our plates – the gristle, the tendons, the assorted nodes and slobber, the oozing yellow balls of fat, and every part of the meat, which the grown-ups enjoyed but set the children's imaginations to run wild as, horror struck, we saw what we had there on our plates. And then someone from the big family table would glance over at our little table:

"Don't pick at that meat. Eat – it won't get stuck in your seat!"

These ugly words, this ghastly verbal concoction, were never spoken by Opapa. He looked out benevolently from the head of the table, as if surprised at the world's immutability: there were always some children who pushed the veins from the meat to the sides of their plates and always some adults there to force them to finish.

Because whoever didn't eat their meat didn't get any *buhtle*.

In the Stubler home buhtle were the regular weekly cakes. For Christmas and Easter, birthdays, name days, and other celebrations, they made special cakes, like tortes, which didn't always succeed, because they were made infrequently and were not a regular kind of cake. Cakes recalled and carried forth countless family sagas, the biographies of aunts who had disappeared and passed on, grandmothers and great-grandmothers who had lived in distant lands, uncles who had never returned from the faraway frontlines of Europe, and it seemed that baking cakes on festive occasions and bringing them out to the grown-ups' and children's tables was a way to remember and tell stories that had been told many times before. Only buhtle did not have their own story. We baked them every Sunday, early in the morning, and all our stories were contained in those buhtle, which is why not a single one is remembered. Thus the Stublers are forgotten. When I think about them, my mind is a perfect blank.

But still I can't imagine living in a world without those Sunday buhtle.

Actually, it's sometimes hard to believe that in all the time after my birth, growing up, and getting older, my Nona baked me buhtle barely two or three times, on the rare occasions when Stubler nostalgia would take hold of her.

In the Stubler home it was Karlo's middle daughter Regina, whom we called Aunt Rika, who did the cooking. She was the meekest of the sisters, believed in God, and followed all the life rules, both inherited and acquired, that made her a good and faithful Christian. By nature openhearted and tolerant, in one thing only did she show signs of a dangerous fanaticism: as far as she was concerned you had to eat every last thing on your plate. Even when some small child, dreading the sight of the monstrous gristle, tried to resist the bribe and forfeit the buhtle she would confront him with the calm and reason reminiscent of an officer of the Inquisition:

"You don't have to eat the buhtle, but in this house the meat and potatoes will be eaten!"

And that would be the end of it: the formulation of "in this house" was unequivocal in a manner that few things in life are, for in it was inscribed a higher authority. You could challenge anyone, your mother, your father, your aunt, but not Opapa Karlo. He did not yell or threaten, he never ordered anyone to do anything, he never "raised his hand" against anyone, although actually once he had, and a half century later they were still telling the story of how Opapa had got so angry, the sin had been so grave, that he'd suddenly slapped the culprit. So though he didn't frown or show in any manner that he supported this irrevocable rule according to which only the bones could lay uneaten, anyone who heard that declaration of "in this house" was still fearful lest they deliver a sinful, abstract blow to Karlo Stubler or to his home. While the home, in actual fact, wasn't even his but rather belonged to Aunt Rika and Uncle Vilko, who had been the ones who built it, while Opapa and Omama only lived there with them.

After the weekly meal, all the collected children would lie down for an afternoon nap. They were led upstairs and put in their beds. The children who lived there were used to this rule, but those who had come as guests experienced sleeping after lunch as a special humiliation.

The grown-ups meanwhile would talk on the lower floor. The women hung about in the kitchen, washing and drying the dishes, jotting down cake recipes on the backs of medical referrals which, when we returned to our homes, would be recopied in school notebooks with greasy cardboard covers. The men would continue to discuss politics at the table while dry breadcrumbs embedded themselves further into the elbows of their sweaters and jackets.

Opapa was an inquisitive man, he knew all sorts of things, and could think for himself, but he didn't always need to be the one controlling the conversation. September 1939 was a rich and beautiful month, the Indian summer would last all the way to November, and the garden in front of the house in Ilidža was filled with scents, colors, and sounds. The birds quarreled somewhere high up in the branches of the weeping willows that Opapa had planted there when he came to live in Ilidža – these one-time saplings would grow to colossal size by the end of the twentieth century, soon after which none of us would be there anymore to see them – thin branches and shaggy crowns that looked in the distance like a head of a bushy green hair. The rabbits tapped on the floors of the hutches with the tips of their nails, the hens beat their wings, running from the frisky young rooster, and everything all around echoed, called, and cried out, as if the earth beneath our feet were breathing. And all in that instant swelled and gave forth life – the year would be rich and full, and everyone for that reason was on the brink of tears, because it seemed to them all that they were actually saying goodbye to this fecund life in which they may have found happiness.

"That idiot will lose the war in the end! But where are we now, and where will we be by the end of it?"

Thus spoke Karlo Stubler, while German troops pressed irresistibly into Poland, which would soon fall and disappear, partitioned between Germany and the Soviet Union, which among the naïve raised the hope that this was in fact the end, and that now Hitler would stop. They were ready to forget that there had once been a Poland and a Polish people, just so this Indian summer could go on forever, and so we Yugoslavs of three kindred tribes might continue to live in the peace and harmony we'd enjoyed up until then. But it was clear to those in the Stubler home that Hitler would not stop.

We would quote Opapa – *That idiot will lose the war in the end!* – after everything had passed and neither he nor we remained, reproducing that word *idiot* in his German accent, in a way that we never spoke otherwise, except when repeating his words.

And in the spring of 1945, when Hitler eventually lost that war, two Partisan soldiers would come for Karlo Stubler to take him off to the Ilidža station and put him into a cattle car whose destination remained unknown. They knew Opapa was a German, and the Partisans had their lists, so why had they not taken anyone else when the house was still full of Stublers? But then with us, both the German blood and the German blame had thinned considerably over the years. We were Croats by now, fit to live more comfortably in the brotherhood and unity of our complex nationalities and ethnicities. But Opapa Karlo was there to atone for our sins, in some deportation camp, where he would no doubt perish, and we'd never learn of his fate, just as Aunt Doležal would never learn what happened to her husband in the work camp in Norway where the Germans had sent him for reeducation. We would have carried him inside our souls like the bitterest of almonds, and never would we, Croats all, have gotten over the loss of our German great-grandfather.

But that's not what happened.

When they heard that the old Stubler had been taken, our Orthodox neighbors rose up. The men and the women ran to the station, the men half-shaven with soap on their faces, the women with their suddenly awakened children – as if they had just leaped from their beds – to beseech the good Partisans to leave Karlo Stubler in peace, for who would be there on Kasindol to protect the people should the Ustaše come back one day? This is not exactly what they said, but this is how it was impressed upon us for our whole lives, and maybe I would have let slip from my mind the wartime actions of my great-grandfather had I not recalled so many times over the past twenty years how Opapa spoke to the Ustaše when they showed up at his door:

"You can't come in here! This is a German house!"

I would have liked to have occasion to utter this sentence at some point. More than that, I'd have liked just to have the courage do so.

I often wonder why after the war Karlo Stubler quickly lost the desire to correspond with his relatives in Bosowicz, why he rarely inquired about his brother's fate, why he was so indifferent, almost apathetic, to Rudi's search for our cousin Regina Dragnev, and why he never exchanged a word about any of this with any of us. After 1945 he pulled back into his Germanness like a snail into its shell. But why? There have been days, months, even entire years when it seemed to me that, in the face of the new era, the South Slav state, and the righteousness of the victors, Opapa contritely lowered his head and died – he too, like another victim – but perhaps the truth is different. Perhaps we were not to be permitted to nestle in this truth as eternal victims of our own suffering.

It may be that in 1945 Karlo Stubler broke off contact with his relatives so that he would not have to share with them their defeat and crimes. For he had never supported the idiot, and maybe they had. Maybe not, but his life had already run its course, and he did not have time for verifications. He remained a German to the very end, but after 1945 he no longer shared his Germanness with us.

When he died, the obituary writer asked Rudi what the deceased's ethnicity was.

"A Croat," blurted out our Nano, frightened.

The Long Missive of Mihajlo Fleginski

Whether his conscience weighed on him or whether he held onto a desire from long before (I suspect that he himself didn't even exactly know which it was), after his return from Vienna, Rudolf Stubler tried studying in Zagreb too. His entrance exams in mechanical engineering were exceptional, and he would take the train there for lectures and tests, something that didn't impose any additional expense on the old man, since all of us at the time, as members of a railway family, were able to ride the train for free. Rudi would spend two or three days in Zagreb, sometimes a whole week, then return home, carefully creating the illusion that he was still hard at work at his studies. He then returned to playing his violin in the Sarajevo movie theaters again, to make enough money for his next journey, or enough at least for his entertainment expenses in Zagreb.

This lasted on and off for a year or two, and then, we didn't even notice exactly when, he just stopped going to Zagreb, and no longer said a word about college. It's possible Opapa noticed, he was the one after all who cared most about Rudi's schooling, but for us it just slipped by. Thus, very quietly, the last embers of Rudolf Stubler's academic ambitions died.

These trips of his to Zagreb would have long ago been forgotten, like all the rest has been, if it weren't for Nano's photographs of that city. Here he is in

Tuškanac during late autumn, with the first snow falling all around. Or on Ilica, a few steps from the outlet onto Ban Jelačić Square, grinning at the photographer. A picture of him in the park below the Kaptol walls, with an unknown lady, behind them the towers of the city's fortifications visible.

Mihajlo Fleginski is not in the photographs, but his story, more than all the pictures or old travel documents, brings to mind Rudi's sojourns in Zagreb. Although we never met the man, we came to learn everything there was to know about him when, at the beginning of the seventies, years after Opapa's and Omama's deaths, a long letter appeared. We began to think about him and through him and, in a different way, we began to think about ourselves, about how fragile and weak the human body is, and how little it takes to be forgotten by everyone. And then, several years later, a very short piece of news reached us: Mihajlo Fleginski's son had notified Nano that his father had died – Mr. Stubler's name was listed by his father among those who should be notified – and that he was buried in X cemetery in Y town . . . As if we were going to visit his grave and light a candle. We were not. Ever. As to why will become perfectly clear.

Mihajlo Fleginski had moved to Zagreb from the Serbian town of Jagodina. This is where his family had lived after emigrating from Russia in 1919: father, mother, and boy. He was already an adult at the time but started college seven or eight years later, once they were comfortably settled in Jagodina and decided to go no further. Perhaps Fleginski had begun his studies in Saint Petersburg and wanted to continue them in Zagreb. But he became a mechanical engineer easily, with due order and in good time, and then returned to Jagodina. He found a good job and married a woman whose name we have forgotten, though she is remembered to have been a Russian.

Up until the war Rudi exchanged letters with Mihajlo Fleginski – the exchange of letters, postcards, and photos was something of a family passion that infected everyone, so much so that we grew restless if a day or two passed without someone writing to us from afar – and perhaps they even saw each other on some of Rudi's train journeys. When the war began, they found themselves in two very distant lands. Rudi being mobilized, made an officer, barely escaped with his life. If he ever thought about Mihajlo Fleginski, it was a fleeting thought, like an envelope with an address and a stamp tossed into the postbox empty.

After having lived through his share of fear, and after the war-time and family misfortunes had passed – the Stublers had lost their Mladen in a German uniform and their Željko in that of a Yugoslav airman – Mihajlo Fleginski ended up among those who had gone missing, disappeared, vanished; and then came the long period of waiting for these missing either to suddenly resurface or be forgotten for good.

Did Rudi in the meantime stop thinking of Mihajlo Fleginski? Even if he didn't, surely he stopped thinking that his friend from Jagodina would ever find him again.

It could have been in 1971 or 1972 that the letter arrived on Kasindol Street in Ilidža, but with the prewar house number. A stamp with the face of Lenin. The name Rudolf Stubler was written out in Cyrillic in the handwriting of an engineer. Mihajlo Fleginski had written to Nano.

Days would pass before he grew calm and collected enough to show us the letter and read it to us. Nano had always been easily moved to tears by just about anything: sentimental movies, the ending of Mann's *Doctor Faustus*, Schumann's *Träumerei*, when well performed, the burial of the household dog, which lived to a ripe old age and was laid to rest in the garden behind the apiary, but this was something different altogether. More serious than affection, something one could not cry one's fill over in the same way.

In minute, clear handwriting, as if along an invisible straight line, covering both sides of eight sheets of paper, Mihajlo Fleginski wrote about what had happened to him since the beginning of the war. With an engineer's precision, he enumerated the events, linked them together, and assembled them into a whole, as if he were assembling an internal combustion engine, a turbine, an electric coffee grinder, without feeling, as if the story were about someone else, except when, after bringing one section to completion, in a very short phrase, he noted that his wife had suffered greatly.

Mihajlo Fleginski had spent the entire war in Jagodina. No one had touched him, nor had he got mixed up in anything, but he had gone on with his engineering work, as valued and useful in wartime as he had been in peace. Machinery deteriorates, engines break down, and someone is always needed to maintain them. Then on October 17, 1944, after several days' worth of hard fighting against the SS division on the Prinz Eugen, the allied units of the Red Army and the People's Liberation Army of Yugoslavia, under the command of Marshal Tolbukhin, entered Jagodina.

Once the euphoria of victory had passed, the city's liberation had been celebrated, and the apprehended traitors of the people had been shot, soldiers from the Red Army came for Mihajlo Fleginski and his family. He did not know, nor would he ever learn, why the soldiers had come. They led his family to the station, crammed them into a train, and for the next three and a half months the family Fleginski traveled along the remains of Europe's railroad tracks toward Russia. In cars for people and for livestock, in first, second, and third class, on racks for coal, in open wagons, before the loaded rifles and pistols of young Red Army soldiers, policemen, and civilians, and then on foot, when the tracks came to an end at demolished bridges, they made their way, with other families until they disappeared, with German POWs, disarmed deserters, and other émigrés, gathered up like them in their sleep and now being taken who knew where, to Russia or the end of the earth, it was all the same.

After 111 days on the road, their train came to a stop, and Mihajlo Fleginski was told that he had half an hour to say goodbye to his wife and three-year-old son. They did not tell him where he or they would be going, or explain the separation. Would they be apart for a day, a year, the rest of their lives?

The journey to Siberia was shorter. Mihajlo Fleginski described life in the camp without fear of the censors, who might read what he'd written and return him to the camps as punishment. Or he believed that no one would do anything to him, for he didn't complain about anything, he didn't write that he'd been hungry or thirsty, or about the cold. He did not describe a single emotion in the story of his twenty years of life in the prison colony, or the eight years he spent as an exile in Magadan, where he had a well-heated room, worked in a machinery shop, and could receive packages and write home as much as he wanted. He could even phone his wife and son whenever the lines were free.

He wrote about Siberia without emotion or complaint, without sympathy or self-pity, describing in a few sentences the trains that took him there, as well as the regions he passed through, and the station where he said good-bye to his wife and son. But in all the minutely written sheets of paper informing Rudolf Stubler where he had been for twenty years, there was not a single description. Only figures, how many people were in the camp, how long the winters and summers lasted (there was practically no spring or fall in Siberia), an array of meteorological details, noted with precision and commentary, the number of teeth lost from his upper jaw (the camp doctor said it was gum disease), Stalin's death, the news of which delayed by months and, actually, never uttered aloud, and then another array of meteorological details: winter, a few days of spring, summer, and of autumn before the first big snowfall, as if he were writing to someone who was about to travel to Siberia and might want to know what the weather was like.

Soon in the Stubler house they would be reading Karlo Štajner's *Seven Thousand Days in Siberia*. And then other books would be published in those years, translated from Russian, English, German, from all the living and dead languages of the Russian emigration, and in all these books there would be many descriptions. These would come to be a comfort to us, to Nano, and to all those who read Mihajlo Fleginski's letter, or had listened to Nano read it aloud.

After Rudolf Stubler died – the last among us to bear Karlo's family name on his tombstone – in the spring of 1976, Mihajlo Fleginski's long missive would be misplaced somewhere and disappear into the oblivion of time.

Perhaps this is a good thing. Perhaps if I were to read it today, I would in fact find a few descriptions of Siberia, or the handwriting would not be so orderly and straight, as if following an invisible line, that eternal horizon of the engineer's eye. Perhaps in this way I would lose a certain contact with that unreachable ideal: of suffering that is not named or described by a single word and that exists more truthfully than any verbal description of hardship. What is passed over in silence, in a good literary text and by a true author, knows how to speak through its white spaces and absences, and what surrounds the white spaces is dedicated to such silent speech. Mihajlo Fleginski had passed over everything in silence in order to tell his friend what had happened to him.

Rudolf Stubler answered his friend's long letter. We do not know what sort of an answer it was: probably it was well written – for Nano had a literary knack – and filled with feeling. He surely evoked God and consolation. Nano was after all religious: he believed as a little child believes in his guardian angel. To his letter, Mihajlo Fleginski responded politely, briefly, formally. Nano wrote again, and Fleginski again responded in the same manner. Everything he could really say he had said in the first letter. There was no true continuation. That was it.

Mihajlo Fleginski didn't return to Jagodina. He never visited Yugoslavia. This was in the time of Leonid Brezhnev. Was he unable to get a passport? Was he too poor? Or did he no longer feel like traveling?

To his son he'd left a list of people who should be notified at the time of his death. Had he also asked his son to mention the name of the town and cemetery where he was to be buried? It is uncertain – we don't remember the name of the town any longer, let alone the name of the graveyard.

Have You Thought About Boras?

And when the liberation was over, the earth atop the graves settled, the avenging forces collected their own and went away. They didn't come for Karlo Stubler again, and it seemed that peace had come for everyone. But then from Dubrovnik, Marko Bašić, an old friend and union comrade of Karlo's, arrived for some sort of work. Though younger than Karlo, Marko too was getting on in years. In truth he was an old man for whom the revolution had not so much meant rejuvenation as a certain reprieve from old age. People at the time believed in a well-being that would come one day, and the years while they were waiting for it stood still. As soon as they began to doubt, they might take on the age of an entire epoch overnight, while those who believed to the end would remain eternally youthful. This explains the phenomenon at the end of communism of how it was still possible to meet hundred-year-old adolescents, heroes older than their rifles had been when they'd joined the Partisans at fourteen.

This was never a concern for the Stublers. They grew older in accord with the years and the family misfortunes, rushing unceasingly toward their own disappearance. We welcomed Marko Bašić as an old friend, though it perplexed us a little that he seemed so young. He ate a lot, spoke in a loud voice, had big plans for the future, invited us to visit him as soon as possible in Dubrovnik or at his other house in Brgat.

And then the two of them sat down to talk after lunch.

Karlo expected that now they would share mutual recollections, and this pained him somewhat. As if Marko would be offering him some poor Turk's halva of flour, water, and sugar. But there turned out to be no need for worry. The guest was completely fixated on the future.

"Have you thought about Boras?"

"No. What about him?"

"He's right there in Gruž. Alive."

"Let him . . ."

"And what d'ya think now?"

"About him? Not a thing!"

"What're you gonna do?"

"What could I do?"

"I don't know. Now's the time. Your time!"

"And what should I do?"

"Get back at him!"

"You know, my friend, whatever I might do to him, it won't give me back my life, or the years he destroyed. It seems to me best not to do anything. It's by far the most practical thing."

"Oh, you're such a true kraut!" said Marko Bašić, laughing.

Maybe Bašić was a little embarrassed, because after that he turned everything into a joke, or he thought old Stubler was thickheaded and that's why he laughed, but that day, and the next two while he stayed in Sarajevo, or with us in Ilidža, he didn't bring up Boras again. Nor did he bring him up the next times he visited from Dubrovnik, when he brought what were in those years precious gifts from the south: oranges, carob, and dried figs.

He came for Opapa's funeral too.

Later, at the wake, the vigil or the long period of sitting together that in Bosnia followed the burial of the deceased, when everyone was trying to say something nice about Karlo Stubler, as part of the conversation, in a joke or little story, so as not to provoke the tears of others, Marko Bašić said that Karlo had not wanted to take revenge, even when it became possible.

And then, over his own words, Marko burst into tears.

He was an old man, suddenly he shed all his youth, finding tender refuge in the fact that Karlo had not wanted to cash in the debt he was owed by Boras.

Everything was talked about in the Stubler home, the same story repeated countless times, expanded upon and enriched, maybe in order one day to be improvised upon, and old Karlo took part readily and often. If he got anything from his resettlement, if all of us got anything, it was this passionate, daily story-telling. In other things he might have remained a Swabian, but in stories, and in the need for stories to be constantly renewed, Karlo Stubler was a true Bosnian.

But there was always one thing he refused to discuss.

Who was Boras? I don't know, nor would any one of us ever know. Marko Bašić brought him up during that first visit of his after the war. He repeated the name several times, and perhaps he pronounced it that night when he began to weep over himself, but he didn't tell us anything about this man. And none of us asked.

Opapa, as far as we can remember, during his conversation with Marko, did not even a single time pronounce the name Boras. Maybe this was just by chance. But when Rudi asked him later out of curiosity about this Boras, Karlo went dark as a storm cloud, and then, completely calmly, answered:

"*Niemand.*"

And that was all. Boras was "No One." Boras was *Niemand* – and this declaration was irrevocable, inalterable, forever.

We discussed it when he was out of earshot, fantasized, imagined, and hypothesized who this Boras could be and what ill deed this he could have done to Opapa such that in 1945, four decades after being exiled from Dubrovnik, there was an expectation of getting even.

Rudi asked Lola. She or Uncle Andrija must have known, living in Dubrovnik. It's not such a large town that you couldn't find out. But they didn't know either.

There were a lot of Borases in Dubrovnik, and some in Gruž too, and even if over the years it was possible to discover which Boras from Gruž had transgressed against Karlo, how could we ever have learned the details of what he'd done?

Something held us back from making further inquiries. Whether because of Opapa's authority or the collective Stubler fear about what we might find by asking questions like this, Boras's role in our lives would remain unresearched.

According to histories of Croatian surnames, the Borases hail from Klobuk, near the Bosnian town of Ljubuški. At the beginning of the twenty-first century, the quantity of such last names in Croatia was 749 – approximately eight hundred souls live by that name. Whenever I hear of anyone named Boras, I still feel a little sting.

Why didn't Karlo Stubler want his children, or his children's children, to know anything about him? Because such ignorance was practical?

Even though he talked at length, and about things that in other families were considered strictly intimate, Stubler was silent about something that had clearly frustrated him, about someone who – we didn't know how or why – had destroyed years of his life. Boras was a central figure in his exile from Dubrovnik, but we never learned more.

In much the same way, after 1945 Karlo had ceased to have contact with his relatives from Bosowicz, had not looked into who was alive or who was dead, as if he had suddenly lost interest in his ancestry. He readily told stories from his youth, described the house where he was born and the village none of us would ever see – not a single one of us have ever been to Bosowicz – talked about what happened to his relatives between the two world wars, but this was only until the end of the thirties. After that they never came up in his stories or remembrances, as if they had all suddenly disappeared inside a statistic, the year 1938 or 1939, inside the closed circle of the numeral 9, as if fallen into a black hole.

Whether Opapa thought about them, just as whether he thought about Boras – how often they came into his mind, how bitter were the memories, of one and the others, none of that could we know, but it wasn't just that he did not talk, his face would go dark whenever we asked, or whenever he knew that we were thinking about something that we shouldn't be thinking about. He'd get angry at us as one does at a small child who sneaks a look into his father's anatomy book.

His daughters and son thought he did this because, like any father, he saw them as children, snot-nosed little kids, to whom he would eventually, once they were grown, do like in the Jovan Jovanović Zmaj poem and "just say it all."

But that wasn't it.

Karlo Stubler wanted his German suffering to remain his alone. He didn't want the questions that tormented him in connection with his relatives in Bosowicz to be laid upon the shoulders of his children. Had these relatives survived in their homes? Where had they been taken away to? Had they been killed or deported to Germany? But also, where were they and what were they doing during the occupation? Had they held the belief that the Banat should be German and that others had no right to remain there? And what had they done if they believed this?

In 1945 Karlo became a private German. He didn't renounce his Germanness yet he didn't share it with his children. He intended for them to become a different people and to take on, in place of German fears and suffering, the fears and suffering of their Bosnian homeland. It would be easier for them this way.

The fact that he chose to become a private German saved his life on two occasions. The first time was when he wanted nothing to do with his compatriots after they arrived in the town in 1941 in support of the Independent State of Croatia. He could not be brought to support them, nor did he come out against them: in both cases he would've been killed. The second time his private Germanness saved his life was when, with unexpected bravery, he hid his Serbian neighbors in his house on the nights when Ustaše ran wild. Had he been less brave then, he would have met his end old and alone in some deportation camp or, if he were lucky, died in a German home, and we would have never known where his grave lay.

Having reconciled himself to the fact that they would not be Germans, and being happy about this fact – for being German in isolation is painful and difficult – he didn't want to expose his children to temptation, either to commit the acts he assumed his relatives had committed in Bosowicz in 1941 or to do what he had done in saving his neighbors. Somehow the two extremes were not so different. They were villains from a feeling of having superior merit, from a German pride and arrogance, but he too had taken the decision to stand before Maks Luburić's drunk Ustaše out of a similarly prideful attitude. Despite the guns in their hands and the symbols on their caps, Karlo Stubler saw them as inferior to himself. And they had bought it, turned, and walked away.

Between the German crime committed against neighbors and Karlo's neighborly beneficence the difference is only in the morality of the action. So even though his attitude might have resembled that of his Bosowicz relatives, it was an underlying morality that set Karlo Stubler apart from them.

Karlo wanted his own family to feel less constrained. He left us to choose our own compatriots, hoping in this way we would be less alone. Who knows whether he miscalculated.

And so, rather than being frustrated at Boras's unknown role in our family destiny, we feel just a slight prick when we hear of someone who bears that name. And then promptly we forget – like everything else, it's all the same to us.

All Our Bee Cousins

Though he never built his own house, Karlo Stubler was still a house-proud man. He created small furniture pieces: with the help of a handy carpentry kit and woodworking tools brought some time in the distant past from Vienna, he made a small wall cabinet for the household medicine containers and placed it next to the front door, so that, in case anyone got hurt working in the courtyard or the garden, he would have bandages close at hand, as well as adhesive tape, rubbing alcohol, iodine, hydrocortisone ointment, acetisal, aspirin, activated charcoal, an enema pump . . . He also made a single kitchen chair, some stools and footstools, and a wooden box for keeping track of various documents.

What he made around the house was more important. The moment the masons came to build the house that he would live in with Omama for the rest of his life, Karlo Stubler planted a weeping willow sapling twenty paces from the edifice. It wasn't any longer than a switch for punishing a naughty child. And that's exactly how it looked: like an ordinary, thin stick. During the house's construction, he was careful to prevent anyone from stepping on it or splashing it with whitewash. Today the enormous, monstrous tree, the most massive on all Kasindol Street, towers over the house in which they'd once lived and can be seen from the planes landing in the airport at Butmir.

Ten paces farther out, he built a small carpenter's workshop and, in front of that, a rabbit hutch. Next to the rabbit hutch he made a chicken coop. Behind the workshop was a garden. In the first part, nearest the house, there were raised beds for berries, tomatoes, lettuce, peas, and beans, and his little plantlets grew in neat rows like a regular Sokol gymnastics parade. They were hoed and watered daily, watched over lest a wild blade, weed, or evil caterpillar approach too close, and from a distance Opapa would supervise our care of his garden, pleased and tranquil at the prospect that everything was growing, sprouting, blossoming, and yielding fruit according to some natural order, free from history and from the lead that seeps out of newspaper headlines, ready for those who would refashion it into bullets, artillery ordinance, bombs.

After the kitchen garden came the raspberry bushes and the black and red currants, from which Aunt Rika, under Omama's supervision, would make juices and preserves for winter. Another ten paces farther were the rose bushes, bright red, pink, deep red like thick human blood, and white. Here the bees' buzzing grew louder, and with a few steps more it would seem as resonant as a thousand tiny tin wings scraping all at once against a round tin drainpipe, which is to say that nothing could be heard but the buzzing of the bees. It was much softer than a human voice and not shrill, but everyone in the midst of it would begin to speak more quietly, to whisper, so as not to interfere with the bees.

Here Opapa built a wooden apiary with six hives. Inside, behind the hives, were the garden tools and, in one corner, neatly arranged, the beekeeping gear. Here too, hung on a peg in the wooden wall, was the mysterious beekeeper's outfit, which at first frightened the children and later attracted them to beekeeping. When he put on the hood, the wide pants and gloves, his face hidden behind the apiarist's veil, Opapa would look exactly like a member of the Ku Klux Klan, who would one day appear on our television sets, though then, in that pre-television age, he looked to us like some sort of a wizard and alchemist holding a device in his hands that blew smoke, and drawing out from the teeming hives, like metal from a forge, chock-full honeycombs with hundreds of living, thronging bees – surely doing something important right then – each honeycomb looking like a factory or like a New York City street where humanity at the pinnacle of its history scuttled in all directions. Like God in a solemn uniform, his face invisible, Opapa Stubler presided over the pinnacle of apian history.

But that was just in our imaginations, for in the forties and fifties, when the number of Stublers was at its greatest, when our social life was at its pinnacle and seemed would not come to an end any time soon, neither Karlo nor his son Rudolf were using the beekeeper's suit anymore. The bees were well acquainted with them, had grown accustomed to the smell of their bodies – they say bees are sensitive to the odor of sweat, it makes them nervous and it's because of this that they attack – and neither Opapa nor Nano were afraid of bee stings any longer, if they'd ever been to begin with. Without gloves, in short-sleeved shirts, they would approach the hives, extract the honeycombs, slide their hands through the heart of the bees' world, and perform all the complex and – to us – mysterious acts described in Opapa's thick German books with their Gothic script. The bees endured this good naturedly, having grown used to their seasonal visits, and perhaps in Nano and Opapa they had come to see their apian gods who would deliver them from every evil, whether famine, illness, or fire. Deliver them from everything that it might occur to people to ask for deliverance from when they prayed to their own God.

A tender image from my childhood – one I have not known how to describe and so has remained unused, unwritten, and from which no novel or string of stories has branched out like the delta of a river – comes from the summer of 1974, 1975, or 1976. In Ilidža, in that overgrown and tucked-away Swabian kingdom of flowers, fruits, and insects, Nano is seated on a folding chair showing a bee to me and my cousin Ladislav Cezner, Aunt Rika and Uncle Vilko's grandson. He's holding it in his palm, playing with it. It seems to us he's pushing it lightly with his finger, and maybe he really is, but the bee doesn't do anything to him. It was friendship.

When a bee stings a person out of fright or when it's trying to protect itself or those close to it, the bee is left without its stinger and its insides; its entrails, which spill out, and that's the mortal end of the bee. Many bees stung Nano and Opapa in their lives – it was said this was good for rheumatism, so what did they care – but each of these stings would stand as a sad moment. Yet another unnecessary death in the long line of Stubler demises. Yet another irremediable misunderstanding never righted.

It appears his seemingly intrinsic knowledge of bees was another thing Karlo Stubler brought with him from Bosowicz. But then he also ordered books – Rudi would bring them to him from Vienna or they would arrive by mail – in which everything people knew about bees and beekeeping was collected. First came the handbooks on practical skills and on errors in traditional and popular beekeeping, as well as books on the construction and architecture of hives, varieties of pasture, and the influence of climate and seasonal changes on the rhythm and variety of the work of bee farming, then came handbooks on bee illnesses and propagation, on the types and manners of healing, along with brief overviews of the largest and deadliest epidemics, as if to say that sickness and death stand at the gates of every metaphysics, of every history of civilization or society. In peace and collectedness, in the lateness of evening and winter, Karlo cultivated his metaphysics of the bees and with a feeling of trepidation imagined a bee history, which, like that of human beings, was no more than the history of plague and evanescence. The difference lay in the fact that the bees had reached the completion of their civilization; reliably, stubbornly, and in perfect order they built their architectonically perfect hive, which had always been the same, over thousands of years, just as the honey and the bee's daily rhythm had been. People should not take bees as their example because people are not complete. It was in the imitation of bees that people became Nazis.

Beekeeping seemed to run in the family. Rudi inherited his father's love of bees.

Franjo Rejc, my grandfather, grew interested in beekeeping and became a keeper soon after he married Olga and became a member of the family. He was still living in various parts of Bosnia, wherever his work took him, and he did not have land of his own – nor would he ever acquire any – so he placed his first hives on someone else's meadow, the rent for which would be paid in pots of honey, somewhere near the little railway station in Želeće, between Nemila and Zavidovići. On days he had off from work he'd take the train to his bees, spend time with them, prepare them for winter, extract honey, sustain them against epidemics, using this trip as an escape from what was tormenting him in his everyday family life. In contrast to Rudi and Karlo Stubler, what the bees afforded to Franjo was this possibility of escape, and as he was more thorough and bookish in his fascination, and knew more languages, books came to him from all parts of the world; he subscribed to several beekeeping magazines, and, through the Sarajevo beekeepers and honey sellers' association, he even engaged in a sort of educational work.

Franjo Rejc was absorbed in this for more than half his long life. He suffered for many years from cardiac asthma. He was nervous and unhappy with his life and its surroundings, and, had it not been for the bees, he would have likely died years earlier. They extended his life, infused him with health, gave meaning to his everyday existence. It is quite probably due to the bees that I even met my Nono and that he was able to answer certain important questions. Though I have an aversion to them, fear their stings, and am incapable of keeping my fear in check, I also suffer them, at least a little, as relatives of sorts, part of my Stubler kin. We became relations and then, like so many others, they disappeared.

Nono kept his bees until 1966, the year of my birth. He'd just turned seventy, and that spring he gave all his hives into the care of a beekeeper neighbor, whose name we no longer remember. This was near the Dražnica station, on the border between Bosnia and Herzegovina. Twenty-seven years later, in a new war, an entire village would be killed in this exact place. The living descendants of Nono's bees would buzz around the open eyes and nostrils of people who would no longer shoo them away.

An orchard grew just behind the Stubler apiary. Apples and the odd short, humble pear, up to the edge of the property. Every little piece of Karlo's land, land he borrowed from his son-in-law and daughter, was attended to, and its purpose and significance was clear to everyone – almost an entire human age would need to pass in order for the earth to forget him completely, to wipe from its surface his choices of what was to grow, and where.

Marija Brana and Vasilj Nikolaevich

Marija Brana and Vasilj Nikolaevich lived in a one-story little house with two rooms somewhere on Sarajevsko polje. His name was actually Vasily. Nikolaevich was his patronymic, and he surely had some sort of a last name, but for the people of Ilidža he was just Vasilj Nikolaevich. Everything else disappeared and had been lost when, in their long exile from home, they settled here, put down their roots.

The two of them also had a son, but the boy died and they persisted alone.

There was also another version of the story, but the Stublers didn't believe in it: the son had joined the Soviets and was never heard from again. This is the more frightening version.

Marija Brana had fallen ill early in life. Even before the war her hips were in bad shape, and she would sit on a sofa all day long. No one ever saw her take a step outside. Anyone who later called her to mind could picture her clearly, seated on her couch, leaning forward like a snowdrop and looking ahead with laughing eyes. Marija Brana was a very kind woman. When she spoke, we imagined her by the side of a train about to set off for Leningrad, on its way to which it would be traveling till the ends of our lives, while she had stopped to say just one more thing to us before she boarded.

Vasilj Nikolaevich had been an officer in the army of the tsar. His long aristo-cratic face fit the part, as did his beard, which was of the sort worn by the Russian upper class, even by the tsar himself. On his legs were officer's boots, to just below the knee, like those German officers would wear in the coming war. Had he come all the way from Russia in those boots? Probably, but this was something beyond our knowledge, for in those years, the late 1930s, we only saw such boots at the theater, in the costumes of French and Russian melodramas, and on Count Tolstoy, in the plate reproductions of an encyclopedia of Opapa's.

The boots Vasilj Nikolaevich wore made him seem unreal. He often appeared in the children's dreams, where he was sometimes good and sometimes evil. When they were awake, the children were a little afraid of him and ran away, for Vasilj Nikolaevich had a strange way of speaking. He would start saying the next word before finishing the previous one. This was how Russians spoke who hadn't learned our language well, and not a single Russian had.

On Mondays Vasilj Nikolaevich put on his shoes and went out to work. He worked as a minor clerk in some railway office. He couldn't get any other job because nobody needed an officer from the army of the tsar. His empire had fallen, and his particular military skills were useless translated to another country. Which in a way seemed absolutely logical to us.

Marija Brana and Vasilj Nikolaevich had not brought any gold along when they were escaping from Russia because they didn't have any. But this is not to say they had nothing: they'd brought tablecloths, bedspreads, wallrugs, and one woven Turkish carpet. We didn't know anything about wallrugs. But in their little house, every free space of the newly whitewashed walls was covered by a rug.

The two of them had some sort of a Russian name for the thing, but we could not remember it. We didn't even really try, because after all this wasn't Russia, everything had to have one of our Serbo-Croatian names for it. And how else would you call a carpet for a wall but a wallrug?

We children told Marija Brana and Vasilj Nikolaevich that their walls were hung with wallrugs. Vasilj Nikolaevich laughed, but by the next day he too was calling them wallrugs.

Later we heard how, during their conversations in Russian, they would insert the word *wallrug*. Maybe they could no longer remember what that thing was actually called in their own language.

If we had told someone in Sarajevo, at school or on the street, about the wallrugs, if we had said that Marija Brana and Vasilj Nikolaevich covered their walls with them so as to be warmer in their house, they would have told us we'd made up a story and it was a stupid story at that. A person, after all, has trouble believing in something he hasn't seen with his own eyes.

For them, the war came and went.

Neither the Germans, nor the Ustaše, nor the Partisans laid a hand on the two of them. The Red Army did not enter Sarajevo, or Ilidža, but even if they had come to take them away like they took Mihajlo Fleginski from Jagodina, even if Marshal Tolbukhin had come to liberate Sarajevo, they would not have laid a finger on them. People fear misfortune, just as they fear poverty.

You only need to have enough misfortune, or enough poverty, for people to be afraid of you, for you to be protected your whole life long, to be avoided and bypassed. This was a kind of misfortune that couldn't be explained or recounted in words for it had no content, it was misfortune plain and simple, well bred, cultivated like an English lawn, all the more horrifying because it could not be made the object of scandal.

All that was known was that Marija Brana and Vasilj Nikolaevich's son had died shortly after they took refuge in the Kingdom of Yugoslavia. That was everything. He would shrug and, folded in on himself, say it was God's will. She would smile like a snowdrop and say not a single word.

No army would lay a finger on such misfortune, for people believed ill-luck was infectious, just as they believed all the wells in an occupied territory were poisoned. They also wouldn't have laid a finger on them because Marija Brana and Vasilj Nikolaevich were invisible to everyone but children and the Stublers.

It's hard to know what our friendship with the two of them was based on. They were émigrés and foreigners, just as we were foreigners in this land. This was perhaps a good basis for mutual recognition.

Vasilj Nikolaevich would come to the Stubler house on Kasindol Street, take the best seat at the table, partake of the coffee, cakes, or whatever else was being imbibed at the moment, and then, most often, he'd be forgotten about. Someone would bring up a story about something that had happened that day or the century before, Opapa would say what he had to say, Omama would insert a couple of words of her own, while everyone else would jump in one after another, interrupting each other's train of thought, which would then be interrupted by someone else, and thus would the pleasant afternoon hubbub proceed, with only the rarest of breaks, unless someone managed to get into a quarrel. Or someone brought up something the others hadn't heard about. Usually a death.

During all this, Vasilj Nikolaevich would be sitting in his place, accepting whatever was offered to him and not saying a word. He'd remain quiet, listening, polite and absent, like some minor god who had created his little world and stepped back from it. Vasilj Nikolaevich, it seemed, had taken a step back from life. But he continued living because it was the decent thing to do. If each person's presence in the world serves somehow to compensate for some kind of absence, and this in turn is the most important reason for that person's existence, then Vasilj Nikolaevich compensated for the world's lack of decency.

So why would he come over to our house only to remain silent?

There are very few things as important as this question. None of us was ever able to answer it. For some this was because they wondered about it only while Vasilj Nikolaevich was still alive and later forgot. Others didn't even try, because they were afraid that behind such a question, as with everything connected to him and Marija Brana, there lay some sort of misfortune which they'd rather ignore. A third group among us never became conscious of the question at all.

For me, having been born six or seven years after Vasilj Nikolaevich's death, the question would come to mind while traveling by train from the West toward East Germany, or across Poland, on the way from Warsaw to Kraków, Katowice, or Wrocław, or whenever my car might land itself in Zagreb's afternoon traffic jam, which would not let you move forward or back. At such moments the question grew to such a fever pitch that I'd turn off the radio and think in silence:

But why did Vasilj Nikolaevich come to the Stubler house, to sit among all those men and women with their children, and be completely silent, like a ghost in our midst?

When I'm bored or have nothing to think about, or when I feel desperate and at the end of my wits – as I do now as I write this novel of the Stublers, whose end is known from the start, a novel out of time and in it, which continues even after it is finished and is finished already by its very first sentence, which reads, "There in Bosowicz, in the Romanian Banat, on his departure for Bosnia, my great-grandfather Karlo Stubler left behind an elder brother" – again I wonder why Vasilj Nikolaevich came to our house.

Atop this question, whose lack of an answer I try to preserve within me, cultivating it like an oak bonsai, a line of equally unknown answers grows, and each is in harmony with its own narrative genre, stylistic format, or perspective from which the same question is always posed.

Vasilj Nikolaevich came to remain silent among us because we created for him an illusion of family unity, and beyond that an illusion of a homeland, a motherland. That is, of everything he had lost when he fled Russia. He was like a devoted paraplegic soccer fan in a wheelchair beside a field on which the world championship was being decided. Once in a while, Vasilj Nikolaevich was flooded with happiness for his lack of a family. This happened in those moments when someone close to us died. He was there when the military notification of Mladen's death arrived and when they telephoned from Zagreb about the crash of Željko's aircraft. He hugged us all, comforting and strong, cried with the women, and was happy that, besides Marija Brana, he had no one of his own and no one he could lose.

But as I've said, the gist of our godlessness was an empty heaven. The feeling that above and below us there is nothing, and that after us there will be nothing. I never managed to imagine how it would be to live with God, a life in which the heavens are not empty and one's imagination is populated by stories about the creation of the world, the apple of sin, or the Immaculate Conception.

If God exists, if his presence is conceivable, then he appears in different forms, wearing the masks of people and animals. God is an actor who through his various roles tests humanity's relation to him, or humanity's relation to itself. He is the negative of a person's portrait. We were hearing from God alongside

Vasilj Nikolaevich, in his silent vigil at the family table through the long years and decades of the twentieth century.

Is this true? No, just as no story from a family history is exactly true, or ever quite right. The truth is in the exchange of answers to the same impossible question.

Marija Brana died first, at the end of the forties.

She'd been sick ever since arriving in Ilidža. Her hips had given out, she sat on her sofa, her eyes laughing. And it seemed that this would last to the end of the world. We buried her in Sarajevo's Stup district, in a graveyard on top of which, forty years later, one of the entrances to the city would be built, a road that from its top takes in the entire cemetery and then, closer to the Stubler graves, flows into an avenue on its way to the center of town. I don't know where in that cemetery the graves of Marija Brana and Vasilj Nikolaevich can be found, under the kindred foreignness of Russian Cyrillic.

Vasilj Nikolaevich continued to visit after his wife's death. He might have even grown more talkative. Good and kind, a retiree with the smallest of office-worker pensions, this solid and upright man of the tsar lived a humble life.

Sarajevo was full of Russian émigrés. Well-off individuals, professors, doctors, forestry engineers, scientists, café keepers and waiters, script writers, indigents, impoverished counts, workers, drunks, good-for-nothings, burglars, and experts on all forms of locks, they were people of various kinds, but for the most part, Russian émigrés did not want to know about one another. Not a single one of them wanted to know about Vasilj Nikolaevich. Let him drop dead – every man lived for as long as he was allowed! While we were sort of surprised by this, there wasn't really any need to be.

Vasilj Nikolaevich died at the beginning of the sixties.

His death was long anticipated. There was no one whose name could be written on the death certificate. No brothers or relatives. And this was a time when every death needed to be recorded on a death certificate, which would be tacked up on tree trunks and telegraph poles. But Vasilj Nikolaevich was by then completely alone in this world. As alone as God.

In the end, he left the wallrugs to the Stublers. Though in the years of confusion, disorder, and disappearance, they were eaten through by moths. He'd also left a pocketwatch issued for an officer in the army of the tsar. The watch too, like everything else, has disappeared.

The Mushroom Prayer;
or, The Use of Learning

Ever since his early days in Dubrovnik, Opapa Karlo had collected encyclopedias. From the first days of spring until the first autumn rainfall, in the cool of the courtyard, sprawled on a deckchair or sitting at the garden table, he would explore the entries that had reached him that day along the river of time. Mahatma Gandhi had died. He looked up his name in the German and Yugoslav encyclopedias, lexicons, and handbooks. Having studied everything there, he moved on to new entries: India, Hinduism, Buddhism. And so on until the next day's afternoon rest, when some new event, a detail from everyday life, would lead him to take up the study of hydraulic pumps, blast furnaces, or Chilean saltpeter deposits.

And thus did the circle of his knowledge widen, knowledge never to be used, unless the use was in fact what that knowledge itself enabled him in contemplation. To his children and grandchildren Opapa Karlo imparted the belief that reading for its own sake was a very useful thing.

On a Sunday afternoon in the summer of 1947, he was sitting at the garden table, teaching his five-year-old granddaughter a song. Sixty-five years later, though she is now a seriously ill, demented old woman, she remembers every line:

The fly agaric's red cap
And all the puffy puffballs
Chanterelle, boletus
Opened their umbrellas
Praying to the Lord:
Rain, rain, give us rain
To make us grow and let more remain.

But she doesn't remember the name of the song. For our purposes, let's call it the "Mushroom Prayer." Mushrooms are, after all, the most mysterious phenomenon. They are only created in the wet parts of the forest, in the shade of deciduous trees. We don't know whether anyone has ever seen mushrooms at the moment of their sprouting.

No one knows in what book Opapa found the "Mushroom Prayer," or who wrote it. But somewhere in the Stubler home on Kasindol Street in Ilidža, under the sedimentary rocks of time, beneath brittle old newspapers, clothing, and documents, the wallrugs of Marija Brana, photo albums, medical test results, the faded X-rays of who knows whose lungs, magazines on gardening and on classical music, surely there still exists a book, buried and petrified, with that song in it, the "Mushroom Prayer."

The disarray of every home is the result of the disorder of people's lives, their intertwinings, attachments, and initiatives. It would be best, if possible, for everyone to move out when the father of the house dies, to go live elsewhere, where they can continue their lives, with new wardrobes and dressing tables and nightstands. The living would otherwise take on the lives and fates of the dead. They would bury their dead, threadbare shirts beneath the neatly folded shirts they still wore, their living shirts, and the house, with each passing death, would be transformed into a grave, the living dreaming the dreams of the deceased, afflicted by their own fears, until the sweet, salty, and bitter tastes of their own disintegrating lives began to settle sourly on their palate.

The disarray of the Stubler house was composed of fifty, or perhaps more, complete and incomplete lives surrounding the figure of Karlo Stubler, our innocent patriarch. That house was never put in order or cleaned out. Every instance of cleaning, or dusting, or purging of old things is an act of violence on a person's being and life. Every instance of cleaning is an accounting with one's own biography and the biographies of those close to us. A moment of our death and a reminder that nothing is lasting and everything moves toward oblivion.

Dusting requires either sheer courage or the complete absence of a soul.

But that disarray is also a grand metaphor for the interests and occupations of Karlo Stubler, something my relatives who continued to live on in that house were unable to throw out. Although the house on Kasindol is not mine, its disarray is still my disarray. If it could be put in order, if I had the strength and will for it, if I had the time, I could write a novel in which not a single name, personage, or event was invented. At its center would be Karlo Stubler, and all around him, chapter by chapter, all the Stublers I know of or would come to know of, those who lived with him and those who knew him well, even if they were born long after his death. Then the story would widen outward in concentric circles, telling of friends and neighbors, of people who lived along Kasindol Street, the long peripheral road that stretches out amid uncultivated land all the way to the new Butmir Airport, of the people Karlo Stubler and his family knew well, of their fates in life, how their fates were entangled with his, and of the fates of all their offspring, up until the present day.

Such a book, were it possible, would put in order the disarray of the house on Kasindol, the disarray of our souls, having sprung forth from a surplus of memory, but also from the fact that we did not clear away the dust. Such a book would leave us clean and new.

When he wasn't flipping through encyclopedias, following webs of associations about useless bits of knowledge, Karlo Stubler would read books on technical know-how. On beekeeping, gardening, fruit growing and agronomy, on steam locomotives, diesel engines, shunting, and a variety of railroad procedures – technical books on anything that might have been a subject of interest to him. And he was interested in anything that could be made, repaired, or transformed with one's hands. Any mechanical system, electrical device, car, truck, or plane interested him so much that he could become absorbed in the study of quite complex specialized manuals and university textbooks, losing himself in the subject as if it were a stimulating crime novel.

When on a hot summer evening, while the men would play preferans somewhere off in the cool and the women would make the rounds of the neighbors' houses for a cup of coffee, he would settle into his deck chair and study the functioning of hydrofoil engines or the use of cement in bridge construction. He never philosophized about what he had read, even if he were asked about something, but would respond somewhat shyly that he didn't know, he wasn't an expert in that. Most of what he studied remained with him, archived away in his head, never to be used. But can meaning really only be about use? Karlo Stubler read about engines and cement with the same sort of interest that one might read *War and Peace,* and no one's ever read that book to become a great general or lover.

He didn't care about card games. He had nothing against the others playing, but he himself didn't know the rules to even a single game. At the time, in the thirties, forties, and fifties, card playing was a very widespread way of using up one's free time, though it was generally thought to be a marker of bad taste, lower cultural or social status, so people often played in secret. Karlo Stubler didn't share the prejudices of his day. He didn't care if we played. Perhaps it even pleased him that we were spending time together that way, that we were happy, and that we'd have something to remember each other by. But about card playing itself he had no opinion at all. He didn't play, and that was that.

Karlo Stubler didn't play chess either. He wasn't inclined toward any social games. He did everything himself and needed others only for conversation. He told stories and listened patiently to the stories of others, trying not to let anything disturb, disrupt, or – God forbid – direct them in the telling.

It was important to him only that the children learn some things that they might remember throughout their lives. Something like a mushroom prayer.

The Balijan Summerhouse

When the Stublers moved to Kasindol Street, down a little farther toward the future tram tracks, there stood a luxurious summerhouse that belonged to the Balijan family. It was designed by the engineer Moravec, husband of Doctor Marija, for his father-in-law and all their family to enjoy. The elder Balijan was an Armenian, or a Jermen, as they said in Sarajevo. He had lived in Istanbul, where he'd obviously done well for himself, such that in 1915 when evil times arrived and the great nation of Osman decided to reform itself into something of a smaller Turkish nation, Balijan ran away toward the West, saving his neck in the process. As he'd set off at the right time, he didn't leave with empty pockets and was then able to purchase a house in his new homeland and continue to live well. He sent his daughter to Zagreb to study medicine, and in Ilidža, in accord with the old customs of Constantinople gentlemen – whose pastoral habits we would come to explore in Orhan Pamuk's *Istanbul* – he built a summerhouse where his family would spend their days from spring to fall. He would arrive as soon as the mountains turned green and stay until the first autumn frosts.

In the golden days of Tito's socialism, when Sarajevo was being built from the money that the large state factories made in Libya and across the countries of the Middle East, high-rises sprouted up all the way to below Stup and Otes, the city joined Ilidža, so that today Kasindol lies right on the edge of Sarajevo. But at the time when Balijan had his summerhouse built, in the thirties of the previous century, one came to Ilidža by train.

The Balijans would gather at the train station in Marjin Dvor, with their bags, suitcases, and supplies for the next several months, and the narrow-gauge local would transport them for the next half hour to Ilidža, from which they would set off on foot or, if they had too much luggage, on a villager's horse-drawn wagon, for their summerhouse.

This way of life was unusual for Sarajevo. People expressed surprise at the Balijans and their habits – and indeed Sarajevans liked more than anything to express surprise about anyone who differed from them – because there wasn't any sort of pastoral culture in the city. Those who kept summerhouses in Stoj-čevac and near Vrelo Bosne, Turks and Austrians, had long since gone away by then, leaving behind only those who didn't share their customs, or those who had thrown off such cultural habits in the intervening years – fearing that someone might identify them with defeated kingdoms or hateful occupiers.

But Nono Balijan had no such problems with historical heritage and cultural practices. He arrived in Sarajevo with the intention of living precisely as he had lived in Istanbul. Here of course everything was a bit smaller, closer, and some-how more practical, but the only thing he really lacked, for complete satisfaction, was the sea. Sarajevo was like Istanbul, captured in a crystal ball, but without the sea, likely because you could never fit such a body of water within the spherical confines of glass. Instead of leaving for somewhere far away, France, Italy, Germany, or America, where the exiled Jermens in fact often went, their children going on to become famous singers, actors, and authors, slightly changing their family names according to their new languages and cultures, Nono Balijan had gone to a place that seemed to him at the time – in the twenties and thirties – the most similar to that bygone Ottoman Constantinople in which the neighborhoods hummed and jingled with all the languages of the empire, each of which any small child understood. Praying to God, too, took place in countless, eternally opposed manners, such that in Constantinople, as now in Sarajevo, each person was of a different religion than, and a heathen to, his neighbor, though they understood one another all the same.

Perhaps Nono Balijan arrived in Sarajevo by chance, through a combination of circumstances, or maybe he chose it in just this manner. We will never know for sure.

Nona Balijan had the appearance of a refined European lady, while her husband seemed to us more like an Istanbul serasker from the previous century. He actually looked a bit like a villain from a heroic epic poem. We were afraid of old man Balijan until we got used to him. And once we'd got used to him, we would make our way down Kasindol to find him. We'd dart around his legs while all our enemies – the older boys, Ilidža's Gypsy kids, and anyone stronger than us – would run off in different directions, afraid of Nono Balijan. He was short, like all our Jermens, and was not particularly strong, nor did anyone ever hear of him threatening someone, but he looked like he could threaten. Later everyone got used to him, and his frightening appearance no longer protected us from the enemy *rayahs*.

Besides Marija, whom everyone called Mica, Nono and Nona Balijan had a son named Ivica. He was a handicraftsman and had neither the intelligence nor the ambition of his sister, but like his father he was beloved in Kasindol. He did not take after his paternal side or have anything Jermen-like or *stambolski* about him, but resembled rather the Sarajevans of his generation, the rather fickle youth born toward the end of the First World War and in the immediate postwar years, in whom was preserved the Ottoman partiality to an unhurried life and small, everyday pleasures that, in combination with the provincial fashions of Habsburg officialdom, produced a ruinous mental blend among all the witty Sarajevo layabouts, of the sort that we continued to see up until the 1980s.

Ivica Balijan fell in love with Štefica Reš – who was actually Stephania Resch – and she became his wife, with whom he would have two children – Alfred (Fredij) and Jasminka. They arrived during two years of the war, a fact that perhaps supports the hypothesis that neither Ivica nor Štefica experienced the war in particularly dramatic fashion. They came through it intact, the trouble arriving only in the summer of 1945. Stephania Resch was from somewhere in Vojvodina, a Swabian, a daughter of the Volk, though in the Balijan household, and even more so for the estranged Jermen that was Ivica, this was in no way an important subject. Perhaps all this was too complicated for him, his experience of the world, and the priorities of his life. If not, it means he was smart enough to know that living with such revelations was impossible while dying from them, God forbid, was quite possible indeed.

That summer Štefica lost all contact with her family. They disappeared as if swallowed up by the earth. She wrote to neighbors in Vojvodina, but they didn't know anything either, or at least they pretended not to. As the story spread through Kasindol about how the Partisans had been marching away Karlo Stubler when the Serbs from his neighborhood came to save him, led by the prominent, influential Partisan collaborator Aleksa Božić, the unhappy Štefica could only imagine what had happened with her loved ones. They'd been taken away, and for them there'd been no one to run to the train station to rescue them.

She was beginning to come to terms with the fact that they had disappeared and she would never see them again when, several months later, her mother appeared. Her husband had died in the camps, but she'd survived, that is if what remained of her could be called a life. The unfortunate woman was beside herself, deranged, lost. She could not finish a single thought, or explain what had happened to her or what she'd experienced. They thought she would get through it, but she never did. For years we would see her around Kasindol, talking to herself, marveling at the sky and the clouds, and strolling along the road beside the traffic marker that in 1992 would become the line of demarcation between warring soldiers, a noose strangling the city. She was always dressed in folkloric garb, which here on the fringes of Sarajevsko polje, in the depths of Bosnia, seemed distant and uncanny, just as the suffering of this woman seemed distant and uncanny. The war came to an end, people were poor, they bought their food and soap with rationing coupons, but everywhere the belief in a better future grew, a future that she didn't embody.

What had Karlo Stubler thought when he would see her passing by on the street?

The architect Moravec imagined the Balijan summerhouse through a twentieth-century vision. In front of the house he built a pool, designed with beauty and discretion, so that the children would be able to swim in the summer. By contrast to the pools of today, his was not visible from all angles, nor did the striking blue tiles clash with the harmony of the surrounding greenery or the earthen tones of the house and its environs. Actually, the entire area's landscape from spring until fall was brown, as in the abstract paintings of Ljubomir Perčinlić, so that the summerhouse and its pool attracted all the colors and nuances of Kasindol Street. In Stubler memory, it was the most beautiful house of the neighborhood, and even though it was foreign, it was there that the Stubler biographies were most inscribed, our family tree, all that we were but also all that we might have become if our fates and separations had not driven us in different directions.

On the cover of the historical-family novel entitled *The Stublers*, which would, like a small stone tossed into a calm pool, widen outward in concentric circles with the stories of the inhabitants of Kasindol Street and, very likely – after years of research, filming, photographing, and roaming around the Kasindol of today, along with collecting statements, memories, photocopies of documents and school diplomas, flipping through photo albums, examining city archives and police records and traveling across the world to speak with the scattered former inhabitants of Kasindol – would comprise several thousand pages and be released in five or six volumes, on the cover of that novel would be a photograph of the Balijan summerhouse, just as it was until the end of the fifties, when the Balijans sold it. But such a photo was probably never taken or was taken and lost forever, just as the novel itself will never be written. I mention it again here not in order to lament the things we've forgotten or remove the weeds from our graves but because I rather like these kinds of novels.

Doctor Marija Balijan and the engineer Moravec decided to move to Zagreb at the end of the fifties. This was a time when many of the Sarajevan *kuferaši* – Czechs, Slovaks, Germans, Slovenes, and Jermens, too – who had in the interim been nationally reborn as Croats – decided to move to Zagreb. They all had some reasons of their own, and all these reasons appeared simultaneously, for life had gotten easier, basic goods were no longer being rationed, the first imported goods were appearing in stores, there was more money, and even the real estate market, as one might put it today, had recovered.

And so the time had come for the sale of the summerhouse, and its eventual disappearance.

Nona Balijan, who was born in 1879, was five year older than Nono, and died before him, in 1956. Nono would die in 1962, outliving the sale of the summerhouse and its disappearance. We don't know whether he was touched by the news – probably he didn't care, what was done cannot be undone, as they said. The Balijans had vanished forever from Kasindol, the engineer Moravec having moved to Zagreb with his spouse. They had two daughters, Višnja and Ubavka. Ubavka died young, but by then the summerhouse had already been long gone.

After her mother's death, Štefica and Ivica continued living in Sarajevo with Fredij and Jasminka. Ivica died in time, in 1982, before the very end would come. Štefica survived this too: she died in 2000.

Their daughter Jasminka lived in Dobrinja. She had two children, Stela and Nikola. In 1993 or 1994, as was the case for most of the war, the city had no water or electricity. Jasminka and her daughter, Ivica and Štefica's granddaughter, went out for water. At the water site, as in a newly composed epic, the turbo-folk epic of Sarajevo's siege, a Serbian shell caught up with both of them, and they were killed.

The granddaughter and great-granddaughter of the Jermen who had managed to survive the Armenian genocide at the hands of the Turks, the granddaughter and great-granddaughter of the German who had survived the avenging hatred of the victors of the Second World War, perished in the genocide that Radovan Karadžić attempted to carry out upon a people to which, in the persistent cynicism of fate, Jasminka and Stela didn't even belong.

And by then, the Balijan summerhouse had long since ceased to be.

It had been bought by people who did not need a summerhouse but the kind of house where honest, hardworking villagers live. Nor did they need the engineer Moravec's architectural design but rather space in which to shelter themselves and their property from the rain, the cold, the heat, and the sunshine. And so they started adding to the summerhouse horizontally and vertically until before long it had lost its shape and become one of those monstrous, eternally unfinished structures we see on the outskirts of all our cities. There is nothing of Balijan left in the house. It's as if it has been swallowed up by oblivion, ravaged by Alzheimer's, and now, in place of the grand pastoral vision of Moravec, there is only fear in an eye that continues to look out but no longer recognizes anything.

In *Istanbul* Orhan Pamuk describes how, during his childhood, fires destroyed the abandoned wooden summerhouses of the Constantinople gentry. The fires broke out by accident, with some unknown homeless person lighting the first flames. But then others (perhaps those who came to replace the gentry forced out of the summerhouses) came and burned the houses down purposefully and methodically to make room and create lots where their own world would be built, with different memories and vistas. Nono Balijan's summerhouse did not go up in flames. While writing about certain people and their destinies, the writer has linked them together with others, whom he didn't know but who in his work do exist.

Confession Before
the Sacrament of Marriage

In the brief biography of Olga Rejc, née Stubler, it is noted that she gave birth to three children, two sons and a daughter. She lost her firstborn son when she was thirty-eight. We shall set to one side the story of the circumstances surrounding Mladen's death, though it was the most important event in the disappearance of the Stublers, an event that came to define us, though this was never uttered aloud, and Mladen's name was never mentioned, even if he, or our idea of him, hovered behind every one of our actions, for as long as Nona was alive.

There were no pictures of Mladen in the house where I grew up. Nona had destroyed them over the years. Whenever she came upon one, she'd tear it into the tiniest little pieces or expeditiously burn it in the stove. She was kept busy in this task for nearly forty years. Pictures tumbled out from all sides: from shoe-boxes in which useless family documents were kept, from old albums, from envelopes and thick books that had sat unopened, from the inside pockets of Nono's old jackets and overcoats, from drawers overflowing with doctor's prescriptions, diagnoses, and employment certifications; they appeared from every direction, and she doggedly annihilated them, taking care to do so unobserved. As if she were doing something shameful, as if she were in the toilet flushing down photographs of her eldest son, and it seemed as if all her work was for nought, for new ones continued to surface.

The last photograph I found was in 1983, in a pre-war Stanoje Stanojević encyclopedia volume. I didn't even know that it was my uncle Mladen in the photo: it showed a grade school classroom, two students sitting at their desks laughing. Their laughter was hysterical, hormonal, their faces distorted out of all proportion. Behind them, in the depth of the perspective, was a third boy with an angelic smile, calmly staring into the lens as if unaware of what was happening around him. That was Mladen.

The picture was almost a miniature, four by three centimeters, which was probably why it had survived so long unnoticed in the house.

I left it lying on the writing table in my little corner of the living room, and in the morning it was gone. That's how I knew it was Mladen in the picture. Nor could he have been one of the two boys with the distorted faces. He was the quiet one in the back. I remembered his face then.

Nona also destroyed all Mladen's school diplomas, his birth and death certificates, his letters, and his homework. There was not a single sheet of paper in the house that might have had his name written on it.

At the bottom of the wardrobe, under the winter things, she kept a wooden box of soil. Several months before her death, Nona spread that soil around the garden. After that as if on their own, odds and ends found their way to that box: postcards, receipts for electricity and television service, unused postage stamps. Grains of soil stuck to their adhesive back. Those grains were the last trace of Mladen in our apartment. It was soil from Mladen's grave in Donji Andrijevci, Slavonia, a grave that no longer exists.

But there were still papers, photographs, and letters among the layers of disarray in the Stubler home on Kasindol. Those she could not burn or wipe out.

Another thing we know of Olga Rejc is that she had at least one abortion.

In the winter of 1945, not long before the liberation, while Vjekoslav Luburić was cooking people alive in the basement of a Skenderija villa, and the Independent State of Croatia was, with the blessing of our archbishop Ivan "the

Evangelist" Sarić, squaring accounts with all those not living in accord with Jesus Christ and the Poglavnik Ante Pavelić, my Nona – who knows where or how in Sarajevo then – had her final abortion. If they had captured her, she and whoever had helped her would have found themselves among those hanging from their necks along the boulevard in Marijin Dvor. Those were the final moments of the Croatian state, no time to be fooling around by throwing some woman into the camps at Jasenovac. Also they were the final moments an abortion could have been carried out, for a month or two more and the fetus would have been too large to dispose of.

When Aunt Jele, Olga's sister-in-law, the wife of our uncle Karlo, once asked, "Good Lord, why isn't Franjo a little more careful?" Olga Rejc, née Stubler, my Nona, sighed and said, "Oh, my Franjo is an empty prick!"

This kind of unintentional wittiness was all the more impressive for the fact that intimate secrets would slip out without any sense of discretion – which among the Stublers was always quite clear and was why they so often betrayed it – and would be recounted in stories for years, even in front of Olga, who could not stand any allusions to the subject of sex.

Slipping out in this way, word got out that after the birth of his second son, Franjo Rejc had begun using condoms. But they were rather poorly made – that technology was just getting started – so sometimes they would fall off or break at just the crucial moment. Their daughter, born May 10, 1942, sixteen months before Mladen's death, was conceived and later came into the world despite the condom.

Just like my mother's, one might say my own birth was made possible by the inferior quality of the work of a certain Zagreb factory division charged with the fabrication of those delicate elastic products.

But perhaps one other circumstance was crucial.

The Independent State of Croatia was, in many ways, the herald of ideas, ideals, and political practices of the state that would emerge within those narrow borders some half century later. And as in Tuđman's Croatia, where the politics of procreation, or of the natural proliferation of Croats, was one of the main factors behind popular enthusiasm from day one, along with church incursions into the intimate life of that hitherto secular society, so in the Independent State of Croatia, following Hitlerite science and by then the multi-year Nazi strategy of procreation, the question of increased breeding was exceptionally important.

Besides this, abortion was punishable by death – a position staunchly supported even by the church fathers, for whom then, as today, the life of the unborn was more important and somehow holier than the lives of the born – and because condoms were in short supply, they would be snatched up the moment a new shipment arrived at the local pharmacy.

Everyday mythology is created and thus, gossip and rumors spread, along with disinformation – this was punishable, once again, by deportation to Jasenovac – but one of the most interesting, slightly humorous, slightly threatening rumors was that certain priests, in collaboration with the pharmacists, or even under the directive of the authorities, were using tiny needles to poke holes in the condoms.

That was a story told around Sarajevo in the fall of 1941. Likely it was made up, a joke, or barroom yarn, whose origins no one can know, but it was revised and elaborated upon through such countless retellings that in the end it started to sound authentic. Even too authentic. So authentic that there was no way it could be true. To the extent that anyone might find even a grain of truth in it, that grain of truth would not be worth accepting, let alone believing.

This is what my grandfather Franjo Rejc was thinking as he was buying condoms through a connection of his at the pharmacy on the city's main street, which in those days, in the fall of 1941, had not yet been named after Poglavnik Ante Pavelić, since the Croatian leaders in Zagreb were still deciding whether it was necessary for every large Croatian city's main street to bear the name of either the Poglavnik Pavelić or the Führer Hitler. Franjo Rejc despised them both, but by no means did he believe that devout priests were going around to the pharmacies in the dead of night to poke holes in condoms so children would be born. Just as it is for a rich man to enter the heavenly kingdom through the eye of a needle, so it is in a dark, godless time for a Catholic or a Muslim, a true Croat, to enter this world, this vale of tears, through the tiniest of rips in a condom. Nine months later, on May 10, 1942, a child weighing barely two kilograms was born in Sarajevo's Koševo Hospital.

Whether my Nono's condom slipped off, or it broke at the crucial moment, he could never remember. Maybe he forgot, although men rarely forget such events, especially when they don't want to have a child.

From my perspective, precisely at the sunset of the Stubler line, in the mystery of my eventual birth, alongside a variety of other coincidental, cryptic, and unlucky circumstances, the following two factors remain noteworthy: the poor quality of Zagreb-manufactured condoms, and the Catholic shepherd yearning for as many lambs as possible to be born by the following spring.

My Nona didn't want to talk about any of this, not even after time had passed – for her all the born or unborn children had become one and the same. Furious, she would say it was all bullshit and only old bullshitters like Franjo's card buddies talked about such things.

On most other subjects, in her attitudes toward life, politics, and religion, she was a liberal. She was far freer of the norms that would hold sway in the social circles in which, a quarter century later, her descendants would live. But on the subject of sex and everything that followed from it she was as hard and closed as an abbess, as someone concealing a great secret or misfortune.

It was usually assumed that all her life's adversity was tied up with Mladen and his death. Her youngest child, that tiny girl born on May 10, 1942, she would never really to the very end accept or come to love. The circumstances of this rejection were perhaps of an instinctual, animal nature.

Like a she-wolf, she unconsciously linked my mother's birth with the death of her oldest cub. And she never forgave her youngest daughter for it. She could not forgive her, for if she did, then her troubled conscience over Mladen's death would have driven her crazy, torn her to pieces.

She was to blame for her son's death.

The little girl's life stood as a reminder.

Everything that was to happen from the fall of 1943 to the spring of 1986, from the day of Mladen's death to the day Mladen's mother, my Nona, died, would be defined by that troubled conscience, by a guilt which for me is deeper and more frightening than any other Croatian or inner human guilt. She had not murdered Mladen, but she'd done something that, according to the undying conviction of the heart, which is carried from generation to generation – wounding some for life, imparting to others one's own sense of guilt – was equal to murder or perhaps exceeds it: she had interfered, as a mother, in his destiny and, as a result, betrayed him to his murderers. Mladen would be alive if she had not made his decision for him.

There was a clear and unbroken line in Olga's case from sex to birth to death.

If there hadn't been those shadowy evenings in Doboj, if Franjo Rejc hadn't caught her unawares and got her pregnant, if Karlo Stubler had not blessed – even if unwillingly – their marriage, if several months later Mladen had not been born, then neither his death nor her guilt would have come to pass.

That, perhaps, is how things looked to her or to her demons.

But in that most intimate form of chattering and burbling after the Stublers were no more, in the sick-bed expansiveness of despair, near the twilight of Olga's youngest child's own life, to the story of Mladen was added another chapter, warped and wound up in the previous one, creating something that was more difficult and complex than any written or spoken story could be, whether true or invented, but which often ends up happening when relaying a person's life, especially after we have thought and spoken about that person from the perspective of their grave.

But before this, and before her church wedding – there could have been no other kind at the time – Olga Stubler had had to go to confession.

This happened in Doboj or Usora. We no longer know the name of the church or of the confessor. But this act of faith before God, or before his delegate, was something that weighed on her heavily, more heavily than the abortion. She cried for a long time that day and again the next. It is not known whether she told anyone why she was crying. If she did, it was not conveyed further. But then, in Doboj or Usora, in the confessional of some little, isolated Bosnian church with all its various superstitions, Olga's spiritual world shattered.

Since her childhood in Dubrovnik she had been religious. As is known to be the case with children who have a strong and lively imagination, one capable of picturing everything, even the good Lord, differently from how it is in catechism, she had a very rich and fanciful inner life, filled with angels, saints, and holy tales. She did not get this from her father, or her mother – Johanna Stubler had a meager imagination and unassertive authority – and while her elder brother Rudi might have taught her something, as he was a firm believer to the end, she would nevertheless develop her own private God and, around him, a picturesque heaven, rich in holy flora and fauna, like a primeval Amazonian rain forest, filled with manifestations, as on the Russo-French battlefields of a Tolstoy novel.

We know nothing about what her confessor said to her or how serious the sins she confided to him might have been. But if we look for clues in our own memories and those of our family to ascertain what really happened, who had what on her or his conscience and what, aside from history, life in foreign parts, and unstable loves, led to the demise of the Stublers, then we can begin to presume what some Bosnian priest, Franciscan friar, or episcopal shepherd under Archbishop Josef Stadler might have said to a sixteen-year-old girl who came to him for confession before the conferral of the sacrament of marriage.

We aren't sure that Olga was pregnant at the time. But still it's unlikely that she was not.

Not even in old age did Nona dissemble or try to soften everyday reality by slight circumventions of the truth. She never lied to me, and she would get angry, more than might be expected, anytime I as a young boy lied even a little. She would be as horrified by this as if a grown man had lied to her. She never attempted to get out of trouble by lying, and she did not want me to resort to doing so either. (In this she ended up doing me a disservice. I lie, it makes me nauseous, and then I must convince myself that what I have made up is true.)

She didn't conceal the motive behind her marriage to her confessor.

The belly, though showing little, continued to grow. As did the powerful, incomprehensible, devastating sin that must have come before it. She did not want to lie, and she had faith in God. That faith was based not on fear but on the personal connection she felt. Had she feared God, she would have remained a believer forever. The bond was severed when the God who she had so much faith in allowed Mladen's death.

What did a confessor in the 1920s in the backwoods of Bosnia, then still in the grips of its Oriental destiny, say to pregnant young girls who had shown up for confession?

Coming after the 1878 departure of the Ottomans and the arrival of Western authority, it was a time of free love. With the Austrians came entertainment with dancing, electric lighting, officers' balls, a postal service, the railroad and telegraph, and everything suddenly started swirling like a merry-go-round, and life, which had been spilling outward from the interiors of homes and courtyard walls, suddenly became public – for Christian daughters as well as sons – for not only did the new authorities have nothing against all this, they even validated the new morality with a certain openness and sociability.

There were no statistics at the time about such matters, but leafing through old newspapers, reading novels and stories by the writers of the day, and above all, listening to family stories, teaches us that in every Bosnian backwater and in every Christian family there were legends, mostly tragic, and memories and accounts of young women, girls really, who got carried away, ended up pregnant, and paid for it with their lives, or gave birth to illegitimate children and, like loose women of the Old Testament, were ostracized by their communities and families, or saved themselves by jumping off cliffs, slitting their wrists, or drowning themselves in a river, or if lucky enough – if this could actually be considered luck – they'd be rescued from the shame of it all through marriage.

What did the confessor say in such cases?

He likely was not compassionate, nor would her future husband be.

This was the moment when the Bosnian priest – whose identity we could determine if we had the time and means to travel to Doboj and Usora and verify in the church records the names of the clergymen serving and confessing people in those parishes in 1921 and 1922 – directed the life and fate of Olga Stubler, the future Olga Rejc.

All at once, in place of her pastoral inner world populated with spirits, creatures, and occurrences, the church's gray walls rose up, frozen and empty. Her God suddenly turned Christian, Catholic, average, becoming like the God and vision of the priest himself and his little flock, and also like so many other Bosnian priests and all their little congregations. When he becomes ordinary, God can make the institutions of the Church powerful and influential, but such a God is also weary, exhausted, and hollow, an old man on the verge of disappearing altogether.

The fact that Nona could not tolerate conversations about sex and was so closed off and resistant that her youngest surviving child, in moments of all-consuming resignation, would say her mother found sex disgusting, must stand in some contrast to the fact that as a sixteen-year-old girl she slept with a railroad worker eight years her senior.

Rail men were well paid, and Franjo must have impressed her from that angle too. He was an upright young man, well built, intelligent, kind, and with a handsome face. There could not have been many such attractive, well-educated rail workers in Doboj, while she, dignified by nature and a Dubrovnik native to boot, a schoolgirl from a German family studying in an Italian high school, must have been looking for someone just like him.

But where in the world, and how, had she so quickly and easily slept with him?

Olga was Karlo's youngest child, after a son and two daughters. He seems to have expected another boy, but it'd turned out to be a third girl instead. The most intelligent, most gifted, most lively in both body and soul.

He was proud of her, more so than of his other two daughters. His son Rudi was an excellent student, but physically he was delicate, more tender even than his sisters. Olga, on the other hand, was strong and solid, as agile as a ballerina. If she had been born in Berlin or Paris, she would have been a suffragette. She took up swimming in Dubrovnik. At the time, during the First World War, it was not yet customary for female children to engage in sports. But she swam and he was proud.

As a fourteen-year-old girl, in the summer of 1919, the year before Karlo Stubler's banishment from Dubrovnik, Olga placed third in a race held in the port of Gruž, for which she won a medal. Her father was beside himself with joy. He would often talk about that great day, even when nothing remained that resembled that summer of 1919.

She was competing then with kids older than she was, the sole girl swimmer among boys. Dubrovnik residents were a little scandalized, but in Dubrovnik, too, Stubler was a Swabian, which meant that for him different rules applied.

In moments of anger, when blaming her mother Olga for her own life's missed opportunities, the daughter would say her mother was – in all likelihood – attracted to women but never dared admit it, let alone act on it. That was why she refused with such repugnance to talk about sex, and the race in the Gruž harbor was just a nice scene from a film or an episode from a novel, not proof of anything, though such stories in real life often communicate something that cannot be proven or verified.

But what about the teacher in Usora she cheated on Franjo with?

Maybe he merely served to prove to herself that sex with men made her sick.

Is all this even possible? I don't know. My job is investigation, into the past, into memories, and nothing in it is real except for the Stublers. And they aren't really real either. We are a family of phantoms and spirits.

My mother, her daughter, thought she'd shock me by maintaining that my Nona was an unfulfilled lesbian. That it would be difficult and painful for me too, as it had been for her, and that she would not be alone in her sickness and the unfulfilled nature of her relations with her father and mother, which, I always knew, were not good.

I listened to her, my mother that is, and it occurred to me that a person at the end of her life, in old age and sickness, might try to continue the quarrels with her own long-dead parents. Perhaps that was how one was able to slowly cross from one side to the other.

And perhaps it was about revenge too: she knew Nona was much more important in my life than she was. Nona's memory shaped me, for from it I am kin to something, or rather what I am by language and culture – the surest and strongest center, the foundation of a separate identity, a house, family, and homeland – is really by grace of being her grandson. Everything else is in flux.

Perhaps my mother was trying to get back at me by saying Nona was a lesbian.

Could be, but this too is an improvisation. The stringing together of memories, living and invented, imagined, false, phantom-like memories with which one fills the emptiness, while the memories multiply, before swallowing each of us up one day. Death is a tiny rip in the universe.

To me, my new lesbian Nona would be just as dear. Besides being pure in her unhappiness and suffering, she confirms, in narrative and in reality, the completeness of my own isolation, a stone with which one more window is sealed up that used to look out onto the wide and all-pervading foreign world.

The thought of her lesbianism is even a consolation compared to the story of Mladen's death and her own. Perhaps this is what makes it seem so implausible – because in fact there is no such consolation.

Germans in Sarajevo

In the colony of huts that began in front of the destroyed temple and widened out along a muddy wasteland shielded on two sides by the rows of buildings along Yugoslav National Army Street and the Obala Vojvode Stepe tramline, extending all the way to the First Gymnasium, there lived Germans from Vojvodina and Slavonia who had been driven out when those regions were cleansed of the servants of the occupier, and of any ethnically unacceptable population. After having collected them all at the end of the war into deportation camps which, in terms of living conditions, in terms of cold, hunger, and epidemics of infectious diseases, resembled Nazi concentration camps, the Partisans attempted, unsuccessfully, to have them transported to Germany. Razed to the ground and occupied by Allied forces, Germany was unable to care for its own citizens, and so the cattle cars filled with people were turned back from the border, or never even set out for that ominous fatherland that these people were being required to accept in place of their lost *Heimat*. Both were their homeland, and the differences in the meanings of these words would be defined afterward by the destinies of millions of displaced persons.

In order not to have to form camps again – since they themselves were probably aware of the uncomfortable associations and ominous similarities with those of the Nazis – the former Partisans resettled the Volk families across Yugoslavia, in barracks and abandoned refugee settlements, where they would wait to be driven away in the end. This would go on for years, while Germany was being rebuilt and renewed, and they would die of misery, despair, and old age, repaying their own debts and those of others, until finally being resettled in a land where they would forever be foreigners while their children would be Germans who had sacrificed their own family memory in the name of collective responsibility.

At the time this story begins, in late summer 1946, these people had been delivered via cattle car to the old train station at Marijin Dvor, from which they were led by military escort to the very center of Sarajevo, the Jewish temple, and to some abandoned barracks whose previous purpose remains unknown to us.

The very next day, the chairman of the Local Party Committee, climbed to the top floor, the fifth landing (the elevator long since out of order) in a building on Yugoslav National Army Street, just next to the Temple. He rang the buzzer next to a plate that said Franjo Rejc and asked to speak to Comrade Olga.

"This is she," she said.

"May I come in?"

And in he came, but she was undisturbed. This might seem strange but we were never frightened when, in the course of the Stubler history, representatives of the authorities descended on our home. I suppose we were slow on the uptake, though as time went on we would glance at one another in silent questioning of what some person wanted from us, beyond what he had said he wanted.

The president of the Local Party Committee knew Olga spoke German and, moreover, spoke it extremely well, so well that under different circumstances it might have been suspect, and he offered to put her in charge of the distribution of ration coupons and booklets for the precinct's provisions. In exchange, her family would be placed into a higher provisions rationing category and would receive better American canned goods and more flour, oil, soap, and powdered milk.

Thus did my Nona get the first job of her life, becoming the main link between the world of the *Volkdeutsche* barracks and the city in which the barracks found themselves. Besides the fact that the corralled Germans lived in deathly fear of anyone who approached them or happened to enter their hidden colony on some errand, these people avoided the most innocent of contacts with the city's residents, refusing even the most casual of kindnesses.

It was as if they were trying to avoid even the possibility of treading on the Sarajevo asphalt or in any other way inscribing their lives and fates into the city's history. There are no newspaper accounts of their stay in Sarajevo, no historical document or testimonial texts. Some seventy years later there is no corroboration that a colony of German barracks even existed. These people never were.

Around the same time as these confined unfortunates, German technicians and specialists began to arrive in Sarajevo with their families. They came from the east and the west of Germany, from destroyed and abandoned industrial centers, as the first postwar European guest workers. Engineers, mechanics, electricians, contractors, and architects, people with university degrees and high-level specializations in their professions, all came to Sarajevo to work and make money, to endure until such time as their countries lifted themselves up, renewed, and they and their knowledge would be needed once again back in Germany.

When they arrived, they were housed in the Hotel Pošta on Kulović Street. They lived there, were provided for, and taken care of. Following the wartime horrors and life among the Allied bombings, following twelve years of Hitler's rule, in the course of which each person well knew how much they each had suffered, or what had burdened their conscience, these Germans must have found their arrival in Sarajevo as a kind of disencumbering of body and soul. The men quickly adapted to the local work routine, befriended the other workers, and little by little learned the language. Of all the Germans in Sarajevo, and the city had observed all sorts and sundries since 1878, these were somehow the most open and friendly. They were overjoyed whenever they met someone who knew German, and our apartment on Yugoslav National Army Street, formerly Tašli-hanski Street, was often filled with Germans. Olga and Franjo befriended them without any hesitation and visited them at their homes, and many years later, as a retiree, Franjo would work part-time as a bookkeeper at the Hotel Pošta (by then the Germans had long since departed) without feeling at all burdened by the horrors of the war years. It wouldn't have occurred to him that one of these people might have committed murder in Ukraine or Belarus, or that one of these skilled engineers might have built the gas chambers of Auschwitz. If they had ever suspected this, it would merely have deepened their own grief and suffering, for Mladen too had died in a German uniform.

There aren't even a hundred steps between the Hotel Pošta and the Temple. There was no wall between these Germans and those, or any visible barriers. It is very unlikely that the authorities kept track of whether the displaced Banat Swabians from their barracks had any communication with the German engineers and craftsmen from the Hotel Pošta. They didn't even have to do this, since fortune and misfortune were so clearly evident among the divided peoples at the time that there was no way of mixing themselves up in it. And although these émigrés were united by language and belonged to the same people, they were as distant from each other as they were from Jews, Serbs, or Croats.

There was, however, another collection of Germans in Sarajevo, the domestic ones, those who had not been compromised during the war and who, after 1945, continued to live their normal lives. By contrast to Karlo Stubler, who had lived on the very edge of the city, whom they would have sent off to a deportation camp had it not been for Aleksa Božić and the Serbs from Kasindol, no one touched the Germans and Austrians who lived in the apartment buildings at the city's center. Of course everyone knew what each of them was doing and where they had been from April 1941 to April 1945, and no one forgave anything of anyone. But if they had done nothing wrong, they continued to live afterward like the rest of the world. And once again in 1946 and the years that followed one could hear German being spoken on the city's main thoroughfare of Tito Street, and in the cafés across town. It was their language, and they spoke it loudly, as Sarajevans do as a rule, so that a traveler might have thought all the town's inhabitants were a little hard of hearing.

These people, like Olga and Franjo, spoke readily and made friends with the specialists from the Hotel Pošta, while the unfortunates from the barracks avoided them, just as they avoided every other Sarajevo resident who might have chanced to approach them or enter their hidden colony on some errand.

In the early spring of 1947, before the Hotel Pošta, with their bags and cardboard suitcases, appeared Mr. and Mrs. Püframent. Tall and blond, Mr. Püframent was one of those ideal Germans who some fifteen years later would come through in their Opel Olympias on their way to the Adriatic, while his wife, an attractive Swabian with a healthy, pink complexion, tried to keep their two children in line, at least until someone from the hotel's front desk might check them into their room, where they could run wild . . .

Mechanical engineer Heinrich Klaus Püframent found employment at the railway works. He was charged with overseeing the repair of steam locomotives and switching engines, and with exploring the possibility of bringing on line the rolling stock that, during the war years, had been utterly neglected and ravaged by the sabotage tactics of the Partisan underground, engineers, switchmen, and technicians from the works. The identities of these individuals were, for the most part, never uncovered and the Party's railroad network was never broken, not even during the several terrifying weeks of Vjekoslav Luburić's reign of terror, and so the engineer Püframent's work was, among other things, to teach the technicians how, in the name of public good, to repair the machinery that, during the war, also in the name of public good, they had ruined.

People welcomed the German engineer warmly, the work proceeded apace, and with the work, social life. This is how the engineer met Franjo – by then a high-ranking railway official in a neat and well-pressed suit, not often seen in the early days of socialism – who spoke *Hochdeutsch* with no accent, so that Püframent, who was already accustomed to the Sarajevans' distorted variant of Viennese German, was so surprised that he assumed Mr. Rejc was a German.

"No, I'm not German, I'm Slovene. My father-in-law is German."

Püframent was bewildered by how having a German father-in-law would enable one to speak the language of Thomas Mann, but asked no questions. After all, in this country, he was a guest with the awkward reputation of a former occupier. Regardless, he did not believe Franjo one bit. He would later confess, laughing, that he'd thought Comrade Rejc was a Soviet charged with keeping this Yugoslav collaboration with German experts under control.

Before long the Püframents began visiting us every Friday. Mrs. Püframent and Nona would oversee the preparation of a poor man's feast in the kitchen and, while potatoes in the crust baked in the oven, would exchange recipes for stew, chocolate cake, and "rabbit à la vild," though probably neither woman hoped to ever use these recipes or believed that there would ever come a time when they might once again eat as they had long ago. Nona would recall times from before the war, while Mrs. Püframent didn't wish to recall anything as a rule, or did not wish to speak about the times she was willing to recall.

At the same time, Franjo would be discussing world politics and the future of the railroads with the engineer in the living room. Afterward, each of them would praise the intellect and culture of the other to their respective wives, but never would they ask each other what they did during the war. The Püframents knew that Olga and Franjo had lost their son in the war, but they didn't dare to ask how Mladen had died, on which side or in what uniform. And Olga and Franjo in turn did not ask the Püframents what they had been doing at the time, or how they'd lived or where.

Meanwhile the children would run wild through the house.

Their daughter's name was Wiebke, and she was the same age as the Rejcs' daughter. Uwe, her little brother, was an active – which is to say, mischievous – child, only ever looking for what he could climb, what he could break, and, in the end, what he could dive off toward certain death.

The girls would run after him, shouting, "No, Uwe! No, Uwe!" just as they had heard Mrs. Püframent do, but he did not hear them, just as he did not hear his mother, and just kept right on climbing the walls in defiance of gravity while the two precocious girls would punish him with slaps on his backside, which Uwe would also defy, and in fact they could thrash him all they liked, he merely wriggled out from under them and dashed off to something else. He would climb the walls, run in circles, cling to the ceiling – No, Uwe, you'll fall on your head! But he wouldn't listen to his father either.

If he hadn't been a living boy, insensitive to pain, but rather a metaphor, then Uwe Püframent would have been a German metaphor. But real people cannot be metaphors, not even the smallest of children.

And thus would Uwe run wild through our apartment every Friday, while no one could stop him. The girl would be overjoyed, for then her family's melancholy home would come alive, and for a few hours no one would think about the irrevocable past or blame anyone for anything, and everyone was dear and loved.

The ration booklets for provisions were distributed on Saturday mornings: sometimes once a month, others every two weeks, still others every Saturday. This depended on the unverifiable, clandestine rhythms and rules of bureaucracy, about which we didn't dare ask.

Olga Stubler, known as Comrade Rejc, would take her daughter with her. From the fourth floor on which they lived – or rather the fifth, since the first floor was for some unknown reason called the "upper ground floor" – there were more steps than from the building's entrance to the first door of the barrack.

As soon as they caught sight of Comrade Rejc and the young girl, the expelled Germans would run for cover inside their huts, hiding and pretending to be invisible. They behaved as if they were the fearful natives of some wondrous, unexplored African territory. Except they were white.

Olga took the young girl with her, hoping in vain that they would not be so afraid and with her help Olga would be able to get closer to them. This never happened.

There were very few adult men in the colony. Some old men, a lame young-ster, another who was missing an arm, and two others who didn't seem to be missing any limbs. The women were all wearing traditional dress. In wide, gathered skirts, with dark blouses and head kerchiefs, they looked completely out of place. Like characters in a book that, by some mistake of the designer and printer, had found themselves in the wrong story and now were unable to escape.

The young girls wore miniature versions of the same gathered skirts with dark blouses and head kerchiefs.

The men spoke our language, but not the women. Either they were pretending not to understand it, or they didn't. This was unusual, since the old people spoke Serbo-Croatian like natives. They had a drawl like everyone from Vojvodina, but their pronunciation sounded completely domestic and attractive. It seemed unlikely to us that Germans would speak this way. If they even knew our language, we thought, they had to speak it somehow more rudely. They had to talk, we said, like the people from Romanija, in the eastern part of Bosnia and Herzegovina, or from Kalesija in the northeast, but not like this. It was almost enough to make a person suspect that maybe they weren't Germans at all, and that someone had made a terrible mistake in driving them from their homes, which were no longer theirs anymore but rather had become our liberated houses.

In September of 1949, in the hungry days when due to Tito's revisionism the country was isolated from the people's democracies and barely accepted in the West because of our path into socialism and attitudes toward enemies of the revolution, Franjo and Olga's daughter was in the same grade as the children of the expelled Germans.

Mihailo, who would become Michael if he survived, was very aggressive. The moment anyone looked at him sideways, he would start a fistfight. Without the least bit of guile that some children have, deprived of any need that others should like him, dirty and covered in welts, Mihailo fought for his life like an animal. Of all the shapes of desperation in this long story of the Stublers, Mihailo's despair is the greatest, even if his family name has been forgotten.

Laura and Maria wore gathered skirts like their mother but removed the kerchiefs from their heads. This was the only sign that they'd started going to school.

Laura spoke to no one and cried constantly. When the other children quickly formed into groups and ran to the courtyard during recess, she stayed in the classroom and wept. At the beginning she cried from grief and misery, but later she cried out of habit, not knowing what else to do. She cried for the same reasons that Mihailo got into fights. But she was reconciled to her own end. If she's survived, Laura is a seventy-year-old German retiree today.

Of the three of them, Maria was the strongest. If another girl took exception to her, she would yank furiously on her pigtail or braid. She was loud and authoritative, interrupted the teacher, spoke up impatiently when she knew the answer to some difficult math question. If we hadn't known whose daughter she was and where she was from, if her name was not Maria, with an accent on the *i*, but instead was Marija, we would have seen in her a typical Sarajevo girl, sharp and promising, soon on her way to becoming a squad leader in the youth work actions of Bosnian Highway '59, or a member of the Communist Party of Yugoslavia, a valued and active participant in the workers' collective . . .

But Maria too was destined for exile.

The teachers treated the young Swabians the same way they treated all their other students. They were strict and impartial, in accord with the meager resources of the day and the proclamations of the proletarian international, guided by old-fashioned pedagogical rules, they publicly recognized the good students and, also publicly shamed the bad ones. But they didn't know what to do in the face of Laura's weeping, which was so out of harmony with the atmosphere of general optimism and which somehow lay heavily on their adult consciences.

The teacher would come up to Laura and stroke her head. And then everyone would see Laura's shoulders heaving. The teacher would quickly pull her hand away, as if she had touched a hot stove with the tips of her fingers. Several days later, having forgotten, she'd again stroke Laura's head. And everything would start over.

In the spring of 1952, Mihailo, Maria, and Laura stopped coming to school. Before the beginning of the first class, the teacher said they had moved away. Where to? someone asked. To Germany, she answered quietly. And that was all, in effect, that would be said for the next sixty years. No one even noticed that the women with the gathered skirts who didn't speak our language had disappeared, along with their fathers and grandfathers with their drawling, welcoming Vojvodina accent.

Suddenly there were no more barracks, renovation and construction were in full swing, new houses had sprouted on what had been a muddy wasteland, and even the Temple would soon be restored. The Jews of Sarajevo would make a gift of it to their city, and it was there that the most acoustically attractive concert hall in Bosnia and Herzegovina would be built. So that it didn't ring hollow when there were no concerts, in the seventies and eighties daily movie screenings were held, mostly action films. And since it was always cool inside, the Sarajevo layabouts and Roma children would cool off and take their siestas at the morning and early afternoon screenings in the hottest days of July and August.

Of the five or six years that the Banat Swabians spent in Sarajevo there is no trace in journalistic accounts, chronicles, or novels inspired by those days. Sad and frightened, they passed through the city like a summer downpour, after which the asphalt quickly dries. Even by the next day no one remembers it. Except for the children who were in class, though they too would soon forget Maria, Laura, or Mihailo, whose pages in her grade book their teacher crossed out, with the help of a ruler and fountain pen, carefully tracing a line from the upper left corner to the lower right, and writing in her best penmanship across the middle, over grades that no one cared about anymore, in science and society, mathematics and Serbo-Croatian: *relocated*.

She did the same for the two girls. The bureaucratic language avoided emotion and any feeling of closeness to those who were no more, and sometimes a gendered pronoun can function as an unnecessary and dangerous emotion for the wary, bureaucratic mind.

At the time of their resettlement and disappearance, the engineer Püframent was still living with his wife and children in the Hotel Pošta. And they continued to come visit us on Fridays. Uwe and Wiebke started school and spoke Serbo-Croatian as we did, and everything was normal and ordinary. Only the coffee was no longer the substitute kind, made from over-roasted barley, but real coffee, Ethiopian.

Franjo and Olga also became friends with an engineer named Petstotnik and his wife, also Germans from the Hotel Pošta, but in 1949 they suddenly had to return to Germany. The *Befehl* came one Friday, ordering them to be on a special train in the early morning on Monday, which would bypass the regular lines and timetables, taking them through Hungary to Dresden, a city so obliterated during the bombing that it practically ceased to exist in 1945. The Petstotniks had been born in Dresden, and their parents were from there. One day in late winter or early spring of 1945 the sirens had begun to howl and the two of them, being disciplined Germans, went down into a shelter. When they came back out,

Dresden was no more. None of their friends or relatives made it, and no one and nothing was left of the city. They did not feel fear or sorrow for their loss, for everything had so suddenly and thoroughly disappeared that a person just did not have time for ordinary emotions. And in the end, fear too was just another ordinary emotion.

The one thing that happened that day and night, and the next day and night, was that Mrs. Petstotnik lost the ability to get pregnant. Neither of them was able to assess precisely the relationship between the American bombs and her fertility, but Nono and especially Nona, took them at their word.

A veil of grief settled over Mrs. Petstotnik when the order came for them to return to Dresden. She could not stop crying when they came to say goodbye early Sunday morning. Mr. Petstotnik was serious and spoke about the next day's journey as something that needed to be undertaken with complete professionalism. Fate was like an engine in need of repair.

They brought us things that they would not be able to take with them in the rush: a porcelain tea service and two monogrammed silver spoons. In the half century that followed the tea service would gradually break – I created a fictional episode in the novel *Dogs at the Lake* that was based on it – and one of the teaspoons would be lost, the other is still around as living proof that the Petstotniks had once lived in Sarajevo.

The suggestion that the Petstotniks stay was on the tips of Olga's and Franjo's tongues that Sunday in February 1949, but the words remained unspoken. Neither of them liked Stalin or Walter Ulbricht, not a trace of their property in Dresden was left, and in these two or three years in Sarajevo they had come to feel completely at home, made friends, learned the language, and so there was absolutely no reason for them to set off on Monday from the old railway station at Čengić vila with just a couple of cardboard suitcases toward East Germany, whose Communist Party had condemned the revisionism of their Yugoslav comrades as a betrayal of the proletarian international and an example of Marshal Tito's grandiose historical adventurism.

Olga went with them to the station. It was not yet dawn when the train carrying the Petstotniks set off. We would never hear anything from them again. They promised to write, but no letters ever came. They left behind a peculiar sense of insecurity and a slight but insistent sense of guilt – the Petstoniks might well have stayed had the suggestion merely crossed the lips of Franjo or Olga.

But the Stublers so rarely interfered with their own destinies that it would have been uncharacteristic of them to meddle so directly with the fates of others.

Frau Maria Püframent had become pregnant with her third child in Sarajevo. For her engineer husband and herself this was an occasion for great joy. Wiebke and Uwe were happy because they would get a kid sister or brother. By contrast to them, their sibling would be a born Sarajevan and true Yugoslav, which would make the two of them a little less German and more *ours*. No one had said anything ugly to them just because they were Germans, but still Wiebke and Uwe so wanted to be thoroughly *ours*.

She was in her sixth month, when one day standing in line for bread. It was no longer the time of the worst postwar hunger and shortages, but people continued to stand in lines and, for luxury items, they would until the very end of Yugoslav history.

Frau Maria, in the meantime, still stood in line for bread, with the memory of the war still quite vivid. In truth, Sarajevo prided itself then as it would a half century later, on never questioning nationality or the particular God prayed to, which explains why the majority of the Germans from the Hotel Pošta grew so easily used to the local customs and mentality and adopted them as their own. And so it happened that, deceived by someone else's kindness, or maybe already having become a little Bosnian herself, Frau Maria ended up in an argument with another woman, a nosy, prying gossip, Christian or Muslim – it made no difference in this case – about who was in front of whom in the line for bread. No one knows who was in the right, nor does it matter.

But when the woman understood from Frau Maria's person or speech that she was German, she kicked Frau Maria with all her might in the stomach.

That same afternoon, in the Koševo hospital, Frau Maria and the engineer Heinrich Klaus Püframent lost a child, whose facial features and sex were already clear. We did not ask whether it had been a boy or a girl.

Maria told Olga what had happened in the bread line. Every detail.

It was unpleasant for her to hear all this, to the point where she almost felt guilty, and she said something ugly about a woman capable of kicking a pregnant woman in the belly and railed against what she imagined that woman's identity to be, or about Bosnia in general, where such women lived.

"You mustn't speak that way," said Mrs. Püframent. "Who knows what torments her life was stitched from?"

She actually said this somewhat differently since the two of them only spoke German together, but the story in the Rejc and Stubler households was passed on so that each time it was told this very folklike phrase, which is perhaps not possible to translate into German, would be repeated: who knows what kind of torments her life was stitched from?

Whenever we came back to this event, and to Nona's exchange with Mrs. Püframent, we would not comment on the backstory. Or perhaps we weren't aware of it while there were still Germans from the Hotel Pošta, among them the Püframents, in our lives. Besides the history was still too fresh, between us and them there was always something we didn't talk about, something about which we kept silent or were simply unable to put into words.

This unspoken something later becomes the impetus for a story, or for literature itself. And had there been a writer there, a writer with talent and time, a saga might have been written, or a novel in frescoes, or a Modernist novel written in stream of consciousness, or an infantile multivolume narration, in the first person, from the perspectives of a chorus of children, or a detective novel presented in several different time periods, as a story from 1952, or one from 1972, or 2012 . . .

Olga was pricked by her conscience for something that had been done in her name, in her city and homeland, while Frau Maria showed a generosity of spirit without which life in Europe after 1945 would have been unthinkable. The price for this reversal of roles was the life of one unborn child.

A year or two later, the Püframent family would move back to Germany. The engineer completed his work, said goodbye to his friends and colleagues at the railroad, and everything proceeded in the best possible order. Who knows how all this might have turned out if their third child had been born in Sarajevo.

By 1955 the last of the German technicians and specialists had moved out of the Hotel Pošta, which continued to operate for another twenty years. Later the only part of the hotel that remained was the café, and after the last war the café too disappeared. The building was all that was left, the same old walls, windows, and gutters.

The Life and Tenants
of Madam Emilija Heim

It was early spring and the peaks of Trebević were white when the soldiers came to evict Madam Marija Peserle. They removed the small furniture in silence and emptied the cabinets and closets amid the clinking of pots and plates. They tossed all this out into the entryway or onto the steps, so that the rare passing tenant could barely get by. But anyone who did would hear Dragica, Madam Peserle's sister-in-law, who was standing out on the steps as if she too were a thing tossed out, repeating, "Oh, good God, good God, oh good God . . ."

Dragica repeated her expressions of grief and despair as if she were practicing to a metronome. She knew nothing else, this old maid and sister of Ivan Peserle, the famous journalist and owner of numerous Croatian and German newspapers from the Belle Epoque. Dragica hadn't lost her mind, but rather for her the time had become the same as the summer when Gavrilo Princip shot Ferdinand – nothing could move beyond it. And when time stops, misfortunes simply accumulate one atop another, like all those items out on the steps that turned completely useless the moment they found themselves outside the cabinets, shelves, and drawers of Marija Peserle's luxurious apartment, as if outside that apartment their very existence lost all its value.

Fortunately, Madam Peserle was a collected and rational woman. About her and Dragica's fate she spoke coldly and from something of a height, as if she were wondering aloud whether to dismiss a messy housekeeper during an afternoon tea with her lady friends, Viennese dames and the wives of royal and imperial generals. While her sister-in-law was cracking her knuckles as she recited her mantra *oh, good God, oh, good God*, she sat in our living room, drinking sweetened wheat coffee as she talked with Olga.

"What will you do now?" Nona asked Madam Peserle, who was the sister of our former landlady, the late Emilija Heim.

"I don't know" – the old woman hesitated for a moment, then said, "I'm thinking it might be best for us to go to the nursing home, in Turbe. Madam Hoffstädter wrote me that it's nice there" – and like that she had decided, in complete calm, as if she were discussing where to spend the weekend.

And what would become of her things?

Actually, nothing. Madam Peserle had packed two large suitcases for herself and the distraught Dragica. She had used them on her travels to Opatija, where she and Ivan used to spend their summers before the Great War. There would be no *inconvenience* or *indiscretion* regarding the other items as she had kindly asked Mrs. Matić from the third floor to put them into her basement as it was the most spacious, or, beforehand, if they liked, Mrs. Rejc, Mrs. Doležal and Mrs. Bilić, as well as the local women and prewar lessors, could look through it all and, without any hesitancy, take whatever they might want or need. Neither she nor Dragica would have any further need for such *rubbish*.

This is the word the old Peserle woman used: *rubbish*.

She looked at her life and fate in this manner, condescendingly, from on high. God forbid if we others had fallen from such heights – we would've all broken our necks.

She on the other hand, accompanied by oh-good-God-oh-good-God Dragica, the very next morning, with her two suitcases, which had been carried before the war by Gypsy porters from Tašlihan, in the company of two male natives of the building, her head held high, in a long blue dress and a hat – spruced up as if it were 1901 – rushed off toward the train station without once looking back.

Several days later, into Marija Peserle's apartment, on the second floor of the building on Yugoslav National Army Street, behind the Temple, moved the family of a colonel whose first and last name we don't remember. He was from the frontier region of the Krajina, a nice man who greeted everyone politely from the very first day, held the door open, offered to carry his neighbors' shopping bags, to help them, give them things, keep things for them, take care of things . . .

His wife was from the city. She too was kind, polite, and discreet. They had a son, his name was Brane, he was in the second grade, and he didn't make a sound. The other kids would run up and down the steps or suddenly cause a ruckus, which, especially during the afternoon repose, would provoke some irritability in the building, but nothing was ever heard from Brane. As if he were walking on tiptoe, kind and considerate, ready to greet anyone politely the first moment he saw them.

At the beginning, the neighborhood took pains to keep them at a distance. And that would well have continued, since the colonel and his wife did not force themselves on anyone, but little by little it was understood that none of that made much sense. After all, they weren't the people to blame, it wasn't the colonel who had forced Madam Peserle out of her apartment, others had done that. Nor was it the soldiers who were to blame – what do soldiers know, they do what the higher-ups tell them to do, counting the days until they can take off their uniforms – and God forbid anyone might say the fault lay with the people from the regional committee or the military command. It was the whole of human misfortune that was to blame, Hitler was to blame, Stalin was to blame, injustice in the world was to blame, history and geography were to blame, for they had determined that we would be born precisely now and precisely in this place. This was a truth one could stand by: Hitler, Stalin, and difficult historical conditions were to blame, not the colonel who had moved into Madam Marija Peserle's apartment.

But this was not the end of Peserle's story.

Several years later, the colonel and his wife along with Brane would be ringing at one door and another, excusing themselves to say that they were going away, moving, as the colonel had been transferred to Zagreb. And everyone said they were sorry to hear it, and were probably lying. But as soon they had closed the doors of their homes after the sturdy farewells, when they caught sight of themselves in the mirror by the coat rack, they understood, with some embarrassment, that there'd been no need to lie since they really were sorry to see the building lose such good neighbors.

Immediately following their departure, that very same month, the large four-room apartment of the late Ivan Peserle, in which he had lived with his wife and sister, was divided four ways. Into three of the newly created studio apartments moved, for the most part, lower-class citizens, the Resch family (Sarajevo Germans who had collaborated with the occupiers), a quiet office worker with his wife and their rachitic son, a stoker from the railway works with his wife and two children – but the fourth and largest of the rooms was returned to Madam Marija Peserle.

From Turbe she returned just as upright and undaunted in her splendid certitude that her life was characterized by something grander than material well-being, more important than money or any form of property. Her stay in the nursing home had neither aged her nor taught her anything she didn't already know or that she wasn't able to rationalize away. The difference being that Dragica was no more. She'd died in Turbe, and Madam Peserle had arranged to have her buried at Saint Josip's, the old Catholic cemetery in Koševo, in the monumental family tomb of the Heims and Peserles, which still today is located immediately beside the sepulchral arcade and the entrance to Saint Josip's itself.

Nona took me through that gate two or three times as a young boy. She would stop there for a moment or two, without faith and without God, in front of the stone memorials for her two sisters and their husbands, and then we would move on, down Koševo or alongside it. I did not ask her why we'd gone in, whose graves these were, or who they were to us, these people whom I would once upon a time recall so vividly, even though they had all died before the year of my birth. We visited gravesites often. At some of them we had our own dead, while at others we did not, but it seems to me that to a great extent I grew up among graves, without fear of death, sadness, or anxiety, in the midst of a world that, I would come to believe, belonged uniquely to me. In today's Sarajevo – today is October 30, 2012 – even just by thinking of a few graves I feel myself at home in my native city.

The tenants of such an apartment, one divided into parts, were called *partaja*. In official bureaucratic language, a *partaja* was "one with the right to co-tenancy for an indefinite period." They all had just one door and entryway, the toilet and washroom were shared, and next to the doorbell was a set of instructions indicating how many times to ring for which tenant. So alongside their other daily tasks and occupations, the *partaja* needed to count the number of times the doorbell rang. They would put the washroom schedule up in the entryway, and, even among accommodating individuals, of which there were always too few, disagreements simmered regarding who had failed to remove their hair from the bathtub or whose turn it was to scrub the toilet.

With the *partaja* system, which was likely invented in the Soviet Union during Stalinism and adapted from there to life in our own cities, the Party had tried to solve two burning problems. The shortage of housing and the surplus of it. To some this might appear mistakenly to be a single problem seen from two different perspectives. But that is not the case. The matter here had to do with two cultures, one that belonged to the past and suffered from a chronic surplus of housing, and another that was dedicated to the future and truly had nowhere to live. Their lack of agreement and mutual unhappiness would last for a long time, for decades even, until both would disappear, past and future collapsing, and in place of communism something else would be promised to the citizens: the end of war, the heavenly kingdom, the exit from an economic slump.

Whenever a *partaja* received an apartment from her or his employer or, God forbid, died, the occasion was equally joyous for others since they would all gain from the resulting surplus of living space. Everything one could live without was still considered surplus, but still, the dead *partaje* were not replaced by new *partaje*.

Madam Marija Peserle died in 1959, and thus did the end arrive for the history of this building above the Sephardic temple, which had been built at the beginning of the century with the money of her sister Emilija Heim and Madam Heim's deceased husband, a Sarajevo restaurant and hotel owner.

In this five-story building, the entire first floor with its vast, high-ceilinged four-room apartment was occupied by Madam Emilija Heim. On the second floor were Marija Peserle and her sister-in-law Dragica, while the ground floor, the upper ground floor, and the third and fourth stories were comprised for the most part of nice, rather spacious, two-room apartments intended as rental space. Emilija Heim rented these apartments out to better-off postal workers and railway officials, to professors, and to Sarajevo's upper crust. She took such things into account because she wanted to have her peace and also for others to be comfortable. She thought, at any rate, it was better for each person to live according to his station, with his own class and race, people of quality with people of quality, workers with workers, poor folk with other poor folk. To her way of thinking this was a recipe for perfect social harmony. She didn't give a thought to revolutions or revolutionaries, they had nothing to do with her, nor did she have anything against communists, or religious devotees, or Jews – to the latter she would have gladly rented an apartment, for, based on her insight into their world, Jews were a very tidy people, even when they were not especially affluent – but, in accordance with her limited means and abilities, she did what she could to ensure that no revolution, whether red or black, ever came to pass, and that people did not suffer for being what they were through no choice or desire of their own. And in fact, up until April 1941, it seemed to all of us that Emilija Heim was quite successful in her historical designs, and her building would remain an oasis of peace amid the flames of a belligerent Europe.

In those times before the war, and even during the war, the stairways were perfectly clean, and from the ground floor to the tops of the building there were bright red carpets spread out on the landings, a little like the red carpets of Hollywood, while the building superintendent and housekeeper made sure that at every instant of every day the walls were perfectly whitewashed. Actually the building's stairways resembled the exquisitely illuminated hallways of a fine European hotel.

Such was the state of the building in which Franjo and Olga Rejc rented their apartment upon moving to Sarajevo. The apartment was on the fourth floor, just beside the attic, and while it might not have been spacious enough for a married couple with two sons, one of whom, Mladen, was already attending high school, this was how the two of them were. Having a smaller, more elegant, and orderly apartment was more valuable to them than having something that might have been larger and disorderly, surrounded by neighbors of all sorts. This variety of civic caution was typical of the Stublers, and perhaps Franjo got it from her, but it had a paradoxical effect on anyone who knew about their social adaptability and, especially Olga's, sympathy for the poor, strangers, and people of other faiths or customs. They lived within this paradox, and probably because of it they never achieved much affluence. Karlo was paying for Omama's treatment at expensive German baths, partly out of the belief that her heart would not last through another spring, partly because he loved the orderliness and seriousness of a world to which he did not actually belong, the sort of world described in Thomas Mann's *Magic Mountain*, while Rudi was spending both his own and his father's hard-earned money on travel, concerts, and Viennese cafés, and Olga and Franjo, why not, wanted to live in the fine, upscale apartment building of Emilija Heim.

Emilija was the eldest and most enterprising sister. Her husband had died relatively young. We do not recall what sort of a man he was because we never met him. When we moved into the two-bedroom apartment on the fourth floor, Madam Emilija was already a widow. She had two daughters, but they had married by then.

One of the first memories of Olga and Franjo's daughter, born sixteen months before Mladen's death, was connected to Madam Emilija.

It was 1945, again early springtime, a night of Allied bombing, in which our own Željko took part, the son of Olga's sister Karla Ćurlin, née Stubler, whom we all called Aunt Lola. Željko would later say to Olga – Auntie, I watched out not to hit our house! – though we all knew that in the middle of the night he could not watch out and this was more like the excuse of a well-raised child than the expression of a grown man.

And while Željko was watching out, we were all in the basement, the building owner Emilija Heim, and her sister Marija Peserle, and her sister-in-law Dragica all curled up, and Aunt Doležal, and Matić with his wife, and the Bilićs, who lived across the way from the Matićs, and all the others who had lived in the building since 1941, and Mrs. Rojnik, who had moved in later with her husband and her daughter Damjanca.

It was pitch dark in the basement, bombs were falling, thundering from all sides, and none of us was able to estimate just how far away the house was above our heads or whether it was even standing at all anymore. Just once in a while the candle in Madam Heim's hand would come alive, or Matić would light a match to look at his watch, and for a moment the entire basement would be lit up and Olga and Franjo's little, not yet even three-year-old daughter would look around at all the faces – she would remember them distinctly for the rest of her life.

At dawn, after a night of terrible bombing, Olga and Franjo's daughter recalled, even as an old woman, that Madam Emilija Heim, cane in hand due to her failing hips, made her way up the steps toward the shelter exit.

All the other tenants stayed where they were. The children asleep, the adults awake, following Madam Heim with their eyes. Of the children, only Olga and Franjo's two-and-a-half-year-old daughter was awake, watching so she could one day remember.

And it was her earliest living memory: Emilija Heim, holding her cane, tall and straight, standing at the entrance to the shelter and looking out. In front of her are the walls of the ravaged Sephardic temple and, beyond that, clear sky. It is quiet outside, the aircraft engines cannot be heard, perhaps birds are twittering, perhaps there aren't even any birds left.

Thus stood Emilija Heim, in the gaze of a two-and-a-half-year-old girl, in her memory, in the memory of a seventy-year-old woman. At the opening and closing of life stood Emilija Heim.

In April 1941, on the low ground floor of Madam Heim's building there lived a Jewish woman. We don't remember her name. We remember she was a widow and that she was very quiet and smiling. To greet her neighbors, she would just smile. As if her throat hurt or as if, for some reason, she was trying to conceal the sound of her voice. And actually, just as no one remembers the woman's first or last name, no one can recall her voice.

The tenants of the building above the Temple do however remember her screams.

Early in the morning, at first light during the month of May, they came for her. They could have been Ustaše, or members of the militia, or even members of the Quisling collaborators. One thing is certain: at that time it was not the Germans who were rounding up and deporting the Jews.

But we do not remember the color of their uniforms or the signs on their caps or if they were even in uniforms or wearing caps at all. We did not see this but rather hid ourselves away deep down under our bedsheets while the voices reverberated on the stairs.

In truth it was variations of one and the same human voice.

It prayed with the devotion of a beggar.

It offered gold to ransom itself, though it had no gold.

I'll go to my sister in Kraków for the gold and bring it back to you, it said.

And when they didn't believe it, it shouted.

It screamed.

For a long time it screamed, but no one heard it.

Though nothing had yet happened to Sarajevo's Jews, and no one knew, or no one wanted to know, of the fate of the Jews of Poland, Czechoslovakia, and Vienna, our neighbor, whose name we do not remember, knew everything. And that was why she screamed, in the voice and the voices of an innocent person being led from her living room armchair to the gallows.

We never saw her again and started immediately to try to forget about her, ashamed at the whiteness and softness of our bedsheets.

All this happened on a Monday.

And on Tuesday, into the apartment of the quiet, smiling old Jewish widow whose name we do not recall and who resonates in the memories of the Stublers and Rejcs only through her screams and imprecations, moved Stanko Rojnik, a senior official with Sarajevo's Ustaše militia, along with his wife and child. The Rojniks entered into the aromas of the old Jewess and were infected, like the people in the Middle Ages who had by some miracle or privilege granted by God survived the plague but then moved into the homes of the dead that still stank of their sweat and fear.

Did Mr. and Mrs. Rojnik talk about the old Jewish woman, upon whose bed, at least for the first few days and weeks, they lay down each evening? I presume they did, but no form of literature and no amount of authorial imagination by any author can reach the content of those conversations, though nothing else would so truly speak to the reality of Sarajevo in 1941, the war, and the Holocaust, as those, probably naïve, worried, maybe even a bit erotic, conversations between Stanko Rojnik and his wife.

He was a gloomy, distant man, usually dressed in a cheap, poorly cut suit from before the war and carrying a leather briefcase that was on the verge of falling apart. It was in that case that he carried his militia papers. My uncles, Mladen, who in 1941 had started the seventh form of high school, and Dragan, three years Mladen's junior, shuddered at the thought of Rojnik and were terrified of his briefcase. Inside it, their still vivid adolescent and childish imagination conjured death warrants and corpses; in that bag there were firing squads, gallows, and concentration camps, laws and mobile courts-martial; in there was everything they were seeing in the city, hearing about from their parents, and especially everything people were silent about and imagined when they were most alone. In Stanko Rojnik's briefcase there was death. Death for the two of them would forever remain the fear of that tattered, worn-out bag ostensibly with nothing but papers in it.

Mrs. Rojnik, in contrast, was a good and decent woman. She must have noticed that her neighbors avoided her, though perhaps she attributed that to the fact that the two of them were actually Slovenes. This was a distracting factor in the lively story of Stanko Rojnik: a high-ranking Ustaše militia official, but also a Slovene. To my grandfather, Franjo, it was not at all clear how this could be possible. Franjo's Sloveneness was idealistic and naïve, and naïveté and idealism are a dangerous combination where nationality and identity are concerned, for they can easily lead a man into trouble with the guileless ease of an opiate.

Ordinarily, early in the morning, Franjo would be making his way down the steps, dressed in his expensive suit, a new bag in hand, and would run into Stanko Rojnik on his way, wearing his ugly, cheap suit, which always reeked of tobacco smoke, carrying that tattered briefcase that was always on the verge of falling apart.

He'd greet Rojnik not a whit more cordially than the other neighbors. And he would look him the eye, just as he did with everyone else. He didn't lower his gaze the way one usually does from the eyes of a policeman.

Rojnik noticed this, and seemed to smile back at Franjo.

Or maybe it just seemed that way.

When he came home one afternoon, Franjo said to Olga, "I saw Rojnik this morning!"

"God knows where he's been!" she said, quickly bringing down his mood.

And then Franjo Rejc sat quietly, in his own kind of fear, wondering what in God's name Stanko Rojnik, that Slovene, did at night. And he could think of nothing good.

The Rojniks spent the whole war that way, in the ground floor apartment from which our Jewish neighbor had been sent to her death. In 1943, the worst time of all, a little before Mladen's death, they had a daughter. They gave her the very unusual name of Damjana. In Slovenia, before the war, there had been Damjanas, but in our beautiful homeland, reborn through the goodness and wisdom of the Poglavnik Ante Pavelić, and with the support of Croatia's great friend and the defender of the Croats, the leader of the Greater German Reich Adolf Hitler, probably not a single Damjana had ever been born.

Mr. and Mrs. Rojnik liked to call the little girl Damjanca. Damjanca helped Franjo, and after him Olga, to take another step toward Stanko Rojnik. Franjo had given his daughter a name that was impossible to find in the Croatian church registries, and to the cautious priests of Archbishop Ivan "the Evangelist" Sarić the name had sounded rather Serbian, even though it comes from the name of a tree that grows in both Croatia as well as Serbia, so it was necessary that the child have a second name. Besides the one from the tree, she was also called Regina, after Olga's sister. And like Regina, the little girl had been baptized in the Catholic Church.

Franjo told this to Rojnik, expecting that he would say something in response. But he didn't. The policeman cordially nodded in acknowledgment but said nothing. Franjo didn't dare say anything more. He was even a bit concerned that Rojnik might have thought that he, Franjo, was insultingly suggesting that Damjanca was a Serbian name.

But then the Poglavnik dispatched Vjekoslav "Maks" Luburić to Sarajevo to straighten things out. It was the end of the war, the beginning of 1945, and an inkling of how it would all end was beginning to be felt, so there was disorder among the municipal authorities, between the soldiers and civilians, which would only become worse and more widespread after the Germans, who had their own worries and defeats on all sides, lost interest in what was happening in the city. They were prepared at any moment for withdrawal toward new lines of defense, about which they were not informing their co-combatants, so that not even the Poglavnik had any idea to what point, to what fateful line, Hitler's troops would pull back. At that time in the city corruption was rampant, the black market flourished, prices soared, and the Partisans strolled calmly about. They would merely put on civilian clothes before stepping out onto the asphalt or cobblestone streets, heading out for a spritzer and kebab. So it seemed to the Ustaše.

Luburić arrived as a grand reinforcement. After him nothing would ever be the same, let alone Croatian history in Sarajevo. What he did in those few weeks, or that month and a half, during his frightening control over the town, would forever be remembered. Each day, in the basement of the villa into which he had descended on Skenderija, he would torture his captives, boy and girl high school students, street traders, postal workers, anyone he'd heard from somewhere might have some connection to the Partisans, the English, the communists, Stalin, enemies of red, yellow, and black . . . He cooked people alive in pots of boiling water, peeled the skin from their backs, tore out their nails, sliced off women's breasts. This was what Maks Luburić did, or what his people did,

Sarajevo perverts, reprobate sons of former Turkish beys, syphilitics, the off-spring of brother-sister incest, the sons of Sarajevo servant girls and high school dropouts from outlying counties, the oafs of Sarajevsko polje come to town for the first time, the God-fearing sons of Herzegovina black market shops, kids from Trešnja longing for adventure, war veterans, good-for-nothings, layabouts, and devout Catholics and Muslims – they tormented people, in Maks's name, until those people confessed and informed against others.

The majority of those captured had nothing to confess to and no one to inform against. But it was enough for a single person who did know something to confess and inform. And there were lots of those people, someone in every entry-way, café, and office, at every Turkish shop window, with reliable information about three communist sympathizers, two clandestine Partisans, and at least one person at the post office, railroad, or police force who worked for the movement.

It was a time when the whole city knew who worked for whom and whom you needed to contact if you wanted to join the Partisans, a fact that Maks Luburić – founder of the Independent State of Croatia's concentration camps, commander at Jasenovac, and one of the worst butchers in Europe during the Second World War – gladly used to identify collaborators in the National Liberation Movement, from nearly all city and state institutions and factories, among the ranks of shop-keepers, town criers, news reporters, and the ordinary, seemingly uninterested people of the city. This was the moment when Sarajevo paid the greatest price for its way of thinking: here each person knew everything there was to know about everyone else, people peeked into each other's living rooms, kitchens, and stomachs, and a series of open secrets came to stand in for freedom, which this city had never really experienced and which was, in a certain sense, alien to its very nature.

And so one day, to the surprise of the tenants of the building above the Tem-ple, they came for the tall official from Sarajevo's Ustaše militia Stanko Rojnik. They took him away and never brought him back. Rojnik was a Partisan collab-orator, a secret communist, inserted into the Ustaše militia in the spring of 1941, a cuckoo's egg in Croatia's nest, in that Ottoman Turkish Sarajevo. Extremely careful and pedantic by nature – this was what was said of Slovenes, that they were pedantic – he played in our building the role of a morose, unlikable Ustaše bureaucrat who brought death, in all its forms and manifestations, with him in his briefcase. How one person can misjudge another. As in the seventies Yugoslav television series *The Expendables* or the film *Valter Defends Sarajevo,* Stanko Rojnik carried secret conspirator documents in his bag, he carried the freedom we would celebrate until the next war.

When she heard what had happened, Olga did something imprudent.

Just as her father had taken his Serbian neighbors into his house, which they would not forget when the time of his need came, so she rushed to the ground floor, her daughter in her arms, to be there for Mrs. Rojnik.

"They took him away!" said Rojnik's wife, repeating what everyone already knew.

And that was really all that happened. For the next several hours they sat in the living room, amid the furniture of the old nameless Jewish woman and the few things that the Rojniks themselves had brought to the apartment – it's easy to imagine what they talked about.

Olga tried to gently console her. She said: "Stanko will come back, he's not guilty of anything!" Mrs. Rojnik certainly had nothing to say to that. Or she kept whatever she had to say to herself. Out of caution and fear, because she too, just as her man, was a secret conspirator. She knew well what his work was and for whom. She must have known why he had stuck around in May 1941 to work for the police, which was then in the process of becoming the Ustaše militia, at a time when his Serb colleagues, and the occasional Croat or Muslim wary of making his nationality known, were running as far away from Sarajevo and that militia as they could, usually toward Belgrade, or into the woods to the Partisans. How could she, a Slovene herself, not have known why Stanko remained among all the Croats to suddenly turn into a Croat and take part in cleansing the city of its Jews, Serbs, and communists?

She knew, without a doubt she knew, just as Luburić knew that she knew.

And then someone rang the doorbell on the groundfloor.

Olga was scared shitless. Her first thought was: Why had she brought her child? She could have left her in the apartment with Dragan, who was hiding in the loft to avoid being drafted. Later she would perhaps not love the child with that mythic motherliness, if she would love her at all. Of this we can't be sure. But when the bell rang, she already felt guilty for what would happen to the child. This is perhaps a protective mechanism of the mother and father: they defend themselves against the fear of death by means of another fear – that something, God forbid, might happen to their child. Perhaps this is one reason why so many people have children.

Someone from the police, in civilian dress, was standing at the door.

He was alone. He showed Mrs. Rojnik his ID: "Forgive the intrusion, Ma'am. They sent me for the radio!"

He left behind a receipt for a confiscated shortwave radio. He said thank you and bowed upon saying goodbye. He was very polite. So polite that Mrs. Rojnik broke into tears. If she had retained any kind of hope until that moment, right then she knew Stanko would never come back alive.

On that April evening when the Ustaše retreated from Sarajevo, and Luburić was already far away – purportedly in the forests near Konjic, along the tree-lined boulevard that no longer exists in Marijin Dvor, near the Church of Saint Josip – secret communist operatives, sympathizers of the movement, and English spies, or those whom Maks Luburić considered as such, had already been hanged. Among the untimely Christmas decorations hanged Stanko Rojnik.

Several months after the end of the war his widow moved to Slovenia. She had no one in Sarajevo and was all alone. She needed someone to help her take care of Damjanca in those ugly, hungry times. This was not a city where she could stay. She lived in fear in Sarajevo, and eventually she saw her fears come true.

The name of Stanko Rojnik survived for a time in the memories of the tenants of the building above the Temple. Perhaps up until 1969, when the Energoinvest high-rise was built immediately beside it, and the majority of the tenants moved to other parts of town. Afterward nothing remained that would remind them of this man, whose name is noted only in some old books in the city archive, among the lists of the "victims of the fascist terror." Nothing was ever named after Stanko Rojnik. Nor would anything ever be. What he gave his life for no longer existed in any form whatsoever.

A decade after the liberation, news reached the building that Damjanca had died somewhere in Slovenia. Not how or why or from what. We merely learned that she had died.

Everyone in the building had shrunk from Stanko Rojnik. Except Franjo Rejc, a romantic and naïve Slovene.

But not a single person had been at all afraid of the Home Guard colonel Bilić and his gracious wife. He worked at the headquarters, spent almost all four years of the war in Sarajevo, only rarely went out into the field, to Romanija and eastern Bosnia, and really didn't give the impression of being a high-ranking officer, especially one from the kind of army that was Croatia's. He seemed like more of an Englishman layabout sent into the foreign service in India, doing the job in such a way as to protect his own hide. From his Zagreb perspective, Sarajevo, along with our building and its tenants, may as well have been India. He and his wife simply wanted to enjoy life without letting anything get in the way. They were superficial and easygoing. Petty riffraff and his lady.

Colonel Bilić had once been a royal officer.

As soon as the time had come and the country was transformed, he became a Home Guard official. Polished and well bred, he was also in his element with the Germans. They had a daughter, Jolanda, who was twelve years old in 1941 and had been born in the Serbian town of Smederevo. They had moved into our building when Bilić was still a royal officer. His historical transformation was as natural to all the other tenants as it was to him. It wasn't a subject for conversation. Bilić was not feared in the least. It's possible none of us even thought about him.

After Mladen's death in the autumn of 1943, once Dragan had graduated in '44 and become old enough for the army and for dying in an Ustaše uniform, we hid him in the loft so that he wouldn't have to do so. Did it occur to Nono and Nona to ask for their neighbor Bilić's protection, to ask him to intercede the first time, when Mladen had been enlisted into the German army, to have him assigned to Home Guard headquarters, to some sort of desk job? Or, perhaps when Dragan was threatened with the draft once again, this time into the Croatian army, it probably never even entered their heads to talk with Colonel Bilić. To him, after all, they were India.

The Bilićs would frequently organize get-togethers in their house that turned into loud parties as the night wore on. The colonel would invite Home Guard officials, as if he were not especially concerned over the bad news from the front lines in 1942, 1943, and 1944, as long as there was an occasion, a holiday, national celebration, birthday, or name day, or for no reason at all, as long as it raised the fighting morale, and they would arrive with flowers and boxes of chocolate, as if it were the most peaceful of times at some tree-shaded villa in Vienna or Zagreb's Tuškanac district, a pianist playing or a gramophone, the latest recordings having just arrived by diplomatic courier from Paris and Berlin.

Unfortunately, the Bilićs' apartment was directly below ours, so it was often impossible to get to sleep because of the colonel's all-night gatherings, especially after Mladen's death, when Olga's and Franjo's sleep was somewhat shallow because even their dreams would be invaded by what they couldn't stop thinking about during the daytime. One such night, in the spring of 1944 – it might have even been the tenth of April, Croatian Independence Day, the partygoers had gotten so carried away, or Nona was so much more upset than usual, that she grabbed the push broom and leaned out the window to knock on the Bilićs' window to see if that might quiet them down a little. And as often happens in the middle of the night, when a person's body is not completely under control, she slipped, knocked too hard against the glass, and broke the neighbors' window.

The three of them almost died from fright.

The party immediately below suddenly grew quiet. The song stopped, all the gramophones and pianos died away, and they all just waited to see what would happen next. Dragan ran back into the loft, Nona wrung her hands – Oh, God, what should we do, Franjo? – but Franjo just hissed back angrily, "Now you ask me what we should do? Now?" and both of them ran up and down the room, as if by running they could make something right.

The torture lasted for some fifteen minutes, but then the celebration started up again. It was even louder now, since Colonel Bilić's apartment had one fewer window pane. Never had the obnoxious singing made us so happy.

Neither the colonel nor his wife ever brought up the broken pane. Either they were too drunk to have noticed the broom when it stretched down from the floor above, or, and this seems more likely, they found one broken window a minor price to pay for not having to go talk about it with people whose despondency frightened them. They must have known the Rejc family had lost a son, that he'd been killed somewhere in Slavonia, as a German soldier no less, and they really didn't want to allow themselves to notice such misfortune if there wasn't an important reason to. Unhappy people are like a magnet and a chasm: they pull a person in and swallow him up . . .

The building's tenants didn't experience much during the first winter of the war: there was still food and heat, Pavelić's kunas maintained some of their value, such that you could even buy something with them. But the winters of '42 and '43, when Stalingrad was in the midst of falling and the war's victor could be sensed on the horizon, especially in '43 and then '44, those winters were cold and hungry. People went to Slavonia on smuggling trips, where from the greedy, self-serving villagers (or rather from people whom God had given the opportunity to enjoy the charms of the market economy), one could, with Austrian ducats and jewelry passed down through the family, buy flour and some eggs, which were valued by those who purchased them as if they had been hatched from Gustav Fabergé, rather than some mangy Slavonian chicken. One went by train to Slavonia, through war-torn Bosnia, through Partisan ambushes, past Chetniks and hajduks, and even ordinary highway bandits completely uninterested in politics, in fear of everyone and everything. But a person didn't have a choice. As always, you had to survive, and since others were taking smuggling trips, Franjo set out as well.

In accord with the architectonic standards of the beginning of the century, each apartment in Madam Emilija Heim's building had a spacious pantry. Before the invention of the electric refrigerator, when every city domicile would prepare its winter provisions with the beginning of fall, and at the beginning of spring would explore methods of ensuring that as temperatures rose the food would not go bad, decompose, dry out, begin to stink, or germinate, the pantry resembled a chemistry and physics laboratory, in which each individual mistress of the house was her own Marie Skłodowska Curie. During the wartime shortage and hunger, the pantries of Emilija Heim seemed wider and more spacious than even the brightest and most expansive living rooms.

Only one pantry was full to the brim.

Our neighbor on the fourth floor was Mrs. Vilma Doležal, who we would call Aunt Doležal. Aunt Doležal's husband had been a jail guard and revolutionary collaborator. He was discovered in the pre-Luburić period and sent to a labor camp in Norway. It was not the Croats who had been responsible for his disappearance, but the Gestapo. He would never come back.

From Aunt Doležal's bedroom window, the so-called maid's room in the Bilićs' large apartment could be seen like the back of your hand. The empty space, the gap in the middle of the building, thanks to which it was possible to peer into the maid's room of our better-off neighbors, was called the atrium.

One day, in the freezing winter of 1943, someone knocked at our door.

Dragan quickly stole into the loft, Nona adjusted her hair out of habit, and slowly moved toward the door while her son managed to hide.

"Who's there?" she asked in her innocent voice, the kind that raised the greatest doubts among the police.

"It's me, Mrs. Rejc, Vilma!"

"Oh, Mrs. Doležal. Why are you sneaking up on us?" asked Olga angrily as she opened the door. (The two of them addressed each other formally throughout their lives, although they were very close. This somehow accorded with Aunt Doležal's sense of propriety and her irrepressible sense of humor, which none of life's horrors could manage to destroy – not the loss of her husband, or the war, or any of the other things that permanently embittered most people and crushed the most resilient of characters.)

"Please come with me. I have to show you something!"

She led her to the window through which the colonel's maid's room could be seen. Beyond the opened curtains and gently separated light drapes was a table with a white damask table cover. On the table, sunning itself in the wintry January sunshine, lay a slaughtered suckling pig. Not even three months old, as if preparing itself to be eaten for Christmas dinner, it lay there completely dead, and somehow alive.

Without thinking, Olga asked, "What are they doing with a pig in the maid's room?"

"Dear Mrs. Rejc, I'm of the impression that they could not put it in the pantry."

From then on, Olga would go over to Aunt Doležal's to see what they had over at the Bilićs'. And she would tell her to wait for her before looking herself because it was only an experience when you looked at it and enjoyed it together.

Aunt Doležal swore never to look without her. And who knows, perhaps she was telling the truth. The spectacle offered by Colonel Bilić and his wife's maid's room was remembered more than anything else. Maybe it was for the suckling pigs, chickens, hams, apples, pears, sacks of white flour and sacks of corn flour, the turkey-hens and geese, the long, thin Slavonian sausages, the baskets of eggs and the baskets of unshelled nuts, and the live carp in water troughs, maybe it was only for all this treasure, this manna from heaven, that those two people and their house were still remembered. It made them immortal. Otherwise, perhaps they'd be forgotten by now.

Colonel Bilić was not thoughtless and crass, however, nor did he give in to despair. He knew well, by contrast to others around him, the guilty and the undeserving, the criminal and the apathetic, the murderous and the future martyrs, just how much each thing costs and how much human suffering was worth. Although he was not the vindictive sort, at least as far as we knew, and did not commit even the slightest offense toward anyone in the building – nor did he help anyone either – Colonel Bilić was nevertheless aware of how heavy and terrible the victor's retribution could be.

No one saw him as he was leaving, and no one knew when he did so. But he left in time, when it was still possible to take one's own car to Zagreb and onward, to who knows where. We don't know what happened to the colonel, but we believe he survived. He was that sort of a person.

Mrs. Bilić, however, stayed with Jolanda in their beautiful, spacious apartment, as the liberation rumbled through. The maid's room emptied out or Mrs. Bilić lowered the blinds, neither Nona nor Aunt Doležal could remember which. Before long, two or three years after the liberation, Jolanda graduated, and the two of them quietly and in orderly fashion moved to Zagreb.

No one in the building felt bad about these neighbors' departures. No one would remember them with good or ill will, for the three of them had in the end been neither good nor bad. They were exactly like the time in which they had lived, to which they gave nothing of themselves. Maybe it was better that way. Empty souls, like circus balloons filled with helium, they disappeared, flying off to Zagreb or the West. At least they forgave us that broken windowpane.

But this is not the end of the Bilićs' story.

Across the way from them on the third floor lived the Matićs. Đuro Matić was a Serb who'd been a pre-war Sarajevo lawyer, later employed in some state institution. His wife, whom we called Matićka – we do not recall her actual name – was from Zagreb. Although she had lived nearly half her life in Sarajevo, she spoke as if she'd arrived just yesterday from Jelačić Square.

They had two children: Girlie and Sonny Boy.

The two of them had other, both civil and baptismal, names for school, but everyone in the building called them Girlie and Sonny Boy.

Girlie was an anxious little girl, matching the time and conditions of life, and differed not in the least from that generation of Sarajevo girls from better families. Neither pretty nor ugly, not especially bright but not at all stupid, Girlie grew up in a disciplined manner and was not a nuisance to anyone. In contrast to Sonny Boy, Girlie did not really need to be brought up.

From the time the Matićs moved in, we recognized Sonny Boy from his shouting and howling: even when he was little, he would scream in the stairwell as if he were being skinned alive, and all because of who-knows-what sort of perceived injustice. Later we heard his voice begin to crack as he grew older and began to curse and blaspheme in an attempt to seem important. And then when Sonny Boy had reached a certain age, he began to lead cheap girls down the hallways, so again he gave us no peace.

It should be said that Sonny Boy was actually just as typical as Girlie was.

An urchin from a *kuferaš* family, his mother's son, impossibly spoiled, as if the entire world revolved around him. And his mama, Matićka, the Zagreb native, who was never at all thrilled with this Oriental mentality, this Bosnian and Balkan sincerity and directness, where everyone addressed everyone else informally, the poor man to the landlord, the pickpocket to the university professor, the patient to his doctor, she tried to instill in Sonny Boy from his earliest years the belief that he was better, more intelligent and capable than others, that he was above the world that surrounded him – for he was from a fine house, his grandma Erika and grandpa Štef were from Jelačić Square, and it was only a combination of strange and silly circumstances that had led to Sonny Boy's growing up here, on Tašlihan, in Sarajevo, instead of where he should have been according to the nature of things and all the laws of people and of God.

The boy was not in fact overly bright, or perhaps it was the environment he grew up in that stunted his intellectual growth, and Sonny Boy grew up to be something of an idiot, a word he might have had some difficulty spelling.

When the war began, as early as the summer of 1941, Sonny Boy did something unusual: he went to join the Chetniks. How the news spread among the neighbors is hard to say. Probably the same way all other news spread around Sarajevo. Or else Matićka, being who she was, complained to the people around her so that soon everyone, and not just in our building, knew that Sonny Boy was in Romanija, then in Vučja Luka, that he was in the king's army, wearing a fur cap with a cockade and a long knife at his belt.

The first thing people around them said was that Đuro Matić must be dying of fright, and that the Ustaše would next be turning up at his door to lead him off to Vraca without his having done anything wrong at all. For absolutely everyone knew for a fact that he'd had nothing to do with Sonny Boy's upbringing. The boy had been brought up by his mother, he was her pride and joy, while Đuro had watched over their daughter. Orderly, serious, and quiet, she was his child. Sonny Boy was entirely his mother's. He was a lawyer, he did his work, and he respected the state, every state – this one too.

Of course the colonel and his wife knew where Sonny Boy was. They couldn't help but know, no matter how uninterested in their neighbors they were, no matter how much they were focused on themselves, their parties, and their slaughtered swine.

The Bilićs and Matićs lived through the four years of the war in peace, door to door. They met one another at the entrance, went down the stairs together, and never was an impolite word exchanged between them. Not a kind one either if the routine greetings exchanged by people don't count.

The fact that Colonel Bilić was not prejudiced toward Sonny Boy for his desertion to the Chetniks would be unusual in some invented story or novel about the time of the Second World War in Sarajevo, but in life, as it really was, there was nothing miraculous about it. The miracle would only come after the war had ended.

The colonel's wartime enemy and, until yesterday, neighbor concerned him about as much as anything else, which was not at all. He was as cool and indifferent toward Sonny Boy's Chetnicking as toward the fact that his neighbors could see the delicacies in his maid's room. Only an evil person or some sort of Croatian idealist would have punished Đuro because his son was a Chetnik. And Bilić was neither evil nor an idealist. The fact that Matić was a Serb also made no difference to him. He had nothing against the Serbs, he had lived among them for many years, and his daughter had been born in Serbia. The fact that he had adjusted and accommodated himself under the pressures and injunctions of great history does not mean that he changed his convictions. He didn't have such convictions, until he needed to. But even then, he was very, very moderate.

The evil of our century was preserved by such moderation.

In the spring of 1945 Mrs. Bilić was alone with Jolanda in one apartment while in the other Đuro Matić and Matićka were holding their breaths about what might have happened to Sonny Boy.

It would not take long for them to find out.

The Partisans had captured him, dirty and lice ridden, somewhere in Romanija, after which, as was the practice, he was put on trial by a people's court in Sarajevo. We do not recall, or we were never told, the length of Sonny Boy's sentence, but he served a good three years. Then he came back home, life in the building continued on its course, Sonny Boy was again Sonny Boy, only a little older, quieter, and more distrustful. We only heard from him when he drank.

By the time Sonny Boy returned from prison, Mrs. Bilić had moved with her daughter Jolanda to Zagreb. While living in Zagreb, Jolanda wrote a collection of poems, which was published by the well-respected publishing house Zora, who had also brought out the selected works of Miroslav Krleža.

Madam Emilija Heim died in 1952. She was old and sick. One afternoon we were all at the gravesite at Saint Josip's, where she was buried in a monumental family vault. We left her to be alone amid those white and black marble confines, covered in their German Gothic script and Silvije Kranjčević poems, as heavy as the first November snow, which falls suddenly, at first light after an unexpectedly warm evening, when the sweet, muddy stench of the city canals is all around and a person might once again believe that winter would never come, that death did not exist.

Das ist rote tane

It's the fourth of April 1945, early afternoon, and everything is unexpectedly quiet. The electricity has been out for some time. Someone's knocking on Aunt Doležal's door.

Madam Emilija Heim, between two German soldiers in full combat gear.

"Mrs. Doležal" – Madam Heim cannot seem to catch her breath – "Mrs. Doležal . . ."

Aunt Doležal leads them into her entry, then into the living room, offers Madam Heim a chair, helps her to set aside her cane, and the two helmeted soldiers with their rifles stand by, embarrassed.

"Please, gentlemen," Mrs. Doležal says at last in German.

The two men brighten, the wall between them and the light having disappeared, and they let go of their rifle straps . . .

"We've been given the task," says one of them, "of keeping an eye on Trebević, and the mountain is most clearly visible from your window!"

And so on the fourth of April 1945 Aunt Doležal, who did not yet know she had become a widow, her husband having been lost or killed in a German work camp in Norway, took into her apartment two despondent German recruits.

They stayed until the next morning, when, with a naïve, somewhat childish goodbye, they left. Only then, as they were making their way downstairs, did Aunt Doležal realize she had not asked their names. If they went away like that, she would have lost them completely, gone forever. She wanted to run after them and ask their names, but then thought better of it. Even if she knew their names, it was not likely she would ever see them again, but by learning them, oblivion would have at least seemed to have been postponed.

Who knew what the two men would have thought, and who knew what others would have thought, had they heard her talking with the German soldiers, just two days before the liberation of Sarajevo. That conversation is no longer relevant to anyone. They went away, disappeared, and were no more.

But let us return to the moment when the two have just entered the apartment, and Madam Heim has sat down, and is catching her breath, drinking water.

There is someone else in the apartment just then.

She's sitting on the floor, playing with a small red tin jug that her aunt has filled with beans, which the little two-and-a-half-year-old daughter of Olga and Franjo is shaking up and down.

She shakes the little toy, the tiny dry beans knocking against the tin, which makes a clanging noise that every adult ear finds unbearable. This is why Aunt Doležal has brought her to her place, given her the little jug and the beans, because Aunt Doležal knows how, whenever anyone in life needs it, not to be an adult. And for someone of her years this is an important thing to know.

As she plays with the jug, the little girl looks at the two soldiers and says, "Rote tane, rote tane, rote tane . . ."

The soldiers look at her. They don't understand what she's saying because they don't understand this language, and four years of war has not been enough for them to learn it. The girl has a bright complexion, light, almost pure-white skin, blue eyes. She looks at them as if she's the only one in the world who knows something about them.

"Das ist rote tane!" she says, and at the same moment their faces break into smiles.

This event would be remembered thanks to Aunt Doležal, who could not have felt indifferent when she saw the German soldiers at her door. Two or three years earlier, we are unsure whether this was in 1942 or 1943, the Gestapo had questioned Aunt Doležal for several days, while her husband, our neighbor Pepi, was deported in a cattle car far to the north, to Norway.

Josip Pepi Doležal was a jailer in the Beledija city authority. Beledija had been an ancient Sarajevo prison, which existed since Turkish times, though its most famous days would not come until the Austro-Hungarians, when members of the Young Bosnia movement and the assassins of Archduke Franz Ferdinand would be interned there. But Pepi was still a boy then, not yet at the prison but instead trying, without much success, to finish high school. That didn't work out. He failed grade after grade. While he wasn't especially stupid, he was the laziest student in the school. This legendary, colossal laziness also defined his life's calling: as a jailer he really didn't have anything to do except keep track of the keys.

But even then, he wasn't able to keep track of them.

Besides laziness, Pepi had another great passion: rakija. He was a notorious drunk, he was always drunk, though in his drunkenness he was also always good natured. Or rather as soon as he was drinking he got that way, became nice. Aunt Doležal lived with him that way, drunk as he was, and besides the eternal smell of alcohol, there weren't any other problems in their life. Their marriage had its own kind of harmonious basis.

They had a daughter who, according to Pepi's desire, was given her mother's name of Vilma. During the war Vilma was already a big girl in middle school.

At the time of the monarchy, Pepi's alcoholism didn't give him any problems at work. Jailers are often dark, difficult people, with some sort of hidden fault or abnormality. They are psychopaths or sadists, people born to suicide, wannabe police detectives or wannabe generals. But Pepi was just a simple drunk. Toward the prisoners he was never harsh, toward his colleagues he was always friendly, ready to conceal at any given moment the consequences of his wayward character. Being drunk, he was blind and deaf to most of what went on in Beledija.

And at the beginning, it seemed that the arrival of the Ustaše and the Germans would not change anything. Pepi Doležal kept on drinking, and perhaps he did not even notice the moment when the prison turned over into a torture chamber. Or perhaps it is just nicer to think he didn't notice.

It will never be known for certain whether the prison guard Josip Pepi Doležal aided the communist Olga Humo to escape from Beledija out of conviction or if it was because of the booze. The fact is that Olga Humo was saved and managed to get to free territory, while her savior ended up in the hands of the Gestapo. She would later fight alongside the Partisans, while he would die somewhere far off in the north, from extensive exposure to cold and toil. His despairing letters found their way to Aunt Doležal, as if either the Norwegian camps were unaffected by the strict German and Ustaše censorship or the contents of the letters were part of some intended mutual punishment.

She soon understood that Pepi would not be coming home. That he could not survive. Nor could even those who were stronger, more resolute, and soberer than him. After the war, Aunt Doležal would receive a commemoration of Pepi's martyrdom in 1941, but she too could never be certain whether the suicidal action that had saved Olga Humo came from Pepi's convictions or from his alcoholism. One day she thought one way, the next the other, and all of it she would recount with a light, laughing air, as if all of a person's life and fate right down to death in a concentration camp could be transformed into a joke.

After the war, Olga Humo lived a peaceful, happy life in Sarajevo with her husband Avdo and with her daughter, who was the same age as the little girl with the little red jug. Well-educated and very attractive, from Belgrade's famous Ninčić family, she worked as a high school English instructor, and later became a professor at the newly opened School of Philosophy. Comrade Olga Humo devoted her life to the ideals of proletarian internationalism, to the enlightenment, consciousness raising, and edification of her neglected and ignorant people, but she didn't remember Vilma Doležal, the widow of her jailer, nor did she ever ask about her. In 1956 Humo moved to Belgrade, where Avdo was a politician in the federal government while Olga was a professor of English at Belgrade University.

Thus did the fates of the postal worker Vilma Doležal and the famous Yugoslav revolutionary hero Olga Humo cross paths, in one of history's least significant moments, never to cross again unto time immemorial.

Aunt Doležal would live another fifteen years in the fifth-floor apartment of Madam Emilija Heim's building, at which point she would trade apartments with Vladimir Nagel, a German member of Sarajevo's tiny Protestant minority, who had become her son-in-law. Aunt Doležal then moved to what had once been Nagel's large apartment at Marijin Dvor, which had, in accordance with the rationalization of living space, been divided into two smaller apartments with a shared entry and bath. The Nagels received the Šleht family as *partaje*, and with them, as had been decided, they would share the good and the ill, mostly the ill, until one or the other moved out or died, after which the survivors would spread out into the whole apartment.

Vlado Nagel resolved his problem with the Slehts, who were difficult, unfriendly, and detestable people, such that he left them his mother-in-law. And Aunt Doležal, being the person she was, endured being a *partaja* the same as she had everything else in her life, with a sense of humor and a sort of almost flippant resignation.

At the end of the sixties, as the Energoinvest high-rise was being constructed and the inhabitants of the late Emilija Heim's building were emigrating, the Nagels moved to Rijeka. Several years later Aunt Doležal's daughter Vilma died there, and Aunt Doležal herself was left alone in the world at Marijin Dvor, among the moths and the Slehts, dust strewn and long ago widowed, without anyone to joke with.

Then the girl who had shown her little red jug to the two German soldiers and repeated, *rote tane! rote tane!*, returned her childhood debt. She visited, brought food, turned the old sick woman in her bed, bandaged her, and in the end accompanied her to Sarajevo's new Bare Cemetery. Peacetime telegraphist, bearer of a 1941 Partisan commemoration, Vilma Doležal died at the end of the seventies. The Slehts then expanded into the whole of Nagel's apartment, and the story was complete.

But all that was still far in the future.

On the fifth of April 1945, the little girl says, "Das ist rote tane!" and the German soldiers smile.

This would have been a nice, comforting end to the war.

Several hours later, troubled by the noise of heavy footsteps above her head, whose force was making the chandelier sway as the cheap glass pearls clinked against one another, Matićka, the native of Zagreb, Đuro's wife and Sonny Boy's mother, went upstairs to see what was happening and found Vilma and Olga in conversation.

"What in the world are you doing in the loft, you two old fools?" she asked, pretending to be angry.

"It's not two old fools, my dear Mrs. Matić, but two German soldiers!" said Aunt Doležal, and for the next fifty years everyone would laugh about that, until they died.

The Germans spent the night in Aunt Doležal's loft. They watched Trebević through their binoculars, observing the tiny figures of people who were no longer rushing toward anyone else because no one could hurt them anymore, without fear of the snipers or their rifles, let alone two such soldiers watching them from a town that had not yet been liberated. They were not afraid, because they knew it was all over – the war, that is – and there would be no continuation, and a new time would soon begin, when they would no longer come into contact with their enemies, for all their enemies would be dead, or re-clothed as tourists visiting the Dalmatian coast, German engineers and technicians, doctors and nurses, perhaps under whose care they would one day die, should they travel to Germany seeking a remedy for some otherwise incurable illness. But before that new time arrived, there would be a pause, an in-between, an intermezzo, when no one was rushing toward anyone else and everyone lived their lives as before, only a little more quietly and slowly, as if just before dying.

And so, from Aunt Doležal's loft window the two nameless German soldiers examine the movements of the Partisans, people walking up and down the slopes of Trebević, talking or nibbling on green stalks as they look down at the city in the valley. They look at them through the binoculars, write something in their black notepads, even though it is already too clear to them that no report will be written and what they're doing isn't needed by anyone anymore.

Aunt Doležal wants to host them with some rakija, the šljivovica that Pepi has not managed to finish off, since the Gestapo took him away.

They say no, German soldiers do not drink alcohol, especially when they're on duty, on watch. They grow serious at her offer, as if the war were not finished already.

Aunt Doležal brings them a serving dish, and on the dish are two Turkish coffee cups, and in the cups there is coffee. It isn't really coffee but a barley coffee substitute, with a little bit of actual coffee added. For every nine spoons of barley coffee, there is one spoonful of real coffee. At least this was what Hasan, the prewar shopkeeper, had said when he brought her a box of the substitute and accepted payment in the form of a gold ring, though maybe he was lying and there isn't even a bean's worth of real coffee in it. It would be fine if that were the case too, for it is important to believe there is coffee in that barley, or that from barley one can make coffee, and that the story about the Ethiopian and Brazilian plant was invented.

The Germans brighten, pleased, thanking her for the honor, and Aunt asks them the same question people would ask the German tourists of thirty years later: have you managed to learn any of our language?

"We have not managed to learn your language, and we have forgotten our own," one of them answers sullenly. This too will never be forgotten, as long as we are alive.

In the morning, looking younger than they are or than they were the day before, the soldiers leave, without Aunt Doležal's having asked their names. She starts after them to correct this, but then stops: someone might think something of it.

And again the beans in the jug go clink, the little girl happy that the noise does not bother her aunt as it does her mother, and she starts up her mantra once more:

"Rote tane, rote tane, rote tane . . ."

The Grave in Donji Andrijevci

A frigid, dry frost without snow anywhere. The bus crawls slowly toward Slavon-ski Brod. Along the road, in the courtyards before the A-frame houses, sliced-open pig entrails hang upside down. The intestines, livers, and hearts are steaming into a cloud, as if the animals are still alive or their animal souls are streaming up into the sky after the horror of the slaughter. It is November 29, Republic Day in the year 1970, and Javorka Rejc – this is the first time we commemorate her by her given and family names – the little girl who until a short while before was jingling beans in a small tin can and repeating *rote tane! rote tane!* is taking the bus on her way to Slavonia, to Donji Andrijevci, a village near Kopanica. For two years now she has been working at a public bookkeeping service, the first job she's ever had. By the time she retires, thirty-seven years from now, she will have worked at the National Museum, in a university's department of dentistry, at the Academy of Cinematic Arts, and in the School of Education, but she cannot know this as she sits in the bus, two rows behind the driver, looking through the window at the steaming pig entrails on this frozen November day. She's twenty-eight years old, separated, with a four-year-old son, but as always there has to be a life before her. This is not the way she thinks or feels; she is unsatisfied, deprived, and unhappy. Some terrible things have happened to her, which we might relate at some point, but it all started late in 1943, when her elder brother by nineteen years was killed – Mladen, whose grave she is on her way to visit.

The story of his death we shall set aside for the end, even though it has already happened and was long ago recorded amid the Stubler chronology, defining their family history not only in the future but in the past as well. This event changed everything: all that had happened and all that would happen; with it, probably, our family history was finished. Although life went on, death had already announced itself, and the end was all that was awaited, in accordance with people's petty biographies and the chronologies that we cannot respect but merely imitate through a more accurate tracing of scenes, temporal flows, and chronologies, and then say that Javorka went on living her life after her family's death, and her own.

That early afternoon in the bus on its way to Slavonski Brod, Javorka was a young, pretty, blonde-haired girl, and none of her fellow travelers would have thought she had just separated from her husband or that she had a child. She wore ugly patent leather boots of the sort that were in fashion that winter, a skirt cut just above the knee, a wool sweater, with a sheepskin coat that was for some reason called a "hunter" thrown over her shoulders. People wear those sorts of coats now, too, but the name has been lost in the meantime. On her lap sits a lady's handbag she will not let go of because it contains a purse with all the money she has. Underneath, in the luggage compartment, is a small suitcase made of fake black leather that was purchased in Stuttgart that spring, which would make its appearance on various occasions in the apartment at 23 Sepetarevac Street all the way up to the beginning of the war, in the spring of 1992, when it too, would at last disappear.

In Slavonski Brod she transfers to a rickety local that will take her to Andrijevci. The bus is empty – everyone's been home for some time now, slaughtering a pig, celebrating Republic Day, and warming themselves up with this year's šljivovica. By evening, the sausages will be made, the meat ground up and packed into the wide, flexible pork intestines, the cracklings will have been salted and left to cool in the summer kitchens on wide, black baking pans, the cats will be gorging themselves around the courtyards on the pig spleens and the little bits of their animal insides that a person cannot manage to swallow, and everyone will be dead drunk, singing Croatian songs about the Fairy of the Velebit and Ban Jelačić, and when the rakija has wiped away their minds completely, they'll be emboldened and shout to the memories of the Ustaše Jure Frančetić and Rafael Boban, and to the glory of the Poglavnik Pavelić, and neither the People's Militia nor any village informants nor spies will be there to report the songs or the singers, for they too will in that moment be feasting on their slaughtered pigs, singing different Croatian songs or maybe the very same ones. For it is the year 1970, all of Croatia has awakened, cheering the Croatian Spring and its leaders Miko Tripalo and Savka Dabčević-Kučar, the rebirth of national heroism, bravery, and consciousness. People no longer want their money to go off to Belgrade – "Croatia toils, Belgrade takes the spoils" – but are instead for a politics of open accounting, so that all will be clear as to who brings what to this socialist collective of ours. People are filled with joy and with anger, which is why they're singing so loudly, shouting out what they would not have dared shout out even a day ago. From their graves long-gone fathers and uncles have risen up, regiments from the battles of Stalingrad and Dravograd in columns of two and four deep making their way toward the shallow mass graves that the asphalt and cement of socialism have not yet managed to cover over; and from their graves frightened Home Guard soldiers have risen up who in the meantime have become heroic as dead men, and they too sing as one with their sons and grandsons; and up too have risen the Jasenovac cut-throats and Croatian martyrs, who in 1942, their fucking swords drawn, ranged across Kozara, burning, raping, and murdering, and they too now join in this grandiose Republic Day pig slaughter, in remembrance of November 29, 1943, when the eternal brotherhood of the Yugoslav nations and peoples was founded in the town of Jajce.

But she rides along in the ancient Mercedes bus toward Andrijevci, looking in front of her at the dirty headrest cover, her stomach unsettled by the mixture of smells: the stench of sweat and children's vomit, diesel fuel, cigarette smoke, and burnt plastic, all mixed together to form the single, unique aroma of traveling by bus. She's trying not to think about anything, taking deep, regular breaths through her mouth. She is alone, on this journey and in life – this is how she feels, and this is how she yearns to feel, awash in self-pity and the belief that everything is over and all her life's opportunities have been lost and destroyed,and that she's not responsible for any of it: her mother, her former husband, and her awful mother-in-law are to blame, as is that little boy whom she gave birth to; it's his fault too that her life is now finished, even before it really was able to start.

It was over when she was barely eighteen months old and the news of Mladen's death arrived.

Ivan Latić is waiting for her at the gravesite in Donji Andrijevci. The caretaker of the graveyard, actually a local villager transformed into a caretaker by the kin of those soldiers collected there who, out of gratitude to him for caring for the graves of these brothers and sons who perished on the wrong side, give him money each time they visit. There are not many graves, just five or six – five from the Home Guard, and the sixth, Mladen's, is German, SS – but those few graves are enough for an illusion of the importance and privilege of one's work.

Latić's is the last house before the graveyard. It's an attractive and orderly village dwelling, with a tidy courtyard, in the midst of which some large boars are just being scalded. The blood has long since emptied out from their slit throats, the cinnamon and cloves give off a sweet smell, Latić's wife is roasting blood sausage, and everything is somehow quiet and solemn, as in a church or at a cemetery. But Ivan Latić is not a typical villager. He doesn't drink and never has. It doesn't agree with him. His father had been a horrible drunk, he says, and he knows the kind of unhappiness it can bring. Javorka solemnly agrees.

He takes her to Mladen's grave, though she could have found it herself. She's been here at least ten times, at first with her mother, then with her father – from the time she was little – and then alone. This is the fifth time since then that she has come, once per year, less for the sake of memory and the soul, more out of fear that if she doesn't visit, the authorities will dig up and plough over this graveyard for occupying soldiers. She's known Ivan Latić since he was a young man and youth organization member who had once looked with disdain on those who lit candles and brought flowers to these graves. He never would have dreamed that one day he would be the graveyard's caretaker. He'd matured, grown older, and had woken up to a complex reality. No, he didn't need rakija to start singing songs that he really shouldn't be singing.

She would spend the night at Latić's. It was this way every time. There were no hotels nearby, and even if there had been, these were not times in which one spent money on hotel rooms. That was for tourists and the affluent, for directors and their chauffeurs, not for someone who came from far away to visit her brother's grave. Her mother too had most often slept at Latić's, as had her father once.

He brought her to a grave with a black iron cross, on which there was a white plate with the first and last name, the date of birth, and the date of death. Latić pulled a few dried-out, frozen weeds from around Mladen's head, displaying his concern for the grave.

From her purse she took an old-fashioned white candle and lit it without difficulty. There was not even a breath of wind, and the flame stood up straight and nearly motionless. Then it was as if she didn't know what to do. She waited at the foot of the grave for some appropriate length of time to pass. This was the time in which believers prayed to God or directed their thoughts to the deceased, calling them to mind, letting some sort of internal movie run in their mind's eye. But she didn't remember Mladen, and she didn't believe in God. Her lack of belief was pure and unambiguous, almost as naïve as some people's faith. God was unnecessary to her because he had not been able to resolve even one of her problems. And she did not know how to dissemble, lie, or live in a lie. When she died, Father Ivo Marković sent me a note of condolences: "I knew her personally and recall her sincere manner of communicating, of the sort that only children have, which is always something to admire. May she rest in Peace." He was the one who allowed me to see this fact: my mother didn't know how to lie like adults, which was only one of her childlike traits.

And that was why she didn't know what to do, but just stood there at the foot of Mladen's grave, a little angry that someone else was standing there because now she couldn't just quietly walk away.

Ivan Latić did not understand her reminiscences. He moved his lips as if reciting a prayer, then crossed himself, nimbly as a rote Catholic. As they were leaving the graveyard, he said something that maybe he would not have said had there not been that senseless waiting or had it not been the year before the *Croatian Spring*:

"The man who killed your brother lives here in Andrijevci. You'll undoubtedly see him today. Would you like me to point him out?"

"No!" she shouted, as if trying to forestall him, or as if Ivan Latić only had to raise his finger and direct it toward someone, though just then there was no one else around.

That night Mladen's sister, my mother Javorka, lay in a spacious bed with the sort of elderdown quilt that could suffocate the unaccustomed, as if in a thick sea, and imagined the man who had killed her brother, but more than that, the man who perhaps had had the most crucial influence on making her life what it was. She couldn't manage to get to sleep before dawn.

She'd continue to imagine him over the next days, months, and years, until Mladen's killer became unimportant. She would go to Mladen's grave only one more time, in 1975. Again it would be in November, when Vesna and Andrija had just got married in Kopanica, and, on the Sunday after the wedding, when the majority of the guests had been felled by a great drowsiness, she went alone to the graveyard in Donji Andrijevci. Ivan Latić was taciturn and suspicious, as if in the interim he had suddenly grown old, and was not ostentatious about his role. He quietly took the money offered, and we never saw him again.

Countless times she tried to recall each of the men's faces she saw in Andrijevci that Republic Day in 1970 before she had gone out to Mladen's grave with Latić. Young men, middle-aged villagers, and the elderly, mostly dead drunk, in open-collared white shirts, bloody from the slaughter, and ribbed-cloth coats. She remembered some of the faces, or so she believed, and others only came to her in dreams. But not once did she regret telling Ivan Latić that she didn't want to see the man who had killed her brother.

Until a few weeks before her death she hadn't told anyone about this. She could not have told her father or mother, or her brother Dragan, who might not have understood. Or if he had understood, then he would have gone to Ivan Latić and asked him to show him the man living with a clear conscience in Andrijevci, despite the fact he had killed someone – an SS officer – in September 1943. But this part was all the same to her. What was important was merely having a story, it didn't matter which one – just a true story to turn her from the thought that she was about to die.

Miners, Smiths, Drunks, and Their Wives

Quartets

Aunt Jele and the
Kljujić Šumonja Family

I

Marko Kljujić Šumonja was an enormous man and a valuable one. He was the type of person who'd rather move mountains with his bare hands than stand around with nothing to do. In the highland colonies he built a house, and farther up in the mountains, above the settlement, he cleared a well. The land was not his, nor was the well. He did it for the community, for everyone's use, so each person would have access to water. What he built here would outlive him and would remain in place through the eighties, by which time all of Kakanj had long since started receiving its water from the water treatment plant. This is why agas and viziers, warlords, noblemen, rich landowners, and all those who wanted to be remembered long after their deaths had built public fountains and improved wells and springs all across Bosnia.

Marko Kljujić Šumonja had two sons. Mato was unlucky in life; he married then separated. In those days people didn't get divorced. After that, he lived alone to the end of his days. The other son, whose name we don't remember, was in the Ustaše. That's how he died. We don't remember when or where. Nor do we know what he was like or whether he ever married. All we know about him is that he was in the Ustaše.

Marko also had four daughters: Aunt Ruže, Aunt Mare, Aunt Luce, and Aunt Jele, who was our actual aunt. Aunt Jele was married to Uncle Karlo. Uncle Karlo was Franjo Rejc's brother. But more about Aunt Jele and Uncle Karlo later.

Aunt Ruže's daughter was named Manka. Her real name is unknown; everyone just called her Manka. Before the Second World War she gave birth to a son. His name was Ivica. Whether he was born out of wedlock or Manka's husband left her is not the important thing here. In the mining colonies just about everything occurred, including extramarital children and runaway husbands, and all of it could be suffered through, hurled forward with a flip, along with those things called "illegitimate children."

Ivica just barely finished the first two grades of elementary school and didn't go further. A teacher might have said Ivica was stupid. The village priest might have said, somewhat more kindly, humanely, that Ivica was simply not very bright. Anyhow, it wouldn't have been right for everyone to be intelligent in the same way.

But Ivica did have one great desire: to become a chimney sweep.

At the time, just after the war, becoming a chimney sweep didn't require any higher schooling. Just a little skill, the courage to walk along rooftops, a black coat, and a brush.

"Don't do it, son!" said his mother. "It's much too high up!"

Ivica listened to his mother and didn't become a chimney sweep but instead became a miner.

Not even six months had passed when, in a very small mining accident, Ivica was killed. He was the only one. He'd been breaking through a rock, and his head had been crushed. An unlucky incident. In such a situation, all the intelligence in the world would have been useless to a person. So it was all the same to Ivica that he had no intelligence.

This was at the beginning of the fifties.

The suffering of Manka's son Ivica, Aunt Ruže's only grandson and the great-grandson of Marko Kljujić Šumunja, who was as strong as the earth and built that well with his own hands, was the sort of event that amounted in the memories of others to an entire biography characterized by pity.

No one could ever remember Ivica without feeling pity.

II

Aunt Luce was a kind woman. She would rush to help anyone in need, without asking who it was or why. She had married a certain Segat, who'd spent about three years in prison after the war. No one asked what part of the law he had violated or what wartime misdeed he'd committed. Serving time was all you needed to know then, it was better not to ask more.

As soon as the war was over, the people of Kakanj would use any excuse to go out to the meadows, which they referred to by the Turkish-derived word *meraja*. The moment it wasn't too chilly and didn't look like rain, they'd pack up for the *meraja*. Miners, rail men, office workers, both men and women, everyone would bring food from their homes, Turkish coffeepots and cups, a bottle of rakija and little glasses, and, somewhere along the Bosna River, have a picnic and tell all kinds of stories. Once in a while they would even spend the night, returning to the Colony well after dark.

On one such occasion there was a trip with Segat and Aunt Luce. Franjo and Olga came from Sarajevo with their daughter, who must have been five or six. Old enough, that is, to remember it all for the rest of her life.

When he'd had a couple drinks, Segat grew expansive and started to tell a story.

Otherwise he was not a big talker. He was normally quiet, sullen, and everyone said this was because of his time in prison.

The more he talked, though, the louder he got, until our people felt like hiding their faces. Both the women and the men. They disappeared, like tortoises pulling their heads inside their shells, waiting for Segat's foolishness to pass. But he didn't stop. He said everything, as if for years he hadn't said a word and this was the beginning or the end. And just when you thought now he had to stop, he couldn't possibly go on, a God-fearing person couldn't talk like this, on he went, sinking lower, growing uglier, more horrible. He talked in such a way that a person felt guilty for listening, as much to blame for the words being aired as the person doing the talking.

This was in 1949 or 1950, in the mining colony at Kakanj, in the summertime, on the *meraja* along the Bosna River.

When he understood no one was going to do anything, Franjo got up, took his child by the hand, arm in arm with Olga, and walked away, just like that, without a word. No one asked where they were going.

Segat was drunkenly shouting out a story of how some Gypsies had been butchered one dawn at Jasenovac while he was in the service there.

For years in our house the question was debated whether Segat had invented his service at Jasenovac as a kind of boast.

That was the last trip to the *meraja* in Kakanj. Segat was not seen much after, only at family funerals. Then he himself died. No one knows exactly when, or from what.

III

There were villagers who worked in the mines. Either they lost their land or didn't have any in the first place and therefore had to go into the pit to feed their families. They didn't last long. If they weren't buried by a landslide, they took the ash into their lungs, or were consumed day after day by alcohol.

There was one fat peasant who would sing the same bawdy folk song every morning as he came toward Kakanj every morning alongside the Colony:

When you give your titties
A little shaky-do
You don't give me no peace
I'm sad through and through.

In sunshine and snowfall, when no one was around or with people every-where, he sang the same song. People got used to him.

Once he was singing *When you give your titties a little shaky-do* when from down the street an older woman in traditional dress called, "Praise Jesus, child!" to which the peasant-miner politely replied, "Praise him everywhere" and then continued, *You don't give me no peace. I'm sad through and through.*

For years on end. Nothing ever changed there – nothing, that is, until the great mine accident down in the pit, the innumerable funerals, and the eventual arrival of delegations from Zenica and Sarajevo.

IV

Aunt Jele was the boss of the home.

Not because she wanted to be, but simply because she had to be. Uncle Karlo was a foreman in the mine, a quiet, helpful person, but he never decided anything on his own. It was his nature. He could have, but he was tired out from always being the boss.

He drank a lot but never became a drunk.

Aunt Jele died in 1970. Uncle Karlo five years later.

It wasn't easy for him on his own.

The Karivans: A Short Tale

I

The Karivan house was the closest building to the Franciscan monastery in Kreševo. Karivan Place was an old smithy where since the Middle Ages they had forged steel in the same way. On this same spot a large public ironworks would be erected after the end of the Second World War – the state would nationalize the land, destroy the smithy, and build something of its own.

No one would even ask about compensation afterward. After 1990, when denationalization should have taken place, the war came. After that it was too late. The Karivan descendants scattered across the world, and no one was around who could still remember the story of the smithy, let alone ask for restitution. Besides, to seek restitution all the heirs would need to connect. And these people, perhaps, didn't want to know about each other.

They had been miners in addition to being smiths. On the whole, for generations, as long as the family had been in Kreševo, their lives had revolved around coal, iron, and steel for generations. One story has it that they'd begun moving to Sarajevsko polje to take up residence because one Karivan had killed a Turk and had been forced to flee. Though it's not a very likely story.

You wouldn't run to Sarajevsko polje if you'd killed a Turk, you'd run toward the sea, where there weren't any Turks and Turkish law was not observed. More likely they'd headed off in search of some sort of easier work. Not everyone is cut out to be a miner or a smith.

And after some left, it was expected that others would follow. So from the end of the nineteenth century, from generation to generation, the Karivan kin had settled in Otes, Hadžići, and Tarčin. And then, eventually, closer to Sarajevo.

Their line was not strong, nor did they give birth to sons, nor were they lucky in life. Who knows what else there might've been at play, but the family name Karivan didn't seem to spread or grow.

II

It was not a large or a rich house.

Made from little mud bricks, not stone or baked clay, the Karivan house in Kreševo, the closest building to the Franciscan monastery, caved in soon after they had left.

The courtyard disappeared too: overgrown, transformed into wasteland.

Only the walnut tree in front remained.

Everyone called it the Karivan walnut.

In Kreševo, in front of a house that once was, and a courtyard that is no more, grew the Karivan walnut.

III

By today's standards, the distance from Otes to Kreševo is not far.

If the road were better, it would take barely a half hour. But the road isn't good.

The part of the family that resettled in Otes, both the men and the women, stopped wearing the characteristic dress of Kreševo and replaced it with that of Sarajevsko polje.

And the Karivan women from Kreševo, in their black Turkish embroidered pantaloons, their white blouses and black embroidered sleeveless jackets, would look so silently at the Otes Karivan women, with their black skirts and differently designed white blouses, while between them a foreign land grew larger and broader. Some thought their daughters, daughters-in-law, and sisters-in-law were growing estranged, while others thought that their mothers, mothers-in-law, and sisters-in-law had been left behind in their sorrow and poverty.

The space that separated them, however, could still have been crossed on foot.

But the distance was the same as if chains of mountains had risen up and oceans had spread out wide between them, foreign languages sealed upon their lips. Everything was over once the first Karivan woman in her Turkish pantaloons saw another Karivan woman in a skirt.

The foreign country expanded, and it swallowed them up.

IV

Uncle Mato Karivan had bought a house in Bistrik, in Sarajevo's Catholic quarter.

This house too was nationalized, then destroyed.

All that was left was a rundown wooden shed full of holes that was for storing tools and unneeded junk. It didn't belong to anyone.

To the neighbors, it came to be known as the Karivan shack.

It stood there for all of fifty years before finally falling apart by itself.

That, or the neighbors had destroyed it during one of the winters of the war, lighting up its torn planks to warm themselves.

Such is the story of how the Karivan shed and the Karivan family disappeared from Sarajevo.

For the Love of Your Goddamn Mother

I

Aunt Mare married Kvesa, a miner from Raspotočje.

When he wasn't down in the pit, Kvesa was busy making kids. Aunt Mare bore nine of them.

Watching over the kids, raising them, teaching them, was her job, but as kids will be, they were a handful. When one of her nine sons and daughters committed any sort of folly, by word, action, or oversight, Aunt Mare didn't punish them right away, but made a mental note.

Then on Saturday before dinner, just after their baths, she would line all nine of them up and have them bend over a bench to spank their bottoms with a paddle, dealing the same number of blows as indiscretions committed by each child during God's good week.

She beat them so they would begin the Lord's Day cleansed.

She was practical, Aunt Mare, because what other kind of person could have kept a running count of the punishments to be meted out for offenses committed by every one of her nine sons and daughters over the course of an entire week? She had a good memory and never forgot a thing. It would not have been fair to one child to forget or overlook something, for another child might then be doubly punished.

Aunt Mare Kljujić was an Old Testament mining mother.

One Saturday she was in the process of giving her most lively and energetic son such a wallop that he shouted, "Dammit, mother, for the love of your goddamn mother, cut it out!"

II

When they were given away in marriage, women became mourners.

They put on black veils, but in a particular way, backwards, so it covered the backs of their heads.

Among the more educated it was believed that in their black pantaloons and black veils they mourned the last queen of Bosnia, Katarina.

Ethnologists believed in this quaint, romantic story, along with the collectors of folk proverbs, sketched panoramas, and photographs, who came from Vienna and Zagreb and fell fatally in love with the provinces of Bosnia and all their hardships.

And perhaps it was really true. Perhaps the bride-mourners mourned for the queen out of some longstanding practice passed from generation to generation down to our own day.

Every daughter of Marko Kljujić Šumonja, except for our Aunt Jele, was given the name Katarina.

In order to distinguish between them, or because of some already existing difference that found expression in a slight transformation of the order of vowels and consonants, they called the Katarinas by different names.

Aunt Ruže called her Katarina by the shortened version of Katina.

Aunt Mare's Katarina was simply Kate.

III

All four of Marko's daughters were literate.

At least enough so that during Sunday mass they could read from the breviary.

They signed documents in a knobbly laborer's handwriting that to the ends of their lives lent their letters a beginner's shape and would preserve forever the impression of being written by seven-year-old girls.

They read the telegrams with news of the deaths of those close to them in faraway places, and then the death lists and newspaper obituaries of their own husbands.

This was how being literate served them.

IV

Aunt Jele gave birth to large children.

Both Drage and Vlado weighed more than four kilos. In 1944 Rezu was born, and he too was big.

When Franjo's wife Olga gave birth in May of 1942, Jele got on a train for Sarajevo to visit them. For some people this would not have been a great journey – it's not far from Kakanj to Sarajevo. But for people from the Colony, both men and women, who did everything they did around Kakanj itself, and only when it was absolutely necessary ventured as far as Zenica, traveling to Sarajevo, a big city in which they had no business, was like setting out for the ends of the earth. And then there was the war, famine, and poverty.

Aunt Jele, though, was very close to Olga. The two of them understood each other. They weren't just sisters-in-law, they were friends. She had to go to Sarajevo.

It never entered Uncle Karlo's mind that he should go too. After all, he had work. Despite the war, in the mine they worked at full tilt. Uncle Karlo was a locksmith at the screening plant.

Olga gave birth to a daughter.

She had her at the hospital, which for Aunt Jele was rather extraordinary.

The little girl was tiny, barely two kilos.

After she was born, she lost twenty grams more.

"Olga dear, I would have been ashamed to give birth to a thing like that!" said Aunt Jele, peering over at the little child in her sister-in-law's arms.

Even today people in Kakanj have a laugh at this, seventy years after the fact.

Aunt Jele was witty and knew the right moment to make a joke, as few people do.

Anecdotes and experiences that were made funny by two or three of her words of commentary were remembered and passed on. For the most part, people would recount them during mourning visits, at the home of the deceased after the burial.

Then they'd laugh with relief. Just happy to still be alive.

Uncles

I

Church was the center of social life in the Colony.

People went to church, those who believed and those who didn't, because of their friends, God, and Reverend Divić.

Divić was handsome. All the girls were in love with him. He was also very mouthy. This was the word they used – *mouthy*. And the miners in those days prized such people.

The way you spoke and the fact that you went down into the pit separated the brave from the cowardly. People to whom God had not given the choice to be brave respected the fact that Divić had been given a choice and that he had taken it. Their black miners' garments were after all sown from the same cloth as Divić's priestly gown.

During the war, the reverend would bless the believers and ask them to pray for strangers, for all those they knew, for their loved ones. And each time he would add, "And let us pray for the ones out there . . ." and he would point to the woods, where in the collective imagination of the congregation the Partisans were hiding.

Reverend Divić was instigating rebellion. The people knew what he was doing and why. There had never been many Orthodox Christians in Kakanj. Neither in the neighboring villages nor around the mine. But there was an Orthodox Church and a priest, Father Miloš.

In accord with their experiences and spiritual interests, the rules of the market, or more probably as the result of a kind of empathy that brings people of similar characters together, Reverend Divić and Father Miloš became friends. The reverend would visit Father Miloš and his wife every Sunday for lunch, helping Miloš's children with their Greek and Latin, such that a firm trust developed between them in this lost, melancholy Bosnian backwater.

The first thing the Ustaše did upon taking power in Kakanj was kill Father Miloš.

Reverend Divić was not able to save him. Father Miloš's ultimate sacrifice weighed heavily on the reverend's conscience. This was why he instigated rebellion.

Maybe it was thanks to Reverend Divić that the miners from the Colony didn't join the Ustaše. A villager here or there who worked in the mine did, but no one from the Colony itself. Instead they prayed for all the living, for the people they knew and those they did not, for their loved ones, and for the people out there.

But when the people out there emerged from out there and liberated Kakanj, it did not take long for Reverend Divić to start being mouthy again. He disliked everything he saw about the communists, and he unloaded it all onto the people on Sundays, encouraging them to think for themselves and decide.

It didn't take long before they came for him.

He spent a month, or two, or three, in the Zenica prison, then they let him out. Reverend Divić came back and continued his work.

Years passed. Some people believed in God, others did not, but he kept on preaching. All the girls were in love with him. The Colony had, after all, never seen a more handsome man.

When the siren sounded, each person would look around to locate father, husband, brother, father-in-law . . .

Then they would scramble.

The men would jump up from their meals, spoons clanging against plates. They would run outside without speaking, heading for the mine, and it would take some time before the air calmed, the scramble came to a stop, and the first words were spoken.

Where's the accident?

Which corridor?

How many injured?

III

Uncle Rudo's wife, Aunt Anica, was a converted Jew. She was born in Zenica and had the maiden name of Jungwirth.

Her people had come to Bosnia from Austria.

There was no synagogue in Zenica and there were barely any Jews. So as not to be alone, or out of fear of remaining alone, the Jungwirths became Catholics.

Aunt Anica looked just so: like a little girl, a young woman, an old woman from a Marc Chagall painting. Any old German or Croatian Nazi would have recognized her had he chanced to come across her on a Sarajevo or Zagreb street.

But neither of them would have thought there might be any Jews in Kakanj, out there in the Colony. Uncle Rudo didn't ask her about such things. He was a carpenter and uninterested in questions of parentage or extraction. He trimmed boards and in his free time made very nice home furniture. Every solid, valuable piece of wood in Franjo Rejc's Sarajevo home was cut and shaped by the hands of Uncle Rudo.

Nor did others ask Aunt Anica about it.

Either they were too embarrassed to ask, or it wasn't yet the sort of subject one could discuss.

In their son Tješo's face you could see hers.

Something distant had been printed and sealed into the roughhewn Bosnian features and the worldly path of the Rejcs.

One could look long at it in Tješo.

IV

Franjo Rejc had three brothers: Karlo, Rudo, and Eda. Franjo's and Rudo's children referred to Karlo using the Turkish-derived word for uncle, *amidža*. But Franjo's, Rudo's, and Karlo's children called Eda *stric*, using the Croatian word. When they found themselves all together, they always knew exactly who was called *amidža* by whom and who was called *stric*, and never did any child make a single mistake. It would take the wars of the nineties for the Rejc children and grandchildren to understand the nature of these distinctions.

Our aunt Marica, Uncle Eda's wife, a good cook and a big-hearted woman with a stormy disposition, was born in Vitez. Nieces and nephews didn't use the word *amidža* for uncle there. Except among the Muslims.

Revelation Through Story

I

Ramadan fell on the summer months in those years.

The days were long, and the longer the days the longer the fasts.

Avdaginica was fasting, with her brother-in-law and five small children in the house. Her nerves were naturally weak: she exploded easily and had a hard time calming down.

Every now and then she'd beat her children. She beat the hell out of them, from being on edge.

Olga said to her in a friendly way, "For God's sake, either stop beating your children, or stop fasting!"

Avdaginica looked at her and said, "You've got a point."

II

Every village had a bey, a district governor of the Ottoman empire. Such had been the custom.

In this village, along the railway, Olga became friends with the late bey's widow.

Their friendship was such that when she would come to their house, she would remove her veil and headscarf. As if Franjo were her brother. As if she were not a woman. And a widow.

The two of them were great friends.

III

The Muslim women remained covered even before other women if they were Christians.

They were afraid a Christian would reveal to her husband what her woman-friend looked like. And she would describe her friend so accurately that the husband would know everything, as if he had seen her with his own eyes. And thus would the Christian woman, living according to her own customs, shame her Muslim friend, perhaps even without knowing it.

The shame came from a different man knowing what you looked like. Whether he was a believer or not. There is something terribly sensual in the fear that a man might discover you, strip you down, and shame you through a description.

This fear contained the deepest human faith one can have in the art of storytelling.

IV

After a short while, Olga began to travel among the Muslim villages wearing pantaloons and a headscarf. She felt comfortable like that, especially at the beginning of spring. Not to mention that it was easier for a young woman to run in pantaloons. And during those times, at the beginning of the twenties, there was no one who didn't feel like running from lightness and joy, or maybe at least in the warm months, in the villages around Kakanj.

Later, one by one, they would grow tired and heavy, as the times would too.

Olga was amazed at the faith of some women.

There was one named Besima who had two daughters.

In spring, one of Besima's daughters died.

In summer, the other daughter died.

Olga went to her, as she was used to doing, for the mourning. There was no such custom among the Muslims. Nor was there a custom of refusing a mourner.

And so they sat there, one before the other, on the floor, looking at one another across the empty table.

Besima was calm, Olga barely kept from breaking down.

"Cry, Besima, it will ease your grief," she said.

"God gave, God has taken away!" Besima answered peacefully.

That was how the two of them mourned.

Thank God, We're Catholics

I

Uncle Mato Karivan married twice.

Both his wives were Albanian. After he became a widower, when he brought another wife home, no one believed he'd not gone out specifically looking for another Albanian woman. But he hadn't. He met her by chance, or perhaps, he thought, it was destiny.

The first had been a good housekeeper, proper and steadfast in everything. She went to church more often than our women did. And people were surprised at that. Some malicious individuals said Arnautka must be terribly sinful to have to go to church every day.

Uncle Mato barely recovered from her death.

"Thank God, we're Catholics," he'd often say.

Everyone found that funny, as if she were not a Catholic to them. Or as if they thought she must be terribly sinful.

II

Between seven thirty and eight at night the Hail Mary would ring out.

Everyone rushed home then. It was late, they said. And who knew what might happen outside. After the Hail Mary, when darkness descended upon Kreševo, life stopped flowing according to Holy Writ. Dragons and witches took control, the dead walked through the center of town, superstitions came to life. One after another people would fall into fitful dreams.

This lasted until about five in the morning.

Everyone would wake up then, in summer or winter. In winter it was still pitch dark at five. But this darkness was not as deep as that of Holy Writ.

III

Bakšić was an official at the mine.

His wife was a traditional Muslim, she wore the traditional covering.

She gave birth to two daughters.

Though the eldest died young.

Fifty years later, when the younger daughter met Franjo's daughter, she would hug her and say, "I'm so happy to see you! It's like seeing my very own sister!"

IV

When the decree against headscarves and veils was passed, Zehra came to complain:

"Olga, dear, I feel completely naked!"

To Olga, Zehra's nakedness was like that of a kinswoman. The revolution had no understanding of human shame. The revolution in Kakanj and Kreševo truly was shameless.

Slaughtering Pigs in the Colonies

I

It is 1956.

Early morning, before dawn, the three of them making their way toward the train station.

The train for Kakanj is full.

Morning coughs, the gurgle and clink of the handheld machine the conductors use to punch the pink and green tickets. Thick cardboard rectangles three centimeters long by one and a half centimeters wide.

The villages of Visoko, Podlugovi, Ćatići. The long train stops at every station, the brakes' metallic squeak, the nasal voice of the Albanian boza vender.

They don't have any gifts for their relatives in Kakanj. It isn't customary. And anyway what could they bring from Sarajevo. It's a time of scarcity, empty store windows, dreariness, November fog.

People are careful about every word they utter, every person they curse.

In the second and third mining colonies, each little house has a courtyard and a small orchard.

In the courtyard there's a hog, with the hog a sow, and all the little pigs.

Every November, before Republic Day, the miners slaughter the hogs.

On Saturday afternoon, the squeals of the "unclean" animals can be heard all the way to the center of town.

There are more than a few Muslims in the colonies, but no one complains.

These are the times. You don't complain unless someone else does.

Before evening, the sow circles the hog, grunting softly, amazed, while above the eaves, their bellies slashed open, her children hang upside down.

The flames reflect from all sides on the faces of the Rejc family. Cracklings sizzle on the tin trays atop the flames, and a soft rakija daze covers everything.

In the mountain colonies a worried mother calls for her absent children to come home, it's late. Though she's worried, when they return, they'll get what's coming to them.

III

Several days back they were cooking some šljivovica.

Neighbors gathered around the kettle.

They talked about mining accidents.

About brothers and sons who hadn't yet returned, whom they'd been waiting for, beside the radio, since the summer of 1945.

About a man who had blasphemed and ended up in Zenica, serving five years.

About who had died just the year before, the names strung together in a list.

And so they got drunk without even taking a sip. As they inhaled the alcoholic vapors, the spirits of the miners pulled back. Sometimes this drove them crazy, and their wives paid for it the moment they asked a question.

There was always a bottle set aside for the ones they were waiting for.

They return to Sarajevo on the night train.

Ćatići. Podlugovi. Visoko.

There are fewer travelers than in the morning, so there are places to sit. On the wooden grating above their heads a drop of blood slowly accumulates. It doesn't happen often, but the children watch in anticipation to see if the drop will fall – right on their father's neck.

They're bringing sausages and cracklings from Kakanj to Sarajevo, and a whole suckling pig, its eyes compressed as if it were asleep, because it's late and long past the hour when children should be up.

It's 1956, a time of scarcity. The women on board are silent, watching over their children, who have only just fallen asleep, one after another. The men are careful not to curse.

There's a bottle of stewed miners' prunes in their bag. For Christmas, or just in case a guest shows up.

Mama Ionesco

A Report

December 2, 2012. Pula, near the Roman Forum.

The second floor, stone steps worn smooth by feet, sculpted by a hundred fifty years' worth of traversing soles. A small servants' room, remodeled into an apartment for tourists. Vertiginous ceilings, white walls, white furniture and bed linen, luminous woodwork and shining floors. On the side of the small wardrobe I'm looking into: a portrait of Modesty Blaise.

The mobile phone on the nightstand vibrates. Her name appears on the screen, but I know she's not the one calling. It's a man's voice.

"My condolences," he says, then, after a meaningless pause: "Mama has died."

It occurs to me that it isn't appropriate for him to call my mother that.

While I speak the words that are needed in such a moment, demonstrating calm and collectedness, answering the small, technical questions – the funeral has already been arranged for Tuesday at half past eleven – I think about that indiscreet use of the word: Mama.

December 24, 2011, Hotel Majestic, room number 600, Belgrade. The phone vibrates. Her name appears on the screen, and I answer a little angrily because I've told her not to call me when I'm in Belgrade – roaming's expensive. She's in a bad mood. She's talking about unimportant things, I've forgotten what they were, and then, after several minutes of conversation, she says she found a *lump*. Where? On the inside of her left leg, just below the groin. It's nothing, I tell her, but this time I sense that it isn't. She was often ailing, usually from little things, and would raise the alarm over false signs, something she had found, traces of blood, negligible discoveries . . . She was always like this, focused on herself and the minor imperfections of her body. She imparted to me this same eternal fear, that in the very next instant something catastrophic might happen. Or maybe I inherited it the same way one inherits eye color.

It's between Christmas and New Year's, a time when one doesn't go to the doctor, certainly not for an exam, and only in an emergency, but this, it seems, is not an emergency.

"Does it hurt?" I ask.

"No. It's like I'm touching a piece of wood, like it's not me, this *lump*."

I come back to Zagreb for New Year's.

Now we can talk. January first, second, and third are mostly not working days. People go skiing. Here they go to Austria, in Bosnia they go to Jahorina and Bjelašnica. I try to get her to talk about that. Someone in a certain Sarajevo periodical said I was an "incurable Chetnik." But this no longer upsets her. It's no longer the subject. She'd rather talk about the *lump*, even if there really isn't much to say about a mere *lump*.

Then she repeats the same phrase, the same words, for the thousandth time . . .

"It's nothing, right?"

"Of course it's nothing," I tell her.

A few minutes later, the same question and answer.

So we begin a year's worth of lengthy telephone conversations.

She has always had this irrepressible need to discuss things about which there is little to say and then repeat the same phrases, the same questions as I respond to them one by one.

She goes to the doctor just before Orthodox Christmas. The doctor is a Serb, such an appointment wouldn't feel as urgent if it weren't Christmas for him as well. But, in fact, this isn't urgent either, even though we talk it all over for a long time. Words flow between us that in someone else's conversation wouldn't make an ounce of sense. Much later it will occur to me that this is how characters talk in Ionesco's plays. Perhaps I should stop reading him, Ionesco, or at least stop seeing his plays. Mama Ionesco.

"He felt it," she says, "the *lump*, but said you can't tell anything from touching. He scheduled tests for after Christmas."

January 14, 2012, Friday. The phone vibrates.

I answer, knowing she was at the exam in the morning, for a biopsy on a small piece of tissue. She's upbeat, as if everything's fine. She's telling stories, talking about who she had coffee with after the exam. The findings, she says, will come back on Monday. And the lump, has it got bigger? No, it's still the same. On second thought, maybe a little bigger.

The winter is snowy and wet. During the weekends I pull back from everything, as if shrinking into a steel cell, one without any exits. The thought is obsessive, always identical, from the moment I wake up in the morning to the second I fall asleep late at night. It's like this until December 2, when the phone begins to vibrate in the white Pula room that reminds me of heaven, and her name is on the display, and somehow I know it's not her. Her illness has been on my mind every waking moment.

On Monday at ten o'clock I answer the phone and hear her cold, distant voice, and it is as if she has been to my school and discovered I've been hiding from her the fact that I got an F in math.

"I can't keep this from you. It's the worst it could possibly be."

The word *lump* is never pronounced again. The strange term *lymph node* has taken its place. We'll grow completely used to it, as with all the codes and bywords that will come to be associated with her entire condition.

She had an exam two and a half years earlier. They saw something then, but the doctor – whose name I now recall with the kind of rage that makes my joints feel as if they're being pulled apart, my bones being ripped asunder – said that it was surely nothing. Then, so that everything was by the book, he sent a bit of that nothing off for analysis, by which it was simply confirmed that the something was in fact nothing. But he didn't look carefully, or perhaps didn't know how to look, at what he saw under the microscope, discerning an abstract image in which distinct signs of death could be recognized among the chaotic signs of life, and he didn't see what had already begun. It wasn't nothing. It was something. And at that point it would have been completely treatable . . .

Is this really the truth, or is it just her way of protecting herself from bad news?

No, it is the truth.

And then she repeats the story that makes my joints separate and my bones break apart, about the careless, alcoholic doctor. You should sue the hospital, she says, get reparations from the hospital, because treatment will be expensive. Terribly expensive. You should hold someone at fault, threaten to write about it in the Croatian and European papers.

Suddenly she sees me as a powerful and influential person, before whom the world will tremble at the threat of my pen. I try in passing during our conversations, which grow longer and longer, to slip in the fact that someone called me an "incurable Chetnik" in a Sarajevo paper, but this no longer reaches her. It's a part of reality that's been removed by the scalpel, without any need to send it off for histological analysis. It's wrong of me to bring up such things: if she could think about them, if there were room in her head for the remark of some Sarajevo poet about her son's being an "incurable Chetnik," she would go crazy. Or perhaps she'd kill herself, knowing in her head as well as her heart that there was no more help for her.

Our perspectives differ: I would like for her to have a little tranquility, for her not to ask things of me that are impossible and crazy, that won't be helpful for anything, and I don't see, I really don't want to see, that she's grabbing onto me like a drowning person, and if I don't keep my head about me we'll both go down.

What does keeping your head about you mean in such a situation?

You would need to call someone in Sarajevo, tell them what was happening with your mother, ask for help, for someone to be there. I'll call H., to whom I can pour out my heart. He'll understand everything in the right way, but I wouldn't even know how to do that: pour out my heart. It seems there aren't any others left . . .

The next day everything starts again: she expects me to blame someone, make threats, find a lawyer, announce to the world what this doctor has done to a celebrated writer's mother and how the medical bureaucracy is trying to cover it up. Then she comes back to the doctor, repeating in detail what happened two and a half years before, *when there was still time*. I listen, say that she told me all that already, but she just says, "So what if I already told you! Do you know what that man did to me? This is about my life, not yours!"

And then she starts the story again from the beginning, exactly as it happened, not leaving out a single detail, as if the repetition contains its own sense and is in itself the sought-after cure.

She was born on May 10, 1942. Her elder brother Mladen – who would receive, a few days after her birth, his recruitment notice, as an ethnic German, to report for duty with Hitler's SS – wanted his sister to be called Javorka. She couldn't be christened with that name, her birth couldn't be registered with it, so the common Stubler name Regina was the one officially given to her.

She was sixteen months old when Mladen was killed.

The environment that grew out of that event would shape her life. She was not a beloved child. Her mother suffered sharp pangs of guilt for having sent her son to his death, for not having allowed him to desert or escape to the Partisans, for she had believed that serving in a German uniform might save him. A foolish belief, but useless to talk about now. And so mostly it wasn't talked about. Instead there was silence, and my mother grew up in its midst.

Her mother, Olga Rejc, was an intelligent woman. She had an artistic spirit, played the guitar, the zither, and the violin a little. After Mladen's death she never sang again. She read, mostly prose, every single day, entire libraries of books, in Serbo-Croatian and German. None of us who followed her ever were able to read as much as she had. She read quickly, totally concentrated and voracious, in all situations. In the kitchen, with mixing spoons on either side, over a batch of dishes that had just been washed, waiting for a cake to bake. She read constantly, simply in order not to have to live or think about living. Although she did not write, her thoughts and sayings turned immediately into literature. She treated her pangs of guilt with literature. Unsuccessfully.

The newborn girl had taken Mladen's place in the world. His reference number, his fate, his breath. It was unbearable. And she refused to allow the girl to take his place. Probably she wasn't conscious of expelling the girl so completely from her life.

As time passed, rather than the wounds healing and all the horror growing diluted in the blessing of forgetfulness, the circumstance of Mladen's suffering remained in our apartment and within the wider family, growing ever more present and alive. Javorka became the very face of Mladen's death. She and her mother's restless, horrified conscience. She loved her, I suppose, as any mother loves her child. And she hated her at the same time, with an inhuman, indescribable, unspeakable hatred of the sort that, unfortunately, didn't exist in any of the novels she read. Such hatred could not exist in literature.

When I was publishing my first books and knew to what end our family story was tending – though I could not imagine the exact circumstances – I thought the trajectory of my mother's life could be altered as simply as if one of the great novelists Olga so loved to read, someone like Pirandello, Dostoevsky, Andrić, Gorky, Tolstoy, Pearl Buck, Flaubert, Bunin, Hamsun, Crnjanski, Bora Stanković, Zola, or Thomas Mann, were writing a book about a mother who blamed her newborn daughter for the wartime death of her son. Had such a novel been written, my mother's and her mother's lives, and mine too, would have taken a completely different course. Perhaps the Stubler family finale would be different too, and the story of Karlo Stubler's moving from Bosowicz would have never come to pass.

Javorka was an excellent student and also attended a music school where she learned to play the piano. She became a member of the Communist League of Yugoslavia at an early age – at the time, in the latter part of the fifties, this was more connected to being part of the cultural elite than to any sort of political gesture – was selected as the 1961 valedictorian of the Second Gymnasium, and studied medicine in college, though she didn't complete her degree, withdrawing after the first year, a fact that, twenty years later, in fits of bitterness, she attributed to her parents' peevishness toward her medical ambitions. Maybe this was true, I don't know, but in this circumstance, and in a long line of others, which would lead to her being alone in the end, dying as she did, in a room that once had a view of Trebević but now faced the white wall of a new building, there were always self-justifications and reasons for seeing herself as a victim to the last day of her life. Death came as a finale – almost as if she had said, I knew it would be like this! – to the stream of monotonous, compelling, mournful stories whose course was set the moment Mladen, in the midst of a Partisan ambush, tried to run from one haystack to another. They killed him like a rabbit, and the story flowed onward in a single direction, as monotonous as a toothache, to her death, or to the moment when the story of her death would be recounted.

That summer, before the end of her first year of medical studies, she fell in love and ran away from home. This episode would become known only much later and never in its entirety. He was a political figure in a youth organization. She probably met him at a conference, celebrating the anniversary of the revolution on Zelengora, and convinced herself that this was her chance to remedy all that was constraining her, that with him she could make a happy life for herself. And of course, she was hugely mistaken.

She felt nothing for this man, by contrast to all her other loves and lovers, for whom she retained passionate emotions, which she would express in her oft-told stories about them, as if they had happened yesterday. She spoke about these former lovers as if they might turn up at any moment, and their stories would continue from where they had left off. She was the same toward each of them but not toward the man who had been her first husband.

I had long since grown up when she confessed to me that she'd had another husband before my father. It was the only time my mother ever expressed shame before me, and truthfully she had no reason whatsoever to feel that way.

That escape from the house had deepened Olga's hatred.

Though she had never run away, as a seventeen-year-old Olga had come to her father and announced she was marrying a man her parents had never met. He let her, of course he had no choice, but he also said, "Now it's done, he can split firewood on your back, but there will be no return to this house," and such a proclamation had pained and scarred her. She never tried to return, she had no reason to, but she could never let him forget what he'd said.

Javorka, meanwhile, came back a little over a year later. But she didn't return in the same way she had left, for she had nowhere else to go. She described what awaited her there with a sufferer's self-assurance, as when the mother of a fallen soldier becomes accustomed to her role, so that it was impossible to believe her story. Not because it was inaccurate but because it was emotionally twisted and impossible to listen to. In telling it she blamed her mother and with her all the world.

The fact that she had come back after having run away provoked in Olga both anger and sadness, more than might have been justifiable. The sadness probably had to do with the fact that returning had been forbidden for Olga herself, even if Franjo had split firewood on her back. He didn't do that – in fact she was always the greater authority in their house – but she still knew that the Stubler home in effect no longer existed for her. Not when her parents grew old and weak, not even when they died – she came to know there really does exist a place to which one can never return.

Olga had a powerful, highly literary imagination and imagined different courses of life for herself. There was always at least one unrealized opportunity, better and happier than anything that actually happened. She must have wondered what her life would have looked like if she'd not met that young rail man in Doboj, if she hadn't fallen in love and run off with him, but instead had remained her father's favorite for but a few years more, if she hadn't had a child early but instead had begun some other life that, perhaps, was more in accord with her nature. Immortality, perhaps, would still not mean anything, but trying out a variety of possibilities in the span of the same human life, the opportunity to return to the beginning and start over again, following a different path, that for Olga would have been the realization of the dream of eternal life.

Instead, several months after haughtily leaving – just as her mother Olga had haughtily announced her marriage to the young railman – Javorka did that which for Olga had never seemed possible: she returned.

My mother was barely twenty years old then.

Her mother, my Nona, had just turned fifty-seven.

First she tried to find a job, but that didn't work out. Next she started a degree in economics. There was never even a word about the possibility of her continuing in medicine. After all that she had done, she couldn't become a doctor. In doctors you had to have trust, and it was not possible to trust her anymore. A stable job for a woman, even a divorcée, would be behind a counter.

This was how things looked to Olga in her anger. Or maybe Javorka imagined this was how her mother saw things, and from there she began to erect her private monument to self-pity. Later, at the beginning of the eighties, when Nona's health was beginning to fail and Javorka's final life loves were in the process of leaving her shattered and broken – though she was hardly forty years old – hysterical fights would take place, mostly on Sunday afternoons. Javorka would erupt with accusations of a ruined life, how Nona had kept her from studying medicine . . . At some point Nona would stop speaking, just wait for it to pass. All this would be happening somewhere around me, the doors slamming, my mother throwing herself on the floor, yanking at her hair – like a child – while I sat silently, always by Nona's side.

Before all of this, in 1964, my mother met my father. I don't know how it happened, I forgot to ask. After she'd died, that same week, when I had come back to Pula from the funeral, I realized that I didn't know how my father and mother had met.

This happened on Sergijevaca Street, on the steps that lead to the Sacred Hearts Gallery. I remember the exact place, and the moment and feeling: it was like when a person remembers he's forgotten his keys at home, and now he has to go back for them. The difference was that I no longer had anyone to ask about what I'd forgotten, or never known. Several days before, until she had been put on the morphine drip, all the answers had been there – one life, and the several lives surrounding it, everything about them could be known – but now it was over, there was nothing, no one left.

I cannot describe the feeling I experienced just then, on Pula's Sergijevaca Street, at the moment when the story closed itself off. That the feeling was intense, I suppose, is evident from the fact that I remember the place and time, the color of the sky, and the weather conditions at that instant, as I realized that the time for questions was irrevocably over.

My father had been fourteen years her senior. He was thirty-six years old when they met, single, an only child, with a difficult mother and a nasty family history. He didn't know his father and grew up in a modest, tiny apartment with a shared toilet in the hallway on Nemanjina Alley, a couple hundred meters from the building on Sepetarevac Street that would be my home up until my departure from Sarajevo. He was an exceptional student, graduated from the First Gymnasium, received his medical degree early, worked first as a teaching assistant, then as a lecturer, then in a hospital, providing part-time care around villages in Romanija, then studied a specialization, got his doctorate . . . And all this, mostly, with an unbalanced, aggressive mother and a toilet in a collective hallway in an apartment that had no proper bathroom.

Before meeting my mother, my father was a hero of socialist labor. An exemplary young man, a doctor who showed by example that nothing was impossible. His successes in life boiled down, for the most part, to his medical pursuits. Everything else was defeat and wretchedness, a bit of luck, a lot of fear, shame, anguish, and then attempts to leave everything to one side and make amends – by his devotion to his work – for the emotional and personal losses of his life.

He was already like that when he met her.

I asked her many times, in different moods and surroundings across the thirty-five years of our conversations about my father, whether she ever loved him. She answered yes. But I'm not sure she was telling the truth. What else could she say but that she'd loved him, despite the fact that he had disappointed and betrayed her, and almost driven her mad? Otherwise, in her eyes, she would've seemed guilty before me. And there was nothing she wanted more than to escape guilt.

Their love was short lived. They never lived together. They would meet in the city, he would take her to the movies, go out sometimes to Pale or Sokolac, where on Tuesdays and Thursdays he received patients in the local clinics. They took the bus because he didn't have a car – he wouldn't even get his driver's license until 1975 – and come back to Sarajevo late at night. On one of these excursions, in September 1965, they conceived me in the Hotel Panorama in Pale. Instead of coming home after my father's shift ended, they had decided to spend the night at the Panorama.

By the time of my birth, their relationship had disintegrated. The marriage that had been quickly arranged, though no one even knew why, in the spring of 1965, fell apart. The question of when the actual divorce would be filed was purely technical.

I was born at the children's hospital in Jezero. The delivery was ordinary, but a portion of the placenta remained inside my mother after the delivery, which caused a serious infection several days later. She barely survived – for this occurrence she blamed the doctors and also her husband, who thoroughly discouraged her from pursuing the issue – so that before completing my first week of life I was separated from my mother. I was breastfed there in the hospital by an unknown Muslim woman, who had just given birth to a girl. The circumstance of having been breastfed by a Muslim woman was something I would recount frequently in the nineties. As if this event defined us politically, my mother and me, at the time of the war between Croatia and Bosnia, and we both spoke about it with a sort of foolish pride.

I never properly met the woman, she died several years ago.

After being separated from my mother then, I never went back to her. Nona took me home from the hospital and began caring for me, which she would continue to do until her death. Olga never reconciled with her daughter – she coldly pushed her away – and was emotionally uninterested in her younger son – Dragan could never replace Mladen – but the arrival of her grandson in the house gave her new life. She gathered herself up around me, raising me and in a certain sense protecting me from the entropy that was growing and spreading inside the walls of our building, in the apartments of Emilija Heim, and also, since the summer of 1969, in our building on Sepetarevac, for which, given her inability to get beyond her son's death and ease her conscience, she was probably the most responsible. I was exempted from the coldness that was growing around me, and it was only just before the war and throughout it, in the months before her death, that I grew conscious of what Nona had protected me from.

Javorka was ill for a long time, first in the hospital and then at home. For the first two months she was not able to care for me and then she found ways of deliberately not doing so. Illness, anxiety, job hunting, taking exams for special classes, arguments with my father – everything was a reason not to take me off Nona's hands. And later, after six months, I showed a strong attachment to Nona and Nono that was unusual for my age. This would be a favorite topic of conversation over coffee, and they'd say, "Oh, what a smart child he'll grow up to be" – and relatives who came to see the firstborn son would laugh at the unattractive baby, the baby that acted like a grown man, who was aghast at not knowing how to speak, expressing what he wanted simply by extending a hand – toward his Nona.

Although I have memories from a very early age – Aunt Mirjana teaching me to walk in Drvenik, choking on a piece of black bread, Nono carrying me across a bridge over the Miljacka while I cry for fear of falling into the river – I don't remember why I grasped after Nona's hands as if to save myself from drowning, or what it was that ultimately so repelled me from my mother.

One night forty years later, when I had returned from a short stay in Sarajevo, she waited up just to tell me on the phone that her heart had been torn to pieces back then when I would cry the moment I saw her, when I looked only for Nona and reached out my hand always to her.

I answered that as far as I knew six-month-olds still couldn't properly see, so I couldn't very well have looked for Nona.

"But you did!" she exclaimed, "whether with your eyes or in some other way."

I didn't even for a minute feel the slightest pang of guilt.

I was seven months old when Nono and Nona took me to Drvenik. It was the end of November 1966, Sarajevo had become plagued by smog, and Nono had begun to suffocate. For years he had suffered from cardiac asthma, waking up at all hours of the night in fits of coughing, unable to breathe or seemingly find air anywhere. His was a frightening illness, filled with a fear that, in the six years we were together as grandfather and grandson, was passed down to me. He taught me about fear, about living with fear, his fear, and that there is no greater gift in life than a strong breathful of pure night air.

His cardiac asthma was the result of a weak heart, which could have been inherited or could have been acquired over time. This wasn't something that was being studied in the sixties, and even if it was, it would have been hard to trace in retrospect the life course of Franjo's heart: whether it was Mladen's death, or all the wartime fears he'd experienced, or messing around with the Slovenian anti-fascist T.I.G.R., or his famous tendency to run his mouth, which had impelled him to speak out against Hitler and Pavelić and afterward almost die from fear that someone might inform on him, or in the war years on that bloodiest of fronts, at the Piave River, where he was saved by being captured by the Italians, or back to his poor, disorderly Bosnian childhood, with a violent drunk of a father responsible for the untimely deaths of both Franjo's sisters, one who killed herself, the other who wasted away – God knew how exhausted his heart was, such that it could no longer pump blood with enough vigor, the left ventricle unable to squeeze out the blood from his pulmonary veins. Nono suffocated gradually every night.

My father treated him with careful attention. The one thing my mother always acknowledged about her husband was his care for his patients, one of whom happened to be her father. They got along well, the two of them, even if their roles were unequal. While the doctor held the authority over his patient, they were both the weaker sides in their respective marriages. My father defended himself against my mother's accusations, ran away and hid from any obligation, and was, as the women of the time would have said, a typical weakling. Nono was incapable of convincing Nona to let Mladen ignore his draft notice and to find connections they certainly could have found that would have allowed him to run away into the woods; nor was he able to convince her to let Mladen desert afterward and, even if through some sort of crazy plan, escape to the British through Dubrovnik. He had been weak, and for that his son had died. If he had been strong, he would have been the one to make the decision, not his wife. Because of this weakness before her, when he'd lost his nerve completely, he was known to reprimand his wife for having sent their son to his doom. This didn't serve to truly unburden his conscience, but it certainly did leave her isolated in the world with her own conscience in the face of Mladen's death.

And so, my father and my mother's father understood each other well. This was why they played preferans together. Nono went a little easy on my father because otherwise the game would not have been interesting, given that he was practically unbeatable. He could only play seriously, without letting up, with three or four older men, Jews and Germans, retirees from the railroad management office. They were joined by his best friend, Matija Sokolovski, but he was such a weak player that even an amateur like my father could beat him sometimes.

My perspective was different from my mother's. I was captivated by the narrative, and I could narrate the story of Nono's card playing, even in the same room, very softly and looking on from one side, when I was three, four, and five years old. I remember everything. At first I remember rooting for Nono, without saying a word because otherwise they would have made me leave. He felt this, it seemed to me, and tried harder to remember the numbers of cards played, calculating until in the end he knew without looking which cards were in the others' hands, and he always won when I was there. They said I was his good luck charm, in their cardplayer jargon, and with me around he could become preferans champion of the world. The truth was that there wasn't any luck in it at all. It was just his way of using his sharp mind to compensate for all his losses and defects of character.

His preferans didn't interest my mother in the least. Her father, by contrast to her mother, wasn't cold to her, he didn't drive her away from him. But when he played, she didn't matter to him, and he wouldn't speak with her. He would talk with me though. This might also have offended her. She could have been jealous. She forbade him to teach me preferans. No child of mine is going to be a layabout, she told him. Preferans is no game for layabouts, he laughed. Layabouts wouldn't have the intelligence or the patience for it. But she didn't listen to him. I cried and begged him to teach me then, though I was still too little.

If he had lived, Nono would have taught me to play preferans, of that I'm sure. Even though I don't have a gift for mathematics, and maybe not even the practical intelligence for the game with its combinations of sums, I would have tried hard not to disappoint him.

That first winter in Drvenik I spent in a stone Dalmatian house heated by a single gas stove. They say little children should always be kept warm, but I certainly wasn't at the time. The Drvenik winters of those years were cold, snowy, with a stiff northern wind, but this did no harm to me. Just as I wasn't harmed by the difficult relationship between my grandparents, which perhaps was not quite as difficult after I came on the scene. Like a peacemaker, a gift from God for all the years of suffering and guilt they endured because of Mladen's death (though, since neither of them believed in God, this last sentimental assertion misses the mark, or else I'm compensating for some inadequacy of my own and in this way resemble my mother . . .).

My mother came to visit us every other weekend. She traveled by train to Ploče, then by bus. In 1966 was the first season of operation for the normal-gauge track from Sarajevo to Ploče. The year before the engine had traveled along a narrow-gauge track, and the trip took some twelve hours. Now the train got her to Ploče in three and a half. Then another half hour by bus to Drvenik.

This was how she was able to watch me grow. In obvious spurts, for a child is visibly bigger two weeks later. I would go back to Sarajevo at the beginning of the following June, several days after my first birthday. Three weeks before that I'd taken my first steps. I remember this. Or I remember the memory of my remembering that I remembered my uplifted arms, which were being supported by our Drvenik neighbor, Aunt Mirjana, a woman from Belgrade who spent several months a year with her husband, Mr. Momčilo, at their vacation house, which they had built just next to the house we were living in.

This woman was important in my earliest childhood: after all, she taught me to walk.

I don't know what happened to her, or whether she's still alive. If she is, Aunt Mirjana would be ninety years old. She too, like my wet nurse, I lost for good somewhere along the way.

Above the bed in the room where I slept with Nona – Nono slept in the basement, where he could cough, gripe, and worry in peace – hung a small, framed reproduction of the *Girl with a Pearl Earring*. I hadn't yet been able to talk when I started pointing at her, saying, "Mama, Mama, Mama . . ."

For some reason the woman from Vermeer's famous painting reminded me of my mother, she felt more accurately pictured in this painting than in any photograph. And she looked out at me from the wall just as the Mother of God looked out on a devout Christian.

Nona was touched. Fifteen years later she would be telling this story with the same strong emotion, and as she told it she would suddenly feel love for her child, because her child had given birth to me, who saw his mother in a Vermeer picture, and there was no way to convince me that it was not her.

I don't remember this, but Nona said the first time I recognized my mother in the picture, she brought a photo of Javorka, pointed to it, and said, "See, here's Mama!"

I didn't contest it. That was indeed Mama – that is, until I lifted my head and saw a better picture of her.

My mother was then twenty-five years old. Only her pale complexion and gray-blue eyes resembled the women in the Vermeer painting, but to me it was her. Even when I was a little older, maybe three or four, it was still my mother. Later, even as a grown man, I would continue to find similarities between Javorka in her youthful photos, where she looks just the same to me as she had in those winters when she would come to see me every other weekend, and Vermeer's *Girl with a Pearl Earring*. That was exactly how she looked when she would appear at our Drvenik house, opening the door at the base of which a folded sheet had been tucked to prevent the wind and snow from entering.

Those winter weekends when Javorka would come from Sarajevo were peaceful and harmonious. There were no fights, harsh words, or reproaches for anyone having done anything to anyone else. My mother would flutter in, on a wind from the north or south, as light as Vermeer's young girl. Sometimes the train took a while to clear the snowdrifts. Once she was so late that the last bus from Ploče for Makarska had already left and she had to spend the night all by herself in the overheated station waiting room. Another time a guy from Tuzla who was on his way to Split gave her a ride. She met him at the tobacco store at the Ploče station, where he was buying cigarettes and she was waiting for a bus that refused to come. He felt sorry for the young girl, already a mother, on her way to visit her son – she knew how to describe her predicament without the self-pity that would surface later on – and he must have liked her. He drove her to our house. I was then three years old and hugged her legs, in my bare feet on the kitchen floor, though it was February, and the man stayed – at Nono's invitation – to have some coffee at least. Did he want a drink? Just one, since he was driving, you know. And then he went back on his way to Split and we never learned anything else about him. Not his name, not who he was going to see, not even what sort of a car he was driving.

When I went to visit her in the summer of 2012 – at the time our story about the Stublers and her youth had not yet begun to be written – I asked her what she'd talked about with that guy from Tuzla during the half-hour drive from Ploče to Drvenik, back in February 1970. At first she couldn't remember the man – what guy from Tuzla, there wasn't ever any guy from Tuzla! – but then I reminded her of how she'd been standing by the news kiosk because there wasn't any bus, holding a big rubber rabbit under her arm because she couldn't fit it inside her bag, and of how her string bag had got torn, and then she remembered the guy from Tuzla.

"Good Lord, bless you, you remember absolutely everything!"

I didn't tell her then – just as I never said another ugly word to her after I left Sarajevo late in the spring of 1993, after which I never moved back and only by some errant miracle found her alive in the midst of all those mortar shells and snipers – that fortunately I don't remember everything. And I hope I'll forget 2012, which flowed through me with her dying, with the torment in my conscience that I wasn't helping her, and with the lie that somehow I could and everything would be okay. For there really was no way for me to help her. I knew it was easier for her to grab me around the neck and pull me toward the water, drowning me along with her, I knew it was easier for her to latch onto my heels suddenly and pull me backward into the grave, for she did not want to be there alone and couldn't stand the idea that someone – except that drunk doctor whom we couldn't do anything to – should not be held at fault for her illness, and that no one could do anything, not without a miracle, to stop her from disappearing. It was easier for her to pull me down with her, drown and kill me, for in her relation to me, her grown son, and now a respected author, she was the child. It had been like this earlier, but in her illness she'd become ever more childlike, dying as very intelligent children die, those not turned into angels by their illnesses – this happens only in the novels of Thomas Mann – but instead grow embittered at the world they are in the process of leaving behind.

I couldn't tell her, but now I say it, without hoping she might ever hear me from beyond the grave, that during the year 2012, in the midst of her illness and our endless phone conversations, I understood how important the blessing of forgetfulness was in life. Until then I'd thought, stupidly and arrogantly, that – since life was really just crossing a field – a man would be happiest if he never forgot a thing. When he remembered every beautiful and ugly moment in life, every circumstance, sensation, and experience, from birth to distant death, then life would stretch across thousands of subjective years and truly be eternal. Her seventy years, if she did not forget anything, would be an eternity entire. This is what I thought, and then, in her company, as she died, I began to understand that this was hell. Not to forget anything, to keep all of it in mind, this was really hell. A person could only be calm and content by keeping this in mind, by eschewing such thorough remembering. It wasn't the same as when memory was formed into some sort of literary fiction, something that could be truer than fact, more transcendent than memory, something that wasn't etched so painfully into the living flesh as memory was.

What was she doing from Monday to Friday during those first two years of my life, before going to work for the Service of Social Accounting in 1968? I asked her, but she didn't answer. I repeated my question a few more times, and then again in the fall of 2012, when we were on the phone together.

"Why are you asking me this?" she asked angrily.

It was during those weeks that she'd stopped being able to go to the bathroom on her own. One woman cared for her during the day, another at night. (I'm not going to tell stories about them: in this report on Javorka's life and her final year they will remain only shadows. They are alive, and they have a right to their own lives outside literature. If I do say anything about them, it will be merely a notch and a bridge to her life. Their strong women's armpits, the forearms she gripped desperately while taking those seven or eight steps between her bed and the toilet . . .) She would soon lose her remaining strength, but still she believed she would recover. And I supported her in that belief, reinforcing her childish illusions and dreams, and trying – quite selfishly – to make my stays in Sarajevo as short as possible, beside her there, on her way to the toilet and back.

But despite her deterioration my mother's voice remained clear and strong for a long time, up until a few days before the end. Her voice had hardly changed from the days when she'd come visit me every other weekend under the Vermeer painting. I can't remember her voice now. I can barely call to mind its high pitch, the fact that it was always a little too loud, on the cusp of crazed laughter, or the beautiful soprano somewhere within it from which, in the seventies, she sang while washing our clothes in the bathtub. The songs I remember from those occasions are "Bethlehem Is Not Far," "Terezinka," "In the Hills," "Far Away," and "U tem Somboru." I remember so much, but my mother's voice is gone, it has disappeared, for the human voice is the first thing we forget. I thought about this as two skilled grave diggers used ropes to lower her into a grave dug in the grayish-yellow Sarajevo clay. It seemed to me then that her voice still lingered in my ear, but it occurred to me it would soon be gone.

"Why are you asking me this?" she snapped angrily, when I'd asked what she'd been doing during those first two winters of my life, in Sarajevo, in our apartment above the Temple, or wherever it was she'd been when she wasn't with me. If she'd only known how to tell me what she really wanted to keep to herself, she might have tried to sound less angry.

I'd started walking very early, and after that no one ever carried me again. The baby carriage disappeared from the Drvenik house, given away to locals who were just then having children. From then on I walked where they did, treading beside Nona and Nono, holding their hands. Before long we were walking to Zaostrog or Donja Vala, neighboring towns some three or four kilometers away. Because of his asthma Nono couldn't pick me up, and while Nona was strong enough to do so, she didn't, for some unstated reasons of her own. When our relatives would come from Kakanj and Zenica, or when Uncle Dragan and Aunt Viola came from Russia, where they were living then, they would lift me up into the air, carry me around the basement or around the courtyard in front of the house. I remember the sensation very clearly: it's nice to be in the air, but after a while it starts to feel unnatural, you want down, you don't understand why they're doing this, what you didn't ask them to do in the first place . . .

I don't remember my mother ever carrying me.

She probably did, but I don't remember it. Every two or three months, once or twice in the course of our winter stays in Drvenik, she'd come with my father. They weren't living together, and I had always known they were somehow separated, but they'd come together and sleep in the same bed. He would toss me into the air but also hug me so tight I couldn't breathe, his face, unshaven, rough as emery board, chafing against mine. It was a pleasant feeling, even if there was something exaggerated in his embraces.

My mother and father behaved toward me the way adults do toward a child. Nono and Nona talked with me like an adult. This wasn't the result of a position they had taken, it just happened that way. I wasn't their child, nor did they always want me around, so they didn't think beforehand about how they would treat me and everything unfolded almost arbitrarily, unselfconsciously. I wasn't long with Nona and Nono – he would die by the fall of 1972 – but my stay with them brought peace, a pause in the mutual, spoken and unspoken dissent, which lasted to the end. Although his asthma tormented him constantly, despite the fear of not being able to breathe in the next moment, and although he spent the nights pacing the basement or, if the weather was nice, the courtyard – because he'd begin to suffocate the moment he lay down – those six years when we were grandfather and grandson were calming and beautiful for him, and for her too. I fit between them as something completely new, as someone who was their own but unconnected to their misfortunes. But was this really the case?

Later I often wondered why my mother had brought my father along during those years. If I'd asked her, I know what she would have said: she did it to preserve for me the illusion that I had two parents. This was a sacrifice for her, for she didn't love him and he was psychologically abusive. This is what she would have said, but I know it's not exactly true. She would often refer to this kind of sacrifice, but never was she actually ready to engage in it. If she had been, I wouldn't have been living with my grandmother and grandfather in a cold Drevenik basement until the age of six months. There was something else too, something in the relationship between my mother and father that was never explained to me and I never managed to discover, not even in the last months of her life, when I asked her about all sorts of things and we had long conversations about the Stublers, the Karivans, and the Rejcs, and about her own life as well.

Once near the end she wanted to tell me about what my father had said the first time he saw me in the hospital. She had only managed to say he was completely horrified before I was able to stop her. I told her this wasn't interesting to me anymore, he was gone, I didn't need stories about him, for they didn't serve me in any way, not even literature. I told her I would be writing *The Stublers* and the subtitle would be *A Family Novel*. When I saw her for the last time, I gave her the first chapter to read, "Have you Seen Regina Dragnev?" It had been some time since she could hold a book in her hands, but she grasped the papers on which the story was printed easily. She was satisfied and didn't bring up my father anymore, or say anything else about how horrified he'd been when he first saw me as a newborn baby.

This episode served her as a way of convincing me she was in the right in that marriage without marriage, and that she was the victim. She also wanted to tell me he really didn't want me. This was something she cared about a lot. She didn't know how to affirm her love, or she didn't feel the need to do so, but she wanted to establish beyond a doubt, in these last months, weeks, days, and moments, the clear and powerful difference that existed between her and my relation to him. She wanted me to know which of the two of them was mine, and which was not, even if I no longer cared. The last time such a story might have interested me was probably when I was twelve years old. But normally she repeated the same stories again and again, even when she knew she'd already told them.

I rejected her, and that could have sounded harsh. I told her I was busy with my writing, trying to offend her just as she had offended me, boiling down the reasons for her confessions to the very utilitarian end of some future book of mine. But it didn't offend her, she couldn't care less how I used her stories, for to her they were at least then serving the most important purpose in the world, more important than the world itself – while she talked, she had the sensation of being outside her own body, as if she were not ailing but living inside the stories.

"I'm only happy when I'm talking to you. But I don't have anything more to say," she uttered, breaking into tears, in that last week before the morphine.

"You do, you do," I replied, and maybe I slipped in some coarse word so as not to seem different toward her, so she wouldn't think I'd become tender just because she was dying. I did not acknowledge her death to her.

She used to take my hand as the two of us walked toward Zaostrog or Donja Vala. This would end badly – she'd start to feel nervous, and we'd come back quickly, because she didn't know how to talk with me. She would answer questions and maybe ask some, but between us there was no real understanding. We talked together as if we'd met by chance. I was three or four years old, and she wanted to talk with me as one does with a three-year-old. This didn't work because no one had taught me to speak in that way. The only people who had spoken seriously to me, Nono and Nona, had not spoken to me like that, and I didn't really understand what was expected of me.

She interpreted this as a boycott on my part.

Such a little kid, but he already understood.

And it would play on her conscience because just after, I suspect, she'd think of how her mother Olga had turned me against her. Or how Olga's sense of guilt was unconsciously being transferred to her.

Whatever it was, the best moments were when my mother appeared suddenly at our door on an afternoon, or evening when the train from Sarajevo was late.

Once she arrived so late that I'd already fallen asleep. She came and kissed me on the cheek. An unusual, beautiful sensation. It had never happened to me before. And it never would again.

When summer came, and the first German tourists with it, we would slowly prepare to go to Sarajevo. Everyone else was heading to the beach, but we were leaving. It didn't seem fair. We stood with our bags beside the highway waiting for the bus to take us from Makarska. We'd loiter in the comfortably fresh air of the train station waiting room for Sarajevo. Nono would study the train schedule, checking what had changed since the time when he was part of creating it.

Summer in Sarajevo was uncomfortably hot. The Miljacka River stank with sewage. I hated the town with all my heart before we settled there for good, after Nono's death.

My mother tried to take care of me. My father came by once a week. Every Sunday, during the summer, we'd go to Trebević. We'd take the closest cable car, just up to the pensioners' home, and later on, when he had purchased some land and begun to build a summerhouse, we'd go by car to Mala Ćelina. In the mountains my mother's head would begin to hurt as she was accosted by migraines. I'd get sick for a little while on Mondays. I'd have a temperature, which would soon dissipate.

Often during the week we'd visit my mother at work. She worked in Novo Sarajevo, in SDK's modern new building. We'd travel by tram. There we would sit down for a little while. Her colleague, a rather fat young man named Novica, would give me a piece of paper with an ink pad and stamp so I could play by stamping up the paper. I think Novica was secretly in love with my mother. Or maybe that part wasn't a secret, but that she'd rejected him. She couldn't stand the man, though he hadn't done anything wrong. She also didn't like the fact that he gave me company paper and an official stamp. She said this wasn't done, a stamp was a serious thing. Out of deference, so as not to make him feel bad, I stamped on the white paper, but we threw it away each time just in case. God forbid someone might misuse a stamp from the Service of Social Accounting. Such were the times. And such was she.

She had not yet turned thirty, the age she would be when Nono died.

In Sarajevo in those years it had become customary to have pictures taken at funerals. Somewhere among the boxes of documents in the apartment on Sepetarevac Street there are still probably a hundred or so black-and-white, ten-by-six-centimeter photographs from Nono's funeral, fastened together with a rubber band. I see my mother, her blond hair done up high like the singers in the B-52s, who were very popular at the beginning of the seventies, crying openly before the excavated grave, in which no one has been placed yet. Nona's standing beside her, in a black coat with a black fox collar and a wide Russian shawl covering her mouth. The air is cold, and this is how she's protecting her lungs. In winter she would always cover her lips with a shawl. Or with an ordinary kerchief. Here she is standing over the open grave, looking down, shielding herself from the cold, or from others' recognizing what she's really feeling. I don't know what she was feeling. She's hiding it, as she always did. I don't know if I learned this from her, or whether it's simply a matter of human nature, but I do the same. When I appeared at the same excavated gravesite forty years and two months after the picture was taken, at the funeral of the blonde woman crying openly in the black-and-white photo, it was important not to let anything show on my face.

The one who arranged for the pictures was my father, who in the photograph is standing next to my mother supporting her arm, though they long before ceased to be man and wife. Or they never were. Everyone at the funeral knows these two are not together, though there has to be a reason – am I the reason? – they're together at her father's funeral. The pictures from Nono's funeral are the most intimate of any of the photographs of my parents together. There are others – one from Pioneer Valley, a zoo in Sarajevo, and another from Drvenik, with the requisite Dalmatian donkey – but they're not so intimate. Also, in almost all the pictures of them together, or perhaps in all of them, I'm included. But I'm not at Nono's funeral. They didn't bring me, believing a child wouldn't yet understand what death was, and left me alone with Aunt Lola in Drvenik. She took care of me, being careful to supervise how much I ate. She thought I was fat and would never let me eat as much as I wanted. She'd take the plate away at just the moment when things tasted sweetest. When she came back from Sarajevo, Nona said, "Ah, you've gone all skinny on me!"

I didn't dare say anything then, because Aunt Lola was there, but I did later. She wouldn't let me eat as much as I wanted. She said I was fat. Later everyone found this funny. It left no bad memories. There was nothing bad to remember. We all loved Aunt Lola, and besides, all of us, including Nona, thought she wasn't really all there.

And why would a person need to be all there?

Both my mother and Nona were disgusted by the fact that my father had ordered photographs of Franjo's funeral.

"It's so primitive!" said Nona.

I don't know what my mother said, but something else bothered her. She was afraid of death and kept it at bay for as long as she possibly could. Three weeks before the end, and two before the morphine drip, she told me with great sadness how the disease had destroyed her physically: "If I pull through, I won't make it even another ten years!"

This was what she'd said, and I answered that one never knew. And it'd be better for her to stay quiet. This was what I said, always pretending she wasn't dying. I took part in the grand illusion. It would've been easier for me then, and it would be for me now, if I hadn't. At the heart of this deception – that there was no death, that the illness was not serious, that miracles happened and were reserved just for us – lay the whole horror of her death. It was something I could never recover from and after which I had aged by decades. It was the kind of delusion the parents of dying young children use. They think children don't know what death is and they lead them toward it as if it were the finale of a Disney film, with good fairies and sorcerers. My mother always believed she would pull through by some miracle. Every kind of suffering was possible, she herself had experienced almost all of them, but there was no death, not for her, there couldn't be! And although she'd seen off Nono in the same room in which she would die, in a bed with the same window and ledge where pigeons roosted, except that he had a view on Trebević while hers was of the white wall of that new building nearby, she was a child who angrily expected her elders to help her and produce a miracle.

She was angry at me for not delivering that miracle. Or for not immediately getting into my car and setting out from Zagreb with one to hand over to her, for she was suffering and in pain. And I lied to her and chattered away, exactly as children do.

I don't remember when I last saw the pictures from Nono's funeral. It was surely after the war. I leafed through them quickly and uncomfortably, as if I were looking at pornographic shots of people I knew in all the poses of the Kamasutra, and then I put them away in the package and wrapped the rubber band around it.

Why hadn't the two of them thrown the pictures away if they hated them so much?

There was a very simple reason: one doesn't throw out things that someone paid a lot of money for. This is the worst aspect of our Balkan frugality. One does not throw away anything that might still be worth something or that is not obviously trash. Actually the pictures could not have been sold, no one would have bought them, and today few people who might see them would even know what is in them, who is being buried.

And my father? He didn't think about it. He paid for something that had been offered. He wanted to be gallant. I don't believe he took any of the photos for himself, even though they were the most authentic pictures of his marriage with my mother.

Nono's death was not prolonged. Nor did he suffocate. Among some heart patients, death is easy to predict, to the week, the day. In the course of August it was clear he was near the end. But my father fought, believing he could do something, even as Nono's legs bulged, the water making its way to his lungs and heart, which had grown so weak that my father did not know how to describe it.

"This is what his poor heart was like!" he said, crumpling his handkerchief and tossing it onto the table.

Nono's heart was transformed into a snotty crumpled-up handkerchief. I kept my eyes straight ahead, hoping no one would notice my presence. Forty years later, it's just a metaphor. A frame from a family film.

In September I started school, and my father decided Nona and I should go back to Drvenik on our own, where I would be enrolled in first grade, while he would try to treat Nono at the hospital and boarding facility of the pensioners' home on Trebević. The fresh mountain air would do him good. He hoped for a miracle.

The last photo taken of Nono was on the terrace in front of the pensioners' home, with Nona, my mother, and his grandson Dragan. My father took it.

He looks calm, his illness invisible. Under the blanket one can see his white shirt and tie. He's looking somewhere to one side of the lens, posing.

Javorka had loved her father more than her mother. Nono's death shook her, and she would often repeat what he had said to her at the very end: "There are thieves all around and just the two of us are left!"

His middle and index fingers, which hung from the bedside, were curved and pressed together as if there was a cigarette between them. He didn't say anything else after that. He didn't answer when she called him. He was sleeping, unconscious, but he continued to hold the invisible cigarette between his middle and index fingers.

He smoked despite the asthma until just a little before his death. After he was buried, Nona put out her last butt, having completed fifty years of smoking. Javorka stopped after her second operation, when she was left with just four months to live.

I completed the first grade in Donja Vala after Nono's death, but then we returned to Sarajevo. I should say returned forever. The time that extends from after what would be my eventual departure from Sarajevo during the war is somehow different, not countable as part of what preceded, and beginning somehow after that demarcated forever.

My mother and I lived together from the moment I turned seven on. Our coming to know one another would last a long time, until Nona's death on June 6, 1986, and onward to my wartime move to Zagreb, her own illness and death. I'm not sure I knew her through and through, or that she didn't deceive me about anything. She was an unusual and unhappy woman. There is no one else whose unhappiness I can attest to with such certainty. My mother was as unhappy as Varlam Shalamov and long tried to change this. But all sorts of things got in her way.

Today I can say calmly: I too was in her way. Perhaps me most of all.

I don't remember the first time I asked her whether I was wanted as a child.

She answered readily, saying I was and that there was nothing she'd wanted more than to give birth to me. And she was convinced she wasn't lying. Later she told me, quite rationally, that abortions had existed then too and if she hadn't wanted me she would have got rid of me. I discovered later that after my birth, in 1968, at a clinic on Skerlićeva Street, she had aborted my brother or sister. And with whom had she got pregnant? My father.

I didn't ask her why this happened, when they hadn't been together for years. I knew she wouldn't answer the question, or she'd lie, say something self-pitying, but either way I knew I wouldn't learn the truth. But the truth didn't matter that much to me – I'd lost the chance to have someone else of my own. Her abortion in the fall of 1968 – which meant the child was probably conceived during the summer, while we were still all in Sarajevo – was proof that I was, after all, the son she wanted.

Or was it that she'd been so disappointed in me that she didn't want another? Did I disappoint her?

Probably. Even though I had only been speaking for a short time and couldn't yet pronounces my r's and l's, I could barely make myself understood with her, because she didn't know the language I spoke with Nona and Nono. She didn't know her own son, and it was as if she couldn't come to know him, for he had learned speech and all the other most important things in life from his grandmother and grandfather. Did she think she wasn't capable of being a mother? It's entirely possible, though she would never have confessed it to anyone. And perhaps it was then that she came to realize I was a fatal burden to her, one which would ruin any chance she might have of being happy.

"Who would want a woman with a child?"

These self-pitying words, more confirmation than question, I heard from her more than once. True, it was always in jest, sitting with her friends at coffee, on a union outing with colleagues from work, and it was always followed by a quick laugh, as if someone had made a tape recording of a laugh and was playing it back.

And they'd say, "Goodness, Javorka, you're still so young! And so pretty! And your son is so smart!"

It made her feel good to hear this, but she'd be waiting for the next opportunity to repeat her question, "Who would want a woman with a child?"

The thought that I might have been an unwanted child didn't bother me. If one believes Freud, this should trouble every adult male. But it didn't trouble me. Nor do I believe it would have bothered me to discover I was adopted and my biological parents were some other people unknown to me. And it would not have bothered me to learn I'd never know who my mother and father were. What was important, what needed to remain incontestable in every respect, was Nona and Nono. I wasn't linked to them the way grandchildren are linked to their grandmothers and grandfathers. I didn't really experience them like that. Whenever I named them subsequently as Grandma and Grandpa in my stories and essays, in fiction and nonfiction, instead of calling them Nona and Nono, it felt false, it seemed to me I was lying, the story had suddenly fallen upon a detail that was fundamentally untrue. These two elderly people, who in fall 1966 when we set out on our Drvenik consociation and I was still a half-blind, tiny, suckling babe, when Nona was sixty-one and Nono sixty-eight, though they were actually each much older than that, meant more to me, I think, than a mother and father mean to other children. In addition to their not having time to talk with me as one does with a child, everything strong and secure in me would be theirs. Every piece of knowledge, up to the present day, would come from them.

This is why the question of whether I was an unwanted child didn't torment me even as I entered puberty. I was curious and wondered just as curiously about it then as I do today. It was probably easier for me to think about it then because Nona was still alive. Today none of them are left, and perhaps it would be comforting to believe I was, after all, someone's realized desire.

Even if it really was the case that before my birth my mother wanted me, afterward she didn't know what to do with me. Nor did she know what to do with herself. Her life was under strain from several directions, and there wasn't any easy way out. Or maybe there wasn't any way out at all.

From Yugoslav National Army Street, the building next to the National Theater, where Franjo and Olga Rejc had lived up to the war as tenants in the building that had belonged to Madam Emilija Heim, which after the war was nationalized, giving the people living there tenants' rights – meaning a kind of part ownership – from that building we moved to Sepetarevac Street. From the twenty or so apartments offered to us, or rather to Nono, as the "possessor of tenants' rights," Javorka chose an apartment in a building that had been constructed and shared by the brothers Obrad and Branko Trklja. Obrad had later sold his apartment to the Energoinvest engineering firm so he could move to Belgrade. In this apartment, she decided, we would live. She was twenty-seven years old. (I always remember how old she was then, because it seems to me she lived her entire active life when she was very young, and everything had happened to her by the time she turned thirty . . .)

She chose this apartment because she believed, naïvely, as it was higher up on a hill, above the center of town, with cleaner air, that Nono would find it easier with his asthma. The calculations were of course completely wrong – the air was the same, and Nono couldn't make it up what was one of the steepest streets in Sarajevo on his own and had to take a taxi. She never admitted she'd made a mistake. And maybe she hadn't – who knows how we might have lived if we'd moved somewhere else.

It is probably an aspect of human nature not to admit one's faults to others.

When I think this, it occurs to me that I haven't ever admitted a major mistake to anyone else either.

Either that or I say I've been mistaken in everything and I would do things differently if I could do them again.

But my mother not only didn't admit her mistakes, she directed her life in such a way as to persuade us all that she had been in the right. And then time would be spent, months and years, life itself, on valueless unimportant things, in trying to repair something that had come out broken. She lived in a past that grew with time, swallowing her up, devouring her, while she tried not to notice. She never talked about what was happening today, about what she was doing to make things better for her – or for me, her ten-year-old son – but rather about endlessly and uselessly analyzed instances of injustice and justice, of mistreatment and abuse, of lives and histories already lived, which would not leave behind any trace of themselves.

As if something were keeping her from moving from where she was.

After two marriages and the birth of a child, barely twenty-four, it was as if she'd been buried. As if her feet were planted in a leaden bog. And she was a leaden soldier. Or just leaden, she didn't move.

In May, before she had grown completely weak, she called me one morning to tell me the dream she'd had the night before.

She had dreamed, she said, that she could no longer move. Not her feet, or hands, or index finger. She lay in the room in which she really was lying, except she couldn't move. She couldn't blink or breathe.

And then she braced herself with all her strength and cried out my name.

She called me but I didn't come.

This was her dream.

I was in Konavle, standing on an old street built by the French, under an enormous walnut tree, looking at the open sea in the distance, and I listened to her dream. It offended me. Not, of course, that she had dreamed it, but that she had had to tell it to me immediately. I was to blame in her dream, and a dream is truer than reality. A person can't overpower a dream, it comes on its own, and from it we learn what we otherwise wouldn't know. I was to blame for not answering her, just as I was to blame for the illness progressing implacably, and for the doctors who continued to react too slowly, and for her unhappy fate. For this last item I was, perhaps, to a certain extent, to blame. But my blameworthiness was not conscious. Rather it was something I'd been born with. Such blame existed only in ancient tragedies. And once in a while in the relations of parents and their fatally ill children.

She was not my daughter. I was her son.

But this, it appears, did not need to be true to the end of life.

Now that she is no more, the dream she offended me with – or I was just waiting for her to offend me with so that it'd be easier on me – has been transformed into a short fairy tale of her life. She no longer moved. She just strained with all her might to call someone who could save her. Or someone who could be at fault in her place.

My mother didn't want to be at fault for anything because her own mother had already blamed her for Mladen's death.

I believe this was the truth. It occurred to me after Nona's death that this was true. Before the story, before the novel, before God – if she really believed in him at the end – before the world, I justified my mother because of this one distinctive need of hers, which made her insufferably selfish. This justification applied universally, in all cases but one.

By justifying her, I took Mladen's death upon myself, to carry with me to the end – I took on the guilt that my mother didn't want, because her mother had blamed her for her son's death. I didn't want to do this. I'm not good. I wasn't worried about her. But such things are passed on without volition.

This also shows how present my uncle's death that autumn of 1943 remains to me at this moment, along with everything that created the context and framework for his death.

My mother knew how to cook, but she stopped in the middle of the seventies, when she was baking sweet bread on Sundays – according to a special recipe, now lost God only knows where – and chicken with potatoes. Nona cooked all the other days of the week.

After that Nona cooked on Sundays too, the day my mother would usually be lying in bed with a washbasin. A migraine. Or she'd be depressed. In which case again she would be lying down all day Sunday. After Nona died, she didn't cook even once up to the day I left Sarajevo during the war.

She no longer cleaned the apartment or wiped away the dust. She only worked at her place of employment. She was a good, thorough head of the accounting department. She followed the rules with Stubler strictness. But did nothing more. She didn't move, didn't care about the state of things around her.

This bothered me immediately after Nona's death, but later on it ceased to. I grew accustomed by degrees to her unhappiness as an aspect of my own family circumstance. We lived together, but until the war all we ever talked about was how badly she felt. During the war in Croatia, she was at the height of menopause. A year or two earlier she'd had a serious hemorrhage. She went three times to have the layer of skin scraped off in order to remove all the blood. I was with her during every instant of this. She had no one but me, so I experienced my mother's menopause from beginning to end in great detail, both the psychological and the physical aspects.

When they attacked Croatia, she was in the depths of depression. She would take her yearly vacation time only to lie in bed for three weeks. It's hard to live with someone who doesn't leave her bed. She said her life had no meaning, she would kill herself. She had no one else, so she had to say this to me. At night she would call a number for help. This kind of line had been working for years in Sarajevo. It was started by a psychiatrist couple. But now it was someone else who answered. The other two had better things to do.

Nor would she move from her bed on the weekends. She'd lie down on Friday afternoon and get up just to head off for work on Monday morning. She would lie in the living room, covering her head with a synthetic Vuteks blanket from Vukovar, while the sounds of the war emanated from the TV at full volume. Generals read pronouncements about the declaration of a state of war, politicians announced cease-fires, an international representative spoke with the intonation of a British tourist on the Adriatic, television announcers reported in hysterical voices on the front lines, explosions and bursts of gunfire could be heard, along with patriotic songs newly rearranged as wartime marches, but she wouldn't hear anything. She'd be sleeping deeply, having taken a few Lexilium tablets, and there was no thunder from even that war that could have woken her.

The siege of Sarajevo happened while she was in a stupefied state. Soon there was no more Lexilium, nor was there a hotline for psychological support, or any phone line. The electricity stopped and then the water, and my mother forgot about the idea of killing herself. She was still listless, often depressed, but she went to work regularly – at the time this was at the Academy of Performing Arts – and she made her way through the falling of the rain and snow and mortar shells, even when others readier to live than she had finally quit because they didn't understand what possible sense their little municipal job might have. Her employment by contrast had that much more sense because it brought her out of her depression.

During all those years at work she communicated with the people around her, often had arguments with her superiors – someone always had it in for her, either because she was a woman, or because she did her work promptly and diligently – while with her female colleagues she had conversations about children, cleaning the house, the prices at the market, ironing, how she didn't really like ironing, almost as if she didn't realize she was discussing things that had long since ceased to have any connection to her own life. She hadn't ironed a single piece of clothing for years. It was mostly me who turned on the washing machine, put our clothes on the line, and brought them in, though I didn't do the ironing because I didn't know how. She had no children she needed to take care of, nor did she go out to the market. She'd always managed to avoid all that.

In her purse she carried a school notebook she'd bought to write down cake recipes. At the time women would exchange recipes at work since the fashion of printed cookbooks and gastronomic contributions to newspapers had not yet taken off. Instead, people believed in secret knowledge and in the sorts of family recipe collections that were collected over years, written down mostly in little notebooks. My mother wrote down everything. Except for tortes with white cream and cakes with sugar icing.

"My Miljenko doesn't like white cream," she would tell them.

And yet not once did she ever bake a cake after Nona's death. Not even for the birthdays that we once had celebrated, not ever. At first she said it was because of her migraines, or periods of accounting reconciliation, or biannual budgeting, or because she had to stay late at work, but later she wouldn't say anything. She just wrote down the recipes.

This made me angry. It made me furious. Because I thought she was hiding the truth from her women coworkers. And lying to them about baking cakes. And lying about caring about me so much. Only after I was no longer in Sarajevo did I start to think of this differently: my mother believed for a long time that all of a sudden by some miracle everything would change, her daily life would be transformed, every day she would prepare lunch, on Saturdays she would bake cakes like other women did, and make sure her son wasn't hungry and his shirts were ironed, just like her women coworkers. All that she did was actually in preparation for the moment when everything would be different.

That was why in 1972 she bought a sewing machine, which to the end of her life remained boxed up in a corner of the living room. She never opened it, but it was there, and from time to time she would arrange the sewing-in-one-hundred-lessons booklets she had purchased on sale in bookstores or from street vendors. She didn't even stop doing this after the war. The last book she bought was probably a few months before she got sick.

She didn't do this out of habit but really believed, even into her seventieth year, that she would one day learn to sew, while a cake with chocolate cream baked in the oven.

Her women coworkers and acquaintances, with whom she would go out, after she'd retired, to the Café Imperijal for coffee and pastries, never learned about the difference between her exterior and interior life, between what happened around her and inside her, what happened in our apartment on Sepetarevac and what she did, said, and thought outside our home.

Sometimes in the years after Nona's death I would reproach her maliciously for that notebook, with which she never parted and in which she very carefully recorded each and every recipe, with an obligatory note – as if cakes too had some sort of authorial rights attached to them – from whom she had heard a given recipe: chocolate cake (Sonja), Mubera's baklava, dried fig bombs (Nadja) . . . Sometimes she'd break into tears, or start screaming, throwing the notebook into the corner like an offended child, and I would leave without a word, slamming the door behind me.

Once she asked, calm on the surface, "Would you feel better if I didn't write down any recipes?"

Her chin was shaking.

I didn't answer. I pretended not to have heard and went into the kitchen for some water. She continued copying into her notebook a recipe she had found at the supermarket on a vanilla sugar bag: for pineapple cake. Even with white cream, I could have liked that cake. Because of the pineapples.

I don't know what happened to her notebooks. She went through about five or six of them. As soon as one was filled up, she would cram it into the drawer of the little table the telephone was on. I don't believe she ever took a single one of them out again. In one of them she had copied down recipes for savory dishes for years. Maybe it's still in the apartment, under piles of paper that don't mean anything to anyone anymore, instruction brochures for independent accounting, issues of the *Gazette*, old appointment books without any appointments in them, telephone directories, bookkeeping forms, old newspapers, file folders, books with financial regulations, economics textbooks, logarithmic tables, blank sheets of merchants paper with a red line down the long edge, boxes of used-up indigo paper . . .

She was formally divorced from my father in 1974 or 1975.

I know this because that's when she changed her last name. Actually she just got rid of the added Jergović and went back to Javorka Rejc. She said she was doing this for the man she might meet later. Other women, she said, kept their names because of their children, but she didn't understand that reason. She talked a lot then about her last name. I remember feeling offended, but I didn't say anything. I was eight or nine years old, having trouble getting used to Sarajevo, finding school painful, as well as life on Sepetarevac, with a new backdrop and a new allocation of roles between Nona and my mother, in an apartment where we were always renting out one room because there was never enough money, her paycheck was too small, and I understood her change of name as a betrayal, a distancing of herself from me, perhaps a hidden accusation about her not having met anyone, remaining a lone divorcée, because she had a child. Other people's children were always a burden, like in Cinderella and all the fairy tales about evil stepmothers and unfeeling stepfathers, and the burden was especially great here in Bosnia where women were looked at disparagingly and a divorcée was already half a prostitute. This was how she talked, finding a frame for her suffering, a social category, and a justification. She was a martyr more readily than a disillusioned woman. She couldn't stand disappointment. It seemed to her that each instance of disappointment was just a new proof to others of her own lack of ability. She went screaming around the house, defending herself even when no one was attacking her. She took pains to make her private unhappiness public.

Or maybe she did this because she knew that Nona really couldn't stand it. Nona always did her best to conceal her private life from others, from family, and from neighbors, who in Sarajevo were always eager to know what was going on behind closed doors. My mother flung open everything that Nona wanted to keep closed.

The divorce was an unexpectedly important event for her, even though she

and my father had never lived together and there had been no mention of reconciliation. In talking about how the three of us should live together, especially
given the fact that he would soon be getting a beautiful, spacious apartment in
a high-rise near the stadium on Koševo (my father acquired this apartment, in
which I would never set foot, in 1974, a few months before they divorced), he was
resolving a problem with his conscience, with some real or invented sense of
guilt. When we would go to see the animals at Pioneer Valley – I loved the animals and our outings to the zoo were important events for me, and I remember
him promising to take me to Vienna and Berlin to see the biggest, most beautiful
zoos in Europe – my father would point to the pansies in the windows of family
homes on the wealthy fringes of the city, where country and city houses began to
mix together, and say, "We'll have flowers like that."

This was how he would put her out of sorts, she would seethe as we looked
at the animals. He did this on purpose, to put the blame on her. Or he was just
abusive to her in that way.

On one such occasion, during a trip to Kladanj, when he had offended her by
some sort of allusion to our future life together, I scribbled down a poem:

The Incident

Late fall somewhere in Bosnia
A pool with a diving board
My mother standing on it
Looking in
Father and I beside the pool
Is she going to jump, I ask?

This was the first text about my mother that I thought could hurt her. She didn't
respond. She liked the poem, as if she didn't notice the cruelty.

Or maybe she'd read it differently.

My mother would humiliate my father by poking at certain painful spots. My
father, for instance, didn't know how to swim. He was an adult by the time he

saw the sea for the first time, and as a child he was strictly forbidden to go with his peers to the banks of the Miljacka. He was filled with a sort of internal shame that prevented him from admitting before others that he didn't know how to dance, ride a bicycle, swim, or speak German well, so there was no way for him to learn how to swim when he got older. Or dance. This awkward trait – or rather this complex, as they'd put it in Sarajevo – I've inherited from my father.

Maybe my mother climbed up on the diving board to show him she could jump in and nothing terrible would happen because she knew how to swim. To torment him.

As always, everything came down to stories, many of them, which would recur in regular succession and, in later years, become a series of verbal ceremonies, mantras, and litanies that were repeated in such a way that it wasn't possible to have a serious conversation – only the illusion of communication was retained. My mother no longer knew how to communicate with me or simply couldn't because I was the only one who could see both sides of her world: the inside and the outside. In her final days her conversations with others were completely disconnected from reality. Everything was invented by that time – just as the reasons for collecting her recipes had been invented. And she could dream about her everyday existence according to the measure of an invented life. I rejected all this vehemently. I did so gruffly. I have no excuse for this. I would have been better able to live with her, and with myself as well, if I had managed to embrace her way of understanding.

She was an attractive girl, with sad eyes.

Blonde.

Recognizing that my parents were divorced to me was exactly like recognizing that the sky was blue, the sea was salty, and Mount Biokovo was full of rocks. I grew up with it and didn't know anything else. My mother was a free woman and would sometimes have boyfriends. She wouldn't call them that, and she wouldn't call them dates or lovers, but rather Veljko, Enver, Firuz . . . That was what they were called.

The first of them, Veljko, was a sailor from a town on the interior of Dalmatia about thirty kilometers from Drvenik. Once long before they had been together. When exactly I didn't know, but at the time Veljko had been working as an engineer. After they split up, he married a woman he didn't love, had two children with her, and went off to sea. Some people get separated, others become sailors.

This was the way my mother talked about Veljko. I don't know whether this was her romantic sense of life or it was really like that. I was five when I first met Veljko. It was in early fall, a little after our return from Sarajevo, when my mother had come for a weekend in Drvenik.

"Veljko's coming!" she said.

Nona was silent. Nono wasn't there.

Veljko didn't come into the house but just stopped for a moment to pick us up. His car was in the middle of the street, so we had to hurry.

A handsome man, a year or two older than her, with a gentle appearance. He drove us to Tučepi, we sat in a local restaurant, and looked at the sea. He put a paper sack in front of us full of grapes from his vineyard.

I took the small grapes and the firmer large ones but avoided the wrinkled ones.

"But those are the sweetest!" he said.

This was one of the things adults said, the sort of thing you hear until you're an adult. There are people later, too, who will tell you something is good that looks bad, but then you don't have to care. Nobody can force on you the ugly, dried-out grapes if you also have the big plump ones to choose from.

It was just so they didn't get wasted. That was why he was saying that. Just so they didn't get wasted, not because a dried-out grape was better than a fresh one.

And I thought he was going to try to convince me and was ready to eat the dried-up ones too, just so he wouldn't keep bothering me.

But Veljko didn't do that. If you like those better, just eat those, and I'll eat the other ones. Then he left me alone.

It was years later when I first tasted grapes dried on the vine. I remembered Veljko. And later in life, whenever I bit into one of those sugary, sun-dried black grapes, sweet like full-bodied prosecco, I couldn't help but think of the man.

I only saw him once. He was still in contact with her afterward, and maybe they saw each other, but then he disappeared forever. She didn't know where he was, on which sea, or if he was still alive. She often said he was unhappy in his marriage, in such a way it was as if his unhappiness made her happy. As if this confirmed her and Veljko's eternal love.

I thought she could be happy, and everyone around us would be happy if Javorka and Veljko had become man and wife, if he had not married a woman he didn't love. This was the great missed opportunity I lamented, imagining what her life and everything around us would be like if things had been different.

But in that case I wouldn't be here.

And all of a sudden I asked myself which was more important: me or the general happiness? Of course there was only one indisputable answer even for a five-year-old. Never in my worst moments of childhood or adulthood was I ever attracted to suicide, or, for that matter, nonexistence. But this was the first time it had ever occurred to me that I was the opposite of happiness. That I meant unhappiness for my mother and maybe for the rest of them too.

A childish thought, harmless, noted in textbooks on children's psychology as something quite ordinary, something that leaves no lasting consequence, and about which no one should worry. But the memory stayed with me, as did the impression that my mother and I had split up right then. That a rift had opened up between us that would last a lifetime, which would widen through other memories and events, and at some point I would come to see her as a foreigner. Everyone closest to me was dead, lying in their graves.

She was never as close to me as when she'd passed into the grave and was covered up with earth.

In the middle of May 2012, in the days leading up to her seventieth birthday, which were characterized by daily psychological breakdowns, when she still had the physical and mental strength, and her rage was such that it seemed the Golden Valley was opening beneath her feet, I had a dream at the end of one of the most horrible days – over the course of which I'd had ten accusatory phone conversations with her – one of the most unusual dreams I've ever had and one that's quite difficult to paraphrase because nothing really happened in it.

I dreamed of a fine, carefully excavated grave, deep and light, in Sarajevo's Bare Cemetery.

At the bottom of the grave grew fine, neatly tended clover. Like in a picture book.

I ran my palm across the clover.

The dream, it seemed to me, lasted a long time.

And nothing happened.

Except for the fact that this was a grave.

Light and deep.

And that I ran my palm across the clover.

Growing at the bottom of the grave.

Enver was ten years her junior, an Albanian from Kosovo. An accountant. Firuz was a friend from school, a professor of mathematics, an eccentric person. They broke up quickly. Zdenko was from Knin and lived in Zagreb. They were together for a long time. He'd visit us in Sarajevo. They met on a train during a trip to some sort of economics symposium. She dozed off, and her head slipped onto his shoulder. She broke up with him just before my military service, and after that there was no one else.

When she broke up with Zdenko she was forty-three. She was never with another man, and she lived another thirty-seven years, healthy almost until the end. Three years before her death she was still going to work every day, socializing with her friends.

What did my mother hope for? What did she expect from life?

The last trip she'd made to the coast was during a summer outing in 1981. After that, right up until the war, every year she would plan a trip and then, for whatever reason, not go. After the war, taking a summer trip never even occurred to her again. While her workmates would be saving for those seven days' worth of Dalmatia, that Sarajevo vacation tradition of which this part of the world was never able to deprive itself, or of going off to the summerhouse they had built long before, driving out post-war squatters by means of the courts, or taking an island cruise in a small wooden sailboat – in Sarajevo after the war sailing was all the rage – she would spend her vacation time at home on Sepetarevac. She would lie on the couch in the living room, dozing, reading novels and self-help manuals, and after her doctors said she might have problems with her back when she got older she would walk to Goat's Bridge and all the way to the border with Republika Srpska, where at a good café she would sit down for a coffee and talk with people. These walks, which in her later years became habitual, were an entertaining exception to her sedentary life. She found joy in walking. The next day she would call me to tell me about it.

But she couldn't travel.

Or didn't want to.

Over the course of the twenty years I lived in Zagreb, she visited me just once. She wanted to come, and she came. She spent five days there and was difficult the whole time. She needed to be looked after every instant. She suffered from migraines. She behaved strangely toward people she'd never met, made me feel ashamed. This was how I experienced it.

That was in 2000, I think. After that I did my best to discourage her from visiting.

Once in a while she would take a very short trip to Zenica or Kakanj to see relatives or for the funeral of one of the last of the *miners, smiths, drunks, and their wives*. She would come home in the evening, only occasionally staying overnight with one of them. Zenica and Kakanj were the places of her childhood, along with Ilidža, where the Stubler home had long stood, and Dubrovnik, where Aunt Lola had moved, and from which she had drawn a bit of her family heritage and identity. These two industrial towns in Central Bosnia – hopeless ecological time bombs in which, since the arrival of the Austro-Hungarians, the native-born and *kuferaš* proletariat had worked and died – were my mother's adopted homelands. By contrast to Sarajevo, nothing bad ever happened to her there.

On one occasion she went to Neum for a seminar on decentralized book-keeping. Another time she went to Mostar, and a third to Međugorje. These were more like union outings than actual travel. Accountants from all across Bosnia and Herzegovina, from both parts of the country, would gather for two to three days in the frigid conference halls of socialist hotels to listen to presentations by foreign finance specialists who organized all this – it seems to me – in the context of the international project of reconciling the estranged Bosnian-Herzegovinian peoples, all under the guise of presentations regarding new tax laws and the use of new computer systems in the field of accounting. And then they probably all marveled at the living miracle of how well these people got along, how they all loved each other.

Two years before her death, she was going to Hungary on a company bus that was to take her back to Sarajevo by way of Zagreb. She would have had to spend one night in Zagreb. I was relieved when for some reason the trip fell through. I didn't want her to come, didn't want to see her in my protected space, bring her into my home, show her the bed where I slept, while she examined everything without interest, looking around for a place to lie down and repeat the same stories I'd heard so many times before – even though today I look on all this with a certain regret.

My mother grew up on Yugoslav National Army Street, which extended from Baščaršija and Ćurčiluk all the way to the new city prison, the Hotel Istria, and the very heart of Austro-Hungarian Sarajevo. Her childhood would stretch from the theater to the First Gymnasium, and from Obala Kulina Bana to Marshal Tito Street. Her Sarajevo was a city where retired Austro-Hungarian officials and elders remembered the time when the Ottomans still strolled the streets. In every entryway lived families that communicated exclusively in German at their Sunday dinners, and who had accumulated misfortunes from a variety of wars. In that Sarajevo there were still displaced persons from the war who had not yet moved on – they were waiting for their moment, for when the conditions might change and the truck would come to take them to Rijeka, Zagreb, or still farther, to Vienna. The truck eventually came while the little girl in her shabby frocks rushed to school, where she was a straight-A student, valedictorian, a paragon for the lowlifes in the back row, who would, each in turn, do better in life than she.

In the early spring, Nona noticed little black dots in the white of her daughter's scalp. Lice, those vermin of the early, poverty-stricken years of socialism, made their attack on the children of postwar Sarajevo every spring, giving rise to clear, legally prescribed procedures in the battle against them. The classrooms were sprayed with DDT, the most celebrated insecticide in our history, which arrived along with American humanitarian aid and so-called Truman's eggs, and which decades later would be discovered to be poisonous to people, not just vermin. But DDT was scarce and often it wasn't possible to wait for all the signatures, verifications, and stamps needed before it could be applied, so the lice were exterminated in various other ways, according to old folk recipes, mostly with kerosene. (Petroleum derivatives for practical applications first came to Bosnia in the fight against lice, and for a long time were not used for anything else. Kerosene lamps came later.)

The procedure against lice used in schools was very strict: complete shaving. This was true for boys – in not a single prewar photograph do her older brothers have any hair – and, in the poorest of times and most depressed of regions, it was no different for girls.

She was deathly afraid of this.

And this was the one place she found an ally in her mother.

Nona would take care of everything, sending Nono off for some very expensive shampoo and cream that he would order at a certain pharmacy on Zrinjevac Square in Zagreb, asking the morning train conductors to purchase them on his behalf and then deliver them when they returned.

The kerosene would make sores on her sensitive skin, so the choice was between shaving or expensive products from Zagreb.

In Vienna lived two brothers, Erwin and Erich Dussel – who require their own story – who are Stubler relations, descended from a common grandmother, Josefina Patat. Though they were not closely related to us, these two men and their sister Dora (with whom Nano was in love, despite their being cousins, and with whom he'd had an affair in Vienna in the wild 1920s) were very dear. So dear that in 1970 Nano, Javorka, and my father Dobroslav spent an entire week at Erwin's, while he showed them around Vienna.

My mother boasted to everyone about how Erwin had purchased the best anti-lice medicine at the pharmacy. One little ampoule, smaller than an ampoule, of penicillin, like a little morphine drip bottle, whose top you removed before drizzling it over your hair. The lice fall out dead and are gone!

Who knew how much Erwin had paid for one of those little ampoules, she told everyone, boasting.

Those were the last lice she ever had, picked up from the headrest in the first-class guest workers' train on the Ploče-Vienna line.

She brought back an album of photographs taken mostly by my father from that trip. The little black-and-white pictures survived times that were disinclined to family memorabilia, when everything was being transformed into garbage that needed to be tossed out of the house, and when many things more valuable than pictures from tourist sites were lost in the chaos that emerged during those moments of the family's withering away – which resembled Marx's withering away of the state, for it reduced a person to his or her own fate.

Like the photos from Nono's funeral, these are of a small format, taken by an amateur who, it's clear, did not know how to use a camera very well. Probably he purchased it just before the trip, never discovered how to use the zoom function, and barely knew how to adjust the aperture. Nearly all his pictures are taken in some sort of general landscape mode, so that only somewhere in the depth of the frame is it possible to make out the tiny figures of people: Nono's bald head is barely recognizable, or my mother in her bright Chanel outfit, her skirt cut above the knee.

In some shots there are no people at all. My father was amazed by the Prater amusement park. He had to get really far away to be able to take a shot of the whole Ferris wheel. And the loop along which the two-person cars came rushing upside down while people's veins flared up with amusement-park adrenaline. But nothing of that is visible in the little photos, only metal machines that resemble construction cranes captured in the eternal black-and-white twilight of a dilettante's photographs.

These pictures should have constituted a sort of family memory, but probably no one ever looked at them again. When they returned to Sarajevo, my father bought an album, selected the pictures that were then prepared at the Ivica Lisac studio, delivered the album to us on Sepetarevac, and that was the end of the memory.

I happened upon the album in 2005 and brought it with me to Zagreb. She didn't even notice it was gone. In general she did not notice I was removing things from her home.

My favorites were the pictures of the monkeys. My father had obviously been fascinated by them. These were a particular species of monkey at the Vienna zoo. He took ten or more shots of them. What was he thinking as he photographed them? Where had Nano and my mother been then? What was so important to him about those animals? Did he want to show them to me on returning? Is that why he took so many pictures? I don't know. But I think about this, about my father's monkey photos, the little things left behind by the two of them, those that are remembered, one day to be forgotten, those that took physical shape – like a photo album from Vienna – only to turn into trash one day. Forgetfulness is like garbage, except with forgetting there is no ecological problem. Forgetfulness is an ecological garbage incinerator. Nothing is left behind. But forgetfulness ravages the person, just as garbage ravages the world. Against forgetfulness there is only story, which must be narrated at the moment before everything is forgotten. Then, before the final forgetting, each story at last comes of age, and a picture of a monkey taken by my father becomes important the moment before it turns to garbage, and it, like everything, is saved by story, and the world is saved by story alone.

Besides her concern about Javorka's lice, her mother didn't really worry about her daughter.

Her daughter would inherit this tendency. It didn't bother her conscience when she didn't worry about me.

Everything had its order and reason for being.

But as a little girl, she'd had willpower. The world was open to her, and at the time she was the very best.

Her class had two women teachers. Marija K. was mean, beat the children, and everyone was afraid of her. But she did not beat Javorka, the best student in class. She praised her and held her up as an example. This made the girl uncomfortable. She didn't like being praised so highly by Miss K. She had a premonition that something bad might happen, the situation would change, and Miss K. would start beating her too.

The other teacher was Nada Vitorović. A kind, good woman, but this is not the only reason I use her first and last name. My mother did not want Nada Vitorović to be forgotten. She pronounced her name aloud, repeating it many times over, whenever she could find a way of threading it into a story.

This was when she was lying in the bed where she would die, telling the story of what would become *A Family Novel*, which was interrupted only by the day of her death. This perhaps makes it an unfinished family novel. Or she just happened to die at the exact moment when it was complete. I had at that time about another ten stories, written in notes, which I wouldn't complete. The Stublers' end was marked by her death, the death of the last of Karlo's grandchildren, the last of the children who had learned from him their first words of German.

My mother did not want Nada Vitorović to be forgotten, perhaps because of the manner of her death in 1992 or 1993. How she died is unknown. She was an eighty-year-old woman when soldiers with the insignia of the army of Bosnia and Herzegovina took her from her apartment. She was living somewhere near Bistrik Street, or maybe in that high-rise near Drvenija Bridge, in the part of town where the old men and women who lived alone were taken away, the Serbs, or those who were presumed to be Serbs by their executioners because of their first or last names. Where and how they were killed is unknown, no one asked after them, and no one, in the heroic history of Sarajevo that began thereupon, which in part constituted the newly christened Bosniak nation and its suffering known throughout the world, no one asked about Nada Vitorović.

In the infantilism of her dying, or even earlier, my mother cared deeply for her teacher. She cared deeply for Sarajevo, and also always for her teacher. Even though her Stubler-Rejc-Karivan heritage was from all over, and in a declarative sense she was one day a Croat, another a Slovene, according to the manner in which the nation had been defined in the Balkans for the previous twenty years, my mother was a Bosniak. In addition to sharing the sentiments of her female Muslim co-workers, she was a Bosniak also in her readiness to speak about the crimes committed by Croatia, to express her outrage, all while asking how people could lock up other people in sheet-metal hangars in one-hundred-degree July heat without giving them any water; she was ready to return ad nauseam to what the Serbs had done in Srebrenica and their bombardment of the city for three and a half years, but about the Bosniak ill deeds in Sarajevo, the killing of Serbs, particularly those about whom no one was there to ask any questions, she barely said a word. This was someone who would say just about anything, even if it took her through a hundred barriers, to get back to the stories of Prijedor and Srebrenica in her next sentence. She would be shocked at the stories about Muslim atrocities, as if somewhere in the depth of her soul she was worried she might be personally responsible for these atrocities. And the more worried she was, the quieter she became, and her strange problem grew larger, though in fact it was not really a problem for her or for me, for my problem would have only been if she felt the need to stay silent about Croatian atrocities. And so I was calm. Like the majority of her neighbors, she had a problem with Serbs. And also with Croats – because they made her feel personally ashamed. And because they continued that story of hers, begun long before, in 1941, which had brought evil into our family. In the end, if those people, the Croats, had not been what they were, then her elder brother would not have died as a German soldier and she, as a little girl, would not have been guilty in the eyes of her mother for his death. Guilty for having been born.

She didn't develop a hatred for the Serbs, even after three and a half years of siege. The Serbs were to blame for massacring the city and killing people, other Serbs among them. She did not hate them, but she readily spoke about their atrocities. As time passed and Sarajevo became a city intolerant of the Muslim and Bosniak majority, might the story of Serb atrocities cease being connected to sentiments regarding the past and begin to create a future? Was my mother aware of this possibility? She was. In relation to the Serbs she did not naïvely take on all the feelings of the Bosniak majority. Or rather, her identity was that of a resident of Sarejevo, the same as it could have been when she started school and was happy that Marija K. was no longer her teacher, but instead Nada Vitorović was, the best teacher in the world. Love for her mother, love for her teacher, love for Tito . . .

For her the progression perhaps began with her teacher, Miss Vitorović, just as it did for me from Nona. Nothing more can be known about this.

I've forgotten the name of her school friend, the one who shared her desk, who suggested to her when they were in second grade that they announce their desire to study religion. I didn't write her name down, or I can't find it in my notebooks, but for my mother this was an important event. Girls mature earlier than boys, and she matured very early, entering a religious phase that I somehow completely bypassed.

The question of God was important and needed to be answered. At least for a while.

Nona and Nono didn't put up any resistance. When she told them that same afternoon that she wanted to take a religion class, they just shrugged. It was 1949 or 1950, the two of them were not believers, but they were far from the Party and all the political opportunism of the time. And maybe they were pleased that Javorka might find something that they'd lost. Like when you lose a fountain pen and years go by before your child finds it.

That would make for a good story: on God and a fountain pen.

The one problem was that the religion course was held far from their house, in the convent at Banjski Brijeg, so her mother gave her a long explanation about how to cross the very busy Tito Street. It was true that along the major thorough-fare of Sarajevo at most twenty cars might have passed, but that was enough for an accident. And they had no idea that a time would come before long when there would be many more cars than that.

They set out for the religion course twice per week. Before the thirty girls and boys the old priest would tell stories from the Bible, always highlighting a moral at the end. And the moral would be that everything was God's will and good always defeated evil, and each misfortune would turn out well, for he willed it to be so.

It was from him that Javorka first heard the name Satan.

The devil had already appeared in her life. Nona and Nono mentioned him, he was present in every story, mostly naïve, mischievous, and clumsy, but Satan was something completely new. That name was impossible to just pronounce and then go on with one's sentence without thinking about and thoroughly com-prehending it. Satan was God's main enemy but in terms of strength or wisdom he in no way measured up to God. Satan could only pose problems for God when he ingratiated himself with people, bewitched them and led them astray, such that they might revolt against their maker. Nothing caused God greater sorrow than when Satan led man astray.

Thus did the old religious instructor speak in the first years of communism, without giving up anything that might have been taken badly from the standpoint of a faithful communist. God could only be of use, as a help and support to the soul, a true companion on the road to communism, a society in which each would have according to his need and produce according to his ability. And everyone would find his place in communism, along with the opportunity to create his personal happiness and the happiness of his family. And this was how Satan would be put out of work, for man would no longer have anything to rebel against. And God, when there were no longer people prepared to rebel and engage in pacts with Satan, would himself become man again.

The religion instructor, of course, did not speak like this.

This was how I interpreted and reformed things as my mother told the story of her childhood religious instruction on Thursday, the eighth of November, 2012. She had less than a month of life before her. Her chin was covered with tumors, like those of a leper, and on her left leg, where the disease had begun, there were small open sores, from each of which several droplets of pale blood emerged. Luckily those wounds did not hurt. The doctors said these were all side effects of the smart drug therapy. The leg was enormous, swollen up like an elephant's. Death had taken up residence there.

But before her leg killed her, God would approach. I still didn't know whether she heard him that Thursday in November. Nona and Nono passed by him mute and didn't hear. Karlo Stubler was an atheist, a convinced Austro-Marxist, a German among Slavs, who professed every day that there was nothing beyond the mirror, nothing beyond life. His wife, Omama Ivana Škedelj, whose actual name might have been Johanna Skedel, did believe in God, and used to ask Javorka after she joined the Communist League of Yugoslavia, "Do you ever cross yourself, child?"

In accordance with church procedure, she took her First Communion in the late autumn of 1950 in Sarajevo's Cathedral of the Sacred Heart of Jesus. There as well, on Tuesday, December 4, at five in the afternoon, a mass for the repose of her soul would be held. The handles and decorative trim on the cathedral's doors were forged by her Slovene grandfather, a smith and drunkard, who had come to Bosnia precisely to forge those handles, and this was one of the conditions for Javorka's birth.

Her godmother was Angelina Bašić, whom everyone had called Deda. Nono's and Nona's friend, the wife of Josip Bašić, an official in the railway headquarters. Bašić was from somewhere on the Pelješac peninsula, maybe from Kuna. It was from there that the first oranges arrived at the home of Franjo Rejc after the war.

My mother boasted about the fact that it was thanks to Deda Bašić that she'd seen oranges so soon during the meager postwar years. She was eating them before she would taste her first sugar cube. This happened in 1948: she received the cube as a gift and put it in her mouth but was frightened when it started to melt and spat it out.

Deda and Jozo Bašić remained family friends to the end of their lives. Jozo died in the seventies, just like Nono, but Deda Bašić lived through the siege.

They had two children: Franjo, whom everyone called Kiko, and Maja.

Maja worked at the railway office and never got married.

She had twins out of wedlock, and she was the only person who knew who the father was. One of the two died at birth, and the other, Boris, survived as an only child. He was born in 1950, a few weeks before Deda Bašić would become Javorka's godmother.

They lived in Marijin Dvor, on one of the streets that shells rained down on when, in 1992, Karadžić was trying to turn the old part of Sarajevo into a ghetto for Bosniaks. He didn't succeed.

When it started, and it usually started in the morning, everyone would descend in an orderly fashion into the basement, where they would remain until evening. Only Boris would go up into the apartment occasionally to check on Grandma Deda, to see if she needed anything, or to bring her lunch.

Deda Bašić was at that point hardly moving. She couldn't make it downstairs and told them to leave her on her couch, for nettles in your pocket will keep you safe from lightning. She told them not to play around with their lives, they would all die if they tried to help her down to the basement every morning.

She was lucid and composed to the last day of her life. She knew very well what she was saying to them, and they had to listen.

And so Maja and Boris went down to the basement.

And Boris came up to check on Grandma Deda.

As he was climbing the stairs up to his apartment, a mortar shell fell in front of the building entrance and killed Boris Bašić.

And thus did Deda Bašić, Javorka's godmother, outlive her only grandson. She died when the war was over. Satan had long since ceased showing up to lead people astray. Probably because he didn't have to.

The building in which my mother attended religious instruction would soon, after 1950, be nationalized and taken away from the Church. A grammar school was opened there and named after Silvije Strahimir Kranjčević. This would be my school.

My mother had her elementary education in the Teachers High School, on Obala Kulina Bana. This was where the instructors from the Teachers High School would come for their student teaching, so the public school teachers were also their teachers. This meant that Nada Vitorović also served as an instructor for future teachers in Sarajevo.

She had two Jewish classmates: Jakob Finci and Isak Kamhi. Blanka Kabiljo, another Jewish student, was one year older than them. No Jews were born in Sarajevo in 1941 or 1942. Years later she would learn why this was the case. In those years – 1949, 1950, 1951 – this was not talked about in school. It was still early, and the crimes and misfortunes were still fresh, so both teachers, the evil Miss Marija K. and the kind Nada Vitorović, rolled out only positive examples, thanking Comrade Tito and the Partisans, while saying almost nothing about the Ustaše. Or the Chetniks. Actually they didn't talk about the Germans either. Only about Hitler.

It wasn't easy for the teachers to talk about the Germans because Maria, Laura, and Mihailo, three Germans from the barracks camp at the theater, were in their class.

Mihailo was a completely wild, desperate child. He fought every day, attacking the other children, taking suicidal leaps from the garage roof onto the playground asphalt. They avoided him, hated him, and couldn't understand why he acted this way.

Maria was aggressive.

Laura wept constantly.

The girls came to school in traditional dress.

Mihailo wore Swabian breeches.

Once he fell asleep in class.

Miss Marija K. dragged him by the ear from his desk and started beating him. She pounded him with her fists, and he dropped to the floor, screaming. She kicked him, shouting at him to get up. Mihailo didn't move, just shouted something in German through his tears. The demon took ever greater hold of her and she continued to beat him like that in front of the class.

"I think it was a nervous breakdown," my mother said. "I think Marija would have killed little Mihailo," she said, "if Blanka Kabiljo hadn't started crying. That calmed her all of a sudden. Or Blanka shouted something or jumped up from her desk. I don't know what happened, but Marija suddenly froze. It didn't enter our minds that Blanka was a Jew and she was crying because the teacher was beating the German Mihailo. Not at all. We were just happy she'd stopped hitting him and we didn't have to watch anymore."

It was in the third or fourth grade that Maria, Laura, and Mihailo stopping coming to school. Miss Vitorović made the brief announcement that they had moved to Germany. And again this was normal and ordinary to everyone. For children everything is normal if they know nothing else. For things to be out of the ordinary comparisons are needed. With the first comparisons some things start to be abnormal. The same goes for suffering. Suffering exists only if some previous times were without it.

In the second grade, for homework, they wrote Tito a birthday letter. (The little Germans too, it would seem.) The very best of the letters from the students at the Teachers High School was written by Javorka. This letter won the competition held among all Sarajevo's elementary schools and was sent to Belgrade, along with a relay baton, for the hands of Comrade Tito.

Perhaps somewhere in the Museum of Yugoslav History in Dedinje, or in the depths of some Belgrade archive, the letter my mother wrote to Tito still exists.

She would remember the letter whenever she was enumerating the proofs of her literary talent. This was important to her and revealed that it was from her I had inherited that gift. She would be jealous anytime Nono's prison camp diary from 1916 was mentioned, written in Cyrillic script but in Italian so that no one could spy on him, or the little diaries he kept in Drvenik, filling up the margins of desk calendars. Or when I would mention the letters Nona had sent me when I was in the service, or the literary essays of her older brother Mladen, or the philosophical and educational treatises of her grandfather, which were published in the interwar years in Sarajevo . . .

She would have accomplished something – having labored diligently, suffering, exhausting herself, destroying her nerves, working herself to the bone – had the one thing she'd managed to do been to impart this talent for writing to me. She would be deserving of a good long rest, having sacrificed everything and remained alone, with no one to bring her tea when she got sick. I mocked her. I'm mocking her now as I write this in my red armchair, the same chair I was writing in when last June the telephone rang and she cried that she had found a new lymph node when she had thought there wouldn't be anymore, and then she said what she'd never say again – that she thought she was dying; and I stop mocking her as I see the same books I saw then, the same window, the same part of the wall with six framed pictures on it, four portraits, a linocut by Daniel Ozmo, and a photograph of the main street in Sarajevo from 1937, and I see that nothing at all in the scene has changed, though a year has passed, and that I'll be able to freely mock her only when forgetfulness frees me from her, from her dying and her death.

At that time she wrote her one and only poem.

The poem tells the story of a veterinarian who cares for all the dogs and cats, those that have masters and those that have no one.

He performs miracles for them.

Then she writes about herself and her illness and how she too, like the animals, deserves a miracle.

She sent me the poem by email. It was the last email I got from her.

She sent it to all her women friends too – up until the end she always had many. My mother was superficial and devoted to her friendships, and it was a kind of friendship people liked. Especially in Sarajevo. She was also indiscreet, didn't hide anything from them, and found little of interest in what they'd say or do.

And then they all put her poem on their Facebook profile pages.

She already had a profile.

Dead people's nails grow for a little while longer after they die, and so do their Facebook profiles. One day several months after her death a friend request came from my mother. I erased the message, but later I was sorry. I don't have a Facebook profile, but it would have been worth accepting her friend request. It would have meant that I had at last accepted her as she was.

It bothered me that her poem was wending its way through the Internet and strangers were talking about her illness. She had always waved off intimate matters with ease. What she would keep hidden was anything that could lead someone to think she was to blame for something.

She asked me whether I might want to publish her poem somewhere.

She said she would like that.

For people to read it, if it's good.

Yes, it's good.

Let them read it then.

And this was how we would talk, repeating the same phone routine whenever she was in a better mood or nothing was ailing her. The conversation about the poem lasted through the summer, until the first autumn rains, as school approached its pupils, and her death approached us. Then, at last, it seemed she forgot about the poem.

She didn't ask me anymore whether I might like to publish it.

Though she would have liked that.

For people to read it, if it was any good.

It was.

Let them read it then.

I told her I would get her poem published, as long as she wrote two more. It didn't matter what they were about. She should write whatever came to her, however it came to her. In the same way that she had written that poem. And I would get it published under her proper first and last name, in a literary magazine.

No, no, isn't there shame in publishing one's first poems so late in life?

Why would there be any shame? There have been other cases.

She said she would write when she felt better. When nothing was hurting. She said that she couldn't write in her state. I was never sure when her dying began. Was I unjust toward her? Is what I'm saying ugly, and is it even possible to be ugly when a person says what he really feels? It can't be ugly to feel.

If I was unjust, I never once raised my voice when she asked whether I might help publish her poem somewhere.

And I wasn't lying. The poem was good. If there was such a thing as a gift for writing, and if this was the result of that gift, then I had inherited it from her. If the gift for writing was a particular kind of indiscretion, eternal talking about oneself, and being unprepared in the midst of such talking to spare others one's most intimate matters, then this was a gift I had certainly inherited from my mother.

By second grade she had started taking music lessons, studying piano. They bought her a small instrument, which would stay in our apartment until 1969 and our move to Sepetarevac. There were lots of pianos in Sarajevo in the early years after the war. They were sold off cheap, since pianists, it seemed, had been among the earliest victims of the war. Or they were the first to escape to the West, to Zagreb, America, and Argentina, and now their pianos had to be sold off.

Buying the piano was no great expense. No one remembers who the seller was, but my mother recalled that Nono paid in three installments. The piano cost less than a large bedspread or a winter coat but more than a fountain pen. At the time, prewar Parker or Waterman pens could be acquired for the price of a chicken's egg, for no one, it seemed, needed them anymore, and it would be years before the socialist offices would be equipped with proper writing supplies.

Nono was fascinated by fountain pens, the little vials with black and blue ink, ink blotters, fine, handmade paper, lead pencils, Japanese brush pens, which used India ink that allegedly was produced from a special kind of ash. Much had been destroyed and burned up in order to make a sea of ink from that ash.

He left behind a fine metal box with twelve Faber pencils with varying densities of graphite for various kinds of writing. Not a single one of those pencils had ever been sharpened. I didn't sharpen them as a child though I'd been tempted to do so. But I had terrible handwriting, the worst of anyone in school either in Drvenik or Sarajevo, so it would have been a poor use of the pencils. When one day my handwriting improves, I'll sharpen one of the pencils from Nono's box. Later I stopped caring about what my handwriting looked like – it remained as bad as ever – and what I wrote rather than how I wrote became the most important thing. The metal box with the twelve Faber pencils with the graphite of different densities that had been purchased before the Second World War in Germany reappeared unopened in some drawer on Sepetarevac when I went to Sarajevo for the first time in 1996. I took it with me to Zagreb, and afterward it traveled with me from one apartment to the next, remaining with me after the sudden, stormy ruptures from the people I shared those apartments with, during relocations when other things were lost, things much more useful in a practical sense. It was that much stranger since the box wasn't even that important to me for such a long time. I didn't know why I had brought it from Sarajevo, and it would have been easy to come to terms with having lost it. I might not have even noticed if it wasn't there anymore.

Today each one of those pencils remind me of the Croatian artist Josip Vanista's painting devoted to Manet called *The Endless Cane*, a dandy's walking stick that forms into crescent handles at both ends. A bewildering cane that was never taken on a walk. Pencils identical at both ends, without point or tip, introverted, sealed up in themselves. Hundreds of manuscript pages archived inside them, an unrealized potential in their graphite hearts.

After they had all died one after another, and after Sarajevo was no more – and I was driven from what rose up in its place – these little things became important. Objects no longer used for anything or, having passed through history, would never be used. Like the twelve Faber pencils. Nono had that box for thirty-five years and never sharpened a single one. They were there in that drawer, which during his life was quite tidy. He saw them every day but, it seemed, never needed them. Or there was some reason why he never sharpened any of them. When he died in 1972, the contents of the drawer remained in the same ugly piece of socialist furniture – under the china cabinet with the liquor bottles that no one ever opened, in the back of which was a mirror that made me think you could creep inside it – and no one ever emptied it, while everyone continued to call it Nono's drawer except that now it was messy. Inhabited by piles of trifles whose provenance it would forever be impossible to discern, Nono's drawer quickly became my Amazon and Polynesia. I explored it for years, really for my entire life in Sarajevo and after – until my mother replaced that piece of old socialist furniture with a new, transitional one – and from it I learned more about life, about the Rejc family, the Stublers, and the Karivans, than from any of the stories they told.

But it was only in the end, when the answers to all questions could be found only in fantasy, that I began to consider why Nono never dipped into the pencil box. Today the silver-colored box with its fine paper label displaying the old-fashioned company logo and the twelve unsharpened pencils, identical at both ends, is some eighty years old. And they shouldn't have lasted long, just so long as any of Nono's stationary supplies and writing materials. Pencils shrink the more you write with them, and Nono wrote a lot – at work in the railroad directorate and then, after he retired, as a part-time accountant at the Hotel Pošta. He also kept a journal about everyday occurrences, who had visited, when they'd installed a new gas canister, as well as beekeeper's journals, a different one for each hive. And he wrote all of them in pencil, such that they are hard to read now. Pale traces of lead against the pale paper.

He used a fountain pen for letters and official documents. The differences between private and public, amateur and professional, and personal and communal were marked by the distinction between Faber pencils and Nono's four fountain pens. The Parker 51 (about which a story was preserved in fragments and so has been transformed into a fiction later in this book), the Ordinary Parker (which may not have been ordinary but this was how Nona referred to it when speaking of Nono's four pens, now lost forever), the Waterman (allegedly the most expensive), and the Pelikan. The Pelikan was always stuck in the inside pocket of his jacket. He would move it from one to another like a handkerchief or a lighter. But the fact that the pen was not expensive but was an ordinary greenish-black Pelikan of the sort carried by every high school teacher did not matter to him, which is probably why he never lost it. A person never loses the objects he doesn't care much about, or the objects he needs for telling a story in the end.

In any case, the purchased piano was ultimately not a big event in the life of the family.

A corner was found where Javorka could practice at her ease, in the apartment's quietest, most soundproof room, which gave access to the attic. She didn't bother anyone, nor did anyone bother her. I don't know if she had a gift for piano. She sang well and worked hard, but probably this wasn't enough for the piano. She finished the elementary school music training and then several classes in middle school, and I assume if she'd had serious talent, something would have come of it.

For she spent all her practice time at the piano on her own.

Once in the midseventies we were visiting our relatives in Ilidža at the house where Karlo Stubler had once lived. I was ill and probably had the flu, so they'd had me lie down after lunch in a darkened room where there was a piano.

After a while she got tired of the company or decided to check on me and see whether I had a fever.

She opened the piano, set aside the green cloth cover, and played a very short Chopin piece. She lost her place, stumbled over the notes for a moment, for she was playing from memory, and went back to the start.

She said what a shame it was I hadn't wanted to go to music school and study piano. It was so nice, she said, while you played. You went off by yourself as if no one else existed.

I was nine or ten at the time and remember it clearly. Probably because of the way she said this, there was something dramatic about it. In any case, she was telling the truth. You could always tell when she was lying, putting on airs, or rehearsing her performance of self-pity. In this too she was like a child.

This was why when she was telling the truth you could feel it so sharply, especially when that truth held some drama for her. These small moments were important to me from as early as the years we spent in Drvenik.

When she said such things I thought my mother loved me. That it was too bad I hadn't wanted to go to music school, because it would have given me an opportunity to be alone.

It was one of the rare occasions when, almost unintentionally, she was comparing me to her. She was confessing her unhappiness to me as if it were my own. And as if I too were unhappy because she was not able to be. Which was of course the truth, but this truth did not, as a rule, get through to her. As if she were not concerned about me, and it really didn't matter if I and the whole rest of the world were unhappy, for hers was an unhappiness that was unique.

The rest of the world and I were simply the stage on which her misfortune played out.

Nothing on the stage was real except for her, who watched it all and for whom the world unfolded as her own living misfortune.

There was nothing else and could be nothing other than my mother and her picture of the world.

It has often been difficult for me to push this away. The world, after all, is something else. It isn't a stage for playing out my own unhappiness. And then I rebel, I write against the petty Croats and the state they are so proud of, just to make clear that I'm alive, though they too are alive and not merely an image or show, or a film with an unhappy ending, those petty Croats, their clergy, and their independent Croatian state, they are real, living, breathing, and dying, just as my mother died, never managing to escape from the steel shell she was locked up in when Mladen perished. And he had perished all because the petty Croats wanted to be great in the eyes of Hitler.

Whenever she wanted to ridicule my father and her former mother-in-law, who had really detested her, my mother would say that Grandma Štefanija had a piano that took up half a room, the only room she had, in order to keep her winter food supplies cold underneath it. After Grandma Štefanija died, she changed the verbs to past tense but told the story just as earnestly. She kept this up until the war and my departure from Sarajevo. When she was depressed or feeling vindictive, she'd tell the story of Štefanija's piano, which really was rather grotesque. In their small room, which was divided into a kitchen, living room, and sleeping area for her and her son – she kept a bed for him even after he'd moved out – stood a large baby grand piano that no one knew how to play, for neither Štefanija nor Dobroslav were musical. I saw Štefanija's piano with my own eyes and wrote about it in my novel *Father*. It was grotesque in the manner of a monstrously large nose on a man's face that has grown as the result of a disease, and I really could write about only that, that piano, my whole life long, for the story of that piano reveals the destiny of a certain Croatian and Catholic world, as well as a part of my family's destiny, and this musical instrument, Štefanija's piano, played a living part in guiding me, as no other piece of furniture did. But anyway, no matter how grotesque Štefanija's Catholic piano might have been, what was the most irritating were my mother's constant repetitions of the same derisive remarks toward her former husband and his mother for being cooped up with a piano like a couple of perfectly unmusical wretches.

Her denigrating my father didn't bother me.

In general it never disturbed me when she said anything unpleasant about him.

She did this quite a lot, in fact.

And when she had nothing ugly on her mind she'd even say she felt sorry for him.

This, I repeat, didn't bother me. But the repetition did. As did the fact that for some time I had been searching in her sentences for things pronounced according to animal instinct, inadvertently, or in connection with some completely inaccessible subconscious, which for the greater part of her life had resembled nothing more than an American prison during a riot: plenty of noise and calamity but without any particular goal except to express a feeling of having been wounded, of injustices suffered.

I asked her why she was telling me all this over and over.

"And who else is there to tell?" she responded self-pityingly, and again was victorious.

This was why it was better not to ask her anything, to act as though I was taking in everything she said, hearing the story for the first time. Like an actor playing the same scene in a family drama for the fiftieth time.

My father didn't know how to swim, he wasn't musical, he didn't know how to dance, he was weak.

She was a good swimmer, she played the piano and had a good singing voice, she had a good sense of rhythm and only needed a man who knew how to lead.

This was how she spoke.

And then during the war, with my departure, something happened that changed her. Or she grew older in the interim. She stopped telling the story about Štefanija's piano. A few years later, during one of my visits, I reminded her of it, thinking I might light a spark.

She just nodded, saying yes, yes, as if it were something that had happened long ago and had nothing to do with her anymore. Or maybe never did.

Back when she'd started school, they asked her what she wanted.

Sandals, she said.

If her parents hadn't asked, maybe she wouldn't have even thought of it, but now that they had, sandals became an obsession to her.

And I imagine, the two of them were saddened by this. It was 1949, the time of the worst poverty, when it seemed unfulfilled desires would last one's whole life. After the world war, four years of slaughter in the woods of Bosnia, people hanging from their necks along Marijin Dvor, the disappearance of Sarajevo's Jews, the death of their first-born son, those sandals of hers fell forcefully on their conscience.

There were no sandals to be bought in Sarajevo.

They had them in the state department stores, a miraculous sort of shop which perhaps didn't even exist and are certainly not mentioned in the books of that time, but my mother insisted on precisely that name, *state department stores*, and was bewildered why no one remembered them.

There they had sandals.

But they were more expensive than a piano. And it would not be reasonable to buy a growing child footwear that was so expensive. Besides, only privileged people could shop in the state department stores, ministers of state, federal envoys . . . Perhaps Nono could have found someone to buy his daughter sandals – this was one of those infectious obsessions that take hold of a whole family, sparing no one, but was it really worth going hungry over some sandals?

Perhaps they would have gone hungry. It was a time when all sorts of things were happening and even some children's sandals could take on the meaning of life. Perhaps Franjo Rejc could have even bought his daughter some sandals – Olga would have been against it but would have refused to take responsibility in the matter. Luckily, he complained to a friend, a Slovene who had a shoemaking shop in a wooden hovel on the spot where the university's department of philosophy now stands.

His friend told him not to worry, he would make the girl sandals, better than the ones they sold in the state department stores.

The Slovenian cobbler shaped and stitched Javorka a pair of sandals that looked like the kind worn by girls in German films set in the Alps. The sort Heidi wore in summer.

They looked frightening, but no one noticed. Nono was moved by the gesture of the Slovenian cobbler, who had managed to buy the leather webbing and the rubber for the outsole who knows where. Nona too, I imagine, was moved, and my mother had her first pair of sandals.

These were the very first shoes made expressly for her.

And they gave her terrible blisters.

My mother stubbornly wore her Alpine sandals to school for days. Tears ran down her face as she made her way along the Obala for those five hundred meters that took her to school, but she didn't give up. They told her she needed to be patient, it took time to break in a new pair of shoes. God knows if she believed them, or if she wore those sandals despite their never getting broken in, trying instead to break in the surrounding world. She fought in a way that she never would once she had grown up. When did she give up? Was it when she came back home after her first marital breakup, or when she gave birth to me and understood that this was for her whole life, and she would forever have me as a kind of completed and final fact of life, after which came dying?

During recess she would play on the school grounds with Gordana Babić.

Gordana wasn't a particularly intelligent girl. She was quite ordinary, though also the daughter of a government minister.

"You have such beautiful sandals!" said Javorka.

"Yours are really nice, too!" said Gordana Babić.

In July 2012, after one of her operations, she was recuperating in the former military hospital when I asked her whether the sandals ever got broken in. No, she answered. What happened to them? I asked. How would I know? Nono probably threw them out. These sorts of conversations helped us kill time while I led her along the linoleum hallways of the hospital, supporting her by the arm as she exercised her legs. She walked slowly, dragging her feet, squeezing my forearm so tight that it hurt. It was hard for her, she had no strength, or all her strength was gathered up in her right hand, which she would draw into a fist, taking hold of flesh and muscle. It occurred to me it was the same with babies – all their strength was in their grip.

I stayed in Sarajevo three and a half days that July.

I slept for the last time then in the apartment on Sepetarevac, among her patient's things, in the bed where she was to die. It was sunny and very hot, and I was alone. It seemed to me that never before had I ever spent so much time alone in that apartment: three whole nights. Someone else had always been there, Nona, Nono, my mother, other tenants. Someone had always been sneaking around in the hallway, flushing the toilet, unlocking the door. Someone's shoes had always been sticking loudly to the linoleum in the entryway. But now there was silence, and I knew somehow it would never be this way again.

I'd go to the hospital every morning, returning in the evening. I went by taxi, as that was the cheapest way in Sarajevo. Most of the cabbies knew my mother. For years she had got rides from them at the Mejtaš taxi stand, some of them since before the war. It was cheap after the war. Half of Sarajevo went where they needed by taxi. Women brought their groceries home from the market that way. People survived by using the rickety old cars brought in from Germany.

And some of them knew she was sick.

They asked me to wish her well. And said she was a great fighter and would surely pull through. She was quite proud when I told her they'd said she was a great fighter. At home, at work, a divorced woman, a single mother, all this worked harmoniously together in a fantastic illusion, in these two words filled with real and ceremonial admiration: *great fighter*.

She held on to this even in her illness. As soon as I called, on those days when she wasn't feeling so badly, she'd steer the conversation to who had said this about her the day before and what words they'd used: *a great fighter, a dragon, a hero*.

I wouldn't tell her what the cabbies had said.

I was never so kind to her as to satisfy her vanity. This, I believe, is the purest expression of love: to always satisfy someone's vanity, without any sort of ulterior motive.

It's not difficult for me to admit that I didn't love her.

Just as I didn't love my father.

But I didn't love my mother in a completely different way.

Not loving him in the end was easy, superficial, like the sadness one feels for a bird lying dead on the asphalt after it has been hit by a car on a forest road. A small part of me was taken up with this absent love. When he died, nothing crumbled. The world continued on without him.

Not loving her was frightening and all encompassing, like a magnet that attracted everything around it, creating devastation and terrible disorder. This absent love left for me a huge mess. Her death shook me, emptied me out, left me feeling as if I didn't even care.

Whatever people said to me now, I did not care.

Even if you are shocked by such a lightly uttered truth – that I didn't love her, that I felt relief when she died but miss all that suffering through all the four seasons of the year, that I have missed her, unloved and unhappy, since the moment of her death – I could not care less. With her death, things turned out to be all the same to me on many counts.

Those three and a half midsummer days in the empty apartment on Sepatarevac had been lovely, when no one was around and she was lying on a hospital bed after her operation. I was leaving for Zagreb on Friday, and she was being brought home from the hospital on Monday. This was known in advance, for there was still a certain order in everything at that point. In the next phase that order would be completely lost. Perhaps the beginning of her death should be defined as the moment when all order in her illness was lost.

The apartment was clean, airy, and light.

The women who took care of her kept it up. Several weeks earlier, in June, someone had had to start spending the night with her. She could be alone for several hours during the day, but at night someone needed to be with her in the apartment. It was harder and harder for her to breathe, and she often had to go to the bathroom.

They cleaned the apartment, those women who took care of her. They created a kind of order in it that had never been there before. With the furniture dusted, the windows washed, the dishes wiped clean, and the floors immaculately swept, the apartment on Sepetarevac looked like it hadn't since 1969 when we'd moved in.

It was the first thing I noticed when I arrived.

For three days I enjoyed this orderliness.

And the silence that was unbroken by a single voice. I didn't turn on the television and instead went out to make phone calls so as not to destroy that unlikely silence, the peace of the walls within which so much had happened.

As I looked through the apartment, peering into drawers, at the overcrowding and the crush of her narrowness, the closet that was about to explode from all the things inside that had long since turned into garbage, the bookshelves on which her biography and mine were frighteningly displayed, along with just recognizable traces of the lives of Nona and Nono, it occurred to me this was where she would die. Somehow I knew this would not happen at the hospital. She had to die here where Nono had, not with Nona at Koševo Hospital, or with my father at the former military hospital. She had been closest to him, her father; he had understood her, though he didn't know how to help her, while Nona and my own father were just figures of her misfortune.

That's why it seemed to me she would die here. In the room that, between two deaths, had been considered mine. This was where I'd lived until the beginning of the war, when we'd had to go into the basement because Trebević was visible from the window and already by April 1992 a couple of anti-aircraft rounds had landed in the room. This was where I had watched television at night – the broadcasts of football matches and the breakup of the last congress of the Yugoslav Communist Party – and smoked heroic amounts of marijuana and hashish without fear that my mother might come in. The agreement was she would not enter my room. The agreement was maintained because she knew what I was doing but didn't know how to take a stand toward it. I was twenty-two or twenty-three, working and making my own money, and I didn't need anything else from her, not even that she rouse herself enough to get up out of bed and stop sleeping throughout the day, and anyway marijuana was good to me. It was kind to me and with a mother's hand led me into the war and the apocalypse.

It seemed during those three July days that the walls remembered all this.

This was my farewell from Sepetarevac.

The next time I came, I would sleep in a hotel, coming here as to the hospital only to visit my mother.

The apartment would no longer be tidy, and this would no longer be my space. Something in it would have changed, or there would be something excessive in it. One might say that two deaths in my room was excessive.

I tried to be as quiet as possible. I looked at the rows of books, lined up just so, according to the orderly sense of the husband of one of my mother's friends, who had organized them the last time the apartment was painted. Lately she'd been able to find people who would carry out such tasks in her place. People were pleased to render her this service, refurnishing and changing the interior of the apartment, and she praised them for it.

She had called me in Zagreb while he was organizing the books. She told me, loudly enough for him to hear, that I would be thrilled. And then she pushed the receiver at him so the two of us would talk. And so I talked with the guy arranging the books in my mother's apartment on Sepetarevac. I never saw him. I don't know what we talked about. We were both uncomfortable.

She liked to do this: call me when someone was at her place and have us talk. I was acquainted with some of the people, others not. Usually we had nothing to say to each other, neither they to me, nor I to them. But for some reason this gave her pleasure. I had become a well-known writer, and these were all friends of hers.

On the third day, when I came back from the hospital, I turned on her computer. I wanted to see what her desktop looked like. The screen was clean with ten very carefully lined up folders, mostly with bookkeeping documents in them. She hadn't installed a background picture of the sort that people put on their screens to provide color in their virtual everyday lives. She was good at controlling her computer, much better than I am. At the beginning of the 2000s she had taken some informatics courses and later got interested in programming. If she had been younger, she would have left accounting to take up information technology. She could sit for hours in front of the screen, exploring the heart of the machine. This gave her joy. She didn't have to think. The computer was like a piano to her. It did not seek anything from her, any sort of emotional engagement. It did not oblige her to anything, sitting down on top of her conscience, but instead transported her simply and painlessly to a different reality. This reality calmed her. Composed of binary numbers, of complex simplicities that expanded into infinity and eternity, like the mirrors in a men's hair salon or the barbershop I had once been taken to at the Hotel Central, computer reality was good for the nerves and the spirit. It contained neither birth nor death. And what was most important: as in piano exercises and études, computer reality contained no other people. It was just her and infinity.

It was so simple, she said.

In summer 1999 and after, during the time of the millennium bug, when it was believed that humanity would explode and destroy itself, because computers would not be able to cross the threshold from one millennium to the next, transitioning from counting with a one to counting with a two, she would call me to enthusiastically explain how simple it all was, acquainting me in the process with the miracle of computers and cybernetic thinking. She didn't care whether I knew anything about it or if I were even interested in computers at all – when I could get a word in edgewise, I told her I really didn't care about them except for the excellent typing machines they made. By then I'd had about two or three years of practice at turning the computer on and off and writing prose and journalism in the simplest of all programs for idiots, and I had even started to write some poetry on the computer, thereby losing the final connection to pencil and paper, but it took her barely two months to overtake my understanding of informatics and to start speaking about things that I wasn't able to understand or even follow.

"You seem to have forgotten I'm not good at math!"

"But this isn't math, it's common sense."

"Then I'm not good at common sense. I'm not interested in it. And besides not being interested in it, I don't understand any of it either."

This conversation took place in autumn of the final year in human history that began with the number one. I wrote it down in a telephone address book – at the time I still had a notepad for telephone numbers because I resisted getting a mobile phone – I don't remember why I wrote down the conversation with my mother (Zgb, 15 Nov, 21:30 . . .), I might have liked how she had reduced the world of the computer and the cyber-galaxy down to a question of common sense.

She had said something that fit her so exactly:

Computers don't have feelings.

Common sense begins where feelings end.

Emotions are a disease or the symptoms of a disease. Family history proves this. The history of her life and the history of the Stublers. They disappeared, leaving no trace, because they were led through life by feelings. If they'd been guided by common sense, or if Karlo Stubler had entered the realm of the computer, the simple language of binary numbers, everything would have turned out differently, and we would not have been born. We would not have been born if Karlo had embraced the common sense that should have guided him through life.

Once she had mastered working on a computer, she learned how to use a program for small-business bookkeeping that she was able to maintain and update herself. At the time when social networks were just becoming fashionable, my mother created a profile on Facebook and began fanatically messaging both people she knew and people she didn't.

After she retired, she would stay up all night on Facebook, responding to messages, friending people, joining support groups . . . She became friends with one of my classmates from high school who now lives on the east coast of Canada. He had tried to get in touch with me more than once, but I never wrote back. I liked the guy but didn't know what we'd have to talk about. I don't like talking on the phone, I don't like sending emails or e-messages. Then my mother sent him a friend request, which he wholeheartedly accepted. When she died, he sent me a message containing the sort of statement of condolences that used to be sent by telegraphs, once upon a time.

In one special Facebook group she gathered together the remnants of the Stubler family, living today in Germany, Finland, Russia . . . She was by far the oldest among them, most of whom were distant cousins. They talked about banal, everyday things – which is, I guess, what chit-chatting on social media is supposed to be about – but also about a fateful discovery of my cousin's, that my mother unintentionally managed to stage an entire theatrical scene. The last great family performance. This was in August of 2011, the last summer before her illness.

At night she was surfing the Internet, researching the life paths of people who she had not seen in fifty or more years, following news stories about wars in distant countries, looking through forums that brought together German refugees from Transylvania and the Banat, asking whether there was anyone from Bosowicz, or using her primitive German to look for Regina Dragnev in Bulgaria. She read what they were saying and writing about me as she wandered around obscure Ustaše sites, trying to fathom how I could have wronged them so much, likewise studying fragments from the works of my leftist opponents, understanding only dimly what they were writing about, and she went through the Facebook profile of the famous Zagreb lexicographer and expert on Miroslav Krleža who had patented his discovery of my being a Chetnik, though she did not send him a friend request, and all this actually made her feel good, including the farcical, scandalous writings about me, her son, including the curses and insults on her own account. She was convinced it all was painless and innocent, and that no sort of trouble could come to her from the Internet.

When they diagnosed her, she carefully researched all she could find about her illness. This was when she discovered the Internet's brutality. It showed her how much longer, according to the statistics, she had to live. In the end she lived according to the statistical average. Almost within a week of what had been promised. She hoped for a miracle. She considered finally that she had a certain right to one, for she truly existed while all around her was mere image and illusion, but the miracle never arrived, though she would never have recognized it if it had. A miracle is only possible if it is noticed by the person for whom it is intended. Miracles could have whooshed by in flocks beside her. And she was angry with me, for I was supposed to be her miracle maker. I failed her.

I repeat it like a parrot, like a novice repeating the same simple prayer. I repeat this litany. I repeat this melody that sticks in your head from the morning when you first heard it on the radio. I repeat it so in the end it will be gone forever, forgotten.

In the last week of her life, she could no longer hold up a telephone receiver. When I called, someone else's hand would hold the receiver up to her ear, and she would cry, pronouncing incoherent phrases, as if she'd been awakened in the middle of the night.

The morphine would calm her, but then her consciousness would fight against the heroin daze and she'd want to talk again. Several times in those final days she fussed about my not wanting to give her my new phone number. She would call me, wanting to tell me something, I was her son – at that point she would break into tears again – but she couldn't call because I'd changed my number.

At the beginning I told her it wasn't true.

"So what's the number then?"

"Zero, zero, three, eight, five . . . ," I would say, listing the digits of my phone number, and she would repeat them after me: "Zero, zero, three, eight, five . . . ," until she seemed to be falling asleep. With each number she grew more distant, and at the end of the fourteen digits of my mobile number she would have given up on the conversation, only to return to it the next time I called or the next time she wanted them to call me.

This way of giving up was rather in accord with her nature.

That's why it was comforting.

I believed it was still her, though, speaking reasonably, she wasn't there. Or not entirely anyway.

On Friday I left for the book fair in Pula. I would work at the fair, presenting books. This is what I said: I was presenting books. I normally wouldn't have said such a thing to her, it's no way to speak to anyone, except small children, or when it doesn't matter what one is saying anymore. When the language I use, for whatever reason, becomes foreign. The next morning my mother wouldn't remember what I'd said to her anyway. The morphine had wiped her away, shaking her memory like flour through a sieve. Some went through, but some remained behind in the mesh. What stayed behind was no longer good for anything. Such was memory on morphine.

As soon as I had said it, I thought how accurate it really was. I was going to present books. And that was the only thing I wanted to do anymore: write stories, novels, books about what was really happening, having sat down, let's say, in a train bound for Sarajevo to spend the long hours writing a book about the journey, taking a few pictures, taking notes in the slow moving train with a fountain pen in a notebook purchased just for this, and doing this for my whole life. Presenting books. Presenting them as they are without rectifying or spoiling anything. As a true reader. That was all I wanted to be, and so it was good that I had said this to her.

Too bad my mother would not remember my words.

She would live just another two and a half days.

On Friday we stopped in Vodnjan, about fifteen kilometers from Pula. We had lunch in a restaurant decorated with the dolls of Italians who used to live there. It was good, enjoyable. A simulation of a lost Istrian world. Except that I had to call her beforehand. My friend Ana sat at the table, flipping through a newspaper, the menu, played with her phone, and I went outside to dial her number.

The caretaker answered, a big, solid Christian woman with a kind expression and a soft, reticent way of speaking. I had never met such a considerate person.

She gave the phone to my mother, and we talked.

I walked during the call. I'd been doing this for the last weeks and months, and during the talks with my mother I covered entire city districts, almost getting lost. I walked through Belgrade like this, and Wrocław, and Graz, and now I was walking through a tiny town in Istria, which had been emptied of all its inhabitants at the end of the 1940s. Here too lived other people, just as in Bosowicz.

She answered in a tearful, sleepy voice. She held me responsible for something I didn't do. Her sentences didn't make any sense, but the emotion in them was very precise. It'd been this way for eleven months. And maybe for a whole life. I was to blame because I was not interested in her illness and I hadn't done anything to help her. What could I do? I never asked this question, for it would have sounded as if I were saying there was no help for her. I didn't want to do that, to suggest that she would die, that her illness was incurable, that it had spread through her insides and would soon swallow her up. I didn't want to tell her that, for I knew my mother lived on childish hopes. Which perhaps were not so childish. Everyone in the end only needs a miracle, nothing but that. Truly religious people are fortunate because they provide their own miracles. The rest hunt for them in the air, grasping at them with their empty hands, rushing after them with waving arms as if trying to catch a fly that always escapes them. Has anyone ever caught a fly with his bare hands? Yes. And miracles have happened too.

That day she was especially aggressive. I couldn't cut off the conversation. She would not stop. It went on for some ten minutes, one sentence after another, without any sense, like Hesse's *Glass Bead Game* and those endless Led Zeppelin songs. I tried in vain to change the subject, get her onto something else. My mother didn't give in, said it was my fault, it would be my fault for as long as I lived, because I didn't go to the pharmacy when I should have, didn't answer when she called, didn't give her my new telephone number.

She would die without my solving the mystery of where this fixation had come from. It must have come from somewhere. There must have been some phrase, some little event, or perhaps a thought – before she had taken the first drops of morphine into her being – that had led her to accuse me for days on end of changing my number and not wanting to give it to her. With that, she thought, our contact had been cut off and that it existed only in these moments, amid her daily distraction, when she could do nothing but cry and implore and chastise me as a mother.

And since my mother showed no sign of stopping, the woman caring for her would slowly move the phone away, and I could hear her wailing, blaming me, and her asking the woman why she wouldn't let a mother talk with her son.

"So, now you know everything . . ."

"Yes. It's hard."

"Yes. Now it's like that. But don't worry about her anymore. We're taking care of her."

I walked away from the Vodnjanka restaurant, no longer knowing which street I was on, which empty little alley of the town, but before I could figure out which way to go, the phone rang.

Mother.

"Thank you for continuing to call," she said, her voice sleepy. "It means a lot to me that you keep calling. Thank you."

I told her to take care, to sleep, and not to thank me. And now I was going to do what I had left to do – present books.

When she got sick, I was writing a picaresque novel about a man lost in time who lives in airplanes and airports. The book's structure was relatively simple, but I couldn't continue. I stopped at the moment when the main character, Babukić, is watching the ants that have marched from inside a sandwich to carry away another suspended ant. I stopped, certain that there was nothing more to get from writing, as long as my mother was alive, as long as she hadn't died or been healed by some miracle. But things became so terrible with time that it seemed to me even after those final moments there would be no more writing. Or even that there would be no more me. It felt as if my bones were being ground up in a mill that turned rock to gravel. And then, four months before the end, there was a sudden change. Mother started to tell stories, and chapter by chapter I wrote *The Stublers*.

And now even that seemed as if it wouldn't continue. I'd managed to write one more chapter, "The Grave in Donji Andrijevci," when she was on morphine and it was clear she would not go on. I couldn't take that book any further after my mother had made this sudden turn. Or rather it wasn't that she had turned into something different, but that she showed me how besides the worlds of the living and dead, there was another world that immediately preceded death. There was dying, which cannot be described in a story because those are feelings and ideas without names.

People don't always manage to come up with words. Dying is impossible to describe, explain. Witnesses try to calm and console themselves, carry on with life which – because of the dying – had been arrested. They try to forget. And I was trying to forget, so I would write a report about my mother, her life and illness. Every story written stops being real life, moves into fiction and fable, even if it is all recorded from reality. There are no stories that deal with so-called true events. There are only true and untrue stories, actual and invented. Andersen's "Little Mermaid" and Shalamov's *Kolyma Tales* are equally true. This is the way I talk now when I present books.

The next day we were in Pula.

It was Saturday, ten fifteen in the morning. It was cold. Heavy snow was predicted.

We were at the Cvajner Gallery. I'd ordered a coffee and now headed outside to call. I crossed the Roman Forum heading toward the sea.

The phone rang three times before a man responded, saying, "Here we are having some coffee. The snow's falling. We're watching the pigeons on the window sill . . ."

As if there were some child involved.

"Miljenko, Miljenko's on the phone. Ah, if only you could see how she's laughing, she's laughing so happily. Here you are."

She cried, yelled at me as loudly as she could, as if the morphine wasn't working at all. It's over, she shouted, repeating it several times, over, over, over. I said okay, calm down, and she said there was nothing okay about it. It's over, over, not okay . . .

The conversation lasted twenty seconds.

On Sunday they told me the funeral would be on Tuesday.

She, my father, and Nano had gone to a very expensive, well-known restaurant in Strasbourg during their 1970 trip. Erwin Dussel had sent them there, saying it was the best place in town and anyone who visited had to go. The Gothic cathedral dedicated to the Mother of God and this particular restaurant. She couldn't remember its name anymore, but she had remembered it for a long time. "If your father were still alive," she said, "he'd remember for sure."

The food was certainly special. She didn't especially like it, but it was honestly special. The wine was magical. You know I don't like alcohol, she said. I get drunk from a couple of swallows, but that red wine took your breath away.

And then she had looked up and seen a huge rat calmly making its way across one of the rafters, in this fine Strasbourg restaurant.

"A rat!" she shouted, spilling wine onto her white blouse. She would have to throw it out because that wine was so red and so real that it couldn't be washed out.

Nano and my father looked up.

Yes, indeed, above their table a large gray rat was walking along.

The waiters did not chase it away. They were used to it.

And in Vienna, when they had just arrived and still had their bags with them and my mother's hair was filled with lice, Nano had called Erwin from a payphone and agreed to meet at a café on Ringstrasse.

Nano got around like it was his home.

He pointed to where the bathroom was for her.

He chose a table by the window where the passing people and carriages were visible.

They looked out at Vienna.

Nano had wanted to meet Erwin Dussel in the same café where they used to get together when he studied here. Fifty years had passed since then, but Nano behaved as if the waiters were the same ones from back then, giving them orders, arranging who would sit where, sure of himself like the regulars in every good pub in the world. They listened to him, followed his instructions, smiling obligingly, ignoring the fact that my mother and father surely looked like a couple of indigent Yugoslav guest workers, and if they happened to say something in German, their German did not differ much from that of a guest worker. The gentleman, however, was simply a regular. Like Nono, Nano spoke fluent German, but whereas Nono had spoken a learned form of High German, such that our neighbor Hans had told him he spoke a lot like the tiresome announcers on the morning programs of German state radio, Nano spoke his paternal Stubler German from the Banat, but wrapped in a Viennese accent and vocabulary, a slightly roguish language from that long-gone time when Vienna, at the beginning of the twenties, had not yet become conscious of the fact that it was no more and that after centuries of glory what remained was the backdrop of a city with a lot of good cafés and hidden whorehouses.

She marveled at his ease in this Viennese café.

She talked about it with wonder forty-two years later, lying ill in bed, although at first glance the only thing of interest in the story was that Nano had felt just as much at home in the old café as ever, even after fifty years, the Anschluss, the Yugoslav occupation, and the Second World War.

And while he could show Javorka where the bathroom was located, which was in the same place as when Jakob Reumann was mayor, Nano was not the same. He was a different man, his movements were quicker and lighter, as if gravity had suddenly become less heavy to him or a heavy burden had been lifted from his shoulders.

She wasn't conscious of it, but she liked her uncle then in a way that was different from other times. My mother loved Nano. She might have loved him more than her father. But not this Nano, a different Nano, one constantly on the verge of tears. This one's eyes were alert, seething. He pierced through the café with them, as comfortable as a pilot in a cockpit.

She could have fallen in love with her uncle just then in that Vienna café.

Though there was nothing so offensive and forbidden in the family as incest.

Since as far back as when Nano had fallen in love with his Viennese cousin Dora Dussel.

I don't know if my mother was conscious of this. She certainly would not have really fallen in love with him, nor would she have acknowledged, God forbid, that she was beginning to have feelings for her own uncle. But still, she never told a story for no reason, without thinking about it. She always had a reason and a point to her stories. The story about Nano's ease in the café where he had agreed to meet Erwin had some unstated meaning.

Erwin arrived, they hugged and exchanged several harsh Viennese expressions, which sounded like Yiddish to her.

Erwin knew my father.

They greeted each other, the Viennese architect and the Sarajevo doctor, as warmly as might have been expected, or even a little more so.

Erwin didn't know that Javorka and Dobro were actually divorced. The only thing they had together was their son. And if they were divorced, then why were they traveling together like this, and without their son? None of the distant relations knew that the two of them were no longer together, nor would they for a long time. Nano wanted them to be together and pretended their divorce hadn't happened, because he loved Dobro. My father impressed him because he was a physician. It was a profession especially prized among the Stublers. The best part of humanity was made up of doctors and engineers, and of course artists: great writers and musicians. Everything else was below that, less important and less reputable. Rail men were, let's say, far above lawyers in this hierarchy. They were the highest of the second tier, just below doctors and civil engineers, bridge builders, electrical engineers, bassoonists. Karlo Stubler admired bassoonists. An ordinary person, he thought, was incapable of learning to play the bassoon, no matter how musical he might be. Bassoonists were like the stylites, those Byzantine hermits who lived for years on the tops of poles. He was persuasive and succeeded in passing his views on to his children and other members of the household, even the strangest ones, like those comparing bassoonists and pillar saints.

And so doctors were highly respected among the Stublers and in all the

Stubler-related households. And so Nano loved my father and pretended to be deaf and dumb in the face of any story about their divorce and any attempt by Javorka to convince him of it. He could not listen and could not allow a doctor, let alone such a fine person, someone capable of playing and losing at cards for hours on end without ever complaining, to leave his home forever or stop being the husband of his niece.

And then Erwin came, and that was where the memory ended.

She only remembered as far as the greetings.

Or she made that part up because the memory was cut off at the point where Nano showed her where the bathroom was. She started toward it, maybe to look at her hair in the mirror, pick out the lice, and throw them into the sink . . . That part she surely didn't remember.

She went on with the story:

In the fifties, Lugonja had moved into the Balijan garage, which Nono Balijan had built for himself long ago, when in Sarajevo and in Ilidža there were neither cars nor garages.

A poor, condescending man, Lugonja was liked by no one in the Stubler neighborhood, nor did anyone think much about him, for there wasn't much to think. His first name was not even known, only his last – Lugonja. Nor did anyone seem to even know he was a Serb.

God, would this be known later!

Nevenka and Naci stayed in Ilidža (Lado was studying in Sarajevo, Regina in Zadar), and the two of them were by themselves.

Nevenka, my mother's first cousin, the daughter of Nona's sister Regina, had already lived through one war in that very house. She'd been a child back then.

Now she was getting up in years, having retired from her work as an architect just before the war, and Kasindol Street was now remembered as one of the occupied parts of the city. News of the slaughter and the forced removal of inhabitants had arrived from that quarter, while shells from all directions fell along the boulevard and troops defending the city rushed down it, but the enemy had pushed them back in their useless attempts to break through the circle and – as people put it then – de-blockade the city.

For a long time we didn't know what had happened to Nevenka and Naci or whether they were even alive. The phones weren't working. Letters and telegrams crossed from one side to the other through the Red Cross and the kindness of foreign journalists, but you had to find someone who could carry your letter to the Red Cross. In Serb-occupied Kasindol, Croats and Muslims were prohibited from moving about . . .

They lived however they could, surviving. Serbian soldiers invaded their homes, then bearded Chetniks like those from a Veljko Bulajić movie, then regular soldiers, and again Chetniks . . . They threatened to cut their throats, but then they didn't, there would be a period of calm, and then everything would start over . . .

One of their neighbors who turned into this kind of a monster was the one who they didn't know was a Serb.

Lugonja.

He was the first one to promise he would cut their throats.

And then he went away, leaving them to wait for the moment when he would fulfill his promise. In an hour or a day, two months or a year. When was all the same – a person who promises to cut his neighbors' throats will probably keep his word.

And then, rather suddenly, came the liberation.

The Americans grew tired of the war in Bosnia, Sarajevo was de-blockaded, and the Serbs dug up their dead and took them away. From Ilidža and some of the neighboring villages entire graveyards went away. This story too would be one worth telling.

Lugonja, however, disappeared, his promise unfulfilled.

He left his elderly mother in the Balijan garage, a widow, not especially kind, dear to no one. It was not the time for people to pity Lugonja's mother. For three and a half years he had spread terror through Kasindolska, and who knew how many people he'd threatened and with what. They had watched as he beat people with the butt of his rifle while throwing them into trucks, never to be seen again. No one could have honestly said that Lugonja was a war criminal, but that he had personally turned many people's lives into a three-and-a-half-year living hell was something that no one could deny.

They didn't touch his mother, neither to hurt nor to help her.

Nevenka asked her what she was living on.

Lugonja's mother shrugged. But she was not moved. As if it was all the same to her, or she was not intelligent enough to grasp what her neighbor was asking and how weighty such a question was.

Lugonja's mother knew what sort of a hero Lugonja had been during the war. She couldn't have avoided knowing. She had raised her son to become Lugonja after all. What he had done was not hidden from her, whether in some other town or even some other street. It was here in Kasindol, right before her eyes.

Nevenka went to city hall to arrange Lugonja's mother's pension for her. And indeed she arranged it, the tiny widow's pension, what was due to her, enough at least that she wouldn't go hungry.

The neighbors asked her why she had done it for the old woman.

Why wouldn't she do it? Nevenka answered.

Lugonja lived several kilometers away, in Lukavica, which was in Republika Srpska. He did not visit his mother. He didn't dare. The wretch thought Nevenka had taken care of his mother's pension in order to lure him into visiting so she could turn him in.

One neighbor, Boro, went to Lukavica regularly. He bought and sold things, surviving like everyone else. He met Lugonja, who asked him had Nevenka said anything? She must have mentioned the thing about the throat cutting.

Boro came back specially to tell her about this.

Give Lugonja my regards when you see him, and tell him to fear God, not Nevenka. This was what she answered.

Whether Boro took the message to Lugonja is unknown, but still he did not come. He had things to be afraid of, and he was safe in Lukavica.

Boro remained in Kasindol. No one touched him even though he had been in the Serbian army. One time he brought Nevenka and Naci a small shaggy dog from the frontline. To keep them safe, to bark when anyone came. They named it Žućo. They would joke and call it Žućo the Chetnik. Žućo lived for a long time, longer than Nevenka. Dogs had long lives in the Stubler house.

As she told these stories, my mother did not feel ill, and for as long as she told them nothing hurt.

By the beginning of May 2012 it was clear the sickness was spreading.

She had to have another operation, after which she could not move freely anymore, though she continued to live alone.

In April she went for the last time to the School of Education, where she had worked until retiring. A little bug needed fixing in the accounting program, and the programmer had suddenly died in a traffic accident. He'd been riding his bike on the coast at Neum and been hit by a truck. Now there wasn't anyone but her who knew the how and what of the computer program's makeup, and the six-month budget report was fast approaching.

Everyone came out when she got there.

The programming mistake was small, but it was there.

They paid her two hundred marks in cash.

She told them they were kind and it was appreciated.

She told them she happened to be ill at the moment.

But she was proud of the work she accomplished.

The next time they would see her she would be in a closed casket.

I said I would not go into the chapel if the casket was not closed. I didn't want to see her dead. And I didn't want others to see her that way. She'd been in such torment that it was no longer her face. There are people who like to look into the face of death. This is why they open the caskets. The waxy gray faces protrude from the piles of white roses or perhaps some less expensive flowers as if to make them more alive.

Throughout May she'd dreamed intently about a special Cuban medicine for her illness that was in use in Albania. When she was feeling better, she said, after the smart-drug therapy (which hadn't even begun yet), she would take a road trip to Albania with friends. Not even at her healthiest would she have undertaken such a trip, but she was dreaming. She described Albania as she'd seen it in some documentary, talked about the Albanians, what sort of people they were, honest people, all the Albanians she'd ever met in her life . . . I participated in this, our phone conversations got longer and longer. Soon my phone bill was approaching two thousand kunas, with roaming in Bosnia even more expensive than in the US, and I had even begun to come up with stories about the fantastical effects of the Cuban medicine. I was lying to her, and these early May lies about the Cuban medical miracle agreed with her, leading her away, even if only in dream, on the road to Albania. These had always been her greatest journeys, in dreams and stories, and this only continued during her illness, which meanwhile did not impart the gift of fantasy, could not lie to her, did not reveal any other reality than hers. This would distress my mother often more than her illness itself. For the first time in her life she had been condemned and bound to a single reality, one in which she could not function and in which she was wretched.

Soon the silver water arrived from Banja Luka.

A certain acquaintance of hers, a woman active in smuggling and altruism, told her about the miraculous properties of silver water. It purified a person from the inside, a little like the way brushes in an automatic car wash cleaned a car, only you had to be persistent enough and drink the right quantities at the right intervals.

She was distracted by this miracle for some time in May but was growing worse and worse. Entropy quickly widened its embrace, the beast growing and swallowing her, appearing where the doctors had not expected it and leaving its ugly, misshapen tracks behind. The findings grew ever worse though the attending physician had a perfected formula for smoothing over their contents.

Nothing unusual, nothing atypical, she said each time.

And my mother, probably like every other patient, believed that it was not bad, it was even good, if it wasn't unusual and wasn't atypical. It seemed to her that death was an unusual and atypical phenomenon in her life.

Then on her seventieth birthday came the medicinal mushrooms. She had been at an exam the day before, a Wednesday, and they had said that the smart-drug therapy would be postponed for another two weeks. This was the second postponement, and her disease was spreading.

She needed the mushrooms in order not to go crazy.

But this had lasted only a short time, not even a week.

We talked once or twice a week. On the weekend there was no phone service, I had told her. In the village where I lived the signal was too weak. I had lied to her that there wasn't any service at all and that I had to walk to another village in order to call. I thought up all sorts of things in order not to have to talk to her on Saturday and Sunday. I thought this was better, she would stop with her obsessive topics, and then on Monday we wouldn't start up again with what we had already discussed on Friday. But this, as a rule, was not true. The very same conversations would start up again from the beginning, as if they'd never been begun before.

She said I should call the authorities in Bosnia and Herzegovina and in Sarajevo, that they should help her, since she was suffering as a victim of medical negligence and sloppiness. She said I should call them to help her since she was my mother and I was an important, valued person in the world. They all knew me and knew the value of my words. If they refused to help me, then I should write about it in the papers and make her case public.

She said I needed to file suit to collect the funds for her treatment. To open a special transfer account, put an ad in the papers, announce how much money was needed. And she had calculated that the smart drugs, if they were not part of an experiemental group, which would make them less expensive, associated with the latest auto-immune therapy, could cost up to a hundred thousand euros. She said I needed to immediately send letters to all my foreign publishers telling them my mother was sick and needed financial support . . .

To distract her from the daily repetitions of the same hopeless demands and requests to make her illness public, I started asking her questions about the past.

Last night, just before I fell asleep, I thought of Omama Johanna, where she was from, what her father did.

"Why don't you know that? Great-grandpa Martin was a joiner. He was from Škofja Loka, in Slovenia."

Then she would talk for a while about Great-grandpa Martin, saying everything she knew about him, everything she remembered. At first she talked without much interest, but still she responded to all my questions. When she had finished, it was only necessary for me to have the next question ready, a new topic, so that she would not return to the story of her illness and all I needed to do to help her.

"What did Opapa Karlo like to eat?"

"What do you mean what did he like? He ate what was prepared for him. There wasn't much to choose from then. Omama didn't cook. She was sick. Because of her heart she wasn't supposed to exert herself, so Aunt Rika usually did the cooking. What did she make? Soup with beef fat, and they would eat that beef later, with homemade horseradish from the garden, and often they had rabbit. You know we had a rabbit hutch back then, and Opapa had kept one since settling in Ilidža."

"Did Opapa slaughter the rabbits?"

"God forbid! He wouldn't even slaughter a chicken. It was Uncle Vilko who would slaughter them, early Sunday mornings before anyone else was up. That was his job. No one knows how he did it. It was on the sly, far from the children's eyes but also from those of Karlo Stulber. Then all the people just pretended. And ate the rabbits as if they had fallen from the sky."

"Did the hutch rabbits have names?"

"Yes."

"So you would eat Bugs Bunny and Long-ears?"

"No, it was only later that we'd notice which rabbit was missing, which one was no more."

"Did you use the same rabbit names over again?"

"I don't think so. A name could have been used again only if we all forgot that there had once been a rabbit named, say, Ðuro."

"So there were lots of different names."

"Yes."

"And you ate them all yourselves?"

"There were lots of people in the household. Two households ate together: the Stublers and the Stevins. Then on Sunday, when we had rabbit, we would come from Sarajevo too, with people showing up from everywhere, so there would be some fifteen people sitting down to eat. The table wasn't big, so we had to eat lunch in two shifts."

"What did Opapa Karlo have?"

Soft-boiled eggs. That was all he ever ate. Aunt Rika would make him about eight of them. If she were out on some errand, he would put the water on the stove himself and, when the water came to a boil, put in an egg to cook for a very short time. Either I was little and it just seemed to me that way, or Opapa didn't ever cook an egg for more than a minute. He would put it on that ceramic stand. I don't know what the deal was with that ceramic stand, but it's probably still in the house on Kasindol Street. He would take it to the table, break off a piece of bread, place everything just right as if it was the beginning of a play, and then with the tiniest little spoon he would flick off the top of the egg. I'll never forget it. That moment and the sound. Sometimes it seemed as if he lived solely so that every evening he could flick off the top of a soft-boiled egg. And he was pleased that I was watching. I didn't ask for anything. I was eating my dinner already, like everyone else, because he wanted to eat his eggs in peace. He loved me. I didn't ask anything of him.

Then the story began to grow, the questions changed the meaning of what she was saying, and I started to jot down her answers. A notebook turned up in my hand, one I had purchased in Belgrade at the Home Army Office at an exhibit of the tragic Serbian artist Sava Šumanović, at the start of December 2011, before her illness. We'd gone to Belgrade twice that month, the first time just for the exhibit, the second, to observe the annual Christmas celebration, as befitting a minority. The first time she had not felt the lump that would, by the second visit, begin this story's report on her illness.

It is a notebook for mathematics, the covers thick, put out by the Sava Šumanović Gallery. It had been printed in the town of Šid by the Ilijanum Press, which is part of the Museum of Primitive Art, set up as a foundation for the peasant painter Ilija Bašičević Bosilj. The cover bears a reproduction of the 1942 painting *Ilok's Road*, one of the last created by Sava Šumanović, before the Ustaše took him away as a hostage and shot him in August of the same year. That same year, 1942, he had stopped signing his paintings, probably so as not to disturb the Ustaše by the written Cyrillic characters of his signature, which was rather childish, like that of an eighth grader. So in the left corner of the painting, in thin black brush strokes, only the year is written.

The road, snowy and hilly, runs along an alley of tall, leafless trees. It meets the horizon at the second rise. It is winter, the road is laden with snow, just like the roofs of the houses lining the alley. There's not a sign of life anywhere, neither people nor cars. The colors are white, light blue, dingy yellow. The grass along the road in the places the snow has not reached has been frozen and burned by the winter.

How that painting might have appeared, what sort of presentiment it might have suggested to the eye of the viewer had Sava Šumanović survived the Ustaše and their intolerance for Cyrillic letters and Cyrillic family names it is impossible to know. And so *Ilok's Road* is a clear intimation of death. This is what the painting says.

But this is not what I thought of when I started writing down my phone conversations with my mother in the notebook, her memories of the Stublers and of her own growing up. I wasn't thinking then about the story of the painting on the cover.

The notebook in which I started jotting things down was not completely empty. On one of its pages, in Trieste, I had written down the short life story of Fulvio Tomizza's widow, Laura Levi, whose great-grandfather had owned a silk mill in Sarajevo in the 1850s. His envious neighbors had set it on fire, the mill had burned to the ground, and the man had gone both gray and blind overnight.

What happened next occurred by chance. But after the notebook took on its new purpose, *Ilok's Road* became an illustration of her dying. I looked at it every day, whenever I took out the notebook during our phone conversations and spread it open on my knees, or in the afternoon or evening, when I concentrated on pulling together the fragments of her story into the chapters of *A Family Novel* under the title *The Stublers*. I did not write out the chapters in the order she narrated them but rather according to the internal logic of the imagined novel, bypassing chronology, outside of any temporal frame, so in the end the story once completed would be whole.

Once she got started, and when she again found in the story her parallel reality, one that her illness neither followed nor respected but was instead unnerving her and killing her off before it destroyed her physical body, I knew my mother would tell the story to the end. Or until the morphine took over. But I didn't know when the end would come, how many stories there would be in the time she had left, and what length might possibly be expected of them, though the difference in this case between subjective and objective time was especially pronounced.

So I began *The Stublers* as a novel that could end at any moment. What was announced in one chapter might never end up being told but would still have its own meaning and its own end. Her stories quickly began outpacing me. I couldn't get them all down. Besides, she had begun to narrate in two parallel lines: one that followed the Karivans, the Kreševo family descended from smiths and miners, and another following the Rejc family from Kakanj and Zenica, Nono's brothers, who lived as part of the industrial proletariat in mining and railroad colonies. These two lines did not belong to the Stublers. Nor did they have the content or consistency favorable for chapters in a novel. My mother simply didn't know enough about them or was not interested in their destinies because they didn't intersect with the important points in her life, her dying. I stitched these two lines into one, the sequence called *Miners, Smiths, Drunks, and Their Wives.* By contrast to a novel, quartets have their own musical structure and rhythm.

When she died, I wasn't able to continue *The Stublers.* I needed to write down the story that she told. In the end, *The Stublers* didn't reveal the most vital part of the story: the circumstances of Mladen's death. While it is announced in several chapters, this great and horrible finale remains outside the novel, just as it had remained outside their lives, like something that happened but about which there was only silence – as if, in the end, there was good reason for Mladen's suffering to be described and documented somewhere outside the rest of the whole.

I did not invent anything in that novel, but that doesn't mean it's completely true. She invented a bit, lied, or narrated things as they seemed to her. I didn't touch any of her skillful lies. But there are not so many.

The Stublers is a collection of stories my mother lived through when her life had become a torment, when she could no longer go on alone. But my mother wasn't confessing, she was narrating. And maybe she was narrating for the same reason that people confess – to make herself feel better, to set her suffering to one side, to live a little more outside the failing of her physiology. She was happy while she narrated, and it was easier for me because she didn't cling to my conscience or ask me to do something I wasn't able to do. These then were our moments of collective happiness. We were never so happy together as when she was telling me her story, never so close. But this was not the closeness of a mother and son, or that of friends, or that of a grown man and a dying child – it was that of the last two people on earth. At the end of each story, each phone conversation, we were no longer alone, and we were no longer close, but each of us was left again with her or his own struggle. *The Stublers* was that vanished world, the story of two happy people. I believe that happiness can be felt in every sentence, all the way to the last one noting her death, even though by that moment she was already gone.

What made her so happy during the telling? It was what makes any writer happy for whom, for whatever reason, literature becomes a parallel reality. My mother was as happy as Varlam Shalamov was when writing *The Kolyma Tales*, despite Danilo Kiš's saying that there never had been a more unhappy man. Probably Kiš was correct, but for that very reason he must have been happy when he was writing those tales.

Love didn't bring us together. That would have been too simple and, after so many years, impossible. Nor was it human compassion for another who was sick, who didn't believe in God, and who was dying without hope that brought me closer to her. That could only have driven us away from each other – and I felt this – as well as the fact that I was alive and, from her hopeless perspective, healthy. Because of this she could have only hated me, especially because I never wanted – or so thought the child in her – to create the miracle that could cure her.

What brought us together was the story, which appeared between us amid the two horrible torments that were killing us. Hers was without a doubt more horrible than mine, but even mine I could hardly bear, even in my dreams I was conscious of it.

That story was an expression of absolute happiness.

My mother was not a writer. This wasn't because she had no gift – about her gift, as I mentioned earlier, I don't know a thing – but because of the sort of person she was. Her life turned into a single, unusually sad story, a novel to the end of which one could not read, so much unhappiness would it bring. And at the same time that very same life of hers, until she got sick, was that of an ordinary city dweller. Seen from the outside, it was an orderly, healthy life, in complete internal disorder amid the disorder of its own domicile. A writer cannot live parallel lives, for writing is a parallel life.

But in the story that would become *The Stublers* my mother behaved like a writer. That was how she talked, taking stock of the details without bothering about the story's frame, which we know emerges on its own, when the person doing the telling has a good reason to stop. And there is no better reason than death.

"I don't know," said the voice that had given my mother the phone to talk with me that Saturday, December 1, "she laughed when she heard it was you, but now she's upset."

"So, now you know everything," the voice said, while she cried in the background, before the line was cut off forever.

Around ten that night she lost consciousness. Her departure took a long time, the whole night. She survived the dawn, when one usually dies.

The last time she had told some of her story was four days earlier, on Tuesday, November 27.

It was the first time she'd had difficulty speaking. She sounded unwilling. I asked her lots of questions, to which she gave one-sentence answers. Either something was especially ailing her or some essential change in her illness had taken place, and everything was rushing to the end. Like a bicycle that has reached the top of a hill and begins to fly down headlong into nothing.

The next morning, her voice sleepy and tearful, she accused me of having changed my number so she couldn't call me anymore. She talked as if it had been a long time, maybe years, since we'd last spoken, and as if I didn't know she was sick.

This was on Wednesday.

But on Tuesday she had wanted to talk about the youth labor actions she'd participated in as a middle schooler.

At the time my mother had been a member of the Socialist Youth Presiding Committee of Sarajevo. But this was not the reason for going on the labor actions. She wanted to get out of the house, run away from Nono's and Nona's mutual recriminations, which usually took place without a single spoken word, through the clinking of the spoons in their coffee cups, the running of water in the sink, and Nona's coldness, directed at her as she grew older and was becoming a young woman. Everything in her life would take place over the next several years, like in a speeded-up film, and then all of it would come to an eternal sudden stop, in a long postponement of the end.

The labor actions belonged still to that world of childhood.

And to her strong, pure faith. At the age of fifteen, in her fourth year at the gymnasium, as a young adult, she became a member of the Yugoslav Communist Party. She was one of the youngest. They wrote about her in some of the Belgrade papers. I had the clippings for a long time, keeping them in a drawer with other documents, but have since lost them.

The next year, when she was sixteen, she went on a labor action in the south of Serbia with the Sarajevo Middle School Brigade. The village was called Džep, near Niš. The action commander was a Montenegrin named Jovan Lakičević.

The following summer, the youth labor action was in Sutjeska. She was the headquarters secretary. An important position. I asked what she did. I don't know, she said. She hadn't answered this way before. She was no longer narrating a story, just listing details, as if I were filling out some kind of form.

I thought: this is the end. Then it seemed to me this was just a bad day for her. They had warned me two weeks before she would at some moment go onto the morphine drip. And then it would be over. There was no more conversation. As if I had done something wrong. Or maybe I was speaking with her about things I didn't need to – stupid things, family gossip, youth labor actions, when the Stubler women had their first periods, in what years they had experienced menopause. Instead of saying goodbye, instead of asking her about serious things, or maybe preparing for what was to come, I was asking her the name of the youth action commander in Sutjeska in 1959. Or was it 1960? What did my mother mean to me if I was asking her such questions?

But I had no better ones.

She couldn't remember the commander. It was on the tip of her tongue. It would come for sure as soon as she stopped thinking about it, but now – no.

"Okay, I'll remind you tomorrow."

"Okay, tomorrow," she said, sighing with relief, as if it had become hard to remember things all of a sudden.

I mentioned to her something that happened in Sutjeska.

I told the story of how she had set out for Perućica with some friends who wanted to show her the primeval forest and one of the places where the great battles for Sutjeska had been fought. It was, in the root meaning of the word, off-road, without shepherds' paths, mountain paths, or any kind of paths at all. They only had a compass. At one rocky pass they'd been attacked by snakes. A frightening number of venomous snakes. They ran into the forest and there, right in front of them, saw a bear.

They lost all desire to continue their excursion and only wanted to go back to the youth encampment.

They had a choice of which way to go back: through the woods where the bears were or across the dry path filled with snakes, like some sort of Old Testament story. (From my earliest memories, I had known this story. My mother had often recounted it as one of the most exhilarating days of her life. She'd had to choose which she feared more, bears or snakes. Her comrades left the choice to her, because she was a woman, because she was the headquarters secretary, and because they themselves were half-dead from fright. On one of the two sides waited death. And perhaps it lurked on both. I read the Bible seriously for the first time in 1979, in a deserted Sarajevo. It was a Zagreb printed book, published by Stvarnost, which my mother had purchased from a traveling salesman. The Old Testament had reminded me of the story of the snake-filled gorge and the bear-filled woods.)

She didn't interrupt me as I told a story she was supposed to tell.

Nor did she add anything to it.

She only corrected one thing: it was a sow with her cubs, not a male.

I wanted to ask her which way they took in the end, the snakes or the bear, for I had forgotten that part in the meantime. But I didn't. Perhaps I thought there would still be time later, or I knew the story would be better without that part. Perhaps I believed I would remember one day.

Her third labor action was the best.

The highway across Serbia.

Again just bare facts without any story.

The commander of the Sarajevo Brigade was Pavle Dutina.

The commander of the Belgrade Brigade was the future historian Veselin Đurić.

The shifts lasted a month at a time.

There were no peasants among the participants.

Only kids from the city.

There wasn't much falling in love.

The relationship was different.

Everything was different.

According to my notebook, the phone conversation ended at 1:40 pm. I only put a date on a few of the last ones, writing the time of day or the exact hour.

When as a journalist I flew out of Sarajevo in May 1993 on a UN Hercules Cargo Transport and didn't come back, my mother remained alone in the apartment on Sepetarevac.

It mortified me not to be returning. This was a grave sin in my world. But for the people around me it was the only possibility. Who would go back to Sarajevo in 1993 once he'd gotten out? This was what they said to me. But there were people who went back to Sarajevo because they had left behind something that was important to them. A bedroom full of comic books on shelves reaching up to the ceiling, a home library, a piano, a father, a mother, a grandfather . . . There were people who had left something in Sarajevo that was so important that they simply had to go back.

What had I left behind in Sarajevo? Who had I left behind?

A mother on the verge of suicide, or on the ceremonial, poorly performed verge of suicide – this was actually never really clear. Since she didn't kill herself, I reserve the right to say it was all bad acting, selfishness, and despair, though would she really have had to go through with killing herself in order for me to admit she actually wanted to?

I left her as she was coming out of menopause. She was fifty-one. Her menstrual cycle had stopped earlier than her mother's. I left her when it was impossible to anticipate what sort of person would emerge from that phase of her life, if indeed she were allowed to emerge from beneath the Serb bombardment and snipers.

When she'd make her way down Sepetarevac toward town, from the hills on the other side men would watch her through the sighting devices produced by Sarajevo's Zrak, which had also produced the optical instruments for the first spacecraft to land on the moon. This was absolutely perfect: my mother in her green Chanel suit and a pair of worn old shoes, her hair golden but not gray – you couldn't buy hair dyes anymore – observed by the eyes of an experienced marksman, who a little before afternoon, at the time when she headed for work at the Pedagogical Academy, evaluated who he would kill or not.

Is this not what happened?

If not then what did? Can anyone ever discover according to what criteria the snipers selected the people they would shoot at?

Once in a while a bullet and then another would whiz by above her head, and mine too when I was still there, lodging itself in a facade or Sepetarevac's steep asphalt.

This was an amateur learning how to kill. Or perhaps my fellow Serbian writers trying their hand. Not long ago, during the year my mother was ailing, one Croatian writer in Zagreb wrote that the Serbs didn't want to waste a bullet on me. One time mixes with another, the years blend together into the past, the future, while people congregate who are quite distant from each other, separated by hundreds of years, and literature exists to bring all this into order and create some new chronology that is close to the nature of the moment. The Croatian writer who today laments the fact that a Serb didn't want to spend money on a bullet with which to shoot me in Sarajevo in 1992 or '93 is an ideal demonstration of my solitude. Thanks to him, and to the blending of distant epochs that his pronouncement made real, I can make my way through Zagreb in the manner that one's eye makes its way across the oils of Giorgio de Chirico – magnificent and comforting is the wasteland of the city, at twilight, when, in late June, the sun has dipped below the horizon.

But what was I thinking about her when I lived in this city then, which was friendlier to me at the time for, in their eyes, I was a victim. People shy away from victims for fear of becoming victims. I assured them I was not a victim because I didn't like being seen as one. This distracted me so I didn't have to think about my mother. In those years I thought more about Zagreb than about her. And once I had at last convinced them I was not a victim, the Croatian writer wrote about me and the wasted bullet. I would have thought less about this and about Zagreb had I dared to think about my mother remaining in Sarajevo, and for a time, a very long time, I knew nothing about her. For a year and a half, until the beginning of 1995, we barely heard from each other. For most of that time I didn't even know if she were still alive. I heard the reports of bombings in the city on the radio, in which Mejtaš and Bjelave were mentioned, and Sepetarevac was right between the two. On TV late at night I would see the images of the killed and massacred from the Sarajevo streets and be terrified by the thought of recognizing my mother, her face, her hair, one of her legs . . . At the time, I was living with a woman who didn't know why I would stare spellbound at the screen, and before my nose got to the point of pressing right up against it she would ask me to get her some juice from the fridge, question me about my day, while I was like a crazy person, like Alice in Wonderland, glued to the screen just a step from falling in. It was really quite enviable how it never entered her head who I was looking for or what it was I was even looking at.

I was frozen by the idea of recognizing her among the casualties, just as twenty years later I would be frozen for eleven months by the thought of her death. I imagined that moment in order to make it easier to bear.

That scene, when at last I moved away from the television, telling the woman, who understood nothing, what I actually saw; that moment when she answered that maybe I didn't see it right and she got all worked up about immediately taking some kind of action, while her eyes filled with tears and she wept because she thought now I ought to cry: the time it took me to calm her, saying I had already lived through this and explaining why I'd been pressing my nose to the screen these past several months, waiting for the news from Bosnia; the next night, when she looked for a way to console me and I was afraid of her consolation, and the next morning, when I headed to the embassy of Bosnia and Herzegovina, trying in vain to verify what had happened, and the day when I phoned everywhere, calling friends and acquaintances, former editors at *Oslobođenje*, to ask them to try and find out through their connections what had happened to my mother, in which morgue she lay, where she was buried, in a park or a cemetery; that moment when at last I discovered what had happened – a shell? a sniper? in the head? blown apart? deceased en route to the hospital? – and the five minutes that followed, when I called everyone who needed to be called – her brother Dragan and who else? – right down to the breaths in and out behind which all feeling would be hidden. I ran through these hypothetical proceedings and repeated them every night before bed a hundred, a thousand times, just in order not to be surprised and shocked, so that she would not die suddenly for me, as everyone in war did.

Had my mother found her bullet or her shrapnel then, as Karim Zaimović had in the last moments of the war, the world would have been filled with sympathy. Zagreb would have been filled with sympathy, my Zagreb, filled with friends who were then sensitive to every Sarajevo death that was so near to them. I can feel the firm, masculine embrace of the publisher of *Sarajevo Marlboro*, my friend, who twenty years later, when my mother really did die, would be the friend of the Croatian writer who published in *Književna Republika* that one doesn't waste precious bullets on the rabble and that any bullet the Serbs used on me would have been good money down the drain. What happened in the interim? We outlived, both of us, our expected deaths, which had functioned as something of an attraction back then. She died after the light of Zagreb's stages had been extinguished, in the long night of Sarajevo, in the darkness of my heart.

By living through the war, my mother freed me of my guilty conscience.

Even when I was a kid, she'd known how to make me feel guilty, as she had for the eleven months of her illness, as she would continue to until I managed to forget or until I turned her life into literature, but never did she once, by word or glance, reprimand me for leaving and not coming back. I will never be grateful enough to her, the unhappy woman, for that. Probably this is why I was never grateful to her while she was alive. Nor do I say this, or any of the rest of it, out of sentimentality. I'm speaking coldly: I was never grateful to her while she was alive, and never did I express anything in the forty-six and a half years we knew each other that might have sounded like filial or even human gratitude. I clearly remember in the second grade, in Sarajevo, when we were writing compositions in anticipation of the March 8 International Women's Day on a simple topic with the title "My Mother," resorting for the first time to true literary artifice. I wrote about another, made-up mother who bore no resemblance to the real one, rather suggesting Nona, but in a masked, hidden way, because as a seventh grader I would have fallen into an abyss if anyone had said I thought of my grandmother as a mother. Not even to myself would I have admitted it, but the resemblance was obvious: my mother was patient, never yelled, told me stories, and when my eyes grew heavy in the evening, she read to me from *The Paul Street Boys* . . . The whole class laughed at my heavy eyes and my mother reading a book to a bumpkin like me at night. The truth was that my mother had never read to me before bed. It was Nona who'd read to me. But only until I started going to school. Then I was supposed to read for myself. Even when my eyes were heavy. Though actually I always wanted someone to read to me before bed, and so I assigned this to an ideal mother. Nona believed I was lazy about reading on my own and that this would pass with time. But even today, when I'm already older than Nona was when she lost Mladen and soon will be older than my mother was at the start of the siege of Sarajevo, I wouldn't mind at all if someone were to read to me before going to sleep.

There was no hatefulness in my lack of gratitude. Sometimes there was contempt, sometimes sorrow – an ugly kind of self-abasement, perhaps a genetically inherited tendency – and there was stupid spite. I never stopped feeling spiteful toward her even during the year of her dying. Though I yielded to her in everything, quietly put up with her demands, gladly lied that I would carry them out all while rejecting them as unreasonable, carried out all sorts of things that were unreasonable, accepted her despair as my own, fell before those who were cold to my distress, put up with the minor, tasteless jokes of Sarajevo's lyrical puppies, complied completely with the role of a son whose mother was dying, of a servant who would be buried alive inside the pyramid along with his pharaoh – still I did not stop feeling spite. And never was I grateful.

When I left, a heavy burden fell from my soul. But it seemed she too freed herself of a burden then. In one of the worst years of the war in Sarajevo, she changed jobs: from the Academy of Cinematic Arts, where she had worked for the preceding ten years, she moved to the Pedagogical Academy. She seems to have finally come out from menopause then, or, with conditions of life growing ever more complex as the tanks rumbled around her, as if the world had suddenly come to reflect her will, and she forgot she had once considered suicide. She didn't really change or become any more diligent, and she would continue to live amid the most spectacular, unsalvageable chaos, but she had turned away from the worst years of her depression. Perhaps this wasn't unusual. Life was degrading and insufferable for everyone. Beginning as early as fall 1992, when any hope that the siege would be broken quickly had been crushed, along with any hope of getting electricity and water back again, people lived in Sarajevo as if it were a slightly more comfortable form of concentration camp. By contrast to the Nazi and Stalinist camps, Sarajevo was special in that the prisoners did not as a rule set eyes upon their murderers and that – though this too was not the rule for everyone – they lived in the same dwellings they had lived in before the war. But everything else, the dying, sickness, freezing, and starving, was like the Nazi camps. The comparison of Bosnia's wars with the Nazi crimes in the Holocaust, which Bosniak nationalists insist on, is completely out of place and aggressively self-pitying.

In a psychological sense, life in this city-turned-camp did my mother good. It was hard for her, she suffered physically, froze and feared for her life, putting up with conditions that were inhumane in every way, but they were the same for everyone. Not just the same. For others they were much worse. This was what consoled and emboldened her, what had strengthened her during the siege, such that when I saw her for the first time upon returning after the war, I saw her reborn. I left behind a ruin and came back to find an off-center, wacky, but rather strong woman. Such was she in 1996, when ghosts roamed the Sarajevo streets and most of the people were gray, skinny, and toothless, still imprisoned in their camps and in their constrained, involuted, internally concentrated worlds. She was an exception then, but as the years passed and the city recovered, she would begin to fall behind and fall apart, dividing her world into the part that belonged to fantasy and story and the part that was real, as both fell into chaos and failure.

But she would never be depressed again.

Nor would she ever care about anything until her illness.

She would be angry, enraged, dissatisfied.

She would believe everyone was against her.

That they didn't value her, that they harassed her. That was her favorite word: *harassment*.

But she wouldn't be depressed.

Or care about anything.

Until the *lump*.

Her wartime transfiguration came about thanks to her last great friendship, which emerged almost by accident, as a miracle and reward for the many good deeds she'd performed in her life. Or actually it was a reward for her insufferable – to me at least – openness toward other people, for that particular kind of indiscretion that one can't stand from people who are close but is actually not such a hated characteristic among people one just happens to meet.

Slavica Džeba, or Miss Cica, whose married name was Šneberger, lived in the basement apartment of her family's one-story building one street number down from us. We would see her after we moved to Sepetarevac in 1969, but nothing went beyond hello. Cica was not a real Sarajevo neighbor woman. She didn't press herself on us to get invited over for coffee, or hug and kiss on the street, and she smiled a lot less than is considered proper in Sarajevo, such that neighbors might have perceived her as odd. She lived with Geza Šneberger, a huge, fat man with heart disease and diabetes, whose black, Clark Gable mustache, given his heavy, tired-out sickliness, was the only thing that made his face appear youthful and tidy.

All that was known about Geza was that he was a musician and that he drummed in the cafés and had played in what used to be the radio orchestra – at the time someone remembered there used to be one. Everything else took place a long way from the eyes and ears of the neighbors, who after a certain amount of time would lose interest in those who didn't need to reveal everything about themselves in public – their background, work, family relations – and such people would soon be called "marginal."

In a certain way, Cica and Geza were marginal, even if it was not possible to say they lived like eccentrics. They were just of a different mold, which was enough to exclude them from the ceremonies of traditional neighborly kindness, or rather, from the sticking of their noses into your business.

Nono had just a little longer left to live then, barely enough to meet them.

They heard him coughing in those summer nights in 1969, '70, '71.

"Poor Mr. Rejc! He's having a rough time."

Nona said hello to them but not more than that.

There was a neighbors' stand-off between us.

In 1985 and the next year we kept a dog named Nero in the garden. He was tied up with a chain, lived in a little wooden doghouse, and was always in the mud. I was not kind to him, a fact that would forever plague me. If I'd been kind, Nero wouldn't had lived attached to a chain but rather with us in the house.

And this could have happened had I just wanted it.

After Nona's death in 1986, we were left alone with Nero.

In December of that year, he tried to jump over the fence while he was still chained, and he stayed hanging like that until he died. It was cold, ten below Celsius. I buried him in the garden. The iron pick broke in two against the frozen ground.

Nero used to bark all night. He wasn't a smart dog, but he was lonely and good-natured. He barked at the cats and hedgehogs on their nocturnal hunts.

Geza had been seriously ill at the time. He could hardly breathe and had been in the process of releasing his soul for months. The dog's barking bothered him.

Cica rang at the door to complain about Nero.

As it happened, this was the day we took Nona to the hospital, from which she would not return. My mother sent her away quite rudely. Cica didn't know, and my mother didn't know that Cica didn't know. When she found out, she was terribly embarrassed. She never complained about Nero again. Geza was destined to listen to Nero's barking every night until the dog died that winter. Then there was silence.

I was angry. So was my mother. We didn't think about his being hardly able to breathe or sleep because of Nero's barking. We had our own worries, just as Geza and Cica did.

And nothing more would have come of this if the war hadn't begun.

She had by then already buried Geza and was living alone in her basement apartment. Although it was the same old Cica and the neighborhood was for the most part also the same, her relations with the world had changed. Or rather, those who were on their own had suddenly been accepted. In those three and a half years of war, within that tiny circle at the top of Sepetarevac at the confluence of three sheltered Turkish alleys, they lived in the midst of all sorts of caprices and oddities, like in some sort of a psychiatric ward. It started in 1992 when the first shells landed in our garden, and then developed and deepened as such cases grew worse and worse. It seemed as if the siege would go on forever, so people needed to make one another's lives bearable and joyous – they had to laugh in order not to go mad. And this was how Cica entered into the social life of Sepetarevac. It wasn't something she ever worked at or set out to do. It was simply the result of circumstances.

People cooked in the gardens and basements, and on the streets in front of their houses.

They died while cooking.

And so, at a certain point, after I had left Sarajevo, my mother came together with Cica around cooking. She would bring food from wherever she could find it, collecting humanitarian aid and whatever she got from work, and Cica would prepare it for the two of them.

Sometimes Mišo, Cica's nephew and stepson who worked as a television production manager, would come from the other side of town. Traveling from the Radio and Television Building to Sepetarevac was like arriving from the ends of the earth.

Cica was a fantastic cook in a way that was unknown in our house. No one in Javorka's family prepared food like this. In the Stubler and Rejc homes they ate their food according to Viennese and old *kuferaš* recipes, with lots of dark rye flour and starch, beef and chicken broth, dumplings and stewed vegetables. It was the same as what they ate in Zagreb and Vienna – unimaginative and, for the most part, unhealthy. But Cica prepared food as if she were observing, through cooking, her and Geza's family tree, which, as in wartime and postwar stories, had grown in all directions, taking on the flavors of different national cuisines, from Vienna, across Bosnia and Serbia, to Istanbul and as far as Izmir on the Aegean.

Geza Šneberger was born in Turkey of a Muslim Gypsy father, and a Hungarian Gypsy mother. His father, Latif Husni Orak, had been a circus acrobat and a musician. When he was young, he had flown on the trapeze, juggled, tamed wild beasts, and for years traveled with his circus family across Asia Minor, the Near East, and along the coast of the Black Sea all the way to Odessa. One cannot live such a life for long. At least this was not the custom in his family, which for generations from distant Ottoman times had been engaged in circus work. Rather, after spending one's youth on the road, working hard and playing hard, the time would come for appeasement and retraining. Variety artist would turn into musician, usually marrying a girl encountered on the road who had run away from home to be with him. Just like a folktale: she ran away with the Gypsies. She ran away to the circus . . .

Latif Husni Orak brought Rosza along from somewhere in Hungary. She birthed him two sons and couldn't have more children after that. They lived a rich and happy life in Izmir, each side observing his or her own faith. Without much consideration for their professional orientation or calling, the sons continued the family tradition. This was the time of the republic of Atatürk, the foundations of society were being altered and transformed, and the family circus suffered. It simply collapsed amid the general modernization and the infatuation with

Western novelties. Audiences in Turkey were not interested in the old Gypsy circus, with its variety-show bits and conventions that probably had not changed since Mehmed the Conqueror. They could no longer travel to Odessa, for Odessa now belonged to a communist paradise, while Russian circuses, which were incomparably better than Orak's old thing, were ranging across Europe, having escaped from that selfsame paradise.

And so the Orak brothers were appearing with small bands of acrobats when the youngest, whom they would name Geza after the mother's father, followed the circus routes to Yugoslavia. In Bitola he fell madly in love with a girl of the Orthodox faith, with whom he would have two children, and from whom he would later be divorced.

She would not be important for our story if Geza hadn't gone to Belgrade because of her and been baptized according to the Catholic rite, taking his mother's maiden name – Šneberger. During the Second World War such performers could not find work even in Serbia – especially those who were known to be Gypsies and whom the authorities, at a minimum, looked askance at – but during the war, more than during peacetime, they did play in cafés and hotel ballrooms, at weddings and funerals, so much so that there weren't enough musicians to go around. This was the story Geza told Cica, who told Javorka, who told me, and which I then asked Cica to tell me in detail, as Geza had told her.

For entire days in the summer of 1998 during the Sarajevo Film Festival, Cica told me the story of Geza's childhood and youth in Izmir, and of Belgrade during the Second World War, about all the places he played music and with whom. She listed the cafés and the orchestras, hundreds of names of people, and wove a great and luxurious tale, and it was as if this story had no end and would never arrive at the year 1945. She knew it all to the smallest detail, as if she'd been there herself.

I didn't write any of it down, fascinated as I was by the story. I wouldn't have enjoyed it as much if I were taking notes. I didn't know then that what she was telling me was important. I didn't know that after her death no one would know the story of Latif Husni Orak and his two sons. Or the love story of a Gypsy musician and a young woman from Bitola, with the embedded story of a baptism in a Belgrade Catholic church, which, though her family staunchly opposed it, had been the only option – Geza could not have been baptized in the Orthodox Church because his mother had been a Catholic. He could be either a Muslim or a Catholic, and this was exactly what he was: Gypsy, Muslim, Catholic. The order might have been different. Cica explained all this as she told the story, just as Geza had explained it to her, and everything was in perfect accord, proper and logical. If the principles of society and civilization could be subjected to logic, then those of Effendi Orak, his Hungarian wife Rosza, and their two sons were perfectly logical.

It's a shame that all this will remain unwritten.

One September morning, on one of those rare days when it seemed to my mother that she was truly getting better and everything was much better than it had been the day before, we tried to reconstruct together, over the phone, the lives of these two individuals and the histories of their families, just as Cica had explained it to us. This was perhaps our longest phone conversation. It lasted for two hours.

Geza divorced his wife after the Second World War. He was in contact with the children but after they were grown, they slowly lost interest in their father. During the siege, Cica tried contacting Geza's son, who lived in Germany. She actually wanted to ask for his help – two hundred marks would have been of enormous assistance – but he didn't answer her. Later she blamed herself for having done that. One doesn't dare beg, she said. The man was in the right. Better that he didn't respond. This she said too. And actually she felt rueful, for she had spent something that was priceless to her. When Geza died shortly after Nona and Nero, she worried about just one thing: what would happen to her? Even though for years he hadn't been able to get to the bathroom without her help, while she had made sure he was clean and well groomed, his clothes were pressed, his hair combed, and everything taken care of; even though all the money that Geza ever earned, including his musician's retirement money, had always been with her, such that she had to make sure he didn't leave the house without any cash on him; even though, in fact, from the very start Cica had taken care of everything while Geza had just played music, she was in a fearful panic that without him she wouldn't know how to live. And that was when he'd said to her, as he lay dying, that if, God forbid she ever needed anything, she could call his son in Germany.

But when Cica had sought this son out, sending a letter through the Red Cross, he didn't answer.

They married at the end of the fifties. Cica was a young girl, Geza already a man of experience in the best years of his youth. It would soon turn out, however, that they were unable to have children. The reason was a common one in those days: illegal abortions performed in sheds and garages, under lurid conditions, by midwives and nurses, retired doctors, and all manner of riffraff without diplomas or credentials, who would have busied themselves with some other kind of crime had abortion been legal. In each case, abortion was something that needed to be survived and if it was, then all sorts of chronic infections followed, visible and not, which ultimately resulted in infertility. Cica was obviously not some old-fashioned maiden. She had given herself free rein in life and was of an amorous nature, attracted to cafés, the theater, and a libertine life. She'd had abortions before Geza. She didn't say how many.

This too would not need to be noted if there had been no Geza, who of course knew why she wasn't able to conceive. She told him, as she might have told him anything else.

"It's good this way," he said, consoling her. "I couldn't survive the fear that a pregnancy might be the end of you, when you're so thin and tender!"

Geza would repeat this to her, saying that children were a worry and a pain, they weren't for the two of them, who loved café life and everything else that raising children didn't go with. He had to console her frequently, wooing her in this way because Cica was one of those women who are made to be mothers. However much she might have drunk, smoked, and made merry, she had an incessant need to take care of someone. First she took care of Geza, then her nephew Mišo, then Javorka, and then me when I arrived from Zagreb, and who knows how many others. There was nothing of the martyr in her caring, nothing that reminded you of those miserable, patriarchal women who lived on

Sepetarevac, who suffered for their sons and husbands and looked as if they were always prepared for some great misfortune to arrive, their mourning clothes ironed and ready.

She was a devoted and authoritarian mother. A sure ruler of the domicile and of the collective family unit. She knew what to do in each situation and was always calm and easy amid courageous life decisions. She was a great, genuine mother, a Brechtian mother for frightening times, and there have been no epochs in the history of humanity that haven't been. Mothers are there to hide their sons behind their aprons. This was the sort of mother Cica was, except that, well, she didn't have any children.

And this pained her enormously to the end of her life. She didn't show it and spoke lightly of her infertility, but it tortured her. And it never stopped. Geza was no more, nothing was important anymore, and soon there would be no more Mišo either – after the war he died of lung cancer, an illness that had long plagued him, but even after his death Cica wasn't able to ease her conscience. Unborn and unconceived, lost to illegal abortions in post-Second World War Sarajevo, Cica's children remained forever an unrealized possibility. They would have had a mother who carried them on her back through the minefields and front lines of all future wars. They would have had what most children do not have: the security and assurance of someone who never failed to have both the will and the strength for them.

My mother marveled at Cica's unrealized motherhood.

She marveled at Cica's ability to act on behalf of others.

A stubborn, difficult, once beautiful woman, sullen and stern faced whenever she passed anyone she didn't know. Her coldness toward her neighbors offered no room for questions and no need for answers. Different from the world in which she lived, in Sarajevo and on Sepetarevac. Different from Javorka, with whom, through a coincidence of circumstances, she became friends during the war. Crazy in her own way, she was masterful at controlling my mother's kind of crazy, holding her own against it, bearing it with the same lightness she bore all who were close to her, with their own kinds of crazy and their own afflictions in life.

Except in Cica's life there had not been great afflictions, other than the deaths of others and illnesses, other than what she herself had no control over. Everything that had been in her hands had passed in complete order. Life had slipped between her fingers like squandered flour.

When the war ended, my mother continued to bring over food and Cica would cook. After lunch, she would lie down on the ottoman while Cica washed the dishes. She didn't tell Cica about her life. Maybe she tried it once but it didn't go well. Cica was able to resolve everything she saw as part of the insuperable conditions of life. Cica easily forgave anyone who had ever made her seriously unhappy. Why torment yourself with other people's wretchedness? It's easy to forget all that. You're still young. Find yourself some nice-looking old man to have some fun with . . .

Instead of my mother telling Cica about her life, Cica told my mother about hers.

Cica's mother had the misfortune of marrying some loafer from eastern Bosnia who would come home, get her pregnant, and then be gone for a year at a time. They lived in Prača, a little town gathered around the train station on the narrow-gauge line that went to Višegrad.

Cica was raised by her grandmother Vida, who had given birth to three sons and two daughters. It didn't bother her that her daughter Anđelka had married a Croat. The only bad thing was that he was a loafer and didn't take care of his house.

Then came 1941: in front of the Orthodox church in Pale, the Ustaše executed two of Vida's sons. The people watched. The third boy, Dušan, ran away and didn't stop until he got to Belgrade. He married a woman from there and after the war didn't come back to Bosnia.

After she had lost her sons, Grandma Vida came to Sarajevo and brought two of her little granddaughters with her. She lived with them very modestly in a basement apartment in the center of town. Out of respect for her deceased son-in-law, she sent the girls for religious instruction with the nuns, celebrated their Christmas and Easter, and was steadfast in raising them as Catholics.

Thanks to Grandma Vida, Cica had all the sacraments: in the photograph of her confirmation from 1943 at the cathedral, in which, far in the background, below the angels in white dresses, can be seen the protective figure of Archbishop "the Evangelist" Šarić, translator of the Bible and composer of hymns to the supreme leader Ante Pavelić. Grandma Vida believed in a God who towered above politics. Being mindful of a human order without which the world would lose its mind and her along with it, she raised her granddaughters in the faith of their father, and of her sons' killers.

She died after the war, her conscience clear, reconciled with the world.

Cica declared herself a Croat on the census and occasionally went to church. The priest would bless her home every year. On the walls of her apartment, off to one side in each room, hung faded holy images.

She was a Catholic, as Grandma Vida had determined.

In the meantime, she celebrated Christmas and Easter according to both calendars, performed Orthodox acts of piety, burned votive candles in the church in Varoš, for Grandma Vida, for her dead uncles, and for her mother Anđelka, and would cross herself each time she was in an Orthodox church.

I asked her how one genuflects in an Orthodox church. She grew perplexed. You know, she said, I didn't think about it. I crossed myself without considering how, the way Catholics do it.

In this too Geza was an ideal partner for her. He didn't ask her the sorts of questions that other husbands surely would have, the sorts that arose among the neighbors as they snooped and gossiped about what faith Geza and Cica really belonged to.

For Geza all this was very simple. As it had been for Latif Husni Orak, the Gypsy performer, circus man, acrobat, and musician, married to the Hungarian Catholic Rosza, with whom he'd had two sons, one Muslim, the other Catholic. Latif Husni Orak loved his Bosnian daughter-in-law. When the couple visited, he would take her to the side to ask whether his son was being good to her.

It was a beautiful and frightening story that spread out all of a sudden before me and my mother. She was already used to it since she was practically living with Cica, but I would only experience it each time I visited Sarajevo. During those ten years, until 2007, I visited often, every other month. Looked at from the standpoint of this story, this was a long period of saying goodbye.

Cica's heart ailed her, but she refused medicine. She said doctors poisoned people and she knew best what was good for her and what was bad. She smoked cigarettes from which she removed the filters beforehand. She smoked each one to the end. She had a torn smoker's voice. Even with that voice of hers she sang well. She drank in moderation, less as the years passed, though when I would come from Zagreb we'd knock back some welcome rakijas. Cica was a café aficionada, and in cafés people's hearts and lungs usually suffer.

My mother brought doctors to her, the best Sarajevo cardiologists.

She brought her other suggestive, talkative doctors, trying to find someone who was able to convince her. And so they tried to frighten her with stories about death. But she couldn't be frightened. She was as cold toward death as she was toward her neighbors. To the doctors Javorka brought into her house she was barely even polite.

She simply couldn't stand them. They'd brought no useful medical expertise when Geza was sick and so long in dying. Then they couldn't help Mišo either.

What use could they be to her now?

In the last two or three years she rarely left the house. She was out of breath after three steps, and Sepetarevac was rather steep.

Anyone on Sepetarevac whose legs failed or who could no longer breathe on the ascent would likely not go anywhere anymore. An ambulance would have to come to take him or her to the hospital. Or the morgue. It had been that way since we moved there in 1969. People would just stop coming out of their houses, and then we would see them for a little longer, leaning, pale and gray, against their windowsills, looking somewhere down the street, along which, if everything went according to the usual order, death would come suddenly.

Then she told Javorka not to bring any more doctors by. If Javorka came with even one more person with her, she wouldn't let her in. If Javorka did that, she wouldn't let her into the house anymore. She'd had enough.

My mother took it badly.

She called me right away and said she didn't want to have anything to do with Cica anymore. So deeply had that woman offended her. It's her illness, I told her. That doesn't matter, she said, illness or no illness was completely the same, she's dead to me. You shouldn't talk that way, I said, laughing. You shouldn't dare call a sick woman dead. It doesn't matter, she said again. You'll go see her again, I said. I won't and there's nothing more to say about it. I have my dignity! Let go of your dignity. You won't get any use out of it. I learned that in Zagreb. What did you learn in Zagreb? That there's no use in dignity. My nerves are not up to this anymore, she began again. I'll take doctors to see her and she . . .

The next morning she was back at Cica's.

She pretended to be mad, but she was laughing up her sleeve because Javorka had come.

And then again Javorka started trying to convince her to take medicine for her heart. First she tried persuasion, for days on end, then she started bringing doctors by again.

At the time, though Cica could walk with difficulty, she couldn't manage the stairs. She would cook lunch and bake cakes, ordering ingredients for cheese pies and *burek* because, after all, I was coming from Zagreb and the only thing I ate was pie. Her ailing heart was considering whether to stop once and for all or keep going a little more, but curiosity drew her on to the next episode, her heart along with her. There are simply some hearts that doctors don't dare treat. This is humbling for them. But if there was anything perfectly healthy and exact in Sarajevo in those last years of my being there, it was Cica's heart.

Of course she rolled out the dough herself for the two pies that would be waiting for me. This was a serious workout even for a healthy heart. It didn't bother her. Or it bothered her less than the thought of not having my two pies baked and ready, one with cheese, the other with meat. My mother tried to convince her to make them out of premade crusts, but Cica wouldn't hear of it. He can have pies with pre-made crusts in Zagreb, she said. It was only the last cheese pie she made, three months before her death, that had crusts bought from the store. After that she couldn't bake anymore. Ana and I brought the pie with us to

Zagreb, inside the casserole it was baked in, a round one of just the sort for pies and *burek*, all wrapped in kitchen towels.

"We'll bring you back the casserole next time!" Ana said

"There's no need," she said.

The round blue casserole with the scorched bottom – for who knows how many pies she'd baked in it – rests now in our pantry, like some miraculous relic that might find its place in a showcase for ceremonial objects if we had one, or in a bookcase for the most valuable of books, manuscripts, and memorabilia. After the pie was gone a couple of days after we had brought it back, we didn't wash the casserole. There was nothing strange about that. Casseroles for pies sometimes sit around for days unwashed until they're needed again. The remains of the dough, the tiny, almost invisible crumbs that crunch under your fingertips like shards from a broken light bulb, don't go bad or become a home for bacteria. And anyway, a strange company had gathered around Cica, so it is completely natural to end this story with bacteria, worms, moths . . .

After the fifth day of not washing the casserole, no one had the heart to do so anymore. Ana said nothing about it, I said nothing about it, but between us hovered, unspoken, word of Cica's death. It is now the end of June, the twenty-fifth day of the month, Maxim Gorky's name day, three and a half years since Cica's death, and her round casserole rests on our pantry shelf, in a nice place among things we don't use. Something prevents us from changing the thing, from affecting the history of our lives by washing it. We don't discuss this. If we need to clean the shelf it's on or get something behind it, we take it out. But then we put it back exactly as it was, as it was the last time Cica held it in her hands. Her fingerprints are surely on it. A dactyloscopy analysis conducted in, for instance, Myanmar or Asunción, would establish that four of us had touched the blue casserole: Cica, my mother, Ana, and me. From the prints it would be impossible to tell what had happened to us in the past three and a half years. As seen from Myanmar or Asunción, all four of us are still equally alive.

Three weeks before she died she gave in and started taking heart medicine. But she did so off-and-on, unwillingly, in fear that the medicine might mess things up. She gave into Javorka because she didn't have the strength to keep struggling and to have the same conversations over and over. Or she felt everything was all the same at that point. The last doctor to come see her, a veteran from the local clinic with rich experience, told my mother it was the end, useless to do anything more. It was a miracle her heart was still beating. But it wouldn't be long, maybe a few days.

Despite this my mother was pleased that she'd been able to convince her to take the medicine. She would call me in irritation whenever Cica refused.

"Here, you tell her!" she would shout into the receiver.

And Cica and I would talk for a bit. About everything but the medicine. She was out of breath, as if she were running across a field while carrying on the conversation with me. She asked if I was writing a new book. I said I was. She asked what I was writing about, said I should tell her because she wasn't going to read it.

"Why not?" I pretended to be surprised.

"I won't have time," she said cheerfully. She was proud of her witticism, like it was the punch line to a joke.

Three days before her death, she told Javorka that on the shelf above her bed, on top of the crossword puzzles under the Daničić-Karadžić Bible, between her reading glasses and her regular glasses, there were two envelopes, and if, God forbid, something unexpected happened, she should take them. One was for her, the other for Mišo's best friend, who had taken care of Cica after her nephew's death.

She called me to tell me as soon as she got home. She was terribly curious. What could be in these envelopes? Although not even at that point, when it was already clear that everything was finished, did she want to admit that Cica was dying – how could she die when she still went to the bathroom on her own and in the morning would sit down on the ottoman and look out the window, lighting up a cigarette to take a couple of puffs before putting it out, how could death come so soon to someone so young? – nevertheless she imagined Cica had written her some sort of goodbye letter, entrusting some great secret to her wartime comrade, requesting a promise of something sentimental: like bringing fresh daisies to her grave every Thursday or lighting a candle for her soul every third Sunday at the cathedral . . . My mother was prepared for such requests and would have gladly satisfied them, whether it was bringing daisies or lighting candles. Someone just needed to ask her. Such duties were outside reality. They were not of this world but of that other one, the dreamed of reality in which she'd lived and found joy as a little girl, while I in my own way had despised her for this. Or rather, disliked.

My mother would die on a Sunday, and Cica died on a Monday. I don't recall the date, but I am sure it was a Monday.

A neighbor called who had been going over to check on her for the past few days and said she had died.

The envelopes were opened. Inside the one with Mišo's friend's name on it was a piece of paper with the words "funeral and wreath." There was precisely enough money for these things. In Javorka's envelope were the words "television, electricity, telephone, rent." And the money for the last, unpaid month of Cica's life.

My mother complained that Cica's character had seemed to change in the last six months of her life. That probably came with her illness. She had always been generous, paid no attention to money, and spent freely in keeping her house. But suddenly she had turned miserly. She had found it hard to give money for meat. We don't need to eat meat every day, she would say. This too had got on Javorka's nerves. How could she live beside someone who had turned into a skinflint overnight? Even if it was the result of her illness. And now everything was clear: she had been saving for her funeral and for a single wreath. From Geza she'd just a small musician's pension. You needed to save up a lot in order to die.

Cica Šneberger had gone to church, celebrated Christmas and Easter, fasted on Good Friday, but hadn't believed something better would come from such a life. She had not believed in anything other than life. Of course God existed. And hell was the disconcerting of the dead. There was no heaven beyond life and outside of the fine, old-fashioned café where Geza played with the orchestra of the Petković brothers, while Ruža Balog sang café tunes and folk songs. That was a heaven in memory.

But still she had left money for the television and telephone bills to be paid, as if in the heavens or on earth someone would be asking about her debts. She had died in such a way as to remain no one's debtor. What people said about this was not important to her. She had never cared about the neighbors. She had left the envelopes for two people who were close to her, simply sending them to an office window to settle the bill.

People say and do all sorts of things before death, but this sort of composure and this sense of obligation toward society are rare.

The apartment she had lived in was returned to the landlord. The furniture was discarded because nothing was worth anything. Cica had had good luck with household appliances: her Obodinov refrigerator was forty years old, the Sloboda Čačak stove was even older, and the TV was a prewar Grundig. The apartment merely needed to be cleansed of another person's having lived there.

She had no more family. I asked my mother to take all Cica's photographs from the apartment. I would bring them with me to Zagreb. She asked what I would do with them. Nothing, but let's not throw them out. In one of them there is a newly married, very ugly couple. Someone from Cica's prewar family. The black-and-white photo had color added by hand in a shop in Rogatica, Prača, or Višegrad. Could there have been a photo studio in Prača before the war? I don't know and there's no one left to ask. When a person dies, her personal effects turn into trash, and humanity is left with a long string of questions that only the deceased could have answered. Humanity of course doesn't trouble itself about this, for all the questions will quickly be forgotten. Like this one: was there a photography studio in Prača before the Second World War, or did people go to Višegrad to have their pictures taken? And then, two weeks later, they would have come to pick up the developed and hand-painted photograph. Around this picture, in which two strangers appear under a light ellipsis suggesting marital union, a single family forms, a structure rises up above them, a home is built, and at least one unwritten family novel unwinds. And in the end what remains is just a picture of two unknown, comically unattractive people that hung on the wall of my neighbor Slavica Šneberger's apartment and not even my mother ever asked her who they were. Or perhaps we asked and then forgot. A photograph doesn't chronicle memory; it notes the moment of death. Each opening of the aperture marks a death.

Cica's passing didn't disturb my mother.

She mourned, her life was changed, she was left alone, but she wasn't disturbed.

She no longer had someone to make her lunch or wait for her to return from work.

She no longer stretched out on the lumpy ottoman in the kitchen.

She didn't yell or fight with someone close to her.

She no longer went looking for doctors for another. Next time she would be doing this for herself and less successfully.

But she wasn't disturbed by Cica's death.

Cica was a cuckoo, she would say, such a cuckoo. She would have lived to a hundred if she had taken her medicine. There hasn't been anybody since the dark ages who died from just letting her heart fall apart. It wasn't even primeval! Do you know how long her heart had been bothering her? she asked. Ten years! God, it had been ten years since her first EKG! And then again, the next time Cica came up, she would repeat the same thing, without sadness, matter-of-factly . . . She was angry with Cica. Soon after, several months later, my father would die, and the story would simply be transferred over to him. At that point she was no longer angry with Cica, and whenever she recalled her she would say that Cica had made a choice about when and how she wanted to die.

My mother was very devoted and reasonable when the lives of those close to her were near their end. She saw them off, remaining beside them when they were conscious, demented, comatose, asleep, frightened, prayerful, faithless, exhausted, sleepless, blithering, silent, angry, kind, agitated, reconciled, sorrowful, cheerful, weepy . . . She wouldn't run away when she was alone at the deathbed. She'd stay to the end, leaning forward as if against the railing of a skyscraper, toward the other world, without the least fear that she might fall. My mother was like a child. She thought death did not have anything to do with her. Or she somehow needed to be the last voice and companion in that final solitude, she didn't mind being the one to stay. My mother ran from nearly all the obligations of her life, but from this one she never did. It's easy to walk away from a dying person. People believe you if you say you just can't manage it. But my mother never said this.

- 301 -

What attracted her to them? Was it just that she felt more alive when she was in the vicinity of the dying and so was drawn toward precisely what made them afraid? It seems to people that death is infectious, that it will suddenly leap from the eyes that are going dull and grab them by the throat, as in a cartoon. This pushes them away from the dying person more than the horror that comes just before the moment in which, contrary to all that a person thinks and feels, a living being becomes a dead one.

She saw Nano off when he lay in the neurological wing of Koševo Hospital in December 1976. He'd grown ill one morning when blood had begun gushing from his nose. He had lost consciousness by the time the ambulance arrived, and then he lay in a coma for days. It was the clinical definition of a stroke, though not everything concurred and some symptoms were contradictory. And then, suddenly, on the last night he started to get better. He was beginning to wake up from his coma when he died. This happened before morning, but she didn't wait for daylight, nor for his relations to wake up of their own volition. Instead she started calling everyone to tell them Nano had died.

While she'd been politically active in the city committee of the Socialist Youth Union in middle school and at the beginning of her university studies, and later was a regular attendee at the Party meetings of the various companies she had worked for, at the beginning of the seventies she became active in the Red Cross. For several years after that she made the rounds of the hospitals and the indigent in our part of town, bringing food and money, taking care of them, visiting social services, finding places for people in shelters and homes for the elderly. She would take me with her – so I could see how the people lived and not be cruel, so I wouldn't grow up pampered. She had a thousand explanations and was actually trying to share with me something of her fascination with human suffering and misery. She was happy only when she was helping people who were less happy than she was. In proximity to death she was alive, ready to run or break into song, do something completely inappropriate, the sort of thing only the living can do.

I hadn't ever thought of this while the two of them were still alive, and it didn't really occur to me until just now, but my early childhood, after Nono's death and our return from Drvenik, was marked by my father's need to take me with him on his rounds in Pale and the mountain villages of Romanija, showing me sick people, their small yellowish-gray heads amid the abundant white down of their peasant beds, and by my mother's need to take me with her on her visits to Sarajevo's destitute. I was eight, nine, ten years old, and these were extreme experiences for me. They shook and changed me, implanted in me a variety of fears. Reality would continue in my nightmares, which for a long time always unfolded in one and the same place. All my fearful dreams took as their backdrop the courtyard of the Church of the Holy Transfiguration in Novo Sarajevo.

I grew up amid my father's sick and my mother's poor.

Perhaps this was why I learned so early that we are all very close to death. I was amazed that we were even still alive, and continual human health seemed one of the most improbable miracles. There were so many sick people and so many illnesses, and the illnesses were all for the most part incurable and appeared out of nowhere, sprouting like nettles inside a person who just a little before was healthy. Since the majority of my father's patients from Romanija had heart problems or lung or liver problems, and were primitive villagers, factory workers killed by hard work, drunks and heavy smokers, their illnesses were part of their destiny. Or this was how my father presented them. Bellies filled with water, livers like misplaced lumps protruding from beneath the right side of their ribs, and those yellow, gray, nearly green faces that would visit me in my dreams – all this was the result of a mistaken life and such a mistaken life had been determined by one's destiny. A grandfather would die of cirrhosis and the next spring so would the son. In the end, by the time I had grown up, the grandson would have been diagnosed with it as well. This happened in a village called Vučja Luka.

I also learned it was a miracle that we weren't poor like the poor.

Sarajevo's poverty was frightening at the beginning of the seventies, in the entrances to Turkish-era high-rises that were about to collapse, made of adobe that eroded under every downpour, in the apartments with rotting wooden floors that cracked beneath your feet, swaying and trembling as if they might break at any moment, in the tiny rooms where the inhabitants were cared for by the Red Cross. To these people they sent my mother, who didn't even know how to take care of herself, but she fought for them like a lioness. She would shout into the phone, threatening to call journalists, to reveal everything to the municipal authorities, to take it all the way to Belgrade if she had to.

Those old men and their withdrawn, speechless wives, casualties of stroke from long ago, would take no notice of me. I'd sit motionless on a little couch, not touching anything, while they described their needs to my mother. Medicine, food from the Red Cross's kitchen, and coal for the winter. Coal for the winter without fail – ćumur, they would say, pronouncing the Sarajevo word like a prayer, the extended hand of a beggar, the word from which all humanity began. The poor feared nothing so much as the winter, something which I had not yet taken notice of. Yes, being cold was understandable, but the fact that the cold could be a source of such suffering, worse than all other suffering, much worse than hunger or squalor, this I had not yet come to understand. In Sarajevo this was learned as part of growing up and part of war, which afflicted every generation of the city.

These people had ordinary names – Jozo, Meho, Sulejman, Roza. These were the names of the poor. The truth was that many rich people had such names, but it seemed somehow natural to me that poor people should have them. Basic knowledge of the world was still being imprinted on my brain at the time: blue sky, fresh bread, bitter chocolate for cooking, good dogs, dangerous wasps . . . The theory of poor people's names belonged to this basic knowledge about the world. Once they gave you the name Jozo, it was somehow expected that the Red Cross would take care of you. Otherwise wouldn't they have named you something else? Because this was the way it had to be, there had to be a poor Meho in the world, and I didn't think anything in all this might have been so audacious as to change. There was a regular order to things and names, there were rules and basic knowledge about the world that children learned – blue sky, white bread, bitter chocolate.

But what did one do when someone destitute, the poorest of all, was called Rikard Goldberger? He lived in a loft on Mehmed Pasha Sokolović Street. Actually he lived in an attic that had a door so low even I had to stoop to get through it. The summer was horribly hot, and the attic stank of shit and one other odor I'd never smelled before. I was uneasy, my heart was thumping as if two drummers were competing at each of my ears. My mother turned white, grabbed me by the hand, and tightened her grip. I thought it was good she had brought me here and not the other way around.

On the floor lay a rotting pillowtop mattress cover with yellow and brownish stains that made it look like a map replete with the seas and continents, and on top of that sat a small, naked man with a scab-covered head. He was looking at us in astonishment.

He was very polite, offered a seat to my mother – I remained standing – but did not understand why we had come. He was fine. He didn't need anything. No, he wasn't hungry. He was healthy. No, he didn't need firewood. There was no stove anyway, look. He wasn't planning on being here when winter arrived. He was waiting for the post office to deliver a letter from his brother with a train ticket for Vienna. The letter could arrive any day. It was supposed to come on Friday, but maybe the postman had had a bit to drink. You know how they are. Always been like that, postmen. He didn't hold it against them since what difference did it make if a letter got there on Friday or Monday? The important thing was that the ticket not have the date and time on it. He reminded his brother, though he didn't have to since his brother knew what postmen were like. They loved to drink. It's not easy for them. People would offer them rakija, and sometimes it was hard to turn them down.

His neighbors had called the Red Cross to help old Riki. He was a good old fellow, children loved him. Generations on Mehmed Pasha Sokolović Street had grown up alongside him. He fed the pigeons in Veliki Park, explained how electricity worked to the kids, and how they built hydroelectric plants. Entire classes would gather around his bench, but that was when his daughter was still alive. After the poor woman died, old Riki had began to decline. But he couldn't just be left to die like a dog.

He had lost his mind when his wife died in 1945. She'd been hit by a military truck near the Markale market. The unfortunate woman suffered for days, and when it was time to record the cause of death, they put down: heart attack! What kind of heart attack was it when she was hit by a truck? Riki couldn't grasp this. They took him off to OZNA, the department of national security, to explain things to him, and it was probably from their explanations that the poor man went crazy. Since then he had been waiting for nearly thirty years for a letter from his brother to arrive from Vienna with a train ticket. The neighborhood wanted to take up a collection and buy him a ticket, but he refused. Afterward someone made inquiries, or rather, an old retired man from the water department, said, "A brother in Vienna? Rikard's parents and brother ended up in Auschwitz. He doesn't have anyone in Vienna anymore." They went to tell old Riki this, to try and get through to him and bring him back to himself because, you see, he had always been normal. He greeted everyone and asked about them, talked about everything like anyone else, only with nicer words, somehow more civilly, like a gentleman, for old Riki was still a gentleman, it's just that some didn't see it anymore, but the neighborhood did and that's why they all felt awful that old Riki was dying like a dog. But when they went to tell him all that had happened in Auschwitz, he just laughed and said, "I know all that very well. Don't you worry about it, child!" And the next day it would start again: he was waiting for a letter from Vienna.

Rikard Goldberger had been an engineer in the municipal waterworks. He'd married a Catholic girl from a devout Swabian family. Getting baptized was all the same to him. Archbishop Stadler himself performed the wedding ceremony. It was Goldberger who hired Jaroslav Černi at the waterworks when Černi returned from his studies in Prague in 1933, while Černi turned Goldberger on to communism. Except that Rikard Goldberger was enclosed in layers of armor, and not only did no one really know anything about him, he even tried to save Černi from being transported to Jasenovac. He made phone calls all around, rousing the German command, calling Zagreb, and none of them were suspicious. There were no secrets in Sarajevo, but it was as if no one knew Goldberger was a Christianized Jew. And it could not have been known that he was a communist. After the war some evil tongues said Goldberger was a double agent working for the Gestapo and this was why neither the Germans nor the Ustaše ever touched him, but for such people it seemed every Jew who survived the war had worked for the Gestapo. The same people said that OZNA had interrogated him because of his collaboration with the occupier rather than because he was asking questions about the military truck that ran over his wife. People were scum. Or perhaps they were ordered to say such things.

By the time Černi came back from the camp, Rikard Goldberger was already waiting for his letter from Vienna. Whether he tried to help him or actually did help him is unknown. Jaroslav Černi soon died, in the winter of 1950, at the age of forty-one.

The visit to the attic on Mehmed Pasha Sokolović Street shook my mother.

What she saw there was devastating, but even more so was the fact that the name Rikard Goldberger was inscribed, even if only marginally, in Stubler history. When Karlo Stubler had been driven out of Dubrovnik in 1920 and the family was living off of union support, Goldberger would come around to see them in their rented little house near Ali Pasha Bridge. He would talk with Karlo and bring him books, though he was somewhat stiff and restrained seeming. They got the completely wrong impression that he looked down on them. Only after the war, in 1945, did Karlo's Dubrovnik friend, the union organizer Marko Bašić – the same man who came to ask whether Karlo would go after Boras now that his own people had come to power, and whom Karlo had told it was too late for all that – this same Marko Bašić revealed to him who had been the main donator of union funds that the Stublers had lived on in the years before Karlo got work at the Doboj train station: it was the waterworks engineer Rikard Goldberger.

Nano searched across Sarajevo to thank him on behalf of his father, but it was as if the engineer had fallen off the face of the earth. He was nowhere to be found. He would reappear only thirty years later, in a rotting attic on Mehmed Pasha Sokolović Street.

I don't know exactly how much time passed, but it seems to me my mother got social services moving immediately, calling the Association of World War II Veterans, and explaining to them Goldberger's situation. Everything played out in two or three days.

The next time she came to see him, the whole neighborhood was roused. A tin coffin of the sort that the homeless were put in would not fit through the tiny attic door, so they had to carry him out. No one knew how old Riki died, but he died like a dog after all.

My mother soon after earned her medal.

The nicely designed medal of patinated white metal with a bright red cross in the middle lay on a small cushion in a blue cardboard case. For years it was spotted around the apartment, on different shelves among old documents and newspapers, popping out from the general mess, materializing in various distant parts of the apartment, as if it were a living thing that moved at night from one room to another, hounding us or else trying to tell us something by its presence. I would come across it after the war too, and in later years when my mother renovated, adapting herself to retirement, adjusting to the beautiful pipe dream, in which I supported her, of opening a bookkeeping service for which she converted one of her rooms to an office. Then too the nameless order of the Red Cross appeared on a variety of new shelves, slipped off, popped out again, and it's probably still there somewhere. In the meantime, objects that had meant something to me disappeared, or ended up by accident in the trash, or my mother treated them as worthless, gave them away as gifts, or simply tossed them out of the apartment, which had accumulated too many private objects, too much family history. The medal meant nothing to her. She didn't see it as an acknowledgment of her talent, activism, or ability. In general she never boasted about her volunteer work with the Red Cross the way she did about things that she hadn't actually taken part in. She didn't recall the people she had helped. It wasn't important to her, and the medal was a piece of useless jewelry that sat around collecting dust, taking up space and serving no purpose whatsoever.

When I brought up Rikard Goldberger, she would immediately begin telling the story of how Marko Bašić had come to Karlo Stubler in 1945, bringing oranges and two stories: the one about Boras, against whom revenge was in order, and the one about Goldberger, who needed to be thanked. She never said anything about taking me to the attic. That was something terribly sad for her, about which nothing more could be said. She watched as the three old-timers tried to force the tin coffin through the tiny attic doorway, cursing horribly when they couldn't manage it. In red pencil on the unfinished wooden door had been written "Rikard Goldberger, Engineer." In case the postman came with a letter from Vienna.

The improbable story of Rikard Goldberger would be, if it were literature, the pinnacle of my mother's need to tend to the dying and the poor. And perhaps the saga of the Stublers could end with Rikard Goldberger if it were written as a fictional story, rather than as a chain of actual episodes sealed by the death of the storyteller. As it is, the Stubler benefactor, the mad old Riki who fed the pigeons and waited for a letter, explaining to the children the wonders of electricity and hydroelectric power, remains on the margins of one story, illustrating an unusual passion of my mother.

Much more important was the death of Aunt Doležal.

Because of her my mother stopped working for the Red Cross, because for two years, in 1976 and 1977, she needed to take care of that woman. Aunt Doležal, as I noted in *The Stublers*, at one point lived in the same building with us, that of Madam Emilija Heim, exchanging apartments after the war with her son-in-law, Vladimir Nagel, and moving to Marijin Dvor. The Nagel apartment was nice, spacious, high ceilinged, and located in an impressive, visually attractive Austro-Hungarian building. But according to the evaluation of comrades on some committee or other, or the city's living space commission, the Nagel family had a surplus of living space, the Šleht family would be accommodated in half of their apartment, and the bath and toilet would need to be shared in comradely fashion.

Perhaps Vlado Nagel really did have too large an apartment, but there were vengeful motives behind this: the Nagels were Germans, Protestants, the war had just ended, and if it were no longer possible to find that they had collaborated with the occupiers and domestic traitors, to put them on trial and sentence them to exile, then at the very least they could be hindered from getting to the toilet. When Vlado married Vilma, Aunt Doležal's only daughter, they decided to exchange apartments. That's how Aunt Doležal ended up with the Nagel apartment and the entire Šleht clan: hearty, healthy representatives of the new age, prepared to live long enough to one day expand into the whole apartment. The *partaja* idea was based on the same principle as that of our entire homeland: to those who can survive and overpower befalls the whole world – along with the bathroom and the toilet.

Thus did Vilma Doležal senior, whom everyone including her contemporaries called Aunt Doležal, after losing her husband – who had been a prison guard and had perhaps helped the revolutionary Olga Humo escape – in a concentration camp in the far north of Norway, end up in a communal apartment, more likely due to the fact that her son-in-law belonged to the enemy German nationality than because he had excess living space. She was punished because of her son-in-law. But she was rewarded because of her deceased husband: she received a commemorative testimonial for his time served in 1941, along with a veteran's pension.

If my mother hadn't taken care of her during her last two years, Aunt Doležal might have ended up like Rikard Goldberger. A decade earlier Vladimir Nagel had moved with Vilma junior and their son Bucik to Rijeka, and Nagel was the last of the evangelical Christians to disappear from Sarajevo. The beautiful Protestant church was sold to the state, which turned it into an art academy. Aunt Doležal's daughter died soon after, so that in the end her only blood relation was her grandson, though he was far away.

My mother had good reasons for taking care of Aunt Doležal. They had to do with the psychological state of her own mother after her son was killed. Nona had been beside herself, in search of a guilty party, someone through whom she could ease her conscience and blame for Mladen's death. These were also the years of her most severe migraines. Her head would ache for days, for a whole week each month, driving her and everyone around her out of their minds. Nona might well have wanted the world to go mad along with her, something which must have been rather frightening for my mother as a little girl.

When her mother was ailing, she had to be very quiet. And her mother's head hurt for so long and so often that the little girl always had to be quiet. She had to be silent, not ask any questions, not utter a word, until the migraine had passed.

So Aunt Doležal would come for her, take her to her apartment, give her the little red can, the *rote tane*, into which she dropped a handful of dry beans, and the little girl could shake the beans to her heart's content, raising a racket for as long as she liked until she lay down and fell asleep. And so, whenever her mother's head hurt, and even when it didn't, Aunt Doležal would come get her, give her the little red can, and let her make all the noise she wanted. This small act was something the little girl would never forget.

My mother believed things would have been much worse without Aunt Doležal.

No one was as kind to her, and while she was capable of forgetting and hiding all sorts of things, she never wanted to fail Aunt Doležal.

As the old woman declined, my mother was by her side performing all the messy jobs that need to be performed for the elderly, those that can be horribly degrading to a person if she has the misfortune to be aware of them. My mother, in the autumn of her own dying, was aware of this humiliation, but Aunt Doležal would not be. She lived as if inside a ball of wool that was being attacked by millions of moths. While we were still visiting her together – up to a year before her death – Aunt Doležal's enormous apartment was overflowing with moths. They would fly all around, mindlessly, crashing into the once quite beautiful Vienna Secession Furniture that, after her death, would end up in a Sarajevo junkyard or be broken up for firewood – antiques were not much valued in Sarajevo at the time – gnawing at the gold upholstery of the ottoman and the armchairs until it completely disintegrated, seaweed began to emerge from the insides, and rusty gray springs began to pop out, eating the blanket she used to cover her always cold legs before moving on to her; first they reduced to dust her old shawl, in which, being a small as she was, she could wrap herself up in completely, then they continued with her sweaters and wool dresses, then they nibbled at her hair, and in the end at all of her, starting from the memory of what had taken place just before, then moving back to the one from yesterday, until they had reduced her, as tiny as she was, down to her synthetic pajamas, which not even moths like, to some distant memory, in which there was neither us, nor my mother, nor the little girl shaking her tin can filled with dry beans repeating *rote tane, rote tane, rote tane* . . . There was nothing left. The moths had eaten everything, and the time was approaching when the Šleht family would engulf the entire apartment. Some thirty years after the revolution came the end of the era of communal living spaces in Sarajevo, with their shared kitchens, toilets, and bathrooms, where other people's hair collected in the drains of the old cast-iron sinks, and the end of the time when the number of rings at the door notified the people inside whether the visitor was calling for resident A, B, or C.

Once Aunt Doležal no longer remembered Nona, we stopped visiting her. It was as if everything grew dark around her, and Javorka was the only one to remain in that darkness, to follow things to their end, and see Aunt Doležal off from this world. This lasted for far too long, and death showed up in a surprising manner.

During her last afternoon, said my mother, Aunt Doležal fell asleep. She slept for a long time very quietly. It was so quiet that my mother went up to see whether she was still alive, and as she leaned over her to see whether she could feel her breath, Aunt Doležal suddenly opened her eyes.

"Oh, it's you, Mrs. Krašovec!" she said in surprise and then died.

She didn't even draw a breath. She just died.

No one knew who Mrs. Krašovec was. My mother looked into it, calling former residents and neighbors from Emilija Heim's building, but no one knew who it could be. There simply were no women with that surname.

They trusted that the words meant nothing, the name had popped out of Aunt Doležal's dreaming the moment before she died, it hadn't actually belonged to anyone, and there never had been a Mrs. Krašovec. Then someone recalled that she had spent the better part of her working life as an operator at the post office, where several hundred names every day went through her head, so perhaps she had once heard of a Mrs. Krašovec there, and this name, without any visible reason or logic, had been the last one she recalled in life. It was the last drop of consciousness that dribbled out of her.

Thirty-five years later, while my mother lay in the former military hospital, I asked her about Mrs. Krašovec. It took her some time to remember. This wasn't important to her anymore.

My mother accompanied many people from life, but Aunt Doležal was the closest to her at the moment of her death. They almost touched noses when she died. It just turned out that way. And while my aunt's death was of little interest to anyone in the world anymore, there remained one unresolved question: who was Mrs. Krašovec?

I was perhaps ten at the time, and the one thing I didn't believe was that the word had to do with someone who either didn't exist or was unimportant. I think the same today: Mrs. Krašovec surely existed, and my mother somehow reminded Aunt Doležal of her. Though she was senile – today it's called dementia or maybe Alzheimer's, but then it was simply senility – Aunt Doležal surely saw something that we did not, something that I don't see when I look carefully at my mother, in the same way that others wouldn't have recognized my mother in Vermeer's *Girl with a Pearl Earring* when I was so sure that it was her.

And so I began to imagine Mrs. Krašovec, searching for her among old photographs, but most often in the stories I told myself when I was bored in the dentist's waiting room, or when we were traveling by train toward Ploče, or in the evening before going to sleep. This was how I took up literature, though I wasn't conscious of it. I had started my first year at the gymnasium when I first saw *Citizen Kane*, which begins with the last word of the main character: *rosebud*. What was rosebud? The viewer learns the answer, but the characters in the film do not. In this way someone knew Mrs. Krašovec and didn't know that it might have been important.

I don't know and don't want to know what my mother's last words were. She didn't say them to me. I wasn't there. To me she just yelled, because I had lied to her about things being all right. That was the last thing. She thought I had tricked her. It got worse and worse, and then she was no more.

My mother died like a child. This was the last great injustice of a life filled with so many other injustices. She believed she had never really been given a chance. Her life was reminiscent of the frustration of a back-up soccer goalie who never got the chance to stand before the goal. At least to try. This was how she consoled herself, drowning in self-pity as if in a bath of chocolate pudding. I taunted her with this, though it was spiteful of me. My petty revenge.

She never had a chance. Everything had gone badly from the start. It had been horrible. And then there had been one false man, another false man, and a son. That son had been a foreigner in life. Half formed by a man she had come to hate. He had taken away the one small chance she had of living. Who had taken away her chance? The man? Or her son? It was unknowable. Later, she couldn't go back. She couldn't start over. It was the end. Childhood, old age, and again childhood. This, all of it, had been life.

Inventories

Kakania

My grandfather Franjo Rejc lived his life in Bosnia. As a high-ranking railroad official, he moved from station to station until, several months before the outbreak of the Second World War, he arrived in Sarajevo to work at the main headquarters with the title of chief railway inspector. When I first wrote about my grandfather's working as a chief inspector, the critics interpreted it as a postmodern inscription for Danilo Kiš, whose novelistic and actual father had the same job. This, however, was not something I was thinking about at the time. I did not compare the life of my grandfather with the lives of heroes in books. But I was still pleased by the critical observation. Anytime anyone would later ask me whether the figure of my grandfather as a chief inspector was an homage to Danilo Kiš, I would lie and say yes. In the end, perhaps it really was. Perhaps the actual life of my deceased grandfather Franjo Rejc was a palimpsest of some written or unwritten Kiš novel. And perhaps the rest of us are living the lives of some future or past literary characters.

But there is something real that connects Kiš's father and my grandfather – the long-lived emperor and king Franz Joseph I. It was under his good leadership that the tracks were constructed where the two of them performed their highly responsible work. The job of a chief inspector is to somehow arrange the movement of trains such that no two trains are ever found on the same stretch of open track, hurtling toward each other. His job is to foresee and avoid all possible accidents and collisions.

From the spring when he arrived in Sarajevo as an experienced railway man to design timetables, until his final days, my grandfather lived in fear of accidents across the territory for which the headquarters in Bosnia and Herzegovina had responsibility. It didn't matter where the fault lay – with a drunk engineer, a broken signal light, tracks in disrepair or inclement weather, a storm, an earthquake, a fire – he believed deep inside that if only one thing were different, if the arrivals and departures of the locals, the regionals, the internationals with people and freight had been planned better, casualties could have been averted or, at the very least, lessened. The network of narrow- and standard-gauge lines were mapped as if onto the network of his nervous system. But as the lines for which he had responsibility were part of a wider structure, the largest piece of which had been planned and built during Austro-Hungarian times, he did the calculations for his timetable and put it in accord with all the others, from the Baltic and mythic Galicia, from the Kingdom of Kraków, from Ukraine and Romania, across Hungary and Vojvodina, all the way to Austria and the capital of the dual monarchy in Vienna. Every accident that took place in this territory was part of his responsibility. Even though the Habsburg monarchy and the Kakania of Robert Musil had been dead for decades, my grandfather Franjo Rejc's native country, to the end of his working days, and then to the end of his life, spread out across the entire landmass of what had once been Austria-Hungary. It might seem a nice metaphor to some, but his country was, before all else, the space of his personal responsibility.

All the timetables were kept in our home, from the first in 1923 to the one for the year of his death in 1972. Even after he retired at the beginning of the seventies, he continued to worry about accidents and schedules, though he no longer worked out the calculations for them. He obviously knew the names of all the hubs from Gdańsk to Doboj and Vinkovci. In truth he knew the names of all the stations from the northern to the southern seas. In his world, the great, luxurious stations like the one in Pest, which was the pride of the monarchy at the time of its demise, or in Warsaw, that ugly and incomplete work of socialist architecture, were less important because it was often the small, provincial, nameless stations that posed the greatest risk of serious disaster. A switchman's wife had died or a station chief had got drunk at his son's wedding and thought the train from Kiev was behind schedule, and there it would happen – a horrid accident somewhere in the depths of Ukraine in which hundreds of people perished and which was felt from Riga to Kovno in the north all the way to Zelenika, the tiny station in Montenegro's far south, at the end of the narrow gauge that completed Franz Joseph's tracks down on the shores of the warm sea. Its finale was like something in a dream – until that bit of track was definitively closed in 1968, the train crossed the boardwalk, passing along the coast before arriving at the final station, right beside the beach where tourists sunbathed, while children with inflatable tubes around their waists hopped back from the locomotive's puffs of steam before saving themselves by leaping into the sea at the last second. From 1904 or 1907, when that part of the track was opened, until 1968, no one was ever killed by the train in Zelenika, though the people sunbathing on the beach would be sprinkled with coal dust from the locomotive's engine. Today this would be considered neither healthy nor ecologically sound.

My grandfather Franjo Rejc's native land extended from Kovno to Zelenika. Though the Austro-Hungarian state no longer existed and the governmental, administrative, and cultural institutions that would have borne its name were no more, and although all of Europe looked on it with disdain and condescension after the fall of Kakania, the most important thing that defined my grandfather's emotional and cultural identity still did exist – the network of complementing, logically linked railway lines of the Habsburg monarchy, as well as his feeling of responsibility and strong emotional attachment to the people who maintained that network. I know of no more precise definition of the concepts of homeland and patriotism than how my grandfather, the chief inspector in Sarajevo's head office, lived his life. I somehow imagine that the other chief inspectors must have resembled him.

My grandfather Franjo Rejc knew the following languages besides his native Slovenian and Serbo-Croatian: German, which he spoke without an accent; Italian, which he learned in an Italian detention camp during the First World War and would remember for the rest of his life; French, because it would be a pity not to study French if you already knew Italian; Hungarian, which he studied and learned well during the last gasps of the monarchy in which all the better-educated Southern Slavs knew Hungarian, too; Romanian – I have no idea why he studied that language; and as a seventy-year-old, having concluded that English was the language of the future, he took up a grammar book and a dictionary and began to study them. I had already been born by this time. He would walk around the house, refusing to communicate in any language but English. Everyone found this funny. Go ahead and laugh, he would say, but this was the only way to learn a language. (As I write this, it grieves me to no end that I did not inherit his gift for languages and even more his courage to attempt to speak in a language one barely knows . . .)

All this was somehow natural and normal. In the world into which my grandfather was born, it was not strange to know a handful of languages – particularly for people from the border. My grandfather was born in 1896 when his father, a Slovene by nationality, was a guest worker in Bosnia. It was a time for big construction projects, and he came from Tolmin, an area of extreme poverty along the coast of what is today the frontier between Slovenia and Italy. He did the metal work for Sarajevo Cathedral, which was then under construction. The door handles and locks of this church were forged and installed by my Slovene great-grandfather. Besides being a good smith, my great-grandfather had six children and was an alcoholic his entire life, a difficult man, and abusive to his family.

Having run away from such a father, my grandpa Franjo connected with his numerous relatives who were still living in Tolmin. He studied at the famous Jesuit gymnasium in Travnik and spent his vacations with them in Slovenia. Even though, from the standpoint of his native land, he was a Bosnian and his true homeland was Austria-Hungary, my grandpa Franjo was a Slovene in terms of nationality. He wasn't happy when, after the fall of the Habsburg monarchy, the border between the Kingdom of Italy and the Kingdom of the Serbs, Croats, and Slovenes cut right through the homeland of his relatives, slicing it into two pieces, the larger part falling to Italy.

And of course, as it was the European custom of the time to give one's life for one's language, homeland, and culture, my grandpa's kinsmen turned toward clandestine organizations. At first they sought their right to be what they were, Slovenes, but as that didn't go over well and the Italians were unwilling to allow them to open schools that taught in Slovene, the demands for cultural and educational autonomy expanded into militant political and irredentist strategies. Thus did my Slovene ancestors, the close kinsmen of my grandfather, turn toward the battle for something that small, European nations would fight for throughout the twentieth century, in different ways and with differing emotional commitments and existential roles, people whose villages and homelands were divided and ploughed through by the borders of newly formed states. The methods were of course always the same: assassination, terrorism, sabotage, concealed explosives.

The largest Slovenian revolutionary organization, which was created by my grandfather's relations and compatriots, was called TIGR (for Trieste, Istria, Gorizia, and Rijeka). As with all true revolutionaries, they chose a quite sentimental name for themselves. The abbreviation spelled out the Slovenian word for *tiger*. I don't bring it up in order to express pride about my grandfather and his relations, but they were in fact the first secret antifascist organization in Europe, for they were formed immediately during Mussolini's rise to power and their program was consistent in its antifascism and irredentism. They printed leaflets, issued proclamations, and shot and threw bombs until the beginning of the thirties, when they were annihilated, driven underground, into the woods, or forced to emigrate to Yugoslavia under the pressure of Mussolini's own state terrorism. Then as now, state terrorism was stronger and more successful than revolutionary, individual, or conspiratorial terrorism. In Italy, several TIGR members, including one of my grandfather's closest relatives, were sentenced to death and killed.

My grandfather Franjo Rejc had nothing against Italians. One could even say he loved both them and their language. He looked at the years he spent as an Austro-Hungarian soldier in an Italian detention camp (from 1915 to 1919) as the most beautiful years of his youth. He made friends among the Italian guards with whom he would correspond to the very end as one by one they passed on to the next world. I suppose he didn't discuss his relatives with them, or the idea that Istria along with Trieste, the Karst Plateau, and the coast to the south, might be split off from the Kingdom of Italy and attached to the Kingdom of the Serbs, Croats, and Slovenes, which in 1929 was named the Kingdom of Yugoslavia. His Italian friends were, I believe, also antifascists, for why would Italian fascists correspond with a Slovene from Bosnia, but, even so, they would not likely have supported the idea of snipping off pieces of Italy, especially since some of them were from Trieste and Istria. How did my grandfather reconcile his devotion to his Italian friends with his loyalty to his Slovene relatives? How did he reconcile his belief that the portions of Italy populated by a majority of Slovenes should be part of Yugoslavia with his cooly acknowledged belief that the Italians were nobler, more cultured, and better educated than we, their South Slav neighbors? How did he reconcile terrorism as a method of struggle for Slovenian freedom with the freedom and right to life of his Italian comrades? I know nothing of all this, having been just six years old when he died and having never had the chance to ask him.

The relation of the Yugoslav authorities to the members of TIGR was strategic. When relations with Mussolini's Italy were bad, they let those people loose and even encouraged them to commit acts of terror. But when at the end of the thirties Milan Stojadinović, who had found in Mussolini his political ideal, became premier in Belgrade, however, the Tigers found themselves under the full force of law. It was even worse at the beginning of the Second World War. The Quisling authorities of the Independent State of Croatia, as well as the occupying German forces in Slovenia, persecuted and killed them, and Tito's Partisans did not have much faith in them. One of my grandfather's relatives, an important leader in TIGR, was even shot by the Partisans. In the battle for the proletarian international, the communists were happy to use terrorist methods, but what they hated more than anything was when someone else was fighting for the same cause they were.

During the war, besides creating railroad timetables and worrying about possible train accidents, my grandfather hid TIGR members who made it to Sarajevo as they fled persecution. He also kept an important part of TIGR's secret documents. Fearing a search, he buried the documents in a field, which was later paved over, so it's not known whether the papers were destroyed or whether they still lie somewhere underground, wrapped in a rubberized tarp or tucked away in metal boxes. They await some future archeologist to discover them by chance and bring them to light. This is how the story of our family's terrorism comes to an end. After the fall of communism and the creation of an independent state, several books about TIGR were published in Slovenia. One was by the widow of my grandfather's closest relative, whom everyone called Uncle Berti.

My grandfather Franjo Rejc would often come to mind when the story of a unified Europe still held a romantic attraction for those of us just coming out of the bloody wars that had begun in 1991 and only ended in 1999 when NATO completed its bombing of Serbia. Though he's been dead for forty years, this sort of united Europe was my grandfather's true homeland. It won't change anything in my life, nor will it become my native country – by contrast to my grandfather, I am a Balkan native, someone who doesn't like to travel and looks at everything from a distance, askance, through books, films, and newspapers. He knew many of its languages and would have learned all the rest if he'd had time. He was a true European, for he created Europe and simultaneously destroyed it. First he worked for keeping the harmony of his tracks, then he helped his relatives in their revolutionary aspirations. Thus did his life unfold in a completely European rhythm of building up and tearing down. Of all this I have only his memory. I have the stories he told me, or the stories about him that others told me, or that I learned from the letters he received from friends, preserved in the back of a Sarajevo closet. His Europe was the "native realm" of Czesław Miłosz, while mine is just the recollection of that other Europe that was his, and probably for me it can be nothing more than that.

My grandfather Franjo Rejc was a more completed European than I. Although I am seventy years his junior, was born in a time of televised, quickly transmitted information, and was formed through and through by the époque of a computerized, virtual, and altogether globalized world, in a figurative sense I am centuries older than he was, less prepared to adapt, more distant from the ideal of a unified world that would stretch from the northern seas to the southern. But I recognize both his railroads and his sympathy for the terrorism of our Slovene relatives. I have a recollection of Europe, but only a recollection.

My grandpa has called to my mind a unified Europe – that is, the European Union – whenever its conception has awakened for me those early romantic and idealistic notions characteristic of people from Eastern Europe and the former Yugoslavia when they were still certain that a unified Europe would be a community of cultures in which the rights of individuals, their basic human rights, would be the basic reason for its existence. Never was Europe so beautiful and exalted as to the wretches of Eastern Europe, to the Yugoslav peoples and the nations ravaged by their brotherly, civil, and nationalistic wars. They honestly believed Europe would return to them their human dignity, that it would heal them of their nationalism, and that by some marvelous enchantment it would make them better and happier. The energy of their disillusionment would be the same as that of their hope. The positive force of Eastern Europe has not been used up, but the effects of the force of disillusionment will continue to be felt for some time to come.

With time I, like others, have come to understand that the European Union is above all an economic corporate entity – a sort of Deutsche Telekom, British Petroleum, or, more precisely, a network of global banks with credit lines, interest on arrears, and marketing-oriented packages of financial services for governments and citizens – and that it is a community of cultures only to the extent that this improves the business of banks, the prosperity of telecommunications companies, the survival of European oil companies in the brutal world market. Just as every large bank publicly boasts of its humanitarian funding and expenditures on culture and ecology, so can the European Union boast of its status as a community of cultures. But the worst and most painful thing is that the basic human rights of a citizen of the European Union depends on having been born in Germany, the Netherlands, France, or, perhaps, Greece, Hungary, or Italy.

How could I have come to see my grandfather as an ideal European? Was it just that he knew so many European languages? Well, today on our computers we have Google Translate, which knows all the languages of the world, in a superficial way. Or was it the Austro-Hungarian railroads and the worry of a chief inspector in the face of possible accidents? How could globalized railroads make someone a European when airplanes have already crisscrossed the sky? Actually, for this Europe of banks I am incomparably better prepared than my grandfather – he lived and died for Europe as a community of cultures, for a Europe of human rights and dignity.

My mistake lies in imagining a unified Europe as a completed and modernized Austria-Hungary, the land in which our kind old king and emperor deemed on principle that he should know all the languages of his monarchy. And his nephew, Franz Ferdinand, whom we would kill in Sarajevo on Saint Vitus Day, June 28, 1914, stated that before ascending to the throne he would speak our own Serbo-Croatian fluently. However much we might ridicule it, Kakania was a community of cultures. And it fell because it could no longer function as such a community. If it had been formed as a capitalist corporation, perhaps it would have lasted until our own day, for in that case it would not have even entered the minds of its small nations to struggle for and win their basic rights to culture, language, and identity. The established illusion of Austria-Hungary as a community of cultures passed through the years and generations of the nineteenth century. When at last everyone believed in it, they took to destroying it. And this was how the shots fired by Gavrilo Princip marked the start of the first World War. Afterward, some Slovene kinsman of mine began shooting at the customs guards and carabinieri in Trieste, for he was fueled by the belief – acquired before the collapse of the great multinational monarchy – that he had the right to his own language, homeland, and culture. And ultimately, that he had the right to his own country.

The Path Through Fury and Despair

The children used to play in the elevators then. Their parents fought with them, threatened them, but they still found some way of going up and down. My cousin was seven and was playing in the elevator with a friend from the building when it stopped between two floors. The space between the doors seemed just enough to be able to crawl out. His friend went first, and at the moment when he was halfway out, the mechanism started up again. Afterwards I could only remember my cousin through that event, especially when we grew up. How could he go on with his life after he came out of the elevator? How often did it flash through his head that he could have been the one to crawl out first? Perhaps his friend was braver or wanted to show off? Maybe he wanted to get out because he was more afraid of getting thrashed by his parents, or perhaps he wanted to do something important? I think about it often because it occurs to me I would have gone crazy in his shoes. And I marvel at how calm and stable he is, how smiling and full of respect toward those he considers more intelligent than himself.

The other big event that took place in his life was when he was sixteen. It was 1993, during the war in Bosnia, inside which there was a second war, between the Croats and Muslims (later Bosniaks). He was living in Zenica with his half-Croat, half-Slovene father and his Serb mother. It was hard, hopeless, so much so that the boy decided to go to his brother in Ljubljana, and his parents had no way of stopping him. They didn't know what would happen to him if he stayed, and they didn't know what would happen to him if he went. They didn't know which of the two was scarier so decided not to interfere in his destiny. With his Zenica personal identity card and no other papers or documents of any kind, he headed across the front lines, the customs borders, and the check points through the soldiers and the war. He used by turns his father's then his mother's ethnicity whenever one or the other served him as an introduction or a justification. When neither of these helped, perhaps his place of birth would be of service. If it looked like he might be conscripted by the Serbs, he said he was a Croat or a Slovene, reasoning that it was better to be beaten for being the wrong ethnicity than end up with a bullet in a ditch. He did the same on the Croatian side. Actually the Croats and the Serbs didn't hate each other that much, they were unified in their mutual hatred for the Muslims.

At the time Bosnia was a rather sizable land. Each locality, district, or village exhibited its own identity, nation, and culture. Every hamlet had a distinct historical memory depending on who was fighting against whom and when. The boy could not know how he needed to behave with everyone but adapted, testing, scrutinizing a hundred times over before setting forth. To get to Ljubljana from the side he started out on, one had to pass through Serbia in those months. Or so it seemed to him. Or maybe he took into account the fact that he had an aunt in a town in western Serbia and thought she might be able to help him on his journey. It appears, in the end, when he reached her, that she didn't help him quite as much as she could have.

He made it through Bosnia safely. It took him weeks to get from Zenica to the bridges on the Drina. When I've asked him how he stayed alive without getting thrown into prison or made into a soldier, he has always answered me willingly, telling the story as if it were a normal thing to pass through the angry Bosnian soldiers, through a thousand and one instances of fury, despair, and wretchedness, across half the land – the half to which Ivo Andrić devoted nearly his entire literary work – innocent and inexperienced, his pockets empty, and with kind and honest intent, heading toward his aunt in Serbia to eventually reach his brother in Ljubljana. What could never be normal to me in my life with my notions of what is real and possible was his life and his mature human resolve. My cousin is not an eccentric young man. He is a simple person, today with a family of his own. He doesn't have a talent for extreme sports and is not inclined to any sort of adventure. It would never enter his head to do any of the things that so many people do during their summer vacations. He isn't an adrenaline junkie. He was just going to see his brother in Ljubljana.

If you were to ask him, I think he would tell you he still doesn't see why his journey is of such interest to me. It's been sixteen years since the war, and he's now twice as old as he was then. Between the two of us there is one major difference: what was life to him can be only literature to me. What he experienced I can write, not in such a way that I am simply listening to and reconstructing his story – I reinvent it. His would be merely the departure from Zenica and the arrival in Ljubljana. Of course, his would be the route and – the most important thing – the time. It took him four and a half months to reach Ljubljana.

My cousin will never write his story. He doesn't believe it is worth telling. And just as I would never have the nerve to set out on such a journey, he would never write such a story. I could be wrong, but it seems to me possible to divide people into those who at sixteen set out from Zenica to Ljubljana across Serbia and Hungary, through war or peace, without money or documents, and those who instead can recognize in this a great story. I've met some who seemed to combine both traits but who turned out to be liars and dreamers. In stories as in life, lies function poorly. Lies demotivate. Lies destroy enchantment.

In war-torn 1993 my young Bosnian cousin, alone and without documents, crossed the country of Serbia and managed to get onto a bus that took him through Hungary to the Slovenian border. This took a long time, months. He was guided by some unrepeatable impulse of life that, I imagine, he would never feel or experience again, thanks to which he managed to pass through the Chetniks, Ustaše, and mujahideen, as well as the Serbian and Hungarian border guards and police officers, good and bad, responsible and not, encountering people who, like me, found it striking that a sixteen-year-old boy would travel east in order to arrive west to his older brother in Ljubljana. If this were a novel or a film and not life, many would be called upon to testify to this impulse of his. Those who understand it and those who do not. Or to put it better: those who feel it and those who do not. They fail to feel it not because they're not musical, have no ear, or aren't endowed by God with something that might allow them to feel the story, but because he gave them something else, perhaps more beautiful and more important. But in all this, feeling is the most central thing. Along with the respect they have toward someone else's great life inspiration. If that did not exist, perhaps my cousin would not be alive today. Nor would he be alive if he had tried to be bigger and braver than he actually was at seven years old. The miracle of life, like the miracle of story, consists in a person's recognizing his inspiration.

Our lives flow at the cleft between living and telling. In vain might we choose to pull away from life, for wherever we run in the world, reality will catch us. And typically everything we most fear and imagine and excuse ourselves for in advance comes back to us, perhaps in our most vulnerable moments. And of course no one would be there to help us because when we pull away from life, people think we are pulling away from them too – they take offense, grow distant, and are no longer there. They don't understand that we tell so we don't have to live, so we can step to one side, anesthetize ourselves, and that the telling is a symptom of some sort of emotional weakness, powerlessness, mental illness, the sort of thing for which other people go to a psychiatrist. If all the weak and powerless, if each person uncertain in spirit and frightened before every coming day, were able to leap across that cleft, that fissure that takes one from storytelling into life, then the psychiatrists would have no one left to treat. Or they would treat only savages.

But if the ones who tell stories were no more, not only would all tongues except computer languages disappear, we would no longer know what was happening to us. Who knows, perhaps this will indeed come to pass. They're already portending the fall of books, the end of literacy and the civilization that rose up from the stories of *A Thousand and One Nights*. If it happened, it would not be true for everyone. Writers would tell stories and books would be published in the richest and the poorest nations. In the first, because they would have been conscious of the results of literacy's demise. In the second, because the news that the book had to die and only the weak and the powerless invented stories would have arrived too late. And outside these fortunate rich and poor peoples, I imagine, would rise up a new civilization of masters and slaves, communicating in some animal computer language, and among the masters there would be eternal war, for by their very nature riches and wealth exist in eternal war, whereas story is nonexistent, or at least the illusion of something worth more than that. Neoliberal capitalism cannot stand such an illusion, and this is why fairy tales and dreams are so bothersome to its defenders, getting on their nerves and interfering with productivity.

But even then, I'm convinced, my cousin would have managed to set out east in order to get to the west.

Christmas in Zenica

My mother calls from Sarajevo on New Year's Eve. I've got a story for you, she says, a Christmas story. She does this sort of thing. Something interesting happens, someone mentions something in passing, or – more often – she remembers something from her childhood, or even better, from a time before she was even born, and calls me up to tell me about it. She really enjoys this and sometimes it's a shame that I'm not recording these conversations. I use some things from these stories of hers, but most remain between us, just something to be remembered.

Here then is what she told me that New Year's Eve.

Just after the war, her brother, my uncle Dragan, studied metallurgy in Ljubljana. He returned to Zenica in Bosnia as soon as he received his degree, where, upon the foundations created by Austria-Hungary, the Yugoslav metallurgy industry was built up. Zenica steel would reinforce Belgrade and Zagreb, resolving the question of Croatia versus Serbia. Yugoslavia's famous shipbuilding industry would be based upon that steel, and from it would be fashioned all those slender bridges across the mountain streams and gorges of that beautiful and accursed land. And from that steel would be forged, in the end, the weapons and implements that would destroy Yugoslavia, first killing Vukovar and then all of Bosnia. My uncle was not lacking in enthusiasm for such great undertakings and ideas, though he was by nature more of a curious hedonist than a believer and missionary of a better future. T. S. Eliot said that tradition is not inherited but acquired, and the tradition he acquired in his home was in no way filled with faith that the future would be better.

Zenica in the late thirties and the forties was a city in which new arrivals from different times and kingdoms mixed freely – Polish and Czech officials and teachers, German engineers, Austrian smiths and blast furnace specialists, some Hungarians, and some surviving Jews, with domestic, pronouncedly eastern Muslim, Catholic, and Orthodox features. The majority of this colorful population circled around the iron works and the neighboring mines of Central Bosnia. Either they worked in them or depended on them for their work, such that the city, regardless of all the differences in status and education, grew unmistakably proletarian. All these people were from the working class. This Zenica proletariat sometimes played an unusual role in conjunction with the city's traditions, which all the Franz Joseph *kuferaši* from the North Sea, Kraków, Galicia, Prague, Vienna, Graz, and Ljubljana brought with them and preserved. Perhaps the Party suspected some sort of danger in this, or perhaps one should not attribute such astuteness to it, but the fact is that social constraint held Zenica together. The simple truth was that one went to prison much more easily in Zenica, and prison was never far off. Even today there it is, practically right in the center of town. At the time, the prison was still full of Ustaše and Chetniks, officials and worshippers of Independent Croatia, and just before my uncle Dragan returned from Ljubljana, some of my own relatives on my father's side were toiling away there. For them it all boiled down to the fact that loving one kingdom too much would get you punished in the next one.

In terms of its identity and traditions, and not just professionally, Zenica must have been an ideal place for Dragan. By heritage he was a mixture of the home-grown and the *kuferaši*, with a half-Slovene, half-Bosnian father and a mother who was half-Swabian and half some mysterious blending of equal parts Mediterranean and Eastern, which the provincials in small countries wittily refer to as Mitteleuropa. As his father, my grandfather Franjo, was a rail man, Dragan was born and grew up in little towns along the tracks before ending up in Sarajevo.

He had a grandfather who insisted that German be spoken in the home and a father who wanted all his children to know Slovene and be conscious of the fact that their first homeland was in the Slovenian town of Kneža, near Tolmin, the same father who, when there turned out to be no Catholic instruction in his son's public school, didn't want his boy separated from the others when they studied God in the Muslim "maytaf" (as he incorrectly called the *maktab*). In the end, it really was as if God had created the boy precisely for Zenica.

He brought his young wife from Sarajevo, Aunt Viola, the most beautiful woman of my childhood, who would not lose her good looks even in her oldest and most difficult years. She too was from a mixed *kuferaš* and local family from the city. In his old age, her father had painted sea panoramas and Bosnian landscapes for the good of his soul. He was a small, kind, warm old man, fascinated like so many of the *kuferaši* of his generation by Bosnia and Dalmatia, regions their destiny had presented to them as gifts. Viola's brother Robert had ended up in Jasenovac when he was an advanced middle school student. He managed to survive, but the camp left him scarred for life. I remember him as a withdrawn, expressly apolitical, and, by his own choice, somehow completely thinned-out person. When I think of concentration camps, he's the first person I remember.

But their love must have been great for Viola to agree in those times, amid the heat of renewal and reconstruction, to go with Dragan to Zenica. It's true that it was only eighty kilometers from Sarajevo, but they were eighty long and distant kilometers that at the time one did not cover often and never without good reason. But as one might expect, Dragan made quick progress and had already become the director of the blast furnaces by some time in the '50s. This was a very high position, one of the highest in the whole of Yugoslav black metallurgy. Of course Dragan had been a Party member by then for some time. It's odd to think that without it he still might have been able to rise to head of the blast furnaces, but either way his professional qualifications would have been more important. Ideas were important, but ideas didn't melt steel – what melted it was something other than ideas. I say this because Dragan had a hereditary notation in his file that would have limited his career options in the majority of other jobs and environments: the brother who had died as an enemy combatant. This had taken place barely ten or fifteen years before. In any case, he needed to watch his own behavior, which did not come easily. Whenever Comrade Tito came to Zenica and, as a preventive measure, all the doubtful characters, sacristans, former Ante Pavelić supporters, and bright flowers of the Croatian people were rounded up, my uncle Dragan would show him around the operation. Somewhere in the house, amid the unexamined chaos of former-life relics, there must still be a photograph snipped from a newspaper in which Dragan is showing the marshal the incandescent inferno of a blast furnace.

In one of those early years of his directorship, maybe the very first, Christmas arrived and Viola was very concerned about getting the tree decorated before the twenty-fifth, rather than for the New Year as the unstated Party rules dictated. And so they managed to decorate the tree very nicely on Christmas Eve, but then something terrible happened: Comrade Saveta Jaroš called to say he was coming for a visit. The two of them were panic stricken, running this way and that, until Dragan picked up the whole tree, all decorated, and dragged it into the bathroom, where he stuffed it into the tub. It was probably only when Comrade Saveta was ringing at the door that they realized the shortcoming of this plan – the toilet was located in the bathroom.

Čedo and Saveta Jaroš were then and would remain later Dragan and Viola's best friends from their Zenica days. Čedo was a Czech by heritage, while Saveta was a Bosnian Serb, former Communist Youth member and now a member of the Zenica Communist Council. This might sound scary today, or at least so ideologically charged as to be unlike actual life, but in their actual lives Viola and Dragan got along really well with Comrade Saveta and talked completely openly about everything except the things one did not discuss with others. Today one might not talk with family friends about sex, but back then it was taboo to mention one's brother who died as an enemy combatant.

Anyway, either Comrade Saveta had quite a good long sit at the Rejcs' that day or Comrades Dragan and Viola were so scared that every minute of her presence seemed like an eternity. Every time Saveta took a sip of her rose juice, a cold shiver ran down their spines because with every swallow she got closer to where they didn't dare allow her to go. Who knows what they talked about. This was forgotten that very day. And who knows if Saveta found something suspicious in their behavior. In the end, everything turned out fine, for their guest did not go to the bathroom and did not confront the ideological aberration of my uncle Dragan Rejc, Director of Blast Furnaces, pride of Zenica's and Yugoslavia's metallurgy industry.

But the story has a sequel.

My mother often saw her doctor, Šerkan Talić, whom she had known for a long time, and the two of them shared stories with each other every time they met. Like many family doctors, Doctor Talić was privy to hundreds of stories and all sorts of human destinies, happy and unhappy, and miracles from the lives of strangers and people close by, such that when he had the opportunity and was not merely acting as a practitioner of his craft, he could be a chronicler of Sarajevo or at least the several Sarajevo streets and neighborhoods where he practiced and from which people would visit him. But as it is with this dedicated variety of doctor, who experiences his work as a sacred calling, Doctor Talić also treated the people in the building where he lived.

And so he told her the story of how on Christmas that year he had gone to see his neighbors, an old couple, terribly nice people, truly beautiful people from a by-gone age, well preserved and clear headed. The man was ailing from something, but he didn't give in to it and the illness didn't bring him down. Christmas was his favorite time of the year. It was too bad it only happened once a year because this was when the two of them brought in their tree. The decorations they placed on it, inherited from his parents, had to be more than a century old. No one had ever seen more beautiful ornaments. They decorated the branches with those candies in shiny perforated paper – you remember, the kind they used to sell some fifty years ago, when there was such poverty that there were no actual ornaments to buy, and it really meant something for the children to take the candies off the tree. No other tree in Sarajevo was as beautiful. And as in every story in which names must be named, Doctor Talić mentioned the names of his neighbors: Mr. Čedo and Mrs. Saveta Jaroš.

And that was the story my mother told me, a Christmas story, as it were, as if it had been shaped by Frank Capra. Today Mrs. Saveta surely would not be angry to learn that the Rejcs had hidden their morally and politically unfit Christmas tree from her in the bathroom tub. Such were the times and customs. It is not healthy to be prideful about one's family and wider relations for that is a step toward pridefulness with regard to one's nation – a much more difficult, hateful, and incurable disease – but still, I am somewhat proud that this story too, was recounted in our family with humor and irony, we were poking fun at ourselves. When in 1998 my uncle Dragan – whom I used to call Tio Dragan – was in a Zenica hospital, he asked me to come see him one more time. It was winter. I traveled from Zagreb by bus. All of Bosnia lay in fog, snow, and mud, and Zenica smelled of thick coal smoke. The iron works were closed. The hospital was like all hospitals. His illness had distorted one half of his face, and he asked, "So do I remind you of Tuđman now?"

Olga's Zehra

She was pregnant by the time they moved to Kakanj in the spring of 1926. Franjo's transfer came all of a sudden. This was how it happened on the railroad: an express would arrive with the posting notice that said on the fifteenth of the next month one should report for duty as the station chief at the location indicated. Mladen was three, a quiet, levelheaded child. He was expecting a sister. He would be disappointed when, three months after their move, his brother was born. If we had stayed in Usora, his father said, it would have been a girl.

Kakanj was different from Usora, and from Doboj, where they met, got married, and conceived their first son. Or perhaps the order was rather different? But this wasn't talked about. It was a small mining backwater that took root around the coal pits and was populated by proletarians from various parts of the fallen monarchy, artisans, overseers, low-level clerks in the mining offices, machine operators and electricians, until people started arriving, the Muslims and Catholics from the neighboring villages, unchanged for centuries before the arrival of Austria, for that most basic of all mining work, which required no schooling whatsoever. They had lived there among the legends recalled since the times of the Bosnian kings and the Turkish invaders, and little of it was true. Surrounded by a wondrous natural world that, like them, had remained the same, untouched by civilization, and boiled down to the turning of the seasons, these people for a long time had little understanding of their own poverty. But once the Swabian had opened the mines and Kakanj began to rise up around them, the people from the legends had something with which to compare their lives. They greedily grasped how that other distant world lived and started heading down into the pits. They began to trade their clean, undefiled want for something they knew nothing about. This was how the miners of Kakanj were in 1926.

A pregnant Olga walked through the little hick town, leading Mladen by the hand. She looked around, went into the mining colony, past the small houses surrounded by rose gardens, and farther up the hill, toward Šumonija Spring. Franjo was never overly friendly and was certainly not in the habit of bringing someone home for lunch to make her acquaintance. And so Olga didn't know how to do this on her own: she'd grown up with two sisters and a brother in Dubrovnik where the house had always been full of people. They went in and out, speaking various languages, stopped in at friends' houses, but only in the course of a walk down Stradun, where again people spoke various languages, and everything seemed so close, because the conversations reached wide-open spaces from Cetinje and Boka to Vienna and Venice and really the whole world as they made their way along Stradun several times like sailors circumnavigating the world. Olga's arrival in Bosnia, to which she was actually returning as a sixteen-year-old, having been born in the town of Konjic in 1905, an event she of course did not remember, was an entrance into silence and solitude, and a very constrained place, where everything took place in a circle of a few hundred meters, the marketplace from which these people had never emerged, and their closest neighboring hick town was a distant foreign land. They had said goodbye to Usora on their way to Kakanj with tears in their eyes, as if they were heading off to a faraway land and would never see each other again. And it was a faraway land. And they never did see each other again.

Franjo was by nature closed off. He didn't need social connections, especially not of the sort one might gain around the railroads and administrative offices, among the *kuferaši*. Or, in Kakanj, among the miners. As the child of a drunk, he detested the society that gathered around rakija. All around him were drunks, ruined, disillusioned people. Out there they drank out of sorrow for the cities of Kraków or Katowice, over here it was for the towns of Zgošća and Kraljeva Sutjeska. You didn't know who was drunker or whose nostalgia heavier. Was it farther from Kakanj to Kraków or from Kakanj to Kraljeva Sutjeska? Kraljeva Sutjeska was farther. You couldn't get there anymore, and so you drank.

He was happier taking care of his books in peace or, later, his bees, than talking with people.

It seemed she needed to be responsible for connecting with others, if others were in fact needed. And it seemed that they were because it wasn't possible to forever be a lone wolf. You always needed someone.

Olga met Zehra just before she gave birth to Dragan.

Olga was twenty-one; Zehra, fifteen. I don't know how it happened, but it was probably the most important meeting of Olga's life. Zehra was the person she trusted the most, the only one to whom she told everything. She knew Zehra would keep what she told her to the grave and never tell anyone else. She also knew it was impossible to shock her. Zehra wouldn't be scandalized by Olga's longings or sensations, nor would she push her away because of them. She would always listen, following every detail to the end.

Zehra didn't go to school. She could barely read, but she was very smart. She was capable of imagining anything and empathizing with everything. Her exuberant imagination was completely under control. In her home, which Olga visited more and more often – though this was not customary, as the Muslims and Catholics of Kakanj did not mix together – the floor was of wood and the walls of adobe. Zehra's mother was proud of her floor and washed it every day so it was polished like a gold piece. For a long time their floor had been of packed earth, but then, thank God, they had got the wooden one, which would last for an entire generation.

Zehra wore a veil. All the Muslim women in Zgošća – for Kakanj was still Zgošća in terms of domestic life – did the same. It was very rare that they would take their veils off in the presence of Christian women. They didn't show their faces out of fear that the other women would describe them to their husbands. This was the same as the husbands seeing the Muslim women with their own eyes. Zehra took her veil off in front of Olga from the very start. She would do the same before Franjo when she came to the house one day. He didn't know what a wondrous thing this was, for at the time he was completely taken up with his bees, books, and useless study.

Olga was a completely liberated woman. She met everyone in town and walked around Kakanj in her Turkish trousers. Some of the *kuferaš* women found this scandalous. She didn't care, and her pride would come out. She despised the world from which she had escaped and which – probably subconsciously – she blamed for her father's being driven out of Dubrovnik, and this was why she went around in those most colorful Gypsy pantaloons. Franjo wasn't bothered. Nor did it bother him that the women talked about her. Relatives would come from Zenica and Dubrovnik, Aunt Lola and Branka came to visit, and they'd go to the Bosna River to swim. Someone brought along a camera. In the photo that's been preserved are Lola, Branka, Uncle Karlo, Aunt Jele, Franjo, Olga, and Dragan. Where is Mladen? Why isn't he there?

And then, once everyone had left, Olga was with Zehra again. They were seen rushing across the market square. Veiled and veilless. Black and colorful. By now Zehra was seventeen.

Why and how Zehra was married to a man from Sarajevo we do not know. Even the name of her husband has somehow been lost with time. We know that his family name was Orman, because for all our lives she was called Zehra Orman, and that he worked as a chauffeur in that relatively early period. And that he was a kind and very dear man.

Shortly after Zehra went away, Olga prepared to go to Sarajevo in order to see what her friend had been married into. This was just how she put it: what she had been married into. She dressed in the most festive clothes she could – the Dubrovnik outfits had been well preserved – and put on a hat that Rudi had brought from Vienna and that she could not, of course, wear in Kakanj, and, thus attired, in white, high-heeled shoes, she set out for the Ormans, on Lower Soukbunar Street, Sarajevo. She went to visit her before, as would have been proper according to tradition, Zehra's own brothers, cousins, aunts, and uncles came to see her. Olga met Zehra's husband even before her own mother did.

What must the people of Lower Soukbunar have thought when, in the autumn of 1929, Olga Rejc, née Stubler, in all her citified stateliness, appeared in their courtyard and asked, "Where is Zehra?"

They must have been surprised. And they might have been pleased, for their Zehra was so distinguished that she had brought a friend from Sarajevo the likes of whom was rarely seen even in Sarajevo. They welcomed Olga warmly, honored her, and made her stay for a gathering, then accompanied her to the station. The young and old members of the Orman household waited with Olga on the platform as they sent off a woman whom, though no one had in any way counted on it, they had acquired as part of Zehra's dowry.

However much people would talk in later years about living together and other trifles, this portion of her dowry was neither asked for nor required. At any rate, was it not those very people, Bosnia's Muslims, who had first given the offensive name of *kuferaši* to that people, letting them know that they would one day leave just as they had come, with Austrian rule, in 1878? The *kuferaši* later accepted the name, using it ironically for themselves and their expected destiny, but we must not forget how it started. Much later, under socialism, people would live together, even intermarrying – at least during that brief period before the nineties and the return to old ways – but in Sarajevo in 1929, the friendship between an illiterate girl from Kakanj and the Catholic wife of a railway worker, was seen as something unusual, strange, and threatening. Like Olga's strolling about in colorful pantaloons from the perspective of the *kuferaš* wives, though for different reasons, it must have been interpreted as a permanent scandal.

But the Ormans were good people and accepted Olga. They loved her because of their Zehra. In the non-hardheaded world, Zehras will always be more important than tenets or customs.

The eight years she spent in Kakanj, before the family moved to its final destination in Sarajevo, were the happiest of Olga's life. She lived a free and full life, raised her sons, found her place among the people, went to swim in the Bosna, participated in the large union outings, played the guitar, and perhaps forgot a little of what separated her from her husband. But the years were happy for him too. He was doing only what he wanted, what he enjoyed. Every summer he went to see his relatives in Tolmin and Kneža, and seemed to be on the threshold of his self-realization with the railroads. He expected to be transferred to Sarajevo, to the main office, as a railway traffic engineer, for he had been the most educated and able of the stationmasters and dispatchers for some time. He wasn't impatient or in a hurry to leave Kakanj, but when the telegram arrived at last with the news, he was euphoric. Though Sarajevo would always make them unhappy. It would be the city of their deaths – Franjo on Sepetarevac in October 1972, Olga in Koševo Hospital in June 1986 – a city of complete and irrepressible family tragedy, but they were not aware of this while they celebrated the fact that at last they were moving to the capital. She would be able to stroll through Sarajevo in her hats, dressed every day as if for the theater, and she could even go to the theater as often as she liked. This transfer would mark the end of the long banishment – after the court had deprived her father of work in 1921 and driven them from Dubrovnik to Bosnia – and it seemed to her that life was beginning again, or at least continuing from where it had been cut off long before. In Sarajevo he would be taken up with what interested him most, what was really the only thing that rail men enjoyed. Rather than being the chief of a single station, he would have an entire network of stations before him, and this network would be linked with other networks, and all together they would constitute an entire world. He found this world thrilling: locomotives pulling cars from Zelenika all the way to Gdańsk. Was it self-important this rejoicing of his? Or did a person not dare rejoice about anything, only weep bitter tears over what made him momentarily happy?

There Zehra and her husband were waiting for them.

He was working as a cabbie by then. This was in the thirties. People were once again coming to Sarajevo from other parts, mostly from Belgrade and Zagreb. Those two cities were competing for the goodwill of Bosnia's Muslims. One side knew that they were from time immemorial and by emotional makeup Serbs while the other knew that they were Croats for the same reason, and they themselves were measuring and deciding which side they leaned toward, just as people do the moment they believe they have a choice in life. Foreigners were coming too. The Hotel Europa was always full, as were the other shelters, and it was as if the city that had enjoyed its brightest moments during the time of Austria, along with a sweet amnesia regarding its earlier history, was recalling a bit of those distant days. Whatever their reasons for being there, plenty of people were riding around in taxis, and Zehra's husband had an overabundance of work.

One after another she gave birth to her five children. There were two by the time Olga arrived in town, and the others were all born while she was there. She told Zehra that she didn't want to have any more children. This was not an easy thing to accomplish because Franjo was pushy. He didn't understand about children, only about his male needs. Zehra understood all this. In general Zehra understood everything and was able to reduce any overlong, complicated story to two or three sentences in which everything was simple, easy, and clear. She was not embarrassed by a single one of Olga's stories – this was important, for her other friends were easily embarrassed – but rather found her way around in each one and managed to say something to comfort her. How was this possible given that Zehra was a Muslim, a very devout Muslim who kept to all the rules of her faith and did everything every day in accordance with it? The answer is strange but simple: Olga belonged to a different world and a different faith. If Olga had been a Muslim, Zehra would have died of shame, run away from her confidences, and never seen her again. But as it was, she not only did not have to run, she could always be helpful. Before Olga's faith, Zehra was always completely free, just as Olga was free before Zehra's. Never in the history of this family that is no more was there a friendship that could measure up to theirs.

They visited one another often in Sarajevo, went to Soukbunar. The Ormans came to Madam Heim's building, climbing to Olga and Franjo's apartment on the fifth floor. Zehra's husband was always available to Franjo in case he needed to go somewhere. As an older, more experienced hand, Franjo would advise him. With time Orman would come to trust him and talk about everything. Franjo listened quietly and spoke of the times ahead, of Chancellor Hitler, who was insane.

Orman continued driving his taxi during the war. There were lots of customers at the start, German and Croatian officers, Italians, businessmen, spies, and adventurers. He saw it all from his driver's perspective. Franjo warned him, told him to be careful. Orman didn't understand what that was supposed to mean. He wasn't doing anyone any harm, didn't criticize anyone, so what was there for him to be careful about? Zehra was wiser. But she needed to watch over her children. All five of them needed to be fed, and every winter was harder than the last. The stores were empty, there was nothing at the market, no more peasants were left in the surrounding villages. They had all been dispersed by the Ustaše.

After Mladen's death, in the early fall of 1943, Olga and Franjo were in the grips of a definitive collapse. Zehra left her children with her sister-in-law to stay with Olga for five days and nights straight. But there was really no help for it.

If I hadn't had Zehra, Olga said, I would have killed myself. And that was the only thing she ever said about Mladen's death.

Perhaps it was true. But besides this, there was no help for it. It was not possible to help those two with what was happening in their souls upon losing their son, not even from that outsider's place that Zehra occupied. For it was not just one death. Others lost sons in the war but were later able to find consolation and peace. This was different. Franjo had been against the idea of Mladen's accepting the summons to serve and going into the German army, but Olga thought her son would be more likely to be saved in the German army than among the Partisans. She thought Franjo was rooting for his child to join the Partisan forces because of his own political convictions. Never did he cease to blame her, even if only in silence, for Mladen's death, and never did she manage to ease her own conscience.

Zehra and her husband continued trying to take care of her for as long as they could afterward. Olga remained mute and closed for a long time, and who knows how much she needed to confess everything to Zehra. In the end, it would be too late.

As the war drew to its end, fewer and fewer people had money for taxi rides. Even the German officers collapsed and fell to pieces. The high Ustaše and Home Guard dignitaries also disappeared, and all that was left were hooligans and riff-raff. The sort who didn't pay even when they rode in a taxi. Franjo told him now was the time to be more careful than ever, and they just needed to hold out until the war was over. My children are hungry, Orman told Franjo once. Good Lord, said Franjo, let them be hungry as long as they're alive! The poor man didn't understand why Franjo was saying such a thing to him. He thought Franjo was talking that way because he had lost Mladen.

Without asking about anything or talking to anyone, in March 1945 Zehra's husband made a fateful mistake: leaving behind his taxi work, because for months he hadn't been earning anything from it, he volunteered as a driver for the Ustaše police. A month later he would find himself in a column headed for Zagreb. He was driving a Home Guard colonel. He supposedly sent a telegram once he got to Zagreb, a day before Sarajevo was liberated. At least that was what Zehra was told. Your husband sent a telegram from Zagreb, they said. She couldn't tell whether they were just taunting her, since a new time had come, or if he really had done it. I swear on the cross, he sent a telegram, said the source.

Zehra's husband disappeared the same way thousands of Croats did, soldiers and civilians, minor officials and major ones, the notables of Independent Croatia. There is an additional irony in the way the event came to be called: "the Way of the Cross." The driver Orman from Soukbunar disappeared during the Bleiburg massacre on the Way of the Cross as he was trying to feed his five children.

The only thing Zehra had in 1945 was a kind and self-sacrificing mother-in-law, who helped her with everything. She supported her, too, in the terrible choice that had to be made. As the wife of an enemy of the people, an Ustaše driver, she and her five children were condemned to ruin. She believed in God, trusted in him and his greatness, and did not shed a tear for her husband, but still she removed her veil and headscarf and went out to the site where she labored as a construction worker. Alongside the men, she carried pails full of cement on her shoulders, that tiny, nearly invisible woman. When she finished her work, she would put her headscarf and veil back on and return home.

They slandered her on Soukbunar Street, the neighbors and the others. This was before the time when it was forbidden for Muslim women to cover themselves and before the time when women would go out on the street with their faces bare.

Oh, Olga, I feel naked before you, she complained.

It was indeed rare for her to complain about anything. She was always smiling, kind, well disposed, and certain that everything would turn out well, and what seemed to us nonbelievers to be turning out poorly, the suffering and death of loved ones, that was all God's will and some deeply serious plan of his.

There was a time when there were no stores and nothing that one might have put in stores. People lived by coupons and tokens that were acquired partly according to need and partly for services rendered. Zehra and her family got what they could, along with fruit from the Stubler garden in Ilidža and the slim pickings brought from Kakanj, but it was all too little.

Olga went to Soukbunar, bringing Zehra ground and powdered barley mixed with coffee. There wasn't any sugar, nor would there be for years. Olga also brought her little daughter, born during the war, even though she swore to Zehra she wouldn't have any more children. But abortions were punished by death in the Ustaše state. The small, blond-haired girl was frightened when she went into the house. Everything was different from what she was used to. The smell was strange. Her eyes were large like those in a Bruno Schulz drawing. Zehra hugged her, though she tried to slip away.

Salko was a little younger than Javorka, so she could order him around. He did everything she told him and seemed pleased. He laughed. Olga and Zehra sat drinking the barley coffee and talking for a long time. They didn't even look at the children. In that moment, they saw only each other.

Okay, now you tell me what to do, Javorka said to Salko. But her mom got up at that point and they went home.

Seven days passed. Olga took Javorka by the hand and they went to Zehra's on Soukbunar. The little girl said nothing, but was pleased.

When they got there, everything was the same, the strange smell, the dark room. But someone was missing.

"Where's Salko?" the girl asked?

And Zehra answered her calmly: "Ah, my child, Salko died."

That was the first time Javorka encountered finality. And only then was it so peaceful. Zehra's eyes remained dry for she believed that somewhere somehow everything was as it ought to be, by God's will. Before Salko the youngest, Azra. That too she had endured calmly. Zehra's children died of poverty and hunger.

It is difficult to discuss such things today. One would need to return to that time in order to see how things were: one day you're drinking barley coffee with your friend, your daughter playing with her son, and seven days later the child is gone.

Three of her children remained: Mehmed, Nadja, and Munira. Her daughters became dressmakers. Her son worked as a porter. She managed to put them on track. Sarajevo's mayor, the former Partisan Dane Olbina, took pity on her and helped by finding her a job as a cleaning woman at Sarajevo's National Assembly. Fortune smiled on her. She came back to herself.

And only when she had completed one thing after another, in those May days of 1966, when the little girl who had played with Salko gave birth to a boy, did Olga's Zehra grow ill. Liver cancer. Javorka's husband, the boy's father, Doctor Jergović had Zehra placed in the very best room of his ward. She was so grateful that she never stopped smiling. They would visit Zehra in the hospital that summer and fall, until Olga and Franjo moved with their newborn grandson to Drvenik because of Franjo's asthma. Olga visited Zehra for the last time on a Friday at the end of September. It was not easy. Zehra smiled and said, "You, my friend, you're headed to the seaside, but now's the time when everyone else is coming back from there."

Zehra died in December. Olga's little sister had died earlier that year, in March. I took Zehra's death harder than Rika's, Olga once said. If she hadn't been there, I would have killed myself.

The Frančićs: Joža, and Muc

Josip Frančić worked as an electrical engineer in the mine. He was there by the time Olga and Franjo arrived in Kakanj. He was sincere and outgoing, always talking with the miners and the ordinary, unlettered people of Zgošća. He did not immediately stand out as a gentleman, but a gentleman he was, having completed all his schooling in Graz and Vienna. There too he met his wife, who came with him to Kakanj and stayed. Her name was Marija, but no one called her that. According to Kakanj customs and Bosnian speech patterns, her nickname was nearly unpronouncible, but everyone agreed to try, even the poorest of people, out of respect for the engineer. They called her Muc.

Olga and Franjo grew close to them very quickly, but no one remembers anymore how that happened. Joža was one of the rare men among the miners who didn't drink. Muc would bring fashion magazines from Vienna, opera-length gloves and hats, romance novels, books by Karl Kraus and Stefan Zweig, crystal services and other things that Olga was interested in, and so, rather naturally, as Joža put it, a "symbiosis" occurred between the two *kuferaš* families. What Olga found in Zehra touched her emotional and spiritual world, as well as her femininity, while what Muc brought was culture and a spirit of Viennese false luxury.

When she thought about Rudi's long years of "study" in Vienna and Graz, Olga envied him a little, so that Muc came to occupy the place of what she might have had herself, had she not got married so early and had children.

Muc had a completely clear, intimate, and adopted Kakanj manner of speaking. The language of the *kuferaši* overflowed with Germanicisms, so hers did too. But as a born Austrian who had not known a word of the local language before coming to Kakanj, she pronounced even the Germanisms as they did in Kakanj. As if they weren't her words and it wasn't her language.

She behaved toward the local women in accordance with her nature – capriciously, such that some of them called her the crazy Swabian. They shut their windows when she went through the marketplace. They covered up their children so she couldn't give them the evil eye. But she made others laugh, the Catholics mostly and some of the Muslims. They found her silly but nice. And they didn't mind if some of her silliness was imparted to them or their children. Zehra said of Muc that even the good Lord was surprised at the miracle when he saw someone like her and heard her speak.

Muc would give birth to two sons in this backwater at the edge of the world.

In the peace and screaming of a birth at dawn, exactly like the women of Zgošća give birth. And never would it enter her head among all her fashion magazines that she might be missing something by not giving birth as they did in Vienna. The eldest son would be called as the eldest son was always called: Josip, like his father, grandfather, and great-grandfather. The younger son was Branko.

Joža had an engineer's mind, Franjo said. Politics did not interest him.

He *paid no heed* to king or country.

He could talk about everything, just not politics.

As the years passed, and everything happened that had to happen along with much that did not, Franjo would go on about why Joža pretended to be an idiot whenever he mentioned Stjepan Radić, Comrade Lenin, or Benito Mussolini. He'd look off to one side, yawn, or asked Franjo in surprise why he was worried so much about things over which he could have absolutely no influence. It was better for him to take care of his bees and the railway schedules. Let other people make the revolution. There were two kinds of fools in the world, Joža said, the ones who set fires all around in order to make people happy, and the ones who put them out. You know how they put out a fire in Dalmatia when the north wind has brought it roaring toward the olives and grape vines? With a counter-fire. They spill benzene on the underbrush in a long line to light it. When the two come together, the counter-fire usually overpowers the other.

Franjo remembered the story, though it didn't turn him away from politics. Why did he tell it? To spare him from something?

The Frančićs stayed in Kakanj for several years after Franjo and Olga left. They moved to Mostar before the war. The bond between them did not weaken, though now they only saw one another rarely. They exchanged letters and Christmas cards, but none of that was preserved. After Mladen's death Olga took pains to eliminate this correspondence too. As if she feared that someone might collect all those papers and reconstruct their own story against her will, from the days when she'd first met Franjo to the moment when the unknown Partisan sighted his rifle and pulled the trigger as if he were shooting a wild pig. Or perhaps she thought she could simply wipe away her memory by destroying all the papers and photos.

The last time Franjo and Joža spoke was by phone on April 6, 1941.

He was sitting in his office at headquarters when around ten in the morning someone announced that all the phone lines were cut and another wave of German bombers was expected. He wanted to verify whether this was true, so he opened his notebook with phone numbers and called Joža Frančić. They exchanged a few words, not knowing what to say to each other, and that was that.

How many months would pass before the Ustaše discovered the illegal communist group whose leader was the engineer Josip Frančić? Time passed differently during the war. The logic of war time is such that soon a person no longer knows when things happen, so neither Olga nor Franjo could be sure when the news reached them that Joža had been condemned to death and was gone. It surely took place before Mladen's conscription into the German army. Olga was convinced that the only important thing was that Mladen remain as far away from the Ustaše and their courts as possible, which meant in the German army. Franjo thought the only place to run from a fate like Joža's was to the Partisans.

He was bothered a little by the question of why Joža had pretended not to be interested in politics all those years. Could it have been the notorious Party secrecy? Or did he have doubts about Franjo's trustworthiness? This sort of thought offended him, and he would grow angry at the executed man Joža Frančić, to whom, were he able, he would explain how wrong he had been by being friends with someone for so many years, visiting him, playing with his sons, while at the same time seeing him as too untrustworthy to confide his faith. It was pathetic, he would have said, but he couldn't. Because Joža was no more. He had believed more in the miners than Franjo. Now this was as clear as day. He had been agitating among the miners all that time. He'd had more faith in the poorest illiterate villager. And Franjo had thought Joža was his friend.

"He protected you," Olga told him.

"From what?"

"From your own craziness around Kakanj and your loose tongue. Joža wasn't pathetic. He saved your neck while you didn't even know who or what he was."

Muc stayed on her own in Mostar with her sons. Toward the end of the war, they were mobilized, one after the other as they reached the legal age. Joža and Branko would find themselves in that endless column of the Croatian Home Guard and Ustaše, office workers and the occasional disguised cutthroat, the same one for whom the Sarajevo taxi driver Orman was behind the wheel of a black Mercedes. They would cover the long route described by the arch of their march, which would in its sense and content remain incomparable in their existential and emotional experience. And the hardest thing was that if they lived through it they would take a lifelong vow of silence about what had happened to them along the way.

They let Branko go first. He was seventeen. Pavelić had dressed him up in the uniform of the Croatian armed forces when he was a student, the same uniform worn by the most hardened Ustaše, the butchers of Jasenovac, in order to assimilate him and the entire generation of children born in 1927 with those murderers. This was how Pavelić led the children under a collective Croatian destiny, driving ·

them forth like lambs into the anger of the war's victors. For the most part the Partisans simply turned away the generation of 1927, stripping them of their uniforms and sending them home.

By contrast to his brother, Joža crossed over from the south of Austria, where he had been imprisoned, to the south of Serbia, where, as one of the rare survivors, he was at last set free, and not even because they'd figured out that he hadn't done anything wrong. It would have been a sin to kill him after he had managed to get to Niš in one piece.

His mother asked, "Did you tell anyone what happened to your father?"

"I had no one to tell."

"How come?"

He didn't know how to explain to his mother that in the thousands of kilometers he had walked, attended by the rifle barrels of the liberators, he had not found a single person to whom he, Lance Sergeant Josip Frančić, could have explained what had happened to his father, the engineer Josip Frančić, in order to save himself.

After the war Muc came with her sons to Sarajevo. She brought them both to Olga and Franjo to tell about what happened to them. This took a long time. They came in the afternoon but didn't leave until the next morning, when they took the first tram. The two boys did not complain – what could they have complained about and to whom in liberated Sarajevo in 1947? They would not recall it anymore. Probably never again.

Marija Frančić lived as a retiree in Sarajevo.

I remember going to visit her with Nona at the beginning of the seventies. When the world the two of them had lived in was gone, Olga stopped calling Marija Frančić Muc. She quit using the name because it had become funny. Or it reminded her of something. In this way, Muc became Frančićka, or Mrs. Frančić. A loud, cheerful woman, she held herself very straight and was a bit loony in her own way. She could not do without men, which made Olga shudder. And when it didn't make her shudder, it made her laugh. She had one boyfriend named Stojan, a farmer from Herzegovina, who would visit her in Sarajevo. She told Olga about him as if she were an eighteen-year-old in love. Olga would watch her as the story unfolded. When it stopped, she would be quiet, waiting for it to continue.

This sentence, which Olga pronounced after Zehra's death, she said only once, and it was in front of Mrs. Frančić: "I took Zehra's death harder than my sister's. If she hadn't been there, I would have killed myself."

And for me it would have been easier if both my sons had suffered, as long as my Joža lived, said Muc, surprised that they were even talking about such things.

Then she sighed deeply, looking at Olga, then at Javorka, and started up again happily, "Now my Stojan . . ."

Marija Frančić died in the midseventies. She was buried at Sarajevo's Bare Cemetery.

Erwin and Munevera

My great-grandmother's mother Josefina Patat, a poor woman from near Udine, gave birth seventeen times, to be left with only two living children. Despite so many deaths, the Patats were one of the longest, most lighthearted and beautiful family connections of the Stublers, especially Josefina's sister's grandchildren. The brothers Erich and Erwin Dussel were, like their parents, Viennese by birth, and besides the thin kinship through their poor Italian relations, nothing visibly connected them to the family of Karlo Stubler, a *kuferaš* rail man from Bosnia. But invisible ties between people can be stronger and more important than visible ones, and we had no better or more devoted relatives than them.

Erich, Erwin, and Aunt Dora, with whom Rudi had an incestuous affair during his long years of study in Vienna, were our link to Austria, to Vienna, and to what Karlo and Johanna, and so their children too, experienced as their cultural and linguistic homeland. The Dussel home, whose door was always open to the Stublers, in a manner that was surprising even according to Balkan customs, was an important place should there be any need – if someone had to leave Bosnia, if anyone needed somewhere to go for a time. No one ever took advantage of this opportunity, but it was important that it existed for nearly the entire twentieth century. So important that one could say the Dussels were a principal guarantor of our civic stability. We had someone to turn to if we were driven away.

The Stublers often went to Vienna before the First World War, when Karlo had a high-ranking position as station chief in Dubrovnik, and continued to do so between the two wars, such that the drawers, photo albums, and shoe boxes contained dozens of black-and-white photos in which Karlo's daughters were strolling about the Ring, posing in front of Vienna cafés in all seasons of the year, all dressed up and behatted like the heroines of silent film comedies.

And so the three of them, Erich, Erwin, and Aunt Dora, started coming to Sarajevo too. Our journey to Vienna was long, but theirs to Sarajevo must have seemed much farther. They were headed to meet their cousins in the Orient, in a great city filled with fatal passions, doom, and dark inclinations that in their imaginations hinted of jasmine, cinnamon, and a thousand unfamiliar eastern scents. The fact, moreover, that this was the city where the Habsburg prince had been killed did not act as a favorable recommendation. But they were curious and did not want to offend their dear relations.

They started coming in 1933 or one of the three years that followed and continued to visit until the late seventies. The world turned on its head during those forty years. Karlo, Johanna, and all their children except the youngest, Olga, died, and the most beautiful love story of the family's history took place.

Erich and Erwin studied and completed degrees in architecture, from which they would derive a good and stable living. Neither had great professional ambitions. Their profession served as a way of satisfying their thirst for pleasure and everyday indulgences. They had no pretensions toward eternal greatness. So they were not interested in politics, and the arrival of Hitler in power, the Anschluss, and the beginning of the war in the Dussels' homeland was experienced at first as something that didn't especially concern them and later as some sort of uncontrollable act of nature, a storm or catastrophic earthquake that needed to be simply lived through without excessive grumbling and theorizing. In this attitude, the Dussels were typical Viennese petit bourgeois.

And being such, they ended up in the battle for Stalingrad.

How they managed to get out of there, what saved them, and by what miracle they avoided a Soviet prison – about these things they never spoke. As a rule, one did not speak with the two of them much about misfortune. In the home in which a son was lost in the war – Karlo's grandson Mladen had died as a German soldier – the war was not spoken of. And never was how someone survived discussed. A story about such miracles of salvation only served to sadden those who had not experienced them.

It was years after the war before it was possible to freely acquire passports and for the Stublers, their children, and grandchildren, to head once again toward Vienna. But Erwin was visiting his family in Sarajevo by 1951. And this is where the story would begin if it were possible. On the street, somewhere around Ilidža, he met a woman who looked as if she were not from this world. She looked that way to Erwin, but perhaps not to others. They told him she was a singer at the radio station. What was her name? Munevera Berberović.

He returned to Vienna. He traveled by train across the devastated, destitute country, across the homeland of his eastern relations, and if until then he hadn't understood them, if on any occasion he had thought that they were living for no reason in the obviously unhappy and pitiful country of Bosnia, from which they would one day have to leave, now his heart was torn as he returned home. Erwin Dussel could imagine the rest of his life clearly on that early fall day in 1951. He would live and die unfulfilled, and as pitiful as Bosnia, for something had happened to him that probably only happens in songs from that land: he had seen a woman, had not approached her, but instead set out on a journey away from her, and now could do nothing but think back to that first glimpse.

He came again the next summer. And then again. And again. By 1954, before even the first Stubler could travel to Vienna after the Second World War, Erwin Dussel had settled in Sarajevo. There he lived a full three years, in Ilidža, employed by some architectural firm, but never would he learn our language. He understood it very well, but could not speak. He would be quiet, listening. And then he would say something in German. During those three years he painted hundreds of Bosnian watercolors. He painted landscapes and cityscapes of old

Sarajevo. Typical of the genre paintings of European travelers to Bosnia. Erwin was probably one of the last such travelers.

We didn't know, nor would we discover, what the love story of Erwin Dussel and Munevera Berberović was like. He was silent about how they met, when they saw each other, what drew them apart. Free from the surrounding life, from all that was ugly and unpleasant, from complaints about differences of faith, nation, and language, from the gossip of loose-tongued neighbors, family scandals, children born out of wedlock and abortions, this love of theirs, until the end of the Stublers and Stubler memory – which took place with the death of the last one to remember Erwin and Munevera – evoked a strange inner light in anyone who recalled it. Though it didn't last long and was ended by their own decision, it was a complete love. So complete as to be impossible to write about.

Later Munevera Berberović went on to sing for our guest workers in Germany and Austria. But she never sang in Vienna. There was no anger or sorrow in this. Whenever she would meet Olga, Rudi, or Franjo in town, or when she met Javorka, who was still very young, her first question was always, how is my Erwin doing? And he would ask the same about her during every telephone conversation, at every meeting. But when he came to Sarajevo, he would not try to meet her. Everyone knew this, and no one tried to convince him otherwise.

Rudi, Javorka, and my father Dobro traveled to Vienna in 1970. Rudi took them on a tour of the places of his youth. They went to southern Germany, visited Strasbourg, but Vienna was the most important. Here Rudi had studied, fallen in love, and, indeed, had an affair with his cousin, for which he was ashamed his whole life. Javorka and Dobro were no longer together, having officially divorced, but they pretended they were. Rudi would have liked things to be different. He wanted to get them back together. He was impressed by the fact that Dobro was a physician. Besides, he was a good man to have as a friend – kind, and it seemed he would be an ideal husband and father. Why this was not the case is a long story. It would take as long as telling how these two newly divorced people found themselves on such a trip that seemed more appropriate for newlyweds.

Rudi convinced Erwin to meet at one of the cafés where he had caroused as a youngster. Even though forty-five years had passed, he would have been able to find his way around there with his eyes closed. He'd been a daily visitor. He knew Vienna better than Sarajevo. He was at home in Vienna.

Erwin arrived. They had a beer together, then went to Erwin's. A large, old Viennese structure in which he'd had an architect's design studio built in the courtyard. Everything was very expensive and luxurious. Erwin was married to Monika, the daughter of a Swedish industrialist.

He asked how their trip was. Javorka said she got lice on the train. We'll fix that, Erwin said, laughing. And before they could run over to the pharmacy, for the best anti-lice medicine in the world, which Javorka would talk about to the end of her life, he asked, "How is Munevera?"

There was nothing melancholy in the question. He did not ask as someone who had missed some opportunity in life or had lived in vain, not having returned to the woman he had fallen in love with. Erwin returned to Vienna, having lived out his love story with Munevera, and the fact that it wasn't lifelong took nothing from the sense of fulfillment. Such a three-year love was enough for one person's life.

Munevera Berberović never married and did not live long. Her name is recalled from time to time in the newspapers. Her voice is preserved on audiotapes of Radio Sarajevo, and some of her pictures have even appeared on the Internet. When I listen to the tapes, I try to imagine the woman my distant relation Erwin Dussel fell in love with. I met him one summer in the midseventies, at my father's vacation home on Trebević. On my way back, as always, I had a fever. The air in my father's gray Renault 4 was a mixture of gasoline and Erwin's cologne. They were discussing something heatedly in German. I didn't understand them. I just wanted to get home as soon as possible. The fevers were short lived.

The Croat

For years I told her to collect the documents and submit her request. It would take at most one morning, and then she would be at peace. It was a precaution. She promised me she would today, then tomorrow, but both of us knew she wouldn't. The one thing we weren't sure about was why. Maybe during the years when she was in good health and all around there was peace, she just didn't feel like going from office to office. In those first years after the war, Sarajevo had become her city, a little crazy, collapsed in on itself, intimate, just as she was crazy, collapsed, and happy, so much so that perhaps she could not imagine the conditions of misfortune and evil in which she would need Croatian citizenship. She was afraid it might be seen as a betrayal, as if she might turn out to be some sort of traitor to herself by taking up that foreign passport and, along with it, like a school report card, that thing they called a certificate of domicile. Half of Bosnia and a good part of Sarajevo's inhabitants, of different faiths and nations, had managed to acquire Croatian citizenship. Even President Silajdžić's minister of foreign affairs had it, along with who knows how many others about whom we just didn't know, but somewhere in a linen drawer, beneath their socks and underwear, they kept their Croatian documents. Everyone knew this, but still for some reason she resisted. She felt more secure with her one identity card and her long-since-expired passport of Bosnia and Herzegovina. Whenever anyone might say something to her, then she could tell them. That's how she always began: whenever anyone says something to me . . .

When she got sick, the question of the papers turned serious. She underwent one operation, then another, and it suddenly became almost certain that she would need to go to Zagreb. And so, at the moment in which her life was breaking down, she became a foreigner. Even though this wasn't the first time she'd experienced it. Her parents had lived mostly as foreigners in Bosnia, her grandfather having been driven out of Dubrovnik to Bosnia as a foreigner; her brother had died as a soldier in a foreign enemy's army; and all of life was the experience of one long foreign journey passed on from generation to generation. But only now did this fact hit her with all its intensity. Being a foreigner meant being a person whose right to existence was protected in some other place. Where was that place? In Sarajevo, the city where she was born, she did not want to get a Croatian passport unless someone said something to her. This is the sort of feeling that is experienced only by someone who feels herself a foreigner in her own city. And because she was a foreigner in Sarajevo, she was condemned to be a foreigner in Zagreb too.

In the consular section of the embassy of the Croatian Republic in Sarajevo, on the fourth day of June 2012, a report with reference number 521-BIH-01/03-EP-12-02 was filed on the acquisition of Croatian citizenship. The report was begun at 1200 hours and completed at 1255. It was a Monday, a sunny, very pretty day of the sort that everyone knows comes along in May and June in Sarajevo, especially when a person is ill or separated by some other misfortune from the comforts of life all around. By then she was having a hard time getting around, but she had good people around her, male and female friends, cabbies from Mejtaš with whom she had maintained close ties since before the war. She knew them all by name, what their lives were like, how many children they had, their life's main anguish, the one they told their first customer about every morning. As a rule, the people who lived on steep streets got close to their cabbies after the war. This surely had some connection to the affordability of the prices.

What happened at fifty-five minutes after the hour in the Croatian consulate at 17 Skenderija Street? It would be easy to reconstruct, for everything is still fresh. We know it well. We know what she would have said at that moment, how she would have captivated the attention of her interlocutor as she took up her place at center stage. But the event itself is not important. More interesting is what was happening inside her head and soul, to which we no longer have access. More interesting is the part we cannot even surmise, no matter how well we knew her, and no matter how much we might recognize some of her motives within us today. How did she feel when she was giving her conscious assent to something she had avoided all those years? She was ill and wasn't thinking about what someone else might say to her about all this. When she was getting her Croatian citizenship, she was feeling that I would be taking her away to Zagreb, to the best hospitals and the best doctors, who did not merely treat people but rather performed miracles. Sarajevo doctors treated people, sometimes even mistakenly, but in Zagreb there were miracles. And this would be hard without citizenship, because getting treatment in Croatia as a foreigner was as expensive as it was in Switzerland.

The record of her declaration reads as follows:

This request for the acquisition of Croatian citizenship is based on the fact of belonging to the Croatian people. On the occasion of this request I have compiled documents proving my and my family's belonging to the Croatian nation. I declare that I am a Croat and that I feel myself to be such, which is clear from the attached declaration and its appendices. It can be concluded from my conduct that I observe the legal order of the Republic of Croatia. I know and employ the Croatian language. I follow cultural events in the Republic of Croatia. I have appended an original work notebook to this request, which I hope will be returned to me at the end of the process. Given that I have problems with my health, I was not in a position to collect additional documents to show that I have consistently self-identified as a Croat. All the appended documents show without a doubt both my heritage and my feeling of belonging to the Croatian nation. Until my retirement I worked at the university's School of Education as director of the accounting department. I thank you in advance for this request.

Kind people were with her. The first secretary at the embassy, who "entered the statement into the proceedings," was kind too. But every time I read these words, I am overcome by a feeling of distress, which immediately turns to anger. Nothing ever changes this, despite the passage of time, and soon I would know by heart the pattern according to which the melody would rise or fall by half-tones upon each subsequent repetition in the theme and variations of her Croatianness before the institutions of a foreign country, before God, and especially before an entire lived life and that of several generations past.

Was she lying? It depends on what one considers a lie. She was a Croat – this was known even by the Bosniak-Muslim poet who, in a drunken tirade outside the Dva Ribara restaurant ten months earlier, before the tumor was yet visible, cursed out her son by referring to his Ustaše mother – and when she spoke of feeling herself to be and self-declaring as a Croat, she touched on her own feelings of guilt. She had not sought out this Croatian citizenship for such a long time precisely because she felt guilty for having a right to it.

When did she become a Croat? Perhaps it was the moment when her uncle Rudolf Stubler had the death certificate of his father Karlo made. It was April 1951 and the time of hardline Yugoslav communism, Sarajevan "brotherhood and unity." When the clerk asked for the nationality of the deceased, fear washed over Rudi telling him to be cautious. Opapa was dead, he didn't care anymore. He said – Croatian. Thus did his father, a German throughout his life, become a Croat upon death. There were Croats among her ancestors, and there were other emotional, cultural, and faith-based reasons why a *kuferaš* in the Sarajevo of the day might have felt herself to be a Croat, but her Croatianness was marked by the Stubler shame. In 1945 the Partisans were leading Karlo off to a concentration camp as a member of the German minority when he was saved by his Serbian neighbors from Kasidol in Ilidža. Here six years later he had become a dead Croat.

Everything in her family that was unhappy and accursed, everything confused, left out, foreign, and rotten, was Croatian. Croatia had made its appearance a year before her birth. Croatia had dressed her brother in a German uniform. And then Croatia had killed him, disappearing from Sarajevo in 1945 and leaving her to live with her Croatianness. So, really, who could better belong to the Croatian nation than she?

She had been a member of the Slovene cultural society Ivan Cankar. Through her work there, she could have acquired Slovene citizenship from her Slovene father, who had actually once been an Italian citizen as he was a native of Kneža near Tolmin. She'd spoken the language a little, having attended some courses and made friends. Just as she had made friends with the members of the Croatian mountain climbers club. She had a good singing voice and was a good storyteller. On one broadcast of Radio Vrhbosna she told the story – in a quite thrilling manner – of the fate of a certain German family in Sarajevo . . .

She was in no way lying before the officials at the consulate when she repeatedly claimed her Croatianness, she was just silent on certain points. Many people are silent on certain points when they claim citizenship, or they attempt to boil down their various kinds of belonging to just one. She had no one before whom to pronounce this final truth, which I will pronounce once more in her place. Everything in her family that was unhappy and accursed, everything confused, left out, foreign and rotten, everything born in Sarajevo only to disappear from Sarajevo, was Croatian.

How difficult this sentence was for her: *I have appended an original employment record book to this request, which I hope will be returned to me at the end of the process.* Still today, somewhere in some drawer of the consular section on Skenderija, sits her little workbook with its gray canvas cover and the embossed coat of arms of the Republic of Bosnia and Herzegovina and the chimneys from which smoke constantly winnows. The day awaits when it will be tossed out and recycled with the other documents that have reached their expiration date, with the old registries and files, the last remnants of the pre-computer age. Although she didn't work a single day of her forty years in the labor force in Croatia, this document will be destroyed along with the historical memory of her dedication when a Croatian institution determines that it should be.

And a second sentence: *I follow cultural events in the Republic of Croatia.* All the rest is simply filling out a form, using repeated phrases that others have uttered countless times around her, but this sentence is completely hers. Who else would say that they follow the cultural events in Croatia while asking for citizenship? But not even she, someone who really was interested in culture, wanted to say that. She wanted to say something else. Something that could not be put into the record but in which she had the greatest hope. She wanted to mention her son and did it by means of this unusual allusion. She believed he would help her.

In sickness and dying a person no longer lives by balancing on the thin thread between past and future. The thread stretches out, becoming as wide as a runway, and for the first time the person lives in the present. She only hopes to prolong it, looking back all the while. This is how it was with her.

Meanwhile, as her body grew ever thinner, simulating a single point of universal pain, hope grew ever more powerful. Hope in the miracle of healing, in Zagreb. The problem, however, was that her illness could only be treated in Sarajevo, using some ungodly expensive German experimental technique. A similar kind of experiment had been discontinued in Zagreb several months earlier.

She was horribly angry with her Sarajevo physician. This made it easier for her. Such an inexplicable, undeserved, ghastly way of dying, and the humiliation of ending a life in such a way, had to be rationalized somehow. Clearly and cleanly, so that all the columns came out equal and every total was correct, like in a well-made accounting report. So the doctor had to be at fault.

I went to see her one summer day on one of the upper floors of the central clinic. An imposing handsome woman, who probably expected me to be a clearinghouse for her patient's anger. In the office space behind her, on a board where offices display nice notes, messages, and photographs, there was a picture of a large, shaggy white dog. It was very old and sick. I asked her about it. In this way, the Sarajevo doctor, whose name was Maja, and I shared our grief. I suppose that dog is no longer alive now either.

I told my mother she would not have a better doctor if she lived in Houston. You mustn't be angry with her, I said severely. I didn't want to acknowledge in any way that she was dying. If I did, hope would disappear.

The illness was quicker than the process for determining whether she belonged to the Croatian nation. After all the files had been filed and the protocols protocoled, the documents were sent to Zagreb according to policy. (Perhaps her workbook is in a drawer in Zagreb?) In Zagreb they might have opened up the package or not. In metaphysical collusion with the sentence "I follow cultural events in the Republic of Croatia," I found a man who could be of help, if I needed it, in the Ministry of Internal Affairs in Zagreb. But in September and October the illness made such progress in its work that such an operation lost all sense.

During her final month, which was November, it occurred to me that maybe the decision by which she would be accepted into the Croatian citizenry would arrive all by itself. The thought reminded me of the end of David Albahari's novel *Tsing*:

The apartment quickly filled with people: women worked in the kitchen, men drank brandy in the dining room. There was nothing to be said: everybody already knew everything. Then somebody rang the doorbell, and when I opened it, a girl asked me if I wanted to buy life insurance She had light hair and bright eyes; I also noticed the rounded shape of her knees. I shook my head and closed the door. Angels always come too late.

But no one called or looked for me to tell me that the case had been settled. Maybe somehow they knew that she'd died? I doubt it. That kind of news takes decades to reach the institutions of officialdom.

Such an ending is in keeping with the poetics of our family extinction. My mother's spirit floats above the thin strip of no-man's-land between Bosnia and Croatia, hoping for a miracle.

But her story does have one other ending, contained in the last sentence of her declaration before the consular officials: *I thank you in advance for this request.* She needed to put, "for your response to this request." As it is, she seems to be thanking the officials for the request without anticipating a response. Angels sometimes reside in grammatical errors. If ever anyone would say something to her, then she would tell them . . .

Hunger, Colored Pebbles

My mother's first memories are from April 1945.

She would be four years old soon, her mother was carrying her to a shelter, the sky was being torn by Allied bombers. They were tearing it like the dark cloth that would be torn into rags on the floor. The little girl wasn't afraid. Going into the shelter was a big event. Everyone was there.

Between Madam Heim's building where we lived and the National Theater were crooked little Bosnian houses made of wood and adobe. Families from those houses came to our shelter. Little Kemo came too. He was a year or two older than my mother and lived in the tiniest of the houses, closest to the theater.

The first memory in my mother's life was Kemo sitting across from the shelter entrance eating a big piece of pie. It was a time of famine. The piece might not have been that big, but she hadn't ever seen one bigger, nor would she ever again.

"Mama, mama, look, Kemo's eating a pie!" shouted the little girl. This was the first sentence she remembered ever uttering.

Next she remembered Mrs. Matić, the neighbor from the third floor, the mother of Seka and Sinek. Mrs. Matić's husband was a Serb, but she was a native of Zagreb.

Sinek was stupid: he went off to the Chetniks at the beginning of the war.

Everyone knew this, but Mrs. Matić and her husband Ðuro were left alone. There she was, sitting in the shelter on top of an army fuel tank, tasting something from a pot she'd brought inside with her.

It could be the same raid or two different ones: one day Kemo was eating a pie, and another Mrs. Matić was scooping from a pot. They were indistinguishable from each other in her early memories. She remembered the food. The spring of 1945 was hungry, and it would be no better for the next several years.

She didn't remember the end of the war, the entrance of the Partisans into the city, or the great changes that took place. As a child, she didn't experience any of that, but then nothing was as memorable as Kemo's pie.

She played outside in the Temple yard. It was a heaven for the kids from our building. It was covered with colored pebbles. She gathered some up and brought them home. Her mother looked away. Her father said nothing. The next time, he took them away and said, "These are not to be played with!"

This etched itself deep in her memory. Even though she hadn't been hiding anything and he did not yell at her, the little girl felt ashamed. She remembered it because of the shame.

In April 1941, during Sarajevo's first raid, before she was born, a bomb had fallen on the synagogue located beside Madam Heim's building and damaged it. A day later a bunch of local riffraff had desecrated the synagogue. I would hear stories about this horrible event, which my Nono and Nona watched from their window, for the rest of my life. What the little girl heard was an argument against each and every form of nationalism and racism, especially anti-Semitism, something her parents had witnessed and experienced and because of which they felt lifelong shame. They had done nothing. What could they have done, oppose the Ustaše?

It went without saying that the Ustaše and their helpers were the ones who had ravaged the Temple. I grew up with this fact, which was spoken of and passed along through time. It defined our attitudes and actions.

Several years ago the Zagreb historian Zlatko Hasanbegović admonished me about the error. Which was not really an error but rather an entire creed written into and certified by family memory. The Ustaše, in fact, arrived in Sarajevo several days after the synagogue's destruction, which took place during the days of anarchy. It had been a spontaneous act of barbarism by Sarajevo hooligans, joined by local Muslims and Gypsies. They took away the menorahs, unfurled the Torah scrolls, threw out the furniture, caroused and plundered . . . It was they and not any Ustaše or Germans whom Nono and Nona had watched from their apartment window.

Nono and Nona would certainly not have survived the reprisal of the Ustaše or opposing their fellow citizens driven to pillage the Temple out of blind hatred toward the Jews – this hatred was obviously something much older than Pavelić and Hitler, and in Sarajevo one did not speak of it. But while it was happening, neither of them knew what the future would bring, and in truth, they, like the other people in Madam Heim's building, were complicit in the evil that unfolded.

But maybe they wiped the truth from their minds because they had to keep on living with those people. Ustaše come and go. Others will always step in to be the Ustaše. They were never our fellow citizens, but the ones who destroyed the Temple would remain there forever. They were locals. They would never be prosecuted by a court, for it was not possible to pass judgment on them as they were not the ones blamed – not Ustaše. Nor were they Germans or Chetniks. Nono and Nona, like all the *kuferaši*, could sense the temporary aspect of their stay in the city. This temporariness linked them to those who had desecrated the synagogue. It was the basis of their fears.

"These are not to be played with!" he said to Javorka as he took away the colored pebbles.

The pebbles were the pieces of a demolished mosaic from the synagogue, which was first destroyed by a German bomb and then was spread in all directions by the hands and feet of those who had entered the Temple to take away its riches. They were in the yard, on the street, and throughout the whole city. Colored pebbles covered Sarajevo. It was a real children's paradise. With them around one even forgot one's hunger. It took great effort for the colors to be driven back from one's consciousness.

The Temple's mosaics were never restored. Nor would there ever be a new Sephardic synagogue. The few Jews who remained in the city after the war all prayed to God in the Ashkenazi synagogue. They continue to do so today, though there have been no Ashkenazi among them for a long time. The pebbles have been dispersed and carried away, and it's been some time since one might find any trace of them. I believe they can be found all over the world. Perhaps people took them along when they went away to the Holy Land to found their Israel, or to America, Canada, or Argentina to find neighbors who would be better to them. The colorful pebbles from the mosaic can also be found in the riverbed of the Miljacka, beneath the asphalt of the streets, in garden clearings, in the city sewers . . . But not one of the thousands of them has been destroyed, for the matter, say those who know, is indestructible. Thus do they remain to affirm the abdicated responsibility of those who witnessed the mosaic's dispersion. My grandfather and grandmother, Nono and Nona, lie together in the same vault at Bare Cemetery along with my mother, the little girl who once collected colored pebbles, but there is still no way to assuage the horror of that day when the mob entered the Temple. The mosaic needed to be pieced together, and the story told as it actually happened.

My Mother Offers Her Hand to Sviatoslav Richter to Help Him Climb onto the Ferry for Lokrum

For years after the war only sick, poor children went to the seaside, along with orphans and the dying, those who the sea air was supposed to restore to life by some miracle. Though it was a time of miracles, these people died, so the registered places of death for many residents of Sarajevo, Zemun, or Doboj were Cavtat, Hvar, and Baška Voda. And especially Dubrovnik. That was where people went at the end of the forties and fifties to suffer and die, which means that in the years when I used to walk around at the Boninovo Cemetery, I would see the graves of children and adults from Sarajevo, Kakanj, and Zenica who had died somewhere in the vicinity and been buried among the gentlemen and eccentrics, and also among Dubrovnik's ordinary folk, who had lived and been buried here in accord with some human, familial, or historical imperative. With their deaths they became incidents, covered over with grass, whose wooden pillars – which at the time were used instead of crosses and tombstones – would one day rot and, like everything else in this story, disappear.

The children born during the war were rachitic and tubercular. They were sick with tuberculosis of the bones and kidneys, or with the other, more common form, pulmonary tuberculosis. They suffered from all the known diseases caused by vitamin deficiency. They had shallow roots and died easily, and society tried to take care of them by sending them to the seaside. Doctor Carole Delianis worked in the school clinic by the Partisan movie theater in the 50s. A distant, elderly woman with gold-rimmed glasses and a completely white frock coat, she was one of those people you couldn't say Sarajevo hadn't accepted; they were the ones who hadn't accepted Sarajevo. The city had left not a trace of itself in her way of speaking, her appearance, or her behavior. She was unselfish and smiling as she sorted and classified the children, looking for a way to give every one of them the chance to live, just as it was proclaimed in the Hippocratic oath and the programmatic documents of the League of Communists of Yugoslavia. Doctor Delianis was charged with determining which of the children would go to Villa Kaboga in Dubrovnik for treatment.

My mother was sent there in 1950. She was eight years old and severely anemic. A tuberculin skin test she'd taken had come back positive. She had little appetite and was quiet and listless. The doctor judged that the sea could help her. The children traveled to Dubrovnik in the company of nurses and teachers, first along the narrow-gauge tracks to Mostar, then by trucks all the way to Dubrovnik. The journey lasted sixteen hours.

The Dubrovnik patrician mansion known as Villa Kaboga had been converted after the war into a rest home for orphans and children of fallen soldiers, but it quickly became a sanatorium and treatment center for Sarajevo's children. The story of Villa Kaboga and the fifty years in which thousands of children passed through its doors, with stays ranging from a few months to fifteen years, is an overlooked "minor history" topic that was described tangentially in Serbian author Momo Kapor's 1976 novel *The Provincial*. Mother spent a full month there, until October tenth, when they returned her to Sarajevo in the same manner, first by truck then by train. From Dubrovnik – whose white walls shone so bright in the autumn sun that one couldn't look at them directly, and for the rest of her life she would recall that city with a pleasant sensation of discomfort at having to squint into the light – she returned to a Sarajevo encased in fog and coal smoke, where the first snow would soon fall. Aunt Lola came with her – she had visited her at the Villa with Branka and Uncle Andrija and taken her to Cela's Place for cake – and at home her mother and father awaited, somber and closed in with their own misfortune and the hopelessness of the *kuferaš* city, from which they would depart only when we were no longer there.

That was her first ever summer holiday. It would be another eight years before the next one. In the meantime, they would travel to Dubrovnik to see our aunt and uncle, but only when it wasn't hot, in the spring and autumn. Once in 1955, they went to Dubrovnik in winter. Uncle Andrija had died at the end of December, so Nono, Nona, and my mother traveled through the snow and ice to his funeral. She was thirteen then, and the trip was so long it seemed that they'd never get there, that they would die of cold somewhere on Ivan Mountain, which the train crossed slowly even during the summer, and then once they did get to Dubrovnik the wind from the north they call the bora was raging. While they lowered Uncle Andrija into the grave, along the westernmost wall of Boninovo Cemetery, the bora was so powerful that whatever the priest was saying was blown out to sea. They could see his lips moving but couldn't hear his words, for they were already somewhere far away, between the islands of Lokrum and Daksa in the half-channel, headed for Italy. When they had all crossed themselves, she extended her hand toward her mother, and Nona slapped her fingers. But that's another story. They returned to Sarajevo for Christmas that year, trudging from the train station through the snow, which continued to fall. She turned around at the entrance to the building, as Nona looked for the key, and the traces of their steps had already disappeared in the snow.

She had her first real summer vacation in May 1958, two weeks at Budva on the Montenegrin coast. Her cousin Nevenka, who would be receiving her degree in architecture in the fall, was taking her fiancé and my future cousin Nacij, or Ignjac, or Vatroslav – whichever you felt like using. Friends of theirs were going with them, Milan Ristanović, Jug Milić and Zdenkica, so it wasn't much trouble for them to bring my mother along, who was sixteen at the time. People in those years were just beginning to take their first steps, quietly and a bit bashfully, into tourism. Five years had passed since Stalin's death, Khrushchev had come to Belgrade as if it was his Canossa Castle, the reputation of Yugoslavia in the world had grown stronger with the definitive victory of little Tito over the Big Leader, and for the first time the standard of living was improving significantly. It was really only young people, artists, and eccentrics who were traveling, and it would take a few more years before Yugoslavia's massive summer tourism culture would take hold, with families heading in droves for the sea.

My mother fell in love for the first time in Budva, with the Belgrade actor who would later play the dervish Ahmed Nurudin in Zdravko Velimirović's film *Death and the Dervish*. This love would not just last the two weeks of the Budva summer but would drag out through her life and into her mailbox slots, being transformed in the end into a legend. When in the seventies and eighties he would appear on the television screen in some film or other, she would stop in passing and say, "Good Lord, he is just so good looking!" And then she'd go on with whatever she'd been doing.

In the years that followed it was hard to coordinate workers action excursions with trips to the coast. For my mother, as for the better part of her generation, workers action was more important. Real life rather than some dream was in those actions, and after each one there was hope that her whole life might be transformed. When that didn't happen, my mother's world slid into an abyss. And then I was born, transforming the abyss into a constant condition.

But she did somehow manage to go to Dubrovnik one week every summer. She'd stay with Aunt Lola until she wore out her welcome. She'd tell Aunt Lola off: "You really don't need to visit me all the time! It's not like I'm sick!" You might think that such a scolding would frighten her away for good, but not two months would pass before Aunt Lola would turn up again at our place in Sarajevo, announcing as she always did, "So here I am then!" My mother kept trying to find a way to slip into the conversation, "You really don't need to visit me all the time . . ." But you couldn't do that with Aunt Lola, so she gave up, and the next summer she would again show up for a week at Aunt Lola's place in Dubrovnik.

My mother was not a big fan of elaborate beach outings. She swam at Porporela, where her mother had once done the same as a young girl, and where, at the end of the First World War, she had won a gold medal at a city swimming championship. This was actually where the other Stublers had used to swim too, until 1920, when they were banished for union activism from Dubrovnik to Bosnia. Porporela is one of the places where you could pinpoint the history of this family. Here in fiction and fantasy, when none of us are around anymore, we could take a great collective family photo with everyone from Karlo Stubler and his heart-ailing wife, our Omama, Ivana Škedelj (or Johanna Skedel), to those of us who, over the next several decades, would depart, reconciling the accounts on their Sarajevo graves.

When I was born, they took me to visit Aunt Lola in Dubrovnik. I learned how to swim at Porporela, in that scary, deep sea that I've never liked because you can't see the bottom. I was three. My mother was happy because, according to her way of thinking, there was a possibility I might never learn, given that my father was not a swimmer. And I'm physically just like him, with several of his peculiarities, including numerous non-talents.

Mother never fell in love in Dubrovnik, though it was full of actors and musicians. Once she offered her hand to Sviatoslav Richter to help him onto the Lokrum ferry. His palm was soft, his grip tough as steel. His long, nimble fingers wrapped around her hand, swallowing it up in such a way that my mother's heart began to race, for it occurred to her that Maestro Richter would discover by squeezing her hand that she did not play the piano well. She had little talent and suddenly felt ashamed for the first time because of it. She kept her hands hidden inside her wide linen sleeves as they sailed to Lokrum. Again she hid them that evening as they listened to his concert at the Rector's Palace.

Every town up and down the coast, from Rovinj to Ulcinj, had its famous summer visitors. Whether they might grow rich or not was not considered important. In fact, the majority of the famous guests were poor on average. But they were artists. From the beginning of the sixties until just before Yugoslavia's collapse – after which my mother never vacationed again – people felt a certain awe before painters, actors, directors, and, especially, writers. They went crazy over the idea that someone might describe this, that this summer, which was like any other summer, might end up in a story, in literature, in an utterance that was truer and more exact than any other, in the utterance of a writer. And maybe a whole novel could end up being devoted to it . . .

A place that did not have its famous writer, painter, and director was insignificant, for it did not qualify for eternity. There could have been such a place on the coast, but it seems to us today unlikely.

But no coastal city could compare with Dubrovnik. On the beaches of Banje and Šulići, and even our own Porporela, some sort of famous person took a swim on a daily basis. Even now I can see the great actor Branko Pleša sitting on a short towel, probably taken from the hotel room, looking out toward Lokrum as if he is trying to remember something. Sublimely dignified, with a thin lower lip that gives his face an expression of satisfaction while it presses against his dry upper lip, Branko Pleša, long since dead and even longer since gone, is probably sitting even today at Porporela while my mother looks on from the side, not daring to start up a conversation though she sorely wants to. She is bothered by the fact that she's here with her child. Luckily, they're both dead, in some eternity of their own here at Porporela, where they are bothered neither by the great cruise ships nor the new masters of this city, whose white summer walls one cannot look at directly.

It is the summer of 1974, and my mother is getting ready for the premiere of Dina Radojević's production of *Hamlet*. A twenty-eight-year-old Rade Šerbedžija is playing the young prince. She takes a long time dressing and is nervous about being late. The production is on one of the terraces at the Lovrijenac Fortress, from which one could fall and die. She comes back spellbound. Three days later there's a consultation about whether Nona will take me with her to the play or go by herself. At the premiere, a boy my age got scared and cried. I assure them that I'm brave, I won't get scared. My world will collapse if I don't get taken to *Hamlet*. I'm only eight years old, but I'll remember every moment of that performance for the next forty. Today, I believe, Dubrovnik feels so low for me because

Lovrijenac then was so high. I don't need to go to a place where my mother still sits, open-mouthed, thinking up something to say to the famous Belgrade actor and after forty-some summers later still hasn't said anything. Dubrovnik is a city of invisible monuments and invisible people, while the real ones, without even noticing it, tread on Pleša's little beach towel and on my mother's fingers, preventing Sviatoslav Richter from climbing onto the ferry, since there was no one else there to offer him a hand.

Kuferaši

Vladimir Nagel was a family friend and neighbor. We lived on Yugoslav National Army Street, in the building above the Temple, beside which the Energoinvest high-rise would be built at the end of the seventies, when we would move to Sepetarevac Street. Some time earlier, the Nagels had moved to Rijeka, but we kept in touch, exchanging holiday cards, and Vlado Nagel came to Sarajevo several times. The last time was in the seventies, when the former evangelical church was being repurposed as the arts academy and some papers needed to be signed. Being that there were no longer any evangelicals – or rather, Protestants – in Sarajevo anymore, he had to come. It's probably not exactly true, but it might be said that our one-time neighbor Vlado Nagel was Sarajevo's last Protestant.

By the early 1880s, after the Habsburg occupation of Bosnia and Herzegovina, people had started coming from various parts of the Austro-Hungarian empire, some looking for work, others as respected specialists in their fields. The greatest number were the closest to Bosnia, Croats and Slovenes, but there were also Austrians, Hungarians, Czechs, and Poles, whose biographies and occupations, and often whose inextinguishable nostalgia for home, one can discover by walking around the Catholic cemetery at Koševo and reading the grave markers. These were the people immediately and abusively termed *kuferaši*: people in Sarajevo called them this not merely to taunt them with their wayward and rootless nature in the place where they had settled, but also because it was the first time they had ever seen a *kufer* – that is, a suitcase. A hundred and more years later, when the original *kuferaši* had died out and their families had spread out into the west or been completely assimilated and acculturated with the local population, the word *kuferaš* would lose its abusive aspect and become a sort of marker of distant heritage.

The majority of these people were Catholics, a smaller number Protestants, and the smallest, Ashkenazi Jews. But the royal authorities built a grand evangelical church on a beautiful spot, striving to maintain in Sarajevo the national, cultural, and religious equilibrium upon which the empire stood. They actually needed to build a new Ashkenazi synagogue since the local Jews, who were exclusively Sephardic, were not well disposed toward their new religious brethren and didn't want to let them into their own temple, referring to them disparagingly as "Swabians" and not really even considering them Jews at all. Beside the class element – for the newly arrived were without exception well bred while the majority of the locals were ordinary poor folk – the Sarajevo Jews, as was natural, acted in all this like all other Bosnians. Very likely they were as yet not familiar with the myth of Bosnia as a place of coexistence and of Sarajevo as a European Jerusalem.

And just as the *kuferaši* had settled in the newly constructed homes and buildings between Baščaršija and Marijin Dvor, and the beautiful evangelical church had been built on the bank of the Miljacka, complementing Sacred Heart Cathedral and the Catholic churches and monasteries, the First World War broke out, and the country that had settled these people in Sarajevo collapsed. During the first few months, in 1918 and 1919, a large number of *kuferaš* families left Bosnia forever, but many stayed, and this was because – contrary to our romantic notions of their having drunk the waters of the Gazi Husrev-beg Mosque and been linked forever to Sarajevo as a result – they simply had nowhere else to go. The homes they had left behind twenty years before or more in Vienna, Brno, or Prague, or some Sudeten or Banat backwater, did not exist anymore. In these zero years of their new identity, when there was no Austria-Hungary anymore, they were a people without a homeland and without a clear sense of belonging. They had become exiles.

It must have been easier for the Catholics than for the others. This was due less to the fact that in Bosnia, and in Sarajevo, they were surrounded by a large number of co-religionists – for there were still great social, cultural, and linguistic divisions that separated them – and more to the spiritual, and, in particular, the political legacy of Archbishop Stadler. This man, who was himself something of a *kuferaš*, advanced rather ambitiously the establishment of a Croatian national framework for Bosnian Catholics, a framework that Poles, Austrians, Czechs, and others fell into, especially in these early days of the birth of the nation. This was not our own Bosnian idiosyncrasy, and even less was it a sign of our backwardness – it was not significantly earlier that the masses of Europe, in Croatia and elsewhere, had been "nationalized" in their own manner.

Those, however, who had not become Croats by 1918 would do so in the coming two or three generations, and this was first of all because the Bosnian religious, ethnic, and identity schema was tightly fixed, and it was difficult to remain outside it. It would have meant you were outside society, and, as we well know, it has never been good to be outside society. But the *kuferaš* identity, at least in Sarajevo, was not simple or monolithic. Besides being a Croat, a *kuferaš* would often have certain Czech, Slovene, or Austrian sentiments. Or his brother might have been born as a different nationality. This was the case with my grandfather Franjo, who was born in Travnik and lived his whole life in Bosnia, moving as a railroad worker from one station to another until he ended up in Sarajevo, but he was nationally a quite conscious Slovene, spoke his mother tongue (which in his case was his father's) fluently, subscribed to Slovene newspapers, and maintained close ties with his family in Tolmin and Ljubljana, while his three brothers, whom he loved and got along extremely well with, were all Croats. There was really no difference between him and them, except that they resolved their *kuferaš* status in ostensibly definitive ways and in a distinctly national key. But both their roots and their uprootedness in Bosnia – our three uncles, for whom we used the Bosnian Muslim word *amidža* – were identical.

In all the countries that emerged after 1918, the *kuferaši* struggled to prove their patriotism in order to cancel out what separated them from the majority. They altered their last names in accord with new ways of spelling, gave their children local, nationally distinctive names, served as the strictest officers in the military and the most unyielding investigators in the police . . . And yet they were never completely accepted, for our society was not capable of accepting those it considers Other, instead assimilating them in part and getting used to them in part. While we thought highly of ourselves, in every kingdom we were our own deep, distant province.

The *kuferaši* were annihilated like every other social minority and vulnerable group by social upheavals, wars, and revolutions, both red and black. The war of 1992 finished them off. They left in buses through Kiseljak and kept leaving, God knows, after the war too, in the era of new, soft ethnic restitution, when they realized that this was the final moment to leave. At this final moment, with the expiration of their own history and the knowledge of their heritage, they sought out and obtained the citizenship of the real and imagined homelands of their grandfathers and great-grandfathers. They were leaving forever, and as a monument to their existence and disappearance, what was left behind was architecture. Everything, or almost everything, that was built in Sarajevo during the forty years of Austro-Hungarian rule, and a good part of what would blossom after – excluding the trees – carries the signatures of an identity that was dying in the city and that really no longer exists. The building of the arts academy – the former evangelical church – is a metaphor for the end of one history. All we await is for some new Vladimir Nagel to put a signature on their gifts.

But there is nothing new or distinctive in this from what happened to others. One can walk through Izmir or Thessaloniki to see cities built by those who are no longer there. Though in such cities, those who left earlier left happier.

Home

I moved, or rather, got moved, for the first time in May 1969. Though I was just three years old, I remember every minute of that day, from closing the door for the last time as we left the old apartment, to carrying our things to the truck, the black leather bags with all my essentials, my whole cosmos back then, over my shoulder, sleeping for the first time in the strange place and my first nightmare. We had moved from an apartment on the sixth floor of a large tenement building above the Jewish temple in the center of town to a building on a hill from which you could see the city in the valley through the windows, and the first thing my grandmother had pointed out the next day was where our old building was visible. Besides being able to see everything from the new place, you could hear more than before too. At night I could hear the steam puffing from the train on the other side of town as it made its way from Bistrik station toward Višegrad.

We left our furniture in the old apartment – a black Biedermeier table and kitchen cabinet, armchairs and ottomans, which I would later wistfully recognize in art deco catalogues and which my grandfather and grandmother had purchased in the twenties and thirties when they were setting up their household as young newlyweds. They had received the chandelier as a wedding present: it was enormous, made of black steel and white glass, and so beautiful and luxurious that it seemed to belong to some wealthier home and better-off world than they or I would ever be part of. I'd loved that chandelier: I would roll back on the ottoman and look at it with my head upside down.

In a flash of optimism, certain that by changing her furniture something would change in her life, my mother, who was then a twenty-eight-year old divorced woman with a child, took out a loan and bought new furniture for the entire apartment. So I would grow up amid the rather bizarre, uncomfortable socialist aesthetic of the sixties. Even today, when I go back to my native city, to that apartment on the hill, and look at the remains of the furniture that she paid off over the course of a good fifteen years, I am always reminded of the loss of my real home, the one whose door we closed for the last time in the summer of 1969.

The first time I felt homesickness was when I was walking by our old building with my grandfather. I asked him if we could step into the entrance hall. I opened the door and smelled the familiar odor. When our old neighbor Džemedžić poked his head out the door of his apartment, I ran away in a panic probably because I thought I was doing something wrong by going back to a place that was no longer my home. Anyway, I was only three. I would always experience the same feeling when I found myself near the Jewish temple and our old building, even when none of our old neighbors were alive. I experienced that first move as something of a banishment, though I was not conscious of this on the day we moved.

I moved for the second time in the summer of 1993, when I arrived in Zagreb during the war. Over the next ten years I would change sublets five times, but I don't remember all that. Cheap foreign furniture collected without order or sense in order to prepare an apartment for renting out, other people's beds for which I felt mild disgust, smells I could never get used to, half-removed Donald Duck stickers on the doors of other people's fridges . . . Today when I pass by the buildings where I once rented an apartment, I experience a mild sense of release and a twinge of happiness, as if I were passing a hospital where I recovered after a tonsillectomy. I don't remember anything good or nice from those apartments, except maybe how in 1995 I used to watch the soccer games at NK Zagreb from my fifth-floor room on Kranjčević Street. Everything in those apartments, especially while the war kept on in Bosnia, reminded me that this was not my home, and that the place I would have called home no longer existed for an array of reasons. I'd begun losing my home when I couldn't look upside down at the great black chandelier in our living room anymore.

In August 2003, I was no longer subletting. From an apartment at the top of the oldest high-rise in Zagreb's Zapruđe district, I looked down onto the beltway where the cars and trams crossed the bridges and then onto the fog surrounding Turopolje, which would not dissipate before noon. Somewhere beyond that were regions that could not be seen, with place-names from Miroslav Krleža's *Ballads of Petrica Kerempuh,* the canonical first edition with Krsto Hegedušić's illustrations. I thought: if this had been my home, I would have coexisted with Krleža's Turopolje mists, like those puffs of steam from the trains making their way toward Višegrad from the Bistrik station. But that train was discontinued in 1974. The past is my home, while the present is for the most part a distant foreign land, regardless of where I might move. Foreignness and sublets.

In spring 2007, I moved with my partner to a house in a village on a hill from which, some twenty kilometers away, one can see Zagreb. I had never lived in a village, and all that silence surprised me. As did the neighbor's neurotic rooster, which would begin crowing at about one in the morning. Here I found a sort of peace in which everything was different from all my previous life in the apartments I'd passed through, closing the door for the last time – in most of them – without the slightest regret.

We inhabited our house without any conception or knowledge of the strategy of making order out of a living space. We established our household, and continued to establish it, slowly, one little thing at a time, whim by whim.

Let me describe the workroom in the attic, so you might begin to understand what I'm trying to say. Against the wall, opposite the window that looks out on Zagreb, there is an extended couch covered in green leather; an attractive replica of an ottoman from the thirties. To the right of it, across the whole wall, stretches a bookcase, handmade by the craftsman Milivoj. Against the wall to the left side of the couch, one next to the other, stands a secessionist chest of drawers, which my friend Vojo brought from Sweden, and a Biedermeier writing desk with an accompanying chair of the sort that not so long ago was found in nearly all of our city's homes. There were big desks for big, rich halls, smaller ones, still smaller ones, and then the smallest of all. Ours is among the latter.

Next to the desk there's a wall and a window. On the wall there's a photograph of Sarajevo's main street in 1937. When I am trying to remember something while writing or just daydreaming, I look at that picture. That past is my home as well, even if I didn't experience it firsthand. It's one of the reasons I write: I can take up residence in a time when I physically did not exist. Above this photo is a portrait of my grandfather Franjo Rejc, sketched in 1942 on the back of a "Traffic Notes" form of the Croatian state railroad. It was drawn by Ico Voljevica, the school friend of Franjo's son, my deceased uncle Mladen; Ico was then a Sarajevo high school student and later became a Zagreb cartoonist. Below it is a photo of the stećak necropolis of Radimlja near Stolac, with a little donkey grazing next to it. Tošo Dabac took this picture in the fifties. A little farther down, at my eye level, hangs a linocut, the third of twenty printed sheets entitled *From the Woods of Bosnia*.

The last time we were in Belgrade, we went into an antique shop on Knez Mihailova Street, where we go regularly. We were looking at the books and plastic-coated topographical maps, panoramas of cities from the nineteenth century, photographs of King Alexander and the Karađorđević family, clippings from Viennese fashion magazines, and other such things that look nice and aren't expensive to frame. Flipping through the pages, two sheets protected in a plastic envelope jumped out at me, I recognized the signature from my childhood, from school trips to the National Gallery of Bosnia and Herzegovina – Daniel Ozmo.

Daniel Ozmo, a Sephardic Jew born in 1912 in Olovo, near Sarajevo, was a painter and intellectual of the Left. He sketched and painted landscapes from his native region, certain of the mission and meaning of socially oriented art. He had a divine gift for seeing what was important and leaving a clear trace of it on paper. He was sent to the Jasenovac concentration camp in 1942 and killed.

Daniel Ozmo does not have a home of his own, and his paintings are worth very little to those who have a homeland. To me they are priceless.

Mejtaš: Description of a Place

Mejtaš is a square above the city. One can see Sarajevo from it, or what Sarajevo was in the 1970s and '80s. It got its name from the square stone on which the coffin was laid during Muslim funerals. A *mejtaš* is a stone for the dead.

But the graveyard was not here on the spot where you're standing. It was located on the hill slope to the left, at the top of which they built the Scouts Association building and the observatory. Several tombstones are preserved there even during our own day. But the *mejtaš* themselves have been missing for a long time, and it is not known what happened to them. Probably they were broken up into smaller stones and used for the walls of houses.

Mejtaš extends width-wise from Mehmed Pasha Sokolović Street to Nemanjina. You get to this square on a hill by way of Mahmut Bušatlija Street, which everyone calls by its old name, Dalmatinska. The narrow Ivan Cankar Street runs parallel with Mehmed Pasha, emptying onto the square and sharing a corner with Miladin Radojević Street. Parallel with that runs Ahmet Fetahagić and beyond that, turning counterclockwise, is another little street called Mile Vujović. This leads to Mejtaš by about twenty steps and then a passageway through an apartment building, which was built in the fifties or sixties and has a supermarket on the ground floor. Then comes Nemanjina Street, then after that Mustafa Golubić.

When you were growing up here in the seventies, at the top of Dalmatinska there was a small pumping station for fuel oil that had two pumps, one of which was always broken. Oil was cheap in those years, or heat pumps had become popular, so most of the Mejtaš area was heated using oil. It was purchased in plastic canisters of five, ten, twenty, and twenty-five liters. Whole families usually came out: the girls carried the five-liter containers, the boys the ten-liter, while mothers brought the twenty-liter ones and fathers the twenty-five. Sometimes they had to wait in line up to half an hour before they could fill up.

It would often happen that winter arrived overnight in the middle of September, the weather turning suddenly cold, and no one had bought fuel in time. Early the next morning, before work, at six or six thirty, the families would come down the hill toward Mejtaš with their containers. The fathers would cough, a cigarette between their lips, the mothers would keep their kids together along the street, and the sounds of empty plastic containers knocking against each other to the rhythm of the children's step would make their way through the closed windows to the sleeping people. It was the sound of fall.

When things were good and frozen in winter and Miladin Radojević Street was like a polished iced-over luge track, it took skill to carry the containers up to the top.

It was probably at the beginning of the eighties, when the world was suffering from yet another oil crisis and the price had gone up, that the people went back to wood and coal, and in the lead up to the 1984 Olympics, Sarajevo was at last completely converted to natural gas. After Tito's death there were few heat pumps left in the city.

Two prodigious poplars, sprouted long ago during the time of the Ottomans, grew above the pumping station. They could have been planted by some pauper who looked after the graveyard for a living. Or perhaps it had been some young people who were running around near the Dudi-bulina Mosque, having a great time whipping each other's bare legs with the thin, flexible switches. They toughened themselves up this way, growing up into future loafers, outlaws, and arsonists, or future janissaries who would defend the empire's borders and perish in

Galicia, Slavonia, and Hungary, defending the land from Christians and infidels. And when they had whipped each other enough, when it was time for evening prayers, without thinking what they were doing that spring day, they drove the switches into the warm, damp earth. And the two enormous poplars sprouted from those switches, healthy and strong, and during summer storms they would often be struck by lightning. It was said they attracted the lightning because they surely grew atop a good water vein.

Toward the end of the Mejtaš oil pumping station's history, the poplars began to dry up. Probably the weak cement tank sprang a leak, the ground was saturated with oil, and the two impressive trees were poisoned. The utilities people came with trucks one summer at the beginning of the eighties and spent a long time cutting them down, days and weeks. When we came back from the seaside, the view was empty and deserted, like the mouth of a toothless man. The poplars were no more. Their story was gone too. The children who grew up near Mejtaš in those years are now in their thirties and do not remember that poplars used to grow there. Those poplars exist in the subconscious of our elder brothers and fathers. They will sprout again on Judgment Day.

One other poplar still stands at the summit of Ahmet Fetahagić Street. Enormous and magnificent, an Ottoman monument, it is a tombstone among the trees.

One day at the end of May last summer, it was clear and sunny without a cloud in the sky, then suddenly in the course of a half hour the sky grew dark, and lightning struck the top of that poplar, burning out all the appliances in the neighborhood. It killed my mother's computer, though she could no longer sit at it anyway. A technician came and took it away for repair, so it would be there should she get better. The computer was returned ten days later, fixed. She had died meanwhile and would never turn it on again. Lightning would never strike our poplars again, for we would no longer be there.

The largest, most beautiful house on Mejtaš, which stands between Mehmed Pasha Sokolović and Ivan Cankar, is a gray, two-story building with plaster decorations in the shape of a menorah and the script of King David. This was one of the seven Sarajevo synagogues, Kal di la Bilava, which was built by one of the Sephardic charity organizations for its own use shortly after the arrival of Austria-Hungary.

At that time, across the way, where the supermarket is today, the Dudi-bulina Mosque still stood. It was old and rundown, a humble mosque without cultural or historical value, but important in the life and standing of one of the city's quarters. Later it suffered in fires several times, decaying further until, probably during the Kingdom of Yugoslavia, it disappeared.

The synagogue remained here until the Second World War. Then the Jews of Sarajevo, one name after another, moved to the other side of the Miljacka, to a beautiful, sad monument in Vraca. We were taught in school that the Ustaše and Germans killed them, but the pitiful truth is that Sarajevo's Jews suffered among other things from the great love of their neighbors too.

In the seventies, the former synagogue was used for city services and apartments for the poor. One boy named Slavenko, who was two years older than us, had a window above which there was Hebrew script carved into the frame.

There is a telephone pole on the corner of Ivan Cankar Street, in front of the synagogue, where death notices were put up with pins. There were notices in green, black, and, saddest of all, blue. The green ones were Muslim, the black were Christian and atheist, with a red five-point star, and the blue were for young people.

An elongated building constructed during Austro-Hungarian times stands between Miladin Radojević and Ahmet Fetahagić. The entrance gate leads to a ground-level apartment where my school friend Behadin, the son of the old white-bearded hajji, lived with his many brothers and sisters. To the left of the gate, by Behadin's windows, was a cobbler's workshop, where everyone had their shoes repaired or their soles rubberized. The grocery Aljo was in front of the cobbler's place. While it was under so-called collective ownership and belonged to a company from Kiseljak, the shop was identified with its managers. Aljo was a graying, skinny man in a blue workcoat who had all the best fruits and vegetables, better than those of any of the other grocers in the area. Or was this merely believed to be the case on Mejtaš? Perhaps across Sarajevo in those years people believed their own greengrocer had all the best produce in town?

You went to Aljo to buy things and to stand around. The Markale market was a once- or twice-a-week destination, usually on Fridays for storing up, but people went to Aljo every working day, for a kilogram of apples, two or three carrots, some okra . . . The standing was done by women in housecoats, with kerchiefs on their heads and plastic pink and blue curlers poking out, and also by a variety of men collecting early disability pensions: depressives, moderate alcoholics, low-level clerks with kidney ailments. They talked with Aljo about their health, complaining about how the prices kept rising on "store-bought goods," as the people who had moved from economically depressed areas said. At the grocer people recounted the most harmless bits of gossip – who had died, who had moved away, who had broken a leg on the ice, and they would learn how some former neighbor had written from the distant part of the world where he had moved to long before, from Alipašino polje across town, or from Belgrade or California. It didn't matter from where, because at the time it was enough to move from Mejtaš to Alipašino polje for years to pass between meetings and decades between visits back to Mejtaš.

Sarajevo was a city that had since olden times reached downward toward its own narrow river valleys. All of it was uphill, you got winded even just thinking about how high up Podhrastovi was, where there was only Sedrenik Street and Jarčedoli, so people as a rule didn't go back to the part of town they had moved away from. They didn't have anything to go looking for there, and no one strolled uphill because it wasn't strolling, it was mountain climbing, and why would anyone go mountain climbing around town? At least this was how it was in the seventies and eighties. I don't know how it is today. Back then everything we needed – schools, banks, shops, clinics – were located in our own valley.

The supermarket opened at the beginning of the seventies. Grand, light, and luxurious, with cashiers sporting new hairdos and work coats that were white as snow. They looked like doctors. About a hundred meters farther on, at the start of Nemanjina Street, the first mini-market opened soon after that. They called it a mini-market when it was larger than a bodega but smaller than a supermarket. The first news kiosk was placed in front of the supermarket in the early eighties.

A phone booth stood at the corner of Mehmed Pasha Sokolović, beside the synagogue. It was an elongated glass box, at first with a black telephone apparatus in it and a fat phone book that looked like a muffed-up encyclopedia. In the seventies it took coins for calls, and when the economic crisis started a little before Tito's death, bringing inflation with it, you needed to buy round metal tokens with a hole in the middle. These were later changed to plastic, and then at the end of the eighties phone cards began to appear. Then there were no more phone booths. In place of them were Plexiglas sheets that barely covered the caller. Phone books too had disappeared by then.

Let's glance once more and for the last time at all seven of Mejtaš's streets. Standing in the middle of the square with our backs to the main part of town. The traffic is light with barely a car in sight and not even the taxi stand by the synagogue is there (it will come only at the end of the eighties). There are no traffic lights . . .

Mehmed Pasha Sokolović is the oldest and the widest of the Mejtaš streets. It's the first one to our right. It once connected Banjski Brijeg, or the Nalčadži Hadži Osmanova neighborhood, with the Dudi-bulina neighborhood, which is today's Mejtaš. In the book *Streets and Squares of Sarajevo*, Alija Bejtić writes that Mehmed Pasha Sokolović was established in its current route probably for the first time in the sixteenth century. The hillside part was called "Banjski Brijeg" because it passed above the Gazi Husrev-beg bath, or *banja*. Bejtić writes that the street name was first used in 1931.

Ivan Cankar is an old, poor street, with small houses made of adobe. These yellow bricks from unbaked clay have thawed out for centuries after every big rainfall but have not crumbled completely yet. A great part of Sarajevo, the oldest and most fateful, was made of mud. The stories told about this town by Isak Samokovlija and Ivo Andrić are stories of mud. One of Andrić's stories takes place on Ivan Cankar Street, in Mejtaš, near the synagogue.

Our Miladin Radojević Street was named after a Herzegovinian hero from Stolac, and there's a nice story about him. An educated man, government official, and member of the then illegal Communist Party of Yugoslavia, he organized an uprising on Mount Trebević. He died young, in fall 1941, in hand-to-hand fighting with the Ustaše near Kalinovik. The Ustaše buried him, but the villagers from Šivolji dug him up at night in secret and gave him an Orthodox funeral in their graveyard.

This was where we moved in the summer of 1969.

My grandfather Franjo Rejc lived here only three years. He died in the early fall of 1972. But even during those three years we were only here in the summer, while winter, fall, and spring we lived in Drvenik. In those years, whenever he would come back from town by taxi – he had to come by taxi because of his asthma – and tell the driver his address, he would immediately know whether the man driving him was an old-timer or someone who had resettled in Sarajevo. At the mention of Miladin Radojević Street, an old-timer would respond quizzically, "Sepetarevac?"

"Yes, Sepetarevac."

This was a memory. It was unusually important to my Nono that people remember. He had nothing against the ones who forgot or the ones who came from elsewhere, but it was important to him that there be those who did still remember around him, and he preferred getting that sideways glance from the cabbie who would ask: "Sepetarevac?" to just being driven in silence to Miladin Radojević Street. His life was a patchwork of memories. He had never had a house built for himself, never made a lot of money, nor had life brought him happiness. The present was for the most part sorrowful, the future, threatening. But the past was luxurious and rich with stories. So even the cabbies who knew to ask "Sepetarevac?" were important. They showed that they too remembered and that memory was important to them as well. They were his brothers in memory.

A rivulet ran beside the Dudi-bulina Mosque that in the spring and fall became a torrent. But in the summer it must have been lovely, beside this shallow, living water, on Mejtaš, in the field, observing the city during Ramadan before lighting the lanterns. The stream was called Kevrin Creek on the hillside, but just a hundred paces farther down the named changed to Buka Creek. Kevrin came from the name Kevra, a famous tinsmith family that had lived somewhere nearby. In

1934 and 1935, during the city's great communal rearrangements, when other Sarajevo streams were being covered over, such as Bistrik and Koševo, this little stream disappeared, too, and in its place a road was built that until just after the war was still called Kevrin Creek. The other part, below what had once been the cemetery and meadow, below the Scouts Association building, where the stream had been called Buka, would become Staka Skenderova Street.

In the sixties the name Kevrin Creek was changed to Ahmet Fetahagić Street, which those in the neighborhood continued to call Kevrin. Not from stubbornness or persistence, and not because of the memory that was so important to my Nono with his cabbies, but to differentiate themselves from people who weren't from our neighborhood. For it was really only the people from Mejtaš, the Mejtašians, who called it Kevrin Creek. It was not one of those strong place-names that have survived the vicissitudes of empires, changes of population, or humane and inhumane migrations.

They named the street after Ahmet Fetahagić – he also had a school named after him where as an eighth grader I won a republic-wide geography contest – a prewar student and fighter in the Spanish Civil War, one of the great Partisan heroes of the Second World War, who died on Christmas Day, according to the Gregorian calendar, in 1944, near the village of Izačić, several hundred meters from the place where the border gate between Croatia and Bosnia and Herzegovina now stands.

At the dead end of Mile Vujović – a small, ugly, nothing of a street with steps that lead down to Mejtaš through a short passageway covered in the piss of the neighborhood's drunks and unfortunates – Nađa and Šerif lived with their child in one of the basement apartments. Nađa was Zehra's daughter, and as Nona did not have a better friend in life than Zehra, she carried over her friendship to Zehra's daughter. We went to Nađa and Šerif's place to visit at least once a month. On an uneven whitewashed wall beneath the low ceiling of their living room hung a tapestry depicting the Kaaba. The black stone building was enormous and around it were tiny people like ants with ornaments surrounding them. We would sit there, tucked up and protected, on the low settees and little chairs. Nona would talk with Nađa, and I would ask Uncle Šerif about his motorcycle.

He had a big black bike with a sidecar. German. Upright and dark-skinned, with a Clark Gable mustache, Šerif was a serious man from my childhood. He died young. But by then they'd already moved away to somewhere in Novo Sarajevo, where people lived that we didn't see anymore.

Mile Vujović, after whom the street was named, a teacher and a native Sarajevan from Nadkovač, was a cultural education officer of the Užice Partisan brigade. He was killed on Zelengora in April 1947 and his remains were brought to the Lav military cemetery to lie in peace.

Like Mehmed Pasha, Nemanjina Street was built in the sixteenth century. It had been a road in the neighborhood of the Hajji Balina Mosque, which the people would remember as Čekaluša. But Čekaluša did not get its name from the word *čekanje*, or waiting, as is sometimes thought today. Originally it was Čegaluša, which probably came from Čegaleu, the name by which Grand Vizier Rüstem Pasha was known, the one who built the Brusa Bezistan and that wondrously beautiful bridge across the Željeznica River.

Rüstem Pasha died in 1561, and if the Venetian ambassador Bernardo Navagero is correct, he was born in some hamlet quite close to Sarajevo. As there was at the time just one Sarajevo hamlet suburb, which was called Bilave, perhaps this was the birthplace of Grand Vizier Rüstem Pasha. This story is actually contradicted by Hazim Šabanović, a dedicated historian and researcher who, on the basis of documentary evidence, maintains that Rüstem Pasha was born in Herzegovina, on Bijelo Polje near Mostar, as the brother of Mehmed beg Karađoz, whose name would be given to the miraculous Mostar mosque, to which Skender Kulenović would dedicate an even more beautiful sonnet.

The street was named for Stefan Nemanja, founder of the famous Serbian dynasty, in 1919, one of those years of ours that were considered years of liberation only to later be designated as years of servitude.

There is one very steep *čikma* off of Nemanjina. The *čikme* are blind alleys, appendices, the sightless bowels of Sarajevo's side streets. My father grew up in a *čikma* off Nemanjina, a one-room apartment with a bathroom in the entrance hall. In the misery and poverty of an enemy childhood. His mother lived here, my grandmother Štefanija. I visited her place only once.

And in the end, before we close out the full circle: Mustafa Golubić Street. It had once been known by the name of the Croatian and Yugoslav politician Ante Trumbić, but in June of 1948, twenty days before the Cominform Revolution, it was given the name of the spy and Comintern assassin Mustafa Golubić. There are several lovely Austro-Hungarian country villas on this street, dilapidated and crumbling, as well as the Militia Building, on the other side of Veliki Park, whose graveyard was transformed in Austro-Hungarian times into a very pretty, well-conceived and constructed square, to which the new Yugoslav authorities had added a public bathroom. They did not think about the fact that this had once been someone's graveyard. Sarajevo is full of graves, as well as disappeared names, individuals, and entire peoples.

They are here no longer and will not be coming back.

Sepetarevac: The Ascent

And now, slowly, up we go on Sepetarevac.

You'll be going up this street for twenty-four years. Until the summer of 1993, when you'll go for a short stay in Zagreb and never come back. It's good you didn't come back, you know that today, but maybe it's not good that you didn't go farther. Though this too is just a game of chance, and who knows what might have happened to you and whether you would still be around, friend, if you had gone farther.

There are surely steeper hills in Sarajevo. Once in a while you climbed one or two of them too, but not one would etch itself in your memory like Sepetarevac. It's clear that the street was named after the crates, or *sepeti*, that were carried – mostly by Jewish porters – up to the shops on Bjelave. One of them, Samuel, was described by the Sarajevo author and pulmonary physician Isak Samokovlija in a short story, which put it on Sarajevo's literary map, a map that must be differentiated from the physical map of the city. The former city exists the way it is described, and only those streets that live in the stories and poems of the better writers are present in it. Some of the tiny backstreets and alleys squeezed between the houses on the city's literary map are more important and visible than the unnamed, pale wide avenues that lead out of town. Sepetarevac is one such vital street.

There are steeper streets in the city, but none is described by its steepness and talked about like Sepetarevac.

Which, in all the time you'll be ascending it, will officially be called Miladin Radojević Street.

No one hurries on this street. Or the only people who hurry are those who don't know it and are not from here: boys on their way to see girls at the Women's Teachers Center on Duvanska Street, or to the trade and medical school on Lajoš Košut Street, or to Bjelave on God-knows-what sort of errand. But this is certain: to be rushing on Sepetarevac you can't be from here, or you have to be so angry that your anger drives you up the hill. Anyone who lives here and knows that he'll have to climb the street again tomorrow finds no reason for hurry. You have to climb so as not to break a sweat and get yourself out of breath, to be able to think while you're climbing, comfortable, resting.

You'll live here long enough that you too will learn at last how to rest while climbing. Leaning forward a little, you can see the street from the kitchen window. And you can watch your neighbors, the ones you know and the ones you don't, slowly creeping uphill. And sometimes you'll meet the ones who fall, collapse, or fly downward. There are people who, for their own private reasons, don't rush down the street either, but the majority dive toward town, taking pleasure in the downgrade as if they'll never have to come back up.

The first fifty meters are the hardest, though this is not the steepest part of the street. You have to get used to it, find the thought that will keep you going all the way up, easing the ascent. The first house on the right, at the corner of Ivan Cankar Street, belonged to a woman whom everyone called the Dalmatian. You never knew her name. If you heard it, you didn't connect it to her. She was a widow, a small woman in colorful dresses of the sort worn in town, and was never very dressed up. In one of those years from the First World War, she had mentioned in conversation she was from Dalmatia. You would run into her as she opened her courtyard gate with that big iron key. Nona would strike up a conversation with her, but she never set foot in the courtyard. There was no reason to.

All the streets that connect to Miladin Radojević do so from the right side except for one. The first, Fadil Jahić Španac, is very long. It's one of those winding streets that cut across Sarajevo's slopes, connecting one climbing site to the next. From Sepetarevac it extends all the way to Hajduk Veljkova Street. In older times it passed through two districts: Sarač Ismailova and Kasim Katibova, which over time merged into the Više Husrev Begova baths. The street was originally named after someone named Hajji Sulejman.

The street got the name by which you would call it in June 1948. It was named after the carpenter and idealist Fadil Jahić, who in 1936 set out from his home-town of Bijeljina to defend the republic. He had been a maker of window frames, doors, footstools, and roof beams, and then, carried away by his faith, he went off to Andalusia, Granada, Castile, Barcelona, gaining through his wayfaring the nickname that was commonly used in our provinces – Španac, "the Spaniard." In it was both a calling and a symbol of faith. It is nice to believe that Hajji Sulejman was similar to Fadil, that he was a hajji in the same way that Fadil was a Spaniard. There is something similar in the two nicknames. Both were achieved with diffi-culty and through great faith.

Afterward Fadil Jahić the Spaniard served as a commander and then political commissar in the famous 38th "Majevički" Partisan Division. He was killed in battle in February 1942, alongside another Partisan hero, Ivan Marković Irac, after being surrounded by the Chetniks. This was in the village of Vukosavci on Mount Majevica.

After Fadil Jahić Španac Street comes the most level part of Sepetarevac, about fifty paces long, before the big steep part, which starts after the bend beyond Džemil Krvavac Street. From Turkish times to today, this street too has kept its old name: Vejsilagin Way. Who this Vejsilaga was has of course been forgotten, though by some miracle on this very street there was an old Sarajevan named Vejsil whom the neighbors sometimes affectionately called Vejsilaga. The name fit the old man somehow especially well, the rhythm and the melody of it, and maybe the sense of it too, with that "aga" at the end, as if he were a minor Turkish lord.

On that street, our handyman Vjenceslav Šulc lived with his wife and son in a lopsided Turkish house of bricks on the verge of collapse in the middle of a courtyard with a fountain and fine round cobblestones. He'd been an airplane mechanic before the war at the military airport in Rajlovac. Before dying at the beginning of the eighties, he would repair anything that broke in your house, except the TV. For that Mr. Fišeković had to be called.

Though I didn't know much about him, I composed a book of poems about Šulc the handyman. He impressed me after he was no longer around. But it was completely normal for you when you lived next to him. You did not know that in other lives there weren't any retired airplane mechanics who busied themselves by repairing all sorts of broken things. Children did not have such knowledge and were not surprised by anything. The time for surprise came later, when you had grown up and everything disappeared.

Džemil Krvavac was an official in Sarajevo's main post office. Your cousin Budo Dimitrijević knew him, the husband of your aunt Mila, on the Jergović side. Budo had been a soldier on the Salonika front in the First World War, awarded Karađorđe's Star and the Order of Saint Sava, and later a respectable and esteemed postal official. And at the time, between the two wars, the post office was the most important civil service organ along with the railroads. Gentlemen worked in the postal service. "Do your work quietly, Džemil, son. Nothing good will come of your doing things so everyone can hear and see them, and you'll suffer for it. Listen to me, son. Work quietly." Džemil was fifteen years younger than Budo, but as he and Aunt Mila did not have any children, Budo called any man younger than he was "son." My uncle Budo Dimitrijević was apolitical, didn't understand communism, respected the emperor, and didn't convince Džemil. Born in Herzegovina somewhere near Gacko, a journalist and aspiring writer, Džemil Krvavac was arrested by the Ustaše police on November 12, 1941 and deported six days later to Jasenovac. He fell in spring of the next year, along with a large group of inmates, during one of the unsuccessful uprisings. Uncle Budo recalled him to the end of his life. Then he too died, while Džemil, the wretch, was turned into a street.

The steepest part of Sepetarevac comes after one passes Džemil Krvavac Street. Here drivers would shift down into first – which was not that simple in a little Fiat since you had to stop the car to shift and then start up again using the emergency break, which was one of the most delicate maneuvers in driving tests from those years – while in winter, with the snowfall and frozen surfaces, and with the children's sleds transforming it into a completely smooth, slippery ice sheet, this part of Sepetarevac was nearly impassable. We all climbed up, young and old alike, by digging our fingernails into the facades along the way. Older gentlemen and strict fathers returning home from work would lose all authority here, in their thick mountain ascent shoes, their hats, their bulky clothes and good coats, trying to remain serious, but in vain, for seriousness led to despair on this most inconvenient portion of Sepetarevac, from street number 19 to 23.

You lived at number 23.

The building was constructed at the end of the fifties by the brothers Trklja – Branko and Obrad. Ten years later Obrad sold his half and moved to Belgrade. In the summer of 1969, when everyone else was at the beach, you moved into his apartment. Professor Branko Trklja taught econometrics and other subjects in the department of economics at the university. A quiet and calm neighbor and an introverted bachelor, unhealthily clean and orderly. He had some kind of secret. You would never discover it.

Several years ago I read the collected works of Franz Kafka, a thick book with completed and unfinished prose works, extremely varied, but all with a detached anxiousness. The main character in all the stories reminded me of someone. I finished the book, unable to remember who it was. Then it struck me: Branko Trklja! Who knows what might have happened, and with what sort of eyes you would have looked at him, had you read the book in time . . .

He retired in the eighties, sold his apartment, and moved to the village of Osijek, one of Sarajevo's western suburbs, where he lived peacefully until the war. He died as a refugee, in a camp somewhere in eastern Bosnia. He had a deep voice and never laughed.

Below you was Franjo Hauptman's garage and below the garage, a three-story building at number 21, an old, unstable, quite dilapidated Turkish structure of yellow adobe. By the time all the wars had ended at the close of the nineties, one wall of the building had separated itself and collapsed. From your bedroom you could see a cross-section of the whole building at number 21, from the ground floor to the attic. They tore down the building several months later.

Milojka lived a little farther down, opposite Džemil Krvavac Street. Alone in an old Turkish structure. Her son had hanged himself one spring.

Once you've passed the steepest incline, there's a little intersection around number 25. To the left, a short street that has no name drops off toward Ahmet Fetahagić, and to the left is Abdičev Street. At the intersection of Abdičev and Sepetarevac there's a nice three-story built in modern times by a certain developer named Čarkadžija, perhaps after the Second World War. We don't know who designed it, but the spirit of modernism is palpable in its shape and can be felt in its balconies and staircases.

Abdičev Street was named after the Muslim family that had several houses here two or three centuries ago. Today it extends between Miladin Radojević and Drvarska Streets, but before the beginning of the twentieth century it went farther on to Bulbulina.

After Abdičev the ascent continues, but for a stretch there are only houses on the right side. It's as if Sepetarevac has been sliced in half here. By now you're quite high above the city. Turn around and you'll see the whole of it, if the valley is not pressed down with the November-December mist and smog.

You'll have to go on yourself from here because I'm not confident in my memory's ascension. I don't have a map of Sarajevo. It would not be of any use to me anymore, so before reaching Bjelave I remember just one street. About three hundred paces or so from Abdičev comes Hadži Hajdarova.

This very old and beautiful side street, sheltered, hidden, and well preserved, gave off an air of some bygone time. Coming up to Hadži Hajdarova was like entering a museum. The street had this sort of aroma, and the people who lived on it had this sort of appearance. You might have believed they never went down to town. Their wives had been very old for a long time. They went around in Turkish pantaloons and wore kerchiefs on their heads strewn with brownish-gold ornaments, while the men wore French berets and short gray vests, or housepainters' slacks and coats with caps fashioned from the liberation of the day before. On Hadži Hajdarova Street it was surely not 1975 or even '79 but some century or two before. It's unclear when time here began to run outside the time in which we were living, but it seems to have happened long ago. Some of the first shells that struck this part of town in April and May 1992 fell on Hadži Hajdarova. The calendars were thus brought into accord, and the time in which the little street had lived disappeared.

For a long time, it was mistakenly thought that the street got its name from Divan Hajdar Kjatib, the court scribe Hajji Hajdar who laid the foundation for the White Mosque of Sarajevo's Vratnik Quarter. But this Hajji Hajdar was older and had been a harness maker at the bazaar. A wealthy, devout man, he had wanted to leave something behind and so had built the mosque, around which a neighborhood arose, which in the sixteenth century acquired the name Saddler Hadži Hajdar's Quarter. It would continue to exist into Austrian times under the name Upper Saddler's Quarter.

After you've passed by Hadži Hajdar Street, Sepetarevac quickly curls to the left before opening onto Bjelave. This long, steep street, on which cars were once a rarity and for as long as you can remember was one-way, though at the intersection-facing Kevrin Street drivers would often pull out the sign, thereby declaring it two-way, belonged like all of Sarajevo's steep streets to the people who lived around it. Nobody climbed it without a particular need to do so. You could live your whole life in Sarajevo without once climbing up to its top. Especially since it was possible to get to Bjelave and Višnjik by a tamer and gentler route, and without being pressed upon by the threatening bunched-up houses on either side of the street and the destinies of the people within them.

During the time of Samuel the porter, they used to go from the synagogue to Mejtaš, from the Jewish workshops up to Bjelave, along a difficult, painstaking path several times a day. I don't know what they thought about or whether they had hope, besides that they might live another day or another year, but the ascent must have had a deeper metaphysical meaning for the Jewish poor. They spent their lives on that pilgrimage with *sepeti* on their backs, and soon it would be as if they had never been there at all, their only memory being in the names of these streets.

But Bjelave, Bjelave is wide and flat. Once long ago, in pre-Ottoman times, this was Bilave, a village that would remain a village even after it became part of Sarajevo. Only in 1530, when a certain Hajji Alija erected a temple, would the village become a city quarter, which Alija Bejtić notes was described in the cadastral registry as "the quarter of Hajji Alija's place of worship, known by the name Bilave."

One went to Bjelave to visit Krunić's bakery, for bread and rolls, and for flat bread during Ramadan. Every morning in those years, when Nona would take you to the eye clinic for your exercises – you were cross-eyed, suffering from strabismus, and they would sit you down in front of a cold metal device with two peep holes and looking through them you needed to lead the parrot to its cage, the green parrot with a big yellow beak – you took a round-about route in order to stop by Krunić's to buy the morning rolls.

Even today I can taste those rolls, and I often find myself hoping I'll taste them again whenever I'm in some unfamiliar eastern city and manage to get rolls from a bakery.

In the mideighties many new bakeries opened in Sarajevo. People had been spoiled by living well and were no longer satisfied by just any old bread, and the bakeries began to compete with one another. Thus did the rumors about Krunić begin to spread: late at night, they said, when no one was watching, someone would deliver piglets to the shop, and Krunić would put pork into the dough for the flat bread. There wasn't a grain of truth in this of course, as anyone who thought about it even a little bit knew, but the rumor had the effect of making the poor baker swear up and down that he was not doing something that everyone knew he wasn't doing. And of course he felt a little guilty because a person feels guilty when people accuse him of something, however unlikely the accusation might be. The guilt wasn't toward those who falsely accused him but toward those who truly believed it . . .

At the time you laughed. Everyone around you was stunned at the sort of world we lived in, at the things people were willing to believe. When you remember this today, you're seized by anger. And suddenly nothing is funny anymore. Everything is a question of human feeling and perspective. What was once funny now seems like a premonition.

Both the laughter and the anger, meanwhile, are real. But if one were to write a novel about Sarajevo in the eighties, it would need to be told from that older vantage point, when the rumor of the pork in Krunić's flat bread was a nasty joke but, still, just a joke.

Zatikuša: Forgotten Alley

A woman wrote me a very kind but admonishing letter to say I had made a mistake: Sepetarevac does not open onto Bjelave, it is separated from there by the street on which, as it happens, she lives. I understood immediately of course, and before my eyes appeared the street she was referring to, the street I had taken so many times. Sepetarevac has a dead end, but instead of bumping up against a wall, it turns to the left, along a street that has disappeared from memory, according to some unfathomable but ever-present logic of forgetting. Nothing is ever forgotten by chance or randomly. It happens according to an order and in accord with a person's internal equilibrium.

Even after twenty years of living in Zagreb, when I dream, and when the dream has a definite setting, the setting is somewhere in Sarajevo. Unless I'm on the road in my dream. The people I dream about are mostly dead, though I dream about them as alive. My uncle, aunt, Nono, Nona, mother, father appear together with dead neighbors, friends, and school teachers in these Sarajevo dreams, telling me something with great liveliness or participating in events that characterize their natures. Events from twenty or thirty years before are repeated, both real and dreamed up, in which the people correct something or make things much worse. I get angry and frustrated with them in the dream, though I usually know they're dead and will be gone again when I wake up. This part is not important. There is nothing sentimental or sorrowful in these dreams. I dream of them somehow conscious of the fact that it is only a dream. And the dreamed Sarajevo does not resemble the city of today, nor is it the city in which I once lived. It is just the city in the dream.

Parts of it are beginning to disappear little by little. Streets and entire quarters are disappearing, as people do. Some parts of this are accessible to reason, others are not. Thus, in the last decade or so, I have parted ways, quite gruffly and in uncomfortable circumstances, with many Sarajevo friends and acquaintances, and with some I'd called friends. It's not important how this happened. They went away and it's done, and while I continue to dream of the dead as if they were alive, I do not dream of these others at all. They have disappeared, like streets I have not walked down for a long time, or thought about. In dream, Sarajevo is a small town, populated by the dead.

In our time Sepetarevac was linked to Bjelave by a little street called Zlati-kuša. Alija Bejtić explains: "In old Sarajevo, which was provided with water by street fountains, individual water sources were not abundant, such that in any of the places where the water was inclined to flow freely, the pipes needed to be squeezed and hindered, the verb for which was *zatiskivati*, so that the water would accumulate in the supply basin. These places were called *zatikuše*, one of which was in the location in question."

I cannot recall that there was a fountain there when I passed by for the last time. That could have been in the spring of 1993, or earlier, before the war . . . They continued to call the street Zlatikuša for a long time, for it takes but a slight revision to adapt an empty word without any meaning to the excessive desires of human imagination. And thus did gold, or *zlato*, appear on Zatikuša, at the top of Sepetarevac.

Now I seem to remember everything. But that of course is an illusion, for I cannot be certain that I really do or, what is more likely, am taking someone else's experience as my own. What has been forgotten cannot be renewed. There is nothing to be reminded of.

Veliki Park

Autumn would arrive around the time of Velika Gospa, as soon as August had split in two and was heading toward its end. While it was never a matter of heat waves, and the sun would not bake things as happens in Mostar, nor would it be steamy like Zagreb or Vienna, and even during the worst July heat a pleasant cool would arrive with twilight, such that you could gather the sense of Muslim evening prayers as in the old folktales. The first signs of autumn would bring a sense of brief easing, for then, with Velika Gospa, came the most beautiful time of the year, which would not last long, until mid-September, when there was nowhere in the world like Sarajevo, and when everything, the climate, the historical moment, and the people, found themselves in complete harmony, and a person would briefly understand why he had ended up here, living in this city, far from the world and from friends and relatives. Then, as September too split in half and suddenly the first morning frosts fell, and the mists rolled up from Otes and Sarajevsko polje, the longest and most miserable time of year would arrive, which was known to last until the end of April, during which the sky above the city would not turn blue, nor would the sun shine, nor would there be any sign by which to surmise that this climactic misfortune would ever pass. For a full seven months of the year a person would not be able to fathom who had ever come up with the idea of putting a city on this crater in the middle of the mountains. Unless Sarajevo had sprung up one year between the fifteenth of August and the fifteenth of September and people had never had occasion to move after that.

After he retired from the railroad central office, Franjo Rejc volunteered as a bookkeeper for the Hotel Pošta. Until 1966 he kept bees in the village of Glavatičevo, near Konjic, visiting them on weekends, until his grandson was born in the spring of that year and he gave away the last of his hives, thereby bringing his apian career to a sudden end. In autumn of the same year he would hand over his accounting books too, and they were so orderly and complete that the entire history of this hotel for government officials could be discerned from them, while their fragments could long be found in Franjo's storage drawers in the fifth-floor apartment in Madam Heim's building and, later, in the apartment on Sepetarevac. These gleanings, half-filled notebooks, hotel ad materials, and yellowed empty pages with memo headings would stick around until 1992 and the beginning of the siege, after which they too would disappear.

Though he worked at it for only a short period of his life, barely seven or eight years after retiring from his position as a traffic engineer, bookkeeping was not something Franjo gave up easily. He was an industrious person. Work calmed him. He found life's meaning in putting things into order, arranging documents and protocols, administering daily life, and turning it into a history, so leaving his work meant a slow withdrawal from life, dying at the front, with the passage of the seasons that in Sarajevo had a fateful effect.

He had to quit bookkeeping because of his illness. He was weighed down by cardiac asthma, and the Sarajevo winter was getting harder and harder on him, such that his doctors recommended he spend it at the coast. So in 1967, with his wife Olga and his grandson born the year before, he wintered for the first time in Drvenik, in an old Dalmatian house that his son Dragan had purchased a few years before. His heart and lungs took a liking to the sea climate, but he was simultaneously faced with his own imminent disappearance and the futility and senselessness of life when one is idle and there's nothing to write. To ease the suffering, he started studying English. In addition to Slovene, Serbo-Croatian, German, Italian, Hungarian, and French, Franjo Rejc in the final years of his life studied English. This, he said, was the language of the future. In his case, it was the language that helped him cheat death.

The move to Drvenik also disrupted Sarajevo's seasonal rhythms. But one of them remained: the first sign of fall, around the fifteenth of August, every year.

After retiring, Franjo went to the office at the Hotel Pošta every day a little after noon. He would usually stay until five, and then, instead of walking the fifty or so steps from the hotel to the building where he lived, he would head down Kulovića Street, then along Marshal Tito Street, all the way to Veliki Park. He walked along the asphalt paths, under the tall trees that have never been renewed since being planted here as little shoots in the eighth year of the Austro-Hungarian annexation, when the park was ceremonially opened in October 1886. After climbing up to Mustafa Golubić Street and the Veterans House, Franjo would sit down on a bench to rest, always the same bench, which does not exist there anymore. He said this spot had the greatest amount of air and was the freshest and most comfortable place to sit in summer. In winter he would just stand next to the bench, listening.

It was precisely here, in the middle of August, that autumn would take its first breath through Veliki Park, inaugurating the finest part of the year in Sarajevo, which lasted such a short time that one needed to know the precise start in order to experience the whole thing.

After resting on the bench, Franjo would slowly make his way home. And so it was every day, endeavoring to slow down the time that, meanwhile, passed ever more quickly.

The Vakuf administration had granted the approximately thirty Ottoman stremmas that the old Muslim cemetery Čekrekčinica had covered to the provincial government in 1885, on condition that the graves remain where they were and that grave markers be created and trees planted around them. This was not in complete accord with the faith. One did not touch burial sites or go walking around the graves for no particular reason. These were modern times now, the Vienna emperor wanted it his way, people had changed, and the graves themselves, to be frank, were very old. Supposedly the area had been fenced off by Muslihudin Čerkrekčija and made into his own *waqf* at the beginning of the sixteenth century. He was buried here as well, and his burial markers are still recognizable.

The plan for Veliki Park was the work of the provincial government official Hugo Krvarić. While he was not a landscape architect, of which there were many in Vienna – they created the plans for the beautiful, luxurious parks in Zagreb – his design was realized and permanently maintained, such that when Franjo sat on the same bench every year waiting for the fall, its state was not much different from in 1886. The paths were identical, the benches in the same locations. Only, in the interim, an ossuary for national heroes had appeared along with a fountain in the lower part, by Marshal Tito Street.

Hugo Krvarić was from Dugo Selo, near Zagreb. He'd been educated in Zagreb and Vienna and moved to Sarajevo immediately after the occupation of Bosnia. He settled here and had a son. Perhaps he died in Sarajevo too, who knows. Hugo Krvarićs's son Kamilo was born in 1894, when the trees in Veliki Park had grown strong. He was born on April 25, at just the time they would have been budding. He went to school at the First Gymnasium, then went to Zagreb. He became a theater critic and was active and respected during the two wars. He moved to Osijek and became the editor of *Hrvatski list*, a paper that was published during the time of the Independent State of Croatia. In 1945 he emigrated and lived until 1958, dying in Argentina. He was a member of Ante Pavelić's circle.

Did Kamilo Krvarić remember Veliki Park in Argentina? In what moments, during which seasons of the year, and how often might he have thought about it? It's impossible to know, and no one has cared for a long time about Hugo Krvarić or his son Kamilo, the wayward theater critic, product of a *kuferaš* family from provincial Sarajevo, who was in between worlds, without a homeland, and who, once in a while, like Kamilo, by means of political radicalism, elevated national and religious emotions, and everyday mental and social gymnastics, tried to become – local. Though almost nothing about him is known, when recalling the August murmuring of the leaves in Veliki Park and Franjo Rejc's waiting there for the fall, it is clear how Kamilo could have become close to Pavelić.

His father Hugo Krvarić had a gift. Thus was a beautiful Austrian park created from an old Muslim graveyard, with a fascinating network of paths that people became so used to that they hardly noticed them. The paths come from all four directions and all four of the streets that support Veliki Park. From the south it is Marshal Tito. From his bench, through the thick treetops and the slender branches, Franjo could see the Hotel Istria, which would be demolished two years after his death. He did not know this and did not care. From his perspective, that structure, named after the largest Yugoslav peninsula, which – as we were taught in school – was returned to its mother country by Tito's Partisans, would always stand where it was on Stjepan Radić Street. Franjo had friends in Istria, comrades with whom he had once participated in conspiracies to free Trieste, Istria, Gorizia, and Rijeka from the Italian administration. His comrades used some methods of terrorism, and Franjo supported them from Sarajevo. They called their organization TIGR.

An engineer named Bonić was in hiding in Sarajevo during the Second World War. He was a TIGR member from Pula who had to leave his native town after receiving a death sentence. If they had known this, the Ustaše would have deported him to their Italian allies, and after the fall of Italy he would have gone to Jasenovac. Bonić bought a house in Sarajevo, which Franjo tried to sell for years once his comrade had gone back to Pula after the war, in the end finally succeeding.

To the right of his bench was King Tomislav Street. Named for the Croatian ruler, whose thousand-year kingdom was celebrated in 1925 throughout the Kingdom of the Serbs, Croats, and Slovenes while today it is marked by marble memorial tablets throughout the territories of the former Yugoslavia. The propaganda of the day created the legend of Tomislav as the unifying king of all the Southern Slavs. It was after him that King Alexander Karađorđević named his second son and also the Herzegovinian town formerly called Duvno.

Mustafa Golubić Street, which borders the park on its hilly side, flows into King Tomislav. Mustafa was a Soviet secret agent, a thug and assassin, whose bleak legend would require a novel, if a feature film was too expensive to make. And if there was an actor who could play Mustafa Golubić and live. The Germans caught him in Belgrade in 1941. They say he was wearing an SS uniform. They tortured him for days, broke all the bones he had to break, but he would not even tell them his name. He could not walk so they put him on a wooden office chair to be shot. The Germans didn't even know who it was they had killed. It seems they didn't care, just as no one today much cares about Mustafa Golubic, a Herzegovinian from Stolac, a Comintern murderer, whose eyes they say filled with tears when, at the age of thirty-something, late one evening in a Prague alehouse, he quietly sang, "Bloom rose, do not fade. Suffer, Ahmed, do not die, for I have no where to bury you."

Veliki Park's fourth side is bordered by such a tiny, unattractive little street that its name has not even been touched, though it's located right in the center of town, where the names of streets, and sometimes those of living people, most frequently and happily get altered. Franjo Rejc never took it because it didn't lead anywhere. Trampina was a dead-end street named after the Trampas family, of whom there aren't any anymore, the family that, Alija Bejtić writes, provided the khatibs and imams for the Čekrekčija Mosque at the base of Kovači, which was built by the same Muslihidin Čekrekčija who separated off the land for this cemetery.

Like Mustafa Golubić, Hajji hafiz Abdulatif Trampa was a brave man, and just as alone amid the great European upheavals and rebellions. He was one of the unfortunates who in the summer of 1878 decided to defend Sarajevo against the forces of Baron Josip Filipović. Those days are described, though not the fate of Abdulatif Trampa, by Ivo Andrić in his story of Mara the favorite wife, one of his most beautiful and most impressive prose works, which even today has more of Sarajevo in it than do all of our memories or anything else on earth, but about him, about this last offspring of the Trampa line, someone ought to write at least a story.

After the rebellion had been crushed, Abdulatif was not killed but was instead handed over for perhaps even greater suffering. He served time in the Olomouc prison, in Moravia, for many years, returning to Sarajevo only when the young shoots in Veliki Park were beginning to take root.

After the war, a taxi might take you down Trampina, which wasn't a dead end anymore, driving quickly like on any other street, past the Park Café. And it seemed to you it was all too fast, the road ran right through the dead end, and its history too, and ultimately would be forgotten. By taking this route, from the Obala Vojvode Stepe across Radićev and toward Marshal Tito, then across that wide sidewalk, then down Trampina, then to the right past the old Sloga printing shop and over to Dalmatinska, the cabbies avoided the busy traffic and the eternal delays on Kulovića, as if by their driving they were trying to make up lost time for themselves and for their passengers. But a person gains nothing by rushing down Trampina so fast that he arrives at his destination without uttering the name of Hajji hafiz Abdulatif Trampa.

Hugo Krvarić's accomplishment has lasted like little else in Sarajevo. Buildings have been destroyed, Austro-Hungarian villas have burned in the many wars, Turkish homes of adobe have fallen apart amid the centuries of rain, hotels have come down and department stores have risen up in their places, one after another. The face of the city has been made uglier more often than more attractive, to the point that for many both its face and the city itself have disappeared. The Trampases have died out, as have the Krvarićs, but Veliki Park has miraculously remained. Except the bench where one might wait for the start of fall around Velika Gospa, that short beautiful moment in the year when Sarajevo has its reason for being, and when it seems to the *kuferaš* families that they were rewarded by God, and by the king and emperor – our Franz Joseph – when he sent them to this place.

The bench is about twenty meters lower now, not where it used to be. But if you know where to look, it's easy to find the right spot. You can stand there or crouch down to wait for what will one day come to us all.

Marshal Tito Street: Dream and Memory

If you were able to describe the streets that occupy your dreamscape clearly enough, you'd start dreaming of a different place in the end, a different city. However simple this idea might seem, it's extremely bold. It's hard to describe a city from memory, and with each detail, each street corner and facade, the place is awakened to such a degree as to be erased from your mind. It is a grand undertaking, which could last to the end of one's life. So it's better to give up and accept the fact that, as if by some curse, dreams unfurl where you can no longer be, where you are no longer allowed to be.

Your world, the layout of memory, extends evenly outward along a hand-drawn line, a bit crooked because the draughtsman didn't use a ruler, from Marijin Dvor to Varoš, where it joins and disappears into the bustle, clamor, and shop windows of Baščaršija. In waking life too, but especially in your dreams, everything else you saw in Sarajevo and in all your future cities, including Zagreb, where you've lived the longest, tries to shape and model itself after this one freely drawn line. Zagreb's Ilica, which is much longer and more meandering, with its narrow sidewalks, constrained road, and the two sets of tram tracks, is in dreams an imitation of this Sarajevo landscape, which was officially called Marshal Tito Street. Tito has completely covered over and swallowed up Ilica, just as it does all other streets, real or imagined, those that once existed and those that will one day come into being.

It begins at the very edge of the city. Everything beyond it is a sort of suburb, alongside which a new town has sprung up. To one side, where the Holiday Inn stands, until not long ago, the 1970s, was the circus grounds. I suppose there are some who still call it that – people with blinders on who haven't noticed that some buildings and high-rises have gone up there with the yellow Straussean cube sculptures in the middle, or those who were driven from Sarajevo so long ago and with such fixedness that from their New York, Belgrade, or Vienna perspectives they can see nothing but the empty circus grounds where over some spring night a tent might materialize. An enormous, yellow-and-white-striped tent of the sort that held Sarajevo's first large movie screenings in 1903 and 1904. In those few seasons the cinema was more of a marvel than the circus.

On the other side of the street that leads into the world, across from the circus grounds, where the parliament and executive council buildings have risen up, once long ago there was a Muslim Eid prayer site, or Musala. It was out in the open, with an optional mihrab and minbar, used for large gatherings that could not be accommodated inside the mosque. This Musala was an open-air mosque in Ottoman times, with the highest vault in the world, bounded by the hills of Sarajevo, an invisible mosque at the entrance to the city.

Here, in times of ancient glory, soldiers would bow down before departing for distant battlefields.

To one side the circus grounds, to the other the Musala.

These two spots are clearly visible from the windows of the building where the city begins. You have never been inside this building or looked out from those windows, but you can imagine what it's possible to see from them.

This is where that line you were talking about begins, to the right side of the building and a bit lower down, at the door to Auntie Doležal's entrance way. It's not completely straight as it is drawn freehand. This is where Tito Street begins.

The route that now runs from the turn into an important little street that bears the name King Tvrtko to Koševski Potok, where Tito grows somewhat wider and more refined, turning into the main street of a city, there was once

a street called Gornja Hiseta. At the end of the Turkish era and before the Austro-Hungarian one, when Marijin Dvor was built, this was a sad, peripheral quarter that would disappear with the first wave of modernizing and Europeanizing
initiatives under Franz Joseph.

The poor of Sarajevo were not clearly separated from the well-off. That was
true in your own time there as well. Unlike Zagreb and Belgrade, Sarajevo did
not have its own residential districts, so everyone lived on top of each other as if
in some sort of a Gypsy settlement. Sarajevo was no metropolis, for a metropolis
has its Versailles and its favelas, while what Sarajevo had was the compactness
of a provincial Turkish town. The last to raise a monument to this culture of
mixture, after Samokovlija and Andrić had already described it earlier, was Emir
Kusturica, who mythologized the Gorica of his youth.

And so Gornja Hiseta did have its wealthier and even perhaps prettier side.
In those same Turkish times, one of the wide streets that led toward the center
of town was called Podmagribija, or "Lower Magribija," after the tiny, nimble
district where the Magribija Mosque was located, which swelled up like a little
tumor outside town. Here, across the street from the mosque, was an office of
the Privredna Banka, where you would open the first bank account of your life.
You would come here regularly until the war to verify whether you had been
paid your royalties. And this was where, when the war began, you forgot about
several thousand Yugoslav dinars or less, not very much money, paid to you for
the rights to publish some of your poems, translated into Hungarian, in a magazine in Vojvodina. That money slipped away, spilling into a crack in time, and
disappeared. It would be interesting to follow its disappearance as the last bureaucratic trace of it was erased . . . During the war, from the fall of 1992 to its final
spring, you would see heaps of savings account passbooks, which the soldiers had
thrown out the windows of emptied-out offices, usually of former banks, where
their staffs were headquartered. In that first year of wartime enthusiasm, Sarajevo
was filled with headquarters. The discarded passbooks contained our stylized
prewar biographies. Lives transformed into money streams, people rendered
metaphorically through savings accounts. The history of each savings account is
one human history, which of course ought to be written down. However many

of those passbooks were turned into garbage, their contents remained precious. You were not aware of it, but your entire prewar life was transformed into heaps of garbage that would soon become precious.

Without recontructing the contents of those passbooks, without that persistent sifting through of the garbage, the landscape of your dreams will never change.

The short but very wide thoroughfare from Koševski Potok to Veliki Park, which in Turkish times had the width of a square, was called Gazilerski Way. It was named after two heroes, or *gazija*, Ajan and Šems, from the early days of Sarajevo, whose memory wandered and changed over many years among the songs of the people until in the end it disappeared completely.

If you went on from there, you often crossed over, from the descent of King Tomislav Street, then along Tito, beside the Parkuša, along the walkway that covers the distance from the old *Oslobođenje* printers, beside the traffic from the Belgrade-based *Politika*, a large, luxurious toy store, the Olomom sweets shop, and the Narodna Banka, all the way to Čeka, the spot where Dalmatinska finally led down into town. That part of Tito Street was called the *žabljak*, or "frog pond."

Here until the arrival of Austria-Hungary was the Hadži Idrisov Quarter, where it appears the people were neither happy nor well-off. The morass of the žabljak was in fact a place for the poor. It was from this quarter, as might be imagined from its nickname, that epidemics of a variety of diseases spread through Sarajevo, as did the misery of the people who found refuge in the swampy backwater among the frogs and tadpoles, a fact the neighbors mocked by giving the quarter its nickname. It was probably only in July and August, during the hottest, driest time of the year, that one could live normally here.

The frog-infested swamps arose out of Buka Creek, which before the Austro-Hungarian regulation of all the Sarajevo waterways, emptied down the course of Dalmatinska Street, while up in the hills above, you recall, it was known by a different name, Kevrin Creek.

There may be no stream in the entire world that had less water in it, but still this one had two names: closer to the source it was Kevrin, and farther down, Buka.

It was such a poor little creek that it didn't have the strength to cut its way through and flow down into the Miljacka. Instead, as it came downhill it trickled off into the frog swamps. Which you remember as the most beautiful part of Tito Street. The part of the city that etched itself into your mind such that you cannot read the word *city*, any city, experienced for the first time, without thinking of it like Tito Street between Parkuša and Dalmatinska, and a little farther down, toward the Eternal Flame.

After crossing Dalmatinska, you can continue without looking where you're going. Your eyes closed, the pebble stuck in the sole of your right shoe tapping against the stones, you point with your raised left arm, while all around you there is no one, for everything is empty in dreams, and all are dead: the Café Unima, shop windows filled with gray, embarrassing socialist clothing, from the time when everyone was running off to Trieste for skirts and jeans, or to the commission shop on Vaso Miskin; the courtyard with Café Lisac in it, where you never went because it was a metaphor, not a real place, having sprung up on the spot where the photographer Ivica Lisac had his studio. All the black-and-white photos of the Rejc and Stubler families were taken with his photographic equipment. Nono, as he crossed the square in front of the theater, smiling at the familiar eye looking at him through the lens. Nono in 1942 in the middle of Ferhadija Street. The only remaining picture of his eldest son Mladen, killed in 1943, taken in one of the classrooms of the gymnasium – Nona destroyed all the others, but this one was hidden away in a book, so she didn't find it – and all our other lost, destroyed, and living pictures, taken in Sarajevo before 1945.

Lisac was a friend of Nono's. It was with Lisac that he carried on his conspiratorial discussions regarding politics. The two of them would sit in the dark room, Ivica fussing with his developing agents. and they could speak freely about what they otherwise would not have.

My grandfather Franjo Rejc was not an especially brave man, but he liked to gossip. Ivica Lisac was eloquent but not chatty. He looked at the world through pictures, not ideas. He was horrified when he saw a photo of a demolished Jewish shop taken somewhere in Germany in Belgrade's *Politika*. He said it would not turn out well. Later, when Hitler invaded Czechoslovakia, it was to Ivica Lisac that Nono first uttered the phrase that would be repeated for years: "That idiot will lose the war!" Lisac probably glanced at his as yet unsmashed displays when he responded, "But we will no longer be around then . . ."

They both survived Hitler's defeat, but Ivica Lisac was in a sense correct that neither of them were there anymore.

It was at Lisac's shop that Franjo Rejc listened to the soccer broadcast of the 1952 summer Olympics from Tampere, Finland. Emir Kusturica masterfully threaded this match through the finale of his film *When Father Was Away on Business*. Fifteen minutes before the end, Yugoslavia was leading five to one, but the Soviets came back to tie it. Those four goals changed history. Yugoslavia found itself at Stalin's feet but in the rematch rose up to win three to one. Ivica Lisac cut out a sketch by Zuko Džumhur from *Politika*, framed it, and hung it on a wall in his shop. Deathly furious, Stalin sits propped on his elbows, holding his forehead. Beside him is a radio split open with an ax.

What would it be like for you to go into the café that replaced his photography studio? Though you were born at a time when Ivica Lisac had begun to shut the doors of his shop, and in your youth, until the beginning of the war, people were going to the café that his son Damir kept, and the place had become important in the lives of the people of Tito Street, for you the time before your birth was what mattered.

Here amid the violet light of the darkroom Franjo Rejc sat on a wooden stool, blowing out a puff of smoke, furiously pronouncing, "That idiot will lose the war!" And Ivica Lisac answered a little absentmindedly as he fished a picture out of the developing tray with a pair of wooden tongs: "But we will no longer be around then . . . " Later, you would no longer be around either.

The Landesbank building, which when you were growing up was the Social Services building, in front of which burns the Eternal Flame – in memory of the city's liberators in 1945 – divided the street like a split end into Vaso Miskin, which turned to the right, and Tito, which continued to the left. This part of Tito Street, all the way to the Gazi Husrev-beg baths, was the famous Ćemaluša: a street and a quarter in which people lived better and more joyfully than in the morass of the Hadži Idrisov Quarter, and where the culture and literature of the constrained Turkish provincial backwater would be born, at a time when that backwater was being transformed into the easternmost Habsburg city.

During your childhood the notorious Hamam Bar was located at the Gazi Husrev-beg baths. On Sepetarevac people called the Hamam Bar a bordello. This was what the worried mothers of boys entering adolescence said, as well as strict female teachers who saw Hamam Bar as a place of corruption for socialist youth, a place where the soul was sold to the devil, a place of waywardness for all men and some women. The Hamam Bar was like a sink that someone had once left unstopped overnight such that all of Sarajevo was being sucked down into the pipes to disappear. There would be nothing left in the morning.

This was how the apocalypse was imagined on Sepetarevac in the midseventies.

Blessed are those who died before 1992, certain that Sarajevo would become something resembling Hamam Bar. Even hell was beautiful to those who only imagined evil.

From the baths to Abdulah Efendi Kaukčija Lane, the street was called "Beyond the Baths."

And after that began Varoš, the Serbian part of town, with the old Orthodox church at its center. On a small bit of the facade that still holds together on an outside wall of one building, though it seems it could fall away with the next downpour, there is a prewar ad for the Uglješa Cucić distillery. Once this facade is no more, and the name of Uglješa Cucić has disappeared, so too will pass the remembrance of the Serbs of Varoš, leaving only the old church, as a souvenir of something that ceased to exist long ago. Souvenirs, souvenirs, souvenirs . . .

The line you are discussing was first drawn after the murder of Franz Ferdinand and his wife Sophie. It was then that Tito Street became one. On November 4, 1914, while the Austrian troops were pressing across the Drina in a punitive expedition, and the Great War's glorious battles were in preparation, the most beautiful part of Tito Street was named after the assassinated crown prince, the extension after the duchess Sophie, and the part from the baths to the bazaar after the provincial governor, Oskar Potiorek.

Only a month after the creation of the Kingdom of the Serbs, Croats, and Slovenes, on January 10, 1919, the entire street, from Marijin Dvor to Baščaršija, would be named after the future King Alexander I Karađorđević. In the middle of April, when the Ustaše arrived on trains and trucks in the city, which had already been occupied by the Germans, and the local riffraff instantly broke into the new Jewish temple and desecrated it, without waiting for any German or Ustaše order. The street was given the name Doctor Ante Pavelić.

After the liberation, on August 20, 1945, the city authorities rendered a decision to return to the street its previous name of King Alexander. At the time the Partisans probably didn't know what to name the main Sarajevo thoroughfare, this line traced by your thoughts and feelings, and so returned its previous name to it temporarily. In this they showed a clear and very important difference between on the one hand, the unifying King Alexander and his class enemies, who established the republic of equal South Slavic nations and ethnicities atop the charred remains of the previous monarchy, and, on the other, Ante Pavelić, a criminal. Perhaps it was not even intentional, but the Partisans did an important thing for the residents of Sarajevo when they allowed the main street to again carry the deceased king's name until April 6, 1946. Those seven and a half months were enough for everyone to examine the palms of their hands, in prayer or not, to see whether anyone's blood might still be on them.

And then, on the first anniversary of the liberation, once their consciences had been unburdened, emerged Marshal Tito Street.

Focht Street; or, the End of Art

It has often happened to you lately that you'll be describing some picture or event and in the middle of the story you stop and grow silent, confused, for it seems to you all at once that you haven't been describing something you actually saw in real life, something that happened, it is some other person's life, and you are telling a story about some other world, which you know perfectly, but which has no connection to the world you inhabit. And then, after a few seconds, you go on talking, certain that you've invented the whole thing. But you have begun to invent. And it is no longer you, since you earlier stopped being me in order to be able to talk about Sarajevo. And then you become a subsequent you, multiplying personas, like the reflections in the men's hair salon near the Hotel Central, and each of them tells a story about his own life, until at a certain moment he cannot grasp how to talk about something that no longer exists. He is silent then, but he's begun to invent, transforming into a subsequent you, who continues to talk about himself . . .

The last time this happened to me I was in Poznań, in a library, speaking to an audience about the public library where I had my first library card. Poznań is a city in western Poland where Jews once lived among the Poles and Germans.

Then the Jews were transformed into smoke and the Germans disappeared into Germany.

I don't know what led me to talk about my first library card, but after the second sentence came out of my mouth I could sense something there, in Poland, among the spirits and absent people, behind the facades in which a disappeared world was reflected through the architectonic physiognomies, that was as comfortable as in its own homeland.

And I heard you talking about the Vlatko Focht Children's Library in Višnjik in 1975. The year before, they had got you a library card and you had started going twice a week with Nona to return your books and get new ones. She would accompany you, but you would finish two books in a single afternoon then want to go back. Taking out more than two books was not allowed. The checkout limit was fifteen days. You spent every weekday that summer in the library, from the beginning of vacation on. When September came and school began, you would continue with the same regularity. It would be like this to the end of the fourth grade, when you were able to get an adult library card. There weren't any books left in the children's section for you.

You didn't think about who the library was named after then. Nor did you think about the names of the streets, squares, or schools until the names started to be changed. The children's library, along with a line of branches, had been founded in 1961. The next year the divisional branch in Višnjik opened. The library bore the name of Vlatko Focht.

That same year Vlatko's older brother Ivan published his book *The Destiny of Art*. And when the library opened, Ivan became an adjunct professor at the philological department of the University of Sarajevo. He lived in a city where he had no relatives and where everything reminded him of their death. The entire life of the aesthetics professor Ivan Focht was a remembrance of death. He was a Marxist and not a Marxist. He was a free man preoccupied by the music of Johann Sebastian Bach. He contained within him a perfect Pythagorean order. In the mathematics of Bach's music, without intending to do so, Professor Focht found corroboration for the material nature of the entire world, and of the dialectics that lead matter toward its eventual origin. Bach's music helped keep him from going crazy.

Ivan Focht studied music and mushrooms, which he'd gather in the woods around Sarajevo. He was the first dedicated mycologist of Sarajevo; his best known work, *The Mushrooms of Yugoslavia*, appeared in 1979.

He retired in 1974. A few years before that he had slowly begun to move out of Sarajevo. He went to Zagreb but would come back every week to hold his lectures on aesthetics. A month after Tito's death, another essay on his life's topic appeared in Belgrade's *Politika*: "Hegel and the End of Art." Here is how it closes: "If art comes to an end soon, it will not be for the reasons given by Hegel, not because it has become too narrow and foreign to the spirit but because spirit itself has lost its battle. Not because spirit has climbed to a higher level but because it has sunk to the lowest possible."

Professor Ivan Focht died at the moment of art's end, on October 20, 1992, in Zagreb. In the city where he was born sixty-five years before, the first winter of the siege was about to begin. One winding, irregular, strangely shaped street still bears the name of the Focht family. Here was the house with a marble tablet where the professor and his younger brother Vlatko were born. On the tablet are a few lines about the fate of the Focht family.

It was on this street that you first happened to lose your way, during one of the first years after moving from Drvenik when you were still trying to make friends with people your age. They rejected you, but you tried. You believed there was meaning in childhood friendships, and in adult friendships, that would last to the end of one's life. Nono and Nona had many friends who had died, about whom they spoke as if they were living.

You were playing one of those hiding games where you would break into two teams and then run and hide in the dark entrances of dilapidated brick buildings, ranging across the whole hill between Nemanjina Street and the Music Academy, all the way to the Sarajevo City Museum.

That's how you ended up on Focht Street and read the inscription on the marble tablet. The next morning you woke up with a fever of 103. Your mother said it was from the previous day's running around. You'd come home all sweaty. Nona said it was surely from all that running around. Nono was by then lying in a grave at Bare Cemetery.

I couldn't tell them I hadn't got sick from running and hiding in the entryways that stank of boiled cabbage, where you had to speak softly and breathe even more softly because in the rooms above, behind the closed doors, someone was always dying, but rather because of what was written on the marble tablet next to the house where the Focht family had lived.

I had looked in through the windows and imagined them there. The unmoving curtains, the light chandelier, the high, yellowish ceilings – everything must have been the way it was in their time. Besides this, perhaps there was a difference between my own time, in which I stood for the first time before that house and read the inscription on the marble tablet. Perhaps inside, I thought, the Focht family was waiting for what was inscribed on the tablet to happen. There was no way to avoid it, it was already written there.

I thought this and then got sick.

You didn't go to school for a whole week. They forbade you from running around like that in the future. Why can't you play quietly? Nona asked. And you answered, "We can!" You didn't think it was really possible, but to such a question there was only one answer.

Josip Focht was a converted Zagreb Jew born in 1897. He fell in love in Bosnia and married Sara Ozma. She was a member of the Ozma family from Olovo. In order to seem less Jewish, or so that her name would be more acceptable to the Swabian ear of her husband's family, she became Charlotte. Their two sons, Ivan and Vlatko, were born in a span of four years. The Focht family resembled the many *kuferaš* families of Sarajevo officials, teachers, and rail workers who had moved there after 1878. The difference began with the fact that the Fochts were of Jewish origin.

They would have survived the war without anyone touching them – for Josip was baptized, and their neighbors on Čadordžina didn't know he was Jewish, and as a rule what the neighbors didn't know the Ustaše didn't know – had it not been for what Josip and Charlotte Focht believed and what they taught their sons.

A history of a somewhat previous or parallel age noted the following fact: equipment belonging to the local chapter of the Yugoslav Communist Party – a roller copier and a radio – was stored in the apartment of Josip Focht beginning in March 1943. Focht compiled the daily bulletins concerning conditions in the country and the world, and events in the Yugoslav theater of operations. He made copies and shared them with trusted messengers, who disbursed the Party bulletins to other trusted individuals or left them in various places in the city where ordinary citizens could read them. Charlotte and Josip carried on an information war against the Croatian propaganda machine and the German propaganda that reached Sarajevo, that city in the southeast of the new Europe, in which Catholicism and Islam were united naturally and through mutual interests. At that time, shortly after the collapse at Stalingrad, in which the finest Croatian sons also perished, particularly those from Bosnia, but before the decisive tank battle of Kursk, Charlotte and Josip also went to war against the Vrhbosna archbishop Ivan "the Evangelist" Šarić, a sworn member of the Ustaše who wrote odes to Pavelić and called on the sons of Catholicism to take part in cleansing Europe – and our beloved Bosnia – of all varieties of the sordid and messy, of the Antichrist, the schismatics, the communists, and who, in the abhorrence of Jews and the faith in one God, found himself on the same side as the Jerusalem Mufti Mohammed Amin al-Husseini, who had taken our Bosnian Muslims especially to heart, more than once making the rounds to visit them across the European theater and encouraging them to hold out in the battle for the righteous cause being pursued by the Führer of the German Reich Adolf Hitler. All this was being broadcast on Sarajevo Home Radio (whose programming could be heard in the city squares and cafes), written about in all the papers, and reported on by all the German, Italian, and Croatian town criers, while against all of them battled Charlotte and Josip Focht using a concealed copier and a radio. What they were doing provoked at least ten death sentences per day against them. They did it out of a faith in universal human values that was much greater than both the confidence in eternal life of our archbishop Ivan and everything Grand Mufti al-Husseini believed in and preached would arrive with Judgment Day. This being the case, it also testifies to the fact that Charlotte and Josip were prepared to sacrifice their two sons for their faith in the equality of all people, and in truth. This accorded with a certain Jewish tradition, described in the *Romancero Judeo-Español*, which in a future that they would not live to see would be compiled by the Sarajevo professor Muhamed Nezirović, but it also accorded with the truth of their times, of which they were both entirely conscious: the lives of their sons would be worth nothing, nor would they themselves have the right to live, if they did not spread the truth throughout Sarajevo with the Yugoslav Communist Party's roller copier. If the lies of Mufti al-Husseini and Archbishop Šarić won out, or those of the man whose name was inscribed onto Sarajevo's main street, Ante Pavelić, there would be no life for them.

The Focht family was discovered on the morning of Wednesday, January 17, 1945. The mother, father, and two sons were arrested. This happened at the same time that an entire clandestine network was uncovered in the city. People fell in the railways, post offices, police stations, and in other institutions where they were hiding. This was thanks to Vjekoslav "Maks" Luburić, general in the Croatian armed forces, founder of a network of transit camps of the Independent State of Croatia, a quite brave and utterly compassion-less man, a criminal and a devil, who arrived in Sarajevo at a time when it was clear to everyone, especially him, that the war was lost. He came to avenge, to hang and butcher, everything that in the preceding four years had conspired against our eternal Croatia, Europe's new order, and the Germans with whom Luburić was forever feuding, for German amenability and their impersonal manner of work irritated his sensibility, while they in turn were horrified by his open and utterly personal bloodthirstiness. He stayed in a modernist-era villa near the top of Sepetarevac while operating in a building that he had selected himself, on Skenderija Street. He chose it, they say, because of the Masonic symbol forged into the facade. He wanted to take revenge against the Jews and the communists.

The Focht family was transferred to a building of the regional police, on what you remember as Boris Kovačević Street. A day later, while they were being interrogated, the eldest son Ivan jumped from the second floor. In this leap, which must have been an act of salvation in suicide, an original philosophical aesthetic came to life. A musical aesthetic above all, though Professor Focht was the first Yugoslav scholar – you would remember this as a bizarre detail – to write about science fiction. In this leap of the seventeen-year-old high school student from Čadordžina Street one hears the *Goldberg Variations* in their most masterful performance, by Glenn Gould, which Professor Focht would of course come to know. In the mathematics of the music, in its perfect symmetries, which permeate with the pageantry of a cathedral, before which even animals stop, spellbound, a wide-eyed lemur, the mentally ill grow calm as do children and penguins, and the good Lord marvels – if it is possible to believe in the Lord – at how a person can create such music. Inside it, in this music, is gathered all the miracle of Ivan Focht's leap, from the second floor, to freedom.

Charlotte and Josip were condemned on March 12 by the wartime military court of Maks Luburić and shot. Fourteen-year-old Vlatko ended up in a transport for Jasenovac. It is not known how he died. Or perhaps this was discovered by those who searched for him. But history stops before such an inquiry can begin in the name of a human hope that by some chance he might be alive. The Sarajevo library was named after Vlatko.

In some future non-time, when you too will no longer be here, in the name of tradition, Focht Street will become Čadordžina, as it was called when the family lived there. Some street will be named after the Fochts on the other side of town, somewhere at the foot of Zlatište, on the slopes of Trebević, where they never set foot. Or perhaps Ivan did, when he was out hunting for mushrooms.

The Church of the Holy Transfiguration:
History of a Nightmare

I completed my first year of elementary school in Drvenik before we moved permanently to Sarajevo. My grandfather had died and without his asthma there was no longer any reason for us to spend winters in Dalmatia and summers in Sarajevo.

That same summer, before I started second grade at Silvije Strahimir Kranjčević Elementary, I started suffering from nightmares. Obsessive, horrible dreams – mostly about death – which repeated and also continued in episodes, like in a TV series, from one night to the next. I had slept poorly in Drvenik too. Most of those dreams would come back, waiting for the next installment. But something had changed: the dreams' setting.

All my nightmares for the next several years would unfold on the same narrow stage, in the courtyard before the Church of the Holy Transfiguration in Novo Sarajevo, and then inside the church. I won't describe the dreams. They were various, touching on my daily fears, whatever had happened in reality, and of course, death. Sometimes some ordinary dream would slide into a nightmare, and then I would suddenly be transported to the churchyard.

And for years later, as an adult, before and during the war, I would occasionally dream of the Church of the Holy Transfiguration. The dreams were no longer as scary, but they were always uncomfortable.

I think I stopped dreaming about it once I moved to Zagreb. Even today most of my dreams take place in Sarajevo. I dream of Zagreb rarely, but even when I do, the dreams begin on Ilica and end on Marshal Tito or near the Health Ministry. But the Orthodox church in Novi Zagreb is no longer in them. I freed myself from it by leaving Sarajevo.

I suppose it might have been possible to speculate for a long time, completely erroneously, about the reasons why my uncontrolled, nighttime imagination chose precisely this stage for all the horrors my consciousness could create.

It would have been an interesting theme for a psychoanalyst.

I have an explanation. As a child I avoided looking at this church. Whenever we would pass by it on the tram, or later in a car, on our way to Ilidža for the Sunday trip to visit our relatives, I would turn my head to the other side. I believed I could erase it from my thoughts that way, that it wouldn't visit me at night. Of course that was entirely wrong. Though I avoided looking at it for a long time, there was no other Sarajevo building I knew so well and remembered.

After the war, arriving in Sarajevo on the road from Zenica, as I made my way down the wide avenue toward Marijin Dvor and the center of town, I would also look intently at it. I had freed myself from my bad dreams, I thought, which was at least one boon of moving away to Zagreb. At the time, at the end of the nineties and in the first seven or eight years of the new century, I would arrive in Sarajevo feeling a kind of radiance, such that I needed a reminder of misfortune, of something bad in this place that I loved. Things changed completely for me later, and Sarajevo did too, but I would still be compelled to stare at the church.

A beautiful, unusual construction.

The Church of the Holy Transfiguration was designed in the thirties by the famous Belgrade architect Aleksandar Deroko. As a stylistic model he used the Church of the Holy Apostles Peter and Paul in Ras, the oldest church building in Serbia, which dates from the eighth century, meaning from pre-schismatic times. Its appearance evokes Mediterranean sacral architecture of the period and is reminiscent of the most ancient Armenian churches.

Deroko of course did not want to make a replica, or through some coarse intervention – of the sort that today has become ordinary – make a larger version of the beautiful, harmonious little church. Instead he reinterpreted it. He used it as a theme – in the manner that Béla Bartók used traditional themes or Thomas Mann reinterpreted Holy Writ to make his story of Joseph and his brothers – and designed a completely new, fundamentally fascinating structure. What first strikes the onlooker – to the extent that she might be conscious of what she's looking at – is how the architectonic idea behind it implies a consciousness of context, of all the buildings and traditions in the midst of which it finds itself. Here too could be the reason the church became the scene of my worst nightmares. For Sarajevo was not Deroko's imagined context.

Like in the miracles of holy books, folk legends, and Latin American novels, the Church of the Holy Transfiguration flew hundreds of kilometers from Split, where the stone foundation for Deroko's structure had already been laid, to arrive here in Novo Sarajevo. The famous architect did not fight it or insist that the project be altered, but the church suddenly found itself outside its Mediterranean context, in a city where, as a new construction, it looked older than the church at Varoš, dedicated to the archangels Michael and Gabriel, which in our lives was known as the Old Orthodox Church at Baščaršija and was built in the sixteenth century on a much older foundation.

The Second World War had been underway in Europe for a year, and that summer the Germans had trampled over France when, on September 8, 1940, the Church of the Holy Transfiguration was consecrated in Novo Sarajevo. The ceremony was conducted with many people in attendance, including the Orthodox bishop, guests from other faiths, and government representatives, and then followed by a great celebration. Everything still looked peaceful and time-honored then, especially in Sarajevo, as if world wars did not concern us, or – as would be the case some fifty years later – as if we were under the illusion that the reasons for which wars began had nothing to do with us, we were far away, beyond the world and its ways, and that's why, with God's help, the war would rumble past us.

A year later everything would be different. As would everyone's feelings. People quickly forgot all that they were thinking and hoping for before the war broke out. There were no longer any believers in Deroko's church, nor would there be any until peace returned.

Aleksandar Deroko had a long life. He died in 1988, on the eve of new wars, in the ninety-fourth year of his life. He had served as a Serbian corporal in the First World War, befriended Picasso and Le Corbusier in Paris at the end of the twenties, designed the Cathedral of Saint Sava in Belgrade (which was completed after the latest wars), and became a university professor. He was a well-known quick sketch artist: in tremulous, very precise lines he created portraits of buildings that in his drawings appeared to dance. He spoke engagingly about architecture on television shows. His houses were alive. It was as if the Church of the Holy Transfiguration was a living, breathing building.

I didn't know anything about architecture when the courtyard of his church became the stage for my nightmares. But I felt buildings the way any child does. That sensation, like everything innate and instinctive, is lost with growing up. The church in Novo Sarajevo was fatal because it was divided from all the other buildings, did not fit its surroundings, was distinct from the other buildings of Sarajevo. This is not about knowing but about feeling. Just as art, when it is successful, and architecture, when it is art, is more about feeling than knowing. Knowledge might help a person to understand what he is feeling. Or it might put him on the wrong track.

In addition to being isolated from other buildings – company for such a church might be the Euphrasian Basilica of Poreč, which was built at the same time and with the same feeling as the little church in Ras – the Church of the Holy Transfiguration was quite animated. Its threatening nature emerged solely from this. The creations of Antoni Gaudí, especially the Sagrada Familia, would also act in a terribly threatening manner on a child, providing the perfect setting for nightmares, for Gaudí's buildings are the most animated of all.

Nightmares aspire to the elimination of the distinction between the living and the nonliving world. Everything comes to life. Everything leads to death.

As chance would have it, during the time of this story the elder of the temple was one archpriest Jadran Danilović. His first name, which in our language signifies the name for the Adriatic Sea. An Adriatic church in the midst of Sarajevo. It is good to have this building today in my memory, just as it was once awful to dream it.

Two Graveyards

For years I entered Sarajevo by road, driving in the late afternoon when the shadows were long and narrow, like Giacometti figures of old men and concentration camp inmates. It's like this in August. By November it is already dark, the mist and smog thick, the streetlights squint like in an Ivan Cankar novel, and everything is long since dead, though it's the same hour it was in summer.

I arrive from either of two directions, by the road through Rajlovac or the one through Vogošća. Either way, I pass by a graveyard. I circle the older one – in which the majority of the Stublers are buried – along a traffic loop that was built directly above the graveyard during the preparations for the Winter Olympics. The concrete half loop joins up with Sarajevo's widest avenue, which leads to the center of town, narrowing and forking along the way, passing by Baščaršija and turning back along Tito Street. I circle almost the whole Catholic cemetery at Stup, looking at it from all angles, and just before the column of vehicles flows on toward the city, I recognize several humble old Stubler grave markers.

From Vogošća and the village of Kobilja Glava, I pass by the glazed votive mosque, from a modern Bosniak benefactor, beside partially industrialized settlements that rose up in the sixties and seventies, during the time of targeted industry, the production of armaments, which were naïvely concealed beneath pressure-cookers that were probably produced in the same operation as artillery pieces, and proceed toward Bare.

Novo Sarajevo's Bare Cemetery was designed, built, and opened shortly after New Year's Day in 1966. It was the first unified Sarajevo cemetery where, in separate, clearly demarcated sections, adherents of all faiths and life philosophies would be buried. It was designed by the architect Smiljan Klaić, while the murals along the porticoes and arcades of the Catholic, Orthodox, Muslim, and Jewish chapels were painted by the Sarajevo artist Rizah Štetić. If it were ever possible to visit Bare for other than a mournful occasion, one could see the great patience and skill, cultured understanding, and respect with which Rizah Štetić carried out his assigned task. He was a good painter, a prewar Zagreb student of Maksimilijan Vanka, Vladimir Becić, and Marino Tartaglia, and a printmaker and sketch artist of Bosnian landscapes and genre scenes with a social orientation. He worked as a teacher at the School of Applied Arts. Quiet and withdrawn, disinclined towards the artistic fashions of the day, probably lacking in self-confidence, but with a powerful artistic and intellectual curiosity, this native Brčko painter is of importance in Sarajevo and Bosnia. The reason does not lie in his work but rather in his meager social ambitions, in the fact that he buried himself in provincial life without the least desire to measure up against the greats of Yugoslav painting. Štetić was an invisible painter, just as his murals on the burial chapels are invisible – burdened with burial ceremonies, we could never really see them.

A website notes that "with thirty-three hectares of surface area, Bare Cemetery is among the largest in Europe, while its terrain and landscaping make it one of the most interesting and beautiful of the large-scale resting places in this part of the world." Sarajevo is not a large city. Neither was it large when the cemetery was built, nor was it anticipated that the city would grow significantly. Limited by the valley in which it emerged and by its position in the middle of Bosnia, Sarajevo is nevertheless as great as any city according to its number of dead and their disposition. The decision to recognize this fact through the construction of a great cemetery was in this regard quite rational. At Bare, in the world of the dead, Sarajevo grew mixed and unified for the first time in its history, perhaps only for a short period. Before Bare, every group had its own cemetery, the dead were kilometers apart from one another.

A period of accommodation lasted from 1966, when Novo Sarajevo's Bare Cemetery opened, until the beginning of the seventies, during which the authorities obliged people, mostly by repressive means, to be buried together in the historic unity to which survivors would proudly refer, mostly in conversation with tourists. All the Muslim graves thus came down from the hillsides above the city to be collected here, in the central and largest parcel, while the Protestant, Catholic, and Orthodox graves, were displaced from Koševo, their traditional resting place since Austro-Hungarian times. At the beginning, it was still possible for people who had leased plots or held family tombs to be buried at Saint Miho-vil's, Saint Josip's, and Saint Mark's, but in 1971 this was forbidden, and everyone needed to be buried at Bare.

At the time when your Nono was buried here in October 1972, Bare was still almost completely empty, so your people had easily acquired a plot some two hundred meters from the entrance, just a short walk during which the old men in the funeral procession did not even get tired. Two plots were purchased at the time, and there was a consultation about whether a family crypt should be built, instead of leaving Nono in the raw yellow clay, where, if everything went according to plan, Nona would lie beside him.

A crypt is a small, underground room, made of stone or concrete, usually with six niches, for six caskets. It belongs to the Christian, mostly Catholic and Mediterranean tradition, and is linked by name to a family. As a rule, crypts are familial, often bearing the name of the person who built them, the family patriarch, and in the six caskets many more than six people are kept, for there is always a body that has completely decomposed, having turned to dust, with only a couple of solid hip bones, an open-jawed skull, and a few stray vertebrae remaining . . . All this is put to the side for the varnish and lacquer of a new coffin, where a body will need twenty, thirty, sometimes as many as fifty years to reduce down to two solid hip bones, a skull with a few black fillings, a spine breaking into vertebrae, into the gravel and stones at the beach in Drvenik . . .

Nono lay in the clay as these conversations about graves and crypts were going on, when Nona at last decided – they would not be building any crypt! But not because building one would be outrageously expensive, or because, already by that point in 1972, it was hard to see the sense in a family crypt given our family's ever-shrinking size, one could sense the day when none of us would be left in Sarajevo, and those six sepulchral niches would be too many for us. It was not this that was on Nona's mind. It was having seen, several years before, in a flooded open crypt in Stup, the remains of someone's life floating in the water. She looked into it and was told that Bare was located on a pronounced floodplain and her crypt, too, would quite probably be constantly under water.

She did not believe in life beyond the grave, felt that death was the end, and ultimately had no one to confess to that June 6, 1986, but at the same time she had a very unusual attitude toward the destiny and decay of her body after death. She was horrified by the thought that she might be swimming around in her coffin as in some kind of Noah's ark, rotting like the bodies Nono had seen floating down the Sava near Slavonski Brod – many years would pass before he realized that Brod was downstream from Jasenovac and that those were the bodies of Serbs, Jews, Gypsies, or Croats who had been faithful to brotherhood and unity among peoples . . . She wanted no crypt. It was more convenient, more humane, to disintegrate into the earth, she thought. But one other thing made her uncomfortable: she had a fear of suffocation, and one cannot breathe underwater. Even dead, she would need air, and in the earth she would still have that. Beyond this, thank the Lord she did not believe in, she didn't know that fourteen years later she would be suffocated by a tumor in her throat.

Thus was it decided that Nono would not be disturbed and disinterred for the construction of a crypt but that she too would be buried in the ground and in the meantime a nice, recumbent, two-part grave marker would be constructed.

It is in black stone, with Nono on the right and, since 1986, Nona on the left. She asked to be lowered, when she died, carefully into the grave, for the marble frame was narrow. The grave diggers should be well compensated so that she would not, God forbid, be placed upside down. She was not indifferent, even if she did not believe there was anything left anymore.

After her death, the next time I would come to this grave was after the death of Franjo and Olga's daughter – my mother. In the meantime, I did not visit for a full twenty-six years. I saw the graveyard from a distance, driving toward town along the Vogošća road, and it seemed to me I could see their graves from the distance.

From whichever direction I traveled to Sarajevo, I had to pass by one of our two graves. Sometimes, descending the Stup slope towards the city's main avenue, among the cemetery's visitors on the rare occasions when there were any, I recognized, I wanted to recognize, a thin, straight-backed woman in black and beside her a child. The woman was Nona, and the child was you, who in the interim, according to the logic of time's distension and the grammar of one's native tongue, have become I. You are dear to me as I look at you across the distance, which has grown insurmountable but whose essence is not in the time that has passed but rather in the sense that this city and this graveyard through which I pass in my thoughts are not for me now, nor can they ever again be what they were for you. I am surprised when an office worker asks dryly from her window: Place of birth? And by my response: Sarajevo? Is that really still possible?

In Springtime When We Air Out the Graves

From the early spring until the first snows, we went once a month to the cemetery. The bus stood at the bottom of King Tomislav Street, and next to it was a flower stand where Nona would buy yellow flowers, narcissus, sometimes even gladiolas. She'd buy red roses too, which were the most expensive, but only for Nono's and Vesna's graves. The other graves were not as important to her. Besides, there was something a little buffoonish about red roses. And if anyone saw her leaving a rose on the grave of someone who was not her deceased husband or her deceased nephew, they were liable to think just about anything. They might even say that this someone had been, heaven forbid, her lover. In her experience Sarajevo was just such a place: someone was always seeing something they ought not to see, and the rumors spread across the whole town, passed along by acquaintances and strangers alike, such that people often came to know each other by means of little bits of gossip.

You liked going with her to the cemetery. After you stopped going to the theater or to the Markale market together, you still went with her to the cemetery. You would continue to take part in this monthly ceremony even after graduating from high school, until the last day of July 1984, when you started your military service. I don't remember when you went together to Bare Cemetery for the last time, probably in June, or maybe July, after school was let out.

By the time you came back from the army, she would be old.

During those fourteen months she had no one to go to the cemetery with and so she stopped. It was simpler to call herself old than to admit to herself and then to her daughter – your mother – what was at stake. She did not want to walk through the graveyard alone, with no one to listen to her stories or to share her silence.

Your next visit to Bare would be on June 8, 1986. They would be burying Nona.

Each year, in the early days of March, around the eighth, when the fog rose momentarily above the city and the earth atop Sarajevo's graves had thawed, she would call and propose we go to the cemetery in a few days. That initial undertaking was different and more complicated than all the others during the course of the year. Instead of taking the bus, we would take a taxi. Nona would buy flowers at Markale on the Friday before, tons of flowers, which she'd place overnight in all the vases she could find in the house, and my mother would get a migraine from their scent.

We would dress warmly on that first Saturday because we knew we'd be standing out in the cold for a long time. Nona would wear her black wool suit – her entire winter wardrobe had always been black – and her light black coat, purchased in Moscow when she had gone to visit her son and daughter-in-law there in 1970, and around her neck she would wrap her fur collar, which we all called fox but was actually more like weasel. The collar had a head with a snout, two glass eyes, and a fastener in the shape of a jaw that would bite the tail when Nona threw it around her neck.

By eight thirty Nona would dial the number of the taxi service to order "a comfortable vehicle." The service was punctual, one waited exactly half an hour for the taxi. Then a black Mercedes would arrive, reconstructed from a 1970s model, or the model you loved most, an old Mercedes Ponton. Or maybe a white or burgundy Peugeot 404. In any case, if she ordered a comfortable vehicle, that was what would come. You would be full of admiration as a young boy, and later as a grown man, for Nona's natural authority – what she set out to get for her money, she got – and for a long time you believed that you too would command such authority.

Besides the armfuls of flowers, we'd also bring a pail for water, along with a small broom, rags, and detergent. Nona would sit in front, next to the driver, and I would sit in the back, covered in flowers, a big travel sack with the cleaning gear between my knees.

The trip to Bare was short, much shorter than when you last drove around these parts in your blue bug at the end of the eighties. There were fewer cars, the settlement at Ciglane had not yet been built, and the wide roads heading out of town were empty. At the beginning of March, the natural world in Sarajevo was still dormant – the trees leafless, the meadows gray – as the two of you set out on your mission.

Just as people go in the early spring to air out their summer houses and their country residences, so Nona decided on the first Saturdays in March to open the graveyard visiting season.

We'd visit Nono's grave first. Although Vesna's grave was on the way, we would come back to it after. The winter snows, smog, soot, and mud would make the black marble plaques impossibly filthy. The scrubbing and rinsing of the headstones took an hour. Nona scrubbed, cleaned, and polished, while I went for water. The fountain was down the hill, beyond the chapel, at the bottom of the Catholic parcel, so it was a long trek. But I didn't mind it: a lot of things happened at the cemetery, quite a few people showed up, we were not the only ones welcoming springtime, others were there to open up their crypts as if they were summerhouses, cleaning them and airing them out for the coming season. Some of them I know, old men and women, I greet them, they ask about Nona – Is Grandma up there? Did Mrs. Rejc come? Say hello to your Nona! Stop by on your way back! – while others I know only by sight. There are few we don't know, we've been coming here for years after all, every March, since 1973, when we had only one earthen grave, around which Nona planted pansies, and it would be that way as long as our above-ground family was there to take care of our below-ground family. Here we all know each other, we smile at each other while standing in line for water, buying wax candles, which are more beautiful than the stearic ones but burn more quickly, we make each other laugh while performing our graveyard rituals and so announce the beginning of another Sarajevo spring. There will not be many more such springs for us, but we don't know that, nor do we think about how many graves there are already or about how our familiar world is gradually moving away from this city into the world of the spirit.

After Nono's headstone – in our conversation it is a memorial; only on paper and in books is it a headstone – has been washed, dried, and tidied up, and after the yellow flowers have been placed into two vases, Nona uses a match to light a candle that's been placed on a special metal stand. If there is no wind, which is usually the case in March, the candle peacefully burns down. If there's a breeze from the north, the little flame goes out but the next person to come around to Nono's grave will light it again.

It is the 1970s, everyone is still alive and strong, the railmen, beekeepers, card-game friends, and their wives are all alive, with armfuls of flowers and pockets full of candles. They know where Franjo lies, his grave is in a beautiful spot, just off the path, easy for anyone to get to, and when they come to see their own, they call on him as well, straightening out their candle and ours too along the way, relighting it if the wind has blown it out.

And so every candle on our memorial burns to the end. Lit again and again, the candle too attests to the fact that we are remembered, respected in this city, talked about . . .

There had been nothing left of Nona's faith for a long time. She was man-ifestly nonbelieving, she had long since discarded the rituals of the Catholic Church and celebrated Christmas only for the sake of her family. You don't think about this, for it has been going on for as long as you remember, you have enjoyed going to the cemetery with her your whole life, for every visit is a great story laced with a number of smaller ones, and nowhere do you hear so many stories about people you have never met as when you go to the cemetery. You don't yet know that all cemetery ceremonies are linked to belief in God or to believing that something exists beyond this life which must be enhanced with flowers, candles, and a forever-clean marble marker. And when you first come to understand this, at the end of eighth grade or in the first years of high school, you don't associate it with her. Other people go to the cemetery because they believe in God, but she does it for a reason you don't think about. If you asked her about it, she would not tell you the truth. I know what she would say: Graves need to be cared for because that's the way things are done! This was her response to everything she wanted to remain silent about: That's the way things are done!

Next followed the tour of the other graves.

To describe that route I would need to follow it once again. Touring today's Bare would be like walking amid ruins, conversing with ghosts. That cemetery is a living world and such must it remain. One solution to this could begin with a precise sketch of the cemetery, a plan of this underground city in which all the graves were registered with all the headstone inscriptions. The plan could be laid out on a sheet of white packing paper, three meters wide by four meters tall, on which I would then trace in red pencil our route through the cemetery after Nono's headstone had been washed, tidied up, and decorated, along with Nona's still-empty plot.

One can arrive at such a drawing after precisely photographing Bare, the way all the larger cities are photographed for the use of satellite navigation in cars. In the next phase, after recording the route, the plan would need to be copied in a reduced version so that it could be placed across the fold on the inside cover of an eventual novel. The book's length is impossible to foresee, but probably about five hundred pages would be adequate for narrating from memory and reconstructing the biographies of those whose graves Nona and I would make the rounds of on those first Saturdays of March. Each gravestone would be its own chapter, graves we passed by for years, beneath which lay people we did not know and who had no connection to the Stublers or Rejcs but whose stories were similar to ours.

We would sometimes visit other cemeteries, for in them Nona had other forgotten relatives and friends from childhood. It would also be worth telling the story of Zehra's grave, which we look at from a distance in one of Sarajevo's Muslim cemeteries, never getting too close, for that is not the custom. Unlike us, Muslims do not walk through cemeteries to visit their dead. Among them, she'd say, this is practically forbidden, lest the dead be disturbed, or God – in whom Muslims believe, by contrast to us for whom God is just a story – cease to show pity for those who are no longer on this earth. This could anger him, for it would show that we don't have faith.

Thus would Nona, staring at Zehra's lopsided tombstone from a distance, unfold her theory of Islam. She knows very well she has told you this before. And you know that she knows, and that is why you listen and wait for the story to come to its usual end.

Even today I don't know why she told that story over again and why she extolled the relation of Muslims to their graves and graveyards. In part, over the years, she had inadvertently invented and elaborated on something that, at its base, had been true. In Muslim cemeteries candles are not burned, and there are no flowers, nor women in black. Overgrown with grass, they had once constituted Sarajevo's natural architecture of meadows and untilled land, sweeping above the city, older than any cemetery and even any idea of one. They had no Latin inscriptions, only white ornaments with Arabic script. This gave her pleasure, for she thought Muslims had something that took the place of visiting graves and telling stories about the deceased. Instead of hating them and seeing them as unbelievers – which was common in her time among the adherents of various faiths, and which today has at last found its legal expression in the reign of terror of the dominant majority against the ever-shrinking minorities – she looked longingly to their faith, the Muslim faith, as a kind of outlet. Besides, she had loved Zehra more than anyone else in the world.

But the novel would not need to end with Zehra. The effect would be tendentious, false, and sentimental. Our reality, especially after it crosses into the past and after it has been crushed by history, often has the effect of being tendentious, false, and sentimental. That is why the novel ought to go on a little longer, ending at Bare in the afternoon, when there are few taxis at the entrance and Nona is not able to choose a comfortable vehicle but instead we take the first available Fiat 1300 back to town. Our hands are empty, no longer filled with yellow cemetery flowers, narcissus, and gladiolas. Our palms tremble from a great disburdening.

Aunt Finka at Saint Mihovil's

Aunt Finka rested in Saint Mihovil's cemetery. She'd never married, and her connection to our family was vague. One could have written several novels about Aunt Finka: she was witty, cheerful, and obsessed with sex, but in an old-fashioned, once-upon-a-time manner, when one did not use the exact names for things but spoke instead in metaphors, and distant – but not the least bit scurrilous – allusions.

She died several years before you were born. While Karlo Stubler's children were still alive, people came to Ilidža every week for a Sunday meal and an outing, and in the summer everyone gathered at Aunt Lola's in Dubrovnik. Aunt Finka was a lively figure in every conversation. People told stories about her, real and invented, jokes, and anecdotes; they even imitated her voice and her speech defect: a gurgled, so-called French *r* that made her sound foreign, as if she were from Zagreb, though she was a born Sarajevan. She would be dead for many years before Krešo Golik's film *One Song a Day Takes Mischief Away* came out. Everyone went to see it and said yes, that film was about Aunt Finka! The writer must have heard her life story from someone. And you too would be told, the first time you saw the film on TV: See, that's about Auntie Finka!

Legend had it that she had purchased the burial plot at Saint Mihovil's before the war. She was in her forties or fifties. She had no one of her own, though she was an aunt to us all, and she purchased a plot for herself and built a nice memorial marker out of cement and stone in the fashion of the day. She would visit it on All Saints' Day, when everyone gathered at the cemeteries, and in the springtime, when it was necessary to wash and tidy up the headstones, and she would sweep around her future resting place, then light a candle and place a bouquet of gerberas in a vase. Gerberas were Aunt Finka's favorite flower. Even today whenever anyone mentions gerberas, you think of her. And you think, God, does her headstone still exist in Sarajevo's Saint Mihovil Cemetery? The last time you went was with Nona in the early eighties, when they were constructing the new road, which ran over a good portion of the neighboring cemeteries of the Holy Archangels George and Gabriel, and passed right through the bones of Sarajevo's Orthodox, whose posthumous suffering and oppression would be passed over in silence.

Saint Mihovil's was almost part of a suburb at the time Aunt Finka purchased her plot. It had been built in 1884 according to the design of one Josef Rekveny, who is himself buried there. In this cemetery, separated from the Orthodox cemetery by an invisible but clear demarcation, all of Sarajevo's Catholics were buried until 1966, mostly immigrants, often of foreign origin: Germans, Poles, Czechs, an occasional Catholic Hungarian, rare Italians, Slovenes, and Croats, the domestic ones and the ones who had been resettled through royal and imperial edicts, from Zagreb, Dalmatia, Slavonia. Nona took you to this cemetery because Finka did not have anyone else in the world to visit her grave. At the cemeteries of Saint Mihovil and the nearby Saint Josip the headstones, the expressions of eternal consolation, recommendations to the good Lord, and sometimes nostalgic recollections of distant countries and homes were inscribed in nearly all the languages of the old monarchy, especially German. It was here that, at a very early age, you got an idea of those who had once lived in this city, who had built it and raised it from the ground, and to whom Sarajevo truly belonged. You had an illusion of belonging to that city, to that forgotten world in which others once lived. When the illusion dissipated, when time swept it away like a fog, the memories turned into fiction, and the city in which you were born was transformed into a fictional phenomenon, a place that existed only in books and dreams.

Some fifty paces farther on from there, or so it seems in your memory, is the grave of Ivo Andrić's mother. This is not an irrelevant piece of information. You never visited Finka's grave without passing it and remembering how Ivo Andrić had been in love with Finka in high school, and how many years later he'd gone looking for her when he visited town. It was 1960 and he rang the doorbell of her house, but she was not home. She was at the pedicurist. He wrote a note on a small piece of paper and shoved it through the letter slot. Finka died unexpectedly the following year, at the end of summer 1961, and two months later it was announced in Stockholm that Ivo Andrić had won the Nobel Prize. When they cleaned out her apartment, which the city authorities had taken over, no one thought to look for the small piece of paper with his note – that is, if that little piece of paper even existed, and if Aunt Finka had not invented it (many of her love stories were imagined). Today, not a single photograph of her has been preserved, though one certainly had existed, a small black-and-white picture I remember having seen, in which Nona and Auntie Finka are standing on the Carev Bridge, laughing. It has disappeared. Nona did not like photographs of people laughing, so perhaps she destroyed it. In general she did her utmost to annihilate all documents, letters, photographs, and memorabilia, so that no trace of her would be left after her death.

The one thing that Nona did not take into account was your memory of it all. You nearly forgot Aunt Finka. You didn't remember her in all these years in Zagreb, or earlier, during the war, or earlier still, when you could have gone out to Saint Mihovil's to see whether her grave marker still existed. Countless times you walked down King Tomislav Street, passing by the Second Gymnasium and then Koševo without entering the cemetery to see whether Auntie Finka was still there. There is probably a reason for this, just as there is a reason I remembered her a few days ago, just before I might have forgotten her forever.

It was early in the morning and I was reading a book by the Austrian author

Gerhard Amanshauser titled *But a Child at Prater* while waiting at the Helsinki airport for a flight to Frankfurt. In one of the micro-essays or fragments from which the autobiography is composed, Amanshauser describes his aunt – who ends up drowning in her bathtub – from whom one had to hide any children's doll that was missing arms, or legs, or a head, because she would have had a hysterical fit if she saw such a thing.

I was not surprised by this but thought all of a sudden that perhaps Aunt Finka had lived a double life: one in Sarajevo, the other in Salzburg. Here she was unmarried, there she had a husband; here she was funny and a little crazy, there she was nasty; here she died in her sleep, there she drowned in her tub; but the one thing that linked the two lives was the horror she experienced at the sight of headless or limbless dolls, which could be found in every home at that time. Regardless of whether there were small children around, you could always locate a doll without a head, or a little plastic hand with painted red nails, or a plastic torso in a short skirt.

Everything else in her life had been clear. The intense sexual desire, her loneliness in Sarajevo among her own people, the loneliness of a whole life; her inability to begin something and spool up a ball of time around it, to gather the patience for it, to set the guidelines for her love, rather than merely subsist without direction; her laughter, her collection of made-up lovers – but however charged it may have been her life had remained light, until some headless, arm-less, legless children's doll appeared before her eyes.

How Aunt Finka reacted to such moments no one knows. No one talks about it. They just spread their arms and say terrible, terrible, then return to their story, about how they would hide their dolls whenever Aunt Finka would visit and how the dolls ended up finding their way out again, even in houses where there had been no young children for fifty years. In any house with a senile, widowed, worn-out, barren old person living in it, some concealed children's doll would come to light: dusty, bald, and – unfailingly – with no hands, legs, or a head. Or else, God forbid, a doll's head would surface, one that still blinked when shaken.

When this happened, and it happened despite the house being cleaned in anticipation of Finka's visit, they would spend the entire day – usually it was

Saturday or Sunday when people came to visit – worried about the fainting aunt. Water and sugar were at the ready, doctors were summoned, Finka was taken for a walk in the park, supported by the arm, in an attempt to bring her back to her normal state, when she would again speak and make jokes at her own expense. After each "attack" precipitated by a sighting of a legless doll, those present would be thrown into a panic that Finka might not ever regain her mind and might forever remain crazy.

What happened to that woman, what she saw in those dolls, no one will ever know. Those who knew are gone. No psychologist would have been able to get the story out of poor Aunt Finka.

I suspect that one grave no longer exists at Saint Mihovil's Cemetery, that of the Sarajevo spinster who was our Aunt Finka. For more than thirty years no one has visited her grave, lit a candle, placed a gerbera into the stone vase. She had done this for herself a full twenty years before she died.

188 Lanterns

Civilization arrived as a humiliation. After the short-lived but bloody uprising against the occupying forces, just after the city had been abandoned by the last Turkish soldiers, Baron Josip Filipović received the surrendering delegation at Konak. "Then," writes Archpriest Nedeljko in his memoir, "Baron Filipović soundly reprimanded the Muslim delegates with these words: 'You, thieves and animals, good-for-nothings and cowards! You and your Sublime Porte, whose every trace stinks of such filth that one cannot walk down your streets. And why did you not declare war openly like heroes rather than like whore-mongering soundrels? I am amazed at how this wretched people could live under such criminals. I will show you the power of Austria, you rebellious animals.'" That was how the Archpriest Nedeljko put it, and knowing the bearing of the generals who brought and then deprived us of civilization by sword, I don't suppose he rephrased or added much. There is, moreover, something in Filipović's words from which you would learn yourself, living some twenty years in Zagreb, something about the nature of that people, small but strong in its provincial fury, which in the East, especially in Bosnia, has always found a real or imaginary space for unloading its anger and its Croatian frustrations. You would find that Bosnia served a unique role for metropolitan Croats and those who gravitated toward

Zagreb in making them great, cultured, and civilized. You would for years travel down Zagreb's Baron Filipović Street, passing the army barracks where all Croat males received their military training, and those words of his reported by Archpriest Nedeljko would pass through your head: "You, thieves and animals, good-for-nothings and cowards! You and your Sublime Porte . . ." And, being a cynic, you'd wonder what in the world those Croats were proud of and whether you too might be proud once you figured it out. But you could never get it into your head or quite sort it out. Over time, as your attitude toward Sarajevo changed and the city itself changed, becoming for you a distant, foreign land, your wonder at the eloquence of a Croatian baron would lose its native quality. At first you had clearly identified with the Muslim deputies castigated by this high representative of the occupying power, and it made you angry. But there's no use being angry. Later that sense of identity was lost, your homeland sailed down the Miljacka, through Bosnia, along the Sava, the Danube, and there it is today at the Black Sea, last spotted somewhere near Odessa, and all that was left was the wonder of it all. As well as the attempt to understand both that Baron Josip Filipović – born in Gospić, frontiersman, inhabitant and fierce son of the Croatian borderlands, member of the always dubious Croatian nobility – and those who came to pay homage to him, the more astute of Sarajevo's Muslims, melancholic and forever introverted, who understood well the logic of history and who, in their heads and hearts managed to perform a great mental, intellectual, and emotional transformation. By contrast to the rebels and heroes, who ended up in prisons or on the gallows, by contrast to Muhamed Hadžijamaković, the sixty-four-year-old leader of the armed opposition, they were able to encompass a long span of time in their thoughts, imagining its extension much further than the life of a man or family memory, and adapt themselves to the great changes taking place in the world. Baron Filipović's insults did not concern them, for in a certain strange way they were the victors. Their imagination far surpassed those who offered futile resistance, or anything Josip Filipović could dream up. The difference between the limitations of the provincial Croat, who became an Austrian general, and Fadilpaša Šerifović, the leader of the Muslim delegates, to whom the baron had offered a seat because of his advanced age before beginning his speech, may be found in military and cultural power and in imagination. The former is on the side of the historical victors; the latter on the side of the defeated. There is often a special franchise in being the loser. Only the defeated, the humiliated, those reduced to despair can write history, and think in breadth and depth, the same way great novels are written. Great history and eternity are on their side, while on the baron's is Croatian temporariness, the servility of the cleaning staff at Croatian summer beaches, the cruelty of the soldiers in Croatian military missions. Fadilpaša was a man from the most distant province of an empire, from the very edge of the Oriental world, an Easterner in the heart of the West, but his world, in contrast to that of Filipović, was far and wide.

Civilization came to Sarajevo as a humiliation. The truth is that each event has at least two versions. Hamdija Kreševljaković was a great collector and a wise archivist of Bosnian history, someone who avoided literary fictionalization, though it would occur occasionally. In *Sarajevo in the Time of the Austro-Hungarian Administration*, which he published in 1946, he cites a different version of Filipović's speech before the Muslim delegates. Muhamed Enveri Efendi Kadić, a Sarajevo writer, was not one of the delegates but from them learned that Baron Filipović had said: "Even if you have seen that the Turkish authorities in the course of these three years have not been able to put down the uprising and establish order, that your roads and bridges are unsound, and that there is no justice, freedom, or equality, you should have welcomed the friendly forces of the great power of Austria, which came to put down the uprising and bring peace, but instead, you took up arms and inflicted great losses on their forces. That is terribly sad. Don't you know – here he raised up his arm – that this iron fist would reach Mitrovica in just two weeks? Go with God!"

The truth is probably that Josip Filipović said both what Archpriest Nedeljko writes and what the Muslim delegates imparted to Effendi Kadić. Merely by relating the two declarations, by comparing the two opposing sets of emotions, we can imagine how things appeared on that twenty-third of August, 1878, just after the Friday prayers when, powerless before the future and preceded by Fadilpaša Šerifović, the Muslims accepted defeat in a war they had never fought. This event would be interpreted in a variety of ways in our school textbooks, depending on the needs of the regime in place, but its real social drama would not be told. The personal drama of Fadilpaša Šerifović, the seventy-year-old man who sat while Baron Filipović delivered his terrifying speech, would never be of interest to anyone, though this man had the experience of ages and generations. Sitting there, he represented a world that was disappearing, a world resigned to defeat.

The leader of the resistance Muhamed Hadžijamaković turned himself in to the Austrian authorities on Saturday, August 24, the day after Baron Filipović had received Sarajevo's delegations. He had been staying in the attic of an accomplice and that day came down from the attic and set out into town. A military patrol intercepted him at the bridge and brought him to the Konak. He was in his most festive attire, already prepared for what was to take place.

He was tried before an Austrian military court and confessed to everything. He expressed no regret and was sentenced to hanging. The baron confirmed the sentence with an order that it be effective immediately. Hadžijamaković accepted it calmly, revealing no emotion. He was executed at the base of Gorica, where, as Kreševljaković writes, the Sarajevo-Pofalići road splits off from the one for Velešići. When they took off the handcuffs before the hanging, the old man leapt up, grabbed a revolver from one of the guards, and fired two shots. The soldiers bayoneted him, he was dead when they strung him up. They buried him in the field across the road from the gallows.

The difference between Fadilpaša Šerifović and Muhamed Hadžijamaković is in their way of thinking. Hadžijamaković could not imagine the world that had just come into being in Sarajevo. Though Fadilpaša could not live in such a world either, he chose self-imposed exile in Istanbul, while Hadžijamaković chose death in Sarajevo. He chose martyrdom, though he could count on future recognition. Fadilpaša could not count on such a thing. Calmly and without struggle he left his world to others, which makes him more interesting in a literary sense. It was according to this paradigm that the history of this city evolved, as did our own family's history. We too are disappearing, while Hadžijamaković's tragic mode belongs more to the genre of heroic poems and the burial monuments of victors, whoever they might be and whatever their faith. Perhaps poetry can only be found in a grave that's no more, which was in a field that is no more, across the road from a gallows that is no more, covered by a layer of asphalt.

Baron Josip Filipović Filipsberški or Joseph Feiherr Philoppovich von Philipps-berg left Sarajevo disappointed, for Vienna did not accept his proposal for the governing of Bosnia and Herzegovina. The baron was stubborn and would not let go of his ideas, which are of no interest to us here. Of interest here is that he left Sarajevo on December 2, 1878. Having passed through Mostar, he traveled to Kotor, from which he set out by ship for Trieste. From Trieste he made his way to Vienna. There in 1882 he was named commanding officer in Prague, where he remained until his death on August 6, 1889. Before his departure, by order of the city council, Josip Filipović was named the first honorary citizen in the history of Sarajevo.

Sarajevo fell under Austrian military rule on August 18, 1878. Just four days later the order went out through the town criers that the shops in the bazaars should be opened and that everyone should get back to work. The shop owners did not know what to do, especially those who had participated in the move-ment against the occupation – perhaps it would be shameful to return to work, a mark of betrayal; would they lose face before their neighbors? And of course they wanted to see what others would do. This was the way of life in Sarajevo: you look to see what others are doing and adjust your behavior accordingly. And so the city's shopkeepers, on August 22, 1878, sent their children to open the shops, with the intention of doing something contrary to rebellion but for which no word can define. On that Thursday, only then and never again, Saraje-vo's businesses were run by children. Serious and preoccupied ten-year-olds, their foreheads creased with worry, sat at the shop doors and windows, biding their time . . . Kreševljaković writes: "Thus were the shops permanently opened, never again to be closed as a sign of protest."

One of the first orders of the new authorities regarded public lighting – after the post-sunset prayers no one was to leave home without a lantern. Years later Austria would invest a great deal of energy and money in streetlights for Sarajevo and Bosnia. Along with the railroad and the postal service, this would be the largest civilizing enterprise undertaken and completed. Light was a metaphor for the West and for Western Christendom, a metaphor for the Europe that in 1878 took the place of an older, long since decrepit Europe, which had been in decline in Bosnia for the last three hundred years. Nothing quite characterized the greatness of the Ottoman empire as its drawn-out demise. Nothing in the history of humanity declined for so long as the Ottoman empire, and this decline was felt nowhere so palpably as in Bosnia. "The mentality of that land, its culture, and its song were constructed upon a downfall." That was Ivo Andrić, and therein lay his literary oeuvre.

In 1878 the streets were lit by kerosene lamps.

From a survey of street lamps conducted by the municipal guard, it was determined that on April 9, 1880, Sarajevo had 188 lamps. Fifteen years later streetlights were introduced. This unheard-of civilizational leap, a transformation unacceptable to people of the old mold such as Fadilpaša and Hadžijamaković, of course had a practical function that today's people are prepared to accept as an absolute. It is in fact hard to imagine the Sarajevo of a hundred fifty years ago, upon which complete darkness would descend every evening, when on its nighttime streets and alleys only crazy people and thieves prowled, and lights only burned where people were busy or unhappy, in the homes of scholars (those few literate imams, rabbis, Catholic monks, or Orthodox priests) or in the homes of the dying. But what else did one need light for? The answer to this question would come from the West, and before long the entire world would be lit up, and Sarajevo with it. Light both real and metaphorical distances us from dreams. And the disappearance of dreams leads to insanity.

The first electric power station of the city was built in 1894, and during the night between the third and the fourth day of April the first light bulbs in Sarajevo flickered to life, "though," writes Kreševljaković, "for a full six years (until April of 1901) the main city streets were served by eighteen bow lamps." Several months before the outbreak of the First World War, gas lighting was introduced, and in Sarajevsko polje, near Čengić vila, the first gasworks were constructed. By then the first members of your family had begun to settle in town, which would soon be overtaken by yet another great upheaval, accompanied by a new misfortune, in which the roles assigned to them by the destinies of one Croatian nobleman and two local Muslims would change little.

Members of the Karivan family arrived, followed soon after by the Stublers and Rejcs. Although the Karivans first came from Kreševo, their journey was the longest. From Kreševo to Sarajevo, in the Bosnia of that time, one had to cross half the world and take leave of a way of life that had lasted for hundreds of years, if not an entire millenium. One had to accept, in the end, a form of humiliation by civilization that was not unlike the humiliation Fadilpaša Šerifović had faced. No matter how hard you might try, you could never describe the Karivans' journey from Kreševo to Sarajevo. It is a secret to you, lost, for they could not tell you stories about it, by contrast to the journeys of the Stublers from Bosowicz and the Rejcs from Kneža, about which you know almost everything. Between those rooted in place and those who have remained eternally uprooted lies your family's history. Any attempt to make sense of it is hopeless.

On a Poem of Mine

Aunt Branka, the daughter of Aunt Lola and Uncle Andrija, lived in Germany and worked as an anesthesiologist. She married a German man, also a doctor, and gave birth to Katarina. She died suddenly in the fall of 1979 from an aneurysm. Without suffering or sickness, without words, she went away.

Aunt Branka's older brother Željko was a royal, then Croatian, then British pilot. He died a little after the Second World War, after taking off drunk from the Borongaj military airbase. Her other brother was Šiško, whom Aunt Lola and Uncle Andrija adopted years after the war to help them forget about the son they'd lost. When I was three Šiško would take me to the Dubrovnik aquarium, the beach at Porporela, and the harbor. He lifted me up and put me on a high, smooth bollard for a picture. I was terrified of falling into the sea but did not dare cry. Šiško was a sailor. Once he had a fight with his foster mother, Aunt Lola, and left the house, never to be heard from again.

Aunt Branka studied medicine in Zagreb. She was a striking woman with an unusual, natural sort of authority. She was deliberate and calm, settling our arguments and solving our problems. And she was funny. Should any of our elderly get really sick, we'd say, Branka will take care of them in Germany. As a child I was particularly impressed by the fact that she put people to sleep before their operations, guiding them into dream, and maybe into death.

In her youth in Zagreb Aunt Branka had been married to the actor Jovan Ličina. Ah, Jovan, dear Jovan, she would say tenderly, sighing. Branka had lived a brisk, stormy life with Jovan. It was filled with celebration and carousing, the years passing quickly as she exchanged them like big banknotes, with no regret or caution, as if preparing for the end of the world. In the end, all that was left was tenderness, and it seemed that she parted from Jovan out of pure tenderness. All around them were horrible divorces and collapses, bloody abortions, and gloom, while her past love shone with pure light and protected her youth against all evil. This was Aunt Branka.

I never met Jovan Ličina, a retired member of Zagreb's Croatian National Theater, though I saw him on the street several times in the nineties. One early morning in one of those years I ran into him on Ilica. We were approaching each other and – had he looked at me, had he recognized me . . . ? But how could he recognize me? He could not know that Branka Ćurlin was my mother's first cousin or that at the mention of his name our Sunday table in Dubrovnik would sigh.

The news of his death shook me. He died on December 18, 2002, in Zadar. I came across an obituary in a newspaper, at the bottom of which was a woman's name, Lada, I think. The text was full of love and adoration. Or at least so it seemed so to me. This unknown woman had loved Jovan Ličina as much as Aunt Branka had. Oh, Jovan, dear Jovan.

There was no mention of his death in the Zagreb papers.

Death of an Actor

For R.Š.

Let those whom the Zagreb actor
Jovan Ličina did harm step forward

Let the floret in the architecture of the HNK, the gala gown
       of Franz Joseph I

And his mallet and trowel, let the cornerstone
And the Theater Café – both of them – the underground passage

The clock on the square and the parking clocks step forward
Let those whom the Zagreb actor

Jovan Ličina did harm step forward
Let the fire equipment and the health inspection certificate
The coal in case of poisoning, the bullet in the revolver
       of the basement gamblers

The placards, posters, the men's and women's hats above the bathrooms
and the white hands of the ticket woman and the entrance woman with the stamp
       step forward

Let those whom the Zagreb actor
Jovan Ličina did harm step forward

Let the beggar woman on the street invoking Christ, who has never
      been in the theater
Though she has always begged at the main entrance, step forward
      if she ever met him

Let the young man with the shaven head getting out of the black Mercedes
        leading the most beautiful breasts by the hand
If he hasn't yet got a bullet in the back of his head step foward, him too

Let those whom the Zagreb actor
Jovan Ličina did harm step forward

Let the tour group from Križevac step forward, the unmarried orphan girls
        from the morning matinee
And those who ran from the winter to the theater and those
        driven to boredom by just love

And the acerbic souls in black with gold crosses round their necks and
        abortion as their greatest sin
And the melancholic prostates of runaway youths and the murderers in
        plain clothes step forward

Let those whom the Zagreb actor
Jovan Ličina did harm step forward

Let the deliverers of pizza at the actors' coat check, the stage
        hands and coat checkers
The café cooks using gas-ring burners, the refrigerators
        named Moscow step forward
And the wig makers, the makeup artists, the pederasts with
        ballet slippers beneath their noses
Let the drunk prop masters and their mournful
        lovers from Borongaj step forward

Let those whom the Zagreb actor
Jovan Ličina did harm step forward

Let the hermaphrodites in the roles of headmasters,
         hysterical divas with bleached souls
And their husbands dawdling as if from Mostar
         step forward if they know God

Let the third-string heralds and esquires, the manicure assistants
         of the baroness of the Castle
Members of headquarters with speaking parts – Chekhov is a genius, but
         it's too bad he was Russian – step forward

Let those whom the Zagreb actor
Jovan Ličina did harm step forward

Let the young scenic appearances who'll play moronic children
         to the end
And the perverse Slovene producers clothing them in women's
         garb – let them step forward too

Let the retired principal players of Croatian theater,
         performers who loose their bellies low
And pass gas during scenes with princely deaths to
         entertain each other, they should step forward too

Let those whom the Zagreb actor
Jovan Ličina did harm step forward

Let professors of stage direction and famous directors step forward
Who speak wisely on the phenomenon of the Zagreb school and
         journalistic insults against the actors' guild

Let the academicians rising up from Grandpa Vidurina's peasant sandals,
        the hagiographers of Krleža with the letter *U* on their caps
Let even those doing research on when and how often Matoš
        spoke about Serbian depravity step forward

Let those whom the Zagreb actor
Jovan Ličina did harm step forward
Let the youth who played Hamlet beneath Pavelić's picture
        in Cleveland
and waited for the applause of the three present, perplexed metal
        workers from Brač – O step forward

Let the kinsmen at the premiere, and the classmates, and newspaper
        critics, hired applauders
and the models with flower baskets and touching tears in their eyes
        first ladies of the scene, alas step forward

Let those whom the Zagreb actor
Jovan Ličina did harm step forward

While the two of us joyously drain our chalices
        toasting him in death

A Calendar of
Everyday Events

Fictions

Christmas with Kolchak

Cold and snowy winters followed the war. The snow would fall around All Souls' Day and would not melt until the middle of March. There was no one to clear the streets, though Marshal Tito Street and some of others in the center of town were cleared by prisoners from Beledija and the central jail, as well as by POWs while they were still around. The rest remained covered and snug, as if under a great quilt that had been spread across all of Bosnia, the people tucked beneath it, resting after the years of horror, and it didn't feel quite so cold underneath it, nor did the pantries, larders, cellars, meat dryers, lofts, and bread ovens feel quite so empty.

In all the years of starved, snowy winters, the winter of 1950 arrived earliest. In his *Calendar of Everyday Events, Income, Expenses, and Meteorological Conditions,* Karlo Stubler notes that the first snow fell on September 11, and that "it was heavy and thick, and under its weight broke the old cherry tree and several branches of the summer apple," but by the next day at noon it had "melted and left behind a lot of damage around the yard." It snowed again on October 5, then ten days later, on Sunday the fifteenth, the first true winter snow began to fall, continuing for the next three days, and "by Tuesday afternoon it had reached the height of the window, one meter and seventy centimeters to be exact, the highest snow since we arrived in Bosnia in 1920 and since, in 1935, with God's help, Vilko and Rika built this house." (Note: as recorded much earlier, Opapa Karlo Stubler was a completely nonreligious person, he did not believe in God, nor was he superstitious, but in his journal he regularly used phrases such as "with God's help," whether for stylistic reasons or for purposes of propriety.)

The snowfall from October did not melt in November, there were frequent winds from the south with heavy morning frosts that made it hard to clear away the snow and beat foot paths around the buildings down to Kasindol Street. The weather turned the snowy mass into ice, the soft quilt grew hard, like an Ivan Meštrović sculpture, and it seemed that we too would turn to stone, becoming memorials of our people's destiny, the pain and suffering before the country's numerous battles. After defending it from the Nazis and the fascists, the home-grown traitors, the Ustaše, the Chetniks, the Albanian nationalists, and the Slovene Home Guardsmen, after Tito, alone in the world, had pronounced his decisive No! to Joseph Vissarionovich Stalin, and after, while hungry, naked, shoeless, and still numb with fear, we had repeated that No! to Stalin and the misled international proletariat with the great Soviet Union at its head, here we were left to turn into a monument, Yugoslavia becoming a sculpture garden for Europe and the world, a land of tourism with no people and no life.

Opapa Karlo would not let himself be turned to stone with the rest of us. He was German, and though old and sickly, he was out breaking the ice in front of the house each morning. As usual he was the first person up, and his quick rhythmic blows with the metal pole against the icy path that led to the rabbit hutch entered our dreams, shattering them, and one by one we got up from our beds.

Opapa waited until the snow melted and died shortly after, in 1951, in the middle of April amid the spring rebirth when the grass had turned his entire garden green. In his ritual of morning snow clearing and ice breaking there existed some primordial fear and belief, which had grown deeper the older Opapa got, that he would not live through the winter but would instead die when the days were at their shortest and coldest, and his hope was at its thinnest. Those who believe in God – and the Stubler home was as a rule half-filled with believers and half with nonbelievers – have Christmas, the day of the child's birth, to safeguard their faith and warm their bones and souls, so they don't have to go out on a morning of Siberian cold to break the ice on the path to the rabbit hutch.

Opapa Karlo loved rabbits. Rabbits reminded him of Bosowicz, his home village in the Romanian Banat, where every Swabian house had its hutch, and all the houses in Bosowicz were Swabian, and there were at least twenty times the number of rabbits as people. When we moved to Ilidža, even before Uncle Vilko and Aunt Rika had started to build their house, Opapa mapped out his model homestead on four acres with fruit trees, a vegetable garden, a chicken coop, and a stable with two cows, a pig, a pigeon loft, and an apiary, but in all this the rabbit hutch was the most important. The greatest number of stories were associated with it, for it wasn't just rabbits that lived there, Opapa's life was there too, within its straw-laced cages, all his memories, as well as his great pangs of conscience.

Karlo Stubler loved rabbits more than people, but he did not give them names. And he would not have been pleased if we had done so. If a certain bunny, through the children and their children's imagination, had become Konstantin, Eleonora, or Moša Pijade (this was a tiny, quick, black rabbit with white spots around its eyes that looked like glasses), Opapa avoided knowing anything about it, for if he knew the animal's name, its fate would have weighed upon his soul and his conscience. This was because it was the destiny of every rabbit in the hutch to one day be eaten at Sunday dinner. Served "wild," or oven baked with fries, or in a goulash, each and every bunny would end up with its hide stretched out on the apiary door, drying for weeks so that one day in a future that would never come it would turn into a fur coat for one of Karlo's daughters or granddaughters. If not for this, the rabbit hutch would not have existed, especially in times of hunger and scarcity. Anyway, no one in Bosowicz kept pet rabbits, to befriend and give names to. All rabbits were eaten. But then Opapa had been a child and he'd had no problem applying himself with an appetite to one of God's creatures, until one day. He would watch as his brother and two cousins slaughtered them before Christmas or Easter, the rabbits screaming in fear like crazed children left out naked in the snow, and it didn't faze him. He had never cut the animals' throats himself, but he'd watched. Now he couldn't do that either. Usually, when Uncle Vilko butchered a rabbit on Saturday afternoon for the next day's meal, Opapa was holed up in his room on the second floor, with the shutters drawn and the light on as he read his Brockhaus Encyclopedia. He would open to a page at random and read the article he'd chanced upon. People said that was how he relaxed. But we knew that was how he hid the sound of the rabbit's death from himself, yet one more murder for which he was responsible, for it was he who had built the rabbit hutch and populated it with beings condemned to die.

Immediately after the war, by the fall of 1945, the Yugoslav papers had begun to report on the horrors of the German concentration camps in Poland, Ukraine, and Belarus, in which millions of people had been killed in just a few years. Opapa had always read all the newspapers he could get his hands on, and in the first postwar years, he would buy Sarajevo's *Oslobođenje* and Belgrade's *Politika* on a daily basis. He felt obligated, as a person, a conscientious union man, and an old Austrian Marxist, to learn everything there was to know about the suffering of the Jews. Hitler's Nazis, they wrote in our papers, had systematically liquidated them, exterminated them, turned them to dust, with the massive support of the local German and European bourgeoisie. Opapa was neither a Nazi nor bourgeois, but he was a German. Why should a German from Bosowicz, or rather a German from Ilidža in Sarajevo, feel responsible for what Germans from Germany had done? No, although such an idea was entirely humane, high minded, and alto-gether proper, it was alien to him. He would more likely feel responsible for the Ustaše and Chetnik butchery, though he was neither a Croat nor a Serb, because Croats and Serbs were his neighbors, his children and grandchildren, sons-in-law, male and female friends, unlike all those Berliners, Prussians, and Bavarians who lived somewhere far away, at the edge of the world. They were Germans, but their German responsibility differed from his German responsibility. That was how he saw it as he read the reports about the concentrations camps.

But he was by no means indifferent when he read that the German Jews, and Jews from Poland, Czech lands, and Galicia, had traveled to the concentra-tion camps by train. He thought about all those switchmen, dispatchers, station chiefs, and engineers guiding their passengers to certain death. All Germans might not be alike, it might not be the same thing to be a German from Kasindol Street in Ilidža and a German from some godforsaken Pomeranian hole, but all switchmen of the world were alike, whether they worked on a narrow-, regular-, or wide-gauge line of the kind that Stalin had used in Siberia. Their procedures were the same to within a hair's breadth, they awaited trains in exactly the same manner, checked the switches, tapped the wheels, and after one of the switch-men had led a train of cattle cars filled with Jews to their deaths, all switchmen suddenly had something in common with him when they tapped the wheels and adjusted the switches, and all the trains traveling along all the tracks of the world right then became that first train, that composite of cattle cars that passed among the switchmen to the camp, the gas chamber, the crematorium, the sky. And above the switchman was the dispatcher, and above him was the station chief, and above the station chief was the headquarters, the traffic engineers, directors, quartermasters, and managers who followed the railroad's strict procedures and traffic rules, repeating the same movements of their hands, feet, and heads, signed the same documents, shared the same fears and anxieties about delays, collisions on open track, accidents, and each of them, Karlo grasped with horror, had guided the hand of that first switchman sending the trains loaded with Jews to their deaths.

Although by then he had been retired for twenty years, along with all his fellow dispatchers, switchmen, and engineers, Karlo Stubler felt guilty. His guilt was incurable, he would carry it to his grave and into the void. Then, he thought, the Jews would save Jesus Christ, and he would save the Jews by helping all the switchmen move their hands in the opposite direction and instead of ending up at the camp the train would come to a stop on a siding, among the Gypsies, crows, and town's poor, where it is gentle and good and there was no Hitler and no anti-Semitism.

Then he read further in *Politika* and *Oslobođenje* and discovered that the Nazis had taken away the Jews' right to bear their own first and last names. Every woman became Sarah Israel and every man became Judah Israel. And when they transported the Jews from the ghetto to the death camps, they weren't called Sarah Israel and Judah Israel anymore but instead had numbers tattooed on the backs of their hands.

Then Opapa Karlo remembered his rabbits and understood why he had avoided knowing the names that the children had lovingly given to them. Every name whether given to a rabbit or a child, is the first act of love . . . With a name we become individuals, sheltered by the emotions and morals of a single society. Loading people into cattle cars and killing them because they were Jews required first that their names be forgotten or not heard. That was the only way, for what sort of a conscience could there be, human, switchman's, railworker's, or German, that could bring death to so many people? When there were no names, only numbers, thought Opapa, there were no people either.

All the rabbits were condemned to one day be eaten. Opapa was not stupid, or crazy, or unstable. He was strict and rational, a true German and rail man, and he was proud to be this way, but the comparison of the rabbits and the Jews never left his head. Animals were not people, and he continued to eat rabbit, but he was truly horrified by his discovery of why he had always avoided the rabbits' names. As the Nazis avoided Jewish names. So why in the world had he built the hutch? For the same reason his parents, and his parents' parents, and all the people in Bosowicz had always built hutches and raised rabbits. But why had they done this? The people in nearby villages, Romanians and Serbs, rarely farmed rabbits. Only when they were following the lead of their German neighbors. Which meant, thought Opapa, that they did not feel the need to keep rabbits in hutches, in cages from which they would only let them out once, when their time to be slaughtered had come. Was there something in his German language, in his Goethe and Johann Sebastian Bach, in what differentiated him from his Slav neighbors, that had led him to do this? If so, he thought, it was perhaps that same something that had led the Germans to turn living people into smoke and nothingness. After the war was over, Opapa was not sorry his children and grandchildren were not Germans. They all spoke German well and continued to speak to him in German, but it was fortunate that they were not German. He believed the rabbit hutch would vanish from Kasindol Street when he died.

The rabbits made him feel responsible for what the German Nazis had done but did not change his position in regard to life and death in the hutch. He was strict and rational, our Opapa Karlo Stubler, and the years were poor and hungry, so every Sunday we continued to eat fresh rabbit. Their hides were saved in the attic, in large and tidy boxes, waiting to be made into fur coats for Opapa's daughters and grandaughters. But the coats would never be sewn, and the hides were eventually eaten by worms and attic vermin over the decades.

On December 24, 1950, early on this Christmas Eve morning, Opapa Karlo was out on the path that led to the rabbit hutch breaking the ice with a steel rod. We didn't venture out into the yard because it was minus twenty degrees Centigrade out there. It was the coldest day of the winter. Convinced that he would not be alive when spring arrived, he was cleaning the path so we would not fall and break our necks when we went out to feed the rabbits. And in case he was not there, he wanted to make sure his rabbits would not die of hunger because we were unable to get to them across the ice in time.

By the time his fingers had turned blue and his toes begun to tingle with frostbite, Opapa had stopped breaking the ice about halfway down the path. He set aside the iron rod, jamming it into the snow for the next day, when he planned to continue, and carefully tread on the snow at the pace of a snail or an aged tightrope walker, making his way to the hutch.

"Regina, Regina, my child!" he called in German to his daughter. Aunt Rika did not respond so he switched to our language, trying to get Uncle Vilko's attention.

"Vilko, goodness, where are you when I need you!"

In the end both slid out in their house slippers, along with the children, everyone falling on the ice and causing tremendous commotion at the hutch, where Opapa was repeating hoarsely:

"The rabbit! The rabbit is gone!"

We had never seen him in such a state. He was agitated, as if he had suddenly lost his bearings or his wits and now had no idea what he was saying, stooped over and old, staring at the open cage in which, just the night before, there had been a fat white rabbit whom we had named Göring. This fat, blue-eyed rabbit had reminded us of Hitler's Reichsmarschall, and it was not only from Opapa that we had to keep this a secret, it was from Omama too, and everyone else, for we would have never heard the end of it if they discovered we had named a rabbit after such a criminal.

We were even afraid the rabbit would be the first to pay for this and we'd be eating him on Sunday if it came out that we'd given him the war criminal's name. Göring was not hard to find. Although the garden was frozen over, the thieves of our fat bunny had left tracks behind. Either they had not been careful, or they had wanted us to find them.

We set out together as a group to the apiary, following the tracks that led across the deep frozen expanse.

Opapa Karlo was not worried about giants or colossi, he was not afraid of anyone anymore, his strength had returned. He was angry and ready to settle things like a man with the rabbit thief, if he could only find him. Filled with wrath, he proceeded at the head of the group. His breath failed him, he stumbled, then recovered, and suddenly it was all funny – we knew we'd find Göring. Whenever Opapa was that angry, whenever he became a real Swabian and took to discipline and reckonings of the cosmic order, we all felt confident, for we knew that nothing bad could happen anymore. We smiled to ourselves and followed behind him as the tracks led us to the apiary. They ended right at the wooden door, as in some black-and-white silent film, and the tracks at the door's opening and closing were visible in the snow. There was no doubt that someone was in the apiary. Opapa stiffened, straightening himself as if he wanted to appear taller, and took decisive hold of the doorknob.

The apiary was actually an elongated hut, about fifteen meters long and three and a half meters wide, which Karlo Stubler had built himself in the summer of 1940 after the old apiary had turned out to be too small and inadequate for all his bees. He had bought the fir planks at a sawmill in Olovo, which he described in the *Calendar of Everyday Events, Income, Expenses, and Meteorological Conditions* in the following note (like all the citations from the *Calendar* this was translated by his son Rudolf): "On March 27 of this year, we set out on the morning express train for Zavidovići and then transferred to a local narrow gauge for Olovo to pick up the treated wood materials for the apiary, which had been cut according to the design I drew up and sent by mail to Mr. Konstantinović. We arrived safely in Olovo at 13:57 (a delay of twelve minutes according to the train schedule), where Mr. Konstantinović and his workers were waiting for us. Loading was orderly, as was transfer in Zavidovići, and we returned to Sarajevo at 21:12 (a negligible two-minute delay on a composite train from Zagreb). The materials were successfully brought to Kasindol the next morning by truck . . ."

Karlo Stubler put together his very precisely designed structure in one day. It took him longer, with the help of his neighbor Aleks Božić and his son Rudi, to cover it with tiles, then brought in nine hives that had previously been in the mountain shelters above Fojnica. And so, according to Opapa's *Calendar*, on August 1, 1940, the new apiary of the family Stubler was solemnly established. Before autumn arrived, Opapa would coat his construction with his own mixture of railroad grease that was to preserve the wood and prevent rot, but quickly, within two or three days, its smell had begun to bother the bees. They drowsily hummed in the garden and courtyard, and Opapa would stand to one side anxiously following them with his eyes and ears, until at last they calmed down and accepted their new home.

For the next ten years beginning in the fall of 1940, the apiary lived its orderly, apiarian and Stublerian life, according to Karlo's implacable calendar and strict apian ritual, which was the same everywhere in Europe if not the world, resting on the same precise orderliness as the railroad. Where the beekeeper was more exact, where he took better stock of the changes in weather and the seasons, there the honey was of higher quality, the bees more satisfied, and life steadier. The same was true of trains, timetables, and tracks, as it was with a railroad headquarters, which resembled a large beekeeping establishment. Except in this establishment the bees had to do all the work, for – in his way of thinking – they lived and worked without a beekeeper, although half the Stublers believed that even at the headquarters there existed a higher-order keeper, in the all-pervading, ever-present person of the good Lord.

Opapa turned the handle and gave a decisive shove to the door. The door opened with a bang and he stood at the threshold, waiting for his eyes to adjust to the darkness.

There on the straw in the depth of the apiary, hiding from the light and our searching eyes, behind the last hives, sat an old man and an old woman, holding our white rabbit on her lap.

"Kolchak, good God, is it you, admiral? And Natasha, heaven be praised, what a wondrous meeting!" Opapa rushed forward as if he had suddenly grown young and kissed the old woman's hand.

"And is that Nikolai, dear Natasha, a grown boy, wow, who would have thought! And here I remember as if it was yesterday how with God's help you brought him into our confused and unhappy world!" Opapa babbled on, caressing our white rabbit as if it were a child and not one of our farm animals.

We turned around and rushed back home. Opapa's son Rudi, our Nano, tried to stop us, he laughed and said everything was fine, that we too should greet General Kolchak and his Natasha, and that it would please them if we caressed their son Nikolai, but we were running and screaming as if the skin on our backs was being torn off, certain that Opapa Karlo Stubler had finally lost his mind.

It was just over an hour, and when we heard him coming in, we went into hiding. We were in a panic, afraid of our very own Opapa, and, peeping from under the couch, from the closet and the attic, from the shadow of the winter garden and the double locked bathroom, we listened as he was cheerfully telling to Uncle Vilko and Aunt Rika that Admiral Kolchak and Madam Natalya had come back, and that it was going to be a lovely Christmas with them and their little Nikolai.

It was the most unusual Christmas Eve in the Stubler home and in our collective Stubler history. Opapa trimmed the tree, jollier than we had seen him for a long time. He took great pleasure in preparing for the Christmas meal, insisting the dining room table be extended for there would be more of us than usual, as the admiral and his madam were coming . . .

That night we dreamed our scariest children's dreams ever, imagining Admiral Kolchak, Natalya, and our rabbit, now a baby named Nikolai, sat at our Christmas table exchanging craziness with Opapa Karlo.

Promptly at one, as on every Sunday in the home of Karlo Stubler, as on every Christmas Day, we were all at the festive table. At its head sat Opapa and Omama, dressed as if they were going to the theater, and at the opposite end, Mr. and Mrs. Kolchak. He was in a tsarist colonel's uniform, moth-eaten and timeworn, and she was in a white dress that looked like a wedding gown made from drapes, holding in her arms our rabbit, her son Nikolai.

We were all silent, our noses buried in our plates, as the adults talked about wars, weddings and funerals, children's ailments, building houses, the climate differences between Saint Petersburg and Sarajevo, about Tolstoy and Dostoevsky, the sickly Pyotr Ilyich Tchaikovsky, who composed the most beautiful music in the world (Opapa was lying, lying like a dog, he didn't like Tchaikovsky), and amid all these stories Admiral Kolchak and his wife behaved normally and rationally, they were even a bit tedious, the way all officers in the world are tedious, and probably they were lying a little too, to please their hosts.

That was our only Christmas without rabbit meat. Two stringy old hens from the yard paid with their lives for the first appearance of the Kolchaks in our house. For as we listened to this ordinary, grown-up, intelligent Mrs. Kolchak and her husband, to our amazement we began to notice a change: our Göring was no longer Göring, nor was he a rabbit, but instead he had become a proper little Russian, a young boy child, a noisy babe, the newborn of this old woman and her husband.

This was how our Opapa Karlo Stubler spent the last Christmas of his life, the Swabian from the Banat, the Austrian Marxist and union leader, who had supported a railroad strike in Dubrovnik when he was its station master and was fired and driven into Bosnia, where we would all be born as Bosnians to await our own exile into some other, still deeper and more hopeless Bosnia.

After Mr. and Mrs. Kolchak disappeared arm in arm into the frozen Ilidža twilight, down the snowy path across the field that led to Butmir, we never saw our fat white rabbit again. Nor did we ask about it. New rabbits were soon bred, Göring's cage was once again inhabited, and life went on. We did not see the Kolchaks again.

Years after Opapa's death, the story was told in our house that we never believed but that deserves to be noted, about celebrating Christmas with Admiral Alexander Vasilevich Kolchak, Madam Natalya, and their son, who was named after the Russian tsar Nikolai, who, God willing, would one day be his godfather.

This is how the story came to light, and though it is superfluous given the story just recounted, it needs to be told in accord with the ethics and ritual of narration established by Karlo Stubler in the *Calendar of Everyday Events, Income,*

Expenses, and Meteorological Conditions: when the wave of Russian emigrants was washing across the Kingdom of the Serbs, Croats, and Slovenes, and when, thanks more to the kindness of the House of Karađorđević than to the fanatical anticommunism of the regent Alexander, all the unfortunates, both well-off and poor, the university professors, generals, writers, musicians, ballerinas, and pharmacists, but also the good-for-nothings and thieves, the reckless, the provincial cobblers, locksmiths, and tailors, were being welcomed in Sarajevo, Mikhail Karlovich Shtark-Kempinski appeared in the uniform of an infantry colonel, along with his wife Natalya Alexandrovna Kruchonykh. The two were lunatics and it was a miracle that they had managed to get there from Saint Petersburg, crossing half of Europe to the Kingdom of the Serbs, Croats, and Slovenes and Sarajevo.

Thus did Colonel Shtark-Kempinski and his wife, whom everyone for some reason called by the Latin "Dona Natasha," remain in the city, whose authorities provided them with a small but sturdy little house in the Gypsy settlement of Gorica. And the Gypsies being Gypsies, easily got used to them and accepted them as their own, despite the colonel's aristocratic and steadfast, one might even say rational, hatred for – Gypsies.

This hatred drove him and Natasha into town, among the city's inhabitants and merchants, where he would pour out his misfortunes at their feet. Dona Natasha had found a child's doll somewhere and would carry it around, saying, "This is Nikolai, my son, after all this is over the tsar will be his godfather! That is why we haven't baptized him yet!"

On another occasion she had found a mangy wandering dog – her son Nikolai.

Then a dead pigeon – her son Nikolai.

A blind cat – her son Nikolai.

During the days when all of Yugoslavia was mourning King Alexander, who had been murdered for the greater glory of God, Dona Natasha was going around with a rather large log held up to her bosom – Look at my Nikolai!

The colonel meanwhile fondly supported her by the arm, for he loved her more than his son Nikolai.

Whether Mikhail Karlovich Shtark-Kempinski and Natalya Alexandrovna had ever given birth to their own son and subsequently lost him no one knew.

But it was strongly believed at the time that Nikolai had once existed, and that this was how they had lost their minds. Whether he had died or disappeared in the flames of revolution, or had been killed by the Bolsheviks, or had met his end in that baby stroller that to this day keeps tumbling down the steps in Eisenstein's film, or whether something even more hideous had happened that in the very same instant had shattered the spirits of the two parents, everyone had his own theory, and everyone could let his imagination run wild, for it was known for certain that the truth would never be known.

For Sarajevans from before the war, Colonel Shtark-Kempinski and Dona Natasha were creatures of the imagination. Their actual human destinies, their human pain, touched very few people.

At the beginning of the war, in April 1941, it was as if the earth had swallowed them up.

They vanished, no one had seen or heard from them. The Gestapo had taken them away, or the Ustaše had slaughtered them as Orthodox believers at Vraca . . . And that was that.

And then they appeared in our apiary on Opapa Karlo's last Christmas, in the year 1950. The day our white rabbit Göring disappeared. And the next day, at lunch, in Aunt Natasha's arms we saw the little newborn child Nikolai, whose godfather would one day be the Russian tsar himself.

The Match Juggler | Furtwängler

"If we had known the train was going to be standing here for such a long time, we could have taken a little walk to Medulić or the City Café for a coffee and a croissant. Is Medulić open?"

"I think so. I don't make it to those parts of town much. When I first got to Zagreb in 1944, it was prohibited and dangerous, and by the time the war was over it had become a habit not to go there. I stick to my neighborhoods in Trešnjevka and Knežija, sometimes go for a walk along the Sava and across to the other bank, to Remetinec, Blato, Hrašće. Have you heard of Knežija?"

"Of course! I lived in Zagreb for a whole school year in 1929 and '30. That was a good time. Youth . . ."

"Right, youth. And you think we're old now?"

He looked back askance, and Rudi had no idea what to make of him. One moment he seemed sneaky and dangerous, the next like an ingratiating child. Like a good, faithful puppy. A skinny, hollow man with a large, fleshy nose bent so far down that it practically covered his upper lip. He'd said his name was Joška Herzl, offering his hand as he entered the compartment. The first thing Rudi had thought was: a pickpocket. One of those authentic prewar pickpockets. He hadn't seen any of them for years since pickpocketing had become an offense for court-martialing. Nor had they reappeared at the end of the war, as if they had all mended their ways or grown old, or as if, God forbid, all the pickpockets of the Yugoslav royal railways had ended up at Jasenovac and in mass graves.

Nevertheless, he wasn't pleased to see the stranger. He checked to make sure his wallet was tucked away securely, and thought about how he wouldn't be able to sleep all the way to his transfer in Vienna. That is a long way when one is tired and sleepy.

But then he thought better since pickpockets don't say their first and last names to people they are planning to rob. Though the name could be fake. What did he say it was?

"Joška Herzl!" he repeated, removing a speck from the end of his nose with his tongue – "in case you forgot, Joška Herzl. Yes, I am of Moses's faith, though I'm actually not a believer. I hid my name for a long time, but now I sort of like saying it. A name like any other, nothing special, Pero, Ivo, Haso, there are all kinds, all more or less the same. Names and more names . . . And you, sir?"

"Rudi. Rudolf Stubler."

"Not you too . . . ?"

"No, I'm a Catholic. From Sarajevo. A Swabian sort of . . . I work for the railroad actually. I'm a railway official."

"So you must have a free ticket! You can travel to your heart's content. Did they give you a passport?"

"Yes. I'm traveling on business."

"On business, how extraordinary!" Joška Herzl made a little jump and repeated the movement with his tongue. It wasn't a speck, he seemed to have a tic. Something inside the man was making him do it. Disgusting, thought Rudi.

"And you? Do you have a passport?"

"Yes, I went to Petrinjska Street to apply for one. 'What for?' asks a guy in a militia uniform. 'Just a moment,' he says and leaves with my identity card. Joška, you poor devil, now they're going to take you in."

"And? Did they take you in?"

"No, the policeman was away a half hour or an hour at most. He came back, kindly returned my documents, and said I should come back in three weeks for my travel document, as they call it. I couldn't believe it. *Can this be true?* I asked myself?"

"And now you're using it?"

"Yes, unbelievable. Take a look." He pushed the little booklet onto Rudi's lap.

Rudi opened the passport. It was the real thing: Joška Herzl. Height: 173 centimeters. Hair color: black. Eye color: brown. Distinguishing marks: none. He looked bloated in the photograph, as if he was about to burst out laughing at any moment.

The train was still standing at Zagreb's main station. There was no one on the platform, but once in a while, at regular intervals, every ten minutes, a switchman with a cigarette butt between his lips made his way from one end of the train to the other. It started to rain, a fine autumn drizzle, though it was the end of August. It was 1954, and Rudi was traveling abroad for the first time since the war. He was being sent to Berlin. In his pocket were two letters: one was a pass, the other a recommendation, both having been processed and signed at the Ministry of Railroads in Belgrade. They were sending him to verify whether an order might be possible for steam locomotive burners for the narrow-gauge line from Sarajevo to Ploče. He had been selected for this mission because he knew German, but he was also going to Berlin for a reason of his own that he had not mentioned even to those closest to him.

Rudi's luggage consisted of his leather student suitcase and a medicine bag, both purchased many years ago in Vienna after an especially successful night at cards, when he had won at preferans the equivalent of at least three months of allowance from his father. In his suitcase was a black suit, the only one he owned, for the theater and concerts, three white shirts, washed and pressed before departure, seven pairs of socks and a gray bow tie with red polka dots, a birthday gift from the young baroness Christine Vogel von Steuben, whom he had known briefly and to whom he had pledged his eternal devotion in his second year of studies at the polytechnic institute in Graz. In his toiletry bag, inherited from his father, were his hygienic necessities: postwar American humanitarian-aid soap, which had sat for years in a closet and retained the smell of sheets and pillow cases; a razor and shaving cream brush; a small bottle of aspirin for headaches;

bits of medicinal coal in a paper sack, in case of stomach upset; a toothbrush and toothpick; and some prewar eau de cologne. Next to the toiletry bag, at the top of the suitcase, were two books: Thomas Mann's *The Magic Mountain* and Ivo Andrić's *Bosnian Chronicle*. He was bringing the Andrić just in case: the customs officials might wonder why he had a book in German with him and what sort of book it was; he planned to tell them that Mann was the German Andrić.

The medicine bag was practically empty. There were handkerchiefs inside: seven clean, pressed handkerchiefs of old-fashioned, geometric designs, these too inherited from Karlo Stubler, and one purple silk handkerchief for special occasions, usually worn in the lapel pocket of a jacket. Besides the handkerchiefs, this bag held only a wooden school pencil case with two sharpened Faber pencils, a sharpener, a two-color blue-black pencil, also Faber, and a never used Parker fountain pen purchased before the war with a small bottle of blue ink and a spare gold nib.

Tucked into the inside pocket of his gray traveling jacket was another pen, a green-black Pelikan, for everyday use, alongside a small metal box in the same pocket, containing about ten metal nibs. The pocket also contained his Yugoslav passport. In his left inside pocket was his billfold, with the money he had received for the trip from headquarters, along with some dinar banknotes of his own.

Before setting out he had sewn fifty dollars into the belt of his trousers.

Rudi wore a gray raincoat over his jacket – prewar, but in good condition – that had since 1939 been lying in a wooden crate in the attic among moth-devoured wool sweaters.

He had ordered a hat from Hlapka's on Tito Street as soon as he learned about the trip to Berlin. At headquarters, they were amazed he had spent half his monthly salary on that hat. He just shrugged and said, "One does not travel to Berlin without a hat." Some may have suspected that Comrade Rudolf Stubler would not be returning from Germany but would emigrate to the West. Many had done it, they simply hadn't come back. And then again, why order a hat at Hlapka's in Sarajevo, when in Berlin, in the West, there were probably better and less expensive hat makers?

"How was your trip from Sarajevo, was it crowded?" Joška Herzl asked, just to change the subject once he sensed that the gentleman with the shaved head was taken aback when he learned that Joška was a juggler. Most people didn't consider juggling a legitimate occupation but rather an idle pastime. He might have told the stranger the truth: the police had come in three times to question him before they had even reached Zenica, that they'd looked through his papers. It was better, however, not to talk about this at all. Rudi had no way of knowing who this stranger was or what he knew, or whether it was by chance that he had come into his compartment.

"What do you juggle?"

"Any number of things," said Joška Herzl, laughing, "bowling pins, apples, hand grenades . . . No, I'm joking. I've never juggled bowling pins. I juggle matchsticks."

"Matchsticks?" Rudi said, surprised.

"Yes, I juggle matches. Matches saved my neck. I'd have rushed into the sky otherwise, turned to smoke, disappeared. You get it?"

Just then a policeman appeared at the door and asked for their documents. Behind him a thickset, hairy man in civilian clothes waited ominously in the corridor. He stared at the two of them as if he recognized them, and knew their secret intentions. As if the examination of their documents was a mere formality.

Rudi felt guilty. He always felt guilty in the face of police authorities. He grew awkward, his identity card slipped from his hand as he was holding it out to the militia, and it disappeared under the seat. His voice shook as he answered the questions.

"Father's name?"

"Karlo."

"Mother's name?"

"Ivana."

"Maiden name?"

"Škedelj."

"Destination?"

"Berlin."

"Berlin?! Purpose of trip! Passport! Documents!"

He gave him the passport and both letters. The policeman went out into the corridor. His back was turned as he showed Rudi's papers to the boor.

They stood there for a long time – too long for Rudi's timid nature. He grew fidgety, imagining what they might find in his papers.

"They're doing it to make you feel guilty," whispered Joška Herzl. "It's what they do."

The militia gave him back his papers in a crumpled heap, and it took Rudi some time to put them back in order, each letter back into its envelope with the fold on the inside.

He gave Joška Herzl back his passport and ticket, asking no questions.

"You were saying something about juggling matches?" Rudi asked to relieve the awkward tension.

This idly uttered question, as questions often are among people who meet for the first and only time in a train compartment, would be fatal for Rudi. What was about to happen over the next three and a half hours while the train to Vienna idled at the Zagreb station would preoccupy him for the rest of his life, and he would relate it in vivid terms to everyone.

Before demonstrating his juggling skill, Joška Herzl told Rudi his sad life's story.

He was born the only son of famous parents, the Zagreb pianist couple Maksimilijan Stinčić and Bosiljka Kamauf Stinčić. Maks Stinčić was, we know, the first Croat to make a gramophone recording, but what is less well known is that from the turn of the century to the beginning of the Great War, he was probably the most sought-after concert pianist in Europe. He performed in America as well, premiering pieces by Debussy, and was at home in all the great concert halls of Germany and France.

His wife, Professor Bosiljka Kamauf Stinčić, was the first pianist of the Croatian Academy and today is still a professor at the conservatory in Salzburg. This perhaps explains why Joška Herzl, her son, obtained his travel documents with ease. The professor often came to Zagreb, gave lessons at the Music Academy, and over the years among the envious and the defeated, rumors spread that Bosa was actually the lover of some highly placed party official.

The career collapse of "Zagreb's Franz Liszt," as Stinčić was called, took place after Josip's birth. When the child was three years old, his father realized to his horror that Josip was tone-deaf.

A happy and spirited child, he was interested in everything, learned quickly and easily, even knew all the letters of the alphabet by the age of four. By all indications he was an advanced and good child, except in what his parents, especially his father, found most important: he could not hit a single note correctly.

His mother would probably have got used to it with time, though it was not easy for her either, as she examined the family tree, searching in vain for unmusical branches, great-uncles on one side, great-aunts on the other, whom the boy might have taken after, but his father was in despair. He started turning down performances, considered committing suicide, and lived in fear of someone discovering that Josip was tone-deaf. He let all his household responsibilities go, spent most of his time alone, and holed himself up in their villa at Zelengaj. Only Mrs. Stinčić would go down to town to take care of the necessities, after which she would return even more depressed, for everyone she met would ask: How is Mr. Stinčić? And how is your boy?

In the end, after it had become clear that Maksimilijan Stinčić would die of sorrow and the time was nearing for the boy to start school, an idea occurred to Bosa Stinčić: announce that Josip had died of diphtheria! There would be a big funeral at Mirogoj Cemetery, the empty casket would be placed under the arcade and into the tomb of Maksimilijan's father, the church composer and organist Antun Svetolik Stinčić, and this would be followed by forty days of mourning, when all of Zagreb would pay its respects at the Zelengaj villa and witness the parents' sorrow. After all that they had gone through, it would not be such a difficult performance.

While all this was happening, Josip would move in with Rozalija Herzl, Bosa's aunt Ružica, a widow who had no work beyond caring for her sweet, feeble-minded daughter Doroteja. She would adopt the boy. Of course, Aunt Ružica was Jewish, and there was no reason Josip could not also become a Jew. He would be neither the first nor the last. The fact that he had been christened at

Saint Mark's in the presence of national leaders and distinguished persons posed no impediments. The boy would not remember it anyway.

None of this of course meant that Maksimilijan Stinčić, our first and most famous piano virtuoso, and Bosiljka Kamauf Stinčić, the renowned professor and music pedagogue, had contrived to renounce their son. This they simply would not have done. They were merely looking for a way to avoid a shame that for both of them, but especially for Maks, was unbearable: a tone-deaf child.

And so did the Zagreb boy Josip Stinčić, who might have become a leading professor of botany – for he was very interested in trees – or perhaps a rival to Krleža and his dramaturgy – for Josip was passionate about the theater – become the Graz Jew Jošua Herzl, nicknamed Joška.

At first Joška noticed only positive changes. Instead of a father who spent entire days in his pajamas, drinking or crying as he sat at the piano, and a mother who, in response to most of his questions – What is the capital of Mongolia? Why do people believe in God? Why does the wheel on a bicycle turn? How many centimeters are there between the earth and the moon? Which one of us would die first? – did not have answers and did not try to find them, he had got a big sister, Doroteja, and Aunt Ružica. And he had also become a Jew! Although Judaism was linked to some uncomfortable experiences, and even a physically painful one, Joška was enthusiastic. Being a Jew meant forever living in a fairy tale, and believing only in the fairy tale, which in the course of the year would continue to bring new excitements and experiences. For Jews not a single day was ordinary. Even cooking was a great adventure . . . Everything he remembered from his previous life now had suddenly become more exciting and intriguing. He was not surprised when, after several months, he came across people who did not like Jews.

While he was crossing the main square with Aunt Ružica, some drunk boys in hunting clothes had called out something foul at them. Are they Catholics? he had asked Aunt Ružica. No, they are nasty and unhappy hunters! Are those hunters Catholic? he had insisted. Well, yes, what else could they be? she had said. And suddenly everything became clear to Joška. He did not hold anything against those Catholic hunters, for he knew they were envious. They knew that for Jews every new day was different from the previous one while for Catholics every day was the same. Jews lived in fairy tales. Catholics drank, cried, and lived in anxiety. Joška knew this, for he too had once been Catholic.

Mama Bosiljka came to visit once a month. He saw Papa less often, maybe once every three months. Mother brought money, which she would leave under the little crocheted tablecloth on her way out in such a way that it was visible to everyone but appeared discreet. He did not like this game, for she would blush afterward every time. Aunt Ružica would tell her, "But Mizzi, you shouldn't have!" and then pick up the money and stuff it into the pocket of her housecoat. There was something ugly about this, Joška thought, and it seemed to him that Doroteja was both happy and smart in not noticing such things.

"When I grow up, I'll be like Doroteja!" he once said to Aunt Ružica.

"No one can become like Doroteja," she answered. "One has to be born like Doroteja."

But this did not discourage him. If you look at something long enough and think that it is you, in the end you'll turn into it, the boy thought, having found in his big sister his first and only life model.

His father's visits were even less pleasant.

He never took him by the hand or tossed him into the air, as other fathers did with their sons. It was better that way, he told Doroteja, because he might throw me up but not catch me. And you'd break on the cement! his big sister said, laughing at her joke, though she of course didn't really believe it. But Joška knew it was true.

One time just before Christmas they suddenly showed up from Zagreb. Papa had brought a Christmas tree. But we're Jews! Joška said. Aunt Ružica just laughed, and Doroteja had already started clearing the corner where the little tree would stand with the gifts underneath it.

To please their guests that Christmas, everyone in the house would be Christian until the new year; they acted like Christians and did things the Christian way. Big Doroteja went around the house with a melancholy expression, the sort Christians wore in the most solemn moments for Christianity, which got on

Maksimilijan's nerves, grating him so much that every once in a while he would whisper into Bosiljka's ear: "Why is that retarded cow mocking the Mother of God?" She was bewildered, for she didn't see mockery in Doroteja's expressions, nor did she believe the unfortunate girl knew how to mock anyone or anything. In the end, Doroteja's attempt to act like a Christian among the Christians even led to a little marital spat, when Maks Stinčić, not paying much attention to whether their hosts heard him, yelled that it was because of her, Bosiljka, that the Jewish grandmother was carrying on. Aunt Ružica and Doroteja actually did not speak Croatian very well, so might not have understood what he was saying, but Joška had certainly understood it.

One other thing upset his father: in the home of Rozalija Herzl, Bosiljka's Jewish aunt, there was no piano. There had actually been one at a certain point, during the life of Uncle Moses, who had played the violin in the Graz orchestra, but after Moses died, Rozalija had sold the piano. She didn't say it, but it seemed that she had blamed the piano for Moses's fate, his serious illness and short life. Maksimilijan Stinčić took this very personally. He hated the old lady, Joška's dear aunt Ružica, and his sister Doroteja too.

And since there was no piano in the house, Maks could not sing Christmas songs. It was the first time he could remember, he said, that he would celebrate Christmas without singing. This was a bad sign: "Song was prayer," he explained to Joška, "and a sung prayer before God was worth twice as much. A person who didn't know how to sing, in all probability, would go straight to hell."

As he said this, he stretched his long, bony fingers up into the air in front of Joška's eyes. Maksimilijan Stinčić was proud of his fingers, so he liked to show them to people, including his son. "The secret of great piano playing lay in stretching one's fingers," he told him, "but you don't know this, and you never will." He sighed, without ceasing to move his fingers as if he were pressing the keys, each finger moving on its own as if they were not connected to the same hand or as if each one thought for itself. Little Joška Herzl found this fascinating. It was then that the desire to enchant his father was born, the way his father enchanted audiences with his playing.

At the start he wanted to impress him.

Later, embittered, he wanted to show his father, Maksimilijan Stinčić, that there was a greater skill than his, and that his fingers could think, each one for itself, and that they could move, each one at its own time, even though there was no music in them and never would be.

"Music saves the soul," said his father that Christmas. "Only those who are able to play and sing well can take Jesus into their souls. All others are lost!"

Joška remembered these words.

And that was how he started to learn how to juggle matchsticks. Rudi asked him several times whether he had heard about this skill from someone, whether he had seen anyone else juggling matchsticks, but each time Joška Herzl did not seem to hear the question. In the end, Joška never told him, and in the long stories about his journey to Berlin, about Furtwängler, and about the juggler of matchsticks, which Rudi would repeat with variations whenever he was in the mood or whenever anyone came to visit the Stublers at their Ilidža home, he was forever equally sorry for the missing detail in the narrative. The biography of Joška Herzl, unfurled in the several hours that the train for Maribor, Graz, and Vienna stood waiting at Zagreb's main station, was crippled and incomplete without the story of how and where the boy had first seen match juggling.

He started practicing between Christmas and New Year's, at first using only the middle finger of his right hand.

He would place a match on his fingertip to balance it there, then, with just a flick of the first joint, he would send it into the air and try to catch it. It took Joška Herzl six months to flick the match once, twice, then three times in a row with his middle finger. This was not juggling. If there had been anyone but big Doroteja and Aunt Ružica looking on from the side, they would not have recognized any great skill in this thing that required ten hours of practice per day. When he wasn't at school or at the rabbi's for religious instruction, when he wasn't eating dinner, doing his homework, or sleeping, Joška was practicing to juggle with that one finger.

After he had managed to flick the stick seven times with his fingertip, he put another one on his index finger and tried to do it with two fingers and two match sticks separately. It seemed impossible. Months passed before he was able, for the first time, to flick two matches into the air, one with each finger. And that was just one time. It was another six months before it happened again, and it was a miracle, for each finger to flick and catch two matches twice.

Doroteja didn't ask a thing. She just sat there staring at Joška's fingers. For her it was a wonder when he succeeded and a wonder when he failed. And Aunt Ružica just knew that the child was trying to do something important and she did not care whether he succeeded, nor did she care what anyone else might think of it.

In the meantime, an unknown noncommissioned German officer named Adolf Hitler broke with his Munich beer hall society, governments fell, prime ministers were assassinated, young poets died of tuberculosis, and the people, hungry and hopeless, looked for someone to blame for their hunger and hope-lessness. And whenever people are looking for someone to blame, somebody thinks of the Jews. This time it happened very fast, faster than Joška Herzl could flick and catch matchsticks with his two fingers ten times in a row. In Germany the first concentration camps were opened, the shop windows of Jewish stores were smashed, and mountains of great German novels and volumes of poetry were burned. The rabbis' beards were shaved off, and their temples transformed into public urinals and stables. Thousands of members of Moses's faith were able to escape from the land of philosophy and song, sailing to Palestine and farther, to America, Canada, and Argentina, before Joška Herzl had managed for the first time to juggle with the four fingers of his right hand.

"To juggle matchsticks," Joška Herzl explained to Rudi, "the hand must be stable. It cannot move the way a juggler moves his hands to catch any number of bowling pins, apples, or balls, for juggling matches is not acrobatic, it is a mental discipline, a philosophy and a philosophical attempt, the first in human history, the first in the biography of the human species, to have the fingers separate from the hand so that each moves independently, in a perfectly harmonious and coordinated symphony of motion, the fingertips always accepting a match and relaunching it so that it never collides with another match, launched into the air from a neighboring finger an instant before.

"The ideal in piano playing," Joška explained, "is for each finger to touch a key independently of the state or status of any other finger, especially the adjoining one. The hardest is with the ring finger, for it is connected by tendons to the next two. It is impeded by both physical and metaphysical factors. Robert Schumann, a tragic composer – " "My favorite!" said Rudi enthusiastically – "longed for piano virtuosity. He had quick fingers, a perfect memory, and was thoroughly musical. He had an ear that recognized tones other people could not, and he heard voices others did not. His perfect pitch eventually drove him to madness.

"But there was something that tormented Schumann more than the voices no one else could hear. His ring finger. No matter how much he tried to think through the tip of his ring finger and impart his soul to it – though the soul for other people of the day was in their chests, for Robert Schumann it was in his two little fingers – the moment his ring finger started to move, so would those damned other two with it, one on each side. To change this and triumph over his fourth finger, Schumann created a mechanical device, which he attached to his right hand, but instead of exercising the finger to make it independent of the other two fingers, he broke the tendon in the hand, inflicting irreparable damage to it. And so, in breaking the will of his ring finger, Schumann broke his own soul.

"He made a mistake, a fatal one," said Joška Herzl, waving his arms in the heat of his story. "He should have got to know it instead of breaking it, dealt with it on its own terms, won the finger over with his charm. If the finger was heavy, let everything around it be as light as a feather!

"This was why one fine day the great Romantic composer Robert Schumann lost his mind. By contrast to Joška Herzl, he had no legitimate reason for his struggle. His reason was that of an artist: he wanted to be a virtuoso, a piano juggler greater than all the others, but that was not sufficient for each finger to think for itself and for the hand to break into four minds with a fifth, great notion in the thumb. To achieve that," Joška shouted, moving closer to Rudi's face, "a man had to have reasons based in his destiny. Only great and true unhappiness could move fingers to each think for themselves.

"A happy man has no reason to be an artist!" Joška said, bounding about the train compartment while the police officers making their way down the corridor looked at him, perplexed. "A happy man will become an unhappy man, troubled and with a broken soul, should he attempt to become an artist for no good reason.

"And what, my dear sir, is art?" he shouted at Rudi, who had tucked himself into the corner, nearly flat against the window, regretting that he had ever entered into conversation with this man.

"Art is juggling with matchsticks! It's a miracle that serves no one and nothing, but is a reason to stay alive, all in the fruitless attempt to attain perfection. Six hours of practice, every day. Then ten, twelve, eighteen hours, merely in order to get the tips of the four fingers of your right hand to juggle the matches ten, twenty, thirty, a hundred times . . . At the beginning I was practicing six hours per day, then ten, twelve, and finally eighteen. I had stopped going to school; the temple had been burned down, and I wasn't going any longer, I had stopped praying in the end, I was just sleeping and practicing. Were there people who admired me? You wanted to ask that, didn't you? Well, go on then, ask, and I'll answer: no, no one admired me. Who in Graz would have been amazed at the skills of some small and insignificant Jewish kid while Hitler's troops were marching through the city? Doroteja? Big Doroteja? You think maybe she was amazed? No, the dear girl, my big sister, was devoid of that gift. To be amazed you have to recognize the wonder, but for my Doroteja there was no wonder. Everything I did was ordinary and normal to her.

On the day – it was a Monday – when the SS burst into the home of Rozalija Herzl and carried her off along with her mentally deficient daughter, Joška Herzl was sitting at his writing desk, juggling eight lit matches for the first time. His thumbs resting on the black veneer, his palms unnaturally inverted, he juggled the miniature torches as if each of his fingers had an ingenious mind of its own, the mind of a great pianist, circus performer, and Buddhist, who knew how to measure the force of each thrust in accord with the loss of the match's weight, which was disappearing into smoke and tiny ash.

The SS men were dumbfounded. The sight so entranced them that they forgot to take Joška Herzl away.

While he was juggling, he didn't notice what was happening around him. He lit the matches, one by one, flicked them in the air with the tip of his finger and waited for the unlit end, then lit another, tossed it, and watched as the match returned, spinning three hundred sixty degrees in its flight, and he did this eight times. He could neither see nor hear Aunt Ružica and big Doroteja as the Germans took them away.

Before all the eight matches had burned down to nothing, they were no longer there.

Joška Herzl never learned what had happened to them, whether they were taken to a camp or died somewhere along the way, but when he thought about their death and disappearance, he saw them both as two whirling matches flying through the air and vanishing. Several seconds had been enough for them to be gone without a trace, except in his memory, his shame, and the guilt that would survive in him.

He thought he might have saved them if he had not been juggling the matches. But was that worth more than their two small and unimportant human lives? If juggling matches was worth more than the two of them, then between him and the SS men who had taken them there was no difference.

After Hitler moved to annex Austria, Joška Herzl had stopped thinking and studying, going to school and synagogue; he had stopped taking walks around town and chatting with people. At the time the majority of the Graz inhabitants had discovered that they were Germans rather than Austrians and that their greatest enemy, as with all the Germans, was their Jewish neighbors. There were not many Jews in Graz – they had never been much liked in the city, so they had avoided settling there – but that did not mean that their disappearance was any less dramatic. In the end, within just a few weeks following Hitler's annexation of Austria, Joška Herzl was the only Jew left in Graz. They left him alone, ignored him and his despair at the loss of his family, or else the truth was what some say today, that the Nazis left one Jew alive in every city as representative of the annihilated race, as a warning.

Joška would sit in the park, his back turned to the fountain, his thumbs pressed against the back of a bench, as he flicked the matches with his fingertips, one after another, miniature torches that would burn out in the air, leaving no trace. They would turn to smoke and dust, just as the Jewish people, in a year, or two, or three, would. But no one would believe this, for who would think of doing away with six million peaceful and unarmed people – small shop owners, moneylenders, gullible bankers, industrialists, rabbis, shoemakers, lottery ticket salesmen, small-time crooks and con men, idealists, communists and Zionists, soft-spoken worshippers afraid of life but even more of what comes after, famous doctors, surgeons, pediatricians, psychoanalysts, disciples of Doctor Freud – whom the Nazis did not kill when they found him in his Vienna apartment, exiling him to London instead, for Doctor Freud too was a match juggler – professors of biology who created the most beautiful herbaria in the history of Europe, archivists, librarians, village teachers whose frightened wives concealed their Jewish heritage, great German poets and travel writers who had journeyed all the way to India and Nepal in order to leave their testimonials to the German culture, circus performers and owners, village carpenters, proprietors of pawnshops and rare books, chemists, manufacturers of poison, barbers, mystics, tricksters of great imagination, quacks who for tiny sums would make the rounds of apartments in the center of town, performing abortions on the underage daughters of the city's solicitous gentlemen, philosophy professors, building custodians, owners of small kosher restaurants at the border of the ghetto where non-Jews were also welcome, maids, servant girls, midwives, authors of the first Aztec, Turkish, and Aramaic grammars, blind and deaf painters, idlers, dreamers, assiduous bookkeepers, industrialists with no heart for their workers or their workers' rachitic children who would not live long, rag merchants, peddlers, roofers, ice cream vendors, loafers, porters, dish washers and dish dryers in communal kitchens, where the Jewish poor found food, philanthropists, sponsors, coin collectors and counterfeiters, false prophets, proselytes and neophytes, who changed faith too late for by then Nazism had come along? Who would have believed that someone would actually come forth and erase the lives and memories of all these people?

Joška Herzl sat on the bench in the park – though Jews were forbidden to enter the park under penalty of death – with his back turned to the world, his thumbs against the bench, juggling lit matches with his fingers. He did not want to think about Aunt Ružica and his sister Doroteja who up to the moment of her death had never had an evil thought, and he wished to be killed right there, while juggling the little torches that burned and disappeared one after another. But no one dared satisfy his wish.

And here the sad life confession of Joška Herzl could end, and it would be the right moment for the juggler of matchsticks to demonstrate for Rudolf Stubler his art, if we were prepared to forget and mislay from the history of the twentieth century that part of the story that touches upon the great Croatian pianist Maksimilijan Stinčić, after whom today, in 2012, a beautiful Zagreb street is named, which until the nineties bore the name of Stevan Stojanović Mokranjac, and upon his life's partner, the famous music pedagogue Bosiljka Kamauf Stinčić. Perhaps we could even forget it, were the two of them not linchpins of Croatian culture and were the story of them not at the same time the story of Zagreb at a certain moment in history, the moment when Rudi, following his unsuccessful studies in Vienna and Graz, spent the last days and months of his youth in the city.

After the fateful Christmas they spent with their son, Aunt Ružica, and her simple-minded daughter, when Maks Stinčić insulted the boy and provoked him into becoming a match juggler, they visited him in Graz whenever their consciences weighed on them. And with the elections of 1933, as Germany began to get back on its feet and once more become a power, their consciences weighed on them less often. In part, this was a result of the difficult conditions in the country, the misery in which the Croatian nation found itself after a Serbian war volunteer shot three representatives of the Croatian Peasant Party at the Belgrade Assembly, fatally wounding the popular leader Stjepan Radić. Neither Maksimilijan Stinčić nor Bosiljka Stinčić had been known for their patriotism until then, but this attack so disgusted and infuriated them that they attended less and less to family matters. They gathered with socially and politically like-minded people, glowered angrily, and by October of 1934 were quietly celebrating the murder in Marseille of King Alexander as a tyrant and oppressor.

They started thinking about their son again in 1936, when reports first appeared in the news about Hitler's possible seizure and annexation of Austria. Probably one of them, perhaps Bosiljka, had thought it would be only natural,

and in line with familial relations, warmth, and solidarity among people, to save
Auntie Ružica and her simple-minded daughter along with Joška, and bring them
all to Zagreb to live in their house in Zelengaj. There was a comfortable little
apartment in their basement in which the three of them could live. It would
not be too crowded – Doroteja could be instructed to be quiet, especially in the
afternoons when Mr. Stinčić was resting, and not to hang around in the garden,
where she might trample the roses that Bosiljka had been growing for years –
but then again, how would they explain to people, what would they tell their
acquaintances at the conservatory, who those three people suddenly living in
their basement were? Ought they to say that they were Jews, or would it perhaps
be wiser to keep quiet about it? And anyway, was it really the right time to be
announcing to the world that Bosiljka's aunt was a Jew and that Madam Elene
Levy Kamauf, her respected mother, had actually been half-Jewish? To Mr. Stinčić
this would not have been a problem, he was a man of the world and for years had
performed with Jewish musicians, and the deceased Mr. Stein-Baruch, Maksim's
manager from the best days of his career, was a Jew who kicked up his heels on
the Sabbath, which was why Maksim did not perform on Friday evenings, but
was this really the time to be explaining all this to people? Might they take it as
a provocation, a political taking of sides, just at the moment when a new order
was being born in Europe, one in which the Croats needed to find their place, if
Bosiljka proclaimed to the entire musical world that her mother had been a Jew
and that, for this reason, she had decided to open the doors of her villa to some
Austrian Jews?

But this was not all. How could Maksimilijan and Bosiljka have faith in Joška's
discretion? The old Jewess would, it was certain, keep the family secret for her
own sake. Aunt Ružica well knew what would happen to her and her child if they
stayed in Graz, if the Stinčićs did not save them, but could they be certain that
simple-minded Doroteja might not tell someone the truth about Joška Herzl's
background? All they had to do was open up the tomb under the arcade and
confirm that the small white casket was empty, filled with dirt, and that the Josip
Stinčić "for whom his father Maksimilijan and mother Bosiljka mourned eternally, praying to the dear Lord God and the Virgin Mary for their only son among

the angels" was not in his grave. And if he wasn't there, then perhaps what the simple-minded girl had said was true.

The people of Zagreb would slowly recognize the faces of the two famous musicians in the monstrous physiognomy of the Jewish boy with the tic. And that would be the end of Maksimilijan Stinčić and Bosiljka Kamauf Stinčić, it would be their social and artistic suicide.

After German troops erupted into Austrian territory on March 12, 1938, and the borders were declared nonexistent between the countries in which the same German language was spoken, Maksimilijan Stinčić and his wife fell into a kind of religious rapture. At first, it seemed perhaps this might be merely a momentary spiritual state evoked by the early onset of spring, a temporary neurosis – as was noted by the popular medical commentators in the pages of the newspapers *Jutarnji list*, *Obzor*, and *Svijet* – and that the trembling would pass as soon as April, May, and June came around, months that are especially pleasant in Zagreb, when, in the mortally ill Kingdom of Yugoslavia, the cultural and civilizational distinctiveness of that Central European metropolis, by contrast to the colors and scents of central Serbia and the southern heart of the Balkans, was most evident.

But the rapture did not pass that spring, or that summer, and in the fall and winter of the final European peacetime year the Stinčićs continued to hold memorial masses in the city's churches, spending their afternoons and evenings at the Mirogoj Cemetery, kneeling at the grave of their only son, incapable of holding back the wave of grief that had suddenly surged forth and about which, in deep sympathy, the Zagreb gentlefolk commented during intermissions of theatrical matinees, where the most significant town discussions often took place. Parents will live in shock for years after the death of a child, incapable of grasping what has happened, the loss they have experienced exceeds any other loss in life, exceeds what a person is able to understand, imagine, and endure, and what cannot be imagined cannot be endured.

Zagreb's well-to-do commented in this manner, shocked by the image of the parents kneeling and praying every evening at Mirogoj, their knees on the cold Brač stone. If until the spring of 1938 there was still hope in the recovery of the great pianist Maksimilijan Stinčić, whose career had been suddenly cut short for reasons largely unknown to the public, after the season of despair and grief, it was clear that his piano playing was over.

After the Anschluss and the disappearance of Aunt Ružica and big Doroteja, Joška Herzl's parents stopped visiting. The letters from Zagreb, which had once arrived with monthly regularity, no longer came, nor did any messengers deliver parcels or money at the Emanuel Café, leaving them with the landlord Hansijo, a Zagreb native from Kustošija. On one occasion Joška managed to go into the post office, though Jews were forbidden to go into the post office, and begged a postal worker to call the Zagreb number 47-39, though Jews were forbidden to use the telephone, but to everything he said his mother Bosiljka answered: "Hello, hello, you've reached Zagreb, I can't hear anything, you've got the wrong number . . ."

Anyway, even if she had wanted to talk with him, Joška Herzl wouldn't have known what to say. For days he had circled the post office, looking for a way to pop inside and ask some kind soul to make just that one phone call, he had on his mind to ask Papa Maks, a famous pianist who had once performed before Marshal Hindenburg – a fact confirmed by the framed photograph that, in Joška's early childhood, hung above the fireplace at the Zelengaj villa – to urge the German authorities to let Aunt Ružica and big Doroteja go, since it was all just a big mistake, neither of them had done anything wrong, but once he made it to the phone he understood how senseless his plan was, for Papa Maks would never have done such a thing for them, nor would the Germans have listened to him.

While he yelled into the receiver and Mama Bosiljka did not hear him, Joška Herzl experienced for the first time a guilty conscience. He was to blame, not any SS men or Hitler, for the suffering of the two human beings closest to him: his cousin Doroteja and Aunt Ružica. He was to blame because he had no musical ear, for if he'd been musical, if his soul had been capable of discerning that greatest of all artistic forms created by man, he would not be a Jew today but a devout Catholic, and a pianist like his father Maks, and he would have saved Aunt Ružica and big Doroteja himself. He could not sing, that was his transgression, but would Joška's soul have grown hard like Papa Maks's, and would Joška have allowed the SS to take the two of them away the way Papa Maks had? He wondered if he would feel less guilt, but in vain.

Once he became aware of his guilt, Joška Herzl reached the height of his match-juggling talent. With eyes open or closed, he flicked unlit or lit matches into the air and caught them with the tips of his fingers, tossing them into the air for as long as he wanted or as long as it took for them to turn into smoke. There was nothing left in the world, nothing in Joška's soul, to stand between him and the matches landing on his fingertips and then returning into the air – there was no gravity, no fear of a slip-up, no awareness. He was free of such thoughts, for since the very beginning of humanity and its ability to feel blame, no one had been as guilty as he, Joška Herzl, was for the suffering of Auntie Ružica and his cousin Doroteja, and for all the Jews of Graz who had vanished with them. Joška was to blame because he had been allowed to live, and there could be no greater guilt than that. If he had thought about it, he surely would have gone mad. And so he did not think, and when a juggler does not think, he has reached perfection.

On Friday, September 1, 1939, the day German troops crossed the Polish border and the Second World War began, a concert was held at Mirogoj, at the tomb of the composer and organist Antun Svetolik Stinčić, by his son Maksimilijan, the famous Croatian and European pianist, who had long since retired from the world stage but who was performing in memory of his forever inconsolably lost only son Josip.

The day before, on Thursday, a baby grand piano had been delivered by truck from the Music Academy, which was unloaded and then carried into the cemetery by five strong Serbs from Lika hired at the train assembly station. Until the next afternoon at five, when the concert was scheduled to take place, the instrument was watched over by students of Professor Bosiljka Stinčić: Irfan Ibrahimkadić from Banja Luka and two natives of Zagreb, Josip Pepi Mrak and Đorđe Steiner.

Before evening it suddenly grew overcast. Heavy, wet, gray-black clouds gathered on Mount Sljeme above the city, lightning flashed up beyond the hill, and it looked as if it would begin to pour at any moment. This event is exceptionally well described in the book *Recollections of a Musician*, by Irfan Ibrahimkadić, published by the Munich-Barcelona based Knjižnica Hrvatska Review in 1981. Joška Herzl in 1954 could not have described things in such detail to Rudi, for he knew only what someone in Zagreb had told him in passing after the war and what he later read in a bound version of the issues of *Obzor* for September 1939, at the home of a friend who worked as a compositor at *Vjesnik*, but we, in this lament of ours on a travel episode from the life of Rudolf Stubler, cannot resist threading into the story what we read about Maksimilijan Stinčić's performance in *Recollections of a Musician*, after Rudi and probably Joška Herzl too, was no longer among the living.

But let us return to that night between August 31 and September 1, 1939, carefully recorded by Ibrahimkadić in a long and inspired chapter entitled "Concerto for Rain and Keyboard."

And so, when the clouds had gathered, and the first two or three large drops had splashed on the black veneer of the piano, Pepi Mrak, the youngest of the three but the most enterprising, rushed to the first villa along Mirogoj road to look for something with which to cover it.

He came back with two military tent covers, a part of an officer's war kit, which Colonel Simović, deputy commander of the city, a Serb from Belgrade, had kindly loaned him. (By including this fact in his work Ibrahimkadić feigns a European sensibility and a lack of national prejudice though he was a rigid Croat . . .)

They covered the piano but knew it would not be of any use if there was a storm or a big downpour. So Pepi Mrak went to the Music Academy, but no one was there. He knocked on the door of the director, Boris Papandopulo, and, in despair, he went to the Stinčićs at Zelengaj, where someone finally opened a door. Professor Bosa Kamaufova – that was what her students called her – calmed her distraught pupil, assuring him that the three of them could in no way be blamed if the rain damaged the piano. The piano was expensive – a personal gift of Prince Paul to the Music Academy – and they would not have sufficient funds for a new practice instrument, which would probably just be a small one, but whatever happened, the students who had volunteered to safeguard the piano overnight at Mirogoj could in no way be held responsible for meteorological conditions.

But this did not mean she was not upset.

Maksimilijan Stinčić was of course not at home. He was probably with friends at some pub drinking rakija and stuffing himself on pork rinds with onions, and likely had not even noticed it had grown cloudy.

Night had descended on the cemetery, lightning was flashing further off, and thunder rumbled from the Turopolje plains. One speaks of miracles only if your piano finds itself under the open sky or if you're getting ready to repair the cracks on the roof of your house. Then the story becomes great and grows to the fifty pages of "Concerto for Rain and Keyboard," that unexpected prose piece by the minor Croatian musician who spent the bulk of his career playing in Buenos Aires nightclubs and at commemorations of the April 4 invasion of Yugoslavia by the Germans. Ibrahimkadić would be a dedicated member of the Ustaše during the war, a high-ranking official in the Ustaše Youth, and an active military officer – at the end of 1944 he had accepted a post in the Jasenovac concentration camp – all of which would qualify him for being charged with war crimes, a warrant for which was issued in Belgrade in 1946, but it seems that nothing registered as intensively on his life as that night between August 31 and September 1, 1939 when, with his two student friends, he had watched over the piano on which Maksimilijan Stinčić would musically commemorate his only son. It is as if everything else in his life was a lie, as if he'd maintained himself through lies and lived on them, this failed musician and pianist of limited talent, for the entire book, with its ironic title of *Recollections of a Musician*, in which for the most part he laments the suffering of his revolutionary Croatian generation and the communist crimes against the Croatian people, is a lie, except for that improbable "Concerto for Rain and Keyboard," which is deeply felt and brilliantly rendered, and in which one recognizes the paradox of an unrealized or unrecognized writer's talent: he wrote then about something that had truly touched him, that one time and never again.

Ibrahimkadić and his two friends were terrified of being thrown out of the

Music Academy for allowing the piano to get wet. And this fear had been strong enough to inspire Irfan Ibrahimkadić to write prose of a surprising power.

What Irfan Ibrahimkadić did not know was that the only thing inside the tomb of the organist and composer Antun Svetolik Stinčić was an empty casket. A small child's casket with a bag of dirt from the Zelengaj garden.

That night, while the German troops marched into Poland, and before Radio London announced the news, the three students of the piano department at Zagreb's Music Academy stared into the dark starless sky above Zagreb. All night long it was overcast, lightning flashed, thunder rumbled, and once in a while two or three large drops fell to reawaken their fears, only to turn into a clear morning, as if someone had wiped off the glass of a steamed-up window.

Đorđe Steiner was mortally afraid, and a man who is afraid finds it hard to call to mind ideals greater than his fear.

In a surprisingly correct phrase, but without any true emotional engagement, Ibrahimkadić notes that Steiner was executed at Jasenovac in 1942. He was a talented pianist, by far the most gifted of the three. He was not a communist, nor was there anything that interested him other than music. He performed many times as a young soloist at the Music Academy in the course of 1940, held Chopin-themed concerts in Osijek, Novi Sad, Sarajevo, and Belgrade, and his last performance was on April 3, 1941, at Belgrade's Kolarac Concert Hall, devoted completely to Chopin – Emanual Saks spelled this out in a proposal to name a Zagreb street after the musician. The proposal was not approved, but Saks's text, typed on a machine with uneven spacing in sixteen stapled pages, is preserved in the Croatian state archive. This document also contains the only biography of Steiner, in which it becomes clear the pianist and his entire family perished in Jasenovac and at Auschwitz.

The war interfered with Pepi Mrak's musical studies. But if it hadn't been the war, it would have been something else. Pepi was a cheerful and simple person – good, kind, and obliging, but devoid of any creative or spiritual imagination, without which there is no artistry. Whoever had known him at the Academy or during wartime – when he was in hiding to avoid being recruited, and ended up with the Partisans in 1944 more by chance than intent – would have made some joke or clever quip with Pepi's last name, *mrak* meaning "darkness." In fact, there was nothing dark or in the least melancholy in Josip Pepi Mrak, nor was there anything that would cloud his sunny spirit. One of Pepi's former teachers at the Academy remarked that "a pianist of such a temperament and spirit could only appear in the circus, as an accompanist to an elephant on a ball or a dog riding a bike, but what do we do with him without our own original socialist circus!?"

Just after the liberation, Josip found himself in Belgrade among the Partisans, where he ended up in the propaganda division of agitprop. He took part in the founding of the national news agency Tanjug as an editor of a culture column in the newspaper *Borba*, and then he disappeared. Even amid the optimistic atmosphere of agitprop and socialist propaganda, Pepi's cheerfulness starkly contrasted with the bleak disposition of the other true believers and Radovan Zogović himself. And so, instead of generating enthusiasism, Pepi's nature had the opposite effect.

And so – as would become known fifty years later, from the testimonials of former communist detainees and prisoners – Josip Mrak was reassigned to the state security sector. He worked in Belgrade, then in Zagreb, on the infamous Petrinjska Street. He was on Tito's prison island Goli Otok, in Sarajevo, and in Tuzla, only to end his career in Pristina in the eighties, where he investigated members of the Kosovo counterrevolutionary movement, Albanian irredentists, and terrorists. He retired quietly in 1987, returned to Zagreb, and somewhere near the town of Samobor had a small house with a large garden full of roses, which he cared for himself, breeding some and buying others from various parts of the world. In 1997, the soon-to-be eighty-year-old Josip Pepi Mrak published the *Lexicon of the Rose* at Matica Hrvatska, with seven hundred fifty entries on different varieties of roses. Except for one Burmese variety and seven varieties grown in South Korea, Pepi had one of each in his garden and had taken their pictures for his lexicon. Numerous political and cultural figures, including President Franjo Tuđman, Defense Minister Šušak, the writers Šegedin and Majstorović, attended the book launch that was held in the Croatian Journalists Home on April 10, 1997, and the old man was so moved that he could not speak. He just cried and cried.

On the first day of 2011, in advanced old age, Josip Mrak, world-renowned author of the *Lexicon of the Rose*, died at Zagreb's Rebro Hospital. A large crowd turned out to send him off at the Mirogoj Cemetery, and the family of the deceased received telegrams of consolation from the president of the republic, the prime minister, and the minister of culture.

Josip Mrak's sunny disposition would be a good subject for a Croatian novel that, as with so many other stories, will remain unwritten. We've already strayed far enough from the story of Rudolf Stubler's voyage to Berlin in the summer of 1954, and of his meeting with the match juggler Joška Herzl while the train stood at the Zagreb train station.

But, as we have already reconstructed the fates of two of the students who, on that night between August 31 and September 1, 1939, watched over the piano that Maksimilijan Stinčić would play, we are obliged to say what happened to the third and best known of the threesome.

Irfan Ibrahimkadić died of complications from an operation for appendicitis, early in the spring of 1990, too early to see the sovereign, independent Croatian state of which he had dreamed and for which he had worked diligently since he left Zagreb in the spring of 1945 as part of the escort of Poglavnik Pavelić. Others grew tired, resigned, gave up, drank, lost their minds, but he persisted diligently, believing and "praying to Allah for Croatia," as the academician Dalibor Brozović put it in an open letter to the family on the occasion of Irfan's death.

But let us take a look at what was happening at Mirogoj that Friday, September 1, 1939, when all of Europe trembled beneath the boots of German soldiers as they marched across Poland.

The weather had cleared, there was not a single cloud in the sky. From the direction of Sljeme came a light summer northerly that spread the scent of blossoms, burnt rock, wax, and stearin, appropriate at the beautiful Zagreb cemetery, where for decades the dead have met and strolled past one another as if on a promenade: the poor with the poor, the rich with the rich, just as they'd crossed paths in life. Around the tomb of the Croatian organist and church composer Antun Svetolik Stinčić, several hundred Zagreb natives were gathered in a wide half arc – one could attend the event only by invitation, jointly signed by "father

Maksimilijan and mother Bosiljka, in anticipation of reuniting once again with their lost son before the face of the Lord." Some quite inappropriately wandered around the nearby graves, "to see and hear the maestro Maks Stinčić play Bach, Mozart, and Beethoven as he mourned his angelic son."

This event in the cultural history of Zagreb, or in the history of everyday life – which might be a more appropriate name for the history of Zagreb's gossip – is recalled in drastically contradictory ways. The concert itself was not reported in *Jutarnji list* or *Obzor*, or written about by any of the musical chroniclers or critics of the time. This performance by Maksimilijan Stinčić, which would turn out to be his last, was not noted by a single historical review of the history of Croatian music, despite the fact that it followed his long silence and that such events, bizarre and outlandish, add spice to the history of European music. The reason for this silence can be suspected: Maksimilijan Stinčić, "with fatherly tears streaming down his face and dropping onto the keys," played horribly. The way he played made everyone want to forget the event as quickly as possible, for it was not only shameful for him, it was shameful for all who had responded to his kind invitation, all who had ever praised his extraordinary skill at the keyboard. After all, Stinčić has always been mentioned alongside Ivan Meštrović, Miroslav Krleža, and Maestro Lovro von Matačić, as one of the Croatian giants, proof of the cultural and national identity of the Croats, and negative criticism on his account could mean undermining what they had in common – their patriotism.

Krleža touched upon the event tangentially in his conversations with Enes Čengić and in a few allusions in his journal ("Oh, the Mirogoj delicacy of the keyboard fingerer Maksimilijan Maksim Maks Stinčić, in whom there is as much artistic truth as in Ribbentropp's arguments against Poland"), but he was not present that Friday at Mirogoj. No one would have invited him, nor would he have gone to such a thing, though, to be honest, he was curious. In the end, Bosa Kamaufova and Maks Stinčić were characters from his dramas and prose pieces – he met with them on occasion, they got on his nerves, but outside of fiction and theater, he diligently avoided them. Or they avoided him. For until the arrival of Marshal Tito and the Serbian Partisan detachments eager for revenge, Zagreb belonged more to Bosa Kamaufova, the expert of piano fingerings and solfège, who knew all there was to know about music and was simultaneously incompetent enough to tell others all they required, and to the Croatian piano-playing genius, her until-death-do-them-part partner Maksimilijan Stinčić, than it did to Krleža. Serbian cannons would be needed – communist or royalist, truth be told – for Miroslav Krleža to at last acquire importance and become an undeniable giant of Croatian culture. To be honest, Krleža was, let us acknowledge this torment to the endemic Ustašoids, a Serbian-occupation writer for the Croats. He was a living monument to Croatian humiliation, to righteous punishment for the camps at Jasenovac and Jadovno, and the Glina church massacres, and this would be true in Croatia for as long as there were those who understood his writing. When those people had all died out, then Krleža would become a great national writer for all the Croatian intellectuals who had never read him. The teddy bear of Croatian literature, as authentic as Croatia's Mikado chocolate with rice, as light and fluffy as Croatian chocolate with rice . . .

Rudi had not read Krleža. He feared him as one might a strict professor. He sensed, without knowing it, that Miroslav Krleža was poisonous to the Zagreb that Rudi had looked down on from the height of a provincial Bosnian who had studied for a good decade in Vienna and Graz.

Unlike Krleža, his critic and co-polemicist, the great Zagreb and Croatian chronicler, the feuilletonist and piteous European liberal Josip Horvat, found himself that August 1, 1939 at the Mirogoj piano recital of Maksimilijan Stinčić. He actually described the event in retrospect, remembering it during the winter of 1942–43, while the debacle of Stalingrad was underway. In Zagreb there was a shortage of anything and everything, Pavelić, with German assistance, was cleansing the last of the Jews from the city, and the municipal police force built and trained by the great war strategist Dido Kvaternik was making early morning rounds in search of Masons and suspected communists for interrogation and internment at Jasenovac. Horvat was terrified that they would come for him too, and for months, mortified but collected, he had prepared himself for this eventuality, searching obsessively, largely in his own soul, for the source of all this evil. In Horvat's memoir of those years, he brightly and somewhat nostalgically tells the story of the Mirogoj recital. He did not receive the mailed invitation either, although, unlike Krleža, he was close to Maks Stinčić and Bosa Kamaufova. Actually, the two of them wanted to be close to him: he impressed them as a social and cultural critic, an author of biographical novels about many famous Croats, a top-notch journalist who had no use for scandals and about whom it was rumored that he was a Mason. They were both terrified of Masons, believing the words of Archbishop Aloysius Stepinac, who claimed Masons were devils sent to the earth, enemies of Christians and Croats, but whenever anyone was referred to as a Mason – and in those years, at the end of the thirties, after the short-lived rule of Milan Stojadinović, it had become fashionable to talk about prominent people as Masons – Maksim and Bosa felt a thrill, a sense of forbidden adventure, a desire to look into the Mason's eyes, make his acquaintance, sit beside him shoulder to shoulder at a concert of the Music Academy, and dream about Masonry as if it were an infectious social disease spread by going to concerts and theater performances or by reading books that had been touched by Masons. Besides, Josip Horvat was a European liberal, it was even whispered that he was English, and the English, however treacherous and haughty they might be, represented a higher race to them both, before which one ought to be humble. After all, one could never be sure that Germany would be victorious in this and every future war, and it was in no way out of the question that the Perfidious Albion might end up the victor.

Even so, they did not send an invitation to Josip Horvat. Horvat does not get worked up about this in his memoir. It never occurred to him that he ought to have received an invitation to such a public event. To the very end he was unaware of his position in small-town Zagreb. Besides, he didn't know the important detail in this story: that the grave was empty.

Horvat describes how he ended up at Mirogoj that day: the first of September was the anniversary of the death of Miroslav Albini's mother, who at the beginning of the thirties had moved to Latin America where he traded in coffee. Before leaving Zagreb, Albini had requested in his will that, if his friend Horvat was in Zagreb, he stop by the grave to leave gladiolas and light a votive candle. How serious Albini was about this request Horvat didn't know. The promise had been easily made, without much thought or certainty that he would actually go to the Albini tomb every first of September. But the following year on the first of September, Horvat remembered Mirek Albini and that same afternoon he went to light a candle at the headstone of his deceased mother. He continued to do this every year, and the outing to Mirogoj became for Horvat a private ritual, inaugurating the onset of autumn. And so it happened that by pure chance, Horvat attended the important social and cultural Zagreb event that day in 1939.

He describes his discomfort at Stinčić's playing. "It was as if the piano had gone out of tune, the hollow marble enclosures swallowing up the sound, and it was creepy and ominous. And worst of all, it made one want to laugh."

It is not likely that Josip Horvat laughed. He was too decent for that, but perhaps a chuckle or a slight grin ran through the crowd of invitees and those who had an ear to hear how Stinčić was playing that day at the cemetery, as the beginning of the Second World War was announced.

In his "Concerto for Rain and Keyboard," Irfan Ibrahimkadić did not write a single word about the actual concerto or the excellence of Stinčić's playing. Only one sentence is devoted to it: "Amid the trampled grass and the scent of rich Croatian soil, our Croatian tragedy reverberated from the fingers of Maestro Maksimilijan Stinčić."

What Joška Herzl could tell Rudi about the concert was limited to two or three terse sentences which contained all the grief of a Jewish youth, but it was this part of the story that led to Rudolf Stubler's obsession with Joška Herzl's life.

As we have mentioned on multiple occasions and demonstrated through multiple episodes from his life, Rudolf Stubler was a believer. Chance (or God) had so willed it: the Stublers were divided into deep, true – which also meant naïve – believers, and utter nonbelievers. Regarding God, there was never any misunderstanding among the Stublers, it was just that for some the heavens were blue and for others they were empty.

Rudi was of the first group, and he believed in everything that a Christian child was supposed to believe to the end of his life. It satisfied his spiritual needs and freed him from the useless and terrible fear of nothingness, and his belief colored his knowledge and convictions. Although he was well educated, rational, and a gifted mathematician, in all aspects of his life he made judgments according to his pure and naïve catechism.

And so the notion that the horror of the Second World War had grown out of Maksimilijan Stinčić's fraudulence unconsciously entered his mind. It was like a story in the Bible: a great evil was evoked by the wickedness of one man, perhaps tiny in relation to eternity, but as striking as an Old Testament moral infraction. The world was punished, Rudi sensed, because a father staged his son's death and then brought people together to watch as he performed Johann Sebastian Bach over his grave.

And what else could God do but release a great misfortune upon humanity, in which good would be clearly distinguished and separated from evil?

During the war, in Zagreb, Maksimilijan Stinčić lived the quiet, retired life of someone who had grown senile, weak, and old. He rarely left his Zelengaj villa, and sat in the garden beneath a century-old cherry tree, watching the fruit ripen, listening to and watching the birds.

That was a Jewish titmouse, poor thing, her call is so ugly.

That was a thrush, a Nordic black bird, the Grieg among birds.

That was a sparrow, ah, sparrow, millions of people dying in this war, from Normandy to the distant eastern seas, and like millions of sparrows, no one knew who they were or what they were or under whose banner they perished . . .

The once famous musician Maksimilijan Stinčić listened to the birds and philosophized to himself, while his wife, Professor Bosiljka Kamauf Stinčić, taught at the Music Academy, traveled every month to Salzburg, Berlin, and Rome, and once visited Paris, where she lectured the gifted young people on the variety of musical wisdom that was highly prized in a plundered and war-torn Europe and because of Bosa's lectures, European and American performance halls were dominated by virtuosi in whose tone something evil and heartless could be discerned, an indifference to human suffering.

How did Joška Herzl survive the war?

There was no great story or miracle here. After all the other Jews had disappeared, the Nazis lost interest in Joška. For them, as for the ordinary, peaceful neighbors, Joška Herzl had ceased to be a Jew. He was no longer a Jew for the Nazis, but in his own mind and heart, he was more a Jew than anyone else could have been, in Graz, in Austria, in all of Europe. Joška Herzl saw his misery in a larger context.

In the winter and spring of 1944 everything started falling apart. Homes crumbled, asphalt peeled away from the streets, and the poorly laid village roads turned into muddy rivers.

As Joška Herzl told his story, Rudi's eyes widened in disbelief. He knew Graz well – he had studied there for a long time, until his father had ordered him home. After Vienna it was the city he knew best, much better than Zagreb or Sarajevo, and he found Joška's account hard to believe, that the houses and people had fallen apart, disappearing into the earthly magma, gummy with stench. "I've got the smell in my nostrils even now!" Joška Herzl shouted, grabbing himself by the throat.

Whatever the case, in the early spring of that year, Joška decided on a completely unreasonable undertaking. He set off for Zagreb to find his father and mother, or else perish on the road. The second possibility was much more likely, but he was not in the least concerned.

He purchased a ticket and boarded a train.

Although the war was nearing its end, the Partisans were creating diversions along the rail lines, the English had bombed railway hubs to the southeast several times, but in Graz everything was as it had once been long ago: lively, peaceful, and fresh. The cattle cars stank of cow droppings, neatly dressed poor people wandered the platforms in search of a train that might take them to their long-lost homeland, SS officers and local police checked the papers of suspicious characters, examining identity cards, searching for passes, taking people aside . . . When he caught sight of them, Joška would run toward them, like someone determined to die, digging in his pockets to show them his Jewish identity card, but each time they would sullenly wave him aside, and let him pass, wanting him gone from their sight. Schizophrenia had become an infectious disease in those days, the SS were afraid of crazy people, and Joška's eyes were those of a madman.

"Look at me!" he said, staring at Rudi. "Do I look mad? Tell me honestly. I can take it! Those people, see, the whole regiment, at the station in Graz too, and on the train, and we went through three checkpoints at least and they made at least ten passengers get out of each car and took them away, while they ran from me as if I was infected, and not only did no one check my papers but the conductor, who could have easily turned me in as suspicious, barely even looked at my ticket!"

Aside from the inspections, from which Joška was exempted, peace prevailed on the railway. No one could disturb it, not the SS officers with their checkpoints or the Partisans or the black marketeers, for inside the train and around it in the surrounding areas of the great stations, provincial outposts and blind tracks, wherever the tracks went, strict railway procedures reigned, upon which no one, not even Adolf Hitler himself, could have any influence. In the spring of 1944, before the wartime victors had started bombing intensively and the defeated were pulling back in retreat, the railways were the last secure territory in Hitler's portion of Europe, where reason, sobriety, and a certain higher order reigned, which it seemed had outlived the tyrant and the two-thousand-year-old faith in Jesus Christ, son of God. Only the railway was spared, remaining exactly as it had been for a hundred years, with the timetable as its sole article of faith.

There, listening to the familiar clatter of the metal wheels, for a brief moment, Joška Herzl wanted once more to be alive. This desire evoked fear and distress in him, but he quickly forgot about it and continued to offer up his Jewish papers for inspection.

"So that saved your life!" Rudi exclaimed with joy.

"What is it you think saved my life?"

"Well, the fact that you tried to force them to check your papers. It's simple. It's too bad for the others who didn't think of it."

"No, you're wrong. My life was saved by the fact that I was already dead."

Zagreb Station had been dirty and full of refugees who mostly spoke in a heavy Bosnian accent accompanied by lots of pitiful nostalgic curses. Ustaše police stood by, preventing them from leaving the station and making their way to town. Why the Bosnians wanted to go to Jelačić Square was hard to know, nor did anyone know who had driven them there. It had once been Serbs, then Chetniks and Partisans, depending on who was around and how harshly they swore, but the truth was – Joška Herzl sensed this as he made his way toward the exit, heading straight for the Ustaše guard who would ask for his papers – that they had escaped from their own hot heads, from something they themselves had caused, most likely because they had embraced Croatian independence too eagerly and allowed themselves to be talked into all sorts of things, and now, well, the times had begun to change and, out of fear of losing those same hot heads, they had come to Zagreb, to Markov Square, to the place where it had all begun, so that those who had started it all would take care of them. But it was too late for them, and before long very likely it would be too late for Croatia.

The Ustaše guard let Joška pass without questioning him or letting him take his hand from his inside pocket.

He made it to Zelengaj but was not allowed into his parents' villa.

A stranger opened the door. He told him to wait and then came back several minutes later, furious, with a wooden club in hand just in case.

"You should be ashamed of yourself!" he shouted. "You defile the memory of their only son. Madam said to call the police if you don't leave right now, and by God I will!"

Over the following months Joška Herzl slept in basements and sheds. He avoided the center of town and the parks, where Jews, if there had been any left in Zagreb in April 1944, were not allowed to step foot, but he soon realized that he was not safe. He did not look like a communist agent. Those people – he would come to understand after the war – were well dressed as a rule. Nor did he give the impression of belonging to a race outside the law. As we have indicated, there weren't any Jews anymore, and unkempt and filthy as he was, he had the appearance of someone who had come to Zagreb in search of something that belonged to him by right: a lost relative, his human and Croatian rights . . . He looked like someone before whom one had to lower their gaze, pretending he was invisible.

Besides, it did not bother him that the buildings were rotting and crumbling here as if they were built of raw potatoes. It was not clear whether Maksimilijan Stinčić and Bosiljka Kamauf Stinčić were aware that it had been their son Josip who called at the gate of their Zelengaj villa that day. It seemed they thought someone was playing a nasty trick on them, mocking them in the ugliest of ways, by reminding them of their dead son. It did not occur to them that he could have made it from Graz to Zagreb alive.

The first time they saw him, at least so thought Joška Herzl – and this was what he told Rudi in the train that stood at the Zagreb Station in August of 1954 – had been in the early spring of 1945.

The day was gray and icy, and the air was dry with no sign of snow, though for weeks the temperature had been dropping below ten degrees centigrade, and a breeze from Sljeme sent shivers down the spines of passersby under their coats, which were gray, threadbare, and eaten through by moths and war. For a long time the kuna had been worth almost nothing, the national currency was experiencing a breakdown, the black market reigned, and the authorities were battling against it, mostly without success, by means of court trials and deportations to Jasenovac. As they retreated before the Partisans, who, with the support of the Red Army from the east, were preparing for a decisive spring offensive, the Ustaše once more took the field against smugglers and black marketeers, creating the illusion among the city's inhabitants that everything was in the best order and the state was standing up for its integrity in the domain where even in peacetime it was most threatened: in the markets, stores, and butcheries. The truth was that, particularly outside of Zagreb, there were no butcheries or stores or markets, but everyone ignored this fact. Anyone who came face to face with it knew the government was counting down its final hours and all the debts acquired in the four preceding years, collective and individual, were soon to be reconciled. But how could we know how much was owed by whom? And who would be in charge of collecting debts?

The only things still functioning, which supported the illusion of the existence of the Independent State of Croatia that it maintained itself, were concerts, theater performances, and cultural life in general. Music was performed at the Music Academy every week. Independent Croatian State Radio held onto its strict seasonal repertory, conceived years before, when the perspectives for European civilization and nations advanced by the great German Führer Adolf Hitler seemed much healthier . . . And so, by the end of winter, encouraged by the insane optimism of Croatian music lovers, the Stinčićs one Thursday afternoon started out for a concert at the Music Academy. A young pianist, a certain Perinčić, whose first name they could never remember, would be playing Sibelius.

They met Joška on a deserted Ilica Square.

There was no one around. People had closed themselves up in their houses, peeking out their windows, waiting for something to happen. For days, shootings were heard from the suburbs, though the radio said the Partisans were far away, somewhere in dark, deep Bosnia and that Croatian knights were holding them back.

They thought they were seeing a ghost.

Maksimilijan trembled as if shaking death off his shoulder.

"Oh dear God!" squeaked Bosa, and the two stopped midstride as if expecting Joška Herzl to pass by without noticing them, perhaps thinking they weren't actually alive but that by order of subcommandant Budak, a monument of them had been cast in bronze right there on Ilica Square.

"Mama!" he said in amazement, though he had been preparing for this encounter for months.

And then he grew immediately uncomfortable. He had addressed her in a way that he shouldn't have, that he hadn't intended. It had somehow been understood that they were no longer his parents and he was no longer their son.

They did not move.

"Joška, child, where in the world are your shoelaces?" she asked, not knowing what else to say.

Maksimilijan Stinčić was silent, staring obtusely ahead as if he were waiting for all this to be over. And how could the son of the greatest Croatian pianist be tone-deaf, unless this pianist, along with the whole, ancient and long-suffering Croatian nation, was just as tone-deaf as he?

And while Maksimilijan Stinčić waited, his face contorted into a grin, a drunken pub keeper's guffaw, for he suddenly understood how funny Bosiljka's question to her son had been: "Joška, child, where in the world are your shoelaces?"

"We're going to a concert of . . . ," he finally said, then stopped short. He could not for the life of him remember what the young man's name was – Peričić? Perišić? Perinčić? – who was supposed to be playing Sibelius, and his eyes bulged, as if a fish bone had got stuck in his throat.

"At the Music Academy they're performing . . ." and then all of a sudden he could not remember Jean Sibelius's name either, the name Grieg was on the tip of his tongue instead. Finnish family names ended with *onen*, and it was riling him up inside that he could not remember that most famous of *onens*.

Only later, when they had reached Gundulić Street, in front of the Music Academy, and he glanced at the placard with the announcement of Perinčić's recital, did Maksimilijan Stinčić realize why he could not remember: Sibelius's damn name didn't end in *onen* at all.

The encounter was brief. His mother babbled on about the laces and his father completed only half of each sentence. Words failed him. He couldn't remember Sibelius's name or that of the pianist, and Joška Herzl thought that his father Maksimilijan Stinčić had begun to lose his memory.

This was their only meeting before the war ended.

For the next three months, the Stinčićs did not leave the villa at Zelengaj though Bosa Kamaufova went out for a ducat or two's worth of supplies. Until the Partisans' arrival, the black market was perfectly functional.

And then came freedom.

In the first weeks nothing happened. A new army marched around the city, formerly prohibited communist songs could be heard, accompanied by the tinkle of Gypsy violins and the swelling of harmonicas, and everything was like the theater, a stage on which a play by Maxim Gorky was unfolding. Bosa Kamaufova and her husband did not like the theater. Not even the opera. Every theatrical presentation contained something false and exaggerated. Even the sets of productions at the Croatian National Theater were offensive to Maksimilijan. Branko Gavella would turn the stage into a living room, with a table, chairs, a couch and armchair in the background, with a cupboard and pictures of ancestors on the walls, and the room reminded him of their Zelengaj salon. Then actors would enter who would, largely on the basis of a text by Mr. Krleža, subject the scene to ridicule, which they both found insufferable. The theater, they felt, besmirched their own cozy nest, it scorned all those in this city and in this land who lived and behaved like normal people. In whose name was this done? And where did this Krleža live with his dramatic muse?

The very thought of the theater enraged them.

They were enraged, as they watched the communists march theatrically through the city and replace their burnt-out Lika and Kozar villages with Zagreb. There was an expression of outright disdain on Professor Bosiljka Kamauf Stinčić's face. She looked at them from above, those little, meaningless red termites, those red worms, which she could have squished one after another if there just hadn't been so many of them. Maksimilijan was somewhat more careful. Or perhaps his fear ran deeper.

It was Friday, June 15, 1945, when they came for him. Two Partisans, unarmed, in neat British uniforms, knocked on the door, for the bell was not working, politely introduced themselves, and led him away. Bosa was utterly lost, not even knowing what to say, her heart in her throat . . . She was neither enraged nor afraid. It was an undefined but quite intense feeling, which completely deprived her of reason. She let him leave in his house robe and slippers.

He, meanwhile, did this demonstratively. Let people see how they led him away in his dressing gown and slippers. Let them see what these liberators were like . . .

Of course if the two Partisans had ordered Maksimilijan Stinčić, one of our first musical giants, who had commanded the stages of Europe alongside Milka Ternina, to put on a summer jacket and shoes, he would have done so without comment. If they had told him to put on a tuxedo, he would have done that too, but since they had already decided to shame him, he was happy to allow it.

At first Bosa Kamaufova did not know where her husband had been taken.

For days she searched for him, making the rounds of the offices on Petrinjska and Zrinjevac, asking people – professors and musicians – who she supposed were close to the communists. Some did not know; others turned her away with contempt. And then she had a life-saving idea: Joška! She would find Joška Herzl, a surviving Jew, whose destiny would open all the doors in Zagreb to her.

Joška meanwhile had also been detained.

They had arrested him at Zagreb Station at the end of May in a raid that was aimed at remaining smugglers and black marketeers, though possibly their net might also ensnare a disguised Ustaše colonel, a Jasenovac butcher, or a priest who had blessed the pistols and bloody knives across Lika and Bosnia.

Joška had just started demonstrating to two elderly citizens – one was a plainclothes Partisan agent – how to juggle lit matches. Someone grabbed him by the collar, the little flames flew in all directions, his nostrils filled with the strong scent of phosphorous, adrenaline rushed into his blood stream, and Joška Herzl went to prison.

Everything he told his Partisan interrogators seemed fantastical and unlikely.

At first he was not afraid; he thought the misunderstanding would be quickly cleared up. For God's sake, he was a Jew, and the communists, the Yugoslav Partisans, protected the Jews, the whole world knew this, and the Partisan units were filled with Jews, the Ustaše press had trumpeted this, Croatian bishops and priests had told stories about it, and it just wasn't possible that all this wasn't true and that he, Joška Herzl, might die for being Jewish . . .

After he had finished his sad story of the old aunt and the half-wit sister taken from the house while he was playing with matches, the interrogators – purely from pedagogical motives for they were certain he was a liar and a stupid liar at that – gave him a thorough thrashing. They thrashed him good-naturedly, as one might a child, with belts and shoelaces, careful not to harm him more than was seemly. Perhaps they'd been touched by the naïveté of his story, or they believed he was mentally retarded, or maybe they actually weren't sure whether there might not be something more serious behind it, something one ought not touch.

Whatever it was, they struck a deathly fear into him. He screamed as if they were ripping the skin off his back. Joška Herzl had long since been ready to die. But he could not bear the thought of being beaten without any intention of finishing him off.

Besides, he did not know how to make them believe him.

And so he decided to tell them the whole truth.

He then had to repeat his story before a higher officer. Then once more before a psychiatrist, who was probably also a Jew. And then three more times before people who came to listen to the tale of the child whose parents denied him because he was not musical, sending him to his Jewish aunt in Graz, who turned him into a Jew.

The last time, the seventh or eighth, Joška Herzl told his sad life's story to Davorin Gubijan, a prewar communist and at the time, in summer 1945, the best-known Partisan prose writer, whose novel *The Bloody Year* had just been printed and would be released in late summer. In that first postwar publishing season, Zagreb was parrying Belgrade, where at the same time two novels by Ivo Andrić, *A Bosnian Chronicle* and *The Bridge on the Drina*, were both published. Although there was no competition, the one who had written his book in the mountains of our proud land rather than in the rented room of a Belgrade apartment, not far from Hotel Moskva, held a great advantage. But let us leave that for another occasion, perhaps a literary historical survey . . . It might be worth noting that Joška Herzl had never read either Gubijan's or Andrić's novels – in fact, he hadn't read anything since his school days, for if he had, he wouldn't have seen any sense in match juggling, or have had the time to perfect it – while Rudolf Stubler was a very careful Andrić reader, loved the author, and kept his books among the German originals of Broch and Thomas Mann, considering him their equal, while he avoided Gubijan like the plague, and never touched his novel *The Psalm of David*, published in spring 1948, whose entire remaining print run was confiscated and destroyed after Davorin Gubijan, that same summer, positively and aggressively refused to comply with the Cominform Resolution of June 28. He was imprisoned at Goli Otok, where he served time twice, almost without a break in between, until the end of 1959, after which his work would for a long time be prohibited and later forgotten. Davorin Gubijan would then self-publish *The Psalm of David* in Belgrade in 1991, but it attracted no attention. Two years later, alone and embittered, this Partisan author and martyr of Goli Otok would die in the ninety-third year of his life.

In prison in Zrinjevac, it took Joška Herzl no more than two or three hours to tell Gubijan his life's story. He asked for a box of matches to demonstrate his artistry to the famous writer, but the jailers did not grant his request, lest the prison catch fire.

In the end, he put Joška's entire story, faithfully and with no digressions of any sort, directly into his novel. He only changed the name of the protagonist: Joška thus became David Šlomo. And of course he changed his profession, but not altogether: instead of a match-juggling, unmusical son of a famous Zagreb musician he became a three-matchbox swindler. In Davorin Gubijan's novel, he used his matches to swindle naïve travelers in stations across occupied Europe. He rotated his three matchboxes on the platforms, and somehow the little ball was always under the one no one discovered . . .

The Psalm of David was scandalous even in that final spring of Yugoslav Stalinism. The dark manner in which Gubijan ridiculed the Croatian petite bourgeoisie, intelligentsia, and Zagreb gentlefok sharply contrasted his depiction of the proletariat in the city's suburbs. Most terrifying was the end of the book, when David Šlomo, after the war, is reborn in a Zenica work-rehabilitation center, where he learns to be a carpenter, a worthwhile worker, a socialist citizen, a husband, a father . . . The story ends with a meeting at which a proud David is accepted into the Yugoslav Communist Party, as he rapturously declaims sentences from the *Communist Manifesto*. This is why the book is called *The Psalm of David*.

When they no longer knew what to do with Joška and were convinced he was not an enemy, German collaborator, Ustaše member, smuggler, or pimp, but simply a habitual liar, a beggar with a Munchausen-like imagination, they set Joška Herzl free. Let him go on his way, wherever it might lead him.

This was at the end of August.

By then Bosa Kamaufova had come to terms with the fact that her renegade son had disappeared – he was no more and could not help her. She sought help from Zagreb's musicians, Partisan sympathizers, Serbian and Jewish, who could guarantee that Maksimilijan Stinčić was innocent. Not only was he innocent, but it was well known to everyone in Zagreb that during the quisling Independent State of Croatia, the most famous Croatian pianist had not given a single public performance. This had been his way of resisting against the occupier and its collaborators. And what else, I ask respectfully, had been available to an elderly man? Should he have taken up a rifle in those times, rushed into the woods, and started shooting? Let us be clear, good people, Maksim was at least ten years older than Comrade Vladimir Nazor, who deserved every honor!

And so, on August 31, emaciated and gray, Maksimilijan Stinčić was released from his Zrinjevac cell. Perhaps all that had separated him from Joška Herzl was a wall. If so, he did not know it at the time.

Before long, Bosa Kamaufova began teaching at the Music Academy and, soon after, through some diplomatic intervention, was given permission to travel to Salzburg as a visiting professor. She would make amends for all that she had failed to do during the war, and her method of musical instruction, amoral, cold, and mathematically precise, would dominate Central European universities and music schools.

Maksimilijan Stinčić sank ever deeper into his alcoholic melancholy, already resembling the bronze bust that would one day stand in the Music Academy's auditorium. He did nothing and spoke to no one. After his release from prison, the once-celebrated Croatian pianist had not uncovered his old piano or touched a single key. When one or another of Bosa's talented students would come to the house – Vojkan Milić, the future director of the studio orchestra of Belgrade Radio and Television, or Husnija Beglerbegović, today a famous Sarajevo pianist and composer, the author of the *Siege Symphony*, which held countless performances around the world in 1993 – Maksimilijan would set aside his newspaper, get up from his armchair, and leave the room with a sigh.

She asked him what was wrong.

He replied that music was no longer to his liking. As if they were talking about a dish that was hard on his stomach.

Gradually, as time went on, they started to introduce Joška Herzl into their conversations. They mentioned him with pity, shrugging and sighing demonstratively, as if they were talking about Mishka the fool. They didn't care that he was living somewhere in the vicinity, God only knew where, maybe in some Vlaška Street basement, nor were they concerned that he might tell someone his life's story and that they might believe him.

In the end, the war had sliced every person's life in two, and what was left over from before the war did not seem to hold any importance any longer. Responsibility had disappeared, debts and loans wiped clean, but few had been as liberated by this break as the Stinčićs. They stopped lighting candles on the empty grave of their only son, they went to Mirogoj only on All Saints' Day, during the Zagreb-wide cemetery parade, but not even then did they feel the need to show people the sadness and despair they might have felt for their progeny.

This is what we know of Joška's parents, what was reported in the Zagreb papers of the time or what witnesses reported in their memoirs. Of course some of it has been added to, invented – Rudi had been the first to add to it, in the countless versions related between 1954 and 1976 to the Stublers and their descendants, friends, acquaintances, and guests at the house on Kasindol Street, and then, more generally and perhaps more tendentiously, the storyteller himself has added to it and reshaped it, and the presumed atmosphere of the Zelengaj villa transported him to such a degree that he wrote dozens upon dozens of pages devoted to the marital conversations and silences between Bosiljka Kamauf Stinčić and her husband, which would eventually end up in the depths of the recycling bin.

Joška stayed on in Zagreb. He lived like a bum, of which there were not many in Zagreb in those postwar years; most of them, like Mishka the fool, were mentally deficient or psychotic, for otherwise the authorities would not have tolerated them. In those years, during Stalinism but also later, once Tito had dealt with its dark spirit, the police had a paranoid aversion to any vagrant, for in every poor wretch they saw a potential British or American – and later Soviet – spy, who surely had a clandestine radio device hidden in his den, by which he was feeding secret information about conditions in Yugoslavia to his superiors. Secrets were everywhere: from the price of bread at the store to the results of the weekly soccer matches, for it was impossible to know what the enemy might be able to use against us. And so it would remain until the end of the fifties, perhaps through the sixties, until the day the Yugoslavs had freed themselves from their ancestral sin toward the Soviet Union and begun to forget the warning that had once been inscribed on every official telephone: "The enemy never sleeps."

Of all these Zagreb urchins, bums, and down-and-outs – of which there could have been four or at most five at the end of the forties – only Joška Herzl was both mentally and emotionally normal. Or so it seemed to him; perhaps on Petrinjska – the Zagreb police street where officers, spies, gendarmes, monitors, and militiamen had had their seat since the days of Franz Joseph – he was considered just as crazy as Mishka the fool.

In any case, whoever had seen the match juggler in action even once would have understood that only a deranged person or genius could flip ten miniature torches on the ends of his fingers until they turned into smoke and ash while the fingers continued to move through the air . . .

"In any case, whoever had seen the match juggler in action even once understood that Joška Herzl was either deranged or a genius!" Rudi would say, relating the story of his trip to Berlin to the Stublers.

"In any case," he said, raising a hand into the air, "whoever had seen the match juggler in action even once was left wondering whether Joška Herzl was insane or a genius!" This was Rudi on November 29, 1970, at the table during Sunday dinner, at the house on Kasindol, this time addressing, in German, Doctor Werner G., to whom Branka Ćurlin, Lola's daughter, had just been married and who was visiting his in-laws for the first time, where this story had to be related to him.

"In any case," Rudi sighed, "whoever saw Joška Herzl juggling matches even once was left wondering if the young man was crazy or a genius!"

This was in the summer of 1976, in the cool shade behind the apiary, as he dealt his last hand of preferans with Isak Sokolovski and two other people now forgotten. What preyed on him, and what was on his mind each time he pronounced these words, was the fact that he, Rudolf Stubler, had never seen Joška Herzl juggle matches.

At the very moment when Joška Herzl had pulled a box of matches from his pocket, the train began to move, and not even he could juggle in a moving train.

"Fine, we'll do it later," he said, offering Rudi the box for safekeeping.

But there was no other opportunity, the compartment was soon crammed with passengers, all heading to Maribor, the train made no more stops, all the track signals were open.

Only after he had ceremoniously bid his fellow travelers goodbye, extending his hand and saying, "We shall meet again!" and after Rudi caught sight of Joška Herzl through the window as he disappeared down the platform in Graz, did Rudolf Stubler realize he had not seen him juggle the matches. He felt a deep sadness, stronger than expected, and considered getting off the train to urge Joška Herzl to come back and prove his talent. He called "Joška!" out the window, but by then Joška was far away and running, as if he had just seen someone he knew.

Here the story of Rudolf Stubler's first postwar trip abroad might have ended. And he would have ended it, if that were possible. Unable to reach the match juggler, he should have just gone home. His trip had lost all meaning: the burners for steam locomotives that, in the name of the railway headquarters in Sarajevo, he was to order in Berlin were no longer being manufactured anyway. The factory had been leveled to the ground by Allied bombing raids, and he knew this before setting off on his trip, but he had kept it quiet at the Sarajevo headquarters and at the Unified Railway Ministry, while Wilhelm Furtwängler, the celebrated conductor on whose account he had undertaken this journey, all of a sudden no longer interested him.

The great German conductor whom Rudi worshipped, listening to his performances on crackling gramophone records, had saved the lives of a number of Jews who played in the Berlin Philharmonic. A bassoonist, an oboist, and even a flutist obtained the privileges of honorary Aryans thanks to the great conductor – Himmler was against this, perhaps Goebbels too, but music, in the end, took precedence over the desires of mere mortals. The great Germany could not allow Wagner's *Ring of the Nibelung* to sound imperfect. The perfection of Wagner's music guaranteed the final victory of the German spirit, and it was not possible to attain that perfection, it seemed, without the Jewish bassoonists and oboists . . . And thus, they said, did Furtwängler save the lives of these Jews and redeem himself for participating in the cultural and musical life of Hitler's nation. The iconic figure of the regime thereby transposed himself in 1945 into a righteous man.

Rudi, too, had read the story of the bassoonist, the oboist, and the flutist somewhere, and was prepared to repeat it word for word should anyone question the greatness of Wilhelm Furtwängler in his presence. If someone investigated, if in Berlin there were Yugoslav spies and someone denounced Comrade Rudolf Stubler in Sarajevo for having attended a concert by a confidant of the fascist regime, he would narrate for the police the moving story of the Jewish musicians. If that was not enough, let them put him on trial, let them send him to Goli Otok.

Rudi was the family coward, but not when it came to Furtwängler. He felt strongly that music was greater than anything, greater than any suffering, fear, or death, and that music would protect him from anyone who had any prejudice against Furtwängler's wartime performances, or against anyone who might infer from Rudi's German heritage a sympathy for the Nazis.

He had not cared about anything before his departure except getting through all the national borders and arriving in Berlin.

And then Joška Herzl, the match juggler, had ruined his plans.

He no longer felt like going to Berlin, to a Furtwängler concert.

So he was not disappointed when there was no concert.

He landed in a city that was raising itself, brick by brick, up from ruins. The streets of new Berlin, whose contours were barely reminiscent of the old city, droned with American and Russian trucks. The nighttime bars rang with Afro jazz music, and all the languages of the occupiers could be heard, while the border between the eastern and western zones was as yet invisible. Soon a wall would be built that would stand as a symbol of the divided world in which Rudi would live the rest of his life, and that world would seem to him as to everyone inalterable and eternal. For the seven days he spent in Berlin, he wandered aimlessly, irritated by the sights, smells, and sounds of the city sprouting up. Nothing there was his anymore, and with the Germans he encountered – at the kiosks, in shops, or at the reception desk of the modest Hotel Hans – he felt less connection than he had with the occupying soldiers and officers during the war in Sarajevo. Toward them he had felt defiance – combined with fear and a desire to avoid them – but they had nevertheless been people he could understand in some deep sense, as one understands the misfortunes and moral failures of others, but with these Germans, who were taken up with jazz and the Russian *kazachok*, Rudi found nothing in common. Hunched and sullen, as if the low northern sky lay heavy on the crowns of their heads, they looked as if some great injustice had been inflicted upon them.

This annoyed him, and at last, years after the death of the family patriarch Karlo Stubler, Rudolf Stuber stopped being a German. He simply no longer felt like one. In late summer 1954, in Berlin, something happened that changed him and solidified in him a different sense of identity, which, at least for the sake of the story, and to get to the point, could be called Croatian. Or perhaps Bosnian, or at best Ilidžan – a Catholic identity, narrow and quaint like San Marino, but still strong and secure enough to last for the rest of Rudi's life.

Since becoming a young man, Rudi had been a little of this and a little of that. Whenever he was really afraid, during the war, in his imprisonment, or later, when they came for Opapa to lead him off to a camp, and later still, as that horrifying event had faded a bit from his memory and their stories, Rudi had felt like a German. When he played cards with the old Sarajevans – Franjo and Isak Sokolovski, along with one or another of his railway comrades – during the long spring and summer Saturdays, in the courtyard beneath the thick canopy in front of the house on Kasindol, people would pass by to say hello. In those moments, Rudi had felt a part of that world, and he'd been a Croat and an Ilidžan. And this was how Rudi's national identity shifted with respect to social conditions, mood, and the time of year. But he felt like a German, usually, when he found himself in the minority, when he was afraid, or when he had read something in the papers about great German war crimes. He was a German when he came face to face with Auschwitz or Jasenovac – though other Germans had no connection to Jasenovac at all – but he would be a Croat when he said hello to the Ilidža villagers or when he took his sister's children to Vrelo Bosne and then, while they went off down the long alley way, he sang softly the lyrics to the song "Jahorina": Oh how high Jahorina, oh gray the falcon that cannot fly over it . . .

He had nothing in common with the Berliners, he did not recognize himself in their eyes but was seized by the urge to grab them by the collar, pull them aside, and tell them what the Germans did to him and his loved ones, how they dressed Mladen up in one of their uniforms, decorated it with the symbols of the

SS, sent him into battle with the Partisans to die as he ran from one stack of hay to another. Haystacks protected us from your bullets, Rudi would have shouted at the first Berliner giving him that self-pitying and accusatory glance, but of course the Berliner would not have understood, no one there would have. They had no idea, for they wanted to forget as soon as possible. They would have only heard Rudi's accent and in it identified his heritage. Oh, those Danube Swabians, they had entangled us in everything with their sick need to attach themselves to the homeland, to become part of a great German empire along with their Romanian and Bulgarian backwaters, a Third Reich, founded on optical illusions and magicians' tricks that would enable those Transylvanian boondocks, the Volga, and Stalingrad, wherever any of those provincials might live, to become suburbs of Berlin! And then our sons – oh, our violated daughters; oh, our dead-and-gone sons – would be fighting in Russia, going all the way to Yugoslavia and Greece, only to enable the ingrates to consider their mangy *Heimat* part of Germany. What an insane geopolitical strategy, what futile suffering, and all because the Führer had wanted to make those people's thousand-year dream come true. Which wasn't at all surprising since Hitler himself was an Austrian and he didn't even have German citizenship, did he? And as an Austrian, he was sentimental about that mossy, dirty world, which had nothing German about it, except that they spoke their own corrupted form of the German language. We had once thought they might be Germans, but now we know they're not. They deported them to us after the collapse in 1945 as additional punishment for what we did and didn't do, as punishment for Adolf Hitler's demented attachment to all those Slavs, Romanians, Bulgarians, to those Mongolians who wanted desperately to have their Mongolia belong to the Third Reich.

Rudi read their thoughts as he wandered around Berlin, stepping into stores for basic goods where everything was too expensive. He knew what any one of them would have thought had he grabbed him by the collar and shouted that Mladen hadn't been an SS officer, a criminal, or even a German, he'd just known the language, or that those feeling sorry for themselves and blaming the whole world for their sins, had protected Mladen from the Partisans' machine-gun fire with a haystack. That's who these people were, Rudi thought, infuriated, they dressed a man in an SS uniform, raised him up to have Aryan honors, and protected him with haystacks!

Rudolf Stubler had completed the work regarding the burners for the narrow-gauge steam locomotive on the Sarajevo-Ploče line by the third day of his stay in Berlin. The factory razed to the ground in the bombing had been rebuilt and now produced oven burners for steam heating. It had the same name and symbol – the symbol contained a tiny steam engine – which probably confused the people at headquarters and the Ministry of Railroads, but they did not ask, nor did they know German well enough to ask whether the new factory would actually produce burners for steam locomotives.

After this, so as not to return to Sarajevo without having accomplished his task, he went to the German railroad headquarters, which was located in the Soviet zone, and there he quickly learned that they had an abundance of obsolete burners for steam engines that were kept at the railway yards in Charlottenburg, and that they would be happy to sell them to the Yugoslavs at a low price. He went to Charlottenburg and discovered that indeed they had enough burners for the next hundred years of traffic on the Sarajevo-Ploče line.

At first he wanted to go back to Sarajevo immediately, though he still had five days left before his agreed upon return date. He did not like Berlin. The city nauseated him – not just the people there, the Germans, or what the Germans had become, but also the repugnant manner in which Berlin was raising itself from the ruins. It repulsed him and also scared him. An enormous, gray cement colossus was rising from a dream, from the dead, reaching for the sky with senselessly tall towers amid the nothingness and the ruins; the hundred-meter-long apartment buildings with thousands of equally sized windows looked like prisons or barracks for a monstrously large army that would remain there forever. On one side of the invisible line, they were building according to American plans – the city looked like a stage replica of Chicago – and on the other, the Soviet architects seemed to be designing sets for a Nikolai Ostrovsky performance. Berlin looked like a scary splicing of America with Soviet communism. And it seemed as if at any moment a new, bigger war could break out. It was as if the Americans and the Soviets did not notice each other, passing one another blindly at the great intersections of the city. Only the Germans, the lumpen proletariat of the big city, provided an awareness and image of the two occupiers, making them visible through their accusatory glances.

Then Rudi decided to stay.

His hotel was paid for, he had the cash he had received from the Ministry of Railroads in Belgrade for his trip, along with fifty black-market American dollars that he intended to spend on a wristwatch and gifts for his family – and it occurred to him that he might never have another opportunity for five free, unencumbered days in Berlin. And who knew whether he would ever be able to travel to Berlin again . . . And so Rudi stayed.

And as he stayed, he thought of Wilhelm Furtwängler at the Berlin Philharmonic. The concert he had initially planned to attend was held on August 1, 1954. The program included the *Pathétique* Sixth Symphony of Tchaikovsky, Beethoven's Ninth, and, as a symbolic climax, Chopin's Second Concerto for Piano and Orchestra. There was no announcement in the newspapers, but it was understood that this concert was being given on the fifteenth anniversary of the war's start, and that the Chopin finale was to serve as a quiet German apology for the attack on Poland in the early morning of August 1, 1939. Rudi had read about this in Belgrade's *Politika*; he then heard about it on a nighttime Berlin radio station, which was when he decided to try and get to Berlin. Everything had gone smoothly – for months at the railway headquarters there had been a great concern over the steam burners, and no one found his offer to try and resolve the situation suspicious, for there were few at headquarters who knew German. And those who did know the language were in no hurry to reveal it.

When he showed up at the ticket office, they told him the concert had been canceled two months before. It had been canceled as quietly as it had been announced – the ticket clerk told Rudi. But why? he asked naïvely. The man just looked at him and said nothing. Perhaps he offered a feeble smile, thinking how stupid and naïve people could still be, or perhaps he thought that this tall man with the shaved head and rather odd accent was a spy who'd come to observe his conduct during the de-Nazification.

"Besides, the maestro is ill. He grew suddenly weak on his return from Lucerne, he conducted the London Philharmonic there, you know," said the ticket clerk, deciding for some reason that it would be important to let the ignoramus know that Furtwängler had conducted British musicians in Lucerne.

"The maestro is getting on in years," he answered, just to say something. "He'll soon been seventy. But so will I . . ."

"A hard life."

"We've all had a hard life, at least in the last twenty years. And before that . . ." he hesitated, as if trying to remember, "before that it was hard too. It has always been hard in Germany."

"Where hasn't it been?"

"That is well said. I'm sure it has been hard everywhere."

"And the maestro, as you say, is getting older."

"I'm afraid it isn't just that. He declines from day to day, as if there's something eating him from inside. All men have their problems, except that in some it develops and in others it doesn't. With me for instance, I should introduce myself, my name is Alois" – he offered Rudi has hand through the hole in the ticket window – "inside me there surely exists an Anti-Alois. But I'm not complaining, I'm in good health, Anti-Alois is still insignificant in relation to Alois!"

He struck himself twice in the chest with his right hand, demonstrating how healthy he was. It echoed hollowly, as if somewhere deep in the woods an ax had hit an oak trunk.

"So you believe the problem is with the Anti-Furtwängler!" Rudi said, laughing.

"Exactly! And don't laugh. I don't think the maestro will be around for long." The old man announced the conductor's imminent demise rather cheerfully.

"Forgive me for laughing."

"And where are you from? You don't sound like a Berliner."

"I'm a Yugoslav."

The ticket clerk was taken aback, but only briefly, and had an answer ready that was inoffensive enough for the conversation to continue without arousing suspicion from any spy – American, British, or Soviet.

"My deceased wife was born there, in Yugoslavia. Actually, the country was called by another name then: the Austro-Hungarian Monarchy. Something like that, no one remembers what its actual name was. The Personal Union of Austria, Hungary, and some other lands, under the rule of the Habsburg royal family. It was all very complicated. That's why it had to fall. People want simplicity."

"And that leads them to war."

"That could be, my dear sir, it very well could. But I wouldn't know anything about that, I was freed from military service long before all these wars. You wouldn't believe it, but I'm flat footed. Besides, I only have one lung. They sliced the other one out because of tuberculosis when I was seven. They thought I wouldn't survive. And look, they were wrong, Alois overpowered Anti-Alois."

Rudi sensed just then that someone was behind him. He turned around, thinking the man wanted to buy a ticket, and he gestured with his hand as one does when letting another onto a tram.

The man was of medium height, but one of those straight-backed old men who appeared much taller than they actually were. He had a thin moustache, like gun fighters in films about the Wild West, a prominent, quite recognizable head, and he patiently waited for his turn.

He smiled at Rudi, who stared at him, astonished, and Alois extended a small packet wrapped in brown paper to him through the opening in the window. "Here you are, maestro!" he said, proud that Rudi was seeing and hearing this.

The old man took the packet with his long, knobby fingers and bowed to the stranger.

"I thank you!" he said then turned back to Alois. "Mr. Stickelburger, please give my regards to Colonel Stewart. Tell him I will send him a letter shortly. He already knows everything else."

From behind he looked much older. He moved slowly. His steps stayed close to the ground, his soles scraping the floor, as if suffering from Parkinson's. A great deal of time had passed before he made it all the way to the exit.

The door scraped closed, the sound of the Berlin streets disappeared, the voices of people and the ambulance sirens, as if the space had been hermetically sealed.

"Go after him, why not. It will probably be nice for him. He hasn't met anyone from Yugoslavia for some time."

Rudi later had no idea why he'd listened to the ticket clerk. He ran outside and almost collided with Wilhelm Furtwängler, who had barely made it a few steps down the street.

"Excuse me, maestro . . ."

The conductor took him afterward to a teahouse, just around the corner, in the building where he stayed when in Berlin.

They sat by the window, drinking Russian tea.

He told him he would soon be going to Baden-Baden. His joints plagued him and the bathwater and climate would help. Furtwängler insisted that suffering in no way proved that a person was alive. Only music can demonstrate that there are signs of life among these crags, Furtwängler said. But even if it isn't so, even if there is no more music, one mustn't be sorry. At least you Yugoslavs have no reason to mourn Beethoven. You have the sea. And in the late summer, the wind comes up before dawn, and the waves wash against the cliffs below the Dubrovnik Hotel, and the sound is worthy of Beethoven, though devoid of musical form and harmony. It is a shame that Arnold Schoenberg – you have heard of his work – did not spend his summers in Dubrovnik. If he had, he would have realized his music was superfluous next to Beethoven's, like the waves that beat against the Dubrovnik stones, producing that completely atonal sound. This is the reason, Maestro Furtwängler said to Rudi, as they sat in the corner teahouse drinking Russian tea, why you Yugoslavs should not mourn Beethoven.

And as for the oboist, the bassoonist, and flutist, I did what I could, Furtwängler told him, but I do not say my conscience is at peace. Only scoundrels refer to their peaceful conscience. And I am sorry for your nephew. So many young people, Furtwängler said, paid with their lives . . . I can only feel sorry, that is all.

And then he told him the story of Karl Holbein, an extraordinarily gifted youngster, the impoverished son of a Jewish baker. There's that Jewish sense of humor, Furtwängler said, so many poor people taking on such last names. Karl

Holbein had perfect hearing: the sound of a mosquito buzzing in the next room would wake him. He was ideally suited for music: he could hear it beyond set tempos and compositional directions, as it had never been played before and as it could be if we all had perfect hearing and musicality, and he also had something greater and more important – he had imagination.

The Jews are more musically gifted, Furtwängler said, because Jews in general have greater imaginations.

Young Karl Holbein imagined Beethoven. And Tchaikovsky, and poor Gustav Mahler, and sweet Mozart . . . But he had a different ambition. He did not want to become a great conductor. He wanted to play first violin in the Berlin Philharmonic.

He was my student and my protégé, Wilhelm Furtwängler said, but I could not protect him. I told him: Son, go to Switzerland, or America, wherever your legs will take you, you'll earn bread anywhere, you'll be a famous, great violinist, and once you've grown up you'll realize that there is something besides the violin for you, but leave this place, Germany is not for you.

And is it for you? he responded impishly.

Germany is for me, yes, but it isn't for you, the famous conductor shouted at the young man, and he shouted at Rudi too, as he was telling him the story.

I don't want all that, Holbein said calmly. All I want is to be first violinist in your orchestra. If you go to New York, or become the musical director of the London Symphony, if you go to the moon, I will follow you . . .

But Furtwängler did not want to leave Germany. He conducted with Adolf Hitler seated in the front row, surrounded by a suite of select German criminals, and the maestro understood how all this would end, acknowledging his sin, but he did not want to leave Germany. He believed that only in Germany would he be able to conduct the Ninth Symphony as he wanted, outside the instructions and accepted conventions of the lax musical spirit of a corrupt Europe. In Europe and America, Arturo Toscanini had been in control for decades, and he was not a conductor but a metronome that waved its arms from the podium just so the musicians wouldn't lose their place.

Karl Holbein did not play the bassoon, or the oboe, or the flute, so all was in vain. He was merely a student of Furtwängler, who procured false documents for him with the name of an Aryan boy who had died in a traffic accident. He walked through Berlin without the mandatory Star of David symbol, until someone recognized him and reported him to the Gestapo. Furtwägler begged them to spare him, insisted he had never had such a gifted student, telephoned Goebbels, but he did not answer his phone. It was in vain because Holbein did not play the bassoon, the oboe, or the flute, so Beethoven could be just as perfectly rendered without him.

If anyone else had hidden a Jew and procured false documents for him, in the best of cases he would have ended up in a camp. No one in all of Germany besides Furtwängler was allowed to hide Jews with impunity.

This was what Wilhelm Furtwängler was told, which he, word for word, conveyed to Rudolf Stubler, who would in turn relate the story during family gatherings, weddings, and funerals. Among the Stublers, as has been recorded and as the finale of this family history confirms, there were many more funerals than there were weddings.

They even allowed him to be alone with Karl Holbein – or Judah Israel Holbein, as his name was entered in the official documents – but the only thing he was able to do was take a sheet of paper from his briefcase and write on it in black ink the announcement that Karl Holbein was appointed concert master and first violin of the Berlin Philharmonic.

The next morning Karl Holbein was merely one among thousands in a cattle car taking people east. Karl Holbein ended up in a camp, Furtwängler did not know which one, and the maestro would spend many fruitless days begging Goebbels, Göring, and anyone close to the Führer to do something to save the German musical genius. Maybe he was a Jew, Furtwängler had said then, and now to Rudi in the little Berlin teahouse, maybe Holbein was a Jew, but the music Holbein imagined was German music. The greatest German music of our time. That was what Furtwängler had said, but there was no one to hear him. The innocent youngster who dreamed of becoming first violinist in Furtwängler's orchestra would forever be on his conscience. For that dream the child had been prepared to die.

Had Wilhelm Furtwängler been prepared to leave Germany, which, after all, is what all of cultured Europe expected of him, Karl Holbein would have remained alive, for he would have followed him. But then an oboist, a bassoonist, and a flutist might have ended up in a camp . . .

"But I'm going to tell you something, dear sir. I've thought about this for a long time, and now I know: Karl Holbein died happy, for his dream was realized in the cell of his Berlin prison. He became the first violinist and concertmaster of the Berlin Philharmonic, and this order was personally signed and verified with artistic honor by Wilhelm Furtwängler. His dream was realized. All that may be small, insignificant, but we as human beings don't really know what the big things are. This is why Karl Holbein died happy, the moment before he would have grown disillusioned with his dream . . ."

As the train crawled slowly through a ravaged, divided Europe, it occurred to Rudi that perhaps it had all been a huge deception. The old man might not have been Wilhelm Furtwängler – after all, would the great conductor have invited him to tea to tell him about his life? Maybe he was an impostor, a liar who had spent a lifetime lying about himself. A good-for-nothing tramp who changed roles and masks, taking up the identities of famous people, living off their genius, suffering, and sacrifices for the homeland. The old impostor had played this last role masterfully, Rudi thought, traveling in his empty compartment on the Munich-Salzburg-Vienna line, explaining to people what Wilhelm Furtwängler should have explained to people.

The one thing that did not fit and that plagued Rudi about the entire affair was that the old man paid for his own and Rudi's teas. You are the traveler, Furtwängler said to Rudi. It's not your place to pay. When I'm the traveler, you can buy tea for me.

The Bee Journal

In the basement of the house on Sepetarevac Street, among the things that remained there after our move, was a little moth-eaten wool bag, a so-called *zob-nica*, found in the summer of 1998, and in it a pencil – the only thing untouched by time and the basement's humidity – a rusty benzene lighter, two pieces of red wax for sealing letters, and a notebook.

The bag, lighter, and wax ended up in the trash – who needed wax for sealing letters anymore? – the fate of the pencil is unknown, but the notebook I kept, because I thought it might contain an answer to the question as to whom this bag, which resembled a horse-feed sack, from which its name is derived (*zob* meaning oats), had belonged and for what it had been used. Where it had been sewn together was hard to say, for its colors and ornaments had been lost to rot and filth, and such bags were used all along the Dinaric belt, from the Karst Rim to Istria, across the Velebit, Dalmatia and Herzegovina, all the way to Albania, wherever there were sheep and men who tended to them.

I was curious to find out to whom the bag had belonged. I often think about lost possessions, searching for answers to questions left over from the past, or trying to reconstruct events witnessed by those no longer with us. I torment myself this way, especially when I'm sitting in waiting rooms, or bored, or lying in the dark with a headache, and I develop theories about everything and everyone. Nothing good comes of this, no literature – only torture without meaning or end. Wittgenstein was lying when he said what cannot be imagined cannot be thought about: oh, yes, it can. Such thoughts hurt at first, then lead into obtuseness and torpor.

I wanted to forget about the bag, so I tried to discover who its owner had been.

Besides, I was thirty-two – the following year I would be the age Jesus had been when he died – and it was too late to change professions. But researching the contents of a bag found in a basement, reconstructing the historical moment from seemingly ordinary objects explained by jottings in a notebook, after having spending years rummaging through archives and traveling to places where the unknown actors in this story lived or visited, I began to piece together the sense behind *minor histories* – the most interesting of scholarly genres – but also the sense behind the practice of scholarship, a practice I unfortunately shall never undertake, for I will remain to the end of my life a journalist and fiction writer who invents things and tries to arrive, by shortcuts, at what scholars get to with much greater certainty. And this being the case, at least this once I should research an object of interest and remove from it all doubt and speculation.

After I had cleaned off the deposits of dust and mold with a small rag, a gray-blue leather cover with simple narrow decorations along the edge appeared with a now barely visible inscription in the lower-right corner. In handwritten letters, with a line underneath as if for a signature, the word *Notes* was printed. Though both the inscription and the decorations, which looked as if they were linked together by staples, were by now barely discernable. Under careful inspection, it was possible to see the traces of gilding in the grooves, and the decorative aesthetic and shape of the letters were consistent with art deco.

The notebook could not have been expensive.

It measured 10.3 centimeters by 15.8 centimeters, and contained forty-four hand-numbered pages, of which two, between 32 and 37, were torn out, and two others were the unmarked front and back pages.

It was filled with writing from page 1 to page 18, then again on pages 21, 25, and 27, all in pencil. The handwriting was minute but clear, except where it had faded with time as the graphite dried and turned to dust. But those parts too, which did not compose more than a quarter of the text, could be reconstructed with a little effort and a magnifying glass. Each record in the notebook had its own entry date, from the first, on July 18, 1935, to the last, on page 27, dated July 14, 1937.

On the inside of the first blank page was an "abbreviations and symbols" legend.

M = queen
D = drone
W = worker bee
C = colony
B = brood
SB = sealed brood
E = egg
← = back
→ = front
O = middle
+ = swarm

The handwriting was the same from start to finish, and instantly recognizable, flowing and distinctive, controlled, small. While it was possible to tell when the notebook was held in the palm of the writer's left hand and when it had rested on a firm surface, the handwriting was never unsettled, nor was any letter ever larger than its delimited space, the so-called cubelets of a mathematics notebook sheet, which had probably conditioned the self-control and balance of the keeper of this unorthodox journal.

Only one sentence was written in a different hand, in equally small letters, on the inside of the second blank page. The sentence read, "Saturday, June 7, Mina visited." As the seventh of June fell on a Saturday only in 1941, the sentence had been written after the notebook was no longer used, although there was a slight possibility that Mina had come on Sunday in 1936.

That sentence had been written by Olga Rejc.

All the rest had been written by Franjo Rejc.

He kept the journal in the notebook with its gray-blue cover for a single bee colony. At the time, between 1935 and 1937, Franjo managed another community, this one in Želeće, near Žepče, where he had nine hives on a meadow not far from the station. There was surely another journal that accompanied the life of this other community. It has not survived, nor are there any living witnesses to confirm the story of the nine hives situated on a meadow belonging to Dušan Zlatković, a switchman employed at the Žepče station. Franjo Rejc paid his rent for the meadow to Zlatković in honey, or "pollen rent," as they referred to it, though Zlatković didn't request it. "It's great luck, good for any normal human to have bees on the land. God loves bees. God's love makes honey heal." That was how Dušan Zlatković talked about bees, according to Nono's memory, or my memory of Nono's memory. While he was only a switchman, he was a devout person – not common among the rail men and track workers, especially the Orthodox ones – he read the holy books every evening, went up into the mountain to chant the psalms, and would forever ask, "What would God think of that? How would God look on that?"

Franjo did not have to pay rent for the six hives at Ilidža, for this bee community was located in Karlo Stubler's garden. Karlo and his son Rudi sometimes looked after the bees, but in those years Rudi would be playing in the Sarajevo variety theater, and Opapa was ailing – late summer allergies seemed to be giving him trouble, at a time when allergies were not commonly known – so care of the bees fell to Franjo. That was why he kept the journal.

His need to note and document was pronounced throughout his life. Perhaps this was the expression of some cocooned literary talent or derived from a need to stop time and save himself from oblivion, or perhaps it was the result of Franjo's bureaucratic orderliness, which drove him to select, analyze, comment upon, and archive everything. He had always kept journals, not just for bees and bee colonies, but for everything else too. He recorded his phone conversations in the table calendar: the date, time, conversation length, whether he had made or received the call. Below that he would note whether any mail had come that day, a letter, a telegram, or a book ordered from Germany. On the little papers he stuck to the worktable he noted what had transpired at headquarters, who had a new grandson, whose boy had graduated from Zagreb, whose wife had died. Later he would file them into a folder, or they vanished on the way to the wastebasket, and no one, not even he, knew what purpose this documentation of reality served. He felt insecure if he was not keeping a journal.

Karlo once asked him why he wrote down what he would most likely remember anyway.

He seemed confused at first but then answered very reasonably: "So people will know what to do with the bees if something happens to me. It would be a shame for the bees to suffer along with me."

Karlo didn't believe him. No one who knew Franjo would have believed that he kept a journal to protect the bees from whatever might happen to him personally. And anyway, when the beekeeper was no more, and when there was no one left to look after the hives, the bees would still have survived. The colony would have changed, the hives would have emptied, there would have been many dead and unborn, the larvae would have rotted in their broods, the acetic odor of death would have spread, but the bees' line would nevertheless have carried on.

Franjo knew this better than anyone, but he could not think of a better reason why he kept a bee journal.

Or why he kept all his other journals.

So this much I was able to discover quite easily: the bag with the pencil, benzene lighter, letter-sealing wax, and the notebook had belonged to my grandfather.

And it was time to step back, to forget the notebook in one of the drawers of my desk in Markuševac, where it would remain so long that the graphite would disappear from the paper, leaving the empty, yellowed pages without any writing at all. Thus in the end would all Franjo's stories and chronicles return to their original matter.

But I still needed to learn two things.

Why had he stopped keeping the bee journal?

And when had Mina visited Olga and Franjo: on Saturday, June 7, 1941, or on Sunday, June 7, 1939? Had Olga entered the wrong day of the week, or had she made the annotation on the inside of the second blank page a full four years after Fanjo had stopped keeping a journal of the Ilidža bees?

The notebook had probably been in the bag with the pencil, benzene lighter, and letter-sealing wax by that time. Did she take it out merely in order to record the date and day when Mina came? Whom did such an annotation serve and for what purpose?

In the August 1998 I searched through drawers and old notebooks, poked around the attic of the Sepetarevac house looking for other bee journals. They were not there. They had disappeared, perhaps they had been burned during the cold winters of the war or tossed out as garbage by Javorka, his daughter and my mother, during that first peacetime spring, carried away by the euphoria of a new day.

I called old people who remembered him on the phone, but they too had forgotten him. They were usually suspicious. In the best of cases they thought I was an impostor and was planning on robbing them and abruptly hung up. But many did, meanwhile, remember who Franjo Rejc was and would tell me all about him.

In Zagreb's Lavoslav Švarc Home for Elderly Jews I found Đorđe Bijelić, who on January 17, 1937, had been appointed to the steering committee of the Society of Beekeeping and Honey Producers of the Kingdom of Yugoslavia. Their meeting had been held in the Workers Hall in Sarajevo. Franjo Rejc had been responsible for keeping the minutes.

It was raining and unusually cold for the start of September.

In front of the building, which was hidden in thick foliage in the eastern part of town where it would not bother anyone, stood a statue of the communist underground agent and martyr, translator of Marx's *Capital* and academic painter of the Munich school Moša Pijade, which had been displayed at an important Zagreb intersection before the war in 1991. Instead of dynamiting it into smithereens – which would have upset the inhabitants of the neighboring buildings – the blackshirts had politely offered to the local Jewish community to have Moša moved to a property where he would not be visible to the indignant public or offensive to the Catholic majority. The grateful Jews had the statue moved to a spot in front of their home for the elderly. No one noticed it there.

It was not lunchtime, but the old people were seated around a common dining table covered with a white tablecloth. Some were drinking tea, but most were not drinking anything. One woman with freshly permed hair wore an oxygen mask.

At the head of the table sat a corpulent, middle-aged woman with a familiar face. A famous opera singer, who had performed for years at the Met in New York, was moving slowly to the rhythm of an invisible orchestra, pressing her chest to the edge of the table, then leaning back into the chair.

She was singing an old song: "My thoughts fly to you mother, across mountains and plains, carrying you a greeting from your only son . . ."

The old people were opening their lips with her, mouthing the words, but their voices made little sound. The permed woman, too, opened her mouth under the transparent plastic oxygen mask.

Đorđe Bijelić was sitting in a wheelchair.

Georg Weiss, son of Joseph Pepik Weiss, professor of mathematics at the Main Gymnasium, was born on January 1, 1901, the first day of the new century. He enrolled in Belgrade's School of Agriculture as Đorđe Bijelić. That is how it is recorded in the *Encyclopedia of Yugoslavia* published by the Lexigraphy Institute of Zagreb. He taught at the same school for several years after graduating. It was anticipated that a great scientific career awaited him. He was a visiting faculty member at the Sorbonne, where in 1933 he delivered the famous lecture "Christianity and the Soul of the Bee," only to suddenly return from Belgrade to Sarajevo two years later. He abandoned his university career, was quickly forgotten in scholarly circles, taught biology in the very same Main Gymnasium, and in his free time occupied himself with beekeeping. And so in 1937 he was selected to serve as the sole Bosnian on the steering committee of the Society of Beekeeping and Honey Producers of the Kingdom of Yugoslavia. He remained on the committee until the beginning of the war, when the society was disbanded, and Đorđe Bijelić fled from the Ustaše to Dubrovnik and then on to Italy. After the war he returned to Sarajevo, where he taught biology in middle and elementary school until his retirement in 1966. He refused a job at the newly founded School of Agriculture but took part in some scientific projects, on his own or in collaboration with Professor Ignjat Pobegajlo, author of the book *Bee Plague (Larva pestis).* In 1976, ten years after his retirement, in an edition put out by the Sarajevo publisher Svjetlost, his life's work was published, the magnum opus of Đorđe Bijelić, and one of the most unusual books of Yugoslav culture, *Plague and Exodus.* This three-volume edition with all of its two thousand pages evoked heated discussion in all quarters, and the editor was quickly replaced, while Bijelić's book was declared a publishing failure at a meeting of the Party steering committee, and it was stressed that the responsibility of individual comrades and links in the chain of worker self-management would be discussed later, but the issue would not be resolved with a simple replacement of the editor in question.

While *Plague and Exodus* was appraised by some as an outrageous concoction, "the product of a megalomaniacal mind," "a work of provincial learning that suffers from delusions of grandeur," "one big prank by a collection of idiots," or, simply garbage, the sort that occasionally appears everywhere as a result of the over-production of books, others, a small number, but more authoritative and powerful, greeted it as an epoch-making book: "the final realization of a brilliant intellectual biography, proof of how the greatest literary works and historiographical syntheses take shape in the solitude of monastery cells, far from university cathedrals and academies, in peace and in silence, with anthropological reach into the depth of our civilization's subconscious, magisterial cultural and historical ceremony and summation, a disclosure of the human and the apian soul, a theological *tractatus* on insects and on flowers, which puts man and God face to face, even for those of us who don't believe in either the one or the other. *Plague and Exodus* is all of this and much more!" This was what professor of aesthetics Ivan Focht wrote about Bijelić's book, but all the polemics were halted and all the derision died when Miroslav Krleža raised his head in defense of Bijelić's work. He was housebound by then, he was old and found it hard to move. He was no longer writing, but he came forward on two occasions, to defend two books: Danilo Kiš's *A Tomb for Boris Davidovich* and Bijelić's *Plague and Exodus.* Both had been written by Jews. One dealt with concentration camps; the other with beehives.

With the bloody Easter of 1991, at Plitvice and then with Vukovar and the bombing of Dubrovnik, no one remembered Đorđe Bijelić and his work anymore.

When the bombing of Sarajevo began and the Serbian ring formed around the city, he was just a barely mobile ninety-year-old Jew who, thanks to his Jewishness, could be transported out of the city. In Zagreb, where no one knew him anymore, he was living in a home for the elderly, where no one visited him. He was a widower without children, his only son Dragutin had died of diphtheria in 1930 in Belgrade. He had been three years old. His wife Blanka, of the Belgrade Albahari family, could never conceive again. She had worked as an English teacher at a school for foreign languages in Sarajevo. She died young, in her sleep, at the end of August 1940.

This was all I had been able to learn about Đorđe Bijelić.

I hope as I write this that someone will nevertheless know more and that my story about him might serve as an opening and through it, perhaps, all that has been left untold and unknown in connection with my grandfather Franjo Rejc's bee journal might be discovered. For this reason it is important that this story touch its readers so that they might spread the word, and it's important that it be translated into as many different languages as possible, for the world of Đorđe Bijelić, the world of Sarajevo's Jews and beekeepers, was scattered across the earth, and their descendants have been scattered three times since, so it is likely that the person who knows the whole story lives somewhere far from Sarajevo and this language, which I call again, in spite of all, Serbo-Croatian. If you hear me, please be in touch!

When the song was over, I asked him whether he remembered Franjo Rejc.

He looked at me, smiled kindly, and nodded.

He did not remember him.

I asked about the members of the steering committee of the Society of Beekeeping and Honey Producers of the Kingdom of Yugoslavia from 1937, whether any of them were still alive.

He didn't understand.

"You know, old Đorđe suffers from Alzheimer's," said the nurse kindly.

"Yes, yes, Alzheimer's!" the old man shouted, as if remembering a word that had been on the tip of his tongue.

After exchanging a few words of small talk, promising I would come back to see him again, and acknowledging that I too was from Sarajevo, though I had felt estranged from it for some time, I made my way to the exit.

And then a question occurred to me, and it seemed important to ask it.

"Mr. Bijelić, why would a beekeeper have taken a queen from the hive in Ilidža in 1937?"

The old man straightened, looking at me as if I had just woken him.

"For sentimental reasons, sir, only that. I can tell you what he would have done afterward. He would have waited for the sun to set, then poisoned the bees with gas, buried them on the spot, and burned the hive."

I didn't understand, I thought the old man was raving. Only several months later, when I had acquired a collector's edition of the 1933 book *Bee Plague (Larva pestis)*, by Ignjat Pobegajlo, published in Belgrade, in the used bookstore Brala, across the street from the botanical garden, and had read about the procedures for dealing with American foul brood, did I understand what the old man had been talking about. But by then it was too late to ask any other questions, for in the spring of 1998 Đorđe Bijelić died. The news was reported only in the culture supplement to Belgrade's *Politika*, along with an essay by Muharem Pervić on the book *Plague and Exodus* and its influence on the intellectual movements in Yugoslavia at the end of the seventies, and in Zagreb's *Bee Messenger*.

When I had understood by reading Pobegajlo's book that Franjo's Ilidža bee journal had cut off when the plague had appeared in his hives, I went to the university library to search the bound periodicals for May and June 1937 for news of an epidemic of bee plague in and around Sarajevo. I leafed carefully through *Politika, Obzor, Jutarnji list, Večernja pošta* . . . But nowhere was there any mention of the disease. At the time I felt resigned, was ready to give up the search, and believed that any further effort was futile and I would never learn what had happened at Ilidža and why Franjo Rejc had taken the queen from the hive in his cupped palms, while all around he smelled the foul, sour stench of bees dying, more frightening to him than the odor of a mass grave or any human suffering.

I probably would have given up if I had not happened to find, in a Sepetarevac drawer, a letter Mina Jelavić sent on May 23, 1941, from Dubrovnik in which she inquired whether Olga thought it was a reasonable idea, under the circumstances, to have consultations with doctors and travel to Sarajevo, for an exam set for Friday, June 6. At issue were "those things," from which it was clear that Mina had an appointment with a gynecologist. Although the letter was addressed to Olga and marked as confidential, there was no doubt that someone other than she could have read it, so about those things Mina wrote cryptically, in code and metaphors, and it was impossible to know what illness she might have suffered from. The simplest conclusion to draw would be that she was being treated for infertility, and this would serve well in some short story or novel, but in reality Mina was unmarried and would remain so, along with her older sister Franica, until the end of her life.

The two Jelavić sisters lived in Dubrovnik's Lapad district, in a ground floor apartment with a spacious Mediterranean garden filled with cactuses and fragrant vegetation, among figs, lemons, and oranges. It was there I first saw garden gnomes, as a three-year-old in the summer of 1969. I recall thinking that someone who had such objects in their garden must be very rich. They were much more valuable, in my estimation, than the monuments to Comrade Tito, the bronze king at the Zagreb station, and all the other monuments I had ever seen. Nothing looked to me as priceless as the gnomes in our Aunt Mina and Aunt Franica's garden.

Mina and Franica weren't technically our aunts, they were distant relations, but Olga, her sisters, and my mother had looked after them their whole lives – from the end of the First World War until the mideighties, when they all died quietly, one after another. The Jelavić sisters were laid to rest beneath a marker in the Boninovo Cemetery, leaving no trace behind them. Soon Olga would die too, the last of Karlo's daughters, and in the span of just a few Dubrovnik summers they were all gone.

The second page referred to the Saturday that fell on June 7, 1941, the day that Mina had visited. The day before, she had been at the gynecologist for an exam and the next day had appeared at Olga and Franjo's.

It was the end of the school year, Mladen was in his final week of high school and Dragan was preparing for his high school entrance exams. That summer

Olga would become pregnant again and the following May give birth to a daughter. The war was just beginning, in Sarajevo it had not been felt except that the Jewish-owned stores had been assigned trustees: Croats, Aryans, mostly Ustaše or Ustaše sympathizers, but it was not yet awful. Not that awful – except that several people had been slaughtered in front of the Orthodox church in Varoš and that someone had smashed bottles at the Cucić liquor store and poured out all the šljivovica so that King Alexander Street had stunk of brandy for days. Everything was normal. Except that King Alexander Street was no longer Alexander, it had been renamed after Doctor Ante Pavelić. And you had to speak slowly and carefully to avoid calling the street by its old name. Not everyone had heard of Doctor Ante Pavelić yet, and there were some old folks living in apartments in the tall, dark Austro-Hungarian buildings in the center of town who believed Doctor Pavelić was a physician who lived nearby. But the healing seemed to have not yet begun. And it was not yet awful, not that awful.

This was how Mina talked, repeating words and phrases. She couldn't do it any other way. Just as some people stutter, Mina had to repeat words in order to continue her sentences, to keep her thoughts going, and make the conversation last. If anyone had admonished her in jest, Mina would have shut down and stopped speaking entirely. Those who knew Mina well found this endearing. It entertained our family, all the Stublers, from Karlo's generation down to me. And when Mina went away, or when we left her large, fragrant garden in Lapad, we would laugh, repeating the words that had served like bricks or stones for Mina that day as she skipped across muddy patches without getting splattered.

Franjo, whose head was filled with words and different languages, was the one who most appreciated the way Mina spoke. He was even a bit jealous of her and would start repeating words and phrases as she did, though he could not be like Mina. No one could be like Mina.

And as is often the case, what made us happy and was for us a unique aspect of Mina's charm, she experienced as a curse and the worst form of spiritual deformity. Olga dear, she would say, my stutter prevented me from marrying. So what, Olga would console her, you sleep more peacefully at night, for by then it was late, the beginning of the seventies; Mina was an old woman, tall and bony, like a dried-up olive tree, and Olga could no longer tell her what she used to say in bygone days, when Mina would complain, Olga dear, my speech defect has prevented me from getting married! Mina, you poor thing, Olga would say, don't say such foolish things. Men find it charming, and anyway they need to be told things three times before they hear. My Franjo needs to be told everything three times, and even then he doesn't hear. And then Franjo would pretend to get angry, and everything would end in laughter. And the words and sensations would be frittered away, as if life would last forever, and Mina was held in a pure, bright love.

Franica was a more serious case. By contrast to her sister, who was tall and thin, she was small and round. She also had a limp. She wore one of those ugly orthopedic shoes, which had always made me feel afraid of her. It gave her a menacing appearance, that shoe.

But Franica never said a word about not having got married because of her limp. Because as a young girl she'd had Pott's disease, and everyone had expected her to die, but she miraculously recovered, and that had made her happy. Her limp reminded her of how beautiful life was and how lucky she was to still be alive. But she had not got married because of Mina. She was the elder sister, and had to take care of the younger one. And later, when it no longer mattered who was older or younger, she couldn't leave her. What would happen to Mina if she got married? First she would forget to turn around the drain tube in the bathroom, and the house would be flooded; then the house would be blown into the air as Mina changed the gas canister; and eventually, Mina would poison herself and, in passing, all of us who had come to visit, for she would have mistaken the hydrochloric acid for the vinegar . . . How could she leave her alone? How could Franica get married?

This was how they lived, the two sisters each unmarried for her own reasons, in their crumbling Lapad apartment and their beautiful garden. They would both take care of the plants, pruning them, fertilizing the soil, watching over the lemon and orange trees, protecting them through the winter, and all of Dubrovnik marveled at their garden. Tourists would come up to their lovely wrought-iron fence

– which they also took care of, painting it every other year – and stood for a long time before the fragrant old grove.

When the two sisters died, one after the other, Dubrovnik's scent changed. For the first time, at the end of the seventies, Dubrovnik's sewer system could be detected in the air. The papers said this was from the pressure of tourism, the sewers having been planned for a much smaller city. The first time the stench arose it was from the fish market, from rotten shellfish and spoiled fish guts. This was due to laziness, to gabby fishmongers, and the fact that people from the interior, from the other side of the mountains, had started working at the stalls, something impossible to imagine. Or so they said in Dubrovnik. Then the rotten oranges from the park below Pile started to stink, and the cats that had multiplied around the Orthodox church pissed on walls at Karmen and Pustjerna, and there was the rancid oil from the restaurants on Prijeko Street, and the dog shit, and the stagnant seawater in the harbor, and suntan lotion, and dead people at the Boninovo Cemetery – all of Dubrovnik reeked, and people could not understand what was happening and what had changed. And then, with time they got used to it, without ever understanding what had changed.

The aroma from the Lapad garden of the sisters Jelavić was no more, and every stench was palpable, as it was in any other town. And that was how the sweet scent of Dubrovnik was lost.

Why did Olga make a note that Mina had visited them on Saturday, June 7?

This was the next question that hounded me, and to which it seemed I would never find an answer but instead go on wondering why Olga had chosen to note in Franjo's discarded notebook that Mina had visited on Saturday, June 7.

It was futile to run from obsessive thoughts. The whole thing was futile from the start. Instead of tossing out the rotten bag, without looking inside it, or if I had looked inside, then instead of calmly throwing it out along with the rusted lighter, the pencil, the letter-seal wax and the notebook – instead of calmly tossing out the notebook without ever opening it, for days and then months and years I had tortured myself in an attempt to answer questions that could not be answered, about the bag and its contents, only to have new questions arise in the place of one whenever I might happen to find an answer for it. Like in fairy tales about serpents and dragons who grow three heads in place of every one chopped off, so through the end of 1998, the number of questions only multiplied with every day I spent on the notebook.

Olga had been barely seventeen when she married Franjo. And she was probably already pregnant by then. She'd come to Karlo, her father's favorite, and told him she was getting married. Her father was disappointed, she was his most beloved child, she'd been a son to him, set apart from his two other daughters and his fickle, gentle son Rudi, and his disappointment showed. She went to confession before her marriage. This was difficult for her. It's likely that she really was with child.

And so her little adventure with the young, handsome rail man, a Slovene, did not serve her well. Perhaps this had made having sex with Franjo nauseating for her for the rest of her life. And she had unwillingly given herself to him. She never talked about it, she was disgusted by such talk, she'd get angry . . . Was it because such stories reminded her of how it had all started? Or because she was a lesbian?

Whatever it was, the two of them had not loved each other as man and wife through the course of their lives. At the start they'd been a couple in which she was dominant, and then after Mladen died, they blamed each other and drifted apart. Even so, there had always been a certain deep devotion between them, a feeling that they had been destined to be together. They were not conservative, did not believe in God, neither was a true wife or husband to the other, though they became mother and father three times, and their marriage was as hard as stone. They had horrible arguments, but neither she nor he ever swore at the other. Or struck the other.

And so they came to resemble one another in many ways. He was obsessed by his little chronicles and journals, he followed the movement of the queen in every hive, he looked into the souls of his bees, and the day when the drones were tossed out of the hive was for him an event equal to the start of the Second World War. And so Olga too, with the passage of years, began to note the dates when Mina had come to visit, and whether it was a Saturday or a Sunday. And she began to imagine the world in his manner, filled with small details whose coordinates, names, and places were for whatever reason important and worth writing down.

The dates should be remembered.

18 IV 35. Frost on the 15th, 16th, and 17th. All the flowers in bloom destroyed. All swarms well supplied with pollen and new honey. Nests spread across 7–12 frames. Drones have hatched. Numbers 1, 2, and 3 received extensions. The pasture has emptied.

2 V 35. They bring less pollen (two illegible words). The supply of honey strikingly reduced. Drones driven out from hive no. 6.

Mid-April freezes in Sarajevsko polje are frequent. They happen every spring. Snow falls in April. The May Day parade, which in the prewar years headed toward Vrelo Bosne, early in the morning, was caught in a snowstorm on the road. The blizzard was so intense they couldn't see where they were going; only a line of trees along the roadside prevented them from losing their way and freezing to death. If the Swabians hadn't planted those trees, Sarajevo's workers and trade unionists would have perished that May Day. But this was not in 1935, it was earlier. Karlo, Rudi, and Franjo were saving the bees, digging the hives out of the snowdrifts. The snow had melted by May 2, and one of the sunniest and warmest springs in the century followed. Perhaps this had been in 1933? It too is described in one of Franjo's lost notebooks.

While the spring did not begin as it should have, the year was nevertheless good. There were no diseases among the bees, and the worker bees had to fly a long way. The flowering plants extended all the way to Stojčevac, Vrelo Bosne, and Mount Igman, so the honey was luxurious and brought with it the scent of distant parts, of the heather, lindens, and meadows around Ilidža's Roman bridge. Or this was just Franjo's imagination as he watched the poor things circling the stunted, wounded blossoms, collecting the pollen left over from before the freeze. It was honey from suffering bees.

He lived for forty years among the bees and knew everything about them he could read and learn. He collected a library of books in all the languages he spoke, and also in those that, with the help of a dictionary, he could read, including the massive *Glossary and Customs of Beekeepers in the West and the East, upon Examination of Religious Teachings Concerning Bees*, by the young Romanian author, scholar, and lunatic Mircea Eliade. And when he had learned all that others knew about these holy insects, Franjo found himself before a wall. He realized he did not understand them. This tormented him, and he would often speak about it, while playing preferans under the tree on Kasindol, in front of the future garage.

Don't worry about it, Karlo Stubler told him. It isn't rational to expect a bee-keeper to understand bees.

Don't go to so much trouble, said Rudi. If God had wanted people and bees to understand each other, he would have given them a common language.

Bees are the same everywhere, in Poland and Bosnia and at the ends of the earth. But people are all different. That's why it's not a man's place to understand bees, Matija Sokolovski philosophized.

That's stupid, Franjo answered. You don't know anything about bees. The bees in Poland and the bees in Ilidža are not the same sort of bees. And you, Rudi, if you think God spends his time thinking up languages, I must say you're wrong.

And that would usually be the end of the conversation. No one wanted to work himself into a sweat over what Franjo expected of himself and his bees. Besides, no one besides Karlo Stubler understood how serious he was about all this, or how much he was joking with them, soothing his nerves with a story and shortening the day with the philosophy of bees. Karlo never played cards; he could not enjoy the game. Cards for him were a waste of time, but he knew his son-in-law was serious. He really would have liked to talk with the bees and to understand their reasoning.

It worried him a bit that he had put the first hives at Ilidža and introduced Franjo to beekeeping.

Don't worry about him, Olga had said.

And then she would tell the story of how Opapa was worried about Franjo's mental health and how he might lose his marbles over the bees.

Everybody thought that was funny, except Karlo and Franjo. They both got angry, each for his own reasons, and neither found anything entertaining in the story.

They both approached bees seriously.

Karlo loved them but looked at them coldly and rationally. He studied bee anatomy, was sad whenever there was an epidemic. If he had to destroy a swarm because of it, he did it according to the rules, and it was important to him that the bees not suffer. But he was absolutely certain that bees had no souls. They did not have their own language, thoughts, or feelings. Outside their swarms, societies, and colonies, bees did not actually exist. They react instinctually, as a swarm, and make decisions as a swarm. In this they differed from people, Karlo thought, troubled by the way Hitler was turning Germany into a hive.

Franjo experienced bees individually. The swarm was the perfection of their organization, which would not have been possible without a bee language. If he could not learn it and speak to the bees as equals, at least he wanted to know something about that language. And to study the language, one had to know what the bees felt.

For instance, what they felt when tossing the drones out of a hive.

Heavy and sluggish, these bees were unfit for life and would not survive outside the hive.

They could not fly. They lived off what the worker bees brought in on their wings, and took pleasure, if bees like people find pleasure, in extending the species.

When their task was accomplished, their voracity and gluttony became a burden to the swarm. Once the bees' feminine nature had been satisfied, the amazing prolongation of the species took place. And so one day in early spring, the time of life's renewal, they started pushing them out of the hive.

Franjo liked to be present when the bees tossed out the drones. He was superstitious and believed this brought him luck. Besides, it was the beginning of a yearly cycle, the time of the hive's renewal and of nature's as well, and a man felt he too was being reborn.

A life's span was not seventy-five short years, but seventy-five re-births, which was nothing to sneeze at.

This was how it seemed to Franjo since he'd become engaged in beekeeping.

But he did feel some discomfort about the fate of the drones. He would lift one up from the grass, let it rest on his palm, flailing its wings in vain. He'd touch its stinger with his thick thumb, and it would bend as if it wanted to sting. But nothing happened.

Then he would put the drone back into the grass, where it would die of hunger, unless some little forest beast had finished it off. The next day the ants would scatter them throughout their anthill, and soon there would be no trace of it left.

Idleness had killed it, someone joked.

After the frost fell on the blossoms in 1935, the year's honey was scarce but good and healthy. The bees had to fly far, and they brought news from distant domains on their wings and legs. It was said they flew all the way to Mount Igman. The pastures on the mountain were always rich. Stubborn, extremely fragrant plants grew there. The plateau of some ten kilometers, which could be encircled by an enormous compass, opened out into a broad, extended world.

Inscribed into the honey was the history of that circle, which because of the April frosts of 1935 was wider than in other years.

Franjo never sold honey. In his forty years of beekeeping he was an expert at overseeing many hives. From 1933 to 1939, he had some thirty hives in three locations, at Želeće, above Bistrik, and at Ilidža, but he divided up the honey among his friends and relatives. It would be interesting to calculate how much honey was consumed in the home of Franjo Rejc from the time his father-in-law introduced him to beekeeping until his death in the fall of 1972, or until the end of the seventies, when the last of the honey jars ran out.

On the pantry's highest shelves were the half-kilogram jars with exemplars of the honey from each year of his beekeeping. The first three, from 1935, had yellowed labels with notes in fountain pen: "Ilidža 35," "Želeće 35," "Ilidža 35 (Falatar)." The third contained honey from Stjepko Falatar, who was ailing in those years and whose story needs to be told, as Franjo took care of his bees, keeping a sample of their honey. Farther back on the same shelf were another forty-three dusty jars in no particular order.

Under no circumstance was that honey to be consumed. When we moved from Madam Heim's building to Sepetarevac, Franjo personally oversaw the transport of the little labeled jars. Although by then he was old and sick, his heart was spent, and he did not have much longer to live, he still fantasized about the bees' language and the secrets of history inscribed in the honey and how he might one day decipher what it recorded. When he retired, he started studying organic chemistry, he would get together with Professor Ignjat Pobegajlo, author of the book on bee pestilence and the most famous Yugoslav specialist on bees, Bijelić's mentor and advisor, and have long conversations with him about deciphering the notes in the honey.

From the honey we would learn what a given year was like, but not just in regard to the climate. For instance, we could compare 1940 and 1941, the last pre-war year and the first year of the war. Everything that had happened between those two years was recorded in the honey. This was what Franjo said.

You might be right, you might be right, Matija Sokolovski would say, absorbed in thought, without letting go of his cards, but you can find all that out by going down to city hall and looking through the old newspapers. Everything is recorded there quite reliably.

Had anyone else said that to him, Franjo Rejc might have got angry. But Franjo appreciated old Sokolovski's comments and would conclude their talks by saying they were two old fools, each in his own way.

But he never gave up on his dream of speaking with the bees and reading history from their honey.

By the end of September 1972 he had fallen into the bed from which he would not rise. My father placed him in his ward at the hospital, but he asked to be allowed to go home.

If you can't help me, let me go home. Don't keep me here imprisoned. Let me go home to die.

This was what he said. And my father let him go home.

Then and later, whenever people were nearing death, they would ask to be allowed to go home to die within their own four walls. There was a reason for this. And there still is. Franjo Rejc would die in the same room where, exactly forty years later, his daughter would die.

On the last night, the one that ended with him saying to her, everyone else is swine, it's just the two of us left. No more than several hours earlier he had said, "That honey should be eaten!"

What honey? Javorka asked

What do you mean, what honey? The honey that hasn't been eaten.

What honey that hasn't been eaten?

She thought he was raving, but until the very end Franjo was himself.

Eat the samples. It would be a sin to throw out such honey.

He told her he feared Olga might throw the honey in the trash. She was like that. She was afraid. She was squeamish. She thought honey could go bad. But it couldn't! It could sit for two hundred years and turn into a single great crystal, but it would still be as fresh as the day it was drawn. Honey was eternity.

This was what he said and again begged her not to throw the honey out.

If you're not going to eat it, I'll eat it all myself, she would tell Olga after Franjo had died.

Surprisingly, Nona did not object. And so, for breakfast, before going to school, I had bread, butter, and honey from 1943.

That honey lasted us for years.

In spring 1993, during the siege, while I was looking through the pantry for alcohol, I found a jar of Nono's honey: "Konjic 1953." It was tucked away in the back of the pantry, which had never been whitewashed, let alone properly cleaned – there it was.

I took the jar to Cica Šneberger so she could make us honey cookies.

A few days later, when I left for Zagreb, from where I would not return until the end of the war, Cica gave me a little bag of honey cookies from the year of Stalin's death.

Thus did we consume a history. I remember the crystallized honey, which melted in just a few minutes on the sunny windowsill, turning limpid and clean. Dark, the color of cognac, shiny like a lemon, the honey of long-since-dead bees. The honey of my grandfather, also long since dead, with all his talents, the languages he knew and I didn't, the books he'd read and I hadn't. His ideas died with him too.

Stjepko Falatar had been a steam engineer for the narrow-gauge line to Višegrad and Ploče. He lived in Višnjik as a renter in someone's house. He was married to Rozalija, a pretty Hungarian with a short leg, which in those days was considered a great defect, especially among the lower classes and the poor. When she stood in one place, Rozalija was one of the most beautiful women in Sarajevo, but the moment she began to move, she was a crumbling house, a train falling with its engine into the Neretva River, a misfortune before which mothers would make a sign to ward off evil from their children. Rozalija would pretend she didn't hear or see, continuing on her way without stopping. When she stopped and stood, again she was the most beautiful woman in Sarajevo. People would admire her, envy her, waiting to see her walk again, so their hearts would return to their chests.

Rozalija gave Falatar five children, one after another between 1915 and 1921. This was a time of war famine, Spanish influenza, typhus, and cholera . . . Of the first three born, two would die. If a woman was pregnant and there was not space in the house for another child, it wasn't a problem since one or another of the children would die anyway. During a time of great death, as around that of the Great War, the world succumbed to animal instinct, male came down upon female – this was how the human species fought for survival – and more children were born than usual. The priests had their hands full, for infants had to be baptized before they died.

It was different with the Falatars. The Hungarian gave birth only to living children, who sprang up despite all the epidemics, and if any of the children did get sick, they quickly got better, and were bigger and stronger. But with each new child, they grew ever poorer.

Stjepko Falatar had originally been from somewhere in central Bosnia, from Jajce or Varcar. He'd quarreled at a young age with his father and left home. His father had summoned him back home, threatening to disinherit him, but Stjepko didn't respond. He was young, full of himself. He had a gift for learning, the friars wanted to educate him, but only if he made peace with his father. He did not want to do that so studied to become an engineer. Austria was just then looking for local people to work on the railroads, and he took advantage of it.

Thus was Stjepko's life shaped at a very early age.

He brought the Hungarian girl from Sombor. It did not bother him that she limped, nor did he care what people might think. He did it out of love and defiance of the world. He continued to be defiant for a time, but then the Great War came, hunger and poverty took their toll, his children were born . . .

To feed his children, Stjepko Falatar took up beekeeping. Perhaps his kids were healthy and strong and were untouched by disease because they were raised on honey. On greens, nettles, roots, rotting potatoes, which had always been around, but then also on vast quantities of honey, which was abundant in the Falatar household. During the early years he maintained his hives in secret, built nests in the woods, came up with ways to prevent others from stealing the honey, and he thought up some fine ones. People were afraid of Falatar's bees. It was said that he trained them, taught them to attack anyone who drew near to a hive uninvited. He himself might have spread this rumor.

Nevertheless, there was something to it. Bees grow accustomed to the scent of the beekeeper's sweat. They recognize it and if someone strange comes close, they grow nervous. They do not handle human sweat well – it drives them crazy, and they make suicidal attacks on its source. But they grow accustomed to the beekeeper – they have known him their entire lives, passing on the knowledge of him from generation to generation.

They met because Franjo had heard from beekeeping friends that Stjepko Falatar talked with his bees. Whether they really believed this or were just kidding the poor guy, Franjo did not know or care. He believed that someone somewhere existed, or in the several thousands of years people had engaged in beekeeping, someone had existed who spoke with the bees.

And so, little by little, they became friends. The two of them only ever spoke about bees and honey.

Falatar kept bees to feed his children; Franjo to be alone. Though their reasons were different, the story led them to the same place. Falatar's children were no longer little when, in the fall of 1934, his affliction came upon him. His eldest son Josip would soon be employed by the railroad, his youngest Ilija was studying at the gymnasium and singing in the church choir, all three daughters, born one after the other, had started school, and it seemed that everything would soon get easier.

But then Falatar saw a pair of shoes in Šnehajm's shop window.

Black lace-ups – exactly like those worn by hundreds of Sarajevo residents, municipal workers, high-level postal and railroad officials, journalists, artists, and actors. There was nothing extraordinary about them, but they were the sort of shoes Falatar had never imagined on his own two feet and they captivated him, evoking a spiritual crisis that all his years of hunger and poverty had not.

He thought about how life had no meaning and every torment was futile when one knew that he would pass by these shoes his entire life and never have the money to buy them. He did not tell anyone this, not Rozalija, not his colleagues from the railroad, not Franjo.

On Sunday, when they gathered at the Želeće hives, for the first time Falatar was not up to talking. He worked dejectedly. He said his stomach was bothering him.

Once all the preparations for winter had been made, the time of bee inactivity arrived. It was the beginning of November when Franjo went to the Bistrik station to ask about Falatar's work hours. They told him he had pneumonia. He was in bed at home. Franjo came looking for him again several days later. They said things had got worse and Falatar was in the hospital.

He grew worried and decided to visit him.

He brought two oranges so as not to arrive empty-handed. But he knew that Falatar didn't eat oranges. He had never seen him eat anything but bread, lard, onions, and honey. That was what he ate at all times of the year, whether it was freezing cold or roasting hot. Whenever Franjo offered him cheese, salt pork, or Wiener schnitzel that Olga had made him for the road, Falatar would refuse.

He said that one mustn't get used to things.

The more you get used to them the more your needs grow.

Good for the children to eat cheese and buttermilk.

They need it for their bones, to get stronger.

Who knows, thought Franjo, maybe one can live on bread, lard, onions, and honey. Once, many years later, after Falatar had long since died, he would ask my father while they were playing preferans how long he thought a man might live on only bread, lard, onions, and honey.

It depended, my father responded, on how strong willed he was. I had never heard him talk about strength of will or any such metaphysics; it sounded more like the speech of a priest or psychiatrist.

There was no record of Stjepan Falatar in the pulmonary ward.

Nor was there any in internal medicine, infectious diseases, cardiac care, or the liver or kidney treatment areas of Koševo Hospital.

Franjo found him in the psychiatric ward. He was lying in a dimly lit room, whose sole window looked out on the wall of another building a couple of meters away, and he was crying. It was a room with twelve beds in it. His was the closest to the door.

The other patients barely made a sound, wrapped in their medications or heavy, sick slumber; the half-dead lunatics breathed quietly. They aren't lunatics, Olga shouted, they're unfortunates, spiritually afflicted. It can happen to anyone! All right, it can happen to anyone, Franjo shot back nervously, but then repeated that he had found Falatar crying in a room with twelve beds where the light of day was barely visible since the only window looked onto a wall.

Well, what's wrong with him then? she asked.

He shrugged.

Did you ask the doctors?

Doctor Besarović said they didn't actually know what had happened to the patient, except that he had experienced some form of breakdown.

In the shop window of the shoemaker Jakob Šnehajm, on Alexander Street, he had seen a pair of shoes he liked. And instead of buying them, though they would have cost half his monthly salary, Falatar had experienced a breakdown. But not because he had never in his life bought a pair of shoes, for himself or for any of his five children – he had had to buy orthopedic shoes for his wife every two years, and those were the only shoes ever purchased in the Falatar home – that was not what had shaken him. It was the thought that his whole life would pass, and that never ever would he put on a pair of shoes from Šnehajm's display window. And when he realized this, the world around him suddenly began to crumble.

If it weren't the shoes, it would have been something else, said Doctor Besarović. The human soul is a deep dark well, he said. We may be able to sense when somewhere deep down the bucket splashes into the water, and on the basis of that sound attempt to guess what might have occurred or shifted.

A pair of shoes.

A deep, dark well.

Franjo was worried about what would happen to Falatar's bees.

The following week when he went to Ilidža, he visited Falatar's hives, which rested on Balijan's land, on the fallow ground facing toward Butmir. It was quiet, the bees were wintering in peace. Falatar had left them enough honey, having prepared the hives for the cold weather, as one shutters the windows of a seaside house at the end of summer.

This calmed him.

By spring Falatar will have recovered.

But that wasn't what happened.

They let him go home before Christmas. They gave him some medicine, told him to walk as much as possible, to rest, and not to fight with his wife. But doctor, he said in surprise, I never fight with my wife. Good, good, just listen to what she tells you, Besarović answered without interest. He had too many such cases in his department. This was in 1934, and the psychiatric ward was filled with men and women he didn't know what to do with. When his division filled up and every bed had contained two patients, the doctor ordered a great purge. Usually this was on Monday and Tuesday. Over two days he would evaluate which cases were most serious, who was creating disorder, drinking rakija, fighting, or, God forbid, slitting their wrists, and all these he would send to mental hospitals. His former patients were all over the place by then, from Zagreb and Popovača, across the island in the Šibenik archipelago, to Montenegro, Kosovo, and Serbia.

This was why his patients were so afraid of the great purge. They would grow calm and quiet, shrinking so that even a bed with two people in it seemed empty, and they would pray to their respective gods for the frightening diagnosis to pass them by.

There were no rules there. Besarović did not look at their charts; he did not care whether someone had been in the ward for six months, was a returnee, or had just shown up the day before a purge. If he found a concealed bottle of rakija or heard someone talking loudly, he would send him off to Sokolac, even if he was the most normal of normal. And anyone who ever entered Sokolac went crazy, they said, though there were no witnesses.

It was said they had once mistakenly picked up a monk as he was on his way back to his monastery by train, somewhere in southern Serbia. He resembled a certain unfortunate by the name of Simeun, a drunk and an eccentric, who spoke in a confused jumble and anyone unstable listening to him went over the edge in a second, so Simeun was kept in strict isolation. But it was hard to keep him there, for Simeun would squeeze through the keyhole. If you locked him in a room with a keyhole, you could be sure that Simeun would vanish in minutes. He had run away from Sokolac twelve times, they said.

This particular time, the story goes, the gendarmes caught the runaway student, which is what they called Simeun because of his education and beard: they had a photograph of him and they recognized him sitting quietly, dressed in a monk's habit, looking out the window of the train from Sarajevo to Višegrad.

As they recognized him, sprang on him, and put the unfortunate monk in chains, and as he tried in vain to tell them they were mistaken, he was a man of God returning to his home, the more certain they became that they had in their hands Simeun the student. Besides, they looked as alike as two peas in a pod, Simeun and this unfortunate monk.

They say it only took two weeks for their mistake to come to light. This was all it had taken for the real Simeun to drive half the Banja Koviljača spa-goers crazy with his stories and get himself arrested.

If this was Simeun the student, they wondered in Sokolac when he'd been brought in, then who was it they had in the cell?

Could he really be Sava the monk, a man of God from the Mileševa Monastery?

They called up the postal station in Pale, from which a telegraph was sent on to Prijepolje so someone could be sent over to Mileševa to ask whether they might be missing a monk by the name of Sava, who had gone to Sarajevo to visit his dying mother. That was what the man had said when they brought him in, chained up: he'd gone to Sarajevo to visit his dying mother.

At Mileševa they said that two weeks earlier they had reported the disappearance of one brother to the police. He had embarked on the train for Višegrad and disappeared somewhere along the way. Murder was suspected.

It took another three days for the news of the missing monk to reach Sokolac and for them to realize who Simeun the student's look-alike was and whom they were holding in the cell without a keyhole.

They kissed Father Sava on the hand and apologized to him in their choicest words. The hospital's director knelt before him and prayed for him to pull himself together, but the man was clearly insane. Seventeen days in the Sokolac mental hospital had been enough for the monk to go out of his mind. All their prayers were in vain, in vain was all his faith and composure, in vain his understanding of the temptations God placed before a man devoted to him. At Sokolac a few days were enough to drive even the most normal of men out of their minds. Even the Almighty went crazy there!

So the story goes. This was the point at which someone's right index finger would rise high into the air above a table covered with glasses, bottles, and ash trays.

Falatar, therefore, was fortunate. They let him go home before Christmas, and on Christmas Eve Besarović conducted a great purge. If he had not been let out the day before, who knows what might have happened to him.

He grew calmer when he saw his children. The Hungarian woman brought him some bread and lard, he would prop up a big jar of honey between his knees so he could take up the honey with slices of onion, peeling it all the way to the green center of the seed-bud. He would bite into the bread and lard, taking up the honey with the onion, until he finished off a third big, healthy, red-onioned head, which, according to the testimony of everyone who visited, brought Falatar back to health and mental soundness. He was constantly hungry, but he would he eat nothing other than bread, lard, onions, and honey. Habit leads to one's ruin, Falatar would say, one must not become accustomed to good things.

He did not mention the shoes, but it was palpable that they were all he was thinking about.

He held out like this until the end of February, and then it grew suddenly warmer as if it were already May – the gardens along the steep slopes of the city began to bud, old people shook their heads in worry while the young rejoiced – until, as recorded in the notebook, a severe frost fell in April.

18 IV 35. Frost on the 15th, 16th, and 17th. All the flowers and blossoms destroyed. All swarms well supplied with pollen and new honey. Nests spread across 7-12 frames. Drones have hatched. Numbers 1, 2, and 3 received extensions. The pasture has emptied.

2 V 35. They bring less pollen (two illegible words). The supply of honey strikingly reduced. Drones driven out from hive no. 6.

On one of those days, between winter and spring, they took Falatar away. He was beside himself. He was screaming, talking with someone others could not see, and the conversation was frightening.

A very tall gentleman in black, as handsome as Jesus Christ, with long fingers and a ring on his left ring finger with a sizable ruby in it, was offering him the shoes from Šnehajm's shop window in a quiet, calm voice. And they were free. All Falatar had to do was nod his head, say nothing, and the shoes would be on his feet. When he nodded, his youngest daughter would die. This was the contract, this was his generous offer: this daughter of his was not hardworking or especially intelligent. She was ugly. No one knew who she took after, for Falatar was not ugly and the Hungarian woman had been born such a beauty that she was hard to marry off. If he nodded and let the girl die, Šnehajm's shoes would appear on his feet, the most beautiful shoes in Sarajevo.

Poor Stjepko Falatar shouted, struggled, waved his arms, pushed the gentleman in black away, in deathly fear that he might accidentally nod his head and his child would die. This was not accidental. Something was pushing him to do it, telling him it was necessary, reminding him of the beauty and happiness he had never experienced and probably never would, of wearing a new pair of shoes.

All he had to do was nod and let his child die.

The hospital attendants could barely control the wretch. Besarović ordered him to be strapped to the bed, and that night for the first time they tried electroshock therapy on the patient Stjepko Falatar. Besarović deluged him with electric shocks, though he did not believe they would be any use. Doctor Besarović did not believe that any serious mental illness could be cured, but it was only proper that new treatments should be tested in the ward. And this would also send fear into the bones of the other patients.

The next morning Falatar was calm.

He did not remember anything. Or he was lying that he did not remember.

He responded reasonably to every question put to him.

The doctor decided against sending him immediately to Sokolac.

.He was at his bedside when Franjo came with the two oranges.

You know I don't eat that, Falatar said. It's not good to get used to good things.

I know, he answered, but it is a courtesy to bring something to a sick person.

Am I a sick person?

Yes, you're in the hospital, aren't you?

The hospital is not just for sick people. There are fools too.

Well said. There are those too.

As he listened to their conversation, it seemed to Doctor Besarović that the two were equally crazy and equally sane. He had known Franjo Rejc for years. He used to play cards with him and was certain that he was not mentally ill. But until recently he had still wanted to send Falatar to Sokolac. And he would have done it just so as not to have to think about him anymore, but he was uncomfortable because of Franjo.

And so the patient Stjepko Falatar stayed for the next two months in his bed in the psychiatric ward of Koševo Hospital. In that time two great purges rumbled through, many ended up in mental hospitals across the monarchy, from Vrapče to Popovača, across the Adriatic islands, all the way to eastern Serbia, but Falatar stayed put. He would cry for days at a time.

In March, before the heavy frosts of April 15, 16, and 17 killed all the blossoms, Franjo came to visit Falatar at the hospital to tell him respectfully that he feared for his bees but that he didn't want to be responsible for letting them go into the wild to die.

There was nothing to be afraid of, he answered, he should treat them as he treated his own. Do whatever he did for his own bees, so the poor things don't feel abandoned. As he said it, his eyes filled with tears. Then Franjo's eyes filled with tears. There was nothing crazy in these tears. They were both thinking of the bees, and this made them feel like crying. And that is normal among beekeepers.

You're saying they won't attack me? he asked as he was leaving, half-joking, but half-serious.

They won't. I told them not to, Falatar answered.

In fact, Falatar's bees were more patient and considerate with Franjo than his own. When they flew around him, they were careful not to let their buzzing unsettle him. If he was hot, they created a little breeze with their wings. If he was cold, they would alight onto his hands to warm him.

When Franjo talked about how in the spring of 1935 he realized that the steam locomotive engineer Stjepko Falatar, an impoverished Sarajevo resident, had spoken with his bees at a distance, Franjo was dead serious. Some thought he was joking and laughed at the story of Falatar, others took him seriously.

Stjepko Falatar slowly recovered after a long stay in the psychiatric ward. He stayed in the hospital until the end of summer 1935, when he was released during one of the great purges. Instead of sending him to Sokolac or Popovača, the doctor sent him home.

Besarović was certain Falatar would come back, but it did not happen.

He was given a pension for the disabled, and continued to look after his bees. His children grew up and married. The youngest daughter, not a great beauty or especially intelligent, and not diligent or good at housework, ended up in acting school in Zagreb. After the war she married a famous Belgrade director, acted in the Yugoslav Dramatic Theater, was a star of the Dubrovnik Summer Festival, playing the best and widest ranging roles, from comic characters in the plays of Marin Držić and Branislav Nušić to Brecht's Mother Courage, which she would play until the end of her life.

Falatar lamented as they sat, each on his own stump on the Glavatičevo meadow in the early fifties, with the hum of bees all around.

By then he was old and considered demented – what else would he have been since they had retired him early and he wasn't missing any legs or arms? – he was just silent and whenever he spoke, people got out of his way.

But Franjo understood what he said and turned Falatar's words into familiar sayings.

The devil offered me a pair of shoes for her life! my grandfather Franjo Rejc would say, whenever he had seen a really good actress at the movies or the theater.

Franjo, my friend, he pronounced one evening at the Kostanić's in Drvenik, the devil offered me a pair of shoes in exchange for her life! They were watching a program on the life and sudden death of the great Serbian actress Marija Falatar Belović.

While he was alive, Franjo fought against allowing a television to be brought into his home.

In it comes and out I go! he would say tersely to every suggestion of buying that devil's machine that "doesn't let a person read, study, or think," and if there were any further questions, he would suggest we purchase a TV as soon as we had buried him.

If the funeral's at three, he said, you'll have time to get it before the store closes.

Just one time did he go with Olga and me to watch TV at the Kostanićs'. It was winter, December 1971, the day after Catholic Christmas, which in Partisan Drvenik in those years was not much celebrated, the strongest storm of the season was blowing. Grandfather held my hand as we made our way to watch the show about Auntie Mari Falatar. He held my hand so the storm wouldn't carry me out to sea toward Hvar, to Sućuraj and farther on, to Italy and Vittorio de Sica, a great director and the only one, Franjo Rejc said, who could have told the story of Stjepko Falatar, a man who had spoken with bees and lost his mind over a pair of shoes.

7 VI 36. Removed two frames with honey and a few bees, and from one frame shook out a full brood into a separate hive that the day after tomorrow I'll use to start a new one with the help of a queen cell I'll get from Mr. Fabiani from Dovlići (see below under hive no. 3).

30 VI 36. Chamber half full of honey. Swarm very strong.

7 VII 36. Adequate honey in chamber. Added one empty frame. In the next to last brood chamber full of honey.

14 VII 36. Extracted honey.

Lucio Fabiani, whom people called Ćućo, worked as a court reporter. And occasionally as a sketch artist, when the judge allowed portraits to be made of the sides in proceedings that were of interest to the public. These sketches came out in all the papers, which made Ćućo Fabiani as happy as if he'd had an exhibit at the Louvre. The additional work was of course not paid, he did it for free as part of his duties as the court employee, but in most cases his portraits in Belgrade's *Politika* and Sarajevo's *Večernja pošta* would be signed at the bottom with his name. He would buy ten copies of the papers to send to relatives in Italy, his godfather in Ljubljana, friends in Belgrade, so that every time the judge allowed sketches to be made of a defendant, his wife Anđa would wring her hands and scream. It was rumored she once went to the door of Judge Fahrija Kahrimanović to tell him that her children were starting school, that she needed to buy coal for the winter, and she didn't know how they would get by or what she would do if his honor continued to encourage Ćućo in his money wasting.

At first Kahrimanović did not understand. What money wasting? And what did it have to do with him?

But when he understood what the woman was talking about, he laughed his head off.

And he ordered that an exhibit of court portraits by Ćućo Fabiani be set up in the entrance hall to the courtroom and he be compensated twice his monthly salary in payment.

Who knows how much of this story is true, except that the court reporter Lucio Fabiana certainly did have an exhibit space in the court's entrance hall, the various dailies reported on it, and the Sarajevo painter and communist Vojo Dimitrijević published a very positive critique of the work of this unusual autodidact. In this account he refers to him several times as "Gentleman Fabiani," and as a result Ćućo acquired a new nickname among Sarajevo's rough and tumble, which his friends would soon adopt. It started from petty rivalry and envy but eventually the name Gentleman Fabiani had grown so much and was so accepted that Ćućo had started signing his caricatures that were occasionally published in the union messenger at around the time when he was to bring the queen cell for Franjo Rejc's hive number 3. And this work would cost him quite a bit, much more than the newspapers in which his courtroom portraits had been published.

How Lucio Fabiani had arrived in Sarajevo no one seemed to recall. My dying mother could not tell me and maintained that neither Nono nor Nona would have known either. People did not ask each other about such things in those days, for it was only natural that some official, rail man, postal worker, or even coffee-house keeper would arrive in town, not knowing a single word of our language, having moved from the other side of the empire to live here. Lucio Fabiani had not even been born a citizen of Austria-Hungary but was Italian, from Umbria, where he had many relatives, seven brothers and sisters, and a mother who would live to be over a hundred and whom Ćućo would mourn when he was himself an old man, while the beekeepers would console him by saying it wasn't even proper for a man of his years to have had a living mother. A man needed to live with the idea that he once had a mother and not die right after her. This was what they told him, but in vain. He had to mourn his mother the way it was believed an Italian did. When my mother died at the beginning of last December, I thought about Gentleman Fabiani and the story of his tears. The time for crying had passed long ago.

The name of the union messenger is not remembered anymore, perhaps it was called just that, *The Union Messenger*. Not even the name of the editor is remembered but what is known is that the outlawed Communist Party of Yugo-slavia had been behind it. Of course, articles were published under pseudonyms or initials, except for the ones signed by Veselin Masleša, Otokar Keršovani, or some of the other intellectual leaders of the workers' movement. Lucio Fabiani, too, was alerted to rules of authorial anonymity, nevertheless he chose to sign his caricatures as Gentleman Fabiani. They told him that was no pseudonym, all of Sarajevo knew it was he himself, and besides, newspaper illustrations were not supposed to be signed. But then why would Ćućo publish his drawings if no one knew they were his?

Amazingly, he had no problems at the courthouse regarding his collaboration with the communist papers. Everyone must have known that Lucio Fabiani was not a communist but rather an ardent and orderly court reporter. Not only was he not a communist, he did not really know what the communists stood for or wherein lay their sin, except for their not believing in God. He did not follow or understand politics. He did not understand what anyone might have against the king, or what the Croats had against the Serbs – when they spoke the same language, with which he would struggle to the end of his life – but also what both had against the communists. At the heart of everything, Lucio Fabiani believed, lay a great misunderstanding. Politics existed only because of this great misunderstanding, in which he did not have to take part, for as an Italian he had nothing against the king, or against his blood enemies. This was how he thought, and for a long time this was how others understood him.

Gentleman Fabiani did not read the papers or vote in elections, he did not listen to the talk in cafés and barbershops, and he had no opinion about Benito Mussolini. In 1936 when runaway German and Austrian Jews began to arrive in Sarajevo spreading the news of the Nazi terror, he genuinely pitied those people and was prepared to help them. With a jar of honey, some money, lunch in the court cafeteria. But he could not listen to their life's stories. He grew restless in the face of this avalanche of human misery, which sounded less plausible than a movie melodrama or a romance. Lucio Fabiani did not understand what these people were saying.

His bees were happy. Much happier than Falatar's and happier than Franjo's. He kept his hives in Dovlići, a small isolated village on the far side of Trebević. He would walk all the way, but it was not difficult for him. Nothing was difficult for Fabiani, except imagining another's misfortune. It was hard for him to read the papers. So he didn't read them. One should live the way the bees did, he thought, without wishing anyone ill, not taking anything of anyone else's away, but slowly and steadily, flower by flower, honeycomb by honeycomb, moving toward the winter of one's life.

This was what Lucio Fabiani said: the winter of one's life. With extra vowels and softened consonants, as in Italian, so that winter was a-winter, once was a-once, life was a-life, and the moment Ćućo remarked on the a-winter of a-once a-life, both his eyes would be filled with tears. Only not the kind that run down your face but that particular kind of stay-in-place tears that did not exist in Sarajevo then, or anywhere nearby, on the pastures grazing lands, among the beekeepers,so people called them Italian tears, and anytime someone might remark in conversation about how another's eyes had filled with tears, they would ask, Italian tears? And then everyone would nod.

And in this spirit Ćućo would forget reality. He'd forget what he was noting down every day as a court reporter only to have this note taking and commentary slip so far away from real life that when on September 1, 1939, the war ruptured all the borders of Europe it seemed to him he was writing Petrarchan sonnets. Or rather their translation into Serbo-Croatian. All those verdicts of first-degree murder, murders of passion, and murders committed for especially base motives, verdicts of pickpocketing on trams and nighttime holdups, thievery of the postal carriage, of high treason and acts against the king and the state, of communist propaganda and harm to public morality, of cursing in a public place, blasphemy, insults to honor, and everything else for which people were being tried in Saraje- vo's courts, all of it he experienced as a highly artificial poetic form. He would fill up entire sheets of the thick greasy paper, delighting in the lightness with which the tip of the fountain pen slid across it, feeling the security of the watermark, in which the seal of the Kingdom of Yugoslavia was visible, with its Cyrillic- and Latin-lettered inscription, and he worked hard to write out the sentences of the court in calligraphy, though for a long time no one had asked him to do this. As the war drew nearer, about which Ćućo knew nothing and felt no concern, his handwriting got prettier and prettier. But then, somewhere in the middle of the term of Milan Stojadinović, the order came down from Belgrade that all court reporting would in future be conducted with the help of Remington typewriters. Most of the royal courts had earlier begun using typewriters, but thanks to Lucio Fabiani and his calligraphy, the Sarajevo court had long resisted modernization.

Although he was promoted to superintendent of court reporting, Ćućo was disappointed. It did not mean much to him that he was trusted in spite of the fact that he drew caricatures for a suspicious union paper, and had been promoted to an important, responsible position, nor did it please him that his salary was doubled, for all that meant little to nothing compared to the pleasure of the nib gliding across the thick state paper.

He found consolation in bees and in drawing.

And then Belgrade was bombed. Four days later came the takeover and the declaration of the Independent State of Croatia, which took fifteen days to arrive in Sarajevo. In advance of the Independent State came the Germans on black motorcycles with sidecars, in trucks, and in Mercedes limousines. When they saw them coming, a raging street mob plundered and desecrated the new Sephardic temple. Olga and Franjo watched it from the windows of their apartment but did nothing. How Mr. Fabiani reacted or what he felt is unknown. Or whether he even knew about the Temple's destruction, at the time he was in Dovlići with his bees.

In the preceding days, during the bombing, while the sky thundered with the Luftwaffe's Messerschmidts, he had hugged his hives in fear, trying to protect his bees from the noise and the shaking. He sang them Neapolitan songs, told them silly stories in Italian – Ćućo always spoke to his bees in Italian to protect them from the war and from what was clearly the end of the world. He cared little what happened to other people – or he didn't believe anything would happen to them – but his bees he tried to protect from plague. And plague would set in if the bees were upset. All the beekeeping books described this; all good beekeepers understood it.

But the moment he went back down from Dovlići into the city, where the Ustaše were already in control, Lucio Fabiani was arrested and imprisoned. At first he was interrogated in the newly established district police station and then the Gestapo took over. The local police suspected him because of his many years of collaboration with the communist union messenger. He was the only collaborator they had managed to apprehend. Others had gone deep underground, left the city, or protected themselves through impenetrable initials and pseudonyms. Gentleman Fabiani was the only one who had not gone into hiding.

But the Germans controlled the local Ustaše carefully, for they were not yet sure of their ardor, nor did they want to lose some big fish, a communist plotter or revolutionary – so they picked up Lucio Fabiani. Besides, the case concerned an Italian, which made it all the more interesting. Perhaps they saw in him an underground member of the Central Committee of Italy's Communist Party, or a spy of Mussolini and their conspiratorial colleague, who needed to be protected from Croatian bungling.

Ćućo never said what the questioning was like in the district police station or with the Gestapo. He never spoke about those eleven months, from the end of April 1941 to April 9, 1942, which he had spent in the Ustaše and German prisons, and then in the camp at Jasenovac, and it had never occured to anyone to ask him, though they were likely curious to know what Fabiani might have told his interrogators about his communist activity. What could he have said about his Sarajevo court reporting and about the court proceedings against Croatian idealists, sworn Ustaše, or the setbacks to Croatian-biased village mullahs and priests? What could he have told them regarding things he knew nothing about? Or had he suddenly come to political awareness in those frightening moments, in the shadow of the gallows and faced with the threat of the one verdict then being issued by the court he had been brought before? In any case, one day he reappeared in town. He had traveled by train from Jasenovac. He was thin and drained, a head shorter than before, as if by some magic he had been reduced to his boyhood height, his eyes dry as desert dust. For a long time they would hold no Italian tears.

What was it like? Franjo asked.

Fine.

What do you mean fine? How could it have been fine?

It couldn't.

So what was it like?

Fine.

Which means awful.

Fine.

Worse than awful?

I tell you it was fine.

So even worse?

Right.

The only thing he once said, long after the war, perhaps after we had broken with Stalin, was that there were no bees in Jasenovac. It was as quiet as a graveyard, he said. Not a bee in sight.

He found the hives empty in Dovlići. Sour and decaying, infested by flies, hornets, and other vermin. But this did not upset him. Ćućo had faith that his bees had found their way. They had fled to the woods with the people. He said he would recognize them by their sound, his bees, but he never did. They must have gone very far.

Only after the war did he renew his hives, again in Dovlići. And life went on for him as it had before. He understood nothing about politics, did not read the papers, and did not mix with the new political order. The communists were prepared to reward him for his conspiratorial work in the Kingdom of Yugoslavia, which, as we have seen, was not at all that conspiratorial. Ćućo was not interested. He performed office-related tasks for the court until the fifties and then retired. From then on he dedicated himself to bees. After his wife Anđa died in 1955 and his children left for other places, from Pula to Belgrade, Lucio Fabiani moved to Dovlići. He built himself a log cabin, stopped shaving, and was easily recognized by his long white beard. Thus did he acquire his third and final nickname – Tolstoy.

In one of the horrid family photographs from Franjo Rejc's funeral taken by the photographer my father had hired, in the third row behind Nona, whose mouth is covered by the black shawl she purchased in Moscow, and behind my mother and father, who were again husband and wife for the occasion, stands a white-bearded old man, slightly elevated, perhaps standing on a neighboring grave marker atop the decayed bones of someone else: it was a very old Gentleman Fabiani, Ćućo, Tolstoy.

I have taken up a magnifying glass more than once to try and make out whether his eyes are glazed over with Italian tears. But it's impossible – the shot is bad, the resolution unclear.

Ilidža 1936. No. 3 has 14 frames on May 22.

I looked for the queen in the sixth frame (this one inserted ten days earlier for breeding of the queen). She's not there, nor is the queen cell. Next to it is the seventh frame, rather weak and empty. Rusty condition. Found queen in frame 9 surrounded by bees. I opened the cluster – queen is very old. Closed the hive. Must examine on May 24, '36.

24 V 36. Checking.

No queen. Took the added frame on May 12 with brood to hive no. 4.

25 V 36. Checking.

Removed one empty frame, took it to hive no. 1, from which removed one frame to place in the middle of the bee quarters, to raise a new queen in this (worn) frame.

30 V 36.

On May 25 the bees had not used the added frame to draw out a queen cell. Probably because there is no young community. Decided to raise a new swarm (read hive 1) and to join it to this swarm with a fertilized queen.

To this end on June 2 placed two honey frames into a special case to add the queen cell on June 4.

3 VI 36.

Yesterday set aside two looted honey frames; found queen cells on the path inserted on May 25 and left them.

15 VI 36.

Queen fertilized. New queen cell.

Examined back of four frames. Bees agitated, lots of buzzing and stinging. Closed the hive. The movement of the drones is noticeable as they take off. More animated than that of the workers. These on taking off move slowly, as if searching for something. Bringing exceptional amounts of pollen.

20 VI 36.

No queen. Only old bees. Added two frames from no. 2 to the center to help raise the queen on June 30. Found closed queen cells in frames added on June 20. They have a big stockpile of honey.

8 VII 36.

Found the queen swarmed under. Freed her. She had only one pair of wings. Annulled it on July 14, shook the bees onto the grass, extracted the honey.

A bee sting is healthy, Franjo said proudly, it helps with rheumatism, protects against all sorts of ailments, serves as an antivenom, and heals the soul. You are startled awake when you are stung, he'd say, it hurts but you are reminded that you are alive. Like coming up for air from deep under water. The moment you breathe again, you feel alive.

He wasn't aware of what he was saying. He didn't suspect he was tempting fate or announcing the illness he would die from. Or he sensed it already, that illness. The first time he had begun to suffocate at night was in that bitter cold winter of 1943–44, the first after Mladen's death. Hungry and wretched, they would stoke the coal dust that would smoke and the smoke would smother the flames in the stove, the chimney would clog, and the smoke would back up into the cold room, and they would all choke from the hellish, sulfurous stench.

That was the first time Franjo couldn't breathe, but he thought it was just from the smoke.

Or perhaps it was the grave in Slavonia, the earth settling in, penetrating the tin cover of the coffin and pressing against Mladen's chest. And choking the father with guilt for having listened to Mladen's mother when she'd maintained with great certainty that their son would be safer in a German unit than a Partisan one. He hadn't yielded to her. He had known since 1938 that nothing in Hitler's hands could be safe and said as much to Ivica Lisac after the Germans had invaded Czechoslovakia.

That idiot is going to lose the war, he'd told Lisac as they sat in the darkroom of his photography studio. And cautiously and rationally, Lisac, the photographer, had responded, but we won't be around anymore.

Franjo had not heard him in his selfish rage. He had wanted to lash out against Hitler, the wretch! But he hadn't been able to protect his own son, letting his wife decide, because peace in his home had been more important to him than Mladen's life. Or had he been afraid of taking responsiblity?

This, he believed, was what was choking him.

He would take Valerian drops to calm himself and be able to sleep peacefully. They helped at first but then it got worse again. He dreamed of drowning in the sea. He dreamed he was in a hermetically sealed box, in which the air was growing thinner. He dreamed of a soundless room in which no one could hear him while he screamed that he could not breathe. Fifteen years would pass before Doctor Rittig diagnosed him with asthma. He needed to quit smoking. But he couldn't. What would he have after they took his cigarettes away? Besides, while he was smoking he didn't feel he was being smothered. He didn't think while he smoked. Then they diagnosed him with cardiac disease, chronic weakness of the heart. The pump was not strong enough to push the blood into his lungs. That was what choked him. The hydrodynamics of the human body. All this is very simple, Mr. Rejc, very simple. The soul is a material thing, the soul is the strongest muscle of all in the human body, said Rittig. When the soul is ailing we call it cardiac asthma.

Doctor Rittig interrogated him about his childhood, asking what illnesses he had suffered from as a child, whether anyone in his family had suffered from heart disease. Yes, said Mr. Rejc, his father-in-law. Doctor Rittig laughed.

Mr. Rejc, he said, keep your bees. It's good for the heart.

That was the only good thing he told him. Everything else he said was wrong. Franjo had hoped the doctor would tell him his heart had collapsed because of great suffering.

But bee stings are certainly healthy, he repeated.

Let the bee sting you, it's healthy.

Olga was allergic to bee stings. That was why she did not dare get close to the hives. And why he was sure he would always be alone with his bees.

Sometimes the bees would smother the queen. This happens often. They gather around her, paying tribute to their sovereign, each trying to get close, and they turn into a ball that can't be disentangled. If anyone tries to move away from the queen the ones on top of her will not allow it. A person can break up the ball, separating the bees from the queen with a thumb and index finger. They won't sting. The important thing is not to be afraid while doing so. In general, it's important for beekeepers not to be afraid of bee stings. Fear makes people release a hormone that drives bees crazy, and then they sting. Or else human fear insults them. A beekeeper cannot be someone who fears bees.

Franjo wasn't afraid of them, but their stings made him sad. They stung when they lacked confidence in him. They stung when he had betrayed them. Or they had betrayed him. Both made a man sad, and then he decided that bee stings were healthy.

Each sting is a death.

After a bee stings, a bee lives for only a few seconds.

How long is that in their measure of time? Human time and bee time are not the same. A person lives thousands of bee years. In the bee Holy Writ, people are thousand-year olds. Bee Holy Writ is inscribed in honey. The top shelf in the pantry on Sepetarevac, where we kept the samples of Nono's honey, was the Alexandria Library of bee civilization. We ate it, for there was no longer anyone who would learn apian speech and writing.

It was a missed opportunity for humankind. One of the last missed opportunities for humankind.

When the telegram about Mladen's death arrived, Olga sat on a chair in the kitchen and said nothing. No one remembers how long she sat there. Aunt Doležal hurried over and took the little girl away with her. Javorka was seventeen months old. She could not understand anything yet, but Aunt Doležal took her away to protect her.

I took you away so Olga would not harm you in her despair.

This was what she said to Javorka when the moths and the Alzheimer's were eating away at her in her last months of life. She spent an entire afternoon obsessively retelling the story of the day when the telegram about Mladen's death arrived. No one had prompted her. Javorka had not asked, but Aunt Doležal could not stop. The next day she remembered nothing. Not the telegram, not Mladen, not Mr. and Mrs. Rejc, to whom a military letter carrier of the Croatian Armed Forces, a young boy, an unpledged Ustaša, a Muslim, proud of his work and his Croatian homeland, certain that all who died on God's path would become martyrs, and that Allah and Croatia were secure on the same path, had delivered his telegram as one delivers an award or a medal.

My condolences, he said, Your son, a German knight, has fallen in heroic battle with the united nations of Europe, under the leadership of the great Führer, said the young Sarajevo Ustaša, reciting his memorized text.

But Aunt Doležal did not remember anything the next day. What she had known the day before in the greatest detail had evaporated.

Some demon, she'd said, drew me out into the hall just as he was declaiming his text to Mrs. Rejc:

My condolences. Your son, a German knight, has fallen in heroic battle with the united nations of Europe, under the leadership of the great Führer!

At that instant Olga did not understand what was happening. The text meant nothing to her, for she didn't understand the word *fallen*. One expressed this differently in her language – perished, killed, lost his life, died – and none of this went with a German knight. She would never have linked that description to Mladen. An armored Teutonic fighter with a lance in his right hand, from a book printed in Gothic script could not have been her son. Anyway, Mladen wasn't German. He spoke German in two very different forms. One that was literary, the language of Goethe, of *Buddenbrooks* and Professor Hugo Elsner-Rosenzweig, of the Upper Gymnasium, who said he could not evaluate the young master Rejc because the boy knew German better than he did, as a native speaker from Prague. He has a feeling for its grammar! he had said to Mrs. Rejc, and the mother was proud. But midsentence, when Opapa came into the room, Mladen would exchange the language of Goethe for the language of a Banat peasant, still German but different and distant, a language that would never be equal to *Hochdeutsch*, the language of his grandfather.

But still, there was no way he could be a German knight, who fell from a horse . . .

And then, with a sharp gesture, the young letter carrier shoved the telegram into Mrs. Rejc's hand.

When she saw what was written there, her face changed. It was more than a grimace, it reflected a very deep feeling. Her face was altered and would remain altered. Aunt Doležal could always tell when one of Olga's pictures had been taken before or after Mladen's death.

It was the face of a different woman, she would say, as the only witness to the moment the transformation had occurred.

But all I could think of at the time was to take hold of you and get you away, so your mother would not harm you, she repeated to Javorka.

She had run past Franjo, who did not know yet what had happened. He had looked in confusion as Vilma Doležal took hold of the little girl, lifted her into the air, and took her away.

He was holding the paper, and his glasses had slipped almost to the tip of his nose. His jaw dropped. He was about to say something.

Olga sat on a chair in the kitchen and said nothing.

Her eyes were dry. The window was open onto Tašlihan Street, a small, narrow window through which one could not jump out.

He shouted: Revenge, revenge, revenge . . .

What this meant, against whom Franjo intended revenge that early autumn afternoon, no one would ever learn. No one ever asked him. Mladen's death was never discussed. Surrounding it there was either complete silence, or, in moments of intense despair, mutual blame.

Mladen had been killed by a Partisan. No one had to say it, it was immediately clear. But Franjo did not want revenge against the Partisans, except perhaps in that instant. He did not believe in God, just as the Partisans did not. He found the Church's fearmongering repulsive. There was no hell, nor could it be imagined out of the emptiness to come, from the heavens above, or Mladen's grave in Slavonia. The Partisans fought for freedom, brotherhood, and equality. This was close to his heart. And they fought against Hitler. He had nothing against the Partisans so not even in that instant had he been likely to cry out for vengeance against them.

Did he want revenge against the Ustaše? Against the Germans? Against whom did he want it?

He took up his revenge, until the very end, against Olga. Just as she did against him. She was to blame for Mladen's death, for she had believed her son would be safest in the German army. He would do a little training there, learn some military skills, like marching and saluting, and before long the war would end. But the Partisans tramped around the woods, rarely washed, their kidneys suffered from the humidity and the cold, they died like flies rushing into a candle flame, so she would never have been at peace if they'd let Mladen join the Partisans.

You want your son to fight for what you don't have the courage to do yourself! That's your problem, she said to him. You want Mladen to join the Partisans in your place.

This, it seems, had been the final argument, with which Olga had overruled and outtalked him. Mladen reported for military service.

Aunt Doležal remembered believing that day that Mrs. Rejc might harm the girl in her despair. The window in the kitchen was small and narrow, a grown person could not jump through it. But it was just large enough to push a child through.

And perhaps the truth was that Olga would have murdered her little girl, who had been an unwanted child, conceived during the war when her mother was already pushing thirty-five and abortion was punishable by a death sentence before the Ustaše court and eternal damnation of the Vrhbosanski archbishop Ivan "the Evangelist" Šarić.

Then this history would have unfolded differently. Someone else would have found the bag with the lighter, the two pieces of letter-sealing wax, the pencil, and the notebook in which the journal of the Ilidža bees had been kept for the years 1935, '36, and '37, or there would no longer be any bag, or lighter, wax, pencil, or notebook. There would have been no story about the Stubler line's extinction, the extraction of its shallow Sarajevo roots, which ended with the new century, when the descendants of that Ustaše letter carrier plucking the last of the *kuferaš* weeds secured for themselves a rose garden for the long centuries to come. There would have been no Javorka or the person who completed this story in the summer of 2013, in an attempt to unravel the mysteries of the bee journal.

How did the bees experience Mladen's death?

Who cared for the bees and closed the hives after that fall of 1943?

There is no information about this, though it is likely that the Ilidža hives were in the care of old Karlo Stubler, while the bees at Želeće probably went wild, dispersed into the woods and disappeared. The following spring, Franjo did not keep bees at Želeće, or pay the pollen rent to Dušan Zlatković.

I had believed Mladen's death was the reason for this rupture, but then, again by chance, leafing through a list of the dead at Jasenovac, I found the name of Dušan Zlatković, occupation railroad switchman, born in Želeće near Žepče, who had landed in the camp in November 1943 and been killed two months later, on January 17, 1944. It is entirely possible for two people in one village to have the same name, but not likely that two Dušan Zlatković's lived at the same time in Želeće and worked as switchmen for the railroad.

And so the owner of the Želeće land where Franjo had kept his hives died at the beginning of 1944. Butchered by an Ustaše soldier, killed with a hammer or a stone, chopped up and tossed into the Sava, liquidated in a manner inconceivable to human reason, an insane manner, for the Independent State of Croatia was keeping careful tabs on its spending. Vlach, Jewish, and communist wretches were not worthy of expensive Croatian bullets.

Franjo Rejc would never return to Zlatković's meadow, though he did renew his apiary in Želeće after the war, but on the other side of the tracks, on a meadow owned by Sava Čekrk, a postal worker from Žepče. He paid him rent in honey too, but he didn't call it "pollen rent" any longer. That name, which sounds like the title of a pastoral novel that ought to be written in memory of Dušan Zlatković, was linked to the man who had first uttered it, and Franjo, whether out of superstition or respect for the dead, did not use it in connection with other people he rented from. Nor even in his own home did he use it except in connection with Dušan Zlatković. It had been that man's expression, and it died, as was proper, with him, in Jasenovac, under circumstances that are not recorded in the book of the Jasenovac dead.

Dušan Zlatković's sons – there were five surviving after the war – sold the land in Želeće at the beginning of the fifties along with all their patrimony, including two houses, a farm, and barns, and moved to Belgrade. It is possible to follow their individual destinies thanks to *The Serbian Orthodox Zlatković Kinsmen of Žepče and Maglaj*, a bound compilation of the Smederevo *Glas pčelara (Beekeepers' Herald)*, and the memoir *Tito's Guardsman*, by Milorad Zlatković, a joint edition published by Rad in Belgrade and Otokar Keršovani in Rijeka. I met one of his sons in Belgrade in 2001, about which there is more below.

Milorad Zlatković, the eldest of Dušan's boys, was born in 1923. An early resistance fighter since the fall of 1941, he participated in the battles of Sutjeska, Neretva, and Drvar as part of the High Command's escort regiment and ended up with Tito on Vis. On his arrival in Belgrade, he was awarded the rank of colonel, though he had only completed middle trade school in Sarajevo. He wanted to study medicine but was not allowed. That was his first clash with his superiors and his first disappointment in the ideals of communism. He was demobilized in 1950, having announced he wanted to take up writing. In 1953 he participated with Milovan Đilas in the founding of the journal *Nova misao* (*New Thought*), whose editor was Skender Kulenović. A year later, when Đilas fell into disfavor with the Party and ended up in prison, Zlatković did not reject him, instead writing the roman à clef *The Man They Were Ashamed Of*. He was jailed for a short time but was not put on trial. From 1955 on he lived in his apartment on Obilićev Venac, not publishing anything or maintaining contact with anyone. When he went out, he strolled in front of the café at the Mejestić Hotel, where the Yugoslav literary intelligentsia and members of the State Security Services sat at the same tables, but he did not go inside and did not greet anyone. He was suspected for some time, then thought of as a crackpot, and forgotten. In the sixties Milorad Zlatković discovered God. He left Belgrade and went to Mount Athos to become a monk. They would not take him; they were suspicious of his communist past – he could have not disclosed it – and considered him as a spy for Tito's secret police. Instead of returning to Yugoslavia from Mount Athos, Zlatković stayed in Thessaloniki and opened a smoke shop, a kiosk of three and a half square meters, where he would sit the entire day, communicating with the world through a little window. When he had no customers, he wrote poetry, ghazals, prayers, and short, standalone works of prose, which would all go into his book *Winter of the Stylite*, published by Svjetlost in Sarajevo a month or two before the beginning of the nineties war. In the middle of the eighties, he happened to cross paths in Thessaloniki with his wartime friend and fellow escort regimenteer Kazimir Finci, a musician, and translator from Spanish and Hebrew. What are you doing here? I'm writing poetry and selling tobacco. You are selling tobacco? Yes. Finci tried to convince him to go home, the century was growing old, he had no one in Thessaloniki – I have God! Let it go. You'll have God back home too – and in the end Zlatković let it go, returning to Belgrade in the summer of 1986. After thirty odd years, he met Đilas on Palmotićeva Street. What they spoke about is not known, for though Zlatković carefully described in several of the concluding segments of *Winter of the Stylite,* Đilas's home, his desk and chair, the decorations and ornaments on the Turkish rug, the mounds of books rising behind Đilas's back and above his head, and the gray, vacant, void ceiling, where there was still no God, about their conversations he had nothing to say. In autumn 1987 Slobodan Milošević made his appearance at the Eighth Congress of the Central Committee of the Serbian Communists Union, and Zlatković paid for a memorial service to commemorate the Partisan fighters who fell at Sutjeska. By then *Winter of the Stylite* numbered five hundred pages. He approached Nolit about publishing it, but they said such literature had no appeal at the time. Everyone was reading memoirs of communist penitents, and he, Tito's guardsman, had not repented. I am a Christian, Zlatković told the poetry editor, and a Christian does not repent before the devil. He made a trip to Jasenovac, to Bogdan Bogdanović's Stone Flower, with two monks from the Dečani Monastery. They were arrested in the middle of a prayer. The Zagreb papers reported on the latest Serb provocation. He said the same thing to the investigators in Zagreb that he had said to the editor at Nolit: The devil is among you, but you don't recognize him! They let him go, and he left for Belgrade with the two others from the Zagreb railway station. On seeing the monument to King Tomislav, he said: Only a wicked man could raise a horse onto such a high pedestal – horses, like children, don't like heights. When Milošević gave his Gazimestan speech in summer 1989, Zlatković told Đilas the man should be killed. The man who knows how but doesn't do it will go to hell, he said. Đilas answered that they were both old. We've killed too many, he said. I haven't, Zlatković said bleakly. He died on December 28, 1991, in his rented Belgrade apartment, on Charlie Chaplin Street, number 36. He had shot himself in the temple.

Sava Zlatković, the second oldest brother, born in 1927, leaped from a train that was heading to Jasenovac at the end of 1943. It was not the same transport that had taken his father Dušan. Some five hundred Serbian youths from Zenica, Maglaj, and Zavidović had been rounded up and told they were headed to Slavonia for work. They would have room and board, and maybe they would make a little extra money. Sava was the only one who didn't believe it, and said he would jump from the train at full speed. You're crazy, said Todor, a young deacon from Zenica. God knows I might be crazy, God grant me that I might be more afraid of work than death. They laughed at him, but they did not hold him back. Soon they would not be among the living, their grave site unknown, and none of their names would be in the lists of the Jasenovac book of the dead. What is known of Sava Zlatković tells us that he used up all his happiness in the leap from the train. On Mount Motajica, a hideous, deformed hill near the Sava River, where Sava had somehow managed to run, he ran into the Chetnik major Stevan Sremčević. He stayed with him. He did not dare go back to Želeće, and any direction he turned would have landed him again on a train rushing to Jasenovac. The others believed they were being taken to Slavonia for work, but Sava had faith in the slight possibility that, once he had thrown himself through the little hold in the train floor and fallen onto the rails, his arms and legs would not be crushed under the wheels and he would not bang his head against one of the wooden ties, cracking open his skull and spilling his brains across the black carbolineum primer. He was lucky that one time and remained whole. And so he stayed with the Chetniks of Major Sremčević. Bashi-bazouks with scythes and ropes, peasants whose harvest had been burned by the Ustaše, village hoodlums, city informants and spies, a few kind simpletons, a few born murderers, the kind who only ever had an orgasm when, late in the fall, they held under their arm the trembling piglet whose throat they had just slit with a sharp knife – these were Sremčević's Chetniks, independent of any command structure, alone and free, they rushed into Muslim and Catholic villages, plundered and burned, but without any goal. They didn't even know who was leading them in their battle. What kept them together, it seemed, was the fact that none of them had anyplace to return to. Men with no families or patrimony, whose birthplaces no longer existed on the newly drawn maps, members of vanished armies, runaway idealists roaming through Posavina in those months, afraid of returning to the Bosnian forests and even more afraid of crossing the river. By the summer of 1944 there was talk about escaping across the border, to the English and American allies, who would be coming to settle scores with the communists. They'd been expected since the fall of Italy but had not come. Sava Zlatković did not have any thoughts on this matter. He was fine as long as there was kasha and cabbage. He would drink a bit too. The rakija went down easy and warmed the seventeen-year-old, making him sure he would come out in one piece even if he crawled through the floor of a train a second time. The rakija made him brave, but only until he sobered up. In April 1945, Major Sremčević was in negotiations with the Ustaše lieutenant Ljubo Miloš, who had guaranteed him and his people the safety and defense of the armed forces of the Independent State of Croatia. Together they would break through to Austria, according to the agreement, where they would join forces with the Allies and take part in the Anglo-American attack on Tito and the Partisans, and the decisive battle against the Red Army, which would take place somewhere on the Slavonian plain or, if they were lucky, on the Danube and the Drina. Again this time Sava Zlatković did not believe the Croats and slipped out into the darkness that same night. And that was the end of his story. Stevan Sremčević proclaimed him a deserter the next morning and sent men in pursuit, piqued that the little peasant would spoil his agreement with Ljubo Miloš, and perhaps behind this he concealed his own fear of a possible Ustaše betrayal of the agreement. The search party came back from its assigned task. Sava Zlatković had disappeared without a trace. No one ever saw him again, nor did his family ever learn what happened to him. He probably died on one of those last days of the war, but it would never be known by whose hands or from which army.

Dušan Zlatković's third son, Aleksandar, was born in 1932. He was eleven when the Ustaše took his father away. He was standing in the doorway, mute, looking right in the eyes of the leader, a boza maker from Zavidovići named Meho Ciganin. What are you looking at, kid? he said, swinging his rifle, as if, having no hammer, he was using it to drive a nail into a wall to hang a crucifix. He struck him hard with the gunstock, and there was a dull thud, as if the nail had broken through a soft shingle of the wall just barely covered with mortar, except that Meho Ciganin had not struck the wall, he had struck the teeth of Aleksandar Zlatković with the butt of his rifle, after which he was permanently mute. He lived mute and without teeth in Rakovica, near Belgrade, and worked as a carpenter. He was married to a Catholic woman named Bosiljka from Bačka, and she gave him five sons and not a single daughter. He died of heart disease in 1996, uttering not a single word since the day Meho Ciganin struck him with his rifle butt, as if he'd been driving a nail into the wall to hang a crucifix.

Petar and Miloš were twins born at the end of September 1939, sixteen years after the firstborn Milorad. Their mother Jelica barely survived this; she did not expect to have any more children, but at the beginning of the war, before turning forty, she conceived again, and in the winter of 1942 gave birth to another son Đorđije. After Dušan was taken away, she was left alone with three young children and the mute Aleksandar. Sava was able to look after them for a little while, but then he too was taken away. His mother discovered he had ended up with the Chetniks of Major Sremčević only after the youth's disappearance. She would hope in him for as long as she lived, waiting for him to reappear, certain that her Sava was alive. For if he had managed escape from an Ustaše train, how could he not save himself from the Sava River marshes and willow trees? Her motherly hope continued to grow until it had developed into a form of insanity after, with Milošević's rise to power in Serbia, a new kind of Chetniks appeared. The tears came when on the screen of her black-and-white TV in her apartment at the top of a New Belgrade high-rise, she saw on the daily news, the Chetnik governor, Mirko Jović, and his followers in Nova Pazova. Now my Sava! And she pressed her nose to the screen to look for him in the back rows of the demonstration. Sava had always been modest, he was somewhere in back, letting others stand out . . . Her son Đorđije, a famous Belgrade cellist, music critic, and one of the leaders of the antiwar movement and the citizens' opposition to Slobodan Milošević, cared for his mother Jelica and visited her daily in her home beneath the sky. At first he tried to see the change in his mother's behavior with humor. Unlike his eldest brother Milorad, Đorđije remained a cheerful person, one made uncomfortable by excessive emotion and sorrow. So he avoided thinking of his lost brother altogether.

"Anyway, I'm trying to be a good person, not do evil, and also not have to share bread with evil people," he told me, in an interview I conducted with him for the Zagreb paper *Globus* in 2002. We were sitting on the terrace of his beautiful, spacious apartment, in a villa in the Senjak neighborhood of Belgrade, talking about music, his deceased brother Milorad, and a little about Želeće, about the meadows Đorđije did not remember, and where my grandfather Franjo Rejc had kept hives, paying his father Dušan Zlatković in pollen rent.

This was when Đorđije told me the story about his mother.

After the first Chetnik gathering in Nova Pazova, when her son Sava had not appeared on the television screen, Jela began wandering across Serbia, then Bosnia and Herzegovina, wherever the awakened spirit of Serbian nationalism had spread, in search of her missing son. Two years before the war's outbreak in 1989, she was a well-preserved eighty-seven-year-old woman. There were stories about her in the papers. Dragoš Kalaić published a four-page piece about Jela Zlatković entitled "Our Mother" in the biweekly *Duga*. In searching for her son Sava, Mother Jela was in search of thousands of our sons who disappeared in 1945 toward the end of Tito's reign of terror and the de-Serbianization of the people. The mother was searching for Jovan, and Milan, and Dragan, she was searching for Dimitrij, and Stevan, Radivoj, Petar, Dušan, and Bogoljub, she was searching for Dobrosav, Milisav, Svetislav, and Dragoljub. Mother Jela was searching for her Serbian flower and, along the way, justice for the Serbia that once had a right to every one of its names but which lost that right in agreeing to the most frightening of all 1,717 devil's names known in Jewish Gehenna, agreeing to a name foisted upon it amid the cold of the Vatican's ramparts, in that deep freeze of human hearts, but also of all human intelligence, a name from the Ottomans, from Tehran, from Kumrovec and Kupinec, a schismatic, godless name, a name beaten into our ears with the tip of an Ustaše blade, a name that for seven billion years to come would be anathema in the Serbian language, the shameful name – Yugoslavia. Once she found her son Sava, Mother Jela would find thousands of her sons, then would Serbia's heroes be reborn from their decaying bones, dispersed across the Aegean Sea, the Slovenian mountains, and the Austrian plains, then would Serbia be reborn even where it had never been before, and all that remained unappeased inside us would find peace, and we would be reassured as people, when Mother Jela found her sons . . .

That was what Kalaić wrote in *Duga*, and along with the article there were pictures of Jela Zlatković, a straight-backed, worn-out, kerchiefed old woman, wearing black clothes and a Chetnik cockade, pinned to the left side her chest, just above her withered breast.

When he showed me the cut-out pages, which I had read back then at the end of the eighties, the famous cellist Đorđije Zlatković, who had hurried over Mount Igman to Sarajevo in 1993 to give a concert and ask forgiveness from the city they were destroying in his name, his eyes were filled with tears.

That was our mother for you, he said.

It was futile to tell her Sava would not be coming back. He had been dead for forty-five, forty-six, forty-seven years . . . Who knew who had killed him. It could have been his own Chetniks. It could have been the Germans, the Ustaše, the Partisans, or maybe he had died on his own. Whatever the case, he had not been around for a very long time, and it was time to come to terms with it. This was what they told her, but she would shake her head, say I know my Sava's alive, a mother can feel when her baby is alive, and refuse to hear them, leaving the house the very next day in search of her son Sava, following the growing monstrosity that was multiplying by simple division in all the regions of the disintegrating Yugoslavia.

Jela Zlatković became one of the emblematic phenomena and icons of the Serbian nationalistic insanity from the beginning of the nineties. Mama Methuselah, the emcee of death, dark prophet of evil, old crow, raven bitch, or whatever else she might have been called, appeared in highly unusual places across Yugoslavia. She awakened fear in people, announcing war and misfortune to come. She was in Vukovar two months before the Yugoslav National Army laid siege to it. She came to Sarajevo, to the Serbian Democratic Party's convention at the Holiday Inn, a day before the great demonstration in front of the parliament of Bosnia and Herzegovina. She was looking for Sava, but Sava was not there.

I asked Đorđije Zlatković whether Milorad's suicide on December 28, 1991, had been at all connected to his mother. He shook his head. Milorad had long since stopped wanting to know about her. No one knew why. It was just that at a certain point, before his departure for Athos, he had suddenly grown distant from her, like an infant weaning itself and no longer caring. He stayed in contact with his brothers, worried about them, but he never asked anything about her. The human connection to the woman who brought one into the world, Milorad had once said, responding to Đorđije's insistence that they talk about her, had been overrated throughout history. Much evil had resulted from it. The bloodiest of wars had been fought because sons imagined something more between those old women's legs than what had pushed them out, along with bloody fluid and internal impurities, getting rid of it all like a foreign body, freeing itself as if from a senseless, benign tumor. The world would be a better place if it finally became aware of this. But that, unfortunately, was never going to happen, Milorad said in 1989, a few days after Gazimestan, when Đorđije had come to him tearful and distraught to ask what could be done about their mother.

The problem was not with her, just as it wasn't with the hundreds of thousands of people like her.

She would disappear when it did. But that was not going to happen.

This was what Milorad Zlatković had said, and the brothers did not speak about their mother anymore.

The twins Petar and Miloš occupied themselves with bees and beekeeping from a young age. Petar Zlatković was a professor in Belgrade's Agricultural School and was the best-known European specialist in the pathology of bees and other insects, while Miloš Zlatković, an art historian, worked with bees as a hobby, though around Belgrade it was said that he knew more about bees and beekeeping than his brother. For years he edited Smederevo's *Beekeepers' Herald*, where, from issue 2 of 1981 to the combined issues 1-3 of 1989, he published the *History of South Slavic Beekeeping and Honey Production Across the Centuries*, in thirty installments. The Zagreb publisher Mladost announced the publication of Miloš Zlatković's book under the same title, but because of the war it did not come out. His manuscript probably still exists somewhere today, but the author, it seems, has forever lost interest in its publication.

After the siege of Sarajevo had begun, and the story of the ninety-year-old woman Jela Zlatković, who followed the Serbian troops around looking for her son lost in the previous war, had made its way to the international press and the best-known worldwide television programs, the twins' life in Belgrade and in rump Yugoslavia, from which the western republics and Macedonia had separated, became unbearable.

They left the country by way of Budapest, but then they had to separate. Petar went to Canada, where he got work at Ottawa's Apiculture Institute, while Miloš traveled to New Zealand. For years he worked as a freelance video artist, and performer, and in 1999 became a professor at the government film school. They never visited Belgrade, as far as anyone knows. Several publishers supposedly, and Vladislav Bajac of Geopoetika certainly, inquired about the *History of South Slavic Beekeeping and Honey Production Across the Centuries*. Bajac even telephoned Miloš Zlatković, who in a curt and not especially cordial way told Bajac that he was not interested in having the book published, that he did not believe that "anyone back there was engaged in beekeeping anymore," and that he had heard the bees in the Balkans had died out at the beginning of the nineties.

Jela Zlatković died in a Belgrade home for the elderly at the end of August 1995. In the final months she found it hard to move. The cartilage of her knees and hips was gone, bone grated painfully against bone, so the greater part of the day she spent in a wheelchair. The attendants would wheel her down the green linoleum-tiled hall and place her in front of the television in the living room, and she would sit with the remote control on her lap, changing channels occasionally, searching, but there were fewer and fewer Chetniks on the screen. In the middle of July, during the worst of the heat, when there was no air conditioning, on a foreign channel she came upon a column of tattered women, children, and old people as they made their way somewhere, men in torn military uniforms and covered in sweat. The screen was snowy, the picture sometimes disappeared, and there was no sound, only the same picture reappearing: a slowly moving column of ragged, filthy people covered in sweat, kerchiefed women with their heads down, as if the glare in their eyes might blind them. She did not know who these people were or where they were going. The next day she was again flipping through and again they appeared on a foreign channel. Except there were more women, fewer old people, the young boys in the torn military uniforms had disappeared, there were no boys anymore, and they all looked much more exhausted than the day before. She did not know who they were. She called a nurse: Kosara, dear, where are all those people off to? Kosara didn't know, but she was left gaping as the picture went white again, the sound grew louder, and the screen disappeared into snow. This went on for days before Mother Jela discovered that they were Muslims from Srebrenica. Turks, said Kosara gloomily, and paid no more attention. Yes, right, Turks, mother Jela tried to accept it, but suddenly something seemed wrong to her. For days she had been watching those women, she thought she had seen them several times, that she had met some of them, watching like that, on a strange foreign TV channel, and she could not just say Turks. It had been different when the impassioned Serbian nation was defending itself from the hills around Sarajevo, threatened from the minarets and the red roofs, for then there had been no people. Mother Jela had not seen them while she was searching for her son Sava. But now, there, she was seeing people. And she had been watching them on those July days, while everything around baked in the summer heat, stinking of ammonia and human insides, of old age and death, while everyone but she lay down and slept, hidden in their rooms, waiting for a breath of wind, the salvation of the first autumn rain. They did not care, nor did they see the long column making its way today, on that foreign channel, but Mother Jela watched them, making out the faces until the picture went snowy, trying to recognize someone she had seen before. A woman leading a seven-year-old boy by the hand – the same age as her grandson Moris, Đorđije's son, who would be starting school in the fall, and then she wondered where, good Lord, would that boy be going to school, the one who had been hanging on his mother's arm for days – she saw her and her son and the next day would search for them. She saw an old man, perhaps older than she was, thin as a stalk, like the typhus patient in that film, and remembered him, thinking perhaps they had met somewhere before. It was true that Želeće was far from Srebrenica, so very far, and she wasn't sure whether anyone from Žepče or Maglaj had ever gone to Srebrenica, and why anyone would, she had no idea, but then she remembered Mr. Rejc, who had kept his bees on their meadow, and she remembered that Mr.

Rejc had been a rail man but not like her Dušan, no, he'd been an official at the headquarters, a railroad sage, and he had inspected all the tracks to see the damage and determine how fast the trains could go on which tracks, and she thought that he, Mr. Rejc, should be asked whether it was possible to get to Srebrenica by train and whether Srebrenica had a railway station. But then she remembered she had not seen him for a long time, not since that other war, sixty years and more had passed, and he was most likely no longer alive. But then the picture on the screen became suddenly clear. It was no longer a foreign station but Radio and Television Serbia, and people were no longer walking but sitting in a tractor trailer. It was Saturday evening, August 5, and Mother Jela suddenly perked up, raised herself from the wheelchair and said – Turks. They're not Turks; they're Serbs, Kosara said, just as gloomily. The TV-viewing room slowly filled with people and soon there would be no free seats. In their wheelchairs, hobbling on walkers with IVs hanging from them, with and without crutches, holding one another by the arm, those who were still in their right minds came to watch the exodus of Serbs from Croatia. Turks, Mother Jela said once more, as if to make sure. They're not Turks; they're Serbs, people croaked near her. Leave the woman alone, Kosara warned them. Serbs, Mother Jela said. Yes, Serbs, Kosara said, sighing, and stood beside her, as if she were her bodyguard. So it is, said Mother Jela. Yes, said Kosara. The heat had subsided somewhat. It was no longer as it had been while the women, children, and old men from Srebrenica were passing across the snowy screen. It was possible to breathe. Someone cursed. The smell of cigarette smoke was palpable. Though smoking was prohibited, one of the doctors had lit up. His eyes were filled with tears. He was from Zadar, Kosara told her. His people were in the column. Mother Jela looked at the doctor. The smoke stung her eyes. Are you looking for your son? someone asked. For Mother Jela was again shoving her nose into the screen. He's not there, she said. It had been a long time since she'd thought about Sava, not since the summer heat had come. My Sava disappeared at the end of that other war, she said. But no one could hear her. They were shouting, cursing, sobbing in front of the TV, as the column neared the border. There were destroyed houses all around, burnt-out car bodies, tank barriers, and tangled balls of barbed wire. One winter night,

Mother Jela whispered, one cold winter night she would unravel every ball of barbed wire and knit her sons' winter sweaters. She would knit her dead sons sweaters of barbed wire one cold night. And all of it had long since been in vain. Her son Sava would not be there, he would never come back, and both columns would soon disappear from the TV screen.

Jela Zlatković, Chetnik mother, died on August 30, 1995, while sitting before a TV that showed the dancing stars of Grand Production, with the remote control resting in her lap. Nurse Kosara tried to check her pulse while a young woman with large, plastic breasts in a leather miniskirt sang the old hit by Snežana Savić: Three kisses is what I want, not one, not two, I'll not take less, for three's the best for happiness, three kisses is what I want . . .

We have narrated this lengthy tale of Dušan Zlatković's, to whom Franjo Rejc for years paid pollen rent, and of his sons and his widow Jela, even though it has no connection to the gray notebook, the *zobnica*, the rusted lighter, the pencil, or the two pieces of red wax for sealing envelopes found thirty years after the move, in the cellar of the house on Sepetarevac. But this story, too, is linked to the bee journal, and to all the other, mostly lost journals kept by Franjo Rejc in his lifetime. In some of the honey jars, where the bees' understanding of Želeće and of the events that took place on the meadows near the home of Dušan Zlatković were archived, but which we consumed after Franjo's death because there was no one left to decipher the bees' language and read their bee history, there must have been stories told, even if only in signs and bee allusions, of the births of Dušan and Jela's sons. From them perhaps one might divine a certain hidden history of our century.

For 1935, remarks on no. 4

The queen moves slowly. The bees are unusually sensitive, react even to breath. Otherwise the nest is well ordered, with broods in all stages.

Ilidža, 1936, no. 4

Swarm extremely animated in early spring. Queen disappeared at the end of April, joined to no. 5 on May 12, 1936. Gradually extracting no. 4 (this line, the transcriber notes, is written more forcefully and underlined).

19 V 36. Survey. There are twelve frames. Saw the queen. Eggs hatching well. She's moving a bit more slowly. Saw the drone brood. Two frames in all. Adequate honey and pollen. Healthy odor. Entire swarm rather weak. Nest is at center of hive; added one frame. Unnecessary to check again before June 14.

24 V 36. Added one frame with a sealed worker bee brood taken from no. 3.

2 VI 36. Thirteen frames. Three frames have empty spaces. Found the queen at the back of frame 4. Entire frame laid heavily with eggs. Laying is proper. The queen moves very slowly; her abdomen has turned rather dark. She's old. On further analysis located fairly mature brood. Since there is no drone comb, the bees have spread out their work and moved out the drone brood. In frame 10, counting in back I found two not-yet-closed queen cells next to mature brood. Removed one empty frame. No need for further checks before 20 VI 36, thanks to quiet swarming.

Franjo stands above a frame filled with bees holding his breath. They are sensitive to breath. They grow troubled, begin to bustle like people on Baščaršija cobblestones, treading one after another, while on both sides of the street Oriental shops open up after the midday heat. The marketplace is lively, but he does not feel comfortable there. He'd prefer to be home with his bees. All is well among them, even on the days when they sting, even then they're better than the Oriental bustle, better than the world of people, whose curiosity and sincerity are smothering. These people see him as a foreigner, just as they see his sons as foreigners, and will see the children of his children, and their grandchildren and great-grandchildren, waiting patiently for the day when they'll all pack up and leave Sarajevo and Bosnia, just as their great-great-grandfathers had arrived with a bag in each hand, thereby keeping the balance above the abyss of foreignness. Nor do they ever ask where we would go with those two bags, where our true homeland might be. Because for them, as they simper and bow from the doors of their shops, the *kuferaš* homeland is wherever there are crosses. There's a wide world to pick from, so go right ahead!

Franjo had lived along the tracks in many Bosnian towns or *kasabas*, as the locals call them. From the first in Travnik to the last, God willing, in Sarajevo, he had crossed central Bosnia backwards and forwards, traveling often by train and sensing each of the rails under the jurisdiction of the Bosnia and Herzegovina Railway Headquarters. He felt at home in a train, on open track, at a station, on a main line or a sidetrack. That was his homeland – he passed through the car freely, along the corridor through the sleeping compartments, and through narrow passages between the wooden benches on trains that ran on narrow-gauge lines; he had conversations with people, paid no attention to how he pronounced the words, writing down their names and addresses in his notebook at full speed, his hand steady, his handwriting ever clear and strong; though he had never worked in a train, had never been a conductor or an engineer, and had never served as chief of a special line, his steps were steady, as if the floor were not swaying beneath his feet, like an old sailor on a stormy sea, and wherever he was, on a train, at a station, or in a waiting room, or if he was pumping a handcar like a gymnast, up-down, up-down, up-down, on some abandoned track in eastern Bosnia, Franjo Rejc was in his element. The moment he came down onto the platform and took those ten steps to the road, to the civilian world, again he found himself in a foreign land. An eternal *kuferaš*, an outsider, an alien born in Travnik as an alien, who would die an alien, it was not clear where yet, for to stop being an alien he would have to go to wherever they sent him, to Slovenia, Croatia, Germany, for he spoke German too, along with both his mother tongues, and there he would have to be a greater Slovene than the Slovenes, a harsher Croat than the harshest of Croats, to live at last in his own land, his own bread and blood, and not like this, troubled, alone, without air. For years he felt he did not have enough air, that the people in the marketplace were strangling him and pressing in on him from all around. Then Doctor Rittig had said it was asthma, cardiac asthma, and he felt lighter. For a brief while it felt better, for he believed he had finally discovered what was smothering him and that it had nothing to do with his foreignness . . . But soon it all started again. He was choking because there were fingers pressing against his chest – an unsightly little secret police inspector had climbed onto a metal safe in his dream and leaped onto his chest, a dream that repeated for years. He was choking because of Mladen's death. He was choking because choking had become his way of life. A crab backed away, a snake slithered between the stones, a whale emerged to take a breath, but he choked and could not remember that it had ever been any different.

Franjo hadn't been able to breathe since 1945.

He breathed as if onto bees that were sensitive to breath.

He breathed as if to avoid upsetting his bees.

He breathed as if with each breath he inhaled hundreds of stingers into his throat and air passage. Hundreds of bee deaths for one beekeeper's pain, for a strangulation that would last for years.

He asked Doctor Rittig if he ought to engage in beekeeping, if honey might be good for his illness. Physical activity was important! Rittig said. But without getting agitated of course, and it seems to me, he told Franjo, that you must remain calm among bees. Of course, Franjo said, bees don't tolerate nervousness. Bees despise agitated people. A bee never will sting a calm person. If that is the case, said the doctor, then beekeeping is very good for you. I must tell you we know nothing regarding honey's medicinal benefits. We do know that honey is not harmful to a person, as is, for instance, white sugar.

Doctor Rittig was a puzzling man. When Vjekoslav Luburić arrived in Sarajevo toward the end of the war, Doctor Rittig was among the first arrested. It was rumored around the market squares that he was a Mason. He was held for a week, interrogated in the house of horror on Skenderija, which Luburić had acquired the day he entered the city. He selected it, they say, because of the Masonic symbol imprinted on the façade so that he might finish off the Antichrist in his chambers. Few believed the doctor would ever see the light of day again. Cries were audible from the house on Skenderija, Luburić's executioners having opened the windows, perhaps to air out their torture chambers or, more likely, to spread terror throughout the city and with it the story of the Independent State of Croatia's survival, of its tormentors and its martyrs. In this Luburić, who was also called General Drinjanin, was very successful.

Doctor Rittig emerged unscathed from the house on Skenderija. He did not look as if he had been tortured, nor had he lost weight. His face was a little pale, which was not at all strange since he hadn't seen the sun in a long time. Whether anyone asked him how he had fared at Luburić's is of course not known. But knowing the inhabitants of Sarajevo, they didn't ask but rather pretended that nothing had happened. If some crackpot had asked him, Rittig would not have answered. He had been silent about even smaller matters. He merely smiled and shared simple medical advice with his patients without even examining them and making a diagnosis. Don't get stressed. Drink plenty of water, it's good for you, water is the healthiest drink there is. Be careful what you wear on your feet, a hat and shawl are not too important. Some illnesses come from your feet getting wet. Give up smoking, just think what your lungs look like after so many years of smoking – like a chimney pipe! Walk as much and as often as you can. Walking is healthy. Drink only in moderation. Trust in God, but go to the doctor when something hurts; God did not invent medicine for no reason. Take shelter from the heat, it's not good when the sun beats down on your head. Pregnancy is not an illness, and you shouldn't behave as if you were sick when you're pregnant. Washing your hands is more important than washing your feet, but if you've already washed your hands, you might as well wash your feet, at least for the sake of stretching . . .

This was how Doctor Rittig talked after getting out of Luburić's torture chamber.

When the Partisans arrived, they made him director of the hospital for a short time. That's not for me, he told them. I'm a born senior *medicus*. They checked on the meaning of *medicus* and before long Rittig was back at his old position in one of the most remote buildings of Koševo Hospital, located amid the stench of the hospital kitchens and laundry facilities. The patients would see the well-known pulmonary cardiologist about not being able to breathe. They would stretch out their chests and open their mouths like fish but still could get no air. Rittig was their last hope.

He never married, living a bachelor's life on Tito Street, in a large, gloomy apartment. After the war his niece Abela came to live with him, a taciturn, slender girl who played the violin and was studying to become a music teacher. Why she came from Zagreb to study music in Sarajevo, when she had passed her entrance exams in Zagreb, is not clear. She must have taken refuge, just as her uncle had taken refuge in Sarajevo. He never mentioned his native Zagreb, nor did he call himself a Croat. About this, as about erotic matters, the doctor was equally without passion. Whenever a conversation turned to nationality, Rittig would take part reluctantly or, in the middle of the conversation, take out a newspaper or a book and immerse himself in it, raising up around him the same Rittig wall that had forever remained impenetrable. He would just smile mournfully, as if slightly embarrassed, and soon drift off into sleep. Are you a German? someone would ask him. Yes, I speak German well. But you're not a German. I thought you were because you have a German last name. You are right, my last name is German. See how words can deceive you.

Doctor Rittig had a country house near the train station in Herceg Novi, purchased before the war with money from a Zagreb inheritance. What inheritance, from whom, how much – he did not talk about these things either.

He spent winters in Herceg Novi from the time of his retirement in 1960. In summer he'd be back in Sarajevo because it was cooler.

So it was while strolling at Herceg Novi by the sea and along the tracks – it was amazingly beautiful – that he met Ivo Andrić. The writer, who as yet had not won the Nobel Prize, was often approached with questions on the streets of Belgrade, so he had retreated to Herceg Novi. It was peaceful there, in the little places by the sea where the people did not pay attention to strangers walking and thinking, and just met them with a friendly greeting. Responding in kind was not hard for him. And so on their walks they started to exchange greetings. The path was narrow and people were few, especially those whose faces one recognized. Both of them were grayish pale, as if they had adopted the autumn colors of the Sarajevo valley, a sky that remained gray for half the year without ever turning blue. At last they were actually introduced, courtesy of Don Niko Luković, their mutual friend and Rittig's patient for a time. From then on they did not pass by each other but set out together, making their way from one end of the bay to the other. What they spoke about, or whether they spoke about anything, we don't know. The people of Herceg Novi saw them walking together for years – supposedly a photojournalist from a Dubrovnik paper took a photograph of them from a distance, but I was not able to find it even after years of searching – and then, one after the other, six months apart, they died. Andrić in Belgrade at the end of winter 1975, Doctor Rittig in Herceg Novi, in the middle of August that same year.

The music teacher Abela Rittig, who lived in his Sarajevo apartment, disappeared in May 1992. She did not pack up and leave. Her Yugoslav passport was found in a drawer of her desk, and she did not take her Bosnian one. No one could say when she left her home. The neighbors could not remember the last time they had seen her. It was presumed that all she had with her was her identity card. Of her possessions in the apartment, during the police search, the only object found missing was her violin. It was not a Stradivarius or Guarneri but an ordinary, quality violin made in Vienna at the beginning of the twentieth century, which Doctor Rittig had given Abela as a gift when she graduated. Where would Abela Rittig, an old woman, have gone with her violin in the days of the city's heaviest bombardment? For years she had not been performing, and now she had suddenly left with her instrument? But the police were not interested in such details. Perhaps they didn't have time. Soon Abela Rittig's neighbors forgot about the violin and the intrigue that revolved around it. So as not to dwell on it too much, it was said that Abela left the city with a Jewish convoy. After telling this story so many times, people started to believe the lie and it soon became accepted that Abela Rittig had left Sarajevo with the Jews. Didn't her name sound a bit Jewish?

Time passed, the destinies of those who were no longer living in the city faded, and the local population, those whom Franjo Rejc used to meet at Baščaršija back in 1936 and among whom he felt like a foreigner, quickly got used to the idea that no one other than they had ever been in Sarajevo. While their solicitous wives washed the windows hanging above the abyss from the facades of old Austro-Hungarian structures, they wiped the faces from behind the glass where those people had lived. Soon all the windows in Sarajevo had been cleaned, all the faces wiped.

There are two notes on the desk calendar for 1966, in the margins of a page for the week of May 23 to 29. Both were written in fountain pen ink, probably with Franjo's Pelikan, in blue. The first, from Tuesday, May 24, reads, "Gave Doctor Rittig a 2 kg jar of honey from G[lavatičevo] to take with him to I.A. in H. Novi."

The note for Saturday reads: "Javorka gave birth to Vuk at about 11."

There for the first and last time I was recorded as Vuk.

But the Saturday note is less important since it does not touch upon Doctor Rittig. On Tuesday, May 24, 1966, Franjo brought Rittig a jar of his Glavatičevo honey, medicinal, strong, fragrant, from the very border of the continental and Mediterranean worlds, which Rittig then took to the author Ivo Andrić. He had told him about Franjo's honey, and Andrić wanted to taste it. I'm not a honey fanatic, for it's hard to find better honey than the honey made from Herzegovian heather, and heather is here at hand, but as you are telling me about that bee-keeper, the railroad man, and about his honey from Konjic, from the parts closer to the Neretva's source, and I somehow feel those places and hear people from a different time, the start of the Austrian administration in Bosnia. And I think that this honey might help me remember them. So if the beekeeper has a jar of that honey, I'd be very grateful to him. That was what Andrić supposedly said to Doctor Rittig. He conveyed these words to Franjo Rejc, who was of course pleased to hear that the great writer expressed interest in his honey.

In the end it was a jar from one of Franjo's last beekeeping years that made its way to Andrić. On Saturday his grandson was born, and he disposed of his last hives. For a time people said he did it because of me, but then the stories changed, grew quiet, and stopped altogether, so that their end was never reached. He perhaps believed he had given the bees to others so he could spend time with his grandson, though the real reason was that he no longer had the strength, his asthma was crushing him, his heart pumped blood ever more feebly, his lungs filling with water, and Franjo was nearing the grave. There was less and less air around him.

Ilidža, 1937. Number 8.

Had drones at the start of April. It was raining from the second half of April to the end of May. Stock of honey almost full, and pollen completely expended. Drones driven out around May 15–20. In that time I fed them sugar. The hardest rains had stopped by the beginning of May, pasture improved enough so that on June 11 I put an extension of five frames from the brood chamber, in place of which I put an empty comb into the chamber.

Placed the empty comb into the back of the brood chamber, while placing the chamber frames into the front honey chamber.

By June 11 it seemed everything would be okay. But actually the spring had brought ill forebodings. It was April. The rain would not cease, as if it were monsoon season in India. After the mild, slimy winter of 1936–37, without snow or ice, which would have dried out the rot and cut back the dying vegetation from the preceding year, came the rainy spring, transforming the meadows toward Butmir into a bog exuding the stench of decay, as the earth could not absorb so much water.

Mladen, who usually didn't get sick, had ended up in bed with a high temperature. What's wrong, my child? Olga had asked, concerned. I can't move my head, he had answered. It hurts. The glands in his neck had been swollen since the morning, and Doctor Sarkotić had come and said – mumps. This was not good. The child was at the worst possible age, when his sexual glands were developing. He could be left impotent. This was in March 1936. Olga paid for a mass to be held for Mladen's recovery at Sarajevo's Church of Saint Ante in Bistrik. She was afraid Mladen would not be able to have children and his good nature and abundant talents would die with him. This was the last mass for the living or the dead Olga would ever request. She went in the evening to Bistrik, knelt in the half-empty church, staring at the child above the altar, and listened to the priest pronouncing the name of her eldest son.

Before long her younger son Dragan also grew ill. But for him it wasn't as serious for he had not yet reached the age of ten and was in no danger of becoming sterile. Besides, Dragan had never been as loved as Mladen. In addition to not being the first born, he was not equal to his brother in looks, intelligence, and especially talent. This was clear even then, while everyone was still alive and all misfortunes were small. Later the differences between the dead and the living son would grow to monstrous proportions. The dead son would be better in all respects than the living, and the living would have to cope with the fact that someone now dead had been so much better than he was. He could achieve it only by dying, but there was never anything suicidal about Dragan. He wanted to live, good and innocent, a lover of women, a frequenter of prostitutes, a kind and an unfaithful husband, as cruel and tender as a child. He would forever remain the younger brother who learned through personal experience that nothing in life could be as perfect as death.

As soon as he was better, at the beginning of April, while the rains fell on Bosnia without respite, Mladen was taken to the doctor. First to Doctor Rittig, who would know what to do next. He told them not to worry, but their concern grew. He said the mumps were not such a deadly disease, there were far more serious childhood diseases, and then he picked up the telephone and called Doctor Damjan Hadžidamjanović. He received Mladen, led him into a room painted from floor to ceiling in shiny white, told him to undress, sat on a chair in front of him and for a long time poked around in his testicles with the fingers of his right hand, as if weighing them on his palm.

I don't think it's a case of testicular inflamation, he said. Are you sure? Olga asked. I think I am, he answered. Her worry lasted until the very end, when something much worse took its place. From spring 1936 to autumn 1943 they were worried about whether Mladen might have been rendered impotent. Then the time of his death came, and that would torment them as long as they lived. Mladen's death continues to hang over us to this day.

Clearly the mumps were a result of the mild winter. Other children's diseases spread through Sarajevo in those weeks, and adults too fell ill from the flu and other inflammations, of the lungs, kidneys, brain. At an earlier time, such a winter would have brought out the plague, which during the rainy spring would have killed off half the city. Even if Bosnia was at the end of the world, and Sarajevo a byway, the epidemic would have found a way of making it to the city. The last plague had afflicted Bosnia some three hundred years earlier. Numerous families had disappeared, and along with them several old family names of the city, but all that transpired before Austria had arrived in Bosnia and with it the "light of civilization."

For seven long years Olga would worry about whether the mumps had left her son impotent. And then she stopped worrying.

In the forty-three years that she survived her son, Olga destroyed all his school report cards, identification documents, photographs, school composition notebooks, books awarded to him as scholastic prizes, and everything else in the house that was a reminder of him.

When in the summer of 1969 we moved from Madam Heim's building to Sepetarevac, she sorted every paper, examined every object, and threw into the trash whatever might have reminded her of him.

She did all this in silence. She did not speak, nor did anyone question her. I never said a word to her about Mladen. No one forbade me, nor was there anything ever said about not speaking of him. It was understood. I learned that one did not speak of Mladen, as one learns the words for home, stone, face, hand, tree, building, sky, flame, knife, gun, earth, death . . . I don't know when I pronounced any of these words for the first time (really, when was the first time I uttered the word death?), but each one entered my speech unobtrusively, along with a story that could not be remembered, a story that does not exist, though clearly it once had to exist. The closing idea for an autobiography would be to find each of these stories about words, reconstruct them, and write them down. To write the story of Mladen, a boy whose name was never uttered aloud.

Several years before Javorka's death, I received a batch of letters on loan that the Stublers of Ilidža had written and received from Mladen, after he'd been sent for training in Stokerau. Mostly they were to his cousin, my aunt Nevenka, who was eight years old and had just started second grade at the time. The fact that he was writing to a child is clear from the tone of his letters.

They are dated from the end of 1942 until August 1943. Along with Mladen and Nevenka's correspondence there were letters that Aunt Rika, Nevenka's mother, to him and his responses to her. A few postcards were also included from Nevenka's uncle Rudolf Stubler, a lieutenant in the Home Guard, which he sent from the barracks in Bijeljina and then from Šid.

Mladen wrote all his letters in green fountain pen. He was making an effort to write in clear handwriting because Nevenka obviously was not able to read the cursive of adults yet. The postcard he sent to Rudi in Bijeljina at the end of the summer of 1943, though neat, was written in a very different hand.

In most of the letters, those he received and those he sent to Kasindol Street, the traces of the military censure are evident: a pale blue or penciled line from the upper left to the lower right corner, the kind of mark writers use to cross out an entire page of a manuscript.

It is Wednesday, March 24, 1943.

Mladen writes:

Dear Nevenka,

Here I am responding to your letter right away. Hearing from you always gladdens me. We too are enjoying fine weather. In the morning, as soon as we get up, we go outside to run and exercise without our shirts on. Then we sing the Erika March. Then we take our rifles and machine guns and shoot paper Russians and Partisans in the woods.

Like you, we have school, except that in our school one mustn't fail and so there is no homework.

It will soon be two months since I was last at Tante Dora's. One week we have exercises, the next we don't, so I don't know when I'll get leave. But the next time I go to Vienna I'll tell Tante Dora that you're studying your Gothic script diligently and that you will write to her.

The radio plays all day long here, but I can never hear it because of the work we do. And just like you, we eat cakes here as if every day was our name day. I miss cornmeal. Once in a while they make a pudding out of it. I've had enough potatoes, we have a lot of those every day.

Maybe I'll get a leave after Easter and come home, and maybe I won't. Maybe the war will end quickly and I'll come home for good, and maybe it won't.

But tomorrow for sure I'll load the machine gun onto my shoulders and get good and sweaty.

Now I must write to Željko.

Greetings to your mother and father, and to Omama and Opapa, and Nano.

With much love,
Your Mladen

Two weeks later, again Wednesday, Nevenka answers. (Curious how in all their letters and postcards, they write out the full dates without exception. In Franjo's bee journal the entire year is rarely included, instead he writes just the last two numbers of the year. Here that doesn't happen. The dates are emphasized as in history textbooks. Perhaps this is accidental, perhaps only a detail of the generally accepted manners or modes of the time, but it may also be that there is a feeling of the historical moment. Or does that ring with too much pathos? Perhaps a feeling that their deaths were imminent and that in the next instant they could cease to be, as in the bursts of machine gun fire the paper Russians and Partisans ceased to be.)

Dear Mladen!

I received your letter. It made me happy because you had not written in a long time. Soldiers came our way. A dreadful division of Germans. The fields were filled with tents, cars, and horses. A major slept at our apartment. Javorka is crawling and by summer will be walking. We're preparing a school assembly for April 10 and I'll be doing a little presentation. We are all well, Mama, Papa, Omama, and Opapa, but Nano was a little under the weather. We're working in the garden but we miss you. I've got a cold but am otherwise well. Nano already has a job in the locomotive repair shop. He's received his first paycheck. It's snowing today, but the sun will come out by tomorrow. The sparrows are twittering under our kitchen window.

Sending you all my love and kisses, ·

Yours, Nevenka Novak
Are you still singing and playing the guitar?

Nevenka Novak, whose married name was Cezner, had rheumatic fever as a child. This damaged her heart. She later became an architect but did not end up designing a single important building. She had a gift for such work, but the times did not favor it. She did not complain much about this. She gave birth to two children who now live in Germany. She was moderately religious, never a Party member. She lived through her second war, the one that began in 1992, under Serbian occupation in Ilidža, on Kasindol Street, in the same building where her grandfather Karlo Stubler had hidden his Serbian neighbors from the Ustaše patrols. She died several years after the war, from a heart that by then had given up. Her heart valves were hanging by threads, the cardiologist said. He may have invented this, but one remembers such a colorful diagnosis. Until the end of Nevenka's life, a wooden apiary that Karlo had built by hand for four or five hives had stood in the Stubler yard. Coated in carbolineum, used to protect railway trusses, it survived two wars and stayed in the same spot for over seventy years. For its last twenty years there were no longer any bees in it. Franjo Rejc had added the carbolineum touch. He had purchased it at the railway works, and asked for a receipt. There were those who took railway materials, including tools, wooden trusses, and even rails, and brought them home without paying for them. That was why Franjo asked for the receipt, which for a long time rested in an envelope in one of the thousands of little drawers and side tables of the house on Kasindol. Perhaps the receipt still exists today, though the apiary is no more.

On Friday, April 23, 1943, Mladen sent Nevenka a postcard. It is standard, thick, rose-colored military paper. In the upper right corner is the word *Feldpost*, or *field post*, and on the left, under the first and last name of the sender, in small letters: "Bezeichnung des Truppenteils verboten. Als Dienstgrad nur Soldat, Getreiter, Leutnant usw. angeben" (Unit name forbidden. Indicate as rank only soldier, enlisted, lieutenant, etc.). The card has three stamps on it: one with a German military eagle, one with the postmark date, and a third with the name Ilidža and the receipt date. The latter is May 4, 1943. The postcard had taken ten days to get from Stockerau to Sarajevo.

On the back of the card he wrote:

Dear Nevenka,

Thank you for your last letter. I have a lot of work to do and don't have time to write. Yesterday I got up at three in the morning and marched all day, with guard duty lasting until eleven at night. And this morning we were up again at five. Today is Good Friday, but we have duty as on any other day. On Sunday I'll visit Aunt Dora. Last Sunday I was in a castle where the emperor used to live. Now we sing this:

Der Spiess, der hat ein dickes Buch
Und drinnen slecht . . .

Ask Nano to translate it for you. Happy Easter to you and your mother and father!

With much love,
Mladen

At the time, Mladen had been in Stockerau for more than half a year. Training was nearing its end, but it was not yet known where his unit would be sent. It was unclear whether Germans from outside Germany, those who did not have citizenship in the German Reich, still needed to serve in their own homelands. Franjo was nervous; he listened to Radio London in secret, exchanging information with Ivica Lisac, who would hear a lot from the German officers. They came to have their photographs taken to send back home, and they would tell him things were not good. The eastern front would have to be reinforced since for months it had been moving westward. The news that Stalingrad had fallen and an entire German army had been taken prisoner reached Ivica Lisac's photography studio in all its dramatic detail, worse than what Radio London had reported. The English were not exaggerating. The Red Army was advancing across Russia's endless expanse as if no one could stop it . . .

Franjo did not want his son to stop the Red Army.

He did not want anyone to stop the Red Army, for it could not be worse than what it was battling against. There was nothing worse than Hitler. Franjo had known this from the start. Hitler was waging war against the Red Army, against America and England, against the West and the East, but also against his neighbor from the ground floor, the Jewish woman who had been picked up and who had called out in the night for her neighbors to save her. Hitler was waging a war on Franjo's conscience.

This was why he did not want his son to stop the Red Army.

Olga did not want to see her son hurt, that was why she resisted the idea that at the first opportunity Mladen might desert. Deserters were punished by death. She was sure that it would be easier to stay alive by reporting to Stockerau and shooting at paper Russians and Partisans than to fight against fascism in the woods of Bosnia.

Olga was deathly afraid of the Ustaše, which was why she could not bring herself to have an abortion in the fall of 1941, even though she did not want to have another child. A wartime child. Archbishop Ivan "the Evangelist" Šarić preached that any wayward woman who got rid of unborn fruit would end up in hell. He was an ugly old man who wrote bad poetry and translated the Bible. She could not have cared less what he said, though she believed in God and went to church. She could not have cared less about his hell, but she was afraid of the Ustaše. The Ustaše punished abortion by death. That was why she gave birth to a girl on May 10, 1942, and, according to Mladen's wishes, they named her Javorka. The Catholic priests did not want to christen her with that name; they said the name was Serbian. Franjo did not give in. Let her name be Serbian! Are Serbs human beings? he asked a young man in a black robe. He blushed and said: We are all God's children! Then he added: But the child cannot be christened with that name. And so she was registered as Regina Javorka.

My mother was born of the fear her mother had of the Ustaše. Had she not been afraid, she would have aborted the child, as she had already done once before, in summer 1940. If Nona had not been afraid of the Ustaše, the hand that writes these lines would have been a mere cosmic conjecture. Should I be thankful to the Ustaše that I was born? I asked myself this in Zagreb in the summer of 2013, on the seventieth anniversary of Mladen's death, at a time of quiet and implicit gratitude for all that the Ustaše did for Croatia. I am not thankful to those who gave me life. Just as I am not thankful to those who welcomed me with such kindness to Zagreb in spring 1993 after I had escaped from Sarajevo. How could anyone be grateful to the Ustaše and not turn into a piece of shit?

My mother was born with her mother's fear, but Mladen was happy to have a younger sister. He mentions her in every letter and postcard, asking all the family members at Ilidža about her, whether they had seen her, how much she had grown, whether she was crawling. Nevenka would answer him, a precocious girl who knew and understood everything at the age of eight, even about the encamped German division there on the meadow in front of the house, in the direction of the future Butmir Airport, and the German major who slept in Karlo Stubler's house – something the old man was never happy about, though he spoke politely with his countryman – and the celebration on the tenth of April, when she too would give a presentation at a school assembly, and her little cousin Javorka, Mladen's sister, and his worry about the little girl he was thinking of far away in Stockerau, where German soldiers were being trained in preparation for the decisive battle for a free Europe, which would begin in the woods near Vienna, where Mladen and his comrades were shooting at paper Russians and Partisans as they jumped out from behind the bushes. From Nevenka's perspective, from her childish motherliness, everything was exciting and promising, as well as a lot to worry about, and she was ready to accept it. Correspondence with Mladen was a game to her, and all remained a game until the next death.

She wrote Mladen for the first time on Wednesday, February 9, 1943. She trembled with excitement and fear, it may have been the first letter she had written in her life. She wrote it on commercial paper in red ink. She wrote the first letter of Mladen's name in lower case, then corrected it to upper case. Someone was obviously overseeing her while she was writing. Probably Nano.

Dear Mladen!

Thank you for writing. I'm happy to know that you are well. Forgive me for not writing sooner. Are you eating Bosnian polenta there? Well, I learned to eat it too and Mara is already eating it a little bit. But just so you know, Mladen, we eat cakes and cookies whenever we have birthdays. Now Nano is teaching me how to write Gothic letters. When I learn how I'll write to Auntie Dora, and when you talk to her next time please tell her I said hello. For Christmas I got a dough maker and platter, a Petrica Kerempuh book from Dragan, and Letters from My Windmill, *and a book for paints and crayons, two notebooks for writing and one for arithmetic, an eraser, a compass, two pencil sharpeners.*

Hugs and kisses from your Nevenka Novak

Nevenka rewrote this letter in a clean copy, correcting the errors, and sent it on its way, but it never arrived. The next letter is dated Thursday, March 11, 1943.

She wrote it in pencil so she could erase her mistakes. It is difficult to read after seventy years' worth of the graphite flaking away from the smooth commercial paper. The sign of the military censor is easily visible, and the number 184415. A censor number was not usually found on letters.

Dear Mladen!

Please answer my letter right away. To say whether you've received and understood everything. Nano is teaching me to write Gothic script. When I've learned, I'll write to Auntie Dora. When you see her, please tell her hello. For Christmas I got the book Letters from My Windmill, *a coloring book, and a Petrica Kerempuh book, a dough maker, and a platter. Just so you know Mladen, we eat cakes and cookies whenever it's our birthday. When I write you funny things, do you laugh?*

With love and kisses, your Nevenka Novak

For the most part this letter is a copied version of the earlier one. Either the young girl didn't know what to write to her elder relative, or her Christmas presents were extremely important to her. She doesn't mention polenta anymore, but the Christmas cakes haven't gone very far from her head. The month is March, the Sarajevo winter is moving to its end, it is still at its coldest at the southern exits from the city, at the base of Mount Igman. The wind sweeps across the Butmir meadows, gathering up the sharp fine snow and slapping one in the face. 1943 was the first winter of real and widespread hunger, when the war was truly felt in the stomach. There was nothing but polenta and potatoes and the promise that there would be cakes and pastries for one's birthday.

The bees were quiet in the apiary. One did not dare disturb them lest they think spring had arrived. Franjo had left them enough honey for the winter, and Opapa made the rounds to check on them and make sure everything was in order and no one had broken in.

Army detachments would pass through Kasindol from time to time. They no longer marched as they had in the summer and spring, but walked normally, making their way on foot like the rest of us, their heads close to their shoulders. With time, in fear and trembling before death, the human body turns into a tortoise shell. The head retracts into it, disappearing; only the eyes stare out in all directions, on the look out for some armed avenger, a Partisan, who might jump out from the snow nearby and start shooting. Soldiers are afraid, and that fear soon becomes their strongest and perhaps their only conviction. What Nevenka was learning in school about military sacrifice for our beautiful homeland, about bravery and patriotism, all this was false. All that was left in the soldiers was fear.

Besides, they were not Croatian soldiers anymore. They had practically all disappeared from Kasindol. Since the beginning of the war until that winter, the Home Guard had passed by, marching, once or twice. The rest were all Germans. In trucks, in armored vehicles, the officers in black limousines, the infantry perfectly organized up in two long lines stretching out like a caterpillar. The German foot soldiers would pass by quietly, without a single word, their eyes fixed before them, until they grew aware of the world around them, and of their fear, and then they'd start to look around, their heads sinking between their shoulders, disappearing into the tortoise shell. This happened early in 1943, as the news of the catastrophe at Stalingrad spread.

At night, during Catholic and Muslim feast days, the Ustaše patrols would come around. Three or four drunk and disheveled young men would break into the garden, treading on the onion beds, shoot rounds into the sky, and blaspheme God in a loud voice. Somewhere below, in the dark, against the white walls of the Baškarad and Pavlović houses, shadows of people were cast, men, women, and children, and then, as if in a scene from Turkish shadow theater, the person observing could no longer tell whether there had been anything there at all. The drunk Ustaše youngsters, who had just returned from eastern Bosnia, from the bloodbath in which people had suffered and died, in which they had butchered and been butchered, but among whom a strict military discipline prevailed, now gave in to release as they tramped across the onion and lettuce beds, and in their drunkenness did not see the play of shadows on the white walls of the Pavlović and Baškarad houses. When they tramped around in the courtyards of the Serbian houses, of which there were three at the top of Kasindol, and pounded on the wooden doors with the butts of their rifles, shouting in the name of the

Poglavnik and Croatia, no one answered from inside. There was no one, not in the first house, or the second, or the third, and Đulaga, Ismet, and Jozo Posušak couldn't believe that the Vlach was not home at that hour of the night, and it was precisely at night that they had set out to butcher him, for it was his brothers who had butchered all the Croats around Rogatica, Prača, and Ustiprača, those who hadn't run away, including a three-month-old baby boy in a crib and his mother, and a blind hajji who was a hundred years old and hadn't done anything to anyone. And instead of waiting politely, which they would have done had they had any honor or respect, had their cross and their christening been worth anything, so they could answer for the child slaughtered in its crib, and the slaughtered mother, and the blind hajji Abdulrahim, also slaughtered, they had disappeared in the night! Đulaga and Ismet were not pleased, nor was Jozo Posušak, and they let their anger fly into the sky with bursts of fire, and then they headed for the Swabian's house, where the Vlach was hiding, everyone in Ilidža knew it, to call him out and interrogate him regarding the butchered Croatian child in its crib, the child's butchered mother, the butchered hajji, and all of butchered Croatia. Fuck him a hundred times over, would he have let his Germany get butchered? That's what they would ask him, Đulaga, Ismet, and Jozo Posušak, three sworn Ustaše and Croatian heroes, who would even ask the good Lord himself the same question, with a round in the face, if he were against Croatia.

Đulaga shook the door with the butt of his rifle, the same door that fifty years later the Chetnik Lugonja shook with the butt of his rifle. His gaze frozen, Karlo Stubler opened the door as if in a dream and spoke to Đulaga. Just as Nevenka opened the door fifty years later, as if in a dream, and spoke to Lugonja, though her gaze was not frozen. She was not afraid, for she had lived through this once, twice, five times before, though then she had been eight years old and now she was fifty-eight. She asked Lugonja, What do you want? I came to butcher you, Lugonja told her. What is it you're doing to the Serbs in Sarajevo? Who is doing that, Nevenka asked, me? Your people, Lugonja said. Where is your son, Nevenka? He went away, he wouldn't wait for you. Go back home, Lugonja, get some sleep. And what could Lugonja do but go away. Just as fifty years earlier

Đulaga, Ismet, and Jozo Posušak had left their work unfinished, though they knew that the Swabian's house was full of Vlachs. They didn't know what to do when a person looked them so coldly in the eye.

It was easier in the spring, when the German troops were on their way east, toward Albania, Macedonia, and Greece, and they had pitched their tents on the Butmir meadow, while their commander asked politely to be allowed to stay in the house. Opapa said yes – what else could he have done? – and it seemed it was easier for him to turn away Đulaga, Ismet, and Jozo Posušak from his house than to take in German officers. It did not matter that Opapa was against Hitler. The officers were not representatives of Hitler to him; he knew all too well how they had become what they were and how they had ended up in Bosnia. He knew they were in the same misery as his grandson. He did not like taking in such people because of his neighbors. Everyone knew in those days and weeks that a German officer was staying at the Stublers. And for Opapa it was important and always would be important what the neighbors on Kasindol thought. At any rate, it was more important than what some Đulaga, Ismet, and Jozo Posušak might think, or what his German compatriots might think. Opapa's life was such, by chance, destiny, and his will, that all that was left to him besides his flesh and blood was his neighbors on Kasindol. They were his people, his home, and his homeland, his entire *Blut und Boden*, for everything else had been split and dispersed, and by then, in spring 1943, there was no more Bosowicz, where he'd been born and where his people had lived for three hundred years. For him there were no Germans, there was no Germany, no railroad, no railroad coworkers; all this had disappeared and was in the process of disappearing, while those people, whose shadows flashed at night across the white walls of the Baškarad and Pavlović houses, really did exist. And he could not think about what they were thinking when a high-ranking German officer stayed at his house.

He confided once in his son-in-law Vilko, Rika's husband, How can you even think that, Opapa? They're happy and have the peace of God, because the moment the Germans set up camp in Butmir, the Usataše will disappear from Kasindol. But this did not calm him. Something here did not sit well with him, like a perfectly made key that did not fit the lock. Just as how he did not dare to think about Mladen, he could not stop thinking about this. Whenever he thought about his grandson, now in Stockerau training to become a German soldier, Karlo Stubler would rush to some other thought. From the start he had known about Olga's argument with Franjo about what should be done. About whether Mladen should report for the German conscription summons, or hide in the attic as a deserter, risking court-martial, or join the Partisans in the woods. Franjo was for having Mladen go to the Partisans. It was dangerous and risky, but it looked likely that in the end they would win. He said as much in June 1942, when things did not look at all hopeful to either of them. And it was true that Olga once said that those who took women from their homes in the middle of the night just because they were Jewish could not win. God would not allow such people to win. If they did, she said, it would be as if there was no God. She still believed then. But even so she was for Mladen's reporting for duty with the German army. The Germans were not the same as the Croats, nor were they the same as the Ustaše. They were a serious army, kept track of the lives of their soldiers, and the most important thing was that Mladen survive the war. This was what she said, and this was why Mladen answered the call.

Karlo, to whom all this was whispered at the table, which still featured the same rich Sunday lunch, looked first at one then at the other. He did not say anything but became rock hard. If he could have spoken, he would have said there was greater security in letting Mladen go to the Partisans. But rocks don't speak. If he hadn't become like a rock, and if words had not collapsed on top of him, like a house built with one's own hands struck by an earthquake, then Opapa would have agreed with Franjo: it looked like the Partisans would win. If that wasn't the case, then it was still better to go to them out of conscience. If they didn't win, life here would not be worth anything, for every night Đulaga, Ismet, and Jozo Posušak would knock on someone's door, and it was better to take your life into the woods than let them take it on the threshold of your house. This is what Karlo Stubler would have said to Olga and Franjo had he not become hard as rock. And had he not been afraid that he would only speak in such a way so as to free himself of his Germanness. He didn't want to be free of his Germanness. That would have been undignified. He had never done anything like that. He could have, and probably it would have been useful for him, to call himself a Croat or a Serb, since there were Serbs in Bosowicz, but he could never do such a thing. And now he had no right to send his grandson to the Partisans so that his grandson might free him, Karlo, of the horror of being German.

And so Mladen reported for duty. Everything was still in order at the time – the hives were carefully opened and the bees returned to the world after the long, tortuous winter slumber. Much had happened since the preceding autumn; the world had performed several somersaults, turning war into something that for Karlo and his family was unrecognizable. He always had his own way of thinking, which he did not hide and which had cost him a transfer from Dubrovnik to Bosnia, but he had lived in a world in which it really did not matter to anyone which side in the war was chosen by the railroad officials, the postal workers and their children, the Orthodox priests and their wives, the court reporters, innkeepers, barbers, grocery store managers, merchants, or the *kuferaši*, who had been tossed from one end of the empire to the other by imperial decrees. If such a person had his own way of thinking, it would not cost him his head. It had cost Karlo his life, true, for he was driven from a city where he was valued and respected, where he lived in a large house in Lapad, and it was likely that from his railway official's home he would have moved to a home he built himself, but that was still within the confines of the old imperial times. Perhaps he had flown off the handle and made a mistake in calling for a strike at a time when the Kingdom of the Serbs, Croats, and Slovenes had just been formed, and perhaps there would not have been the same consequences if he had done it five or six years later, but whenever it might have happened, Bosnia was never that unkind to him. Opapa consoled himself, but then came the war, and with it, suddenly, a time when the decisions of ordinary people became important, in such a way that it seemed we were not living our own little lives but a series of ancient tragedies, where the individual was in the hands of the gods who would decide his destiny, though it was up to him to oppose them. At times Karlo Stubler no longer knew whom to oppose. But he could not think about the decision they had made for Mladen. Such thoughts would have led him to madness. That was why he preferred not to think. Or to maintain that a mother and father knew what was best for their children.

But everyone agreed that it was important for Mladen to stay as long as possible in Stockerau. And he had already stayed for a long time, much longer than the training lasted while it seemed things were going well for the German forces on all fronts.

Everyone was writing to him then, making their characters and their nearly palpable anxiety evident in their letters. We sense it some seventy years later, as latter-day readers of letters not addressed to us. Mladen did not sense their anxiety. He was naked to the waist, sweaty, marching all morning, at target practice all afternoon, playing the guitar, and singing German songs. The Erika March too.

On the same commercial paper, Olga's sister, Aunt Rika, wrote him on January 1, 1943. She wrote in black ink, her handwriting hardly legible, the letters thin and sloping to the right, like a burnt pine forest.

Dear Mladen!

We received your letter. It makes me happy that you remembered us. I haven't been to see your mother in Sarajevo. I don't know when I'll be able to and I only know how they are from what you've written. We live here like hermits. We can't go to Sar. without a special permit. You seem to have found your way there. You wrote that you have not heard from us. I did write, but it seems you have not received my letter.

We spent Christmas as humbly as you can possibly imagine. We didn't even have sugar for cakes. I wrote you that Onkel Vili was sick, now he's better and will start his service on May 11 in Prača.

The one thing for now is we are all healthy again, and we aren't refugees like last year but are back in our apartment, small as it might be.

As you know, the Germans have left. Opapa wanted to leave, but his health would not allow it so he is nervous and everything irritates him.

Željko was here on Christmas Eve. He is well. He's gained eight pounds. Not at all surprising. It's not good here, but it's worse in Dubrovnik, so the poor fellow ate a lot of Srem cutlets. They were hanging around Fruška Gora while there were grapes on the vines, and he said he'd never eaten so many in his life.

Otherwise nothing has changed here. We have some eggplant. The poor bees have buzzed themselves out, but your papa can't come to see them because he can't get out of Sarajevo without a special permit. And they won't give a permit on account of bees. Opapa takes care of them the best he can. So does Onkel Vili, though he does not quite know how. The bees know that your papa isn't around and they don't like it. They'll give honey anyway. I'm sorry Aunt Dora hasn't been able to visit you. Maybe you'll be able to go to them. Say hello for us. Write again soon.

With best wishes for your health,
Your Tante Rika

On the other side of the page, Uncle Vilko writes:

Dear Mladen!
Here I'll just add a couple of words. As Tante Rika mentioned, thank God I'm back to health now, but for a while there I was quite sick. The climate here is fairly mild, so I won't have to spend the whole winter in Prača. Your mother told me when I was at her place that you would come down as soon as you have a few days of leave.
I see from your letter that you've become a veritable soldier and it isn't a hardship for you. If only this were a different time and everyone could be home. Otherwise, there's not much to report.

Wishing you well,
Onkel Vili

Nevena is writing and will send her letter separately.

The modest Christmas would continue to be the subject until Easter, which would also be modest, and which, in 1943, would be celebrated by Catholics and Orthodox on the same day, April 25. Aunt Rika was "Tante" as she had always been, while Uncle Vilko was "Onkel Vili." They liked that Mladen referred to them this way. Or they might have also thought that it would please the German censor. In the part of the letter written by Aunt Rika there was at least one detail written expressly for the censor: "As you know, the Germans have left. Opapa wanted to leave, but his health would not allow it, so he is nervous and everything irritates him."

When at the end of 1942 the Germans in Sarajevo and Ilidža were listed for repatriation with the aim of firming up the German national territory, those who made the lists were not as forceful as in other parts of the country. People were allowed to choose whether or not to move to Germany, where, it was true, they were promised a house, mostly in the cities and towns of Silesia and eastern Prussia. Old Stubler was thus offered the opportunity of settling in Lemberg, Polish Lviv, which after the war would belong to Ukraine and become part of the Soviet Union. Karlo politely, in the name of his entire family, thanked them for this offer. Some maintain he had explained that two of his daughters were married to men from the local community, one a Dubrovnik native, the other a Travnik native, and not even the third, Regina, could say that her husband was a true German, so it made no sense for an old man to move to that beautiful, far-off city. Others claim that he said nothing, just signed the paper that said he was not moving.

Those who signed such a paper were merely warned that by remaining where they were they might no longer find themselves under the protection of the German Reich, but would instead share the fate of the local population.

In the end, few Sarajevo Germans or Austrians accepted the call for repatriation and resettlement in Germany. Those who had thought of going had left after 1918. Besides, they were secretly listening to Radio London, news and rumors were spreading fast and what was happening with the German armies to the east was not reassuring. Those who did end up leaving, and from whom nothing was heard ever again, did not so much answer the call of the Greater German Reich as decide it was better to escape the Ustaše and the Ustaše regime – which was more of an illusion of a regime, since all the neighboring woods, mountains, and suburbs of the large cities were full of Partisans and Chetniks – and they did not know when the Independent State would run out of Serbs and Jews and the

Ustaše would turn their anger against them, the *kuferaši*. These people made the same fateful mistake Olga and Franjo made when they led Mladen to report for the call of duty. They felt that the German soldiers, particularly in comparison with the Ustaše, were polite and proper in every sense.

Aunt Rika was a kind, happy woman, the most reasonable of Karlo's daughters. She accepted the conditions of life as they were and tried to find a way to deal with them. Where Olga and Aunt Lola were prepared to engage in crazy things and to rebel, she looked for solutions as to how she and Uncle Vilko might make it through life and the frightening twentieth century. She looked after Opapa and Omama, and after Rudi, who needed looking after, as he would never become his own man. When Karlo lost his strength, or when he drew back into a sort of internal seclusion, Aunt Rika took over as head of the family. She did not choose this role for herself, rather it fell to her with the drama which the Stubler family spun to the end of its history.

Aunt Rika did not have any distinct talents, again by contrast to her sisters and her brother Rudi. She was average in everything, balanced, ordinary, as if she were more closely tied to her Italian grandmother, Josefina Patat, who made her way with a sure hand through the immense poverty of her entire life, giving birth to children for as long as God expected it of her, and never asking him to settle her life's accounts. Seventeen times Josefina bore a child, fifteen of whom died before the age of seven. Mostly from poverty and childhood illnesses. Omama survived with her sister, who later got married in Mostar, but she too was not long for this life. Josefina Patat lived with her son-in-law Karlo Stubler and her daughter Ivana, and they took her with them as they moved farther into Bosnia, approaching but never arriving in Dubrovnik. She died in Konjic, where Olga was born. Her grave was there.

Simple like her grandmother, Aunt Rika was very funny. She was ready to turn any misfortune into a joke, fooling around, and trying to trick the authorities in minor ways, ingratiating herself with the German military censors, showing that she was a good German, our good Tante Rika, who with Onkel Vili, represented a brave, self-sacrificing, and sober-minded German family, about which one might even make a movie.

The language of her letter is odd. The vocabulary along with her lexical eccentricities were evident since her adolescence in Dubrovnik, where the Stubler children attended school. Aunt Rika did not read much, except for Holy Writ and humorous books in German, so she wrote the way she had learned in Dubrovnik at the beginning of the century. There is something touching in this lovely blending of old Ragusan and Volksdeutsche petit bourgeois poetics, transplanted to Ilidža's Kasindol Street in Bosnia. Although Aunt Rika didn't care much about identity, but rather tried to adapt to the times and her family's surroundings, her letter is a metaphor for all our impossible Stubler identities.

Between Sarajevo and Ilidža there was a police checkpoint with a border, which was more heavily guarded than the future borders between states. In the winter and spring of 1943, to get to the other side one had to produce a *special permit*. Obviously at that point it was not just a formality, for if it had been Aunt Rika would have gladly applied for permission, received a permit, and gone across to see her sister in town. The border was put there to keep people in a state of fear and could result in the murder of anyone who, on whatever basis, might take it into his head to request a special permit. In writing to Mladen, and hiding her fear of what might be happening to him, she twice mentions the permit. At the beginning and at the end. First she can't get to Sarajevo, so she doesn't know what is happening with Olga and Franjo. And then Franjo can't get to his bees, so Opapa and Vilko have to take care of them.

Uncle Vilko was a cheerful, simple man, like his wife, but less adept at life than she was. He was a rail man and the son of a union activist who had taken in Karlo Stubler and his family after they had to leave Dubrovnik. The Stublers had even lived in his home for a time, which was how young Vilko fell in love with Karlo's daughter. Although everything evolved from self-interest, given that Novak had saved the Stublers from homelessness, it very quickly turned into an ordinary form of young people's love and then a marriage that resembled so many other marriages. Though the Stublers had arrived at the Novaks' hearth, no strife arose from this, nor was there ever any question about who had come into whose home, or who had arrived as dirt-poor folk from Dubrovnik. If there were any problems in their marriage, they were never related to this. They built a house together, into which their mother and father later moved. This was not a problem either. For years before the war, and then at its very start, Uncle Vilko had worked in Prača. He was a communications specialist and repairmen for telephones and other communications technology. He had two trades, and he was good at both and prized for them. But Prača was a tiny, lost, east Bosnian backwater, which had slowly begun to develop after the Austro-Hungarians built the tracks that lead to Višegrad. (In school it was taught that this track had been placed so that artillery could be transported in the future war against Serbia, but this, from whichever point one looks at it, was an exaggeration.) For a long time this track would remain the only connection between Sarajevo and the greater part of eastern Bosnia. The roads were old, Turkish, muddy, messy, and narrow, so the way one got to Višegrad was along the slow, narrow-gauge track.

They say it was good to be working on the railroad in Prača in the late thirties. A quaint place full of fresh air, water, and greenery. Whoever moved there had no worries other than keeping the trains arriving and departing on schedule, maintaining the track, and making sure the telegraph and postal traffic was working properly. Everything else was godly peace, sweetness, and a slow-paced life, with long days such that everything happened in its own good time. One could chat with people, have a coffee, a glass of rakija, wait for the train, watch the people get out of the train cars.

Bad news took a long time to reach Prača, or never reached it at all, so that not even the news that war had broken out in Europe made an impression. People knew about it, they read the newspapers and listened to the radio, but in that meadow, among calm, reasonable people (and only such people lived in Prača, for anyone unreasonable took immediate flight) the war seemed terribly distant and foreign. To those living in Prača in 1939 or during March 1941, when everything was still covered in snow, it was not easy to imagine all the horrors of the world. To those living in paradise, the stories people tell about hell appear exaggerated and implausible.

Nevertheless, in the middle of April 1941, Uncle Vilko and Aunt Rika sent Nevenka to Ilidža to stay with Omama and Opapa. It would take several months for the war to reach Prača and bring to an end this idyll.

It so happened that in 1941 several well-known families were waiting in Prača and their journeys decades later would intersect with ours.

The station chief was Ibrahim beg Mulalić, an unusual, quite elegant man, a foreigner in the land where he was born. There are such people: they do not put down roots or become accustomed to a place, even the place where they are from. The Mulalićs acquired their Turkish noble status after the Ottomans lost Hungary. They had been Hungarian Muslims who resettled in Bosnia, where they were foreigners, and Ibrahim beg had, centuries later, inherited something from that time of wandering.

Ibrahim beg married Štefanija, a Habsburg Pole and lifelong Catholic believer, whose faith shaped all her identities and feelings of belonging but which did not prevent her from enjoying a true and lasting love. The couple loved and respected one another, and Prača, with its remoteness from all civilization, was an ideal place for their life.

Štefanija's parents had escaped from Poland in the nineteenth century. They were escaping from farther east, from the Russians in who knows what war, and they brought with them just two religious objects: a crucifix and a painting of the Mother of God, reminiscent of a Russian icon. The Christ on the wooden crucifix was made of porcelain. With time and their various moves, the wood rotted completely. The Son of God remained with his wide-open arms, without a cross. This was how Štefanija would bequeath it to her granddaughter Mirela upon her death in the '70s. Mirela would wait out the new war and the siege of Sarajevo in her Hrasno apartment. The Christ was attached with thin nails to the wall of her bedroom, where a grenade landed in spring 1992. Nothing was left of the room or the wall but the porcelain Christ, which gently landed onto a demolished ottoman amid plaster, dust, and pieces of concrete.

The families Novotni, Misirlić, and Lončarić also found themselves in Prača in the spring of 1941. Rade Džeba, the father of our Sepetarevac neighbor Slavica Šneberger was there too. Josip and Beba Lončarić were friends of Olga and Franjo's. They had three children. Their son Mladen was named after our Mladen, after he had been laid to rest beneath the earth of Slavonia.

At the beginning, nothing was out of the ordinary. The trains heading for

Višegrad proceeded according to schedule. The Germans were hardly to be seen, and the Ustaše had taken power only to depart quickly. It was a beautiful, rich, yet ominous summer. From the banks of the Drina one could hear bursts of machine gun fire at night. Rumors spread – no one could confirm them – that the Ustaše had burned down and slaughtered an entire Serbian village. They had done this, apparently, out of revenge, but no one said what the revenge was for.

And then in one day the world shattered.

The Chetniks poured into Prača, booming and shooting from all directions, and everything came apart with such lightning speed that the railway workers and local Muslim population barely had time to escape, and they fled with empty hands. The small squad of Ustaše charged with protecting the station and the post office building quickly broke down, taking little account of what would happen to the people. The Chetniks were hungry for revenge, and they seemed to take revenge on anyone they could. They fired at the innocent people, who ran along the tracks, which was for many their only point of orientation, since all around was forest. Although many had been in service in Prača since Austrian times, they knew nothing about the forests, the mountains, or how to travel except by thoroughfare, road, or track. They had remained the same city people they were when they had been assigned to live in this heavenly realm, and so they stuck to the tracks, making them easy and entertaining targets for those who had come to exact their revenge.

Rade Džeba was fortunate; he escaped all the way to eastern Herzegovina, from where it was later easy for him to return to Sarajevo. But he did not live much longer. It was said he was working on a track somewhere, washed his hair, and while it was still wet went to run a handcar. From this he became ill and died. It was 1942.

Tante Rika and Uncle Vilko set out in the opposite direction, toward Pale. How they fared no one actually remembers. Those who knew the story have all died. The exodus of Tante Rika and Uncle Vilko, in all its horror, happened within the reality of a war. Then it turned into a story the two of them enjoyed telling, then into a family story, which everyone else passed on, and then into a legend. Tante Rika died in 1966, several months before my birth, then a decade later Uncle Vilko died. The legend paled with time, for people were no longer concerned about the Chetnik offense against Prača. Only Olga's pronouncement would be remembered: "My sister escaped from Prača with a naked fanny."

The station chief Ibrahim beg Mulalić did not escape but, calmly, in accord with his old Turkish and Viennese sense of duty, waited for the Chetniks at his railway post in the deserted Prača. Everyone else had run away, and for good reason. The Muslims of Prača escaped before all the rest, because the Chetniks were angriest with them, for it was against them that an entire array of vengeful acts had accumulated in the course of an epoch, recalled with the help of the gusle and the epic ten-line poem known as the *deseterac*.

Like an honorable sailor who remains on a sinking ship, Ibrahim beg did not flee Prača with the rest. He calmly accepted it, without ceremony or a farewell, though there was no longer a state. Nothing was left, including those who might have remembered and praised his actions, nor anything that could absolve him of his responsibility to his position. Ibrahim beg could not surrender his charge of honor; he quietly accepted what destiny had determined for him. There was no great story in this, nor would there ever be.

In their fury the Chetniks rushed into Prača. In this war, people were transformed in accordance with the symbols on their caps. It was a Biblical tempest, but each apocalypse was distinct from the others. Countless family memories were destroyed and it was not possible to record and memorialize all of them.

But they did not touch the stationmaster. He waited for them in his uniform; they knew his name well, but when they spoke with him, they did not address him by name but like everyone else by his title, Ibrahim beg. He responded exactly as was required. For the entire time that the Chetniks were in Prača, before they were driven out, Ibrahim beg Mulalić performed his duty. If there were no trains, and there could not be any since the line had been cut, he maintained the station so that everything would be ready for the next train, in accord with the railway timetable and the regulations of service, which never changed among employees of the railroad. Once he had been transferred to Sarajevo and later retired from service, Ibrahim beg Mulalić would calmly accept this change too. It was enough for a paper to be signed, countersigned, and registered in order for people to carry out what the most disciplined army in the world could not, let alone an unruly band of Chetniks. The man's personality had been formed in an unusual blend of Kafkaesque bureaucratic zeal and Oriental calm. This was how Ibrahim beg was in life, and that is how he should be portrayed in the novel that ought to be written about him. His dramatic climax and finale was not the moment he received the Chetniks in Prača, nor in their departure from the place, which would never again be as it had been.

After the war Ibrahim beg Mulalić and his Polish wife Štefanija, whose family had been driven from their Polish homeland in a way equally horrible as certain people today are being driven from theirs, lived in peace and tranquility among their own in Sarajevo as their final days arrived. And then after Štefanija's death Ibrahim beg decided to convert to Catholicism. He did this after having lived his life with integrity and in an orderly fashion, keeping to all the rules that were proper to him as a Muslim. But when the end came, it was important to Ibrahim beg that he lie beside Štefanija in the same grave. This was the sole reason he wanted to be christened as a Catholic. He did not want to work through connections and shortcuts, expose his children to risk or burden them with how or where to bury him but instead organized everything so that it would all be according to the law – to the state's and then to God's. His desire was satisfied, and he lies in a Catholic parcel in Bare, awaiting the day of his resurrection.

The last preserved postcard that Mladen sent from Stockerau to Ilidža is the only one without a date. There are two stamps on the paper: a German one dated May 7, 1943, and one from Ilidža dated May 17, 1943. The fact that the post office placed its stamp after the military censor's examination is clear from the ten days it took for a letter to get from Vienna to Sarajevo in May of that year. The year before the same journey had taken half as long.

The postcard is made of yellowish cardboard with a design similar to peace-time postcards, with an equal number of lines of the same length for writing the name and address of the addressee but without a designated space for stamps.

Instead there is the word *Feldpost*. No longer are there any sweeping warnings about the rules of military correspondence. Instead, diagonally across the space shared by the address and the message are the words "Entnommen aus 'Soldaten-blätter für Freizeit,' herausgegeben vom OKW," and beneath this "Offsetdruk: Bibliographiches Institut AG., Leipzig, Graphischer Großbetrieb." By contrast to 1942, the printer had made a small addition to his 1943 postcards. In the lower left portion of the obverse a small, seasonal cartoon had been appended. Two German soldiers in helmets and winter coats stand under a smiling sun as an abominable snow monster melts before their eyes. On the right side of the picture, the leaves on a tree reach up into the sky where a wild goose is flying, perhaps returning from the south.

Surprisingly, the drawing is signed. The artist Hugo Frank, who did the illustrations for both the winter and the summer postcards, was born in Stuttgart in 1892 and died in Gerlingen in 1963. His drawings can occasionally be found on Internet auction sites. Prints of military postcards from 1943, with cartoon illustrations by Hugo Frank, can be purchased for five euros a piece. The content of a postcard does not affect the price.

Dear Nena,

I'm writing you again because I have time. Tell Nano that I didn't get the newspapers he sent, but he should send some again. It makes us happy to get the Sarajevo papers. Are you planning to start swimming soon? We'll soon be going to a great big lake and we'll be able to swim all summer. What is Opapa doing? What grade are you going into? Say hello to your mother and father, and to Omama, Opapa, and Nano. And Javorka when you see her.

With much love,
Your Mladen

He was distracted and not quite up for writing. He writes that he'll be going with the army to a lake that he'll swim in throughout the summer. He made this up.

He writes "great big lake" because that's how one speaks to children. "A *greeaaat biiiig* lake, bigger than the ocean . . . " When he was in good spirits and could concentrate, Mladen spoke with Nevenka as if she were an adult.

In 1942 during the first period of wartime famine, the family in Ildiža prepared a Christmas package for Mladen. They acquired special licenses, brought food to Sarajevo, baked hardtack that would not spoil on the road, and in the midst of all this activity, they forgot where Mladen was and what soon awaited him. He would be defending the Great German Reich with rifle and machine gun. Then we would disappear and the war would finally be over. And no one would remember that our Mladen had defended the Great German Reich, shooting at paper Russians and Partisans and marching upon the asphalt trails in Stockerau.

There had to be enough in the package for Mladen to share with his comrades. In the German military there were strict rules – the rule of solidarity in everything. Franjo would send him two jars, one with honey from Ilidža, the other with honey from Grabovica. The Grabovica honey was from 1940, our last peacetime summer. He would share it in the morning with his comrades, each getting a spoonful of honey as they lay in their bunks, remembering what peace felt like. It was not good for a soldier at war to forget what peace was like. Franjo knew this. He had fought in the last war and been taken prisoner in 1915, thank God, by the Italians. As soon as they had changed sides, betrayed the Habsburgs and gone over to the French, English, and Americans, they had taken him prisoner. He did not hold it against them.

He wrapped the honey jars in newspaper so they would not break. Mladen unwrapped them on the evening of December 23, 1942. Nothing was crushed or broken. The package had been wrapped in the blue packing paper from which his mother had once made protective covers for his school books and notebooks.

Mladen unwrapped the jars with honey, but he did not throw out the sheets of old newspaper in which they'd been wrapped. Franjo had wrapped one in the Cyrillic print pages of *Politika*, from October 23, 1940. Mladen pressed it out with the back of his hand. That evening he would have something to read.

His father had wrapped a piece of honeycomb in a white handkerchief and sent it to him – it was good for a sore throat. Mladen broke off a sticky piece and put it in his mouth. He sensed the distant flavor of honey and the flavor of the most perfect architecture in nature, more perfect than anything a man could create with his hands. More perfect than the Sistine Chapel and its ceiling paintings, the pyramids of Egypt, the skyscrapers of Chicago, Westminster Palace, Paris's Notre-Dame Cathedral, even than Sarajevo's own Vijećnica. Every honeycomb was a perfect structure. Its flavor was a dull sweetness. The next morning little pieces of honeycomb would remain stuck between his teeth, and he would not be able to brush them out for a long time.

Winter apples, tiny and gnarled, from the Ilidža garden. Mladen smells one. The apple smells of them all, and now he sees them all more clearly than ever. Opapa, Omama, Aunt Rika, and Uncle Vilko, "Uncle Vili," as they're now calling him, his father and mother, and the rabbits from the Ilidža hutch, and the bees . . . The buzzing of thousands of bees envelops the garden on Kasindol. A three-dimensional picture of the garden emerges, in springtime and late summer, when the winter apples begin to ripen, amid the buzzing and the scent of the apples, and before his eyes the figure of a stooped old man with a beard appears, plucking weeds among the strawberry patches. This is Opapa; it is because of Opapa that he is in Stockerau. If not for him, Mladen would not be a German. Just as he would not be a Slovene if not for his father. Nor would he be a Yugoslav if not for the Great Boys Gymnasium across from the Officers Home. On the young king's birthday, and on the anniversary of the resurrection of the country of the Southern Slavs, they would sit at their desks and sing: Yugoslavia is our mother and our beautiful home . . . Only two years later everything would change, Mladen would be a Croat, and everyone around him in the Great Boys Gymnasium would suddenly be Croats. The Jews would have disappeared, hiding out in the woods above Betanija and Jagomir, and up on Trebević, or they were not saving themselves: they were simply not around. A year later Mladen is a German. This is the last thing he would be in his life, but this he does not know before Christmas in 1942 as he sniffs the apple from the Ilidža garden.

On Saturday, May 23, 1943, in the early afternoon, when Opapa was in his deckchair in front of the poplar, leafing through the 1910 edition of the Brockhaus Encyclopedia, a messenger in a Home Guard uniform arrived and asked for Rudolf Stubler.

Rudi's eyes filled with tears as he signed the summons.

He was to report at the assembly point in Butmir on Monday at seven o'clock.

Sunday was the last day of Rudi's life. He did not speak to anyone, he just walked around the garden. He called his bees and they came to him. They were not bothered by the scent of his sweat. It wasn't important now that Franjo wasn't there; they were parting in their quiet bee way. They touched his palm with their little legs, and Nano experienced it as a special and final tenderness in his life. Self-pitying, wretched, and alone, Home Guard Second Lieutenant Rudolf Stubler was saying farewell to the world. He was saying farewell to the bees who left their pollen along the hollow lines of his life and happiness, which he would pass on to the handrails of the train cars that would carry him to the north of Bosnia. He was parting with the garden and the meadows of Butmir from which the bees had collected pollen, and with his parents and sister and with the rabbits that were even more afraid than he was.

Nano's final Sunday, after which he did not sleep the entire night.

In May, it was still dark at five a.m. Rudi turned on the light and put on the Home Guard uniform that had been issued to him several months earlier. In the interim he had got work at the stokehold, an important responsibility, without which the state could not function, he thought, consoling himself that this work would free him from the army.

Rudi, my son, his father comforted him, a complete idiot can work at the stokehold. It's better for everyone if an idiot is not in command of an army.

I am a complete idiot, Rudi answered.

Unfortunately for you, you aren't.

Opapa worried about Rudi. He was his son after all, but it bothered him that Rudi had constantly been whining since being called up for military service.

He would be alive at the end of the war. Everyone knew this, and no one believed that anything would happen to Nano. His eyes were filled with tears;

Franjo called them Italian tears. They were a sure guarantee that Rudi would live through the war unharmed.

They were all on their feet before he left.

They hugged and kissed him, told him to take care of himself.

Omama.

Opapa.

Vilko was in Prača; he was not around.

Rika.

Nevenka.

Nano did not lift her in the air but instead leaned down to kiss her, as if he had grown weak or Nevenka heavier.

A yellowish postcard with a counterfeit two-kuna stamp with a picture of the Zagreb Cathedral, taken from the eastern end of Tuškanac. The trees of the Archbishop's Palace on Kaptol are visible as well as two guard towers. The stamp is red to match the braiding that crisscrosses the upper quarter of the card, disappearing beneath the cathedral and then reappearing and continuing to the edge of the card. On top of the braiding, in the left corner, is a Croatian coat of arms in the shape of a shield and above it, the letter *U* in a more intricate braid, atop which are the words *Independent State of Croatia* in all caps. The name of the printing press is not indicated.

Nano writes in blue ink. His handwriting is much more attractive than Mladen's. He still has the handwriting of a youth – he pays no attention to the rules of penmanship, thin and sloped, thick and straight, but rather writes in a free and unbridled manner. One can tell by the shapes of his letters whether he is in good spirits or preoccupied.

Nano's writing is skilled, harmonious, beautiful. Nano wrote the uppercase *N* in exactly the same manner as Javorka. (They are no longer alive, and I surely look at it now in a way I would not have if they were. I think when she was a girl she saw how Nano wrote his *N*, copied it, and practiced it for the rest of her life. Many of our letters appear as if we copied them from someone, even when our handwriting is poor.)

Dear Nena, here I have safely arrived in Bijeljina. The trip went well. It is beautiful here, but Ilidža is prettier. It looks as though I'll be staying here for a long time. The garden will ripen and you and Opapa will have harvested it by the time I return. We won't be going for a swim in the Željeznica or going for bike rides. Write me sometime if you remember.

With warm regards,
Your Nano

And then, a line below:

Dear Rika, I arrived without complications. I had to spend the night in Šid. The conditions here are not nearly as good as they once were. Everything is expensive or impossible to find.

Regards to you and Vilko,
Rudi

By contrast to Mladen, Nano tries to use the newly introduced root-based spelling system, and he does a good job of it. He was interested in such matters and understood the etymological roots of words, the formations of sounds, grammar, and orthography. He had taught these, as well as mathematics, to generations of Stubler children. Whoever started school acquired Nano as a tutor for the subjects that were not going well: math, physics, chemistry, grammar and orthography, solfège and music reading, Latin, Greek, and German, botany and zoology, pressing plants for the herbarium.

Mladen writes exactly as he did at the gymnasium. There must be a reason for his stubbornness. In his military trunk from Stockerau he carried a book with him that several months earlier he had asked be sent from home. The author: Antun Bonifačić. The title: *Paul Valéry*. The Valéry monograph is one of the few possessions of Mladen's that Olga would not hide, throw in the trash, or burn. It would be waiting for me in the library at our home when, as a thirteen-year-old, I became interested in French poetry, in Valéry, and in my uncle who had died as an enemy combatant. In the upper-right corner of the title page, written in green ink, is "Mladen Rejc 1943." He wrote his first and last name so his comrades wouldn't steal the book. In the year 1943, at Stockerau near Vienna, the Bosnian soldiers in the SS unit composed of Volksdeutsche and *kuferaši* were reading Paul Valéry. But why had he written the year next to his name? Could he have had a premonition that this was the year he was destined to die? Perhaps so. On every available scrap of paper, in his letters and in his books, Mladen wrote the date with the year. After the war these numbers would be magic. 1943. That number meant more than any word of the Croatian language. Of the Serbo-Croatian language, whose rules of orthography he had studied, as I would.

Nano too was interested in Valéry, but not for the same reason as Mladen. Nano had no interest in politics. Or he was afraid of politics, the way every minority member or misfit fears politics, if he is aware of being a minority. And Nano was very much aware of his minority status, which was why he would write "Croat" on Opapa's death notice under nationality. This would happen after the war, and thus would Karlo Stubler become in death someone he had never been. Reflecting on the summer of 2013, with the approach of another long winter without them all, it seems to me that grandfather and grandson traded places in death. Mladen died as a German, Opapa as a Croat, while in life Opapa was the German and Mladen was the Croat.

Mladen was not afraid of politics.

We have sold our flag.

He wrote these words in a letter he sent from Vienna after visiting Aunt Dora. The letter did not pass through the military censor. Olga burned it along with all of Mladen's other letters after the war, but they remembered this sentence of his. Jovorka would repeat it to me on her deathbed, when I asked about her brother.

No one knew what flag Mladen had been thinking of. But it was clearly understood that the sentence concerned politics. Out of all the letters Mladen had written to his parents, this was the one phrase that endured. All the rest burned up, or died along with those who might have remembered them.

In late spring and early summer, Rudi was in Bijeljina. Željko had not yet been transferred to Rajlovac but was in Šid and Fruška Gora for training. Mladen was in eastern Slavonia, near Županja.

They were near to one another but did not once meet.

Nano's letter to Nevenka arrived first:

Dear Nena,

I received your card today. Thank you! You made me very happy. I was glad to read your news. It's been raining here, I can't go out. It's hard because I don't have anyone close. It's evening. I've lit a lamp and am talking with you, even if by the post. When I can I look for lice, for I've got those here. I've only just arrived here and can hardly wait until I'm back home again. How are you? Do you go to school? Are you studying hard? Are there soldiers at the school? How are my bees, are they getting along without me? Has there been any plague? It would make me very happy if you wrote again. If I can, I'll send you something so you can buy yourself some cherries. Say hello to your papa and mama.

A big kiss.

Your Nano

Second Lieutenant Rudolf Stubler, I Section Verification Bijeljina

Nano complains to his little niece, telling her that he exterminates lice when he has the time. That was his way: he spoke about whatever was hard for him, by contrast to Mladen, who was heroic. Everyone was proud of Mladen, and in their pride they forgot about the war and who was fighting whom. Nano was fearful, and so his part in the war was not taken seriously. It was as if Mladen was sending his letters and postcards from some distant future time, which they still had to live through. He did not talk about hunger or lice. Perhaps German soldiers did not have lice.

When the rain had let up, the Croatian Home Guard under the command of Second Lieutenant Stubler dug trenches in the plain, cleared the stubble so the enemy could not sneak up on them, and reinforced the defenses of the main city of Semberija. Bijeljina was vulnerable from all sides and difficult to defend. Then it started to rain again and the second lieutenant withdrew them to their barracks. The trenches filled with rainwater, which flooded in from all sides, and large, well-fed lice came out of the straw to tuck themselves away in the soldiers' chests, in their armpits, between their legs. They shaved their heads , not out of military discipline but because of those accursed Serbo-communist lice that swam through the trenches from the east, crossing the Drina, the Danube, and the Sava as they moved toward Bosnia to consume their souls. Second Lieutenant Stubler did not need to be shaved like the majority of others. He'd been twenty-two and twenty-three when he lost his hair. At first it had turned soft as a baby's, and then, slowly, in the course of a year, he went bald. He shaved off what remained on his crown, and it did not bother him at all to appear before the beauties of Graz and Vienna without hair. Nor did it bother Dora Dussel, the aunt who visited Mladen when he was in the barracks, and whom he would visit in Vienna whenever he had a free day. Rudi had fallen passionately in love with her though she was his cousin. Rudi was nearly thirty and by then had spent his youth in cafés, nightclubs, and bordellos, never finding time for his studies, when the news that he had taken up with Dora reached Karlo Stubler in Ilidža. Karlo wrote him a letter ordering him to come home immediately. He had no choice but to obey. It was a great big scandal, although they were not such close relations that were they to marry it would be against the law.

Rudi had shamed him, but this subject was never discussed, though everyone knew about the affair that ended Nano's education. Probably Mladen did too – it was impossible that he could not have – when he went to visit Dora at her apartment to take a shower and wash off all the military filth. Did he picture Dora as Nano's lover? What did she look like then? Not fifteen years had passed since the affair, so she could not have changed all that much. Like Rudi, Dora Dussel never married.

While exterminating lice in the barracks which stank of kerosene, wet wool, dirty socks, and men's bodies, Rudi thought about his cousin Dora. It was impossible for him at that moment not to think about her. Dora was the first of two women Rudi fell truly in love with. With the second, a Muslim woman from Mostar, he fell in love, and fatally so, in the middle of the thirties. He wanted to marry her and went to Mostar to propose, but her family wanted to kill him as he was of a different faith. As far as love was concerned, that had been the end. For a long time after the war he did not travel to Mostar. At the time, on that rainy June afternoon of 1943, he still believed he would never again go to Mostar. He did not want to think about that woman, whose name we don't know. He committed himself to celibacy. Never again, never again, for he could not bear the thought that she had rejected him in the end. He proposed that they run away, live somewhere far off, free from family. She did not want that. She would rather die.

This was why he thought about Dora. He had been a disgrace at Ilidža, for a long time he could not look his father in the eyes, but now there was no longer anything to be ashamed of. While exterminating the lice in the Bijeljina Home Guard barracks, which smelled of kerosene, wet uniforms, and men's bodies, Rudi talked with Dora Dussel. He complained to her, his eyes filling with tears. He shouldn't have listened to his father and gone back home. This was his and Dora's life, regardless of how angry Opapa might have been. With courage, they could have lived their life.

Then he took a postcard and wrote: "I've lit a lamp and am talking with you, even if by the post." He wrote to little Nevenka, not to Dora. Rudi's letters to Dora Dussel, which must have been numerous, were likely destroyed. Even if they happen to exist, they are probably in the possession of some tradesman who deals in military letters from the Second World War. Written in German, a language better suited to the sort of sentimentality to which Rudi was inclined, these letters would be especially valuable.

Nano was worried about the bees. Like Franjo, he had an idée fixe about the beekeeper and about bee civilization. The beehives were nations of their own, nations that belonged to human civilization. They had grown accustomed to the bees, to the feel of their little feet on their palms. No two bees were alike, just as no two human beings were. To stop the spread of infection, they would be killed at twilight with gas, burned, and buried in the garden. The longer the war continued, the more this image came to Rudi's mind. A summer evening, the stench of rotten bees, black smoke whirling into the sky, then a shallow grave, and that would be the end. Whatever was destroyed in the face of the plague, for which there was no cure other than destroying all the bees, always meant the end of one bee civilization. It was as unrepeatable as Atlantis. To save the other bees and beehives from the epidemic, it was essential to destroy the infected ones.

He asks the girl about the bees, more to complain to her than for her to actually respond. What could she know about the bees anyway?

"If I can, I'll send you something so you can buy some sweet cherries." This "something" is apparently money. But this is a word one does not use in polite conversation. He mentions lice, he mentions plague, but money he refers to discreetly as "something." Money for the Stublers was a dirty word, which is perhaps why they never had it.

Karlo Stubler planned the yard at Ilidža according to all the rules of a good and well-ordered garden, beginning with beds in which he planted green onions, beans, peas, snap peas, lettuce, and Macedonian tomatoes, beds with sweet berries, and then, closer to the apiary, beds with black and red currants, raspberries, and gooseberries. Then apple trees, placed according to variety and time of ripening, in military four-deep files, and then a couple of pear trees, several Damson plums, a sour cherry tree close to the fence, and a walnut tree right at the border, so it would belong to both the Stublers and the Pavlovićs. For a half century Opapa nurtured his garden kingdom.

A thick receipt had been preserved, two and a half centimeters wide and the length of a postcard, the date June 15, 1943 on the seal, the place-name: Bijeljina. "Receipt may be removed," and beneath that, "Remittance due," and then in green ink: "100 Kunas." Payee: Second Lieutenant Rudolf Stubler, I Sec. Verif. Bijeljina. It is interesting that on the postal seal and below is written Bijeljina. On the back of the receipt, "Space for message":

Dear Nena, I received your letter and it made me very happy. And the picture is nice! Here I enclose something for you to buy cherries.
Greetings to you, your father and mother
For now we have no bacon, nor can packages be sent.
Your Nano

The rains continued throughout June, and the trenches and ditches dug one day filled with water the next. The mangy, coughing, lice-infested Croatian Home Guard in their muddy uniforms dragged themselves through Bijeljina, attracting sympathy. Looking more like camp inmates than soldiers, with their shaved heads that made it seem as if they had all suddenly emerged from a collective womb. At the start, the local people were afraid of them, especially the Serbs, of whom many remained in the town, but that fear quickly waned and was replaced by indifference. And then people started to feel a little sorry for them. These Home Guard soldiers had appeared in town as if they had no fathers and mothers, brothers and sisters, but had instead been born to serve in the army of the Independent State of Croatia, digging trenches around the town and living there in rotten wooden barracks inherited from the army of the Kingdom of Yugoslavia. It seemed as if these unfortunate Home Guardsmen would one day vanish along with the rest of the country.

Second Lieutenant Rudolf Stubler inquired among the Serbian peasants regarding the availability of smoked bacon. They said there wasn't any. They would bow low and make themselves small in front on him, smiling politely, and repeating over and over, there isn't any, there isn't any, there isn't any . . . He thought that there was some, that hams and sausages were hanging in their attics and smoke shacks and the villagers were lying – they wanted the soldiers to die of hunger! If they acted like this with him, how on earth would they respond, Rudi thought, when the Ustaše asked them about bacon? There isn't any, there isn't any, there isn't any . . .

Rudi did not know anyone in Bijeljina. There were hardly any Catholics in town and no acquaintances from the railroad or the post office, but at the end of June 1943 Opapa asked him to visit Mrs. Gertrude Seghers-Stein, convey his best wishes, and leave her with as much money as he possibly could. He would reimburse him for this at the earliest opportunity.

Rudi hadn't even known that Mrs. Gertrude was in Bijeljina.

He had not thought about her for nearly fifteen years.

On his first free day, when the rain made it impossible to dig trenches, he set out to visit her.

Gertrude Seghers-Stein was the widow of the Dubrovnik postal director, Maximilian Seghers-Stein, who had been there to meet Karlo and his family when they relocated to Dubrovnik, showing him the city in which he would live the best years of his life. Seghers-Stein was a tall, powerful man, with a roughhewn face and bright blond hair which his hat would barely cover when he went for walks down Stradun on Saturday afternoons. Saturday afternoon was not exactly the time to be strolling down Stradun, but Seghers-Stein had his reason. As with everything else, he had secret reasons, about which no one asked for they knew he would never tell. If someone actually did ask, he would just smile, shrug, and say, "There are all sorts of idées fixes, my dear; it's not worth asking. There are as many idées fixes as there are people."

Maximilian Seghers-Stein was an utterly distrustful person but at the same time quite convivial. He knew everyone, frequented pubs and inns, and took part in social gatherings, of which Dubrovnik traditionally had more than other towns of the monarchy at the time. These two characteristics combined in a strange and unexpected manner. Dubrovnik's inhabitants respected him and loved him in a way. Mr. Maksim was as straight as a mast in his bright hat with which he tried, in vain, to cover his unruly hair – a Viennese eccentric dressed in the clothes of a Croatian dignitary. The former pleased them while the latter impressed them. It flattered them that the emperor and king Franz Joseph had sent such a representative to Dubrovnik. They perceived him as a personal emissary of the monarchy, though any intelligent person would have known that the emperor did not personally appoint postal directors.

In his free time, and there would be more such time at the beginning of the century than at any point later, Master Maksim played the violin and the cello. At first he performed only in shows put on by nonprofessionals or when accompaniment was needed for visiting guest soloists from Zagreb and Vienna, for he believed that a postal director shouldn't be too ambitious in his artistic endeavors. What would a citizen whose letter to his son in the army that had been lost in the mail have said about the postal director's musical activity? What would they have said in the Viennese ministries or the head offices of the imperial postal system when the word got around that in his free time he played the cello? With the years this concern passed, or perhaps he received word from Vienna allowing him to take up such artistic work and music making more seriously, for in 1910 he held his first solo concert in Dubrovnik, and afterward he continued to perform at state festivals and religious celebrations in nearby cities. Over the next two years he was invited to perform in all the larger towns from Zadar and Split to Mostar,

Kotor, and Cetinje. These prewar concerts, where he played from Vivaldi's or Mozart's violin concerti, to the folk or religious repertory, to modern German and Italian love songs, would end up having a major impact on the life of Master Maksim, his Gertrude, and their four children. In fact, when 1918 arrived, and one empire collapsed only to have another rise up in its place, Maximilian Seghers-Stein did not experience the fate of the other directors, chiefs, and officials who had been appointed by imperial decree, nor would he be in any way demoted. Instead the new authorities renewed his position as postal director, for in all those early years, from the moment he gained the courage to perform on his own, he had played by invitation at all the Serbian religious and national celebrations, just as he had when invited by the Croats and Catholics, and for that matter anyone else who had need of his musicianship.

On the occasion in honor of the liberation of Dubrovnik and the return of the City to the Empire of Dušan and the Kingdom of Tomislav, Maximilian Seghers-Stein played the mournful song of the Serbian soldiers who escaped to the island of Corfu, "Tamo daleko." At the sound of his instrument, the hardest and most unenlightened hearts stopped, and the musically knowledgeable (of which there were not many at the time) were mesmerized and stunned by the musical talent and the meticulous musical training of this unusual postal official.

The name of Gertrude Seghers-Stein can be found to this day in musical encyclopedias and historical surveys and chronicles of Viennese high society at the time of the fin de siècle. In addition to being the first woman to study music under the Habsburg monarchy, and the fact that many important contemporaries, including the young Gustav Mahler, spoke highly of her sinfonietta and her collection of songs for voice based on young Viennese poets, Gertrude Seghers-Stein (formerly Gertrude Morgenstern) was an important figure in the social and cultural life of the capital at the turn of the century.

But then Maximilian, for reasons that will remain to the end a mystery, received a transfer to Dubrovnik – perhaps as a reprimand – and thus did Gertrude's role in the cultural and musical history of Vienna come to an end.

In Dubrovnik, Gertrude Seghers-Stein gave birth to children, kept the household, and walked through the woods in search of medicinal plants, but she did not engage in music, at least not publicly. Perhaps it was not suitable for the wife of a postal director to present herself as a musician, or perhaps she was not able to carry on such activity far from Vienna, in that divinely beautiful part of the world which, as she would say, could bring the dead back to life.

Why would people, who saw such lovely hued parrots every day, paint? What was Mozart to those who heard the sounds of birds beneath their windows every morning, or the sound of church bells amid the perfect acoustical shell of the city?

That was how Gertrude Seghers-Stein explained the absence of musical and artistic interest among the inhabitants of Dubrovnik.

For reasons of their own, the inhabitants of Dubrovnik called her Mrs. Danica.

In addition to being the wife of the postal director, which was in itself worthy of respect, she was known and appreciated in the city for her interest in medicinal and edible plants. From her Viennese books Mrs. Danica had derived an understanding of any plant life that might be found in Dubrovnik and in its environs, on the islands of Lokrum, Koločep, and Lopud, in Župa and in Konavle, or right there beneath the city walls among the rocks. And every plant, as had been proved long before, healed something. There was no plant that just grew there, nor weeds that were just weeds, and also no poisonous plant derivative that, if properly dosed, did not cure some disease or other.

Another passion and another important body of knowledge concerned beekeeping. Probably through plants she had naturally come to bees. And thus to Karlo Stubler, Maximilian's friend, who knew all there was to know about bees. He kept his three hives on a hill a little above Saint Mihajlo's Cemetery. It was more that he fed his bees than that they gave him honey, for there was no pasture, and the poor things had to fly far away for their pollen but brought back more sea salt on their little legs than flower dust. Karlo's honey in those years was thick and bitter, from the salt, heather, and bee sweat, and it boded ill. But instead of the bees teaching him caution, instead of his learning something from that Saint Mihajlo honey, Stubler was enthralled by the poverty of the workers and fell in love with it in exactly the same way that a young man falls in love with a beautiful but ill-fated girl.

When they drove him from Dubrovnik, he left his three hives at Saint Mihajlo to Mrs. Danica. This was how Gertrude Seghers-Stein, the first woman to study music in Vienna, also became the first woman in Dubrovnik to keep bees. There were not many beekeepers in the region then, the honey came to the markets in the old town and on Gruža from Trebinje and eastern Herzegovina, but there were some, especially among the railway workers who after arriving from Austria had placed hives above Zvekovica and on the upper slopes of Konavle, along the tracks leading to Herceg Novi and Zelenika. But all this yielded little, and not much would change in the future either, so that after Mrs. Danica it is not clear whether any other woman in Dubrovnik engaged in beekeeping.

But there was something else that would link the Stublers and the Seghers-Steins.

Mr. Maksim and Mrs. Danica would be Karlo's children's first music teachers.

She would teach them how to read music, and before long all four children would be able to decipher any form of written notes. Thus they would learn to hear music without instruments, and Karla, Regina, Olga, and Rudi would learn to play Mendelssohn, Brahms, Chopin, Mozart, Bach, and Schumann. Olga and Rudi had such a keen sense of imagination that they could discern every instrument in the orchestrations, imagining even what was not in the notation: surprise, coughing, the heavy breathing of old conductors, street noises near the concert hall, the sounds of the epoch that poured across the paper notations like a sudden summer rain, melting the colors. But then the electricity would go out, the bora would blow out the kerosene lamp, bringing on the darkness.

Mr. Maksim taught them violin and guitar on Sunday afternoons, and sometimes during the week, after which he would return home for a little nap. Mrs. Danica tried to teach them the basics of piano, but she had neither the time nor the nerves for this.

As soon as I come close to the piano I feel like crying.

Why do you feel like crying? asked Omama Johanna, surprised.

My wife is quite sensitive, said Mr. Maksim preemptively.

And so they did not learn to play the piano. Anyway, the children of railway officials did not play the piano. Railway workers settled along the tracks, moving from one station to another, from one town to another, and could not carry pianos around. Jews and railway workers played the violin, Opapa would say. The piano was for the children of well-to-do folk, who still didn't have an ear for it.

Maximilian Seghers-Stein liked very much the idea that Jews and railway workers played the violin:

Would you allow me to write down this thought? May I say that it was Mr. Stubler who said it?

Why wouldn't you when it's the truth? Opapa said. The cold truth like cold gold. Though I'm an exception in that regard. What I mean is that in our Bosowicz home we had no violin, given that in the Banat at the time it was generally considered that only Gypsy music was performed on the violin, and our parents were not inclined to allow us to play Gypsy music. They thought that would put us on the road to becoming coffeehouse layabouts and, in the end, drunkards and good-for-nothings. This left me with a hunger for the violin, Gypsy music, and coffeehouses. All my life I haven't been able to get my fill of sitting in pubs or listening to czardas, but I've never picked up a violin. No, Mr. Stein, I won't touch your instrument. I refuse! As your good wife expressed it, it makes me feel like crying. I played the piano quite solidly, but after going off to the railroad, I could not have one of those, and so of course it was the flute. I've played the flute for almost my whole life, from the age of seven, and not a week has gone by, except for my few months of military service, that I did not practice the instrument. Or rather that I haven't played for myself or, more rarely, for others. The flute has been my path to music. I improvise, play a variation on some random fragment, something that has crept into my ear, and then I hear the whole universe. While I play a simple phrase from a Christmas song on the terrace on Christmas Eve, in the distance, from the Elafiti Islands, I hear Johann Sebastian Bach coming toward me.

From a yacht? asked Mr. Maksim in jest.

This is called composition, Mr. Karlo. You are a composer of sorts.

No, Madam Gertrude, I am just a railway worker.

The week Karlo Stubler was to leave Dubrovnik with his family, Maximilian

Seghers-Stein went all around the city, seeking out the mayor, the city council president, the town's military commander, asking them to intercede, calling Belgrade, sending telegrams and begging to have the decision reversed and Stubler pardoned because of his impeccable service, in which there was not a single blemish or error, asking that he be absolved for having supported the workers on strike.

Perhaps he could be forgiven, said one of those from whom he sought intervention for his friend. Maybe they could even pardon Karlo Stubler, if only he had been less diligent in his service. You surely know which government he served. Given this fact, why do you bring it up?

The two of them never met again.

Rudi would travel to Dubrovnik, since Karla was of age and had not wanted to leave the city. He would visit her, especially after her marriage to Andrija Ćurlin. By then her real name had been forgotten, and everyone called her by the childhood name given to her out of love by her parents: Lola. This was what her father Karlo had called her because of her character, her unique feminine stubbornness and self-confidence, never dreaming that the name would stick with her for the rest of her life. He had wanted to ridicule her, punish her in his Swabian manner, by calling her after Lola Montez, the dancer and lover of King Ludwig of Bavaria, a synonym for a courtesan in those days. Any other girl, and either of her two sisters, would have been insulted to be called Lola. But she accepted the insult and remained forever Lola.

In spring 1926, the eldest Seghers-Stein child, Emil, had completed his medical training and was living in Vienna where he worked in a psychiatric clinic. The next in order, Rozalija, had married the Ljubljana architect Bogdan Lipovšek and moved with him to Slovenia. At the end of March, the youngest child, ten-year-old Adrian, was lying ill in bed with a high fever. He was hardly breathing while they watched over him day and night and Maximilian had gone for the doctor Karel Karel, an old Dubrovnik pediatrician who had come to town at the same time they had. Karel Karel told them he could not help Adrian and they should pray to God, if they still believed in God, for the next five days would be critical.

If the child was still alive on the sixth day, he would live. They should not hope, just pray. It was only by a miracle that one survived this kind of diphtheria. This was what Doctor Karel Karel said to them, but neither of them believed in God. Maximilian Seghers-Stein never spoke about God, but a secret world grew from his concealed beliefs.

And yet, Mrs. Danica went to the Jesuits to order a mass for Adrian's recovery.

Don Emanuel Prpić, Father Manojlo, a Roman doctor of theology, a handsome young Bosnian with slightly odd, feminine gestures, accepted both her money and the prayers of the parents without comment. His eyes were filled with tears, he knew the boy well from the church choir.

You believe in God? asked the mother when she saw the tears.

He nodded.

The days of Adrian's illness, which Doctor Karel Karel had called critical, rolled onward from that Sunday, March 28. Whenever she dozed off, overcome by horror and fatigue, falling into a deep sleep, Gertrude would clearly see the moment of her child's death. He would cough once or twice, then stop breathing. She would wake up, not having slept even two minutes, and check whether Adrian was still breathing. For six days Don Emanuel Prpić prayed continuously for the boy's health. People said that not once in those six days did he close his eyes or take a rest. He prayed until around five in the afternoon on the sixth day, which was a Friday, when he finally passed out. When the sisters roused him, Don Emanuel Prpić was blind, and tears of blood were running down his face.

He would see again on Monday morning, the day of the child's funeral.

Adrian Seghers-Stein died on the seventh day of his illness, after a sudden and brief reprieve where it seemed to his parents he might actually recover.

It is impossible to bring this story to an end, without talking about Don Emanuel Prpić, Father Manojlo of Dubrovnik. In this way we shall postpone and somewhat dilute the destinies of Maximilian Seghers-Stein and Mrs. Gertrude, rendering them more bearable to those who hear about them for the first time.

Don Emanuel was born in Otes near Sarajevo in 1898, to the family of Ilija Prpić, a school custodian, and Mara, whose maiden name was Pamuk, a washerwoman in the city hospital. His baptismal name was Marko. He grew up in poverty, in Banjski Brijeg, where the family rented an old house across from the monastery. The sun never made it to their lower level; the windows were sheltered by a tall building that Archbishop Stadler had been allowed to construct, in the hope of strengthening the Catholic faith and Croatianness in Bosnia. His father would leave the house early for work at the Main Gymnasium, and his mother worked at the hospital, so the boy remained at home alone from an early age. They watched over him as much as they could. They could not live on Ilija's custodian's salary alone and still make their rent, and if they went back to Otes, where they had a nice, proper little house, he would not be able to keep his job since the suburban train was irregular and there wasn't any other way for him to get to the school every morning. Just one absence on his part could throw the instruction into disarray: there would be no one to ignite the charcoal in the classrooms, light the stove in the common room, and take care of all the things that needed to be taken care of before anyone else arrived. And if he lost his job, what would they live on? They had no land in Otes and in Ilidža it was impossible to find work, so to live in Banjski Brijeg and work from morning till night six days of the week was their only solution. And on the seventh day, Sunday, they went back to their home in Otes.

As one is telling the story, it appears that their poverty was terrible. The damp walls of the bedroom in which the little boy slept, the windows up close to the ceiling, the stale Sarajevo air that seeps into a person's nostrils, brain, and soul, and the long aimless seclusion. It is hard to imagine how long those ten hours felt for the five-year-old boy, from six in the morning until four in the afternoon, when his mother came home from the laundry. That time cannot be measured by any adult concept of time, for it is much longer than the longest period we can imagine in our own lives. In the course of ten hours a child can transform, change, and become someone else several times over. The Marko they left would never again be the same Marko.

Only one thing did not change: every day, the boy gazed out the window at the gray monastery wall, and up at the church spire. Very early the child understood the most important physical reality of his entire life: but for the wall and the tower, the sun would enter into his house.

Who told you that? his father asked in surprise.

I told myself that, and it's true.

Yes, it is, he said, you are right.

His father was a gentle, quiet man. And very shy. He sang well but only when he thought no one could hear. He had a good sense of humor. When his mother felt sad, his father would always say something that made her laugh. Don Emanuel did not remember the jokes – how could he since they were adult jokes? – but he remembered his mother's laugh. He remembered all 743 moments of laughter, and the 743 times his mother had returned home sad from the hospital.

I've seen enough of death, she would say.

What death, dear, you wash bed linen all day long?

It's the bed linen of the dead. The living don't soil them like that. When they bring me a sheet to wash, I know whether the person who had lain on it was dead or alive.

Why do you look at them so much, dear? One could go mad from looking too closely at bed linen. Wash, dear, but don't look too hard!

I would if I could.

Listen to yourself! Professor Mitrinović told me the same thing. I tell him, let the suffering of the world go. Live while God has given you life; be happy you're healthy. Suffering will always be there, you don't need to hold a candle to it. And he gives me the same answer: I would if I could. And then he tells me a story about a German, a famous wise man and philosopher who lost his wits, because like you and Mitrinović, he looked too hard at sheets . . .

By this point Mara was laughing.

You just caught me when I was tired . . .

Wait to hear the rest, dear. When he saw he was going to lose his wits if he didn't get a hold of himself, the wise man goes to Italy to have a good rest there. Italy, the sea, the sun, laughter – he thinks it will help. When he gets there, it's foggy and ice cold, a gloomy city, big like our Vienna. Nobody on the street but a coachman beating a tired horse. He's beating it with all his strength, brutally. And what can the beast do? It doesn't know how to cry or talk; it is the way it is. At this point the wise man loses his mind, if he ever had one, runs over, wraps his arms around the beaten horse's head, and starts shouting: I won't give it up, I won't give it up . . . He yells until they put him in shackles. From then on he is in the madhouse until he dies. He never recovered. He just shouts, I won't give it up, I won't give it up. Mitrinović told me the story, and to tell you the truth I was a little frightened by it. I don't know which one I felt sorrier for, the horse or the man. And he asks me, so what do you say to that, Ilija? Was it from too much looking at books or from something else? I tell him, my dear Mitrinović, that was a gentleman's misfortune. What do you mean? he asks me. Well, sir, only fine gentlemen can take a long trip to Italy. You can see all sorts of things on the way. I too would go crazy if the same thing happened to me. But where am I going to find the money to go to Italy? When I'm on edge, Mitrinović, I stare at the wall. There's nothing frightening in the wall.

This story made Mara feel better.

She didn't laugh as she had those other 743 times, but he did frighten her. Maybe that fear gave her a frisson of pleasure.

When Don Emanuel wrote his autobiography for the Church, which would eventually be read by Archbishop Šarić himself, he doubted the devotion of his parents. They went to church as often as they could, prayed as much as was needed, did not blaspheme God, and were kind toward other people, but when things were hard for them, they did not call upon Jesus Christ or the Virgin Mary or the good Lord. It simply was not their way. He was surprised the first time he heard someone at school invoke the Son of God when the man struck his finger with a hammer. It was a carpenter who was repairing a window in the classroom while the teacher conducted class.

Simple human kindness was more distinctive from any angle in their natures than faith was.

This was what Don Emanuel wrote in his autobiography, and for years this apparently simple sentence was the subject of discussion at church gatherings, from the pulpit, and in monastic gathering places, until both the priest and his statement were forgotten and the two Prpićs had long since been laid to rest in Stup Cemetery.

Marko had just turned five when he finally gathered the courage to leave the house, cross the street, and knock on the monastery door. An elderly nun opened the door, and he asked her by what right the wall stood in front of his window. She did not understand and frowned, and the boy explained that it was evil and wrong for the monastery wall to stand in front of his window, blocking the sun from shining on it.

She asked him to follow her. She led him into the kitchen, where she cut off a piece of bread for him and sprinkled it with sugar.

But I want to know . . .

The boy was persistent.

From that day on the boy would cross the street every day and knock on the monastery door. At first it was to ask a question or two, and then simply to visit. The nuns and the priests began to expect the boy's visits. They grew worried oncewhen he did not show up for two days – Mara had got a leave and went with Marko to Otes. Among themselves they called him Komšo, "neighbor boy." This nickname would follow the boy through his young adulthood, remaining with him until he was ordained and had long since left Sarajevo.

It took his mother and father several months to discover what the boy was doing when they were at work. They were upset, tried to stop him from going across the street, but it was too late. Marko knew what he wanted and was well liked at the monastery. The day was long in a community that devoted itself to God; all was regulated to the hour and the minute, which strengthened the subjective experience of time and lengthened it. Monks' time and children's time were almost of equal length. In this, priests resembled children more than they did adults.

We've grown accustomed to him, Mr. Ilija, let him stay with us while you're at work. We'll care for him and feed him, and perhaps he'll learn something useful.

That was what don Izidor Štok said to Ilija Prpić, and Ilija agreed. This removed a great burden of worry from the boy's mother Mara.

From then on, everything proceeded as if anticipated.

The boy proved to be unusually intelligent and gifted in many ways. Everything interested him, and he acquired knowledge with ease. On Banjski Brijeg he was surrounded by the care and love of those who could not have children of their own. He went through elementary school effortlessly; he never experienced the cruelty of his peers. There was nothing to learn there, for he had long since known everything. He would pass through the Travnik gymnasium and the seminary in a similar way, finding himself at the gates of Rome before he realized he had not made a single important decision in his life – everything had happened on its own, according to some previously designed order, which neither he nor his family had resisted.

Don Emanuel never told his mother and father that he would be ordained as a priest, nor had they ever thought that it would be otherwise with Marko. He'd been born, lived in a dark basement, and crossed the street to knock on the monastery door, all in order to become a priest. Ilija Prpić, the janitor at Sarajevo's Main Gymnasium, and Mara Prpić, née Pamuk, had not thought their son would continue their line. It would end with them and continue in heaven. If there was a heaven above the two of them.

We shall skip over the part about don Emaneul Prpić's schooling and his particular interest in dogmatic theology, for doing so could cause the story of the bee journal and the gray notebook found in the basement on Sepetarevac to slip away for good. Emanual Prpić prayed for five nights and six days for the health of Adrian, Maximilian's son. Maximilian Seghers-Stein had been waiting for Karlo Stubler when he arrived in Dubrovnik and bid him a sad farewell when Stubler was banished. He and his wife Gertrude Seghers-Stein taught music to Karlo's children. And so one day at the end of June 1943 Home Guard Second Lieutenant Rudolf Stubler received his father's letter in Bijeljina, in which his father asked him to visit Maximilian's widow at his earliest opportunity to provide her with as much money as he could. In this story, don Emanuel is just one circle in its expansion and in the long search for an answer to the question of why in spring 1937 Franjo had tried to save one queen bee from a hive infected by the plague and all that this action of his brought about.

After he had mesmerized the professors and monks in Rome as well, and had been accepted among the Jesuits as a miracle born only once in a century, Don Emanuel Prpić made his first big mistake. Instead of obediently accepting the decision of his superiors to take up service in Madrid, he resisted it so strongly that he was transfered to Dubrovnik instead. Perhaps they decided that there was something not quite right with the young man, that behind his enormous erudition and imagination and his pure and rather naïve Oriental devotion, which the study of dogmatic theology should have rectified, or even developed into a creative cynicism, there was mental deficiency lurking, a hereditary disorder that manifested itself as genius. All this, they thought, is just a lucid interval, but before the deterioration continues it would be better for him to be as far from metropolitan affairs as possible. Let him be, for instance, in Dubrovnik, where they knew how to hide and treat the sick.

We don't know of course, unless one day the Dubrovnik church archives are opened, what sort of messages arrived from Rome in the sealed letter that Don Emanuel carried with him. He was told that the letter was important and that he must deliver it by hand before he sets foot in the Church of Saint Ignatius to pray. He found this a strange instruction, smelling of superstition or conspiracy, and it was unclear which of the two was worse: that the church fathers in Rome were superstitious or that they had used him to send a letter that condemned him.

Several times he had the letter in the palm of his hand, as if holding a fistful of desert sand, and he looked at the seal of red wax into which the symbol of the Jesuit order had been pressed. If he broke the seal, opened the letter, and read it, he would know all he needed to know and could act accordingly. But he would be betraying the secret entrusted to him, and this secret would not make it to Dubrovnik. This is what Prpić writes in his *Recollections of a Hermit*, a book published by the Serbian Orthodox Society of Chicago: "If I had only found a piece of red wax in my pocket then, I would have given in to temptation, opened the letter, then sealed it again, and acted in harmony with what I had read. And probably my destiny would have been different. But who would ever think of carrying a piece of letter-sealing wax around?"

Thus did Don Emanuel Prpić complain, while fifteen years later and some three hundred kilometers to the northwest of Dubrovnik, Franjo Rejc carried two pieces of letter-sealing wax in his beekeeping bag everywhere he went. What purpose did that wax serve?

Don Emanuel was received in Dubrovnik with pomp, with the smiles mandatory among the Jesuits. There was something overly theatrical in Don Emanuel's brothers. They received him all too exuberantly.

After they had given him a good dressing down, the Jesuits assigned this Roman PhD in dogmatic theology to direct the diocesan boys' choir. Whether there was a devilish intention in this is hard to say today, but in a photograph published in *Dubrovnik, Centuries of Culture and Patience*, a 1995 edition of the authors collective Matica Hrvatska, in which we see Don Emanuel Prpić enthusiastically conducting three rows of young boys in white shirts, their mouths wide open in song, one can sense what will follow.

At the time when don Emanuel Prpić cried tears of blood after having prayed five nights and six days for the recovery of Adrian Seghers-Stein, this business had not yet erupted among the Jesuits. And by then don Emanuel had already been given the Serbian Orthodox sounding nickname Pop Manojlo, with which the next phase of his suffering began. It is unknown whether they called him this because of his Sarajevo accent, which probably reminded them of the Vlah tribes on the other side of Mount Srđ, or for some other reason, but there is no doubt whatsoever that with it they intended to insult him. He didn't mind. He even let the children in the choir call him Pop Manojlo.

Regarding the conditions of Don Emanuel Prpić's exile from Dubrovnik, little is known. If we set aside the gossip and pornographic fantasies of those who banished Don Emanuel, the citizens of Dubrovnik, and certain church higher-ups, one could say that nothing is known. Except for the name Frane Bogdan, a fourteen-year-old orphan, cared for by his uncle, a retired ship's captain by the name of Lazar Vuk Paštrović.

Frane found himself alone with Don Emanuel in an unheated classroom at dusk on a winter evening before Christmas, when a storm was blowing so hard along the city walls and off the red roofs that it seemed they would be carried out to sea, and no one so much as peeked out from under their comforters, let alone left their houses, unless the need was great. When the door to the room suddenly opened, the candle flames flickered and a puff of wind blew one out, leaving the smell of the wick and partially burned tallow behind. That scent would forever remain in the nostrils of the witnesses, and each time they smelled it, what they had seen before their eyes would come back to them. But we do not know what they had actually seen, for the accounts differ in accord with their individual erotic fantasies. Those who were not present at the instant that the door opened, the candle flames flickered, and one went out would add something of their own to the sight, to compensate for something they did not see themselves. That is understandable. But how to understand the fact that the people standing at the door saw such different things? One said Don Emanuel was standing, staring upward, and little Frane was kneeling before him, his hands clasped together as if praying to God. Others said that Frane was standing, and Don Emanuel was the one praying. A third saw the priest – Manojlo – leaning over a bench, as if reaching for a prayer book that had slipped behind, and little Frane had approached him from the back to help. A fourth said little Frane was the one reaching for the prayer book, and it was proper for him to be the one to do this and the priest to help him . . .

They cut off one of Manojlo's ears, which an innkeeper from Pile by the name of Jozo Novokmet kept for years in a jar with alcohol on his bar. When the Partisans liberated Dubrovnik in 1944, Jozo was executed for having collaborated with the occupier, and a Montenegrin, just to show off, drank the alcohol in the jar in a single chug, chewed up the priest's ear, and spit it out. Thus did the last remaining bodily trace of Don Emanuel Prpić disappear from Dubrovnik.

Years afterward, the one-eared wretch, a vagrant, lunatic, and hermit, wandered through eastern Herzegovina, sleeping in caves, crawling into karst crags to pick through the bones of animals and humans, living off the charity of a people widely known for their lack of charity. The news of Don Emanuel and his sin had of course spread far and wide. They recognized him as Ostoja the One-Eared – his nickname in the new chapter of his life's novel – and beat him up in Trebinje, beneath the plane trees, in Ravno, and at the railway stations along the track leading to Čapljina. The figure of Ostoja the One-Eared, censored, rewritten, and somewhat consoled appears in several short prose works of Mirko Kovač, and his novel *Womb's Gate*. He also appears in the pages of two other

Belgrade writers. It is not certain whether these two – both of whom were, like Kovač, of eastern Herzegovinian heritage – ever met Ostoja the One-Eared, or just heard stories about him.

In his wanderings, say those who know, Ostoja the One-Eared would go all the way to Foča and Višegrad, and then down to Bileća and on to Nikšić, returning all the way back to Mostar, but he did not cross the Neretva River. Why he did not cross is unknown. There is no mention of this in *Recollections of a Hermit*, only the following: "This was a time in which the Lord tempted me and when I myself, human worm that I am, tested him, doubting in God's existence, only to have the Lord then appear to me in all his greatness."

Utterly exhausted, he was taken in by the monks of the D. Monastery near Trebinje in winter 1939. He was feverish, coughing blood, and raving, and they were simply waiting for him to die. When he had appeared at the monastery gate, the monks knew who he was. The story of the Jesuit Don Emanuel Prpić and his hideous sin with the boy Frane Bogdan was known to them. They even knew the boy's name, as the story had come to the monastery almost daily several years before, in its numerous versions, according to different witnesses (let us say, in the end, nine witnesses – seven monks and two laymen – who said they had witnessed the sight of Don Emanuel and Frane with their own eyes), spread by turns as if the devil himself had sent them, first one version, then another, then a third, until there were nine, and then it started over. The monks consulted briefly, the prior asked each to be certain and willing to accept the wretch under the monastery roof. If even one refused, they would turn him away and let him find some other place to die in. That was a wise decision on the part of the prior, for no one dared put his own conscience to such a test, and so Ostoja the One-Eared was allowed to live and die in the D. Monastery, as was God's will, with the approval of each and every member of the community.

When a tubercular patient coughed up blood, the rule was that death would come soon. There was virtually no chance of survival once the lungs had filled with blood. A man usually died when panic gripped him amid the suffocation, he lost his presence of mind, and no longer breathed with that little bit of the lungs that could still take breath, instead trying to take big gulps that would kill him with his own blood. And Ostoja the One-Eared was burning up from the fire of that disease and was unconscious.

The next day, around noon, he again started coughing up blood. This repeated several times before evening. The entire bed was covered in blood. Only Brother Arsenije approached him, wiped his sweaty forehead, and tried to help, while the others stood to one side, watching in stunned silence and praying to God for the soul of the unfortunate man. And then they prayed for the Lord to at last take him and cease his torment. This slow death was wearing them out too, they thought they were losing their minds.

But then the ailing man grew calm. He stopped coughing up blood, and the gurgling and rattling had almost ceased completely when someone said, There it is, he's departing! Several times they placed a hand mirror before him to see if he was breathing, and each time the mirror grew foggy.

He woke in the morning.

What's your name? Arsenije asked him, to check his state of mind.

Marko, he whispered.

You're not Emanuel?

That too, he said, as if recalling.

A Jesuit.

I was.

We have one Marko, a man from a village. We don't need another.

Marko looked at him sadly.

No, that's not what I was thinking. Instead, we shall call you Ignjatije. Just right for a Jesuit.

Ignjatije was no longer a nickname but a new name and the next chapter of his life's biography. Don Emanuel Prpić, whose christened name was Marko, at first was Komšo, then Pop Manojlo, then during years of suffering and temptation Ostoja the One-Eared, and finally Ignjatije in the D. Monastery near Trebinje. At first that was what they called him, but then he grew healthy and was miraculously cured, his tuberculosis disappeared, he accepted vows in the Orthodox Church, and took the name of Ignjatije Bogonosac, after Ignatius of Antioch.

They believed that he did this merely not to have to change his name again.

There were those who believed that deep down he remained devoted to the order of Ignatius of Loyola, but looked at from the end of his life and with the knowledge of how the monk Ignjatije Prpić concluded his existence, there was divine intention in this. Whatever they believed in, the name of Ignjatije Bogonosac reversed and redirected his destiny.

In teaching his disciples about humility, Christ took a child into his arms and said: "Whoever takes the lowly position of this child is the greatest in the kingdom of heaven." That child was Ignatius, the future pupil of Saint John the Apostle, and later the Bishop of Antioch. There he introduced the antiphonal manner of church chant. The Roman emperor Trajan, meanwhile, when traveling through Antioch on his way toward Persia to start some war or other, heard about Ignatius and his gift. He tried to turn him away from his faith, offered him the position of a Roman senator, and when Ignatius refused all these worldly honors, he ordered that he be sent to Rome in chains and thrown before the lions. This was done, and all that was left of Ignatius of Antioch was his heart and, inside it, his love for the Lord.

At the end of 1940, for no apparent reason, the affair resurfaced in Dubrovnik. One of the nine who had seen everything when the classroom door was opened fell ill in bed and announced that none of it was true. He asked for the bishop to come, but the bishop either did not want to or could not come. Then he went before a Dubrovnik lawyer named Jakšić and two witnesses swore that it was all one great ploy they used to get rid of Pop Manojlo. They didn't expect it to spread, that the story would make its way into town, that the wretch would be banished; they only wanted to blackmail him so he would leave town of his own accord. They had foisted the boy Frane Bogdan on him, who had previously robbed the church donation box, and they told him they would not report him to his uncle if he did what they told him to do. They would not report him to his uncle, and the good Lord would forgive him his great sin of stealing what belonged to the Church.

That was what one of the nine testified, dying immediately thereafter.

The lawyer Jakšić went with the two other witnesses to Risan, where they found Frane Bogdan, who instantly confirmed what the deceased had said. He added, moreover, that he was prepared to testify before any ecclesiastical or secular court, for his life too had been ruined by the affair. The lawyer took his stenographic transcript to the bishop of Dubrovnik, who begged him not to make the matter public. This was in February 1941, even as Ignjatije's right ear floated in a dusty jar of alcohol in a bar in Pile. The innkeeper Jozo Novokmet would brag to every customer how he had personally taken his razor to that human vermin and beast, in the name of the Father, the Son, and the Holy Ghost, and then, waving his right hand in a wide arc, he would cross himself at the end of the story.

At the end of March, a day or two before the Kingdom of Yugoslavia's accession to the Tripartite Pact, a secret delegation of the Dubrovnik diocese set out for Trebinje, where they stayed for a brief time in the rector's house before continuing to the D. Monastery with the rector. It is not known what offer they made to Ignjatije, or whether they arrived with a humble apology, or simply made some sort of settlement. Nor is this meeting mentioned in *Recollections of a Hermit*, or corroborated by the diocese. All that is known for certain is that the meeting took place. There is even a photograph of the emissaries, taken with the rector seated in front of the hotel under the plane trees. Many years later, the rector confirmed that he escorted those people to the D. Monastery, but he would not say why he had taken them or whom they had gone to see. "Know one thing," the rector told those who were questioning him, "a part of the shame belongs to everyone, and if you continue to force me to talk, the serpent will poison anyone it pricks!"

"They entreated me to come back once they discovered that the shame was theirs and not mine. But I did not want to, since I had given my heart to the true faith, to Jesus Christ, and to the brothers who saved me." This is what he writes in *Recollections of a Hermit*, but he does not say who issued him the invitation or when. Nor is it clear whether he would have returned to the Jesuits or to Dubrovnik.

As is customary in our part of the world, matters that are kept silent are the ones people know the most about, so it was that everyone in Dubrovnik knew about the affair. Jakšić the attorney refused to comment, and the two witnesses disappeared: one died suddenly, the other moved to Split. Even so, all was known, and all was kept silent. In the meantime war broke out: Italian forces took over the city, the Ustaše turned up, and the period of terror began, when no one dared ask questions. They tried to kill Jakšić, but he managed to escape to the Partisans. With him came a panicked fear that everything might become known. By the end of 1941 all five of the false witnesses regarding Don Emanuel's sin, those still alive, had been transferred to Zagreb or Rome.

As dead mouths don't speak, the only person left to silence was Father Ignjatije.

By the time the Ustaše arrived at the D. Monastery, he was no longer there. They had threatened to burn down the monastery and kill everyone inside, unless the renegade was handed over, but it was futile. They turned the monastery inside out, looking for him in drawers and cabinets, as if Father Ignjatije had shrunk to the size of a porcelain figurine that had to be shattered, but to no avail. He was not there.

What is he to you? Why are you hiding him? the Ustaše commander asked the prior.

He is our brother. But he would not let us hide him and have us and this house of God suffer. He is not here.

His ear is still on display in Jozo Novokmet's tavern in Pile, the Ustaša taunted. Maybe he's gone to retrieve it.

The prior did not respond.

They left without burning down the monastery. There would be other opportunities to do so. Long would the time last when buildings were freely set on fire and people murdered.

When he thought the Ustaše had gone, he came out of his cave, climbed up the hill and looked in the direction of the monastery. Clean, white smoke puffed from the chimney. They were cooking lunch. The brothers were bustling around the courtyard, just like any other day.

In an empty place in Father Ignjatije's heart, in place of the Jesuit Don Emanuel, an avenger appeared. He told his brothers he would not wait for the Ustaše to come back to slaughter him in his sleep. He did not want to expose them to his fate but would settle matters with them on his own. The prior told him to watch out. It was easy, even for right reasons, in the name of goodness and truth, to go over to the side of evil. A man was not perfect, remember that, he told him. He also told him how things were sometimes not what they seemed. People got carried away by anger and then cooled down. But it was often too late. The worst was when anger fueled more anger. Ignjatije heard none of it. The prior's words were a rustling of dry leaves in a late summer breeze. The rustling is forgotten.

The next stage is described carefully in *Recollections of a Hermit*. Let us say that Ignjatije joined up with the first rebel unit he encountered, the Chetnik division of Major Karanfilović. From him the Chetniks wanted a blessing, and from the Chetniks he wanted a rifle. They gave him a dubious looking machine gun, a piece of equipment from the Italian army in Ethiopia that had already jammed several times in battle. No one wanted to use it anymore, they suspected a bullet might explode in the chamber and blow back into the face of the shooter. That was why they gave him this particular gun, while he gave them a sullen blessing. They drank and celebrated and had no idea what they were doing. War for them meant making others afraid of them, making Muslims afraid of them. Ignjatije Prpić found this unpleasant, and as they climbed like a bunch of chamois around the Herzegovinian karst mostly without any purpose, he carried his machine gun on its strap with bandoliers strapped across his chest. Bearded and shaggy, his eyes aflame, he looked like a madman out of a Dostoevsky novel.

He stayed with the Chetniks of Major Karanfilović for two months and then disappeared. In his *Recollections* he writes that he left them their machine gun and ammunition. All he took with him was his canteen. And thus he set out for Bosnia. This was in the spring of 1943, during the time of the great German offensives against Tito's Partisans. He appeared among the burnt-out villages like a holy fool, some saw in him a devil and ran at him with pitchforks, but Ignjatije would simply vanish. Twice the villagers had him surrounded, but when they tightened the circle and stabbed the bush they'd seen him hide behind with their bayonets, he wasn't there.

In the mountain villages around Sarajevo they gave him the nickname Pop Avet, the Ghost Priest. Probably the first to do so were the Muslim mountain villagers of Bjelašnica. But word of him and his name spread. The Serbs thought Pop Avet was a Catholic priest who had gone mad, while the Croats from Stup saw in him a mad Serbian priest whose prior had been slaughtered and who was now revenging himself on the people in their dreams. Anyone to whom he appeared would go insane.

But near Trnov he was captured by a Partisan unit. It was summer, so the first thing they had him do was bathe under guard. Then they shaved off his hair and beard, clothed him, and proposed that he be shot as a class enemy. Father Ignjatije broke into a sweet laugh at the suggestion of the regimental commissar Jovan Bjelobabić Kompanjero.

Why are you laughing, Reverend? Kompanjero asked in surprise.

Because I'm a priest, a servant of God, and not your class enemy.

We shot your kind in Spain.

What kind?

Clericals. We shot them because they led the people astray.

Perhaps that was a mistake on your part.

The mistake is yours if you think there's a God.

Maybe. I don't say it isn't. Maybe it's a mistake. But that doesn't concern me.

What then?

I'm concerned with loving the good Lord and praying to him.

How can you love someone who doesn't exist?

Through faith, how else?

Even when he's not there?

I have faith that he is.

And yet you admitted not long ago that it could be a mistake.

Lord save us, it can't be a mistake that I have faith. All I said was that there could easily be mistakes in what I think.

I don't have faith and I battle against those who do.

The first one is right, the second one is a mistake. There is no way, brother, you can win if you battle against those who have faith. Perhaps that's why you lost the war in Spain. You shoot all those who have faith, and you're lost, for no one is left. Do you understand what I'm saying to you?

Do you understand what I'm saying to you?

I do, how could I not understand you?

What do you understand?

That it's hard for you as now you no longer know what to do with me.

This would be the word-for-word disclosure of Jovan Bjelobabić Kompanjero, who in 1950 was proclaimed a hero of the people and ten years later ended up in Lepoglava Prison, for enemy and counterrevolutionary activity. At a union of fighters congress he stated from the podium that he would have personally shot Tito and Stalin in the war, and every one of the present communist leaders, because of how they were acting now, in peacetime. Then he went on to spell out the reasons why he, hero of the people Jovan Bjelobabić Kompanjero, would have shot Tito, but before he had finished his exposition, the organs of orders appeared to arrest him. They offered him the opportunity to be pronounced mentally incompetent, due to head wounds suffered during the war. He refused: he was not wounded in the head but in the chest and in both legs. They proposed that he emigrate, upon which he said that would not be seemly for a national hero to leave the country he had helped create. They took away his designation of national hero. He laughed, saying that was not something that could be taken away, either one was a hero or not. In the end he was sentenced to life in prison, which was commuted to twenty years hard labor, for conspiracy to assassinate Comrade Tito. "You might as well have shot me," he said, disappointed. "As a class enemy," he added, and laughed. No one knew why Kompanjero was laughing. They thought he was insane.

Jovan Bjelobabić Kompanjero was obviously obsessed with shooting.

Ignjatije Prpić, in his *Recollections of a Hermit*, writes that he investigated, as much as was possible, whether Kompanjero had ordered and carried out executions during the Spanish Civil War or the People's War of Liberaion in Yugoslavia. He did not find a single verification that he had. Except that all the witnesses confirmed that Kompanjero, both as a divisional commissar and later as a divisional commander, was constantly threatening to have people shot. But he kept as far as possible from all trials, saying he was a soldier and imperfect student of French language and literature, not a lawyer.

Perhaps he enjoyed witnessing people's fear.

He looked the man he was going to kill directly in the eye. He had done this countless times. People reacted in different ways. It is a shame Kompanjero did not become a writer, or at least that he did not write his memoirs when, in 1977, having served seventeen years of his sentence, he left prison – though a more interesting book would have been one containing the record of their names and what happened to them afterward, or a description of what the eyes of a man look like when he has been told he will be shot. No one knew this better than Kompanjero did. And after the collapse of an entire world and order, after the destruction of the ideals for which Jovan Bjelobabić Kompanjero had fought, if anyone was interested in what this man had actually been doing for all his life, it would be accurate to say that he had persistently dispensed false assurances to people about their mortality. And all of them, as it would become clear in the end, had been immortal.

Father Ignjatije spent the summer of 1943 with Kompanjero. The dire circumstances around them didn't seem to touch them. Kompanjero followed Father Ignjatije around, trying to make him change his faith. There was no God, there was no God, there was no God, he repeated to the rhythm of his confident steps, and with time something of his audacity passed over to Ignjatije.

If there is no God, then there is no death either, he said, to tempt him.

Well, there you have a nice thought, said Kompanjero, contemplating it.

The life of the novice and martyr Ignjatije Prpić, who alternated lives and names and who, because of his companionship with the Partisan commissar, gained the nickname the Spanish Priest, would have gone off in a different direction if, when they were in the vicinity of Tuzla near the famous village of Husino, Jovan Bjelobabić Kompanjero had not been summoned to Ozren to take up a divisional command, from which he would later be dispatched to the high command. They parted like old comrades, and Father Ignjatije continued on alone.

The group of Partisans crossed the Sava and arrived in Slavonia. Flat land, rich and menacing. The Ustaše still held positions, the cities were secure, the people there loyal to the regime, the Partisans few. There was no Partisan warfare if you were looking for cover in corn stubble.

It was the end of September, and the long, beautiful Michaelmas summer stretched on as God showed himself even to those who did not believe. The spring had been heavy and rain soaked, which was why the autumn had to turn out this way.

Some lay in ambush along a trail where a German patrol would be passing. These actually were not Germans but our own young men, Bosnians, largely from Sarajevo, of German heritage, or else they knew the language, and were enlisted into some sort of fake SS units instead of being sent to the Home Guard. They were told this in confidence by peasants from Andrijevci, Croats, but partial to the Partisans. They would not lie. They said there were around a hundred. Three platoons, one company. Considerable. They had come directly from training in Austria but it was as if they didn't know where they had arrived. Not a real army. This was what they were told. So maybe it was better to leave them alone.

And so for days, they watched them coming and going from the ambush. They took aim at their heads, the point between their eyes, their chests, and their backs. But they did not fire. Such were their orders. And perhaps it would not even make sense. You could kill all three platoons, and then what? This isn't forty-one anymore, the platoon commander Husnija Mehmedagić said. It doesn't make sense now, right, Spaniard? he asked, and the Spanish Priest nodded. It was true, he believed, it made no sense to kill a German soldier who maybe was not even a German soldier.

Just as the German patrols that used the same trail were shifted, so were their ambush counterparts. On a particular day, whose date is no longer remembered, it fell to Ignjatije Prpić to go to the ambush with two Bosnians and Jakov Matić, a Split native and prewar communist who had not completed his studies in philosophy, along with a certain Perica, a local youngster from Andrijevci, who would sometimes spend the night with the unit and sometimes go home. And it all again looked not particularly serious.

Perica lay down on one side of the path the Germans would approach from, and the other two lay down on the other. They took up their positions together because they had things to talk over, while with Perica there wasn't much to cover, except for pigs and the differences between oak and maple wood.

And so the time passed, maybe the Germans were a little late, and Ignjatije had started up a conversation with Jakov of the sort one usually starts with a stranger on the train or a person in a railroad waiting room reading a book and, instead of nosing up to see the book, asks what the title is, and then the story starts.

Schopenhauer, Jakov whispered.

Ignjatije laughed quietly. It would be more appropriate for some swaggering gymnasium student to be praising Schopenhauer than a person of your age, and you, a communist to boot.

You say that because of the faith issue, of course. Schopenhauer's pessimism doesn't accord with faith.

No, he's a believer. Pessimists are believers, but he's a child's philosopher. A good child's philosopher. He's not for adults.

I have a question for you.

Go ahead, Matić.

Is there an idea that is more valuable than a human life? Or even the life of an earthworm? Think about it and tell me.

I don't have to think about it.

No, I insist. Think first.

What happened next was as if in a dream, and it lasted for a long time. At least this is how Prpić presents it in *Recollections of a Hermit*. The next thirty seconds he describes over twenty-seven pages of the book, longer therefore, than he needed to describe his entire wartime journey.

The moment the German patrol arrived, the rifle of the peasant Perica fired. He later maintained that the rifle did not go off accidentally but rather one of the Germans saw him – the one who would later perish – or that he accidentally turned his weapon toward him, and Perica fired. He did not hit anyone, though it was barely five meters to the German patrol. (For the majority this was proof that his rifle had actually fired accidentally.) At that instant, Jakov Matić had not yet completed his sentence:

You cannot know whether there is an idea more valuable than a human life until you have killed a person. Looked him in the eye and fired.

The villager's shot covered Jakov's last words.

Ignjatije thought Jakov was the one who had fired.

The Germans, the three of them – sometimes they patrolled in fours but not that day – jumped back like a buck surprised by a hunter and scampered for cover. The first two ducked behind a low wall that had once fenced the courtyard of a master house. There was no longer any building or any courtyard, only this wall, next to which there probably had once been a wooden fence.

The third German, the one who had been bringing up the rear, threw himself behind a haystack.

From the stack to the wall there were no more than four meters.

All of it was close, or it seemed to Ignjatije that all was close and that they were close to the others. A German behind the wall shouted. The word was in our language, but Ignjatije, probably from the excitement, didn't understand. It was a fairly common Serbo-Croatian word he recognized, and even the accent was familiar. That swallowing of the vowels, that hard, sharp sound with which he had been born and raised. Only in Sarajevo did they speak that way, nowhere else. But he could not decipher the word. He heard it clearly and could have even repeated it, but his heart was pounding in his ears and he was in no condition to grasp what the word meant. This unnerved Ignjatije, and at the same time he could not stop thinking about the question Matić had asked, before he had interrupted Ignjatije and answered himself.

Ignjatije was thinking about this, as if dreaming, at the instant when the third German, thin and long armed, like a spider in a green uniform with a helmet on his head, jumped out from behind the haystack and took his first step. In perhaps two more steps he would have been able to throw himself down among his own people.

Ignjatije was fully aware of the instant he pulled the trigger, in which a perfectly straight line was traced between his muzzle and the man's neck. As in geometry, a tangent touching a circle and then going off into infinity. Perfection contained in the question as to whether there is an idea worthy of the death of this very human being. Jakov Matić had not emphasized this part, and here he had unintentionally deceived him, this human being. As the young man fell, his helmet flew off, he was fair haired – perhaps a true German? Ignjatije was already in a hell from which there was no exit. There was no idea for which it had been necessary to kill him. Someone else perhaps, but the one lying now on his back in the dust, grabbing his throat to try to stop the geyser of blood, gagging in his death throes, he should not have been killed.

This was the second and also the last shot.

The Germans did not look up from behind the wall.

The Partisans did not fire anymore.

Not even Perica.

I had their asses in my sights. Both of them. I couldn't see their heads, or their legs or arms, just their asses. And I didn't shoot. How can you shoot a man in the ass?

This was what the peasant Perica said, who had not killed anyone. After the war, he would quietly go back to Andrijevci. And he'd drunkenly boast that he had killed a German. His grave was over there in the little German military grave-yard. Judging by his name he wasn't even German. But maybe Germans had names like us sometimes.

As soon as he sobered up again, however, Perica would say Ignjatije killed the German, the priest who after that day never spoke a word. And then he disappeared from the unit. He must have deserted. Or just vanished.

When the wounded man stopped gagging and grew suddenly calm, becoming a dead thing and a dead object on paper, they jumped up from their cover and rushed toward the corn. Jakov Matić and the peasant Perica. Ignjatije walked slowly, his palm against his forehead as if in the next moment he would wipe away the sweat. Had they only peeped out from behind the wall, the Germans could have killed him.

At the end of 1949, Father Ignjatije Prpić was living in Innsbruck, caring for Serbian refugees, runaway officers from the former royal army, Montenegrin and Bosnian Chetniks. He did not ask who did what in the war, just sent them across the sea. He provided them with false documents. Asking no questions, he would also help the odd Ustaša or lost Home Guard colonel. He did not ask them for money or about what they had done in the war. Neither the just nor the guilty would tell the truth.

All the while he had one thing on his mind: by saving criminals and butchers, he would save at least seven innocents, who would have been executed if not for his intervention. Seven innocents could testify before God for him. God existed, that Ignjatije knew, for he had seen him in the bullet-pierced neck of that soldier. His bullet.

The money for this operation was vouchsafed to him, as he writes in *Recollections of a Hermit*, by Fra Krunoslav Draganović, directly from the Vatican treasury. Draganović was busy saving Ustaše criminals and, occasionally, an innocent man. He is known to have saved Chetniks too, and people from the puppet regime of General Nedić. God only knows whether there were innocent people among them, but Father Ignjatije was forever grateful to Fra Krunoslav. He did not pass over him in silence in his book, nor did he ever deny having received help from him. Had it not been for Fra Krunoslav, Father Ignjatije Prpić would have gone mad before the image of the neck from which blood spurted.

While in Innsbruck, Father Ignjatije Prpić gained an unsavory reputation in Yugoslavia. And anyone who became notorious also acquired a detailed and substantial dossier compiled by UDBA, Yugoslavia's National Security Agency. His probably still exists today, somewhere in Belgrade, in an archive or perhaps among someone's private store of documents. Very little, I believe, is as valuable as these files and reports – at any rate as I imagine the dossier of Father Ignjatije to be – and if it were possible, though it isn't, and if I could place an ad in the papers, I would sell my soul to the devil and pay pure gold for UDBA's dossier. Those papers alone would amount to an enormous book, much bigger than Vasily Grossman's *Life and Fate*, the original manuscript of which just recently, at the end of summer 2013, was presented by the Russian secret police, heir to the KGB, at a press conference and made available to researchers and the literary public. (I write this, spoiling my story, in the sheer hope that the person who holds Ignjatije's dossier might make himself known to me by phone or email . . .)

We cannot determine what inspired the dark and nameless UDBA chiefs – for this is about them rather than about real people such as Aleksandar Ranković or Svetislav Stefanović – to send killers to Chicago, where after his Austrian adventure Father Ignjatije was living in peace, prayer, and austerity, not taking part in any public or ecclesiastical work. If his crime was having saved Chetniks and Chetnik butchers who had escaped from Yugoslavia, ministers of Nedić's government, and a few Ustaše, it is odd that an UDBA assassin did not take aim at his patron, Fra Krunoslav Draganović, who was freely traveling across Italy and Germany, taking part in public events, lecturing, and holding mass, and who could have easily been assassinated.

Perhaps Father Ignjatije's crime was deeper, older, and more serious than what is usually attributed to UDBA's victims. The intentions of Tito's secret police, whose activities no one could be completely familiar with, including the marshal himself, obviously did not concern the physical manifestations of a crime. After he had investigated the facts surrounding Father Ignjatije, Pop Avet, Ostoja the One-Eared, Pop Manojlo, Don Emanuel, Komšo, and Marko Prpić, they understood that they had to kill the man, for he knew much more than others and was acquainted from all angles with the world they defended. They were not afraid he might use this knowledge – they knew that he was incapable of such action and that his soul had been turned inside out and his heart broken seven times over when he killed a German soldier – but they were afraid of what he carried in his eyes.

That was why the invisible assassin shot Father Ignjatije and cut off his head. The head was never found, so the body was buried without it. As befits Ignjatije Bogonosac, the heart was by some miracle embalmed. When his tomb was opened years later, on the occasion of the old Chicago prior's burial, his headless skeleton was found with a perfectly preserved heart in the middle of the rib cage.

On the table, in the little room where Father Ignjatije Prpić was killed, lay the manuscript of *Recollections of a Hermit*. It lay in the middle of the table, the assassin saw it but did not notice. Even though the book was discussed in Serbia too, after the fall of communism when the story of UDBA liquidations of Serbian emigrants living abroad became widely known, to this day the book exists only in the single Chicago edition.

Thus ends the story of the Jesuit who prayed for the recovery of Adrian Seghers-Stein, son of the postal director in Dubrovnik Maximilian Seghers-Stein and his wife Gertrude, whom Dubrovnik natives of the time called Mr. Maksim and Mrs. Danica. Adrian was buried at Boninovo Cemetery on Monday, April 5, 1926. He was buried quickly, the day after he died, and no one from the Stubler family was able attend the funeral, though the Ćurlins, Lola and Andrija, were there.

Lola sent a postcard to Sarajevo:

Dbk. 6 IV 26.

My dears,

I'm writing to you all without naming each or sending you each greetings, except for mother and father. Are you well? Mutti, is your heart loping along as it should?

We were at the burial of little Adrian S-S, who died on Sunday. There was no saving him. The diphtheria snatched him away. A sad occasion. There was a large crowd. There wasn't a dry eye. The casket was lacquered, small. Only Maksim was like a stone. He supported the mother by the arm. I don't know how she managed. They did not have their own crypt, none of the S-S family had died in Dbk, so they buried him in the ground. The sound of the earth and rocks tossed onto the casket are still beating in my ears.

Everything else you know. A. is working. I'm caring for Ž. It has been hot for April. Who knows how it will be in May.

This wondrously musical and intelligent child had grown up amid the greatest promise and his parents' expectations. It was clear he would be a musician and would make amends for what both his mother and his father, through the confluence of circumstances, had lost the chance to accomplish. He would write the symphonies Gertrude had not written, play with the greatest orchestras in the world, travel to America, whose heights Maximilian Seghers-Stein had only

dreamed of. His dreams had the sharpness and peaks of the towers and skyscrapers of New York and Chicago, which beckoned from inside them, from within
the dreams, along with the Statue of Liberty, that wondrous hermaphrodite that
all the immigrants saw first on arriving in the harbor that was called America
and the island that was called America, where they were examined by American
doctors and nurses with cold hands, before whom, luckily, they did not have to
remove their clothes lest all their poverty become visible; from within Seghers-
Stein's fatherly dreams the emigrants beckoned too, the willowy youths from
Bukovina, the knock-kneed children with big heads whom God had given, the
little monsters, a wondrous gift for music, and could therefore go away, escape
from the Grand Duchy of Lithuania, from Galicia, Belarus, Ukraine, from the
small, ugly shtetlach where a great danger lurked, though no one yet knew what
kind, and where a centuries-old hatred hovered and the jealousy of their neighbors – why the jealousy? why the hatred? who could envy a knock-kneed midget
with a big head if he had never heard him play? Seghers-Stein thought of all
this in his dreams, the nighttime composed of all his daytime fears. He wanted
the child to become a great violinist, for he had not had the courage to do so.
Instead he had continued to live with his everyday fears, as the postal director
in Dubrovnik continued to be afraid that someone would at last examine his
dossier and read in it what all the ministers and imperial chiefs, the regents and
deputies and compulsory wartime directors had skipped over for years. And he
was thankful for every historical or elemental storm, war, accident, or Spanish flu
outbreak, anything that might distract the officials from examining the first page
of his dossier, on which was written his first and last name, his country of origin,
nationality, faith, and the date of his entry into the service.

Adrian's death seemed impossible to both parents, as if it were an error that
might be quickly corrected, for with his disappearance they were left naked
before the world, along with the desires of their unrealized life. And thus naked
they would go to their deaths, or to Boninovo, before the freshly dug grave into
which his casket would be lowered.

Within the short interval of time that followed, Gertrude and Maximilian
Seghers-Stein were deciding what to do with themselves. Dubrovnik had changed

from a place of secure refuge, where Mr. Maksim managed to be inconspicuous, to a place of great misfortune. The city had suddenly shrunk, collapsed onto itself and reduced down to a limited string of symmetrically aligned stone buildings beyond which one could not escape. That was when Mr. Maksim understood that the old town had the shape of a labyrinth of the kind English noblemen built for their amusement around their castles. There was no logical exit or path out of the labyrinth. One would have to cross the red roofs, jump over walls, and vanish.

On every corner of this suddenly shrunken Dubrovnik, in every alley in the old town, but also in Lapad and in Gruž, he saw Adrian. Here the child was playing, there his mother was taking him by the hand so he would not fall into the sea, here she was taking him to see the fish in the city aquarium, there the Ćurlins lived, Lola and Andrija, up those steps all the way to the top, and he climbed them because he did not like to be carried. He'd been three years old then. Later he would go on his own, with his violin, to visit Uncle Andrija and play a concert for his name day. It was cold, the end of November, the bora was howling. It took some time to warm up his fingers, but he didn't want to wait. He was impatient. And he despaired when his violin squeaked beneath his bow. He broke into tears. He thought he didn't know how to play anymore.

That was what Mr. Maksim remembered.

And there was no place in Dubrovnik that did not remind him of the child.

He considered putting in for retirement and moving. But he could not go back to Vienna.

Then he reached the time limit before the next misfortune arrived. And with it the final collapse.

Wolfram Justus was named after the famous Wolfram Justus von Barsewisch, who had died on the day he was born. Gertrude had earlier proposed the name Nicolas. The child's father did not feel strongly one way or the other, though he didn't want his children's names to stand out too much from the ones around them.

With such a name he could become a bishop, he said.

She seemed to sense disappointment in his voice.

Or an organist, he said more cheerfully.

Wolfram Justus Seghers-Stein was not, in the meantime, destined to become a bishop or an organist. Vuko, or Vukota, as he was called in Dubrovnik, was a tall, strong, guileless boy, built like an athlete. He was not without intelligence, he even sang beautifully and played the guitar. He did well in Latin, learned it easily and quickly, and he would have done all this learning and playing and singing well if only he could have done them all on the move. Or while swimming to Lokrum and back, or while walking along the walls around the city. There was something in him that prevented him from standing still. He had to move.

It was the first warm, sunny day of June in Dubrovnik, though still too early for swimming. The gentlefolk from the interior had not yet begun arriving by train from the interior to open the shutters and windows of their villas and summer apartments. The Gruž station was deserted. The only visitors were Herzegovinian cheese and milk merchants, small-time tobacco smugglers, the occasional district inspector, a gendarme, a spy, a Czech poet in the final stages of tuberculosis . . . Wintry frost coated the stones, moisture dripped from the walls, and Dubrovnik emerged from its slumber. With the arrival of Austria, it had become a summer city, and would remain so for the next hundred years.

Wolfram Justus begged his father to take him for the first swim of the year at Banje Beach. If it had been the middle of summer, if Wolfram Justus had not suffered all spring from a bladder infection, if Doctor Karel Karel had not said that it would be dangerous if it spread to his kidneys, and – above all – if it had not been for Adrian's sickness and death, Maximilian would have let his son go swimming on his own. He had gone swimming on his own the summer before, all the way to the middle of November. Perhaps this was how he had got the infection.

The day before, Maximilian had taken an afternoon nap. Maybe he was only asleep for a few seconds, when he felt something like a stone column pressing against his chest. He couldn't breathe, couldn't move, and the ceiling spun around his head, as he opened his mouth in a vain attempt to call Gertrude. He thought he was going to die. And then it stopped in an instant. He jumped up from the bed. He paced around the room. He went into the hall to examine himself in the mirror. What happened? she asked. He said nothing. If she asks again, he thought, he would tell her he'd had a bad dream.

This was why he didn't want to go swimming with Vuko and instead sat back in a deck chair under an umbrella and immersed himself in a book. The book, *A Short Lexicon of the Post, Telephone, and Telegraph*, published in an edition of Belgrade's Knjižarnica by Professor Dimitrije Mita Maksimović, which had been released just a few months before, remains to this day the best and most comprehensive historical compendium of the postal service in our region. The long-serving director of Dubrovnik's post office was captivated by it, for many people he knew were mentioned in it, as was he himself. His vanity gave him no peace, and as he leaned back in the deck chair, he proceeded to count how many mentions there were of the directors of post offices in Sarajevo, Belgrade, Zagreb, and Ljubljana, as well as his friends, current and past postal ministers in the capital and in the metropolitan areas of the former monarchy in order to compare them to himself. He was pleased that he came out quite well in these comparisons. He was mentioned in more places than any other postal director in the Kingdom of the Serbs, Croats, and Slovenes. This distracted him from darker thoughts, from Adrian and his death, and from Wolfram Justus, his Vuko, who was swimming from one horizon to the other, having made his way out toward Lokrum and half way back . . .

He looked up and saw a ghostly empty sea.

His heart seized up worse than the day before.

It stopped short in a way that promised it would not stop once and for all, he would not die.

Instead he would live forever in that bleak horizon.

Guilty for Vuko's drowning.

What happened, Dad? Vuko asked, as he approached, all wet.

My heart stopped. I thought you had drowned.

Me? Drown?! the boy said, laughing.

The anxiety was short lived. It vanished in the few seconds of true happiness, the sort one experiences only in the proximity of a great life's loss. Or when death hovers over his head, only touching him lightly with the tip of its robe.

He continued to read calmly. Then he wondered, distressed, how he could have regained peace of mind so quickly. It was inexplicable, and the distress would grow to envelop his life. Maximilian Seghers-Stein lost his reason and quickly died in a mental institution near Modriča, in Bosnia. That was why Gertrude had moved all the way to Bijeljina, to be close to her dying husband, who did not recognize her anymore, or his children, or anyone else.

His mind's eye must have been the bleak empty horizon of the sea. He knew that he was no more, that he had drowned, yet his heart did not stop short. It could not, for one's heart cannot stop short twice. The adrenaline cannot gush through one's veins twice in such a short span of time. He'd had the chance to save his son but didn't take it. God had granted him a warning not to read a book while the boy was swimming in the sea. But Maximilian had not taken advantage of it. That's why he had taken yet another son from him.

For a moment he did not know whether perhaps the two events had merged into one. The boy had come up behind him all wet and asked, What happened, Dad? That was a ghost. Just as now it was a ghost standing wet before him, grabbing him with his cold claws, keeping him from running away, shouting, What's wrong, Dad? What's wrong, Dad?

How Maxmilian Seghers-Stein lost his mind would remain one of those eternal Stubler riddles. No one would express curiosity about it – rather, they would remain fearful, or watchful, of sudden insanity, which did not arise from a mild psychiatric disorder, neurosis, or depression, but erupted from nowhere, clouding a person's mind. It was only because of Mr. Maksim and his frightful destiny that the Stublers had an aversion to psychiatrists and avoided them as children avoid dentists. This aversion would only come to an end with Olga and Franjo's daughter Javorka, who, ignoring the family story of Maximilian Seghers-Stein, would start visiting a psychiatrist to discuss her suicidal tendencies.

He drove Wolfram Justus away the way one drives a ghost away. The child was distraught, and for a long time his despair would mark him, darkening his otherwise light and simple character, for he did not understand why his father had pushed him away. Before he went into the sea, everything had been fine, as on any day or month or year before . . . His father was a composed, peaceful man, withdrawn and reticent before the world but gentle with his children and devoted to the point of submission to his wife. Why had he so suddenly yelled at him, shoved him, taken up a rock from the beach to strike him in the head. It was great good fortune that Vuko was strong, and for some time stronger than his father, for had he been weaker, his father would have smashed him, killed him, and crushed him in his frantic conviction that his real son had just drowned in the sea.

He asked that the boy's body be searched for along the beaches and in the harbor, and when it was found, that Wolfram Justus be buried at Boninovo beside his brother Adrian. They did what he asked, hoping that afterward he would recover his sanity. More people attended the funeral of Wolfram Justus Seghers-Stein, who had drowned in the sea near Dubrovnik, than had attended that of his younger brother. Many more. The first time those who came were truly mourning the boy – family friends, colleagues and acquaintances from Mr. Maksim's work, neighbors and people who respected the old postmaster – but all of Dubrovnik came to the second one. Everyone who wanted to see the burial of someone who was actually alive, the empty casket, half-filled with wet sand so the grieving father would not be suspicious, and all those who wanted to measure their own sanity against Maximilian Seghers-Stein's madness and feel reassured afterward came that afternoon to Boninovo. It was probably the biggest funeral ever held in Dubrovnik, one that would not even be outdone three years later when the whole town turned out to see off their poet and playwright, Count Ivo Vojnović. The only one absent was the unfortunate Vuko. He could not be at the funeral, even if he had died and turned into a ghost.

Deep into the fall of 1926 Gertrude Seghers-Stein continued to believe she could save her husband and return him to his right mind if only she fulfilled all his requests. She went with him to the cemetery, cried over the graves of their two sons and the plaque with their two names on it, Adrian and Wolfram. Afterward she would quietly speak to her son, consoling him: You didn't even like being called that name. Now the name is buried, and you are Vuko.

He would officially change his name to Vuko Seghers-Stein when he was twenty-one. We come across the name in *Politika* in May 1936, when Vuko Seghers-Stein was named representative of the Kingdom of Yugoslavia for the upcoming Olympic games in Berlin. He did not, however, end up attending this largest of sports competitions. No explanation for this can be found in the newspapers of the time.

There is no cross etching on the plaque above the grave with the names of the two brothers. The grave is located in the largest Catholic portion of Boninovo, which means that according to the rules of the time, Gertrude and Maximilian Seghers-Stein had to demonstrate proof of belonging to the Holy Roman Catholic Church to the parish priest. It is perhaps possible to find a few other grave markers in that part of Boninovo without Christian designations, but they are exceptions.

The war would find Vuko Štajn in Belgrade, where he worked as a swimming and fencing instructor. Some say he was connected to a clandestine cell of the Yugoslav Communist Party. Others swear they saw him in public with the Comintern conspirator Mustafa Golubić on Terazije Square and Knez Mihailova Street in May 1941. Golubić was in the uniform of a Wehrmacht colonel, while Vuko Štajn was in civilian clothes. But all these are probably false leads, lies, and inventions of the Belgrade busybodies, that over the years would spread through theater lobbies and literary cafés, and among the UDBA officers and frequenters of the Saturday matinees at the Hotel Majestic. It is more likely that Vuko Štajn was arrested at the end of May of that year because they suspected him of being a Jew. The baptismal document he provided was counterfeit, a fact verified through phone calls, first to the Ustaše commissioner under the Italian occupation force in Dubrovnik, and also to the office of a Catholic parish in Vienna, which unambiguously confirmed the Gestapo's suspicions regarding Štajn's Jewish heritage. Vuko Štajn died in a gassing van, a moveable gas chamber built by the SS officers Götz and Meyer who David Albahari describes in his novel of the same name.

How the news of the death of yet another of her sons reached Gertrude Seghers-Stein, the definitive death of one whose name had died before his body, a name etched above a grave in which the body would never be placed, we cannot know. Here the story returns to Rudolf Stubler, the Home Guard second lieutenant who, at the behest of his father, would visit Gertrude and insist on giving her all the money he had on hand.

On Saturday, June 30, 1943, it was raining hard across the territory of Semberija.

The Home Guardsmen had permission to go into town, but only the bravest ventured to do so. Or the most desperate. The others sat around on their bunks, played cards, or, like monkeys, picked the lice off one another. They had been quietly discussing since the morning why it was strictly forbidden for a Home Guardsman to carry an umbrella when it rained. Yes, it made sense not to go to the front with an umbrella; that would be strange and dangerous. How would you reload your rifle if you were holding an umbrella above your head? But why was it prohibited to open an umbrella if you had a valid leave notice to town signed by all the appropriate higher authorities? Was it the same in other armies? Well, the Germans didn't carry umbrellas either, but they were Germans, and everyone knew how Germans were. The Italians? It could very well be . . . Actually, it was quite likely that Italian soldiers, during their down time and when they received leave permission did in fact open red-white-and-green umbrellas. The English, too. In England, the rain fell all year round, it didn't ever stop, so what would happen if the English army was forbidden to open umbrellas? The war would have been over long ago; Churchill would have capitulated, the fat belly bowing his head before the Führer. Proud Albion would have had his nuts sliced off in Berlin if such a moronic law existed in England . . .

Second Lieutenant Stubler listened to the laments of the Home Guardsmen, then got up from his work desk in the corner of the sleeping quarter, wrapped himself in a heavy cloak, and went outside.

He walked to the other side of Bijeljina and knew that by the time he got to Mrs. Gertrude's apartment he would be thoroughly wet. But he could no longer listen to the Croatian Home Guardsmen quietly breaking wind, tossing cards onto the worn blankets confiscated from the army of the Kingdom of Yugoslavia as the most significant Croatian wartime booty, and discussing umbrellas. Anyway, he would dry out at Mrs. Danica's. She would look after him, as she had looked after all of them long ago, when the four of them went to her for their music lessons. He dragged himself across town, trudging through a yellow mud that seemed to be a mixture of Saharan sand and the shit of sick people. But for the moment at least, he was content.

Gertrude Seghers-Stein lived in a Habsburg-era three-story building with a peeling facade. The dark stairwell stank of cabbage and cat urine. The light didn't work. Mrs. Danica lived on the top floor. The name Seghers-Stein had been etched in cursive on the bronze door plate. Only the last name and with a hyphen. Rudi was certain that Mr. Maksim had not written his last name with a hyphen. The engraver had made a mistake, and Mrs. Danica had not objected but instead quietly accepted the hyphen.

My Rudi! she cried, opening her arms wide and hugging him, as his drenched undershirt clung to his body. He felt a chill down his spine. It was dark, cold, and stifling all around. As if it were winter rather than the middle of June.

The wooden armchair under him creaked but held. He decided not to ask for anything but just sit there all wet. He merely took off his military cloak, which ought to have been waterproof. "Officer's mantle of rubberized canvas" was the official name for this article of clothing. But it was soaked through with rainwater like everything else. It could have been wrung out.

In Zagreb they called it twist-drying, he thought, or something like that.

He reached into his pocket and pulled out a wet stack of paper notes bundled with a rubber band. He had collected 1,500 kunas.

My father sends you this, he said.

But why, Rudi? asked Mrs. Danica in surprise.

Have you heard from Emil and Roza? he asked, just to say something but instantly regretted it.

Yes, Emil was here in the spring. But you know how it is. He's got so much work he doesn't know where his head is. And then there's this war, hard to stay normal. And Roza is Roza. She's fine. She invites me to come to Ljubljana. What would I do there? Ljubljana, Bijeljina, Dubrovnik, it's all the same to me, my Rudi.

She was lying, it was clear, but years would pass before Rudi understood what constituted Gertrude's lie. Do I need to say, or should I leave this part of the story untold? Or should we begin yet another story, composed of two ellipses that cross paths in two places and postpone what has been postponed throughout this story: the event from the early autumn of 1943? We shall avoid this and tell the story of Emil and Rozalija another time.

In short, only this: the Viennese neuropsychiatrist Emil Seghers-Stein is the author of the cult post-psychoanalytic novel *The Eternal Fatigue of Katharina von Obervellach*, which is the story of a Vienna laundress of Slovenian descent with the gift of precognition. Katharina tells the psychiatrist, a bachelor, whose laundry she washes each week that the world will soon lose its soul and that he will escape with his patients, for the insane will be the only ones saved. Emil Seghers-Stein's novel would be translated here and published in 1955, in an edition by the Zagreb publisher Zora, under the title of *Katarina the Washerwoman from Gornja Bela*.

Emil Seghers-Stein, as noted in the first edition of Krleža's *General Encyclopedia*, experienced a nervous breakdown in 1939 and was hospitalized in the open ward of the institution where he had until then practiced. He stayed there until spring 1943 when, along with several hundred mentally ill patients, he was deported to Auschwitz.

Rozalija Lipovšek, Gertrude and Maximilian's only daughter, escaped with her husband after the April war of 1941 to Argentina, from where she never sent word to anyone, so it was long thought they had disappeared in the middle of the ocean, got lost in the primordial forests of the Amazon, or simply been swallowed up by that large foreign continent. Meanwhile, when the city planner Lúcio Costa and the architect Oscar Niemeyer were speaking on April 21, 1960 at the inaugural ceremony for Brasília, which they had imagined and designed as the capital of Brazil, behind them, among two or three coworkers, stood Bogdan Lipovšek. His Ljubljana students recognized him on television and in photos, after which he was invited from Belgrade to return to Yugoslavia and contribute to the development of his homeland. But Lipovšek was not interested, nor did he ever agree to speak with the Yugoslav press. Like Costa and Niemeyer, he lived a long life. He died in 2003 at the age of ninety-five. Rozalija was supposedly still alive at the time. She is mentioned in the obituary published in the *Folha de São Paulo*, the largest newspaper in Brazil, as "the maestro's eternal inspiration, the life partner who preserved the memory of the Slovene language from which he had sprung."

The destinies of Gertrude's two children could grow into two elaborate works of reportage. But I will have difficulty enough disentangling myself from the Bee Journal and from all the connotations deduced from the rotten wool *zob-nica* discovered in 1998 in the basement on Sepetarevac, in which there was but a pencil, two pieces of sealing wax, a rusty cigarette lighter, and the gray notebook.

My father sent you this, he urged again.

But why, my son? I don't need money!

In the end she took the stack of bank notes to let it dry out on the table. She laid out the bills on the tablecloth, which was eaten through by moths, as if she were laying out cards for a game of patience.

You'll take them after, okay? she said, smiling.

I can't. Father would disown me. As it is he doesn't trust me.

Really?

Yes. He lost faith in me when I flunked out. Now he doesn't trust me at all. Especially where money's concerned. He thinks . . .

That you're going to spend it on women?

Exactly, he said, laughing.

Oh, my dear, my dear, he lives in the past. There are no women in this war. At least I don't see them in Bijeljina. And I don't think there are any even in Berlin or Moscow. Are there any in Sarajevo?

No.

See, there aren't any. That's the kind of war this is. Horrible. But in the last war, when your father was young, wherever the army camped, in war or in peace, women would show up. They would fly in like doves and stand up in a straight line. One more beautiful than the next, and all you had to do was choose. That's the way wars once were and armies too. That's why there were no deserters. The boys rushed to join the army, rushed to death, for they knew that before they died their doves would be there, all lined up one after another, at the telegraph station near camp, as news from the front streamed through the lines. Ten, fifty, five hundred, a thousand dead . . . Now it's different. There are no women.

No, there aren't.

I'm composing.

She hopped up as if milk had started to boil on the kitchen stove. Drago liked my sinfonietta, she said.

It's a pity he will not hear this, she said, opening the piano, which was missing several keys and produced hair-raising sounds. It was as if glass was breaking and china exploding, the walnut groaning amid the frightening rupture of Gertrude's melancholy notes. The chords poured from the sky like crushed glass that cut into his skin. He opened his mouth and wanted to scream. He did not, for he was ashamed. And he felt sorry for this dear woman, whom he had known all his life, who had taught him to read notes and understand music. Gertrude Seghers-Stein had taught Rudi what counterpoint was. Counterpoint was a lack of harmony that sounded harmonious, three kinds of chaos that flowed along three riverbeds, merging into a sea of clean, universal music. That was counterpoint, she told the child, and his eyes opened wide in wonder, and he understood nothing, but remembered it all. And later, through life and through music, he saw all phenomena through Gertrude's theory of counterpoint. If there were no God and there were no music, Rudi understood, the world would be chaos. Gertrude taught him music and made him religious.

This was why he was gripped by such horror at the sounds emanating from the dilapidated piano, as this transfixed woman with fists that branched into bony gray fingers, struck her chords, in which there was no longer even a hint of melody.

When he understood that this would take some time, for Gertrude Seghers-Stein, the first women in the Vienna Conservatory to study composition, was just then performing one of her symphonies for piano and her foot was banging against the rotten oak parquet floor, Rudi eventually calmed down. He got comfortable in the armchair, and no longer felt cold. His trembling subsided and he was quickly prepared to sit there for hours. For as long as Gertrude felt the need to play her symphony, which, judging by the volume of the notation paper she had placed before her, was no longer a sinfonietta.

At that point, Rudi began to take note of all the advantages of his situation. Instead of dawdling with the Home Guard in the barracks and listening to the dreary stories, which, like his own, boiled down to fear of death, and not feeling or thinking anything other than fear, fear, fear, here he was sitting and listening, in complete peace and mental harmony, which enveloped him and eased any discomfort and evil thoughts. He felt the uniform drying on his body, blood coursing through his veins in a normal rhythm, the newly created cells in the organism replacing those that had died, and the toxins slowly steaming out of him with the moisture, and it seemed to him it would always be this way. Time flowed by him in reverse and left him next to the train that was leaving the station while he stood firm, both feet planted on the platform, and knew the train could not come back for him.

At what point he actually began to listen to the *First Symphony for Piano and Foot Pounding Against the Rotten Oak Parquet*, by the forgotten Viennese composer Gertrude Seghers-Stein, Rudolf Stubler was not able to recall. The music had completely engulfed him. He was drowning in it as in a dream, captivated by the out-of-tune little piano, as if it were a new instrument, unrelated to the piano. This was an instrument created in Bijeljina in the summer of 1943, for a piece of music that could be performed on no other instrument. In Gertrude's little piano could be heard the scraping of Slavonian well pipes, the banging of the freight wagon doors closing before the eyes of humanity while the last bits of light strained through the uneven boards, the thunder of the artillery from the other side of the horizon, the motors of a thousand tanks rumbling to life at the same time on an early winter morning, somewhere far to the east, the scrape of Gypsy violins, the discordant, raw sound of tiny blows hammering against the dusty wires, thousands of smothered women and men who remembered Mozart before losing consciousness, the sound of the earth drumming against the coffin.

Overcome, mesmerized, he listened to his music teacher, who he'd thought had gone out of her mind, as he listened to the magnificent *First Symphony for Piano and Foot Pounding Against the Rotten Oak Parquet*.

When he got up from the chair, the clothes on his back were dry. The bank notes on the table had also long since dried.

Please, Mrs. Danica, accept this. What would I say to my father?

Ah, Drago, Drago, he was always so generous.

She was the only one who called Karlo Stubler Drago.

When you come next time, she said, the *Second Symphony for Piano and Foot*

Pounding Against the Rotten Oak Parquet will follow. Prepare yourself and be patient. I wrote seventeen symphonies. Seventeen is a lucky number. Only you will hear them.

In July and August the sun and the rain alternated. As if by some rule of order, a sudden summer storm would hit. The wind uprooted trees and carried freshly washed sheets through Andrijevci, slinging them high in the air and letting them drop slowly atop the old oaks far to the east. It would suddenly grow colder and seemed the fall had arrived in the middle of July, but then the next day it would again be sunny and would remain hot for two or three days. The army had been camped in the vicinity of the village. No one knew why they had been posted there, out in the open, unless it was to serve as bait. There was talk among the soldiers that this was all temporary and they would soon be sent back to Germany. Or maybe to the east, some would add morosely.

Mladen's last letter to Nevenka is dated 13 VIII 43.

As always it is written in fountain pen, but no longer in green ink. It is ordinary blue ink. The handwriting is even, so the letter must have been written on a table, perhaps in the Andrijevci tavern, the only one in the vicinity of the camp, which the soldiers could frequent given special permission. Mladen sounds absent, as if stringing sentences together to finish the letter as quickly as possible.

Dear Nevenka,

I'm sure you wanted to hear from me. I haven't written because I've come to Croatia and don't have much time. If only you knew how many pears, plums, and apples are here for us to eat. Lots of grapes too. We German soldiers are well liked here and are given everything for free.

We might soon be going back to Germany, but maybe not. Have you been swimming? It's very hot here, but there are no rivers so we can't swim.

Have you heard from Željko? Has he taken off, or is he still in Borovo?

What is the news of Nano?

With greetings to your mother and father, to Omama and Opapa, and with much love to you,

Your Mladen

In the course of 1943, after Easter and then again after their arrival in Croatia, Mladen had two three-day leaves. The second time, in late spring or early summer, he even went to Kasindol Street in Ilidža. Somewhere in the Stubler house there is a record of this visit: some ten photographs, small format shots taken in front of the house and in the garden. Mladen is in the uniform of a German soldier and around him the whole family. Only Franjo is not there. He was at work or for some reason did not want to have his picture taken.

Mladen in a garden chair, his elbow leaning against the table, while Nevenka stands beside him, proud. She has placed her arm hand around his shoulders. The unknown photographer told her to do this to make the picture more dynamic. Around the table to each side, standing or sitting, are Karlo, Johanna, Rika, Vilko, and Olga. Nano is not there either. He was in Bijeljina by then, overseeing the trench digging around the city.

Mladen next to the apiary. Alone. Karlo had built the wooden structure with Rudi's help, then painted it with the carbolineum used for coating railroad tresses, which Karlo's son-in-law Franjo had purchased at the railway shop, requesting a receipt so no one would accuse him of having stolen it. The apiary was supposed to be a temporary structure until a stronger, more solid one was built, but it stood on the same spot for seventy years. It was beautiful, and so generations of Stublers and Stubler grandchildren had their pictures taken beside it. Mladen must have walked with the photographer across those two hundred meters, along the raised beds with the strawberries and green lettuce and the red and black currant bushes to have his photo taken there. Mladen walks through the garden in the uniform of a German soldier, with symbols and epaulets of whose importance we are unaware, the photographer with his camera and stand behind him. When the family heard that Mladen was coming home, they had probably brought over one of the two photographers who had studios in Ilidža during the war: Alfons Kafka or Đuro Karlović. Probably it was Kafka, for Karlo Stubler had known him for years, and for a time they had frequented each other's homes.

Mladen standing beside the round garden table. Again everyone is around him. There are two unfamiliar people. Probably neighbors whom, at the time when we looked at these photos – a year or two after Olga's death – no one remembered anymore. A bowl of apples on the table. Where had apples come to Ilidža from in May or June? Or had Mladen been on leave at the end of July when the Petrovka apples were ripe? But the apples in the picture are not Petrovkas. I wracked my brain over this question for a long time: they are large peacetime apples of the kind that never grew in the yard on Kasindol, and the year was lean 1943. The figures in the picture are careful not to obstruct the view of the bowl; the apples were there to be seen, just as was Mladen in his neatly buttoned uniform.

They are artificial, plastic apples, that had come into fashion in the last years before the war. Housewives used them to decorate their tables. They did not rot and were prettier than real ones. When the family had gone out to have their pictures taken, they had taken the apples out to the garden with them. The year was 1943, but they did not want to look hungry in the photos. For them that year was not terrible. It was a page from their life's calendar, and one had to embellish reality. Let it be seen that in honor of the grandson's visiting on his leave they had brought out the best apples.

If Mladen had lived, perhaps these photographs would have been compromising for him. Or if the family history had unfolded differently, if after the war people from the picture had ended up in important positions in the new society, these pictures would have been dangerous. But as it was it made no difference. The Stubler family history unfolded outside social and political history, and after 1943 they would never intersect with it again. The truth is that both political and social history would end at about the same time. The Stublers would disappear, as would Yugoslavia, the last country in which their *kuferaš* biographies might have found their reason for being.

When I looked at these photographs for the first and last time in 1987 or the year after, it seemed to me that everyone in the picture, and not just the young girl, was proud of Mladen's uniform. It was an uncomfortable thought and I did not speak it out loud, nor did I ask any questions. How could I have asked, when they all sat there beside me, staring at the photos, smiling sweetly, as if they were in the presence of a little Christ in his mother's arms. They mentioned the names of the people in the pictures, adding information and dates. I could have asked whether Kafka or else Karlović had taken them, but there was no way I could have asked why the people in the pictures, why Mladen's close relatives, suddenly seemed so proud of his uniform? A senseless question. They strove for order, filled out all the necessary forms properly, stood before the office windows, produced the necessary documents, had their pictures taken, produced evidence regarding their employment, and – aside from that one fatal mistake of Karlo's, when he supported the workers in their strike – spent their lives in bureaucratic rectitude, hoping the state would express to them its gratitude protecting them from danger. Nothing in 1943 seemed so certain as the uniform of a German soldier. To everyone but Franjo.

During this leave Mladen arrived with an elaborate desertion plan. Instead of going back to camp in Slavonia, he would take the train to Dubrovnik. All he needed was a well-made counterfeit pass, and he already had someone who could do it for him. In Dubrovnik he was to be met by Uncle Andrija Ćurlin, who, through his connections, would dispatch him by boat to the English. The idea was bold, youthful. The English had not yet even landed in Sicily, but Mladen had patiently worked it all out. An acquaintance was to provide him with a pass. Actually, it wasn't an acquaintance but the first cousin of Mladen's girlfriend. Franjo was to call Uncle Andrija in Dubrovnik from a phone that could not be listened in on. Uncle Andrija had already promised Mladen he would hide him if he deserted. The idea of joining the Partisans was no longer mentioned. Why?

Olga was horrified. She hissed around the apartment, shouting under her breath, in fear someone might overhear. She forbade Franjo to call Andrija in Dubrovnik. She told Mladen she would kill herself if he deserted and was arrested and shot. She would kill herself, let Franjo and the Partisans worry about Javorka.

The arguments and recriminations about something that had yet to happen continued for three days. She threatened and threateningly imagined Mladen's death. He would jump from a train somewhere near Konjic or Jablanica, they would shower him with rounds of gunfire, and he would fall dead into the Neretva. They would hunt him in Mostar and Čapljina, in Trebinje and Gruž. He suffered and perished several times, and she would furiously tell it to his face, pressing him to return to the German camp at Andrijevci and everything would be right, in accord with the protocols and rules, in keeping with how a citizen ought to behave before governmental and military authorities . . .

Calm reigned on the final morning. He was dejected, his great plans had fallen through, his father had not called Uncle Andrija but looked at him sadly, leaning against the kitchen door, saying nothing. His mother was kind, as if all was good, peaceful and quiet, as if she were sending him to Sokol camp and would accompany him to the station. Don't, he said to her. L. will see me off. His mother had only met her once, when Mladen was in the seventh grade at the gymnasium and L. a year older. This is my girlfriend, he had said to his mother. She extended her hand to her. The girl shook it firmly; she was beautiful. Olga had been proud of Mladen's choice. Daughter-in-law, she joked to someone, that's our daughter-in-law. But she had thought it would quickly pass. High school love affairs were short lived.

L. J.'s name was never spoken in our house, though we all knew it. It is unclear how, but in the years when this was contemplated, people knew L.J. was our secret relation. Mladen's first and last girlfriend, whom he was with from the seventh grade until the end. Olga had shaken her hand once; her grip had been firm and decisive. Franjo never met her. We did not exchange a word with her. No one. We would just smile at her as we passed. She would smile back. That was how we expressed our sympathy to her and she to us, with a smile. When I grew up, I would smile at L.J. too, and she would smile at me. Did she know Mladen had been my uncle, even though I was born twenty-three years after his death? Probably not. Sarajevo was a small town and someone was always smiling at L.J.

She was from an old Tašlihan Serbian family, with a quite famous surname that appears in all the old Sarajevo chronicles and histories. In 1878 her great-grandfather had greeted the Austrian troops in the name of all the Orthodox of the city, not to express subservience to Baron Filipović but to ask the representatives of the empire, which he believed would remain in Bosnia for a long time, as long as Turkey had, how he and his people might be of help. That had not been subservience – rather, the old Serb, who was a businessman, considered this to be the easiest way to prevent harm from coming to his people and to continue their affairs, which had been briefly interrupted by the war. The Austrians were able to respect such an attitude, just as the Turks, while they ruled over Bosnia, had respected the head of the Tašlihan family, and his reputation with the new occupier only grew, as it did both among the locals, those of his faith and those of others, and among the *kuferaši*. The family's wealth grew over thirty-five years of peace, and L's father and uncles all studied in Vienna. Only the murder of the prince, the event that triggered the Great War, destroyed the peace of the wide J. courtyard with its Turkish cobblestones and tall white walls, while the shop windows were shattered, their promissory notes fell in value, and a portion of their bank holdings disappeared. The walls drew in misfortune like moisture. But only for a short time. Although during the war he dispensed the majority of what he owned, the gold, money, and goods, L.'s grandfather was still on his feet in 1918, upright, with a black Christian fez on his head. For the liberators, though they were of his faith and language, he did not express overmuch enthusiasm. He said in public that toward others one should be open and toward one's own cautious, and for this statement he was reproached. He said what he thought, but with clarity and measure, so his words did not cost him. The J. family would never again attain the wealth they had had in Austrian times, but they would remain one of the two or three richest Serbian families in Sarajevo. They could have achieved more, but their grandfather did not conduct any business affairs with the government or allow the family name to be overly used before the authorities. It would not be good if anyone in the marketplace thought the J's were doing better because there was a Serbian king. That would not be good at all, said her grandfather, and her father and uncles did not give it another thought, proceeding instead as if the old man was always correct. J.'s grandfather died in the middle of summer 1940. The entire Serbian marketplace was at the funeral, which was conducted by the bishop of the Orthodox Church of Sarajevo. The funeral of the elder J. was the most important social event in Sarajevo during the last summer before the war.

After the Ustaše arrived in Sarajevo at the end of April 1941, they took control of the J. family's shops, but their homes were not touched, nor did any of their family members experience harm. L.'s father skillfully avoided offers of expressing loyalty to the Croatian authorities, though as a Croat of Orthodox faith, he could have taken part in the expressions of fidelity that began to flow toward Zagreb after the first great crimes, thereby improving the Ustaše's reputation among the Germans, who had criticized them for unnecessary crimes against the Serbs, and also for the living conditions of his own compatriots in Sarajevo. He didn't want to take part in this at any cost; he didn't want to assist evil.

L.'s father knew she was going out with Mladen. Probably he inquired what kind of home the young man came from, though this was not a problem in Sarajevo. Did it bother him that he was Catholic? There is little likelihood that it would have troubled him, given that his younger brother, L.'s uncle, was married to a Catholic woman, a Pole, the daughter of Emil Streche, professor of Latin at the Great Boys Gymnasium. Mladen and L. were together for three years. If it had bothered him, he would have done something to separate them.

Was it useful to him that his daughter was going out with a German soldier in 1943? Maybe so. They did not hold hands in public – Mladen did not want that – but they were seen walking together along Ferhadija Street. He was tall, thin, and blond, straight as a German triumphal obelisk; she a highbred Tašlihan girl who resembled the future Claudia Cardinale, her hair long, flying in all directions, dyed with Istanbul henna.

Why didn't he take her hand? They would walk side by side with their shoulders touching so that not even a sheet of paper could have slipped between them.

Was he perhaps afraid someone might call her a German slut? A Serb and also a German slut? This was quite possible in Sarajevo. Although he would write to little Nevenka, "We German soldiers are well liked here and are given everything for free," and maybe he believed these words while he was writing them, still Mladen understood well what German soldiers were in Sarajevo. And why they liked them in Slavonia and gave them fruit at no charge. He could imagine that one of his gymnasium comrades, some Young Communist, might call L. a German slut, as perhaps he might have done under different circumstances. Or no, he wouldn't have.

What is known: he confided in her his plan to desert and make his way to Dubrovnik. L.'s first cousin would help with the papers. After the war B.J. worked in the Federal Executive Council and then went into diplomatic service. He would become a Yugoslav ambassador somewhere in Latin America. At that time, in the early summer of 1943, he was a member of the communist underground in Sarajevo. He would remain in the city until the arrival of the Partisans, one of the few who did not fall victim to Luburić's police. A bright, cheerful person, calm and collected under all circumstances. Mladen had probably talked with him during his previous leave. What had B.J. told him?

L. accompanied him to the station and was the last to see Mladen alive. The last of those close to him. After that some letters would continue to arrive – letters Olga later destroyed (only Mladen's letters to Nevenka survived) – as would some postcards – also destroyed, and then came the end.

Mladen died between two of Nano's postcards. He was no longer sending them from Bijeljina but from Osijek, where he was transferred for a short time. Judging by the address, he had been placed in someone's private apartment. Actually the addresses are strangely different. The first postcard is signed "Second Lieutenant Rudolf Stubler, I Division," housed at Crkvena 26/I, whereas the second one reads, Cvjetkova 26/basement. Whether these are two different addresses or the same one written in two different ways is hard to know.

On the first, written in black ink, the date is 21 IX 1943:

Dear Nena, I haven't written to you in a long time. I miss you and home. How are you? Are you going to school and studying hard? I know you've always been a good girl. I feel fine here, but I would still rather be digging up potatoes than be here. The weather has been nice and sunny these last days. People were swimming in the Drava. But just now as I am writing to you, it's grown overcast, there was a flash of lightning and a strong wind has picked up. It's going to rain. The fall is coming, and Mladen is in the war. I've been to see Željko and he's come to see me. Now he too is leaving Borovo. Perhaps for Rajlovac. Give my best to your father and mother.

With love and kisses,
Your Nano

Six days later, another postcard, written in pencil, the text faded after seventy years, on August 3, 2013, the invisible graphite dust lingers on my fingertips.

Dear Nena, here I am writing from Mladen's grave. I am sad and sorry. I swallow my tears. He won't play or sing or visit us anymore. He is dead. Aunt Olga was here a little before me. I'm so sorry we missed each other. Now I'm here waiting alone for the train. How are you? Did you recieve my card? Write me and make a little drawing. Is Javorka at Ilidža? How are your father and mother? Has the piglet grown? Are you eating the rabbits? Warm greetings to you and your parents, Your Nano
     Andrijevci 27 IX 1943

Mladen was killed and buried between Tuesday the twenty-first and Monday the twenty-seventh. Regarding the date of his death there is no one left to ask anymore. Until not long ago I thought he had died in October. Did L. ever go to the grave in Andrijevci? Probably not. The love of a Serbian girl from Sarajevo and a German soldier, which ended with his death in the last days of summer or the first days of fall 1943 could be an interesting story for a film. Or a novel. But this happened in reality, and nothing about the two of them can be invented. L. was the only love of my eldest uncle, and if things had worked out differently, if the path of one bullet in Slavonia, near the village of Andrijevci, had been different, they would probably have married. Or not . . .

After the war L.J. studied philology in Belgrade. She worked as a teacher in Sarajevo's middle schools. At the beginning of the sixties she went to Canada, intending to stay, but several years later she came back. She was a secretary in the editorial office of a literary magazine. And then again a teacher, of Serbo-Croatian in a high school. She never married. Some suspected that L. J. was attracted to women. Tall, redheaded, without even a single gray hair, an eternal Claudia Cardinale, she did have a masculine way of moving. In her youth, they said, it was not so. But as she matured, it was as if the masculine side in her became more prominent. She remained strong in her body and face, which had no wrinkles, eternally youthful. As if the aging of her movements transformed her gender.

She would smile at me as if to say everything would be fine.

She left Sarajevo on the bus convoy in June 1992 that transported the Jews out of Sarajevo, along with those who would declare themselves Jews until they got to a place where bombs were not falling. Nothing more was heard about her afterward. She was seventy at the time, though she looked twenty years younger. On her departure, her hair still set fire to the woods at the base of Mount Igman. If she is alive, she is over ninety. But I believe she is no more. In a phone conversation last fall, Javorka suddenly asked me about her, about where I thought she might be. I think she died, I said. I did not want to tell you, Javorka said, but I dreamed she was dead.

2 VI 36. Thirteen frames. Three frames have empty spaces. Found the queen at the back of frame 4. Entire frame laid heavily with eggs. Laying is proper. The queen moves very slowly; her abdomen has turned rather dark. She's old. On further analysis located fairly mature brood. Since there is no drone comb, the bees have spread out their work and moved out the drone brood. In frame 10, counting in back I found two not-yet-closed queen cells next to mature brood. Removed one empty frame. No need for further checks before 20 VI 36, thanks to quiet swarming.

There is no information in the bee log regarding an examination of brood number 2 on 20 VI 36, but there is no doubt that it took place, that the quiet swarming was successfully and securely carried out, and that a new life cycle was initiated. The bee world, in contrast to the human one, is not preoccupied with individual deaths. The bees each have a soul, which lives and dies. Bees demonstrate love and hate, but mostly they are indifferent, like people, traveling from one end of the horizon to the other. If there is bee writing, then bees too create travelogues. People grow enraged many times; bees do so just once, and for that one rage, they pay with their lives. The death of one bee means nothing to other bees. That is the difference between bees and humans.

When he understood that he could not save the queen from the plague-infected brood, Franjo Rejc folded his hands and crushed the queen mother, but she did not sting him. She could not sting him, for she had not the least bit of anger in her. Or was it that the queen does not have a stinger? Who would know better? It is impossible to establish where he acquired the feedbag, for that happened before the plague. The plague wiped all bee memory clean. The plague alters the memories of the beekeeper.

After the war, Mladen's wartime comrades – who went into war in German uniforms and came out of it in Partisan ones – said Mladen had thrown himself behind a haystack while the two of them had ducked behind a little wall. He was left alone when they fell into the ambush, and he was trying to run to them. The one shot fired hit him in the neck. That was what they said. They didn't know who had fired the shot. It wouldn't have changed anything if they did.

Parker 5i

Franjo Rejc's acquaintance with Colonel Carl Schmitt, namesake of the German jurist and theoretician, began by chance at the end of August 1943. The colonel grew ill and collapsed at the door of Franjo's office. Franjo caught sight of the upturned face of a German officer foaming at the mouth, eyes rolling back into his head, and he jumped up from his desk, knelt down beside the unconscious man, and in one sure motion pried open his jaw and pulled his tongue out, which had fallen back into his throat. If it had not been for Franjo Rejc and for the knowledge he had gained as a soldier in the Bosnian regiment of the Royal and Imperial Habsburg Army regarding what to do in the case of a seizure, Carl Schmitt would have died.

When they had taken the colonel away in the ambulance, Franjo continued the letter he had begun earlier:

Dear Andrija,

A man just collapsed before my eyes. A tall German officer lost consciousness, foaming at the mouth. An epileptic seizure. I got his tongue out, turned him on his side, just as it's written in the manual. We were all unsettled. I won't tell Olga what happened. She would immediately think of Mladen. What would happen to him if the colonels around him all collapsed.

We're all fine. Javorka is growing. She started walking but not talking yet. She only says Mama, Papa, Tante Jika. We can't go to Ilidža. For going one needs to get special permission, explain the reason for traveling. What's the reason for traveling from Sarajevo to Ilidža? In my case it's the bees. In Olga's it's green lettuce, fruit, strawberries. How does one make that into words that will be understandable at the police checkpoints? A more difficult task than it seems at first glance. If I knew how, I'd be a writer rather than a rail man.

How is Lola? How's Branka? Željko sends postcards regularly. He says maybe soon he'll be transferred to Rajlovac. Olga was happy, but I told her you need a special pass to get to Rajlovac too, so it's the same to us if he's in Borovo or Rajlovac. It's as if we're in prison.

I've been trying for days to catch you by phone. I've been calling in the late afternoon. They say the line has been cut. Let's hope for better times.

Best regards to all, Lola, Branka, Mina, Franica!

Your friend and brother-in-law,

Franjo

This had taken place on Friday.

On Monday at about eight o'clock, Colonel Carl Schmitt returned to headquarters in a black Mercedes-Benz, cradling a small package wrapped in blue packing paper. He asked for a tall, slender Herr with a gray suit. Although the majority of those who worked there, or passed through headquarters on a daily basis, wore gray suits, and after two years of war it would have been suspicious for someone not to be slender, they somehow knew that the SS colonel was looking for Franjo Rejc.

When Carl Schmitt entered his office, Franjo was in pain. In late summer and at the end of winter Franjo would suffer attacks from a chronic illness. Every year a painful fistula would form near his tailbone, which would bother him as he sat down and stood up, and, once it was well developed, would need to be drained by a surgeon. Franjo would suffer from this affliction for his entire life.

Because of his pain, he did not stand up when SS Colonel Carl Schmitt came into his room. He offered his hand, and the guest could have easily mistaken the grimace on Franjo's face for contempt.

Schmitt was surprised when he heard him speak.

You're German?

No, Franjo answered curtly.

He did not explain what his heritage was or why he spoke German so well, which the colonel might have also found suspicious.

When the slender Herr in the gray suit did not get up from his chair to greet him and answered his question dryly, like a military prisoner saluting an enemy officer, Carl Schmitt offered the package in the blue packing paper without a word and left the office, closing the door behind him.

They had not shaken hands on taking leave and this troubled Franjo.

He opened up the paper without tearing it and took out a bottle of French cognac with a note attached. Translated from the German, it read:

Dear Sir,

The Engineer Carl Schmitt, Schutzstaffel Colonel, is obliged to express his thanks for saving his life.

That was it. No signature.

He put the bottle into his briefcase, while the note, after an hour's search, was found by Olga in the lapel pocket of his jacket.

The Ustaše police arrived on Friday in the early morning. They banged the butts of their rifles on the door of the fifth-floor apartment. As they led Franjo away, the creaks and groans of the parquet floors in the other apartments were audible, along with the clicking of the peep hole covers and the clinks of the door locks.

Olga was scared to death. She sat on the top step in her nightgown, struggling to light a cigarette as she trembled.

What happened? asked Mrs. Doležal.

I don't know. He must have been shooting his mouth off somewhere, she said.

They interrogated Franjo at the Ustaše police station but did not tell him what he was being charged with. He did not dare ask. First name, last name, father's name, mother's name? Place of birth, place of residency, faith, nationality? (He lied and said he was a Croat.) Where had he been on such and such a day at such and such a time? He said he did not know. The inspector repeated the question. He said he did not remember. The inspector got up from his chair and repeated the question. Franjo said that on such and such a day at such and such a time he was at work at the railway headquarters. Why didn't you say that immediately? Why did you lie?

He spent the night in a cell with twenty other men. They slept on the cold cement floor. Franjo did not close his eyes until morning. He sat in the corner, right next to the container for shit, where there was more space, and he reflected on his crime. And as soon as he came back to himself, he thought of Mladen. He would call on his son, the German soldier. He was the proof of his loyalty. Before the dawn sun had warmed the prison gates and the morning roll call became audible, Franjo had brought to mind every occasion when he had said something about Adolf Hitler. Besides what he might have said at the pub, playing cards, or at a beekeepers' meeting, he could not for the life of him remember anything that would have made him appear suspicious before the Ustaše. It tormented him. It would have been easier if he could remember something, some sort of evil deed, that might have landed him in this place.

That night and the next day Franjo Rejc was dying of fright over what he had said about Hitler, and about God, in whom he did not believe, promising himself that if he managed to come through this in one piece, he would keep quiet about politics to the end of his life.

Olga was running around town, trying to find out what had happened to her husband. She left Javorka with Mrs. Doležal, while for Dragan she left a note on the table with instructions about what he should do when he got back from town. If she wasn't there by the next morning, he was to run however he could to Opapa's and Omama's in Ilidža. He should leave the key with Mrs. Doležal. She would know what to do with Javorka and with the key. He just needed to run and not ask any questions about his parents.

Dragan read the note early in the afternoon. It was maybe half past one. Outside it was a sunny day. Voices could be heard through the skylight. Colonel Bilić's wife was explaining to someone how to wash the windows. The sound of a truck was audible from the river bank. The air was filled with the scent of blueberries and rotting apples. It was the end of August 1943.

Several times Dragan asked Olga what she was thinking when she wrote that he should run to Ilidža if she was not there by the next morning. He asked her ten years after the end of the war and then again in Drvenik, on the terrace of their house by the sea, at the beginning of August 1976. She answered him that she didn't know why she had written that, it was wartime, people disappeared in the war.

In the late afternoon two Germans in civilian clothes came for Franjo. They drove him from the prison in a black police car without windows in the back. They headed toward Marijin Dvor. They did not speak. He did not ask anything. He tried to listen in on what they were whispering but could not make it out.

In the improvised prison cell in the basement of one of those tenement buildings in Marijin Dvor, the air was cold and damp. The cell had no windows and no light. Only through the peephole in the nailed up door, a tiny hole of a half centimeter, did a sharp, thin ray of light penetrate, travel diagonally across the interior, and stop on the wall. A round point of light, which did not grow wider or illuminate anything. It seemed to Franjo that light would cut through his palm if he raised it up.

Several hours or several minutes later, the door opened. He felt a sharp pain in his eyes. The light was painful and when he tried to close them, it was as if his pupils had been filled with atropine. Someone took hold of him under his arms and led him into the corridor.

Mr. Rejc, did you write that German officers are epileptic?

No, he answered. And then he remembered that he had. He wrote it in his letter to Andrija Ćurlin, but how did they know that?

I did, he said, correcting himself.

Wipe his eyes, said the voice. He still won't be able to see. And only then did he feel the tears come out.

He was in the dark, he said, as if justifying himself.

Everything is fine, said the voice.

Then Franjo saw a young German officer, barely older than Mladen, in a black uniform, with the symbols of the SS.

And so, you wrote that German officers are epileptic. Why did you write that? Do you consider German officers to be epileptics?

No, but one colonel experienced an epileptic siezure in front of the door to my office. I had to help him. This moved me, and in the midst of the impression, I wrote it in the letter to my brother-in-law.

Meaning German officers are epileptics?

No, just that the colonel probably suffers from epilepsy. It's a disease like any other.

Are you a doctor?

(This scared him. He felt the adrenaline rushing through his veins . . .)

I am a railway worker.

And as a railway worker, you diagnosed epilepsy?

Yes, as I learned in the service.

Which service?

Austro-Hungarian.

What unit?

Bosnian regiment, first brigade . . .

That's enough. And so you claim that German colonels are epileptics? Crazies and epileptics?

No, but that colonel suffers from epilepsy.

Which colonel?

The one I helped.

What is the colonel's name?

Franjo could not remember the name Carl Schmitt. He had a good memory for names. Faces he forgot immediately, did not even remember those of people with whom he'd had much contact, but he remembered every name. Just then, however, all of a sudden, he could not remember. Was it fear? Nerves? What would happen if he could not remember the name of the colonel whose life he had saved?

Carl Schmitt, he pronounced, almost unconsciously.

Carl Schmitt, said the investigator, trying in vain to hide his surprise.

They did not return him to the basement. For the next two hours Franjo sat in the corridor, in a chair brought for him from the examination room. They served him coffee and homemade rose juice. The scent of the roses was enough to encourage Franjo to think nothing bad was going to happen to him anymore. The thought came to him, and he immediately believed it.

A car was waiting in front of the building.

It was not a police wagon but a beautiful, elegant Mercedes-Benz of the sort high-ranking German officers rode around town. A soldier opened the door for him.

Bitte . . .

The leather seat had a nice aroma. The scent of leather, gasoline, and jasmine. The driver wore a gray, very expensive suit, with a tie and a diamond pin. He had never seen such a driver. Where are we going? he asked in German. I'm taking you home, the man answered. I can walk, he said, it's not far. I have my orders, said the driver. Besides, curfew starts soon. It would not be good to be caught on the street. People have been nervous lately.

This was their conversation.

What happened? Olga asked upon his return.

He looked at her as if he were seeing her for the first time. Her nose stood out like the beak of a bird of prey. The sort of nose Jews have. He had not noticed that before.

He told her what had happened. He said it was lucky he eventually remembered the colonel's name was Carl Schmitt.

The next day he was back at work.

He sat at his writing desk and wrote a new letter to send to Dubrovnik:

Dear Andrija,

I have reason to believe you did not receive my letter. Times are hard, and we can no longer be completely certain about the mail. I'll write again the most important parts from the last letter. Everyone's well. Javorka is growing. It will soon be time for Dragan to go back to school, and we haven't seen or had news from our Ilidža relations in months. It's as if they're on the other side of the world. I don't know what's happening with my bees. Opapa is taking care of them, but he's old.

How are Lola and Branka? Željko keeps in touch by postcards. Will he get a transfer to Rajlovac? He hasn't told us anything about that.

Warm regards to all! Franjo

P.S. I'll try telephoning, if the lines are not down.

He thought about it and crossed out the postscript then made a clean copy of the whole thing. It was stupid to write in a letter that would get to Andrija in a week or two, if it got there at all, that he would be calling if the lines were not down, because that would happen before Andrija had read his letter anyway.

He was distracted. He kept looking toward the door. He had the sensation that what had happened a few days before would happen again. He would hear the thud of a head against the oak door and before his eyes would be the upturned face of a German officer. He would jump up, and the story would repeat. (Except this time it would not turn out well.)

Andrija's reply arrived around the twentieth of August.

Dear family,

We are all well. I'm working, Lola's taking it easy, and Branka goes to school. Everything's as it should be. We have enough food, thank God. Željko writes to us when he remembers, which is not often. You know how he is.

Lucky you know how to handle an epileptic.

Greetings to all from Uncle Andrija

So he had received the first letter. But it was as if he was hiding it, keeping quiet, speaking in riddles, like that sentence: "Lucky you know how to handle an epileptic." Andrija did not talk like that. No one did. Franjo was upset and afraid. The censor had read the letter but instead of holding onto it as proof had let it go on to the addressee. Why? Were they following Andrija in order to arrest him?

Franjo's concern did not last long.

A few days later, a telegram arrived. Olga opened the door. A man's voice said, I'm sorry, and she collapsed into a chair and went silent. Mladen was dead, buried in Andrijevci. Olga would visit her son's grave. There she would cross paths with Rudi for an hour or two. But that is no longer important.

Horrified by his son's death, Franjo forgot to warn Andrija Ćurlin that they might be following him, even though he knew Andrija was stirring things up in Dubrovnik, using his influence in the city, the reputation he had among the Italians and the Ustaše, helping people get to the Partisans, and maybe meeting with British spies. If they arrested him, he would be lost, and there would be one more death to drop onto him like a stone and drive him mad. Fortunately, no one arrested Uncle Andrija Ćurlin. And what remained was the story, that dream of Mladen's, of deserting from the German army and fighting for the English. He had come to an agreement about this with his uncle . . .

Franjo lived in grief, and thought of hanging himself. But he did not have the strength, and he felt sorry for his other son, who at first hid in the attic to avoid being drafted and then worked as a miner in a Kakanj coal mine under a false name. He did not want to leave his daughter without a father, his little girl who was not yet conscious of anything. So he continued with his life, and started to think about his bees again. When he did not think about them, he dreamed of hanging himself and of Olga finding him. At that instant, Mladen's death would fall completely onto her soul. And when he grew fed up with this, disgusted with himself and his own cowardice, for he did not dare hang himself, Franjo would again think of his bees. In his thoughts he would build hives, arranging them in Želeće, in Ilidža, on Glavatičeva . . .

In the first days of January 1944 Franjo ran into Colonel Carl Schmitt once again. He saw a tall, worn-out man on the street, resembling one of the spectral figures in a Alberto Giacometti painting. He swerved as he walked, as if he was about to collapse at any moment. He was not swerving like a drunk man, but like someone whose feet felt the earth slipping away with every step. He did not look at his face. He did not know any German officers and did not care to meet any, and he would have passed him by had Carl Schmitt not grabbed his arm as he passed.

Now you're sorry you saved me?

He raised his eyes in surprise. At first he did not recognize him.

I'm not sorry, I just don't look around when I'm walking.

Don't worry.

I'm not worried.

How is it you're not worried. Aren't you a patriot?

No, not in any way. My son died.

As a Croatian soldier?

No, Mr. Schmitt. As a German soldier.

I'm sorry.

It's not your fault.

When did this happen?

At the end of August, in Slavonia.

People passed them as they stood there in the middle of Ferhadija, a few paces from the city market. The street was suddenly full, and like in a nightmare, all the people were acquaintances. They pretended not to see them, but Franjo could tell they did. And he knew they would talk about how they caught him talking, smiling, and joking with an SS colonel. With Carl Schmitt.

They said goodbye after the German once more expressed his sympathy. Franjo found it unbearable to hear this. He went away without saying almost anything. The colonel looked after him, his mouth partly open, as if he was going to call him back. It was cold and sunny. One of those rare sunny days in Sarajevo without fog or snow, without smog.

Do you know who Carl Schmitt is, you poor sot?

Matija Sokolovski was upset and afraid. The devil only knew who had told him he had seen Franjo in the middle of Ferhadija discussing something with Colonel Schmitt.

"I don't know and I don't care. Why didn't you tell me who he was when I was pulling his tongue out of his throat? Maybe I'd have thought better of it. But you just stood there and said nothing."

Sokolovski looked at him with worry and shook his head.

He worked in the next office over from Franjo's. He'd been at headquarters longer than Franjo. When he had arrived at the Chief Inspectors Division, Sokolovski had been there to meet him and show him where to sit. Matija was a Pole, a quiet, withdrawn man, a nonbeliever. It was unusual that a Pole should not believe in God. But he was excellent at preferans. He would have been the best if he did not usually sit at the same card table as Franjo. Nonbelievers were unbeatable at preferans. God did not get in the way of their mathematical games. God despised mathematicians.

He told Franjo everything about Carl Schmitt.

Where do know this from? Franjo asked. He didn't believe him. He thought Sokolovski was trying to shock and scare him. This made him angry. Matija wasn't like this usually. But maybe he had changed. Many people had changed lately. The winter had been hard. Hunger. Everyone treated him differently since Mladen's death. They were waiting for him to do something. They shrank from him. Maybe they were expecting him to hang himself, wondering why he hadn't already. In evil times people were evil. But if Matija Sokolovski had turned evil, there was no one left. Who would he play cards with?

How do you know all that about Carl Schmitt? he asked angrily.

Matija Sokolovski looked at him with his moist blue eyes, which seemed to be welling up with tears. What was it with Matija that his eyes were so wet? Were they this wet before the war? He didn't remember that.

I know, Sokolovski answered, touching his arm as if to calm him.

Franjo did not like it when people tried to calm him. And he did not like to be touched.

But he put up with that too. He calmed down and didn't yell at Sokolovski. He agreed to listen to his story, not because he was interested in Carl Schmitt, but because he didn't want to lose his preferans buddy.

The engineer Carl Schmitt had been an activist for Hitler's party since the time when the National Socialists were preparing to take power. Until the beginning of the war he had worked as a designer of furnaces for the Kruppove Steelworks, and then in the fall of 1939, on joining the SS, he was given the rank of colonel and took part in the eastern operations. He was seen in Poland, Lithuania, and Ukraine. The traces he left behind could be described by only one word: silence. Whoever saw him even once would dream about him until the end of his life.

But what does that mean? Franjo interrupted.

I don't know. It's what I was told, and I'm passing it on to you.

Schmitt was wounded in the winter of 1942 when he fell into an ambush with his driver and two adjutants. This had happened in Ukraine. It was unclear where. They were killed; he was riddled with machine gun fire, but he survived. A Red Army soldier shot him in the head at close range to put him out of his misery. The bullet blew apart the bone above his right eye and came out the back of his head. He lay in the mud for twelve hours until they found him. They thought he was dead, so they were in no hurry to get him to the hospital. Only the next morning, when it was time to start burying the bodies, did someone notice that Colonel Schmitt was alive.

For several weeks he lay dying, and then, over the next six months, his condition improved. His brain's right hemisphere, which controls the left side of the body, was dead. All sorts of other things were also dead in Carl Schmitt. The centers of his brain responsible for memory were not damaged. He even remembered things he had not remembered before.

It was unbearable for him to sit at home. His wife was afraid. His children were small and did not understand anything. There was no one he could speak to about what had happened to him. When everyone would go to the bomb shelter because the British bombers had appeared, he would sit in the apartment. He could not go on for long like this. He asked to be returned to service, sent somewhere at the front, where his own death would feel at home among the others. They took pity on him and sent him to Sarajevo. In Sarajevo he would not bother anyone.

It was unknown what Carl Schmitt's assignment was in the city, who reported to him, or what his goals were. Schmitt's appearance, more than his SS rank, which gave him absolute control over all the German officers in town, as well as every Ustaše *and* Home Guard commander, even of the highest rank, aroused fear and a certain strange unease among people. They would lower their heads before him.

Some people believed Colonel Schmitt was the grim reaper of Sarajevo, and some pitied him, an invalid sent to Sarajevo to die in peace. Or they believed Carl Schmitt was bait for communist assassins – if anyone killed him there would be retribution, and the Germans would raze Sarajevo to the ground.

The winter of 1944 lasted a long time, extending to the end of April, when it suddenly grew warm, the sun burning as if it was already summer. A long, parched Sarajevo summer followed, which dried out the vegetable gardens and orchards. Only the walnuts ripened, as they did every year without regard to wars. Franjo did not know how he passed the time between Mladen's death and the end of the war. He did not remember anything from that time, except that everything was hunger and apathy and there was no life in anything around him. This was how it seemed to him, and this was perhaps how it was. He rarely recalled Carl Schmitt. Did he ever think that after the war someone might look badly on the fact that he had stood in the middle of the street talking with SS Colonel Schmitt? Probably not.

In the first days of April 1945, when the Germans had for the most part pulled back from the city, the Ustaše remained to take bloody revenge against all who had worked for their downfall. The Partisans in the neighboring forests were just waiting for the day when they would all emerge. The attack on the city had been planned for a long time, and they had long known the day would be theirs. They just needed to live to see it.

Franjo was returning from the night shift at headquarters and he was tired and a bit crazy from all the news and rumors flying all about. He could hardly wait to lie down.

He went into the entrance hall, climbed the steps, and at the top step, in front of his door, found Carl Schmitt sitting, his legs before him, his elbows resting on his knees, as if he had been there for a long time.

He held out a rectangular box of brown Morocco leather.

Franjo held it in confusion. He did not ask anything, waiting for the colonel to get up so he could go into his apartment.

You're not going to open it?

What is it?

Open it. Look. It's a stylograph. A very nice one. If you recall, I was once in your office. When you saved my life. I am certain I saw a stylograph on your work table. So I thought you might be able to use this. I used it only for official signatures. Nothing else. I signed perhaps twenty times in all.

He opened the box. A fountain pen lay on a small pillow of red silk. The pen body was also red, while the cap was gilt.

Try it, Schmitt urged.

He removed the cap and wrote down, in the notebook that was offered to him, in blue ink, his first and last name and his place of birth: Travnik.

See how nicely it writes. It settles quickly into your hand.

He said this as if he were talking about a living creation.

Why are you giving it to me now?

Don't worry. It's not a sign of gratitude. You shall be rendering me a service if you accept it. Where I am going I won't need a fountain pen, and I would not like it to fall into the wrong hands.

He extended his hand and stood up. His steps resounded with an improper rhythm, as if a piece of furniture was tumbling down the stairwell. Franjo stood there without moving until he heard the stairwell door close. A silence came that would last until the early morning, when the alarm clocks in the apartments began to ring. After that the first morning siren was heard: the signal for aerial danger from the last Allied bombing of the city.

Franjo Rejc rarely used the fountain pen he received from SS Colonel Carl Schmitt that early morning of April 2, 1945. He did not take it with him to the office. He signed his name perhaps two or three times with it, considering what might have been written on the documents Colonel Schmitt had signed. Once, in the summer of 1945, it occurred to him that the Partisans might have robbed the SS colonel of his things and found his notebook with "Franjo Rejc, Travnik" in it. This concerned him. But then he forgot about it.

The name of the stylograph was Parker 51. Franjo emptied and cleaned it, and intended to keep it for a time when no one would be burdened by his story, for no one would remember Carl Schmitt or think of the documents he might have signed. When his grandson was born in 1966, he decided that if the boy turned out to be kind and intelligent, he would give him the fountain pen as a gift. It would be a valuable gift, a great treasure, and one unused stylograph produced in 1939 on the occasion of the Parker anniversary, would at least find a hand to which it could become accustomed and follow. The unique hand of a fountain pen. People differ according to fountain pens and fingerprints.

He was afraid of thieves. They could break into the house and take the fountain pen. He was not worried about other valuables. Nothing but that pen was valuable anymore. For this reason he decided to carry it everywhere with him. It was the only way to be sure no one would steal it.

It was the last year of his life. He walked down from Drvenik to Zaostrog, sat down at a bar, and ordered a glass of rakija and mineral water. He felt healthy, as if he could live for another hundred years. Everything was good, all misfortunes far away from him. As he was taking out his money to pay, the edge of his wallet caught against the stylograph. He did not notice, not even as the fountain pen popped out of his coat and slipped lightly and silently to the floor.

He returned to the bar in vain, asking about his lost pen, telling the waitress a story of how it wasn't just a question of a fountain pen, it was something much more important. She listened to him the way polite people listen patiently to old folks.

But she did not remember his story.

Sarajevo Dogs

I got to the room late.

A cramped hotel, adapted from a rather large family home, at the top of Baščaršija. The polite receptionist, a psychology student – I could tell from the open book on the counter, which was underlined in different colors of pencil, green, blue, and red – told me how to get to room number 17. Breakfast was from seven thirty to ten, she said. She did not recognize me, which was good.

I tried to turn off the heat, at least for a half hour. I twisted the knobs on the radiator left and right, first in one direction then in the other. They spun around like endless tape reels, without meaning or effect, but the air in the room stayed as warm as it had been. Hot and dry, fifty degrees centigrade, by contrast to the twenty degrees it was outside.

When I opened the window, the frozen air rushed in, but as with a broken shower nozzle, it did not mix with the hot air in the room, so I sweated and froze at the same time. The cold air went in one nostril, the hot air in the other, and half of me cooked while the other half congealed. This corresponded perfectly, in a certain paradoxical and unnerving manner, to my life's circumstances at the moment.

Besides this, whenever I opened the window, the barking entered both the room and my head. Not just of one, two, or three dogs, but of the hundreds and thousands of them up in the mountains, in the valley with its dirty little river, in the famous city at the edge of the world, the city where I was born and where I was sleeping in a hotel for the first time.

I don't know how or when I dozed off. I don't know whether I had in fact dozed off when, very clearly and vividly, a dream woke me. I'm not sure if it was an actual dream or a hallucination suddenly erupting in parallel with the hot little room in this tiny Sarajevo hotel.

I'm sitting in an armchair, reading Péter Nádas's *Parallel Stories*. A huge, difficult book that makes my arms hurt. I'm in my Zagreb apartment, sheltered by its care and patience as snow falls outside.

The telephone rings. My mother. I answer, scared, and she tells me from the other end, in an accusing voice, that by some medical error she's been buried alive. They did something wrong, miscalculated the therapy, the cytostatic drugs didn't work, we didn't have enough money for the entire treatment with those so-called smart drugs, and they ended up killing her. She'd been buried quickly that afternoon.

Okay, but why didn't anyone call me? I ask.

How am I supposed to know! she says and starts crying.

Where are you now? I ask.

In the grave, under Nona. Do something! she shouts.

What can I do?

Call someone. Dig me up. You can at least do that much for me!

Okay, I say. I'll call back when I've got things worked out.

Hurry, she says. I'm running out of air. The coffin is shut tight. It's like I'm inside a jar. I'll suffocate, she says, crying.

I place a bookmark with "Dubrovnik" written on it between pages 178 and 179. She comes in from the kitchen and asks who called.

No one, I lie.

I can't tell her the truth because if I do, the horror won't just be shared between us, it will be multiplied. That's why it's better if everything stays with me. But how? My mother will call again, and I don't know what to say to her, how to put off things until the moment when she'll be just as dead and in her grave as the doctors foresaw.

There isn't anyone in Sarajevo I could call to dig her up. There aren't any phone lines to Sarajevo, besides this one to the grave in Bare.

I know my mother will suffocate in her grave even if this very instant I get into my car and head for Sarajevo. She'll suffocate by the time I'm nearing Derventa or Doboj.

Morning came before the telephone could ring a second time for me to once again hear her tearful reproofs. The same heat enveloped the room. Through the thin plywood door I could hear the voices of people leaving their rooms, driven forth by the savage climate.

I got dressed and went out quickly. At the reception desk there was a different staff person, smiling, just as young as the last one, probably a student. She asked if I had slept well. I answered in the affirmative. I was in a rush, and even if I hadn't been, what was the use of explaining? It was too late.

I caught a taxi at the end of the street.

It was an old, nearly decrepit red Fiat. The driver asked me how things were in Zagreb and then, without waiting for a response, started telling his story. There wasn't any snow yet, he told me, but there would be soon, any day. It always came down when the snow service didn't expect it. The snow service and the beginner drivers. If you asked him, there should only be professional drivers. Those others should have their licenses taken away. Then there wouldn't be any more accidents or afternoon jams, and the cabbies could make good money . . .

His story wasn't making me feel better, but I wanted the drive to last as long as possible, so I could put off the moment when I'd see her and she'd surely begin to cry. She was alive and unburied. In the morning, when I'd first woken, that first moment I'd felt grateful that this was the case. I had come in time, I thought.

The old Fiat could barely make it up the street where I had grown up. But this did not interfere with the driver's story in the least. His daughter had passed her driver's exam, but he would never let her drive his car. Hell, so she could wreck it?

And then what would we all live on? This was his means of production, he said, proudly emphasizing each word in the old Marxist phrase, and then he reminded me that we'd been in the same philosophy class. I hadn't recognized him.

On the way back I walked down the street, feeling a boundless joy that all of it had gone by quickly. I rushed, crashing and tumbling down Sepetarevac, and then along Mejtaš and Dalmatinska, passing by familiar buildings that in the meantime had grown dilapidated, falling in on themselves and emptying out, where no one lived anymore who used to, my schoolmates, their drunk fathers, and old Bato Narančić, who'd fallen down the elevator shaft and survived. I ran, sped into the valley so as not to meet them if it turned out they were still there, happy as if it were the end of the story and there wouldn't be any continuation and from now on everything would unfold much more happily.

The sky was gray and low. The valley was filled with mist and smoke, rusty and dense heavy metals, and 250,000 human bodies, sweating in the heat, evaporating and stinking. The familiar stench of burnt Bosnian charcoal in the stoves of 250,000 people, as it had once been, when I was one of the 250,000.

It was daytime and the dogs were dozing, balled up in front of building entrances or stretched out in the middle of sidewalks. Passersby patiently avoided them, stepping into the street to continue walking up the hillside.

Now I'm on Tito Street, where one, two, three, four cars zoom by at dangerous speed as if it's a race. Rickety old jalopies from before the war. Backfires resound from their rusty, sunken tail pipes, but no one is disturbed. No one turns, ducks, or speeds up their pace. In the distance, from Veliki Park and the Public Health Office, their firing carries a nostalgic ring from the good old days.

It's November 7, 2012, the 105th anniversary of the October Revolution, I rush along Tito Street as if I've got some sort of work to do, trying not to see a single human face. I aim my eyes at chest level, but my glance, agitated by the open shirt front of some beggar, drops down to their knees, and when it can go no lower, slowly comes up, from some wide women's hips, across half-open flies and the flow of belts and straps, up to the men's bellies, yearning for life, and I rush forward like that, trying not to meet anyone, for if I meet someone, if someone crosses my path, puts a hand on my shoulder, calls me by my first or last name, or, God forbid, hugs me, I'll have to talk, say how long I'm there for, until what day, whether I'm there for work or just personal reasons, and then, probably, they'll ask about her. And if they ask me this, I won't know what's behind the question – whether they know that last night in my overheated hotel room I dreamed she had called me from the grave, whether they know she's terminally ill and are checking up, enjoying the experience of asking and their own condolences, or whether it seems to them that they just saw her yesterday and had a good chat with her, they asked about me and she told them, that it was so nice to see her, that they invited her for coffee but she was in a hurry, that she said next time, when in reality there was no next time and would not be a next time in this world, unless they hurried, had their coffee beside her sick bed, with the joking that humans have used in this town for some five centuries to make themselves laugh, that put off every pain and every thought of death, and that was better than morphine, which, thanks for asking, she hasn't yet started to take but will any day now.

A woman I know is selling newspapers in front of the market. I turn my head to the other side and increase my pace. She sees me but is just then taking money for an *Oslobođenje* and returning the change and she doesn't manage to call out to me. Then I almost run into a tall toothless old man, as dried out as a locust tree, and when I try to escape he stops me.

I know you! he says, brightening, and taking my arm.

Now I think he's going to ask me for money, a mark or two, say he's hungry, cold. But he doesn't.

I knew your father too. And Madam Štefanija, your grandmother. She was godmother to my Antuns.

And on mentioning the Antuns, the old man cries out, tears run down his cheeks, and I no longer know what to do.

I'm standing in the middle of Ferhadija, a street that in my time was named after the underground Partisan and union activist Vaso Miskin, face to face with a man in tears, a head taller than I am and almost twice my age, and I feel everyone's eyes fastened on me. They pierce me from right and left, but especially from behind, like a bullet in the back of my head, and it's only a question of the moment when someone will recognize me . . .

Upset, I invite him for coffee.

I drink tea, says the old man through his tears.

I find the most hidden place, a table in the corner of the empty Ćumez, the eternally smoke-filled coffeehouse where we went after school as high school students. Here, I hope, no one will find us.

The old man orders a mint tea. A cloud of steam rises from the boiling little pot, enveloping the frozen surroundings. Only then do I realize how cold it is. Ćumez isn't being heated since there are no customers. The waiter is the same one who's been here for the last thirty years: Nune. But before he was just the waiter, now he's the owner. He stares at me. I seem familiar to him, or he's waiting for me to say hello and is angry that I haven't.

Your grandma Štefanija was a spiritual woman, the old man begins, while the tears dry on his cheeks or in the deep dark wrinkles, sinking somewhere under his skin, a spiritual and proper Christian. There were few like that in Sarajevo. This was never our city – he grows darker as his says this – it was all Turkey, the Orient, halva, salep. Sweet poison! And she saw this, you know. She felt it, my dear sir . . .

I listen to him talking about Grandma Štefanija, a frightening woman about whom I've written on more than one occasion, without the least bit of joy, and try to decipher who this man might be, where I could have met him. He did not introduce himself, probably assuming we were already acquainted, and as usual in such situations I am embarrassed to ask and instead just kept pretending we know each other.

When my Antun was born, the first Antun, it was 1941, springtime in Sarajevo, the twenty-second day of May, everything was sprouting, blossoming, people pouring out from their homes with naïve, foolish purity. And what name should I give my son but the one that was being pronounced so often then, from the purest Christian love? Let him be Ante! Not Ante Padovanski, but our Ante, the one from that time and our kin, the springtime one. We had the friars baptize him at Saint Ante's, in Bistrik. And your good grandmother Štefanija was Antun's godmother. The little boy was three months old when he died. In his sleep. He just stopped breathing. I touched his little face with my index finger and it was cold. His cheek was cold and moist like an inkblot. We buried our Antun in the cemetery at Saint Josip's.

After that my wife could not conceive because of the fear. How she had found her dead child was always on her mind, the poor woman. And how easy it was for a living creature to suddenly stop breathing, without any visible suffering. It was in her head and on her soul, and there was no way for her to conceive again. But your grandmother Štefanija consoled her, called for blessings upon her, gave her prayers, recommended her womb to the Holy Virgin, until my unhappy wife conceived and gave birth, again in May, in the year 1945. And again it was spring, again everything was sprouting, blossoming – people rushed outside, joyous and singing some new songs just as naïve and pure and innocent.

When we went to city hall to record the birth, I didn't know what name to give him. Then some Partisan named Pavle, seeing me hesitate, says, let him be called whatever you like, brother, all names are nice, Pero, Jozo, Mustafa, just not after that criminal Ante! And as he said it, my first born came to my mind, three-months old, the little angel, when he drew his last breath, and when that Partisan asked me again what name I would give to my son, I said – Ante.

I suppose he scowled. I didn't look at his face, but he wrote as I had said: Ante.

We baptized Antun with the friars at Saint Ante's, in Bistrik, in July of the same year. He died six months later of diphtheria.

My wife was insane. I was insane along with her.

And your grandmother Štefanija sends us letters from her prison in Zenica, comforting and encouraging us, and from her consolations my wife conceived a third time.

Our third son came in November 1946. It was cold, and snow was falling. I carried him from the hospital wrapped in cloth and bandages sewn together with hospital bed linen. I was happy, not suspecting a thing, not then and not on the Feast Day of the Holy Innocents, December 29, when we baptized our son with the brothers at Saint Ante's, in Bistrik. That fall your grandmother Štefanija had got out of prison, but we still asked her to be the child's godmother. It would not have been right or respectful not to. It would have been as if we were afraid, as if we had changed our minds and renounced her because of politics, or scorned her consolation, from which our Antuns were born. And so we named our third son Ante. But by then it was all the same. There wasn't any Partisan named Pavle or anyone else to be bothered by that name or hear in it the name of a criminal.

It was the end of February when our Ante died. Again in his sleep and again I touched his little face with my index finger. It was taut and as cold as a knife. By afternoon, taking turns with two grave diggers, Savo Vlaškalić and Nurija Idriza, I had dug a tiny, shallow grave for our Ante. The ground was frozen and stone hard and would not take anyone inside it. All the other funerals scheduled for that day had been canceled. It was negative thirty degrees centigrade, but Savo and Nurija did not want to stop. It was a matter of honor for them. People might have said they could not even dig a single, shallow child's grave.

We didn't have any more children after that. And old age without children isn't easy. You don't even have anyone to make you tea and bring you a cup. The old man finished his monologue and greedily started drinking his tea, which in the meantime had got cold. There was not a trace of the earlier tears. He drained his cup, hopped up spryly, muttered some sort of an excuse, and nearly ran out of Ćumez.

Balo, eh, Balo got you too? Don't worry. He skins everybody at least once. You didn't get off bad. You bought him a cup of tea. He might have taken you for some ćevap. Or for cognac. Before four Balo drinks tea, but after four it's cognac. That's his rule. Well now you know, and welcome back to Sarajevo, friend! said Nune, charging for the old man's tea and my coffee.

He had said "friend," which meant he did not remember my name or didn't remember who I was. Which was good.

I didn't ask him who Balo was or what he knew about him, though this would torment me later. As I was leaving, I tried to leave the impression of being a tourist. This probably went off badly because it seemed to me there was something ironic about Nune's gestures and the way he pressed the cloth over the bar.

I stepped carefully onto the street, as if shells might come down from the sky, then quickly continued toward Baščaršija. I avoided the faces, looking at the level of the larynx, and then again lower, down to the wide hips of the forever discontented service-window workers, and then lower still, to their knees and the tops of their shoes . . .

That toothless old man, that tall, straight twig had swindled a cup of mint decoction out of me, which people here mistakenly refer to as tea. Let him. He had paid for the mint with his fantastic story, which was obviously invented, but there was something in it that still bothered me: how had he known that my grandmother, my father's frightening mother, was called Štefanija and that she was a God-fearing Catholic? Maybe he had read about her in a book of stories – which again through a swindle and on the basis of false friendship a local newspaper publisher and fighter for human rights from Sandžak had wheedled out of me – sold on the streets by the news venders for two or three marks apiece, but if that were the case, if the toothless Balo had read the story of Štefanija, one had to admit he had inserted his own figure into it with talent and storytelling skill and had made it into his own.

As I had listened to him, I could see Grandma Štefanija going to Saint Ante's in Bistrik three times, serving as witness three times for the baptism of each of the newborn Antuns, the sons of a single set of parents, all three of whom would die before they learned to talk or walk. The first had become Ante on the wave of national enthusiasm for Ante Pavelić. The father had named the second Ante so as not to betray his fatherly responsibility toward the first. And the third had acquired the same name because of the first two. In this story of Balo's, in which there was nothing true whatsoever, for such stories are always made up in Sarajevo, the unhappy mother and father were not Ustaše but poor folk, sad mournful Sarajevo Catholics, janitors, waiters, and bodies to be slaughtered, carried away by that April of 1941, and later they had not known how to turn from what had carried them away, but had given each subsequent son the same name, the name of the Immortal One who even today lies so life-like in Madrid, in a casket of gold, waiting for the hour of his resurrection. It has been twenty-two years now since his Croatia was reborn. But however made up the old man's story might have been, my grandmother was not made up in it. Everything around Štefanija was false and fantastic, but she herself was truth, while in the moment of her epiphany, thrice, like the three raised fingers of Jesus Christ at the top of Sarajevo Cathedral, and the three raised fingers in the Poglavnik's oath before God and the people, and the three divine parts of the godly unity, Štefanija bore witness to the birth of a new Ante.

And as I thought about the three Antuns and Balo's invention, I quickly sank into the passersby on Ferhadija, unnoticed and anonymous.

In the hotel room I again tried to shut off the heat. When I got tired, I fell across the bed. I wanted to relax and rest, but sleep tricked me. I slept rigid, without dreams and without consciousness of the passage of time. Only occasionally, when my sleep grew shallow, the same idea would come to me that sleeping was healthy and that, by sleeping, I was growing healthy. But I didn't know what I was ailing from. I didn't know anything in my sleep, and this made things easier.

Things grew so much easier that the first clear, waking ideas were a shock, when facts began to organize themselves and my working memory loaded up, and the world on my shoulders grew all the heavier. I got up from bed, hunched over like the Atlas who carries the balcony of that Marijin Dvor building on his back. Sweat was pouring down mine. I remembered everything I had forgotten while I was asleep: why I was in Sarajevo, why I was sleeping in a hotel, not in the house where I had lived . . . I knew it all, and there was nothing good and there could be nothing good in this knowledge. That was my illness.

It was past five, and I had promised my mother I would be at her place by five thirty at the latest.

There was no one at the reception desk – just the psychology text – so I couldn't tell anyone it was hot in my room and I couldn't turn the radiator off. I rushed to the taxi stand at the top of Baščaršija. The icy air burned my lungs, mixing with the scents of coal smoke, ćevapi, fresh-baked somun, cat piss, and dog shit. Zagreb was without scent, I thought, and for the first time in the twenty years since moving to that cold, Catholic city, I was moved by the hungry cur of nostalgia. I wanted to be there, where there was no odor, color, or scent, and where I didn't yet know anyone.

I got into the first taxi in a long colorful line of cars waiting for customers.

It was an almost brand new Mercedes with sheepskin-covered seats. Instead of Islamic prayer beads, a soccer club banner, or a picture of Marshal Tito, from the rearview mirror hung the most ordinary air freshener – a little green pine tree with the scent of Zaostrog on an early fall day in 1975. The driver, a heavyset older man of maybe seventy, had an unhealthy yellow complexion and an expensive Rolex on his wrist.

It's real, he said, and I realized I'd been staring at his watch.

Sorry, I didn't . . .

It's okay. That's why I wear it.

All sorts of people have them.

All sorts? That's not a good word. I'd say no sorts!

Well put.

I earned the money for it in Germany – he said, showing off the watch – and I made enough for lots of other things in Germany too, in Rostock. That used to be GDR, the German Democratic Republic, as it would be called officially.

Isn't it a little dangerous, with the watch like that, at night?

Dangerous? That's another weak word you've got there. It's not dangerous, it's deadly. But nothing has happened to me yet. It's been a year and a half since I came back from Germany and started driving, like this with a new Mercedes and a Rolex, and still, nothing. You wouldn't believe. Last winter, when that big snow fell, I'm driving a guy toward Trnovo. A young tough, strong, packing, with a shaved head, gold chain around his neck, sits in back so I can't see him in the rearview mirror. That's it, I'm thinking. Now he'll cut my throat and toss me into a ditch, into the snow so I won't be found till spring. And then nothing. Even thanks me kindly for driving him, and leaves me a ten-mark tip. No one besides me, he says, would have driven him in this mess.

We had already reached Sepetarevac – Stop by that no parking sign, and you'll be able to turn around toward Kevrin Creek! – and as I was getting out, he said, Goodbye, son, and God willing we won't meet again! I was a little stung by that, but it was too late.

I was in front of her house.

The key slipped easily into the lock, the hinges squeaked in a familiar way.

Night was falling by the time I made my way back down the street. In the lit up living rooms, kitchens, and bedrooms I recognized the chandeliers and kitchen cupboards, and the range hoods and refrigerators purchased in the middle of the eighties, in the golden age of this city, when the apartments and the dreams of Mejtaš and Sepetarevac were being renovated with money earned on construction sites in Iraq and Libya. And while I'd been peering into the homes of my former neighbors, I had failed to notice the pack of dogs following me. Only when I got to Mejtaš, in front of the traffic light, and turned for the first time, did I see them, a few meters behind, waiting for me to cross and continue down Dalmatinska.

At the front was a Dalmatian with the head of a Labrador.

A beautiful, graceful dog with large, sad eyes. When I turned toward him, he jumped back in retreat. The ones behind him, five stub-tailed, hungry, muddy desperados, backed up, growling, as if they were prepared to attack if I continued. But they would not take his place in the lead. That timid, uncertain one was the absolute leader of the pack.

Was I afraid of them?

I don't know. Maybe I was, for only after making my way down Dalmatinska near the park, above the observatory where, in 1981, eighty-eight trees had been planted for Comrade Tito, at least half of which had then been cut down during the cold wartime winters, only then did I notice the nighttime sounds of the city. Somewhere in the distance, an old diesel Golf was furiously revving its engines, and this was the only remaining sound of civilization. All around from the hills surrounding the valley could be heard the calls, cries, yelps, and despair of hundreds, thousands of dogs. The people had closed themselves up in their homes, covered their heads with quilts. It was cold. The frigid winter was coming, the autumn mists lay atop the valley, and the night, painful and hungry, belonged to the dogs, who came down in packs toward the center of town.

Once more, near the development that used to be called the Sun, on a street that had been named after Staka Skenderova, I turn and go toward him. He looks at me just as sadly.

Good boy, good boy, I whisper to him so no one else can hear me.

I'm on Tito Street, in front of what used to be a drugstore. My canine pack continues to follow. There are few people out, so I don't hide my face. Drunk kids, carefree and emboldened by beer, shout at each other from one side of the street to the other.

Near the old JAT high-rise, which today is called the Vakuf Building, in front of the window of the Cultural Center of the Islamic Republic of Iran, beneath a photograph of the imam Ruhollah Khomeini, a rather young woman sits bent over on a piece of cardboard from a Rubinov Grape Brandy box. A French beret lies in front of her for handouts.

I've never seen a beggar out this late. They usually scatter at the first twilight or start lurking in front of the best, most popular restaurants, but never, not even in Sarajevo, have I seen someone out begging just before midnight.

Especially not a woman.

I can't see her face. She's leaning forward, nearly touching the cardboard she's sitting on with her nose, mumbling Arabic prayers for peace unto us, her speech filled with shame. After I pass, about twenty paces later, I hear her hiss, "Get lost, mutt – "

And then the dogs start growling in the pack's harmonious multiple voices. I don't turn around, but I know the pack's leader – the Dalmatian with the Labrador head, all timidity and goodness – has not started growling but perhaps just jumped to one side at the harsh, leaden human curse.

They follow me to the end of Ferhadija. Then at Slatki Ćošet I turn around again. The pack is gone, but he is still there.

His glance seems familiar to me now. I can't remember whose eyes those are, who looked at me like that, but it's a memory from Sarajevo. Those are not eyes from any other city, any other place I've traveled to by train or car.

I suppose I made some movement as if I was going to approach, or I just looked at him longer than I should have. The dog again jumped back, then turned around and went back down Ferhadija toward town. I stood and looked after him.

I turned back.

Once more.

And again.

I had turned around four times before he disappeared in the direction of the cathedral.

We would not see each other again.

This saddened me at the moment, but as I continued my way along the empty Sarači, I developed in my mind a story about what would have happened if the dog had not gone away forever like that.

I would have taken him back to my room at the hotel. They surely would not have allowed him into the room with me, so I would have spent the night with him in the courtyard outside the building. It was sweltering in the room anyway and impossible to sleep. Or I would have paid just to have them put up him for me. In the morning I'd have taken him to the school of veterinary medicine – I think I could have found a cabbie in Sarajevo who would have allowed the dog in the car – and there they would have examined him and vaccinated him, printed out the necessary documentation and permission to take the dog across the border into Croatia.

And if he hadn't run away, he would have been my dog.

Before the Sebilj was an open market. In front: bananas graying from the cold, pale Spanish oranges, okra pods, and two crates of dark red apples.

I went inside. The small glass-enclosed space stank of gas. A young woman, her hair covered in accord with Islamic custom, handed me two small bottles of water – "Bosnian mountain spring water" – and gave me my half-mark of change. She didn't say a word. This was good. If I lived here, I would come to this shop every day.

It was the first time since arriving that this phrase had even occurred to me, *if I lived here* . . .

It was so hot in the room I had to open the window. I stood with my elbows on the sill, looking into the pitch darkness at the wall of the neighboring building, probably built after the war. Nothing was visible, but I knew what that wall looked like, as well as the little courtyard, its cobblestones perfectly smooth from centuries of rain.

I imagined what those stones would feel like against my palms. I heard the barking of dogs from every direction. I drank in the darkness, my eyes wide, not seeing anything but the darkness. I enjoyed it, enjoyed the fact that, like the blind man in Abdulah Sidran's poem, I had opened my eyes wide and saw nothing but the darkness, the darkness of the city in which I was born, for it was precisely here, two kilometers to the southwest, in the hills, that the woman who'd given birth to me and whom I had come to see for the last time was ailing. The night's darkness was majestic, wondrous, and deep. If death in Sarajevo was the darkness in which dogs were audible from all directions, thousands, a countless multitude of dogs barking like the angels on the Day of Judgment, all of them flapping their wings, if this was death, then one could without the slightest fear or sorrow die on this night in Sarajevo.

Suddenly and unexpectedly I felt a sweet affection for Sarajevo. I nearly collapsed from this sensation. There is no place for death in the world as gentle as Sarajevo, no other darkness is the darkness of death, and nowhere else does one hear the dogs barking, the angels' wings fluttering . . .

From morning to afternoon the guest didn't come out from room number 17. At 12:30 the clerk at the reception desk, Almira H., a student of psychology at Sarajevo University, knocked on the door with the intention of informing the guest from Zagreb, the Croatian citizen M. J., that according to hotel policy he would need to vacate the room or, in the opposite case, be charged half the cost of an additional night's stay, and if he did not leave before 16:00, an entire night's stay, but the door did not open and there was no response from the guest. The reception clerk waited until 13:45 and then used the spare key to enter the room. By doing so she injudiciously violated the terms of service. She ought to have summoned the hotel manager and entered the room in his company or, if the manager so determined, call the police to officially be present during the entrance to room number 17..

Instead, Almira H. on her own came face to face with the dead, already stiffened, body of the hotel guest M. J. She found him leaning on his elbows against the window frame. It looked from behind as if he were alive. He had woken up, opened the window to air out the room, and remained there lost in thought. But one detail led the girl to the suspicion, the certainty, that she was looking at a dead man.

On the head of the individual, in his long, disheveled hair, stood a gray Baščaršija dove, lazily pecking at the dandruff.

That's how the doves landed on the bronze heads of the honored Bosnian writers in the park across from Svjetlost Bookshop, she thought. On Branko Ćopić, Isak Samokovlija, Meša Selimović. In this run of quick associations down the line of cast busts of dead authors, which had been set off by M.J., for he too was a writer, once Bosnian and then Croatian, and later no one's, the reception clerk at that moment understood that he too was dead. The dove was a symbol of his death.

At that instant Almira H. screamed.

Her scream, clear and penetrating, had no one to hear it. They were the only people in the hotel. It was a small hotel, a quiet time of year. She was alone with a dead man.

Word was sent to the Croatian embassy. Then someone phoned the writer's mother. The woman who was taking care of her answered. Then another woman, who watched over her at night. Then her friend, a visiting nurse, and a nun from a nearby convent. Each of them was told the same thing: M.J. had died, it was unclear from what or how, and someone would need to tell his mother.

To each of the five women this telephoned news seemed strange and impossible. Just last night he had been there, talking with the sick woman, interrogating her about her childhood, confessing her in some insensitive, foreign manner of his own. As if he were not her son but an author. And now this. Now everything was returning to some set framework of human destiny that was always frightening, unbearably horrible, but every time it seemed we had heard about this destiny before.

The mother was dying of cancer.

The young, healthy son who had traveled from far away to visit her had died suddenly, without suffering.

We had heard it many times. This was why it sounded so improbable. These women did not know about commonplaces in literature, but commonplaces in life they knew quite well. Those were words that were never true even when they were accurate. These kinds of events that were impossible even when they occurred.

So they didn't know how to tell her. They searched for some sort of evidence, something new.

Or they thought how in that long exertion, that cheating of life that came with a heavy and incurable illness, in the deception by which they were easing her departure, it would not be too much extra to withhold from her the fact that her son had died. To say he had called, he had to get back to Zagreb immediately, he'd been notified that he was being awarded some great literary prize. But how to excuse the fact that he did not call again? This they did not know. They didn't have the heart to lie to her and say her son had suddenly given up and was no longer able to bear her suffering as his own and decided to forget her. It was easier to tell her he had died.

A writer had suddenly died in a Sarajevo hotel, a Croatian citizen, quite known but not particularly beloved in the official circles of Zagreb, which was, of course, a nice subject for an official ceremony, useless and irritating like an opera production with lousy singers.

Before the body was transported to the Pathology Institute of Sarajevo's Central Clinic, police detectives were on the scene, as well as the Croatian embassy's first secretary Domagoj Antun K., and a woman from the Sarajevo mayor's office, who was also a friend of the deceased's mother.

They were crammed into the room, which suddenly seemed smaller than a pantry, while M. J., dead, stayed in his place, bowing before the window frame. It was as if they were waiting for some sort of forensic inspection team, but there was no way anything like that was coming, since those only appeared in Sarajevo on TV screens in American crime dramas.

But what was there to do, how were things to be moved forward "from this dead end," as the man from the Croatian embassy put it, a very unlikable, thick-set youth with feminine, dainty movements and a pronounced east Herzegovinian accent, who spread around him the strong scent of Gaultier eau de cologne, which made everyone present choke. The room was unbearably hot, despite the open window.

"How can we move forward from this dead end?" asked Domagoj Antun K. angrily, upon which the woman from the mayor's office burst into tears.

"How can you, sir!" she said to the man accusingly through her tears.

The first secretary, put out, immediately shrank back, as if he had sneezed loudly during mass, though actually it was not clear to him why the woman was accusing him. It wasn't clear to the others either, but they didn't show it. Nor were they troubled by it; they were pleased the woman had taken the little carnation down a notch.

Two coroners broke in on the scene, strong older men in green, dreadfully filthy work coats, who, without asking anyone anything or verifying whether the police inspection had been completed, took hold of the body and lowered it, folded up as it was, onto a stretcher.

It was so stiff that they could not straighten it.

Its eyes were open, enormous, grayish blue, like the sky above Makarska when at any moment rain might begin to pour down with a rumble of thunder.

The woman from the mayor's office was sobbing.

The police officers seemed to be snickering. The deceased really did look funny, doubled up like an apostrophe and tossed onto the stretcher.

The first secretary from the Croatian embassy Domagoj Antun K. mournfully folded his hands in front of his groin. He looked as if he might start crying too. M. J. had been a citizen of his country after all.

The body was covered with a sheet from the twin bed and then, passing the teary-eyed receptionist, carried out of the hotel. The carriers in the dirty green coats used the specially designed rails to toss him and the stretcher quickly into the Volkswagen coroner's van. Behind M.J. they closed the doors of Sarajevo forever. Once they had taken him away, he would find himself in the green car port of the dissection department, at the very threshold of the underground world. The unbeliever and wretch would have no one to carry him into the sky, from that leaden valley traversed by a shallow, smelly vessel of dirty water that from time immemorial had worn the old Slavic name – Miljacka.

At the moment when, covered with a white sheet, he was squeezed into the van, just one street dog continued to follow him. Warming itself in the frigid November morning against the door of a closed shoe-repair shop, it blinked lazily toward the stretcher. A gentle breeze swept toward him from Kovači, carrying with it the odors of the scene. Man knows little about dogs and canine perspective, and it is hard for him to imagine the picture of the world transmitted through a dog's nose. We cannot know what the dog thought or how it took its leave from the Sarajevo-born writer who had taken up residence in Zagreb, the shaggy, long-haired mutt with short legs and long face, the distant offspring of dachshunds, Scotch collies, and who knew what else, in whose nature were mixed and complemented contrary instincts and drives, prenatal and collective memories, reminders, and frustrations, distinct according to heritage and identity, blended, conflicting, and damaged, in effect, just like the heritage of that dead, displaced man.

Of course, not even the autopsy could take place in an ordinary peaceful manner. The first finding, which was signed by Doctor Fahrudin Karaosmanović, stated that "the patient expired following cessation of the heart, produced by a coronary shock brought on by the low temperature." Or, more clearly stated, Doctor Karaosmanović was suggesting that M.J. simply froze while, leaning against the window frame, he was staring at the wall of the neighboring building and the remains of an old Bosnian courtyard.

In answer to this, the Croatian embassy sent a very sharply formulated request to repeat the autopsy in the presence of a Zagreb pathologist. At first, the offended Doctor Karaosmanović – with the written support of the clinic's director, Doctor Salčinović – responded that as far as their institution was concerned, there would not be any repeated autopsy since the first one had been conducted with the greatest care and according to the highest scientific standards, even more in fact, given that, the words of the reply read, "the matter touched upon our fellow citizen, a great writer of this city," and if the gentlemen from Zagreb doubted the findings of Doctor Karaosmanović, a pathology specialist and department chief with three long decades of experience, they should make arrangements to repeat the entire procedure according to their own abilities and in their own facilities, but after someone from the political sphere (probably from Bosnia's Ministry of Foreign Affairs) got involved, the decision was changed, as was the tone of the electronic communication with Zagreb, and the message went out that Doctor Fahrudin Karaosmanović and his team would be very pleased to host a colleague or colleagues from Zagreb and repeat the autopsy of the deceased M.J. together with them, or, if the gentlemen from Zagreb so desired, simply assist them in repeating the procedure.

The body of M.J., along with the slides obtained and the documentation from the first autopsy, were temporarily put into refrigeration in the hospital morgue.

In the late evening hours, the Ministry of Foreign Affairs of Bosnia and Herzegovina received word from Zagreb that Doctor Emil Steinbruckner, a pathologist, and two forensic scientists, Đoko Firaunović Antolić and Igor Meisner, would be arriving on a regularly scheduled flight to Sarajevo the next day. This information was promptly conveyed to Doctor Salčinović, who immediately telephoned Doctor Karaosmanović.

Doctor Fahrudin Karaosmanović knew Doctor Steinbruckner well. He had for a short time been his mentor when, in spring 1996, Steinbruckner came to Sarajevo for specialized training under the auspices of an American foundation, which intended to use the numerous mass graves – and the fact that all across Bosnia and Herzegovina an entire executed humanity was literally rising from their shallow tombs – for scientific research on pathology and forensic science and as part of this initiative had also funded some local specialists. Steinbruckner had quickly distanced himself from his mentor, made friends with the Americans, and found other ways of arriving not only at a specialization and a doctorate but even at a certain measure of renown in scholarly circles and in the media, which, again because of so many mass graves from the previous war, had grown interested in pathologists and forensic scientists.

Karaosmanović remembered him as a friendly and energetic young man, very polite in his communications and full of respect both toward his older colleagues and toward the city where he had arrived. For years afterward he received New Year's cards from Steinbruckner, which of course he did not respond to – because who sends New Year's cards these days? – but he was still pleased at each of these contacts, and he happily followed the news of professional and public acclaim for his younger colleague. On one occasion he defended Doctor Steinbruckner when some of his colleagues were scandalized that he had taken part in a Croatian TV talk show.

Karaosmanović was shocked when Salčinović called to tell him the man was coming from Zagreb. The moment they finished their call, Karaosmanović turned on the computer and Googled the names Firaunović Antolić and Meisner to see if he could discover what lay behind Steinbruckner's visit.

All sorts of things occurred to him in the meantime. Even the most banal possibility that Zagreb intended to put the sudden death of one of its citizens to a politically instrumental end.

He found that Đoko Firaunović Antolić, was born in 1968, graduated in criminal justice, volunteered in the Croatian Homeland War of the 1990s from the time of the so-called Bloody Easter at Plitvice, defended Vukovar, was held captive in a Serbian concentration camp, and trained on the job as a forensics specialist. His name appeared in an array of media noted cases in the search for mass graves throughout eastern Slavonia, Lika, and Dalmatia, but also in investigations linked to individual murders or the reopening of cases of violent crimes connected to political controversies. Nowhere was any statement or interview with Firaunović Antolić available, and the overall picture gathered from the least reliable means of unearthing information about people – by Googling them – was unnerving but in principle positive. However strong his aversion to the excessive patriotism in the biographies of famous contemporary Croats, Karaosmanović nevertheless found Firaunović Antolić impressive.

Regarding the other forensic scientist, Igor Meisner, almost no information could be found, except that he had completed two degrees, one in medicine, the other in criminal justice, and that he was born in Zagreb in 1985. So just a snot-nosed kid of barely twenty-seven. And the name Igor Meisner could also be found in the world of social media, on Facebook, but as these references appeared to be about an individual who presented himself as a rabid fan of Dinamo and a supporter of the charismatic Catholic Zlatko Sudac, Karaosmanović suspected there might be two Igor Meisners.

Steinbruckner, Firaunović Antolić, and Meisner were installed in the Hotel Europa, the oldest and one of the most expensive hotels in the city. Doctor Karaosmanović considered whether he should invite them to one of the better Sarajevo restaurants in Sedrenik, where better-off Sarajevans would charm foreign guests, but decided against it. He continued to be tormented by the question of what was behind the Croatian request for a second autopsy, for which they had sent such a high-level but also rather mysterious delegation, and what a specialist in mass graves was doing at an autopsy for an individual who had died in a hotel room.

He met them a little before nine in the office of the Central Clinic's director, Doctor Salčinović.

He shook hands warmly with Emil Steinbruckner and introduced himself to the other two. He was mesmerized by the appearance of Đoko Firaunović Antolić. A rather short, bowlegged, unbelievably ugly man, with slanting, Mongolian eyes, wide shoulders, a high chest, he looked like a gangster from some old Soviet movie. But when he spoke, his voice was soft and gentle, very cultured, and – most surprising given what he had found on the Internet – Firaunović Antolić mixed western and eastern forms in his speech. He did this somehow naturally, without correcting himself when he pronounced certain Serbian words, but continued smoothly as the words flowed from him without any regard for language rules, or state boundaries, or wartime traumas.

He almost didn't notice Igor Meisner. A tall young man in a hooded cotton shirt, *awkward and silent, in the twenty minutes that coffee with Salčinović took, he didn*'*t say a word. He just stared straight ahead and occasionally twiddled his thumbs like a bored old man.*

Steinbruckner was no longer the young man Karaosmannović had known. He'd grown flabby and thick, his head having turned into a pear in which his little eyes were pulled so far back that to Karaosmanović it seemed he was speaking with someone who had already left, moved out, and what was sitting on the other side of the table was a mere ghost.

This saddened him.

Where, good Lord, had that handsome, ambitious young man gone, whose ideas, words, and phrases had overtaken each other in such quick succession that it was hard to listen to him? In the interim he had grown sluggish, like an old cassette tape player whose batteries were low.

He did not find this picture amusing.

Karaosmanović was on the verge of tears, right there in Salčinović's office. He gazed at Steinbruckner, nodding as if he was listening to what was being said, and thought a little bit about him and a little bit about the body that was waiting for them in the dissecting room, and about the man to whom that body had belonged, the author M.J., whom he seemed to have met before the war, as a young poet and promising journalist at Naši dani, then disappearing and moving to Croatia in the midst of the war, after which he did not often enter his mind, until he saw him dead, strangely bent over, with wide open eyes that it was impossible to cover up. That youth, who at the moment of his death had long since become a middle-aged man, had had blue eyes, but it was as if in dying or earlier, during his life in Zagreb, those eyes had somehow turned gray. Pathology, especially working on dead bodies, was for him a crossing from science into art. Dead bodies were divine sculptures and it rested with pathologists to marvel at God's work, to respect him during the autopsy and look past the illness, deformation, and much-vaunted causes of death to see their beauty too. About the beauty of the body that had belonged to the writer M.J. he knew nothing, for those eyes would not leave his head. The gray that had once been blue left him feeling bereft. And who could understand all this? Who could grasp what went on inside a person who thought one way about something one day and something very different the next? He too would have felt differently about this man the day before yesterday. He had not liked his newspaper articles. He hadn't read the books. It had been a long time since Doctor Karaosmanović had read books in general. But articles, yes, and he hadn't liked them because they were somehow . . . Croatian. No, God forbid, he didn't have anything against Croats, they were people like everyone else. He had Croat friends, he loved Zagreb and Croatia, and what had happened in the war had happened and not come back – but he could not bear, he couldn't understand, that someone born in Mejtaš might write articles that were somehow . . . Croatian. He would not have known how to explain this. His intelligence was that of a doctor, practical, not literary, journalistic, or artistic, but this was how he felt. And he was certain that what was really true was in the way a person felt. Yes, he had not liked him when he read those articles of his. It seemed to him that the man was taking something from him with his writing, a part of his life, what had existed twenty years before. Back then Karaosmanović never would have imagined that the young man could ever write articles that were somehow . . . Croatian. More than this, then he could not have known, or understood, how something disconcerting or false might be referred to as . . . somehow Croatian. As he thought about M. J. and looked at Emil Steinbruckner. Living and dead, the pathologist and his corpse, they had both once been boys.

The autopsy was conducted in good order. Nothing new or atypical was discovered. Steinbruckner agreed with his elder colleague in everything but proposed that the two of them jointly sign the document indicating that M. J. had died of a heart attack.

Why? asked Karaosmanović in bewilderment.

Because no one will believe us if we announce that he froze to death because he was thinking about something while he looked out the window.

Meisner laughed hysterically at this. Karaosmanović grew convinced at that moment that he was the same Igor Meisner who was a rabid fan of the Dinamo soccer team and a follower of a certain charismatic Catholic priest.

But the truth is he froze. It's not up to us to evaluate how probable that might seem to others.

I agree. But it's enough that we know he froze. The public doesn't need to know this. They won't believe it, and some sort of circus will certainly come out of it.

It's not a circus, it's the truth!

The truth is, dear doctor, the biggest circus of all.

He said this and smiled as if he had just delivered the worst diagnosis to a patient and now he was smiling by way of apology.

There at the gate of the old hospital built during Austro-Hungarian times, Doctor Karaosmanović took leave of his guests from Zagreb. Gone was the desire to take them to dinner, point to the city in the valley through the windows of the Kibeta dining room, to all of Sarajevo as it had once been. He no longer had the strength to talk. He wanted to go home as fast as he could, lie down and not think about anything at all.

Why Doctor Emil Steinbruckner, one of the most promising Croatian scientists, and also one of the most popular public figures in the country, had come from Zagreb, and why he had brought with him the forensic scientists Đoko Firaunović Antolić and Igor Meisner, perhaps might be told on another occasion, in some different story in which Karaosmanović will barely be mentioned and the corpse of the writer M. J. will simply serve as a convenient pretext and justification for some new story, which might be told about who knows what, provided it isn't forgotten by then.

The report on the second autopsy was on the desks of Ambassador of the Republic of Croatia Tončijo Staničić and First Secretary Domagoj Antun K. by the next day. The ambassador was flustered, as if something big was taking place and guests whom he had to meet were on their way, though the actual results of the autopsy were not terribly interesting to him. To him it was somehow normal, even expected, that a man of those years should die of a heart attack. You collapsed as if lightning had just struck, and that was that.

But the first secretary was dissatisfied.

Actually he was furious.

And mad with disappointment.

He'd been expecting this sudden hotel death to change his life. He'd envisioned a case of poisoning – Islamic fundamentalists, Islamic extremists, al-Qaeda had placed poison into a Croatian author's tea; he saw suffocation by pillow, murder by trickery, liquidation, death, the suffering of a Croatian martyr that would find its way to the headlines of the domestic and international papers, and he would give interviews in English, French, *and German for the European television stations, the world humming with this frightening event, and, somewhere in the back, he would be the only visible face in this enormous affair.*

Domagoj Antun K., with his lively imagination, perverted character, and weak mind, had momentarily imagined the continuation of his diplomatic career, sensed it gliding forward upon the wave provoked by the death of a celebrated author, carrying him into the world, to Berlin, Paris, London, far from this fucking backwoods, where he found himself against his will, through the cynicism of some dark, incomplete history that had determined the Croatian Republic should have an embassy in Sarajevo, which made no sense, had no logic to it, for what was Sarajevo? A bazaar at the edge of the world, a backwater market town similar to the ones in deepest Anatolia, in Kurdistan, in Nowherestan, where the novel Snow by Orhan Pamuk unfolds, which Domagoj Antun K. had been reading that summer on Palmižana Beach, while he waited for the officials on Zrinjevac Square in Zagreb to decide where to send him and to which diplomatic mission to assign him. And it did not occur to him then, under the palms and pines, in the courtyard of Madam Dagmar Meneghello, that there could even exist in the world a capital like this horrible snow-swept town, not in Turkey or the depths of Asia, and that he would find his own mislaid claustrophobic version of the Turkish town of Kars barely five hundred kilometers from Zagreb, covered in mist and smog, beneath a snow that at some moments fell gray and black from the smoke and soot, where the people sat in tiny tea shops, drinking Turkish coffee and over-sweetened, thick salep, talking with one another only in half sentences, sighs, glances filled with darkness, despair, hopelessness, and a sort of dull meanness that he, with his silky soul, was afraid of because it actually attracted him. He would toss himself out to them across their little wooden tables, among their Turkish cups and demitasses, to let himself be torn up, used, and tossed away, pierced through like Saint Sebastian, to let them sully him, and he would take pleasure in their filth and lay himself flat like the asphalt of the highway to Zenica, which would never reach where it set out for, with a viaduct leading to a chasm, to the Bosna River, to mud and snow, and the deviant desires born in man in such claustrophobic spaces.

He had thought, the first secretary, or actually he had dreamed, and in his dreaming came to believe in the eventuality that the dead author might bring him salvation and deliverance from this horrid place.

And now there was nothing, everything had fallen through, the author had died, they said, from a heart attack.

This could not be. Maybe he had frozen, as that eccentric with the tearful eyes had written, the toothy Doctor Karaosmanović, but he surely had not died from a heart attack.

And then they needed to decide where and how the body should be buried.

The first secretary angrily called the Sarajevo mayor's office. From the mayor's office they called the author's mother – again they did not reach her but some unknown individuals – and then the embassy, telling the first secretary they didn't know what to do, so he should call Zagreb. The first secretary, in a furor, hung up on them midsentence. But then he called Zagreb, where, to the surprise of the first secretary, they were very sad over the author's death. He could not have dreamed that M. J. might have been so important to them. No one had ever told him he needed to read his books, but fine, if he was so important already, it would be better if he were buried in Zagreb, with all the state honors lit up at Mirogoj Cemetery . . .

But even that wasn't possible just like that. First the closest relatives would have to be consulted, in this case, the mother of the deceased. She needed to be asked where she wanted her son to be buried.

And thus did Domagoj Antun K. set out on foot for Mejtaš, up Sepetarevac, to talk with the woman. If no one else was going to, he would tell her she had lost her son . . .

I'd been leaning on my elbows against the hotel window for half an hour, my upper legs burning from the heat of the radiator, my stomach, chest, and head freezing from the ice outside, and every bone aching from the unnatural position while I looked out into the darkness. It would make no difference whether I was in a hotel room in Sarajevo, or Zagreb, in Warsaw, Graz, Dubrovnik, or Rome, the news coming from the receiver would be the same. On this score there was no doubt. It would be morning. All the Stublers had died at dawn, or more precisely, at the moment when the night had passed but it was not yet light. The sun just slightly below the horizon, beyond the high hills that surround Sarajevo, that moment between night and day stretches out and most people are not aware of it. For them it does not even exist. But for the Stublers it always existed. It was the time they came to death, ceased breathing, had their hearts stop, and their godless, foreign *kuferaš* spirits would slip quickly through that crack between the night and the day, such that it was unclear which side they had ended up on. According to spatial, earthly categories, that time between night and day is clearly reflected and has its correlative in the belt of no man's land that divides states and belongs to no one. This, I imagine, is the reason why the Stublers died at that time of neither night nor day. It was their time, their temporal homeland.

She lay there barely moving from the bed. She needed help getting to the toilet, and when the telephone rang, it was easier for her to talk on the mobile, as it was a little lighter than the cordless receiver. Soon, I knew, she would not even be able to hold that tiny, barely visible little phone, with which she could no longer call anyone since her fingers no longer obeyed her.

She lay there, mostly crying. She didn't know what else to do. Or she stared out the window in silence. She shouted that she needed to go to the toilet. Sometimes she groaned. Her voice continued to be strong. When anyone called from far away, they thought she was healthy and was complaining and crying because she had always been like that, with a tendency to dramatize every life situation, especially illnesses.

No one who knew her well could have said how much pain she was in. Or, as they express this in the world of patients, where it hurt and what kind of pain it was. Among patients, and sometimes among physicians, pain had ceased being a state and become a phenomenon, a material that was living or dead. Pain was no longer singular, it was plural. There were many different kinds. They grouped themselves together and attacked, not retreating from the positions they occupied, remaining to the end, as long as the person lived.

No one who knew her well could have said how numerous or varied, how strong or maddening all her pains were. Those who knew her only in her current state knew this better. Her current dying state.

Was she dying?

Was my mother dying now?

The question made me nervous. I was sorry I wasn't a smoker. If I smoked, I'd have lit up and collected myself somehow. I just stood, closed the window, walked like a caged rat around the hotel room, to the door, around the bed, into the bathroom. I like hotel bathrooms and toilets because they're so clean, and people can overflow the water when showering, use up towels unconscionably, wipe the floor with them, because someone will put it all in order, clean and mop it up. Someone will come in after I've gone out and wipe all the traces clean. In hotel bathrooms people heal themselves from the work they've been doing and from the petty daily tasks and obligations that have been killing them, but in that instant as I tried to drive the terrible question – was my mother dying? – from my mind, like one drives away an ugly, tasteless radio melody, something by Jelena Rozga, some Bižuterija song that the Croats are as proud of as if it were a great achievement of their culture on the field of battle against Oriental folk singing and Serbian turbofolk. As I tried to forget about my mother and think about something else, it would have been good if I'd been able to clean the bathroom, wipe the floor, scrub the toilet bowl, if I'd been able to wash the dirty dishes, dust the shelves, stuff the dirty clothes into the washer, open and close the windows to air out the apartment, oil the squeaking doors, it would have been good if there was a door squeaking, if I could have changed the light bulbs, changed the shower hose, if I could have done anything, if I could have thrown myself to cover from the shells, crossed a street being shot at by snipers, just to get the melody of those four words out of my head – was my mother dying?

But what was frightening in this?

I had known for ten months that she was sick, that it would end just like this.

I had even known when it was most likely to happen.

Why was the idea of her death so overwhelming to me now?

My mother was dying.

We were not close. But perhaps, a son is never as close to his mother as when he utters the words *my mother is dying*.

We did not choose each other but were rather condemned to each other, she to a son, me to a mother, according to the laws of probability and the rules that structure all the living world on earth. The link we shared was founded on folk traditions and beliefs, church teachings, legends, and superstitions, cultural heritage, accepted social norms, so why was the phrase so scary?

I was not able to lead Domagoj Antun K., first secretary of the Croatian embassy into the house on Sepetarevac, into the apartment where I had once lived, which was now filled with people because my mother was ill. If he had crossed that threshold, he would have been entering directly into my entrails, and with him so would the very Croatia that has been trying for all these years to spit me out, and I would have had nowhere left to hide.

Although he was invented and could be snuffed out if I wanted, Domagoj Antun K. never did dare to set eyes on that place. He did not pass through that hall where the parquet floor still creaks, hear the door closing behind him, the same sound I heard for forty years, though I don't remember the voices of the people who lived in that apartment, the Stublers and the Rejcs, and soon I will not remember her voice either – the eight paces to the room that was once mine, in which on the right side of the marital bed of her deceased parents lay my ailing mother.

I could not allow him to approach her and offer his hand, serious and quite official – they were good at this in Zagreb and no one knew how to be so dutiful as they – although it might perhaps have been good if I'd had the courage to do it. He would have extended his hand to her, but she would not have reciprocated. She would have screamed that she couldn't, she was in pain, and with her clear, nearly boyish, childlike soprano she would have shouted upward into the ceiling and the heavens, a cry and an accusation that she could not help and that, actually, would have been completely plausible. My mother, in other words, was no longer capable of raising her right hand for shaking. Her left hand, puffy and blue, appeared as if it had been the first to pass away into the dying that had already begun.

It would have been hard for the first secretary to carry out his ceremony when something so unexpected happened. But I'm curious what she would have said, how she would have responded, if Domagoj Antun K. had actually managed to break the news to her. The continuation of the story, or of my life, would depend on the words she spoke or did not speak.

Whatever she might have said, at that moment my mother would have felt utterly abandoned. She had mostly felt this way during all of her seventy years. Now she would feel complete isolation and abandonment. Regardless of the fact that we did not choose each other, and that by contrast to the majority of other mothers and sons, during the greatest part of our life together we felt clearly that we were not good for each other and that our relationship was one of pure and improbable chance, I was for her, at least since the time she got sick, an exception to her loneliness.

I hug the pillow and think about my mother. I came to Sarajevo to visit my sick mother, probably for the last time. It was unbearably hot in the room. It was dark outside. The sounds of dogs barking were audible, and the only things that existed in that impenetrable Sarajevo night were the smooth cobblestones beneath the window.

I'm alive again now, trying to get to sleep on the rock-hard bed of room number 17. Death would pass by in a minor key. Not even this thought stopped me short. The mattress was as hard as a tomb. The room would soon become unbearably hot . . .

When at last I figured out that it was impossible to fall asleep, I opened my eyes. I wanted to get up, maybe open the window and stare into the dark, or get dressed and go out, but I myself don't quite remember now what I wanted to do because what I saw then horrified me so much.

In the middle of the room, closer to the bathroom door, stood a dog. It looked at me morosely, but its glance was filled with reproach. The eyes were no longer those of a dog, they were human eyes, the eyes of someone I knew. I cried out and jumped over the bed, but it just backed up a little bit. It took a few small steps back, enough to find itself in the florescent light of the bathroom, which I had left on before getting into bed so the room would not be completely dark.

What are you doing here? I shouted. I understood it was a dog and it wasn't in the nature of dogs to respond to such questions. (Goodness what had become of Sarajevo, with dogs walking at their leisure into hotel rooms! I remembered *Mama Leone* and the sentence with which the book begins: "When I was born, a dog started howling in the fronthall of the maternity hospital." What year had that been? 1997? I invented that bark so the entire story would sound like a fairy tale. As if I had known . . .)

I wanted to get up and go down to the reception desk, threaten that cheeky little girl, the psychology student with the colorful pencils, tell her I'd cause a scandal, sue the hotel, write about it in the Croatian papers . . . if they didn't immediately get that dog out of my room.

But I couldn't because I felt guilty.

The dog's stare reminded me of something else. I didn't know what that might be because I couldn't remember whose glance it was, where I knew it from, who had looked at me that way. At me or someone else?

I realized I knew this dog.

A Dalmatian with the head of a Lab. The leader of the pack that had followed me earlier that night to Slatki Ćošet. It was good I'd changed my mind about taking the dog home. I don't know how I could have lived with a dog that looked at me this way.

I moved toward it.

The dog began to growl. Its look was no longer so gentle. Its eyes were steely blue, like Helmut Berger's in some film never made by Visconti. I backed away, the sheet slid away from me, and I saw the most frightening thing a living person can see.

I was not me.

My eyes, which were perhaps not mine, saw a body that was surely not my own. I knew this because the body – strange, even painful to say – was that of a woman.

Dear sweet Lord!

The voice was a woman's too. It was a voice I knew. I jumped up to run to the bathroom. I needed a mirror more than air. I was choking, breathing through someone else's lungs, but it prevented me, baring its teeth. It would bite me if I took a step.

Let me go just to look – I began, and then, from the past, from the deepest of memories, I recognized the voice. Although I heard it from inside, just as a person hears his own voice, and although the last time I'd heard it was twenty-six years before, in the spring of 1986, I knew it was the voice of my Nona.

My dear sweet Lord! I said again, just to check.

The dog was growling quietly, and then it grew calm and again looked at me with the sad, reproachful glance.

It occurred to me that someone had looked at Nona that way, not at me, and this eased my mind. But I still didn't know how the expression could be familiar to me. She would be going to say goodbye to her daughter at Sepetarevac in the morning. I would not be going to say goodbye to my mother. This eased my mind.

Not for a moment had I thought it was a dream. I woke up, bathed in sweat, in the middle of the red-hot tomb of the bed, relieved by the knowledge that I was again me and this was my body.

I decided not to try to go to sleep again before the morning.

I dressed and went out.

The young woman was sitting at the reception desk, engrossed in her book. She wore reading glasses, which it was clear she was a little ashamed of.

Oh, you scared me! she said, taking the glasses off with a swift movement.

I smiled and made some senseless gesture with my palms as if telling the earth to stop spinning. Nothing that night between the two of us meant anything. She smiled back. And I was already outside, on the street that sloped down gently toward Baščaršija. On one side of the street were old buildings from Turkish times that had been renovated and now had private rentals inside and small boutique hotels. On the other side were new three-floor buildings, ugly and gray, constructed in the final decade of socialism. These had branches of several foreign banks, small shops, dirty and empty display windows with For Rent signs. Though it was August and deserted, without any cars or people, I walked along the narrow sidewalk, making my way around the uncovered manholes and the after-effects of inclement weather and underground water, which were eating away at the foundations of the road, foundations laid when there were no cars and when only horse-drawn carriages, or an occasional rider returning from the far east, from Pljevlja, Novi Pazar, Istanbul, or from still farther away. Now the pedestrian had to look continually beneath his feet, between them, and up ahead, so as not to fall into some hole created by the fact that the weight of the world that traveled along Sarajevo's streets had long since become too heavy for them. This was how it was that night and how it had been in my childhood. I had always walked looking down, to see where I would place my feet. This habit had stayed with me after moving to Zagreb, but then with time I slowly began to lift my gaze. Still today it is Sarajevo's paths and sidewalks I know best, the potholed asphalt of the tiny roads and side streets of the sloping portions of town have remained the same from when I used to walk to school. The buildings have changed, the old ones having collapsed on their own, for no one lived in them anymore, and in their places new ones were built, which came to be inhabited by some new, foreign world of people. But the sidewalks and side streets remained unchanged, exactly as they had once been. If someone wants to look up to see what the weather might be like, if it might rain in the afternoon, first they have to stop, just as we, once upon a time, had always stopped.

It was past midnight, but still there were three taxis waiting for fares, one after another at the stand at the end of the street by the market square. It wasn't likely that any fares would turn up before morning. But they waited because this was their job. It was cold out, and the drivers were shut up in their cars. The driver of a white Golf 2, falling apart and at least a quarter-century old, was dozing, wrapped up in his leather jacket. The reddish light of the car radio glowed, probably the late-night program of Radio Stari Grad. The driver of a red Opel Kadett, a middle-aged man with a shaved head, in sweats, sat behind the wheel, reading a newspaper in the glaring light under the rearview mirror. And the third, the driver of the nicest car, a nearly new Mercedes. I realized it was the same old man who had driven me, the one who had pulled back his left sleeve just enough for his silver Rolex to flash. He was just looking forward, waiting.

I crossed the former Tito Street, which now bears the name of the mythic founder of the city Isa-beg Ishaković. Beneath my feet there was no longer asphalt but uneven, slippery stone slabs that had been laid at the beginning of the eighties for the Olympic games in order to evoke the impression of an old Turkish road. People kept falling and breaking bones here for several winters before they got used to it. People can get used to anything with time. And then there was so much time that the mechanisms of all Sarajevo's alarm clocks and wristwatches could have been used to build electric plants. It passed slowly.

If there was ever anything about Sarajevo that I missed – and it seems to me today there is – then it was that long walk through the portion of town where I wasn't looking down at my feet but could raise my eyes in search of someone I might meet. The day before, I had passed through looking at people's stomachs, their half-open flies and knees, trying my best not to be recognized by any of them.

I stopped in front of the Sebilj.

The barking of Sarajevo resonated from one end of the valley to the other, bounced off the slopes of Trebević, Sedrenik, Pothrastovi, and Bjelave, rushing down to Igman to drown in its dark pine forests, its black verdancy so deep that for thousands of years all the known and unknown history of the world had sunk into it and disappeared, all human destinies, ceremoniously resettled to this isolated city in the greatcoats and uniforms of the military hordes of General Filipović, the destinies of the rainworms, maggots, the night moths, the flying ants, the destinies of bacteria, bacilli, viruses, all the tiny entities discovered in laboratories in Paris, Vienna, and Zurich, all sank into those Igman forests and vanished, so Sarajevo would never stretch out beyond that mountain and the Sarajevans, whether they were humans, beasts, or house vermin, would never go down toward the sea, and this city would forever be closed off in all directions, with its only escape route toward the heavens.

The city was squeezed between the hills, situated and concentrated around a shallow, dirty river that was yellow for most of the year, but in the eighties, in the early afternoons, especially on Fridays in summer, when everyone had gone to the coast, it would change colors and become bright rose, green, and yellow and then, over the next half hour, the rose would turn violet, the green would become the color of the Igman forests, and the yellow would turn to crimson. People would gather on the bridges to watch this unusual natural phenomenon. They superstitiously associated it with their hopes and desires, anticipating that the colors might do for them what the good Lord, in whom they believed and did not believe, had not done. They quietly prayed to the greens and the yellows to change their destinies, replace theirs with some other, like one might replace a too small winter coat at the store on presentation of the receipt. The Miljacka would grow so colorful that it looked like a Benetton sweater – the brand was fashionable in those years – and this was the only time in its long and unhappy history since the Ottomans had built the city that the Miljacka had produced a happy and pleasing effect. This river stream, too small to support an entire city on its banks, would turn into a vibrant, living being during those summer afternoons.

Tonight, standing in front of the Sebilj as I waited for the cold to drive me from my spot, I thought about those people on the bridges above the colorful Miljacka. It seemed to me that they'd been unfortunate, that they had expected from some unusual natural phenomena, from games of chance, from fortune-telling dregs at the bottoms of coffee cups, or from the lottery what is now expected from God. But this was probably also why it seemed to me they were better people: with their own kindness and human propriety they had had to contend with so many factors and considerations, which otherwise might be coldly categorized within the rubric of chance, dice, cards, the dregs in a cup, the lottery wheel, and the Miljacka in a thousand watery colors, while the people of today, God-fearing according to a new nature, needed to contend with just one factor – the good Lord, in whom they only believed to a certain degree, if at all. And that God, especially when he came down into the Balkans, particularly into Bosnia, rarely got around to matters of human kindness. Those who had managed to ingratiate themselves to him knew this well.

The Miljacka stopped changing colors one summer once there were no longer any people on the bridges putting their faith in its kaleidoscopic effect. This happened in 1992 when no one was crazy enough to stand on a bridge, for there were no longer any bridges that enemy snipers didn't aim at. But that wasn't why: the little river didn't change colors because the plant that had been flushing its colors into it had shut down. I never found out what sort of plant it was. People said it was the Ključ Sock Factory, but I wanted to believe the Miljacka had been dyed by a rug-weaving mill that had been moved to Bistrik in 1892 by order of the local Austro-Hungarian authorities. Only women worked in that factory, using the most modern looms of the time. The wise imperial and royal authorities had a two-fold intention with this industrial operation. In Sarajevo at the time of their arrival, that mythic Orient of the *Thousand and One Nights*, of sketches and vistas, and of the accounts of travelers through Constantinople and Asia Minor was both coming into being and disappearing, and all this fired the imaginations of Viennese and Budapest ladies and gentlemen, disrupting the distances and boundaries of that captivating, far-off eastern world. Sarajevo suddenly found itself in the suburbs of Samarkand and Bukhara, and it seemed natural to open a mill for Persian rugs. The second reason for the mill was quite practical and rational: it got the women out of their houses, their courtyards, and kitchens, and sent them to work in a factory. This was the real revolution. But within ten or fifteen years, these same women would find themselves, like their European comrade sisters and fellow sufferers, on the long road to freedom and general equality: they would be organizing strikes and charging at the police with their bare fists. They were hungry, they no longer knew how to feed their rachitic children, but they had always known how when they cared for them in their kitchens and courtyards, behind the high garden walls.

They moved the factory to Blažujska Street in the southern suburb of Ilidža, where the road to the seashore begins. This happened long ago, so long that even the oldest among the living don't recall that the factory was once in Bistrik. But the dead surely remember. It pleased me to think the Miljacka had been dyed by the rug mill in Bistrik and that the colors released from the fabric, threads, lamb's wool, and sheep's wool a hundred and more years earlier had floated down it.

Things were hurdling toward their end, the crown of the Stubler family tree would be cut, no longer producing shoots, and almost all its members had died, while I waited for the morning on Baščaršija, unable to go back to the overheated room, I happened to remember the colorful river as I looked at a stream of water as thin as a hair.

As I circled around the Sebilj, I did not notice the dogs gathering a stone's throw away. There were three – three, wasn't this the smallest number for a gang among both people and dogs? – one bigger, shaggy like a Tornjak, while the other two were small, wiener-like mixes that looked like dachshunds. They were standing by the tram stop, looking at me. I turned in the other direction without thinking: four more at the start of Sarači, next to the door of a souvenir shop, across the way from the Carigrad ice cream store. The leader was a Staffordshire terrier with a broad chest, crooked legs, and enormous, wideset jaws that it opened with every breath as if preparing to speak; its expression was sneaky, its eyes narrow, that evaluating glance I remembered well, for it had followed me for a long time, half my life, the Sarajevo half. I had almost forgotten it and wouldn't have remembered if not for this ugly, painful occasion. Next to it was another terrier, larger and shabbier, with a bitten-off left ear, maybe stronger than the leader, but not as smart. Next to it lay a tired-out, gray-bearded mix of a Schnauzer and some sort of slender shorthair, an Argentine herder maybe. It looked toward me with compassion and understanding, like a priest who to his own chagrin was professing his faith in a language I didn't understand. If I understood him, I would know salvation was there, I just had to kneel and pray. The fourth was a mangy brown hound, the blood brother of the Fido that Professor Dragutinović used to take around Dubrovnik with him in seventy-something until they poisoned it and its heart burst.

Fido boy! I whispered but then felt ashamed.

From the other side, in front of the mosque, came five more: a white bitch, her nipples hanging down, as if she were still feeding, and her two pups, which she was trying to push away. And one completely black dog, maybe a purebred lab. And then a slightly thicker male poodle. Strangely, he was the leader in this pack.

I was afraid.

Not that they might attack but that I had recognized Fido, the "mangy brown hound," and I remembered that this was what Aunt Franka had called it whenever she saw Dragutinović passing by on the Lapad shore. This was what frightened me, and I turned with the intention of getting away from them all.

I started off straight toward the white female and her group. The two overgrown pups, which had long before become adolescents, crowded up next to her so she would protect them, and she didn't know what to do first. She growled at them, then at me. The poodle rushed forward to defend them all together, mad and bold, as only little dogs can be, small in stature, just frenzied enough to be leaders, but before it could seize me by the leg, I leveled a hard, angry kick into its ribs, upon which it cried out in a voice that sounded utterly human and staggered away as if it had broken a rib. The moment I struck it, that very instant, I understood I shouldn't have and I would be haunted by the memory for the rest of my life. But I wasn't thinking about the dog, I was thinking about this city that had spit me out, where my mother was dying.

This is why I am writing. It's the real reason for the story, its central place, after which will, I hope, come a descent, a calming and consolation, until, I hope, the story will fade out into that silence from which everything began. In the end only one question will remain: did this really happen or was it the fruit of a writer's imagination? Yes, all this is the fruit of imagination, and when we've come to understand this, the writer's conscience will again be at peace.

The gray poodle had collapsed against the mosque's fence. It continued to whimper softly. The white female with her two good-for-nothings ducked back another two meters, as if this were no longer her pack or her world. She was not concerned with its suffering. She didn't have time, for she was again in the decisive moment a mother caring for her pups. She would have sacrificed herself for them and died defending them if need be, but one should not expect her to also concern herself with the fate of the pack or to take sides. If it were up to mothers, there would be no war.

I made my way around them and set out toward the Petica ćevap shop. I had gone there often after the war, as soon as I could travel to Sarajevo. It wasn't open at that time of night, but at least I could walk past it.

I didn't turn around to see if they were following. But the barking did not stop. It came from all sides of the valley, both banks of the Miljacka, and with it my life and theirs continued to flow, in this city without people, for they had lain down to sleep, protected from the thick, suffocating, hazy November fall, and the winter that in Sarajevo one always lived through with the idea that one had to wait and survive, with God's help, until spring.

In order not to torment myself in an overheated room, I would spend the night walking through the world of dogs.

Once in 1991, the summer before the war, near the Oslobođenje high-rise, I saw a car fly into a dog as it crossed the street. It was thrown several meters to the side, the cracking of its spine audible, the sound of a dry branch breaking. The car, a dusty white Golf, swerved but continued on without stopping. The dog had stayed where it was for a moment, surprised, and then continued crossing the street. It had set off, broken in the middle. I looked at it as if it were an optical illusion – with a desperate hope that everything would be okay. It took several steps and then collapsed. It raised its head, trying to stand, but only its front legs obeyed. It wasn't conscious of what had happened to it or what sort of conse-quences it could have. Some man ran into the street, took hold of it, and dragged it to one side. He tossed it into the weeds beside the road, then went back to the sidewalk and continued quietly on his way. The dog stopped moving while he was dragging it. It was already dead.

The poodle reminded me of this. It wasn't conscious of what had happened to it. Nor did it know that a great injustice had been perpetrated against it, or that this would mean its death. It lay down against the mosque fence to rest. Between a dog and a dying man there is no difference. There's a difference only for the person present at another's death, who is witness to the horror. This is why faith exists. If there were no death, there would be neither faith nor God.

Across the stone threshold at the entrance to Petica lay a brown wire-haired female. She was hardly bigger than a mole. One of her eyes was shut, pasted over with yellow discharge, but the other was completely alert. In it, like in a round black mirror, the little street was reflected with its Turkish shop windows and ćevap houses, Kod Mrkve and Kod Hodžića, the Abdulah Skaka barbershop, where everyone in the marketplace had been circumcised, the little souvenir shop across the street, and looming above this tourist side street, I stood as large as the mountain spirit of Rübezahl, reflected in her eye, staring to see whether she too was dying.

Although everything in the dog's eye was distorted and my face looked as if I were staring into a teaspoon, my nose enlarged, my cheekbones wide, my forehead narrow, tapering to a point like a burnt match, and although the shops and stores with their names and advertisements were distorted and nothing was as it was, still everything was in that eye.

She lay quiet, looking calmly and without expression. The eye did not move, so the same twisted picture remained, steady, motionless.

To somehow atone for having kicked the dog, I squatted down in front of her to be able to see better what was reflected behind my back. There in the depth of the picture, in front of Skaka's barbershop, two figures appeared. I turned but there was no one there. I looked again in the eye and saw that they had stopped in front of the barbershop. Again I turned, but the street was empty. There was no one, and there would surely be no one. But then I saw two figures: one tall, male, in a gray coat with a hat, and another, youthful – a little boy of perhaps five or six years old – go into the barbershop. The man, in a practiced gesture, removed his hat before he went inside. If I turned to the left, I could see them in the dog's eye: they had sat down at a table behind the barber's back and he had taken up a pair of little scissors like those used for fingernails and was trimming the small mustache of the man who'd just had his hair trimmed. It was a Hitler-style moustache, narrow and compact as if issuing from his nostrils, but it had been in fashion since before Adolf Hitler, and it would outlive fascism. These sorts of little mustaches had been brought by the railroad workers, the switchmen, engineers, and minor railway officials who – at the end of the century before last – had neither the time nor the money to attend to the luxurious, raised gentlemen's mustachios of the sort made famous among the local inhabitants – annoying them at the same time – by imperial and royal officers, the director of the bank, the city museum, and the main gymnasium for boys. A particular set of cosmetics was necessary for such expensive and extraordinary mustaches, which one ordered from Vienna and Zagreb, and nothing separated people by level and class so much as a mustache, which always showed whose place was where. Mustaches determined facial expressions, emotions, and moods. One could gauge the spiritual state of a person by his mustache.

The small, thin, daily trimmed mustache of the railroad worker was a sign of orderliness, and of faith in the good Lord and his son Jesus Christ. It was sported by the conservative *kuferaš* world and would continue to be until the end of history. The Romanian Orthodox and Fojnica Catholics would trim their tousled moustaches into this shape when they moved from their poverty and wretchedness to Sarajevo in order to then become its citizens. God forbid they shave them off because of Hitler or the horrible fratricidal war, or later, when the criminal's name had been wiped out. Even then his mustache remained in Bosnia, and no one connected it with him.

The rail man's mustache would disappear with the railroad, when in 1965 the narrow-gauge track toward Ploče was replaced with a normal-gauge line and then, finally, ten years later, when the line toward Višegrad was discontinued. This was the moment when one great generation passed from the tracks and from this world, and with it disappeared the civilization that had brought the tracks to Bosnia. The mustache went with it.

Good, respectable barbers did not charge for mustache trimming.

Skaka was a respectable barber, perhaps the most respectable in Sarajevo. And this was old Uzeir Skaka, whom I didn't remember. He died before I was born. I remembered Abdulah and Abdulah's son, but here was Uzeir too, I was looking at him. He had finished with the trimming and was now applying eau de cologne to the customer's face and patting it two or three times. He slapped it jokingly, while the man in the chair blinked, grumbled, and said something to him, at which old Skaka gave him one more slightly stronger slap. Flushed and smiling, the rail man jumped to his feet and wanted to turn the tables on the barber, who had just given him a good slapping, or, maybe, let him know about the birth of his grandson, who would need to be circumcised, and in this town, in this bazaar, no one did a circumcision like Skaka.

Mainly Muslims came to Skaka's. This was a custom but not a rule. Swabians, Catholics, the Orthodox, and Jews got shaves and haircuts and had their mustaches trimmed there too. This rail man was also a Muslim, who had picked up the fashion of the Viennese mustache from his comrades, but that gentleman with the hat and his little boy, they weren't Muslims. They waited quietly. The gentleman rarely spoke, did not allow himself to laugh at the barber's slaps and his customer, and held himself as if it were his first time there. The little boy was scared. He had pulled his head down between his shoulders like a hunchback, a tortoise . . .

I changed position. My knee had stiffened up from squatting. I lost sight of Skaka's barbershop, and from the other side of the dog's eye, on the other side of the street, I saw a crowd in front of a bakery that was located at the spot where the *ćevap* shop Kod Hodžića should have been.

I turned around, frightened.

Extinguished, cold neon lights glimmering in the storefront window, the empty glass of the meat refrigerator, a blinking, half-dead advertisement for Sarajevo mineral water: the Kod Hodžića *ćevap* shop.

I looked for it in every direction of the dog's eye, but it was no longer there. Just the bakery in front of which was a terrible crowd. The men were in the front, the women behind them, and with their hands above their heads they carried a carved up roasted ram. They pulled it apart in their greasy fists, in the air above them, such that the animal diminished and then disappeared completely once the women's hands had taken hold of it. Then another ram appeared. They could barely get it through the wooden, unglazed door. They tore at it and carried it forward. The whole ram's head ended up in a frighteningly large man's hand, and his finger had stuck into the eye socket as he grabbed for it. The eye popped out like the cork of a champagne bottle and fell into the crowd.

I turned away. The sight was painful.

In the middle of the road, step after step, gentlemen with ladies were making their way as if heading toward Vijećnica. Something was happening there. They had formal clothing on as if for an officer's ball. As they passed, they looked contemptuously toward the bakery, before which the tearing of the roasted ram still continued. This was fortunately no longer visible in the dog's eye . . .

Albert "Berti" Plaschka managed all the restaurant cars on the territory covered by the Sarajevo railroad headquarters.

He was born in 1880, in the Czech village of Bitov. He studied in Prague, where he met Milena Panenko, the daughter of a poor baker. They fell in love and eventually married in the first year of the twentieth century. Berti's parents disowned their only son at that point. The father, a rich industrialist, told him that he could repent and come home but only after he had left that slut of a girl. He would wait patiently, he said, for as long as he was alive. But if he should die before the boy's repentance, Berti must know that he would inherit nothing. And the old man Plaschka had been, and still was, a rich man. So rich that Berti would not have had to do anything for the rest of his life if he didn't feel like it. But that wealth was not such that Berti could marry the daughter of a poor baker.

In spring 1905, an order arrived from Vienna that all the large passenger trains traveling through Bosnia should include restaurant cars. Especially on the longer lines and if it was likely that among the passengers there would be more foreigners. Initially, three specially built cars would be included from Zagreb on the regular routes and tested through the end of summer 1905, and if the need was demonstrated, if the public showed interest, the service would be made permanent and a manager would be named in the Sarajevo headquarters.

From Vienna, into a gathering of waiters at Sarajevo's City Café who had been selected for an unusual sort of job, to work in that moving inn, café, and restaurant, came Albert Plaschka, a former philosophy student and young maître d' of the restaurant at the Hotel Plank, which was under the direction of the royal and imperial railroad.

He brought with him his pregnant wife, who would, with God's help, deliver a baby in a rented room in Bistrik that summer.

This wondrous novelty introduced by the Austrians – an inn where one ate, drank, and picnicked, like in any other inn, except that you started the picnic in Sarajevo, were drunk in Doboj, and were hungover in Brod – turned out to be one of the few that Bosnian society enthusiastically embraced since the Austrians showed up in 1878. People started traveling, even when they had no reason for it, just to see if it was possible: people would start gabbing at Marijin Dvor, singing in Zenica, sleeping in Vranduk, and waking up near Usora. And it was true – one could do just that! The world had never seen a greater wonder.

In the end, during those few spring and summer months there would be a clamor and frenzy for those three restaurant cars. People would take legal action after they had purchased their tickets and the conductor had taken them to their cars and seats and found that there wasn't any meat or rakija anywhere and it was all a lie, a trick, false advertising, for there were people who thought that the train – that satanic instrument of the unbeliever, "which distracted the devout from the path of Allah," as one hajji in Visoko put it – was composed of a locomotive pulling five cars, each of which had a restaurant inside. And some of the idle people were sorely disappointed to find that certain ordinary cars served only to move people quickly from one place to another. If that was the case, then the railroad made no sense at all, since a horse- or ox-drawn cart could do as much, and one could even ride on a donkey! Well, yes – the young rail workers explained with enthusiasm, not removing their uniforms even when they were off duty – but the route that a horse could cover in three days the fastest train could cover in three hours! Only here would the opponents of the ordinary cars dig their heels in that this was all about the most ordinary of tricks: how in the world could a person be in such a hurry that he would change three honest days of riding into three hours? This was one of those questions for which there was no answer, nor would there ever be.

Three times Albert Plaschka telegraphed Vienna, three times he asked what he should do, how he could turn away travelers from the restaurant car, for every now and then "a fight would erupt between those who had gone inside and those who were trying to get inside the car," and the crowd was so large that it was impossible to follow and observe the rules of proper service and maintain gentlemanly order, to which the trains of the royal and imperial railway were accustomed. Three times he warned that the restaurant cars entrusted to him had come to resemble "cars for the transport of livestock," "man's thigh was pressed against man's thigh," which wasn't even moral. To these lively dispatches, into which Plaschka poured all his alarm but also the enthusiasm of someone just starting out on the job, the response from Vienna was always to raise the price of the rakija, for this would turn away the excess guests. So three times Plaschka doubled the price, until the restaurant cars thinned out a little bit to the point where even the odd foreign traveler might be able to find a place in them.

And so in the spring and summer of 1905 the deadline for the trial period of restaurant cars in the trains of Bosnia passed, and afterward, in an office in Vienna, it was decided that henceforth Bosnian trains of longer than three cars would be equipped with restaurant cars regardless of their connection points. Consequently, five cars needed to be sent to Doboj for outfitting and these would be introduced into circulation over time. Thus did five additional wandering inns arrive in Bosnia.

At the same time, it was decided in Vienna and ratified in Sarajevo that Albert Plaschka should be appointed as the first manager of all restaurant cars at the railway headquarters of Sarajevo. By then his and Milena's firstborn son was three months old.

David was a sickly child. He was tormented by painful bladder infections, which spread to his kidneys, such that his father and mother constantly worried over him. The child would not be long for this world, Berti Plaschka feared, but he didn't dare say this to his wife. Also David was ill because Sarajevo's water was unhealthy. He believed his son would have been healthy had he not been greedy and taken the offer of directing all the Bosnian restaurant cars but instead had continued to live humbly and poorly in Vienna. David would have been born there, gone to school with the children of workers, grown up as a shoemaker's apprentice or a small tradesman, but he would have been healthy. In this place, however, even with all the pay of a high-ranking state employee, Berti was losing his child.

He said nothing about this to Milena.

And Milena said nothing about believing David's illness was due to something slightly different, though equally incurable. He had been conceived from her poverty and his wealth as a half-Czech, half-German, and they had brought him into this land that until recently had been called Turkey, and he simply had not taken to it, just as a seedling did not take to weak, poor soil. This land was barren for her son.

She could not say this to her husband because she believed he would answer that people weren't trees. Children were not planted and transplanted. And what could she say in response?

In spring 1914 David fell into a fever that lasted two full weeks. One night he became delirious. Milena and Berti were at an official reception held by General Oskar Potiorek in honor of the impending visit of the crown prince, who was beloved in Bosnia and Herzegovina, and they had left the child with his nanny. She grew frightened when he spoke, with eyes closed, about events unknown to her. The child's voice was almost completely clear as he told a story about something that, she understood, had happened long before. Frau Rosie Steinhuber did not understand the local Bosnian of the town very well. She had learned it, by virtue of being exposed to it over the last two years, since coming to

— 751 —

Sarajevo, so she was spared the ghastly content of David's story. If she had understood completely, it would have been said later of Frau Rosie, who was of a sensitive and delicate nature, that she had lost her mind.

The next day too, and the next evening, because of an increase in his mysterious fever, David would fall into that state of delirium during which, in the most serious of terms, he was outside himself.

On the first evening, before his horrified father, since Milena had been so worried about the child that she'd been accosted by a terrible migraine, David had pronounced a sentence in which Berti recognized the words of his grandfather on his mother's side, Rabbi Samuel Haller, whom he had never met. The rabbi had not even wanted to know about his grandson, since his most beloved daughter Mirjam had run off with a nonbeliever, for which she had become the equivalent of the whore of Babylon to her aggrieved father.

David was saying Jewish prayers in his delirium, in languages he did not know, in Yiddish and Czech, then he addressed some unknown people in German, men and women, whom he called by name or by rank and title, and among them the distraught father recognized some people: the rabbi's brother, his great uncle Moses Haller, a famous Prague sign painter and portrait artist; the old nurse and midwife Mitzi Glovatzki; Doctor Artur Silberstein, a well-known Prague physician and philanthropist. David was speaking to them in his child's voice, advising them about financial questions, asking about their loved ones, providing short instructions regarding what was and was not kosher, telling them in fear about the horrors of Gehenna, and in the end, his voice weak and pitiful, telling them the story of how his daughter Mirjam had betrayed and broken faith with him. She would end in hell, like all harlots, but let the dear Lord take pity on him, her father, and let him replace her in Gehenna and all be forgiven her.

This was what David said, sighing deeply, before falling into a calm, healthy slumber.

The next day, at the same time, when it had grown dark and the fever had flared up, David again lost consciousness and, after a short period of groaning and suffocating, as if he were sailing away from himself, he again began to speak. But now he was no longer Rabbi Haller but his wife. She was speaking in German, complaining that her bones were aching, that she couldn't lift a spoon to eat.

Milena was present too, panicking and frenzied, crying about what was happening *with her son and, dear God, would he come back or die . . . And then, suddenly, she grew quiet and almost lit up with joy.*

Old Helena! Berti, that's Helena!

Helena Panenka, her great-grandmother, had died the year Milena and Berti married. She was 103 years old, as old as an ancient oak or an Old Testament elder. For years she had lain on an Ottoman in the living room. She just ate, smoked, and complained about her aching bones. Everyone had grown used to old Helena as if she were an old piece of furniture that had always been there and would never be replaced, the Panenkas being poor bakers who had no funds for new things. If there had been funds, old Helena would have been replaced a long time ago. And when in the end they were able to live a little better, since Milena had run off with Berti and there were fewer mouths to feed in the house, old Helena couldn't lift her spoon anymore – she was too weak, her bones ached. Soon she wasn't able to chew or swallow the food that others put into her mouth. And so she died of starvation. The poor woman had suffered like a famished child in the Belgian Congo.

Have pity, she had said. I'm hungry. Oh please have pity! she had wailed on the last day of her life.

Have pity. I'm hungry. Oh, my child, take pity on my hunger! David repeated, then suddenly stopped, stiffened, sighed deeply, and fell into a peaceful, righteous slumber.

God, that's how our old Helena died! Milena said, her eyes filling with tears.

At twilight on the third day, the same thing was repeated: David fell into a delirium, left his child's role, and took on the role of Uncle Ernest, brother of old Plaschka and Berti's only uncle on that side of the family, a queer and happy-go-lucky fellow, who lived his life outside the family, and better Prague customs, doing whatever he damn well pleased with each living day in joy and pleasure. He did not hide his inclinations for young men and boys, which were such that he was often caught in bed in the company of gentlemen, one, two, even three of them, always in a different room of the Plaschka family's spacious house. The adults in the house, Berti recalled, had always opened doors with anxiety, or blushing beforehand at what they might see and at their own imaginations, which were fired by the idea of Uncle Ernest in all sorts of the most unlikely erotic poses, stretched out on the cross of his passions, happy and smiling, in a perpetual rush toward a final moment of life's happiness, in which, like the sun's rays in an optical lens, all its lived minutes, days, and years would be collected into one.

As he was dying of a heart ailment – or of drinking and young men, as he himself put it – Uncle Ernest told jokes, stories, and anecdotes from the Prague beer halls. David repeated all this, then heaved a sigh and slept like a child.

The same thing happened over eleven evenings, but with different characters. David would become delirious then, in different languages both known and unknown to him, he would pronounce the final words of Berti's and Milena's buried uncles, grandfathers, and relations. They recognized everyone in David's travels into the world of the dead, except for one man, who spoke a completely incomprehensible language. Berti thought it could be Geza the Gypsy, a violinist who, according to family gossip, had been in love with his great-grandmother. If this was the case, and if those coming to David in his sleep were only his relations, then Geza the Gypsy could have been Berti's actual great-grandfather. If that was true, it meant the merchant and money lender Manfred Plaschka, who'd once killed a Russian for not paying a debt, was really nothing to him, a false great-grandfather. This pleased Berti for some reason. Actually, what pleased him was the thought that in that case his real last name, and with it his real identity, was unknown, insofar as he did not know the family name of his newly discovered great-grandfather, Geza the Gypsy.

He did not dare admit it to himself, let alone to Milena, but it was as if he was more fascinated by the discoveries in the child's delirium than fearing for the boy's life.

Milena ran to the church and, all in tears, confessed to Don Serafim Balta that in her heart she no longer felt any love for her son, because for her he had already passed to the land of the dead, from where he was now transmitting such thrilling reports that she's lost sight of her role as mother.

Don Serafim told her not to worry, this happened to every mother and every father, and after some time it would pass, and everything would again be as it had been and as it was supposed to be. To understand what maternal love meant, one needed to feel its terrible absence. Don Sefarim had the impression that God also would sometimes get lost in the world of the dead, and forget all about the living. And the world then was ravaged by plague, fires, floods, wars . . .

It will pass, my child. Simply be patient!

She was patient, she did not entrust her pain to Berti, just as he did not entrust his to her.

On the twelfth day, David was suddenly better. They didn't know he was better until the evening when, instead of falling into a delirium, he remained awake. Happy and talkative, he was constantly asking questions, as befitted a child.

They were disappointed, for they both knew it was the end.

Just as Don Serafim had said, Milena's sense of motherly love did return after a few days. Fear took hold of Berti, and he took his son to the doctors so that they might examine the boy and tell Berti what had been wrong.

He mentioned only that David often had urinary and kidney infections and that his temperature had been high for two weeks, but about the delirium Berti said nothing. Doctor Markus Freud merely nodded without saying anything, then asked the father to leave the examination room so that he might be alone with the child.

He had not even managed to sit down when the doctor called him back.

Phimosis, he said, not quietly, and not looking Berti in the face.

What is that? asked the father in fear.

Doctor Freud explained in brief terms that the foreskin had almost completely enveloped the glans, the skin having simply grown all around the head, and this was most likely the reason for the frequent infections.

The diagnosis was quite simple. The child would need to be circumcised.

Is there no other way? Albert Plaschka asked, panicking. Anything at all?

Doctor Freud looked at him, and in his look there was something that made Berti feel uncomfortable.

Normally for simple problems there is but one solution. Circumcision. Nothing else.

He took hold of the boy's hand and escaped from the exam room without saying goodbye. As they made their way along the edge of the park toward the exit from the hospital circle, Albert Plaschka felt as if he would die of shame.

He lifted David into his arms and ran. The boy was heavy, being nine years old by then, and one did not carry nine-year-olds in one's arms, so the patients sitting and smoking on the wooden benches stared, but this didn't bother him. He just wanted to run as far away as possible and forget about it all.

Did there exist in this world, the despairing father asked himself, even a single circumcised David who was not a Jew?

At the time of the boy's birth, they had been poor and young, just having arrived in Sarajevo, hoping nothing more than that they might survive. He had instructed the waiters in how to serve while the train was traveling at top speed, told them about the distinctions in waiterly tone and bearing, about the rules that applied when there was firm ground beneath one's feet and when the earth would not stay still beneath them. He had never imagined that they might place him in such a high position or that he would so quickly become constricted in Sarajevo and almost completely forget about old Plaschka and his ransom. He had not been thinking of anything when, free of any intention, he gave the child the name David.

And how could he have known about phimosis?

This time he told Milena everything. She listened to him quietly and was not in the least concerned.

You really think someone's going to order David to pull down his shorts to show whether or not he's circumcised? You think such a time might come when men are so intimate with one another? Or that maybe women might do this?

This calmed him a bit, but going to that same Doctor Freud to have David circumcised was out of the question.

So take him to some other doctor. He's not the only doctor in the hospital.

Going there is out of the question! Completely out of the question!

And so it was decided that Berti would ask one of the Muslims who worked for him, best of all one of the old, serious ones, where they circumcised their children. And this was what he did.

You're a chifut! Hasan Soha exclaimed in shock, and then bit his tongue.

Plaschka took this as an insult and a confirmation of his fears, but he explained to Hasan very calmly and collectedly that he was not a Jew, he was an Austrian and a Catholic, but that his son was suffering from an illness that required circumcision for him to be healthy.

Ah, it's too bad he wasn't born a Muslim, said the old innkeeper softly, almost to himself, and then he indicated to the director the best man for such things, the neighborhood barber Uzeir Skaka, who was from a family that had been performing circumcisions for hundreds of years – on children, that is – and never had there been any problems. If necessary, he would recommend him to Uzeir and tell him about the child's illness.

This happened at the beginning of summer, and there was no time to wait, because it was usually in summer that the child got sick. His ureter would become infected, barely a drop would come out, and then his kidneys would get infected, and the distress would drag on until fall.

He decided to take him to Skaka on Sunday so as to make an arrangement for the barber that very evening, if possible, to come to their house and take care of it. Why Sunday Berti did not know. He couldn't even tell Milena why when she asked. But he knew that only Sunday was an option.

Sarajevo was bustling that Sunday. The crown prince was visiting the city. Everyone had dressed up in their Sunday best and headed out to the market squares. The local community, old-time Muslim, Catholic, and Orthodox inhabitants, did not take their wives with them. But the Swabians, Austrians, and other kuferaši set out with their ladies on their arms, as if they were going to a ball or the theater.

In the prince's honor, the bakers were handing out Turkish flat bread. First it was given to the poor, then later to anyone who wanted it. Whenever a baker saw that the people wanted to honor the prince, he too, no matter how much of a skinflint he might be, had to take part in the celebrating. And when the other tradesmen saw what the bakers were doing, they didn't want to be left behind. Especially whenever an Orthodox shop owner saw what a Muslim shop owner was doing, he would set out to double the offering lest anyone, God forbid, believe he was against the emperor. And it was known around Sarajevo, especially during recent months, that the Orthodox were against the Austrian emperor, since they wanted all this to be Serbia and for the three tribes and four faiths to be one and the same people, which all together, at least when considered from the shop owner's window, was not accurate. Only the unemployed could think such a thing, workers unhappy with their wages or students from the Main Gymnasium.

But Berti, oh Berti, was not thinking about such things as he held David's hand, dragging him through that mass of people. All sorts and sundries, rich and poor, perfumed and stinky, male and female, of all the faiths and languages that one could hear in Sarajevo, who had crept outside to see whether they might profit somehow from this great occasion, this celebration outside all the usual holidays and saints' days, when the shop owners threw their cares to the wind. They spent and scattered, shared and yanked away what was theirs as if Judgment Day were coming rather than the crown prince.

They had just managed to get through to the front of the bakery, where a huge roasted ram was being passed along by a group of men. It had been cooked with the horns on, and the hands passing it along were tearing off meat as it went by. The sight was gruesome. People cried out as if they were being skinned alive, uttering the worst curses in all their languages. In addition to the local Bosnian – which in Vienna they called Serbo-Croatian – one could hear curses in Turkish and Hungarian, all of it furious and desperate, since the ram was sliding out of reach from the hungry hands. Even though they were tearing at it, shoving their fists deep into its innards, the majority of hands were unable to hold anything. The greasy meat slipped through their fingers and they cursed to the tenth generation both the ram and those who had managed to pull meat off it.

Berti was barely able to get the child through that mob. He was distraught, trying to hold back his tears. He would have started crying, but how could he before the child? Something horrible was going to happen, he thought. Something horrible had to happen to people who do such things. It was all the same whether God saw them, whether he existed at all, whether he would punish them or they would be punished according to the natural order of things, the evolution of Mr. Darwin, who had courageously proved that man had come from beasts and that all life on earth had come from proto-life and proto-vegetation. Something horrible was going to happen, he thought, repeating his litany as he tried to free himself from the image of the roasted ram that grew smaller as it made its way across the street.

And now he had stopped in front of Skaka's barbershop.

Berti entered and said hello. The child followed behind. The master, leaning over a man's nose, was just then giving the final shape to a small, nondescript mustache. He smiled, still bent over, and returned the greeting. Berti did not have to explain who he was or why he'd come. All that had been taken care of by the old headwaiter Hasan Soha. What had he said to the barber, how had he announced them? Berti felt better not knowing. This was a strange world, and he wasn't going to understand it no matter how long he lived with them: indiscreet, coarse, and outrageously open, filled with a sort of flippant hatred in which there was nothing particularly personal because every difference and similarity here – every reason for hatred – had to do with someone's faith and heritage. At the same time, whenever anyone needed to do someone else a service, resolve some problem, perform something for the closest of kinsman, a great favor or a family obligation, they did it easily and quietly, without great ceremony, so that the person for whom the service was being rendered also accepted it with the utmost ease. This was how

Hasan had proceeded. It was clear from Skaka's smile that the barber knew everything he needed to know. And nothing beyond that.

And this is our hero! he said, patting David lightly on the shoulder after the customer with the mustache had left the shop.

Come in, come in. No need to be concerned about me. And what is there to be concerned about? On such a day, when the future emperor is coming to the city, what is there to be concerned about! Isn't it true? Yes, of course it is!

Uzeir Skaka made an appointment to arrive at their apartment at Marijin Dvor promptly at six. There needed to be hot water and ice for numbing the pain. All the rest was his concern, he'd said.

On his way back home, Albert Plaschka sensed that the outside world had become strangely agitated. There were as many people out as earlier – they hadn't stayed very long at Skaka's – but it was as if they had been replaced with others in the interim. Hurried and distrustful, they darted furtive glances, both gentlemen and townsfolk. The women seemed to have virtually vanished, just the odd elderly municipal judge or financial director, puffed up and red in the face, passed by quickly with his wife.

Moods shifted in this town like lightning, thought Albert Plaschka. This was a characteristic of the Orient, he had read somewhere. Here, every moment of enthusiasm and every regret manifested itself collectively. God forbid someone might feel something on his own and be happy when the whole town was crying, or sad at a moment when everyone around you was celebrating. You'd be suspicious to the police, gloomy to your neighbors, and your closest relations would have doubts about your common sense. Sarajevo was one enormous Greek chorus. In this amphitheater among the mountains, this crater left from a long-since extinguished volcano, the main characters were madmen, eccentrics, martyrs, hermits, heretics, dervishes, rabbis, friars, and crazy monks from Romanija, ax in one hand, icon in the other, intending to reconcile the world, even though they couldn't reconcile their own two hands.

That afternoon, before the arrival of the barber Uzeir Skaka, who was coming to circumcise his son David, Albert Plaschka felt a sorrow that eclipsed his shame. And the need to analytically approach the world around him would set him free forever, to study and note down his experiences in Bosnia and the Orient, mostly negative and devastating for anyone who might want to visit that land. He would bring his notebooks with him to

Vienna only to immediately forget them behind a row of books in the small library he had built in his workroom, just as he would soon forget both Sarajevo and Bosnia, completely occupied with the monotonous duties of managing a second-tier Vienna hotel.

Although the situation was extraordinary, the windows of the Orthodox-owned shops had been broken, there was hysteria through the city, pursuits were underway for anyone remembered by the mob as a good, proud Serb, Judgment Day was drawing near, and anyone would have abandoned any work he might have started, still Uzeir Skaka honored their agreement. He arrived promptly at the agreed-upon time and efficiently, and almost painlessly, performed the delicate operation. While he did everything as any surgeon would, skipping the entire, long folkloric and religious ritual that accompanied circumcisions of Muslim boys, still, at the end, he gave David a gift, precisely as a family member or friend, according to custom, would give a gift to a Muslim boy: a handkerchief with the initials D.P. embroidered on it.

In early spring 1919, while Trebević was still white with snow, the first and last manager of all the restaurant cars in the history of Bosnia, Albert Plaschka, departed from Sarajevo with his wife and son on the regularly scheduled train for Zagreb. No one saw him off, nor did he take leave of anyone in particular before his departure. His parting with Sarajevo was unexpectedly cold.

During those weeks and months many kuferaši were leaving the city. They traveled for the most part to Vienna, where they tried to arrange some other government service for themselves, and when they were not successful, as almost no one was, desperately defeated, melancholic, and lost, they returned to their distant homelands, which were now located in newly established countries, where they lived out the remainder of their lives in sadness, as people who no longer belonged anywhere and who could no longer experience a single city, village, or country as their own homeland. With the disappearance of Austria-Hungary was born a small European nation, without a common language, faith, or state, but which, more strongly than any other people, was linked to a shared sense of not belonging, rootlessness, and sorrow for their youth, a resilient, vital memory of cities that no longer existed with their street songs, poems, and bards, of the distant and far-flung provinces of the former country they had lived in, where everything had taken place outside the logic and reality in which all human and social communities functioned. This had been something different, these provinces with their wondrous, strange names had been something else: their memory resembled that of a fairy tale. Mournful and joyous, scary and enlightening, but always a fairy tale, which took away the gift and the possibility, from those who had experienced such a life, of ever experiencing any future state as their own. Some of them self-medicated from this melancholic lack of belonging, trying to forget everything. Rare were those like Albert Plaschka who really could. Others made peace with the sadness of the life they had lived, took pleasure in it, and sometimes even passed it on to their children and grandchildren.

This small European people, whose name is unknown but who in Bosnia were abusively referred to as kuferaši – only to have the abusive aspect of the name disappear over time, as the abuse turned into the essence of an identity – gave birth to great literature and music in Europe, but in such a way that it was impossible to know to what or whom their last works were dedicated.

It was to this people that Berti and Milena belonged as they waited for two days and one night on a siding track in Doboj in a train filled with kuferaši, with its two freight cars filled with luggage and the smaller household furniture they had elected to bring with them, as a bigger engine came from Vinkovci to take them to Zagreb. There as they waited, they each thought for the first time of how their life had been divided and split into two separate streams, like a river that by some miracle was split into a number of smaller rivulets that proceeded to flow along new courses, growing ever more distant from one another until the parts soon lost any mutual connection and perhaps even the memory of the great channel from which they had all come. There as they waited in the Doboj station – asking the unfriendly platform workers, porters, and boza venders whether they knew, or whether there was any talk around the station, about when the engine from Vinkovci might arrive – they felt intensely that they had ceased being Sarajevans, Marijin Dvor Swabians, and Bosnian transplants: Berti was no longer a high-ranking Viennese figure, a gentleman director, a worldly man with the manners of Vienna, Milena was no longer a lady with a white hat passing along the river walk, leaving behind her the aroma of cedar, rose oil, and some unusual Caribbean fruit that Sarajevo would see for the first time a hundred years later, after the memory of the Paschkas had faded completely, and in the wartime fire all the documents detailing the life and work of the first and last manager of the restaurant cars of Bosnia had long since burned. Instead of what they had been, the two of them, already here in Doboj, were

Catholic Czech Germans, a bit Austrian, too, with a circumcised son named David, who carried in the pocket of his small gymnasium student's coat a beautiful handkerchief with a monogram.

Berti was even sure that his son was coming to look more like a Jew with every day. This obsession, which only increased in intensity as they sat on the siding in Doboj, such that he could not think of anything else, overpowered the horrible newfound sense of homelessness. He did not want to talk about this with Milena. He didn't want to upset her. Besides, when he once told her in Sarajevo, in the foyer of a newly opened theater where they were waiting for the second act of some boring Nordic drama, that it seemed to him something Semitic had begun to appear in David's features, Milena had started laughing as if she was going to lose her mind. There had been something furious and desperate, something hysterical, in that laughter of hers. It wasn't joy or surprise at what he had said, just a sort of sick convulsion. Or so it had seemed to him.

David did not notice anything but his father's frightened, questioning glances. He looked at him as at a stranger, but this did not disturb him. He learned to see his father's glance as akin to when the weak and powerless look into your eyes. Though he was still bigger and physically stronger in the same way that the majority of fathers are stronger than their fourteen-year-old sons, the glance he cast on him was that of a scared weakling, like the look of a good-natured Indian gnu before a wild dog half its size about to bite its foreleg tendons so it would kneel down far enough expose its neck. David would come to understand why his father looked at him like that and what he saw in him. This provoked a rage in him that would grow over time.

The next day, a new engine arrived at the Doboj station and came to an exhausted stop. A rusty, dilapidated shunting engine pulled the Sarajevo train from the siding and, with a cough and a rattle from its diesel engine, quietly disappeared from the stage of history. It was its final job. For some time after, there would be no need for a shunting engine at the Doboj station, and when in the spring of 1920, the railway traffic in the new kingdom was at last arranged, to such a degree that an entirely new timetable was created, one that would govern all the trains in its territory, the Doboj station would acquire two new German switchers.

The cars were connected quickly with the engine from Vinkovci, and the train for Vienna set off. Though they could not know that this was the end of all their misfortune and tough times in the former royal and imperial railroads, both of them, almost in unison, sighed. They felt no wistfulness of any kind. A darkness fell upon Bosnia. By the time it again grew light, the country would be far behind them.

No remembrance of Albert "Berti" Plaschka, the first manager of restaurant cars in the province, would remain in Sarajevo or in Bosnia. His name no longer appeared in the papers or was spoken in public. Perhaps his work was remembered through the gestures, manners, and fixed smiles of the waiters in the restaurant cars of the Kingdom of the Serbs, Croats, and Slovenes, and then in the Kingdom of Yugoslavia, but this too probably faded in the passing decades.

If he or one of his two dear ones had died, God forbid, he would have been buried in Saint Josip Cemetery in Koševo. Then he would have remained forever in Sarajevo.

David Plaschka grew up to become a lowlife good-for-nothing. He completed gymnasium in Vienna, studied at a technical college in the twenties but never completed his degree. He grew ever more estranged from his father. His mother would take care of him during the intense hangovers that would follow multiple-day bouts of drunkenness in the dives and darkest portions of the city. He avoided the center of town, strong light, and sunshine. He was attracted to dark alleys, frightened women, and eccentric old unmarried men, petty clerks and wretches, the smell of urine in the entrances to their buildings, the poverty of workers, their children, their little girls who, while their fathers were at work and their mothers waited for customers on the street corners, would run outside with their little First Communion skirts on with nothing underneath. When Germany occupied Austria in 1938 and all this – from the northern seas almost to the Adriatic – became one great country, in which everyone spoke German, David felt for a moment like a participant in a great event and an adherent of the idea of European unification and collectiveness, under the mantle of the great Führer. Actually, he was stimulated by the fear of Jewish people, by the fact they would get off the sidewalk and step into the street when he turned up, he a Viennese idler, a person who was seemingly no one, but still here he was so respectable and important that Jews would step into the street before him, not even looking to see if they'd be run over by a tram. He would stare each time at the wretch, marked as she or he was with the symbol of David, to see whether his glance had somehow penetrated their consciousness, whether he could sense what they were feeling at that instant. This excited him.

But soon his desire for all this left him. Or the Jews disappeared from the streets where he walked. The dream of the great nation that would spread from the northern to the southern seas and in which everyone would live together scattered and disappeared. Soon everything became so unbearably empty that David Plaschka no longer felt like going out. Not even the entryways smelled of urine anymore.

No one ever took off his pants to check whether he was circumcised. His father had stopped worrying. He was buried in his work in an ugly hotel for small-time bureaucrats, an inn for the unfortunates who came to Vienna under some compulsion, and he no longer thought about David. He didn't want to be reminded.

And his mother flipped through the pages of prewar magazines, bewildered. It seemed that she had never been young. How could she have ever married that man?

When I moved my hand closer to pet her, the little dog – hardly bigger than a mole – recoiled in fear and huddled in a corner of the doorway. She didn't try to bite me, didn't growl. She just curled up into a corner and pressed herself against the wall.

You're not there, I whispered, and her ears barely visibly pricked up.

She was listening for the tone of my voice, whether I was growling, threatening, or, maybe, whining, though I was so large and strong. She didn't dare look at me anymore, but dropped her gaze and stared at the tattered edges of my trouser leg, then slowly, so as not to upset me, turned onto her back, exposing her neck and soft belly. She had given up.

But all the same, her ears were cocked as she listened, still curious. I could have crushed her with my foot, there in the corner of the doorway.

I stood up from my crouch, and at the same instant, she jumped up to her feet, ready to follow. She'd forgotten all danger.

She had forgotten it not because her memory was short and superficial but because she couldn't imagine death. However many times she had seen her male and female comrades dead, run over on the road, torn up by other dogs, their insides riddled with rat poison, she didn't grasp the idea that before her was her own fate, that death came to everyone, including her. The canine freedom from death is something that should be envied. This freedom is an immortality given by God. If I believed for an instant – in Sarajevo, completely alone, as my mother died – that God had created the world and that he directed the destiny of each of his creations, I would think he had made dogs happier and more complete than he made people. Dogs do not need God, for dogs do not know death.

In the early days of my mother's illness, this thought had often occurred to me: in the café where I go every morning to drink my coffee, a large, beautiful golden retriever comes with the owner and is sweet and friendly with everyone; I imagine my mother will grow healthy miraculously if I kill that dog; I have a half hour to do it, otherwise the spell will fade away; I glance around the premises for something to crush it with, something that will kill it relatively quickly, before its owner – a pretty, long-haired French teacher – can prevent me, or before the men seated at the neighboring tables can grab hold of me . . .

I see an older lady, a retired professor, walking her little dogs alongside the farmer's market. It's Sunday and everything is deserted. A few kilometers farther on there's a metal container burning. Smoke wafts up from it into the sky, flames reaching outward, blue and yellow at the edges. It would be easy to tear away the dog and toss it into the burning container. My mother would be cured in that instant.

Early autumn, the beginning of September, that time of year when nature loses its orientation in the calendar for a moment and the city smells of ripe Maytime spring. Somewhere by now the grain has begun to turn, the early cherries are ripening, and soon the scent of lindens will begin to spread . . . I'm standing on the pedestrian overpass above Frankopanska Street. In front of me a boy, strong like the earth, balances on the edge of the walk, his tattooed shoulders bare. As the tram approaches, I hear – she'll get better if I do that. It would be enough to give a little push, almost without trying, and he would lose his balance and fall onto the tracks. His dismembered body would end up in the morgue and in the newspapers. Perhaps no one would see that I was the one who pushed him.

Since my mother became gravely ill and I began to prepare for her dying, which would be long and painful, ending with a morphine drip – by then my mother would be speaking nonsense, like a hippie on heroin in the old Kaktus disco club – and everyday, in my thoughts, I sacrificed at least one dog, cat, or person for her to be healed; I would grab the child from the carriage in front of the convenience store and smash it against the ground while no one was looking at me, and with this I would grow calm, exchanging one horror for another, which would grow more bearable. Her sickness and death, the way she assailed my conscience in our daily phone conversations, as if I could make her well or as if her illness came from me, this I could not survive for long. I'd had to swallow my fill of her death, like someone who can't swim swallows his fill of the sea before he learns to swim. For me to start swimming, the miracle of healing would need to occur, or I'd need to believe in God. I would need to test it out, like a broken old mixer that suddenly starts to work when someone accidentally switches on the power. But it would be easier to push the man under a tram, in the belief that his sacrifice would heal her, than to start believing in God.

It wouldn't take much to do it, to push him. Muscular and strong as he was, with a Croatian coat of arms tattooed on his shoulder, the youngster would be a tough piece of meat for the tram's sharp wheels. Maybe he would live and be confined to a wheelchair, maybe the wheels would sever his head.

It was the beginning of September, the linden scent beginning to spread, and I thought about how, according to the plan and program of her illness, she would not live to see the next spring. And how I would experience all manner of things before she ceased to be. How she would drag me with her, forcefully, like the time when I was fourteen and barely managing to stay on the surface of the sea and she had pulled me hard by the leg, to teach me to dive, get me used to seawater in my bronchial passages, or from sheer cruelty.

And then the little dog seemed dear to me, I leaned down, caressed her head. I did this from a guilty conscience. She pulled back, curled up, became even smaller, a guinea pig, a mouse; she was unaccustomed to the human hand.

Her hair was strong and sharp, like a garden hedgehog. In my childhood, in Sarajevo, we had hedgehogs in our yard, beneath the window of the room where my mother was lying.

Let's go now – I said to her, and she followed obediently, as my mother never did. The three steps leading to the road were long ago cemented over. I checked to be sure the dog could make it up them. I recalled a boy sitting here drinking a beer he'd bought in the shop across the way in March 1992, a month before the war began. Now he was already a dead man they had called Čelik. They killed him at the top of the cable car on Trebević. He'd been the caretaker of the car, which today no longer exists.

She was whining, scratching at the cement as she tried to climb up. I wasn't going to help her. If she couldn't make it up, she could stay there. We would eventually have to part ways anyway. The sooner the better, before too many shared memories had time to accumulate. There were few memories to move me from when she'd been well. Especially from before the war. She was always somewhat nervous and awkward. Or she wouldn't believe me when I expressed sorrow about something. Or some suddenly expressed need of mine proved diffi-cult for her. Once, on Tito Street, at the pharmacy Zvijezda, I desperately needed to use the bathroom. But she took her time, picked out some Plivadon tablets for migraines, some bearberry tea, blood pressure medicine, relaxation pills. Then came the long climb up to Mejtaš. Once we had made it by the children's playground, passed along the edge of the buildings above it and the intersection that leads down to Staka Skenderova Street, and had started up the steepest part of the incline, next to the meadow at the foot of the Ćolina Kapa observatory, I said – I can't hold it. And the shit ran down my shorts. Soft like pudding, it quickly made its way down my legs as I walked. The feeling was both pleasant and embarrassing. That shit changed me, I would never forget it. Only years later, in Zagreb, after I had come out of the war and bombs had fallen on Sarajevo, did I think for the first time that, if she had wanted to, my mother could have taken me to a bathroom in one of the cafés on Tito Street. After the war, once when I'd come to the Sarajevo Film Festival, I happened to remind her of this. She laughed and so did I. Or it was the other way around: I laughed then she did, uncomfortably. We have always hidden things from one another.

I wasn't going to turn around. Let her scratch and whine and call me.

I continued toward Vijećnica and didn't hear her anymore. I thought she had forgotten me and found another purpose for her life, but then I heard a quick patter approaching from behind. My bodyguard and my only acquaintance in this city, other than the one who – I hoped – was sleeping without any pain.

I was climbing the steps that Crown Prince Franz Ferdinand had once climbed. Or maybe he hadn't, I didn't remember this from the photographs, but now I needed to believe it. With difficulty, she climbed with me, step by step. They were not as high, and she conquered them bravely.

The doors of Vijećnica were still nailed shut. One could not go inside even during the daytime, though the exterior had been renewed. It had been repaired brick by brick after an enemy shell had damaged it in August 1992. Blessed have the times of bloodshed and war been when the enemies have been known. The tired shades and ghosts of firefighters and librarians lingered among the newly painted pillars, along with those of fighters from the first, second, and third wars. The heavy stench of cat urine and tiny mice carcasses was palpable.

She had managed to make it up and was standing next to my left leg, as if she'd been trained. She worriedly sniffed the air, her nostrils flaring. She wanted to leave this place but wouldn't leave me. She was afraid, clinging to my lower leg – God, she'd peed on my trouser leg! – but what could be the source of her fear if she didn't know what death was?

I shook out my pant leg, took a paper napkin from my pocket, leaned down, and tried to clean off her stream. As I did so, I happened to turn toward the street. On the embankment, on the other side – dogs. They were silent, still, waiting. There were fifteen in the pack. I had never seen so many. In the middle of the street, a few paces in front of the others, stood a large gray longhair, like the one from the Branko Ćopić story. Its tail was raised as he looked in our direction.

Then he lay down on the asphalt and emitted the deep sigh of a fatigued leader but his head remained erect, prepared to leap up at any instant.

I've never been afraid of dogs. I can imagine them leaping onto me, biting and howling, while I brandish my left foot then my right, kicking them savagely . . . I can imagine their attack, yet I am not afraid of them.

She was shaking and I leaned down to take her into my arms. The moment I touched her, the pack's leader, the longhair, jumped to his feet and started growling. I pulled my hands back quickly.

The leader yawned and lay back down, almost uninterested. Though his head stayed up like before, he blinked as if he might fall asleep at any moment.

Tough day, I said under my breath.

Once during our daily phone conversations, my mother said in an accusatory tone that things weren't good. A foreign body was growing inside her, it only had to reach her brain, she said. Or her lungs. The worst would be her liver or her pancreas. Then there wouldn't be any more medicine, she said. As if there was still medicine that would help, but I was not being a good son by just sitting around in Zagreb instead of going out into the world to find it.

I pretended she wasn't there anymore. I couldn't explain it to her, for she wouldn't have understood. We lacked a basic understanding, like between a person and an animal, light and darkness, a voice and an echo, because I was going away and she had to stay, or she was going away and I would stay, saved.

There was an agreement between me and the pack: they would let me go, and I would go away, leaving her behind. I would not turn around, for whatever I might see would not make me happy. I descended the steps toward the former Tito Street and heard the tapping of street-calloused paws behind me, hundreds all at once, then growling, a brief bark, and silence.

I didn't turn around and don't know what happened to her.

I tried to forget that I'd left her.

Time would pass, and this event, I knew, would free itself of everything inessential. The signs, colors, and voices would peel away, layer by layer: first I would forget the constant barking, to which I had already grown accustomed, while step by step I left the Vijećnica behind me, in its perpetual shadow, where the night was darkest and the smell of subterranean moisture was thick; then I'd forget the stench of cat urine around the pillars of that final piece of Habsburg kitsch; I'd forget the amateurishly painted and nailed entry doors, and about what I was reflecting on – this I had already forgotten – while I ran my fingertips across the door handle and the heads of the rusted nails, one nail askew as with Christ on the cross.

If the thick fog of Alzheimer's envelops me in old age, I will remember only that I'd betrayed her and that my betrayal had killed her. Once at the beginning of her illness, she called me in the early morning to relate the dream she'd had the night before: she said she had dreamed she couldn't speak, and she would choke any time she tried to say anything. This had lasted for a long time, she said, and then she had screamed and woken up. I could not hear her in Zagreb. She was alone. No one else was there to hear her, except the neighbor maybe. She had been screaming Miljenko, Miljenko, Miljenko . . .

She told me about her dream, and a horror began to take hold of me. When she was no more, she would remain a burden on my conscience. I told funny stories about her illness, said she never wanted me, she wasn't capable of being a mother, just as my father was not capable of being a father, or I said I was ready for her death since the moment I learned the diagnosis, but none of this was really the truth. The horrors had been accumulating inside me, and all at once they would become a petty, bitter mortification of the spirit.

I dragged myself along the sidewalk of the former Tito Street, looked at my feet, making my way around the small, uncovered manholes, each one barely larger than a foot in diameter. Where in the world, I wondered, had all the covers gone?

Before the street opened out onto the Baščaršija plateau, a hundred paces nearer the bend where the former Obala Vojvode Stepe melted into the former Marshal Tito Street, there was a tall, four-story building with two memorial plaques on it. Both noted that in this house the poet Silvije Strahimir Kranjčević had lived. The first had been erected long ago, more than forty years back, right next to the entrance gate. The second plaque was high above the first, where a person's hand could not reach, and was bigger and more beautiful. The Croatian cultural association Napredak had put it up after the last war. In some other city and some other land, the first plaque would have been taken down when the second one was put up. Some socialist cultural-educational community had put it up when Kranjčević was a communal poet. Their cultural-educational community was as far from this world as the headquarters of the royal and imperial railroad with its officials and clerks in formal uniforms and suits awaiting the Crown Prince Franz Ferdinand, and even the prince himself was as far off as the socialist cultural-educational community that put up the plaque for Kranjčević. They had placed it low, within reach, for then there weren't yet any hands that would have swung a hammer at a plaque for a poet.

Everyone had come from Zagreb for his funeral on the eve of All Saints' Day in 1908. The trains had been full, it was said, and not even a needle could have fit into the compartments, for everyone in the literary world of the day was on his way, invited or not, those with talent and those without, lyric poets of various political persuasions, people of the right, republicans, coalitionists, Hungarian sympathizers and Austrophiles, all were headed for Sarajevo to bury the greatest among them. After that overlong train trip, which was likely also the most famous Croatian death by beauty in history, the great Croatian literary consort hailed with great cheering the decision that made Silvije the most important Croatian poet ever.

While he lay dead in the Sarajevo morgue and had begun to smell a bit from the damp, humidity, and rot of the building with the two memorial plaques on it, while he waited for them to bury him solemnly and with all the reverence of the marketplace and the nation in Saint Josip Cemetery, the unfortunate poet could not know anything about his greatness. For just yesterday, or the day before, six months earlier, a year, two, he had been much less. So much less had he been, not just to that majority of Croatian culture, which was typically worldly, Austrophile, or Hungarophile, but even to his own right-wing political allies, who, the moment they were pressed, would extinguish all their nation-building, Ante Starčević zeal, proclaim themselves Germans, and, with a deep bow to the royal and imperial crown, play their farewell waltz, while Kranjčević they suppressed, as if he wasn't even a poet, or they simply didn't understand modern poetry well. This was how poor Silvije ended up in Bosnia, in Livno and then the great village of Sarajevo, first on a temporary basis, later on a permanent one, in an exile for which, again, those to blame were not in Vienna or Pest but in Zagreb, with all its political shades and nuances. The poor guy tried to go back to a more narrowly defined homeland for himself, but it was hopeless, for there was not a place to be found for him anywhere. It seems there were too many cultural giants for the Croatians to keep track of. There was no room for the living Silvije yet just enough for his coffin. It took some time for Silvije's name to stand apart from the herds of all those lyric poets (who emerge from their obscurity only in the fat editions of Croatian biographical encyclopedias, publications of the Miroslav Krleža Lexicographical Institute). For all these national cads and dilettantes need to be written about, and so Silvije had to kick the bucket for the Croats to set out, as if for an Austrian ski trip, for his funeral in Sarajevo. On this journey, which stretched over an ungodly length of time, there was time to raise him up above all the other corpses and proclaim him their greatest poet. I sometimes lament the fact that I was too young – I hadn't even been conceived yet – to have been there together with them, the immortal Croats, to witness the burial of the poet Silvije Strahimir Kranjčević. With them and with Silvije's Sarajevo pals, with the Catholics, Muslims, and Orthodox, who would, when the time came, spread love, understanding, and tolerance above the open graves.

With Kranjčević began the glorious tradition of Croatian literature according to which – it is worth mentioning that this was unique in the broad European context – all the greatest poets were sent into exile. This was not something performed by the wielders of power, the monarchs, ministers, or city police chiefs. Rather, it was their weak and powerless colleagues who drove them away, those glorious Croatian impotents, whose literary greatness lasted as long as a dragonfly's life. They did this in order to find a place for themselves on Parnassus, as renters and short-term residents and, in the end, to await the exiles in their coffins, or visit their funerals in the graveyards of Belgrade and Sarajevo.

And as I was gripped by fury, in the middle of the frozen November Sarajevo night in 2012, only then, for a moment, did I not think about my mother and her illness, or my guilt, which would endure as long as I lived. As I thought about the Croats, that tribe to which I belonged by an unfortunate tangle of circumstance, because my forbears, like dolphins caught in fishermen's nets, hadn't known how to extricate themselves. As I thought about them, I was free from every humiliation, free from pain and unhappiness, which for me had always been private. I'd never shared in collective happiness.

The Erzurum hostel stands across the street from the Baščaršija taxi stand. A light was shining inside, and several men were seated at a table in the corner, near the improvised reception desk. I was feeling cold and I wanted to write down the story of the train making its way from Zagreb to Sarajevo on All Saints' Day in 1908 for the poet's funeral, so I decided to go inside. I was struck by the warm air, the scent of butane from the two ignited gas heaters, and the smell of men's sweat and Bulgarian rose oil. The door squeaked, and all four men at once turned to the entrance, looking at me in surprise as if no one had come in for years. I nodded to them – these days, no one said good evening or good night anymore – and they all quickly turned back to their work. They spoke in a language I didn't understand, their heads crowded together over cups of thick salep. They were sitting with their coats on, though it was warm inside. It was as if they were waiting for someone to come for them and they might jump up at any moment to rush outside.

I took out a new notebook from my backpack and wrote:

November 8, 2012

He'd been sick for a long time. Ella had hoped to the very end that he would recover, but then she went to Don Serafim Urlić, the old priest from Makarska who had been living by then for several years in Pale, near Sarajevo. There he confessed the believers and walked around Mount Romanija, certain that the mountain air would prolong his life.

The waitress appeared, a dark-skinned young woman with too much make-up and bleach-streaked hair.

Her voice was deep and raspy.

I ordered a salep. I hadn't had one in more than twenty years, since before the war, but that wasn't why. I wanted the men in the corner to take me as one of their own and leave me alone. Their speech was filled with sighs and guttural sounds and it was difficult to gauge their mood. The only thing one could know for certain was that these people were close, their conversation was not obligatory, and they weren't chatting about the weather or the meaning of life. Their heads drew ever closer to the center of the table where they were sitting.

For days Don Serafim had been hesitant and unable to make up his mind. He had put off meeting with the sick poet, running the risk of committing a grave sin should the sick man die without confessing his own guilt. He justified himself before God every morning and evening, thinking he was old and his memory often failed him, though he was still on his feet like a younger man, and thank God for that.

One day he wouldn't go out because he apparently forgot. The next he didn't feel well, it seemed to him he had coughed up some blood, and he'd got scared that a cavity had opened up again. But fortunately this wasn't the case and it had only seemed so. On the third day Don Serafim had work to do in Pale, he was dead tired that Saturday as never before and he couldn't make it down to Sarajevo. The next day was Sunday and on Sundays Don Serafim didn't do anything but rest his soul and pray to God.

On Monday he had nowhere he needed to go and couldn't think of any other excuses, so, unwilling as he was, he went to the station, bought a ticket, and set off for Sarajevo to look in on the poet.

Don Serafim composed verses, all to the glory of the good Lord and the Lord's mercy, and had some years before sent a potpourri of them to the journal Nada, *addressed to the main editor, Mr. Kosta Hörmann, with a request that they be published, if they were worthy of it. In the accompanying letter, very polite in tone, filled with Latin humility and contrition, he asked the high office to request the expert poetic evaluation of Mr. Silvije Kranjčević of his work. Don Serafim also noted that he, like our great poet, had been born in coastal realms, in Drašnice, "while Mr. Kranjčević was from Senj, from which the glorious uskoks and hajduks had hailed."*

He wondered whether this last part might be overly ostentatious, whether the poet might take them as a sort of imposition from a fellow countryman – though they weren't even countrymen since it was farther from Senj to Drašnice than from Sarajevo to Zagreb

– or whether the editor Hörmann might see it as excessive and inappropriate, or whether he would even show his work to Kranjčević.

Several times he began rewriting the letter from the beginning, but he would get stuck at exactly the same place and toss it into the waste basket, and several times he hesitated as he tried to make a clean copy, but in the end, after all this, he left everything, even "from which the glorious uskoks and hajduks had hailed."

In complete despair, he put the papers into an envelope, seven pages of poetry and an eighth with his letter, which he then sealed with wax using his personal seal. After he had taken the envelope to the journal's office and given it to a tall young gentleman, from whose name he concluded that the man was in all probability a Christian of the eastern faith – he was called Lazar – Don Serafim understood that in that unfortunate and prodigal addition to his final sentence there might be something that could offend the authorities and Mr. Hörmann, as a sentimental Habsburg.

Would it seem to him that he was praising the uskok pirates and the hajduks? What if Mr. Kosta Hörmann thought, heaven forbid, that he, Don Serafim, was counting on a hajduk or uskok connection with the Vienna authorities and presenting it as an account-ing in blood, lead, and gunpowder? It did not scare him – he was already an old man – that they might take him to the constabulary because of this or, how dreadful, evil, and backwards, imprison him without guilt or regret. Rather, he thought Hörmann would be insulted the moment he got to that part of the letter, crumpling it up and tossing it into the garbage.

Or he would test the poet and his patriotism by sending him the letter in jest and then waiting to see whether Silvije would act in accordance with what had brought him to Bosnia and publish the poems of the priest who, contrary to Vienna and Pest, praised the uskoks and hajduks or, instead, as an alert defender of state interests, throw it in the garbage.

Don Serafim was prepared to return to the Nada office and correct his mistake in order to avoid potential misunderstandings, but it was too late. He also did not know how to explain why he returned for an envelope with poems inside that he had just delivered for publication and the letter in which he recommended himself to Messrs. Hörmann and Kranjčević. He would only become suspicious at that point, he thought. Only then would they read his letter with special attention and discover what was in it. Otherwise, perhaps they would not notice anything.

Or maybe the mention of Senj's uskoks and hajduks would not be seen as disrespectful or awkward in regard to Vienna's gentlemen and the interests of state? Those people had revolted against Venice and the Turks, thought Don Serafim, consoling himself, not against Austria.

For nights Don Serafim Urlić had not been able to sleep in peace. One after another imagined and unthinkable variations on this event came into his mind in sequence, and sleep would not come to him. And each would proceed to its end, weaving itself into his destiny in some new but always unpleasant manner. Don Serafim hardly believed anymore in that one simple possibility that his verses compiled for the glory of God might be published in Nada.

Months would pass before he grew calm, years before he was able to forget, until that first time – it could have been during the winter of the year when Silvije finally ended up in bed – he opened an issue of Nada *and looked for his own name in the table of contents among the listed authors.*

Don Serafim Urlić's poems were not published in Nada *or any other journal or newspaper. He continued diligently writing them, linking them together over-methodically with his meter and rhymes, and he would write them until the end of his life (he died in Pale in 1937, several weeks before his hundredth birthday), but never again would he send any of them to even a single editor. He gladly gave them to people to read, but just to the sisters of mercy and some of the younger priests, who would marvel at his devotion and his poetic skill. To each person he would mention offhandedly that poems such as these were only for the eyes of believers. Stories and novels were for unbelievers who did not have access to what God had created, while love and lyric poetry was for unhappy and unbalanced people, which was why, he said, he avoided mixing with both groups. Thus did he console himself for this debacle in his life – that his poetry had not been published in* Nada *– and lift from himself the longtime worry that had cost him his spiritual peace – namely what Hörmann and Kranjčević might have thought when they read that final fateful line of the sentence, whose origin has long since been forgotten, that "Mr. Kranjčević was from Senj, from which the glorious uskoks and hajduks had hailed."*

He did not recognize the poet's young wife when she suddenly appeared at the door of the wooden house where he lived in Pale, though she had been pointed out to him several times before, at official evening parties, receptions, and processions in Sarajevo. He had probably tried to forget her, since she was linked with events he did not want to remember. (This too should not be forgotten: once, near Christmas time at the end of 1906, knowing nothing about their secret connection, the banker Dušan Plavšić, Mila's sister Ellen's husband, had wanted to introduce Don Serafim to the poet after some function. They had shaken hands, but Kranjčević had not reacted with recognition when he heard the name Serafim Urlić. About this too he had thought a great deal, and it had kept him up nights.)

He was shocked when she told him Silvije might be on his deathbed.

He had heard the poet was ill, afflicted, Don Serafim learned, by Sarajevo's humidity and fog. But it had not occurred to him that all this could happen so quickly. A young man. It had even been to his youth that he attributed the man's nonchalance toward the manuscript he had sent him. This had been one of the kinder explanations he had come up with for why his poems had not been published in Nada. The fact that the poet might truly be dying so young shook and disturbed Don Serafim. Suddenly everything around the poet became grave. Suddenly Kranjčević seemed older than he was, and not only did the soul of the poet find itself before the gates of heaven, so did Don Serafim's poems.

For all this time, in the depth of his soul, he had nevertheless hoped to discover what had happened with his poems, and whether they had remained unpublished because of that obviously inappropriate phrase.

Now he was going to be offered the opportunity to ask.

In the course of 1907, Silvije Strahimir Kranjčević's illness had become public knowledge in Sarajevo. It was that sort of a town: whenever anyone took ill, everyone wanted to know what with. Some were interested so they could commiserate with the sick person, others were interested so that they might offer him, even if through some intermediary, some medicinal remedy that cured everything, and others, unfortunately, just wanted to enjoy someone else's misfortune. The biggest group, however, were those who wanted to know because such was the custom, the valley was narrow, the neighborhoods cramped, one house didn't end before another one started up, somebody's living room was in your kitchen, and in his kitchen was somebody else's, pardon me, toilet, and all this was close to each other, in hate and in love, so it was somehow natural to know what someone was ailing from, even if, honest to God, not even in Sarajevo did anyone ever learn why that same other person might have been healthy.

As the poet's illness proceeded, and he did not give in to it but every day, if he had the strength, went out onto the street and made his way from the top of Baščaršija toward the cathedral, or turned back toward the Nada editorial office, so did Silvije Strahimir Kranjčević quickly become more known among Sarajevo's residents for his sickness than for his poems. Actually he was almost not known at all for his poems. He was spoken of as a national teacher, carrying around the affairs of the poor, a good, respectful Croat in Austrian service, to whom members of the local population, whatever their faiths might have been, were dearer than the Swabians. He had a nice, proud mustache, which gave him the appearance of a rebel, and Sarajevans shrank from that sort the moment they were caught, but they were happy to accept them into their community while there was peace and tranquility. Though Kranjčević was not even all that sociable. This was the way people in his circle were, people said. Warm and respectful, but about their business.

In his illness, it was as if his soul was being turned outward like a glove.

He would stand and talk with everyone, and men of any faith, position, or status would stop him. To ask after the poet's health, recommend some Eastern Bosnian herb, quack, faith healer, priest, or village sorceress, who could cure with a glance, and her glance was like a deer's, so beautiful you could fall in love with it.

In these exchanges, they all pretended to know everything already, so they didn't find out the main thing. Opinion was divided in the neighborhood: some said Silvije, the poor man, could not urinate, which was why he was hurting like Jesus Christ; others said he was pissing himself out completely.

When he went to Vienna, and this he did two or three times to visit the Vienna kidney clinic, where he once had an operation, they were concerned he would not make it back alive. Silvije Strahimir Kranjčević would die in a foreign land, as many already had, going off to Vienna because of their health, and he would be buried in Vienna or in his native land, near the sea. This was what people thought then, and people were gripped by a certain wistfulness, a sense of pity, a feeling that would not have been the same or so powerful had someone been able to tell them that the poet would be buried in Sarajevo.

The question of where a person would be buried was much more important than the question of getting well. While getting better from an illness was just a postponement of something inevitable, and in such a postponement the neighborhood didn't really experience much feeling – unless one's own death was in question – the question of burial was a question of eternity. Not just for the person who was going to be buried, or even for those who would be in mourning, this was important for all those who would attend the funeral. It made people feel more secure, and the idea of their own mortality would be somehow easier to bear. People died and were buried in an orderly, beautiful manner in Sarajevo's various city cemeteries, one after another, in the company of an Orthodox priest or a Catholic friar, a Muslim cleric or a rabbi, the order being the same as with us, the rites and presentation slightly different, but with the same work and the same end, dying and burying so that one's own death would become easier for the living. Sarajevo is a city of the dead, and everything here is assembled around death and the need for burial.

The dying here easily get used to dying, for everyone supports them in it, taking part in their dying, and themselves dying a bit along with them.

During his last trip to Vienna, the doctors let Silvije know that he could not be saved. They did not say this to him directly, but he understood it.

And he had understood well, for around Sarajevo, too, people noticed the poet looked to be close to the end.

Don Serafim Urlić did not go to the marketplaces, and he didn't know much about all this – about Kranjčević's illness or Sarajevo's character or its customs. He walked around Mount Romanija, visited Novak's Cave, heard what the local people had to say about that wondrous cavern, but did not learn anything about Sarajevo's character either from these conversations or from the confessions of the small number of Catholics in Pale and the surrounding area. The light was different up here than the one burning down below in the market town, and though it was barely twenty kilometers to town, the actual distance between Pale and Sarajevo was greater than anyone might have thought. Each person deceived himself who thought he understood something about the people in the valley, about their nature and motivation.

He walked up the wooden steps to the second floor and rang the bell.

An old woman in black pantaloons, the Kranjčević's servant, opened the door. The moment he had stepped inside, she clasped his hand, kissed it, and murmured, Bless me, father!

Never mind, never mind, he said, waving her away as if he was shooing a fly, but to her this probably seemed as if he was making the sign of the cross in the air.

The apartment stank of medicine, disinfectant, and something Don Serafim could not place. It was a heavy, chemical odor that he would smell whenever he turned his head. That stench would not leave his head for days afterward, he would remember it clearly, and would only ever smell it one other time in his life. But that is for the end . . .

Silvije was seated in an armchair just beside the window. When he turned, he could see the street, people passing, making their way toward the markets, carrying baskets with goods inside. He could see the horse- and ox-drawn wagons, the first trams – that wondrous invention for frightening people and animals . . .

I saw you coming this way from Vijećnica and wondered whether this was the person coming to see me, he said joyfully.

His voice was like a healthy man's. This encouraged Don Serafim in his intention to ask about his poems at the first opportunity.

I heard you have been ailing, as they say in Bosnia, and thought I would come around.

You don't have to make things up. She asked you to come. I know that, he said, with a melancholy laugh.

His mustache was no longer as in his pictures and as it was the one time when they had met before. It had got thinner and less shiny, droopy like the sort that those strange beasts in northern seas had. Or like the one Fra Grgo Martić had in olden times.

And if she asked you, she did it to help me. She would do anything to make things easier for me. She was like that from the start. At first she eased my disposition without intending to, and now she eases the pains of my affliction.

That is why God created woman . . . Don Serafim blurted out, and immediately thought he had said something inappropriate, something that would lower him in Kranjčević's eyes. Someone who wrote poems would not dare say anything so obvious and ordinary.

Perhaps for the first time since being ordained he was thinking of himself not as a priest, not as someone who wanted to be seen in the eyes of this man and the good Lord as worthy of his pastoral and comforter's calling. What was important to him was being perceived by Kranjčević as a poet. Nothing else.

Yes, yes, he said, looking again toward the street. You're right, completely right. That is why God created woman. He created man to suffer and endure in his wretchedness and humiliation, and her he created to be a constant vision before him so that he might not notice how wretched he was and how low he had fallen. Is that what you had in mind? he asked, casting a glance on Don Serafim that was somehow caustic and almost wicked.

In sickness people became mean, and should be forgiven.

I wasn't thinking of that, the priest responded.

Woman is like the cinematograph for man. Have you heard of the cinematograph?

I must admit I have not.

Go have a look if you get the chance. There will be a new tour in the spring, on Circus Square. Moving pictures. It's interesting. Look at them and remember me. In heaven.

Would you like to lighten your soul?

So fast? the poet asked in surprise.

Whenever you like.

If I lighten it too soon, I'll race up to heaven like a hot air balloon! he said, laughing.

Laughter heals the soul, Don Serafim acknowledged.

Would you like Mara to make you some chamomile tea? Mara, Mara dear, please make the reverend some chamomile tea!

The smell of chamomile quickly covered over all the other smells, including the heavy, inhuman chemical stench whose source he could not determine. But it seemed to him the stench would put an end to his life.

He sat down on a shaky dining-room chair across from the sick man's armchair, his elbow on the table. For a moment the two were silent, and he had a chance to examine him better. Although it was warm in the room, perhaps even too warm, for Mara kept putting coal into the large stove, certain in her Bosnian manner that every illness could be cured provided that the sick person was just kept warm enough, Silvije was covered to his neck with a gray military blanket. His small, bony fists were poking out from the pockets of a sweater of thin, peasant wool. It was not easy to look at him, suddenly so small beneath all those wool layers.

A small, pale woman came into the room. Her face was pretty, but her body resembled that of an old woman. Two Chinese porcelain cups were on the silver platter, along with the same type of teapot and sugar bowl.

He knew much more about Ella Kranjčević than he did about the poet. He had known her father Franjo and had prepared her grandmother Madam Slava for eternal repose. The quiet, humble family of a customs officer, bestowed with an abundance of piety, but also with a thirst for some distant world, for escape from Bosnia and from Sarajevo. Franjo Kašaj spoke perfect French, taught the language to Ella and her younger sister from their earliest years, and secretely dreamed of moving to France.

Don Serafim had not had such dreams, but he had a heart for the unfortunate border guard Franjo, and for all those similar to him, whom he met during his work, most often on their deathbeds, who had one desire all their lives, frequently something ordinary and banal, around which, like a climbing plant, they twisted and bent their earthly lives, often allowing that desire to shape their destiny. Such people, he believed, were dear to God.

She put the platter down on the little table he was leaning against.

They were both uncomfortable. She didn't know whether Don Serafim had admitted to Silvije that she had asked him to come. Don Serafim was troubled about how to greet her, with what words, as people who know each other well, or recalling her only as Slava's little granddaughter?

A beautiful teapot, he said.

Yes, Silvije said, laughing, Chinese porcelain, made in the Czech Lands. Isn't it strange that Chinese porcelain should be made in the Czech Lands?

It does seem strange, Don Serafim agreed, slurping his tea loudly.

What do you think, my sweet?

Ella did not answer him. She laughed and waved Silvije away. As if he was teasing her, and she was defending herself.

Don Serafim was on the verge of asking, but he was bothered by the fact that Kranjčević had not shown in any way that he remembered him.

Serafim Urlić was not an ordinary name, not one he would have easily forgotten after reading the letter and poems. If he had read them. If the esteemed Mr. Hörmann had not been so offended by the contents of the letter and the invective expressed in it that he had thrown it immediately into the trash.

He considered mentioning that he too was from the coast, from Drašnice, an old Turkish village near Makarska, using the opportunity to repeat his surname, but immediately gave it up. It was embarrassing and unbecoming of someone who thought of himself as *a poet. And of course unbecoming for a priest who had been invited to give confession to a sick man too.*

You know, reverend, the archbishop himself also came for a visit. He delivered some sort of a prize, a recognition, or what not. They could hardly fit in this little room, there were so many of them.

You deserve it.

Do you really think so? Tell me why you think I deserve it. It was not long ago that the very same archbishop, during the fast days before Easter, was sermonizing on my poetry. And he wasn't finding good things to say. What changed in the meantime? Were His Eminence and His Eminence's escort awarding my poems, my work as a teacher, my contributions to Nada, *as they said, or were they perhaps awarding my death? If that's it, I have to tell you, I don't deserve any of the credit for it.*

Whatever anyone might say, Silvije, you are a great poet. Making a mistake can happen to everyone, even to the archbishop.

You're right about that. But I don't think he made a mistake. At least not when he was making sermons against my poems. He made a mistake by changing his mind. Do you think he was showing magnanimity? No, dear sir, the archbishop was afraid of death. Whose death? Kranjčević's!

Don Serafim Urlić looked at him in fear. He didn't know what to say and just wanted to escape and not appear again before this man. This is my punishment, he thought, for coming with the intention of asking him about my poems and not that of confessing him. The confessor is protected from anything a dying person might say to him, from every sorrow, but also from spite, meanness, and eccentricity, from every crime he might pour into his words, like fiery molten lava into a sharp knife, for he is on the other side, and the words cannot touch him while it is God keeping the accounts. But this was something different: a conversation between two poets, one of whom was genuine while the other was concealed.

Or was it maybe that Kranjčević had not realized he was addressing him that way? This thought frightened him, and he suddenly wanted to hide what just before he'd been about to reveal, that he had once written poems and delivered them to the Nada *office.*

Don't take what I'm saying a . . .

I'm not taking anything you're saying amiss.

The bitterness has built up inside me.

It would build up in anyone.

When I'm not in pain, I'm bitter. And when I'm in pain, the bitterness gets aired out. Then it just hurts. I don't know which of the two is worse: when I'm in pain or when I'm not.

I understand.

I did not want to stay here. From the time I came to Livno, all I've done is look for a way to leave Bosnia. They drove me here as punishment, and from God's mercy this was where I met Ella. I wanted to learn French, and she taught me. Me and one of my friends. We got married on my thirty-first birthday. It was snowing heavily, the first snowfall of '17, in February. We could barely get through to the cathedral. Reverend Josip said it was a good sign, that big snow. And I was happy, though I don't know how a priest can believe in such superstitions, let alone pronounce them from the altar.

He wanted to put you in a good mood.

Well, he didn't need to do that, he laughed. My mood was already good enough as it was.

Now it is again.

Yes, for the moment. When I'm talking with someone, I forget, or when I close myself away in this old armchair, which Mr. Studnicka, the bookstore owner, let us have. Do you know him? Or when I look at the people crawling by on the street. I think it's easier for me as the one looking at them than for them going by with their cares, and right away I feel better. I look at the people, the horses, the trams, the dogs making their way down the street. But rarely does anyone I know pass. When you look like this, you almost don't see anyone you know. And then, for a moment, I'm happy we stayed and Sarajevo is the place where I'll die. It goes easier here. Nobody gets all worked up about death like in Senj, my hometown, or in Zagreb, where they die in high style. One can fall from on high into a burial tomb too. And then I turn in the other direction, toward that wall there, I don't see the street, and again my old torment takes hold, or my pain returns, and I think, God, why did you leave me in Bosnia, on my Bosnian cross? Why didn't you let me go home when everyone else has already done so?

That's why it's best if you don't stop looking at the street, Don Serafim said, trying to be witty. The poet laughed enough to be polite or so their talk would not turn back to its morose thread.

Last year in May, when I was visiting Vienna for the last time and was at the hospital, I dreamed I was going back to Zagreb. Doctor Jelovšek had mentioned to me that somewhere on Pantovčak a splendid villa with an orchard was for sale for six thousand florins. It had been on the market for a long time, he said, the price was suitable, but there were no buyers. Far from Gornji Grad, far from the square and the city throng, and on a hillside. If it were in the center, it would sell immediately for three times the price. And from the moment he mentioned it, from one night to the next I started thinking how nice it would be to collect the money, take out a loan, and buy that house. I'd get better immediately, it seemed to me. And the more I thought about it, the more it all seemed not so much an empty dream but something to accomplish. And the longer my sleeplessness and fantasies continued, the more attractive Zagreb became. I see now that after my death there might be debts worth more than the cost of the villa on Pantovčak. Illness is expensive – it shames a person in every manner, morally and physically.

The soul is eternal, Don Serafim whispered.

What?

I said the soul is eternal, the body we leave to time's passage.

Silvije drew his hand from under the blanket and offered it. It was hot. He had a fever. A man could not stay that hot for long, Don Serafim thought. He stopped asking him if he wanted to confess. Nor did Kranjčević bring it up.

Ella accompanied him to the door, teary eyed. Her face was calm. He wanted to console her. He offered his hand as he was leaving. She had long fingers, but her hand was unusually small.

As he went out onto the street, the air rushed with all its force into his lungs. Pure, cold, late-autumn air. The thick, chemical smell that had covered all the other odors in the Kranjčević home disappeared.

He did not see him alive again.

He saw her from a distance, at the funeral, which was thronged by thousands of people. Kranjčević was disliked in life but in death was beloved.

He had turned ninety-five and was no longer making plans. He was nearly deaf, could not hear confessions. Many would confess only to him, it was hard for them to accept the younger clerics. He continued to walk every day from one end of the area to the other.

He would go out to the newly built hotel, sit on a terrace at a table from which the view opened onto the entire region. This was what he had done that morning. It was a Monday in the summer of 1932. He was sitting, watching the broken line of the horizon where the tops of the hills separated from the sky. The dark green, almost black forests, and the light blue August sky with its rare gossamer traces of fog, which, perhaps, was not fog but scattered, destroyed clouds, angels that had sung their last and suddenly puffed into Nothing. When his glance had passed over the entire route, from one end of the horizon to the other, he would go back to the start, like the drum of a printer, covering the same route again, trying to see differences and changes, something he had skipped over or something that appeared in the interim, a cloudlet, an eagle flying above the valley, breaking the line of the horizon, its invisible integrity, constantly crossing the border between sky and land.

He could have stayed there until the evening and deep into the night, when the horizon's line would be just as visible, illuminated by the starry sky except without the colors, but he didn't dare stay too long since his housekeeper Ruža was expecting him for lunch. And Ruža was a strict woman who did not tolerate tardiness. She was especially strict with him, a confessor and pastor of the Lord. Sometimes she would scold him, call him a whippersnapper, but afterward she'd be sorry. She would come to ingratiate herself to him, like a mother to a child after giving it a whack on the bottom, and he would be prankish and pretend to push her away, just like a child. Ruža had become like a second mother to him in his old age, even though she was a half century his junior. Sometimes he would get to thinking and lose himself, but then suddenly he'd feel like drinking a glass of milk.

Mother! he shouted, then realizing what he had said, he would appear to sigh as if from some great heaviness. Oh, dear mother!

Upon which she would appear and say, Reverend, you're just complaining. It's a good thing the woman is deceased with how often you call her.

And that morning he was thinking that his time was limited, by eleven he needed to be at the table for lunch. Ruža was proud of each of his ninety-five years. She thought he had reached such an advanced age because of her good, healthy food.

Those prayers would not help you, she told him, *if you started eating what you cooked up on your own. Not even the good Lord has any patience to heal such unhealthy children who don't pay attention to caring for their bodies.*

He would just have time to cast his glance another few times slowly across the length of the horizon, gaze once more at the little town in the valley, the small houses in the settlements, and the wooden hillside huts that only his practiced eye could make out among the green and brown shades of the mountain slopes before he had to go.

At that instant he detected the scent.

That same heavy, chemical stench that had penetrated and enveloped Kranjčević's home on the day he had gone to confess the poet. He could no longer remember what the dying man had entrusted to him in his confession. Could one forget that?

He no longer remembered his intention to ask about what had happened with his poems, why they had not been published in Nada. Don Serafim had forgotten about those poems, like the majority of things that embarrass a person. His bad reminiscences had evaporated, and he was happy.

He wrote poems about insects, wild animals, and the plants of the forest. About the line of the horizon and the good Lord.

But still he was gripped a bit by fear because he thought at the moment that this was the stench of his death.

And then a crazy idea came to him: that scent was detected when it was a poet's turn to die. And the fear passed immediately.

Only then did he notice that two Germans, a young pair of newlyweds whom he saw every morning, were seated at a neighboring table. The man was reading the paper. The woman was dipping a little brush into a bottle to paint over her red fingernails. As she drew the brush over them, the color disappeared.

Excuse me, madam, what is that in the bottle?

Acetone, answered the woman kindly.

Don Serafim nodded sagely, as though he knew what this was. For the next five years, until the day when, blessed in Christ, he was buried, the old priest thought about acetone. While he did not know this had been the stench at the Kranjčevićs', he had been able to live with the mystery of the scent, but now he could not get it out of his head. The thing that bothered him most was that he had not looked at Ella's nails to see if they were red.

He entrusted none of this to anyone, not to his old housekeeper, or even to the good Lord, who knew everything anyway.

What are you writing there, sir? asked a voice, calling me up midsentence. I hadn't written half the story of Kranjčević's death and the arrival of the train from the main Croatian city. If I stopped now, I knew the story would be lost.

An old man stood in front of my table, no taller than a meter and a half, with a white beard and lively blue eyes. He was carrying a bag of newspapers on his shoulder. A newsvendor.

I'm writing something I'll forget by the morning, I answered, sullenly enough to make him go away but also decently enough so as not to feel I was being unpleasant.

Eh, well morning's a long ways off. It's not even one thirty! Is what you're writing important?

It is to me.

What's it about?

It's something about a poet.

What's the poet's name. Is it Sidran?

No, not him. Silvije Strahimir Kranjčević.

Oh, him! Eh, he was a real bard. The moment I open my eyes in the morning, to make sure I get enough sleep, I think about that "behind low-hanging lashes"! And I go right back to sleep. Just imagine it, dear sir, how beautiful: low-hanging! Not closed but low-hanging! If he had just written that one word, and not a whole poem of them, he'd be a great poet. The greatest one who ever lived in this town. Poor guy was sickly, always in a foul mood, had some sort of torture inside him that couldn't get out. I told him, Mr. Silvije, you mustn't agitate yourself so. Everything's fleeting in this town, all of us are fleeting. Only your poems, here, are eternal. All this will go away, terrible misfortune will come, famine, plague, war, this building will be razed to the ground, but your poems will remain. So you mustn't get all worked up, dear Mr. Silvije!

The old man was twisting and bending as he spoke, as if he were on stage, an old ballet dancer, a choreographer showing the youngsters a scene, a vorspiel, as they say in the basements of theaters and cafés, and his eyes swam about, back and forth like a swaying boat, and one couldn't tell what he was looking at, if he was looking at anything at all. Perhaps they were focused inward, his eyes were those of a madman.

It was the fall of 2012 and I had come to Sarajevo to visit my ailing mother and to see her, probably, for the last time.

In front of me an old man stood, swaying, a figure from Oriental intarsias or vedutas, telling a story of how he had tried to return Kranjčević's self-confidence. Kranjčević had died in 1908, but maybe the old man didn't know this. Perhaps he was not crazy, just a pathological liar, a thwarted author, for whom the tiniest little key word could serve as the basis for a great, extended lie. It was understandable how unaccomplished people, especially men when they lacked status, could invent stories that all had the same goal and point – to show that the teller was important.

May I sit down? he asked. I can tell you all sorts of things about Silvije firsthand.

Not knowing what to do, I gestured for him to sit. This was the way things worked in Sarajevo, even in these times when the city was empty, still someone might turn up to sit down uninvited at one's table and irrevocably interrupt a person's train of thought.

He called the waitress, ordered a rakija for himself and a salep for me.

Jahja, Jahja, what are you going to use to pay for this? she complained to him.

That's not your business, woman! Have I ever left here owing you?

He wasn't bothered in the least by her indiscretion. His face was calm, his eyes swimming with each of his movements. Insect eyes.

He was a sweet man, Silvije. But I can imagine how he might have been harsh and complicated to his family. You know how it is when you live among women – and he had two of them, Madam Ella and little Višnjica – and you're working on all sorts of men's affairs, politics, the nation, and revolution, and you start to act like a drunk father, like, God forgive me, the sort of tyrant who is either hungover and hangs himself or drunk and slapping around everybody in the house. But

Silvije never struck anybody, never even raised his hand against a person, let alone against those two. I don't want to say it, but I'd say the nation and revolution, in those times especially, meant violence against any kind of intimacy . . .

I was surprised to hear him use this word: *intimacy*. As if it did not accord with the old man's appearance. He was too refined and sensitive for a street newsvendor. But maybe this was the way things were when a person read newspapers every day. He ended up learning this word too: *intimacy*. And some instinctive, rudimentary talent taught him to insert such a word in just the right place, more skillfully than a single local writer could. Was there actually in Sarajevo a single living poet who knew how to use the word *intimacy*?

That's what Ella died from – the old man continued. At first for years she took care of Silvije, pampered him, and then in the middle of the worst part of the illness, her mother fell ill too. Madam Slava, a lovely woman with a gentle soul, was weak of faith and afraid of death, so Ella, the moment she had buried her husband, needed to go to Zlatar, near Zagreb, to be there for her mother's final days. The poor woman was terribly afraid of the emptiness, the void that comes after a person's last breath, and she burdened the poor girl with her fear. She went from one deathbed to the other, her mother's after Silvije's. When she was leaving for Zlatar, I told her to take care of herself, however difficult it might be with her mother, in the most difficult moments of her life. Ella, my dear girl, don't let her take you to the grave with her, I said. And she answered, Ivan, you mustn't talk that way. She's all I have now that Silvije is gone . . .

Ivan? Aren't you Jahja? I asked, catching him up in a white lie.

Well Jahja is Ivan, and you know it! said the old man, laughing. But let me go on, not cut off the story's thread like you did your own when you invited me to sit down at your table. And so, Ella, the poor girl, did not listen to me but instead plunged into her mother's illness, and never came up to the surface again. She did not come back to Sarajevo alive. Consumption, a disease of the city and a certain epoch, had already taken many, and now it took her too, Ella Kranjčević, whose maiden name was Kašaj. But it wasn't tuberculosis, my dear sir, it was rather that the young woman had accustomed herself to death, immersed herself in it without any fear whatsoever, and died, like Silvije, easily, as if there was nothing more natural, as if nothing else besides death and dying held any meaning! Madam Slava took her with her so she wouldn't be alone, so she'd feel less lonely in her dark grave. I was at Ella's funeral . . .

That was in 1911! I noted sarcastically.

You are correct. It was the beginning of the month of April. The spring had come early, and with the spring, in a morning train that had come through the night from Zagreb, in the luggage car, was our Ella, in a cherry wood casket, the most beautiful and luxurious piece of furniture in the Kranjčević apartment. She had received it as a gift before her final journey, from the gentlemen patriots and writers of Zagreb for the young widow of a Croatian poet. They had wanted to demonstrate their gallantry in the face of death, and that, I must admit, they accomplished. Croats are gallant people. You know that better than I do since you've lived in Zagreb for a long time.

Yes, by force of circumstances, it will be twenty years soon . . .

Force of circumstances? Hmm, you shouldn't speak that way. Please don't. It's a beautiful city. They are a gallant people.

You recognized me then?

Well everyone knows everyone here. And everyone knows you. Of course some people might pretend they don't. You're right if now you're thinking I intentionally stopped you in the middle of your story. I did it because it's not a good story about Kranjčević. You mustn't ever write about human bitterness. Those sorts of stories never work. You see, we're all bitter in the same way, especially in this town. And your bitterness is the only thing that connects you to your birthplace. Only when you've rejected the bitterness will you become calm and, with peace in your soul, be able to leave this place and never come back.

You're wrong . . .

If I am, you can forget I ever said anything to you. It's easiest for me when I'm not in the right. Then we just go on to the next subject. Or we can go back to where we were before. It was April 7, 1911 – a Friday – the passenger train from Zagreb was pulling into the old Sarajevo station at Marijin Dvor. It was early morning, and there were a lot of passengers. That weekend would be Palm Sunday, and the Catholics were recognizable by the olive branches they had been collecting in Zagreb. People were coming home for Easter. Students were arriving from Vienna and Graz, a few from Zagreb, and the atmosphere was festive, the sort of holiday you can't even imagine nowadays, especially in Sarajevo. We were standing to the side, waiting for the train to empty out and the travelers to leave the platform so we could open the baggage car and take out Ella Kranjčević. This is what they do with coffins, you know. It's an ancient traveler's rule that has existed as long as there have been railroads, and now they do the same with airplanes. Coffins are transported out of the travelers' sight, for people would not be pleased to know that a dead person was traveling with them.

You yourself carried out the casket with Ella Kranjčević?

No, I didn't. I didn't have the right build. Four young men from the Croatian Cultural Society carried the casket. If you gave me some time, I might remember their names . . .

It's not important.

Yes, it's true. Today it's no longer important. They happened to be at the Napredak building when they were making the arrangements regarding Kranjčević's widow's death, and they agreed to come. It was chance.

They sent you as well?

No, my dear sir – the old man again let out a gentle laugh – I was there under a different authority. But to continue: there beside the road, just beyond the threshold, waited a hearse from the Croatian Catholic undertaker Pokop, with two beautiful horses hitched to it. One, I recall, was an extremely beautiful white steed without a single dark spot, a real general's mount, the sort that would later be very highly prized throughout Europe. I'll never forget that white Lipizzaner hitched up to a Sarajevo hearse. That, my dear sir, was the Belle Époque for you, the Sarajevo of once upon a time – a city in which the most beautiful parade horse pulled a hearse. The funeral was held that same Friday, April 7. Ella was placed into the Kranjčević tomb at Saint Josip's. But there weren't many people at her burial. To be honest, there was almost no one. A few people from Napredak and the other Croatian associations, a couple of state officials who had known Silvije, but no one from the Muslim or Serb communities. The people had had their fill of Catholic funerals, or they'd forgotten about it. From among her kinspeople, there was just Ella's dear sister Mila, her Dušan, and of course Višnja. Oh, the unfortunate child, she hadn't even started school yet and she had lost both her parents. It was a great tragedy – said the old man, those eyes of his racing to and fro – a great tragedy.

From the start it had seemed to me that this all might be some distasteful Sarajevo joke. He had recognized me. He surely knew why I had come to town. My mother was not at all discreet. She spread word about her illness in all directions, and soon the whole town would be on its deathbed along with her, and he had just been waiting for the moment to catch me unawares. He had probably come up behind me while I was writing and made out Kranjčević's name. That was the keyword he needed.

And then it seemed to me again that the old man was completely mad and that he believed in what he was saying. He had no problem with the fact that Ella's death had taken place a hundred and one years before. He'd been at her funeral. He'd forgotten a little, but most of it he remembered. Best of all he remembered what sort of a day it had been: early Sarajevo spring, not a cloud in the sky, warm like May, and only far off on the snowy caps of Bjelašnica and Igman was it clear that winter had only barely passed and might return to drop snow on her fresh grave. He recalled the heavy scent of the coal smoke, filled with sulfurous stench, that authentic reek of this land, the occasional, noble scent of ignited pine logs, and the perfume of burning resin. He remembered the budding lindens next to the cemetery gates. And he remembered the patients who had escaped from the Koševo insane asylum and who mixed together with the funeral procession, letting themselves weep bitter tears – there were four of them, three men and one woman – because the deceased was leaving us forever, and theirs were the only tears that Sarajevo spent for Ella Kranjčević . . . The old man remembered all of this. It had always been this way in this city with its beggars and holy fools, whose faith depended on the people who they were trying to get a coin or two from.

But most probably he was a fraud skilled in his trade who had used the occasion to warm himself up and have a couple of rakijas at my expense . . .

Another rakija?

Ah no, I won't put you out for another. One'll be enough for me . . . But maybe another salep for you? Woman, one more salep for the gentleman! he shouted, and she waddled grumpily over. Now she was looking at me as roughly as at him, displeased, probably, that I hadn't driven Jahja away from my table.

That Friday, my dear sir, the Kranjčević family came to an end. Dušan Plavšić took Mila away to Zagreb. Little Višnja was in their care – they might have actually been better for her than her own mother and father, if the wretches had survived. Later, at the end of his life, Plavšić went bankrupt. He was a banker, you know. And Višnja worked for a long time as a secretary at the Croatian National Theater. The managers changed, but she stayed on for decades. If they hadn't helped the father, at least they could help the daughter. Besides, it was through her kinship that Kranjčević was with them, for everything else that was his had stayed in Bosnia and Sarajevo. Graves, graves, graves, my dear sir, it's all just graves. The work was in vain, all those arguments and explanations, in vain did I tell them all that one day they'd be sorry, the poet would not be long for this world, and it would be nice if they accepted him in Zagreb, helped him to die there when it was already too late for him to go on living, that they might bury him under the Mirogoj arcades and let him have his own large grave. Graves, graves, graves, my dear sir. But they didn't listen to me. They didn't care until he died. And after he'd been buried with all that false Sarajevo pomp, after all those false tears had been shed, the letters, prayers, and orders started coming from Zagreb, along with the envoys who requested that Silvije be removed from his grave, like an eye from a living head, and that his dead body be moved to Mirogoj in Zagreb. Ella was still alive then, caring for her mother in Zlatar, but they didn't ask her anything. This happens. It wasn't for the widow to worry her head over important national questions. It wasn't for a woman to think about where, in which grave, in which country, the body of the bard of Croatian poetry would decompose.

You sell papers?

Yes, but what does that have to do with anything? It was the first time he had flinched, and his eyes suddenly grew calm. He looked at me with concentration and patience, like a chemist staring at a slide before putting it under a microscope, the way people look who are completely certain of themselves. This man completed his schooling, I thought, both the regular kind and the prison kind . . .

It doesn't, I said. I'm just curious.

Yes, I sell newspapers: *Oslobođenje, Dnevni avaz, Vesela sveska* . . . Are you interested? Here, I still have got a copy of *Dnevni avaz*. The others have sold out. The world is more literate today than it used to be. I used to sell barely ten copies of *Nada* in a day through all of Baščaršija. And not a single paper was as sought after as *Nada*, but people were not interested in reading. You wouldn't believe me how every issue was sought after and how people would look to see whose poetry was being published that day. There was one vender in town. His name was Haim Albahari, a good man, a Jew, and Jews in Sarajevo didn't much care for *Nada*, you know. Haim was an exception. He was born that way, for poems and stories, not for life, but what can you do, from a poor household, and it had fallen to his lot to make buttons and combs from animal bone. And that, my dear sir, is hard work. Making buttons is harder than breaking rocks in a quarry, friend. And you're invisible, you never meet anybody. The buttonmaker's is the hardest work after the miner's. That's what people who know say. So this Haim Albahari was the only Jew who would buy *Nada* from me. There were certainly others who were subscribers, but that was a finer, more educated Jewish society, especially those who were in government employ. Our Jews here didn't recognize them, called them Swabians, for a long time wouldn't even agree to use the word Jews for them. There were surely those among them who read *Nada*. But this Heim of mine wouldn't just buy the paper, he'd call me over after work, around eight or half past, and then I had to read him the poems. I can't see them, my boy. My eyes are weak! His eyes were weak, but he made the tiniest buttons and figured out exactly how to make them fit into the hole! I saw Haim Albahari wasn't telling me the truth, but I thought: he likes hearing my voice, he enjoys recitation. It was years before the old guy admitted in his shame that he wasn't lettered. Didn't know a single letter but loved poetry. We had that sort too back then, amongst all the various and sundry, somebody like Haim Albahari.

That was a long time ago, I said. More than a hundred years.

It was, it was. For some people it was a long time ago, for some not.

A man lives on average seventy-five, eighty years . . .

There are those who don't even make it to fifty and are already old.

And you were selling newspapers a hundred years ago?

I was. So what?

Well, God, then how old in the world are you, man? I asked finally.

You know, I'm not sure. I counted up to forty, then stopped. There's no point! What use is pushing time to pass, unless you're in some violent rush to get somewhere? I haven't been rushing. There's nowhere I need to go. I'm here where I am. That's the way it is with time, see: if you don't push it, it stops passing. The wheel stops, and stays where it is.

His eyes were again dancing to and fro. The old man was not mad; he was a swindler, once a prized occupation in Sarajevo. I knew some of them in Mejtaš in the seventies. They had swindled me too, though I'd been a child. They had done it to teach me. I knew I didn't have the right to get angry or feel offended by the fact that they'd cheated me. This was their job, and just as Mama was a chief accountant and Papa was a doctor, they were professional swindlers.

I felt a bit relieved when I realized the old man wasn't mad. I let myself relax and started trying to catch him up in mistakes. I watched for when he might make a false statement, asked him questions he had already answered, looked for inconsistencies, tried to get him to lose pieces of his story, but he was unflappable and didn't make a single mistake. He understood what I was trying to do but didn't get angry. He was patient and could answer the same question several times over, in both roundabout and direct ways, with endless variations on the Kranjčević theme and without showing the slightest fatigue or frustration. I stopped when it seemed he was ready to go on till the end of the world, with thousands of different variations on the same story.

But eventually he got tired of it:

My dear sir, now I've grown quite tired! I have to go. You should leave Kranjčević and his bitterness alone for your own good. That story isn't worth anything to you. Silvije was much gentler than you've presented him. You don't have a right to his bitterness, especially not to justify your own bitterness through his. It's true that Zagreb is a foreign land for you the way Sarajevo was a foreign land to him. But you won't see any good come from your own bitterness once you've spread it around in your stories. That is futile. All human bitterness is alike, and there isn't any artistry in it. I had to tell you this. It's why I came. And I was ready to tell you about Kranjčević, what he was like in his soul, what he smelled like, what sort of teeth he had, whether he had a feel for music or went to the theater. I could have told you lots of things because there wasn't anyone as close to him as I was, but, well, you were interested in trivialities. That too is the price of bitterness. Something for you to consider when I leave, something to keep as a remembrance.

As he said this, he placed a photograph face down on the table in front of me, next to the notebook in which I'd been writing the story "Costly the Illness of Homelands," which had come to me as I looked at the two memorial plaques with their two nearly identical texts on the building where Silvije Strahimir Kranjčević had lived.

On the yellowed back was a cursive note in faded black ink: Sarajevo, October 31, 1908. Funeral of S. A. Kranjčević.

I examined the yellow cardboard, which was lined with traces of glue from someone's photo album, and instead of looking immediately at the picture, I waited for Jahja to go out, like a child silently obeying the rules of a game.

The moment he had crossed the threshold of Erzurum and stepped onto the street, I turned over the picture.

I was a little disappointed: a black-and-white photograph, fifteen by twelve centimeters, in a format that was not common at the time, taken through the heads and backs of numerous men in dark coats, bare headed or with fezzes. Atop an excavated grave stood an older, gray-haired gentleman with a half cylinder on his head and, in his hands, a cross on which the poet's name was written in black handwritten letters. Behind him, where by my time there were already broken old grave markers overgrown with weeds, there was fallow empty land. Beyond that was a newly constructed cemetery wall.

It took me perhaps five or six seconds to notice the reason behind his leaving me the photo. I shuddered with horror and the sudden rush of adrenaline, jumped up from the table, and ran out after Jahja.

But he was no longer there, not down the street toward the tram station or the Sebilj, not up above toward my hotel. It was as if he had vanished, for he couldn't have left the field of view so quickly. He had probably guessed what I would do so had quickly ducked into one of the numerous courtyards or building entrances.

It was three in the morning, and I wouldn't have been able to find him even if I'd known where to look.

I went back to Erzurum.

The waitress was leaning triumphantly against the counter.

See, I told you! Jahja gets everybody like that once. He won't a second time.

I went back to the table, but the photo was gone.

Excuse me, where's the photograph? I asked her.

What photograph? she asked, scowling as if I was accusing her of stealing something.

I waved it off.

I closed the notebook, which was still open to the last sentence of the story, that I would probably never finish, packed up my things, paid the bill, and left Erzurum.

Those people were still sitting there, chatting in their incomprehensible language, their heads pressed toward the middle of the table, and didn't seem to have noticed a thing.

The photo had captured the moment when, with the help of two lines, the men in black, some distinguished persons, others grave diggers, were lowering Kranjčević's coffin into the grave. The one whose face was most clearly visible at that instant when the shutter opened was looking directly into the camera, a white-bearded, small old man. None other than him. Jahja or Ivan, who on that thirty-first of October 1908 had been just as old as he was today. Probably he had been the one to write the words on the back of the photograph.

Perhaps Jahja had enchanted me, slipped something into my salep, made me lose consciousness for a moment, and I had imagined the whole thing.

The barking had become less pronounced. They always got quieter closer to morning, having curled up somewhere to warm themselves against one another and have a short sleep.

I passed by the taxi stand again. The wakeful, stocky man with the Rolex on his left wrist was waiting for his first customer, his hands on the wheel of his new Mercedes, the sleeves of his white shirt rolled up high. Behind him were four other cars with four sleeping drivers. Either they had lost hope that anyone would turn up or sleep had snuck up on them before the morning. After midnight, around one thirty, when the first cocks begin to crow, a mystical time of the night begins when something changes and rearranges itself in the human spirit and body, or when God, if he exists, takes account of people and dogs. Sleep overcomes some at that time, while for others, the sick, it is death that arrives. They suffocate and rattle, their hearts stop, rest for a bit and then start beating again, or they fall into an ever deeper coma, become nothing, disappear in an instant, without prior notice, easily and quietly, as if the angel Gabriel had passed across their face. Between the hours of two and six people die in hospitals, in their homes, on the deathbeds of their marital suites, and the weight pushing down on them from above becomes all the heavier, and all the more forceful grows the urge to depart, and thus does the battle between breathing and not breathing continue, the soul separating from the body, the world splitting in two, each time anew, each night from one thirty until the morning, in order for everything then to return to the normal daily rhythm, for to those remaining from the previous night it seems a little better, the color returns to their cheeks, they breathe more peacefully, as if they were just sleeping, and by around afternoon they've sort of returned to being themselves, and then, with the approach of evening, they go back to their pre-death state, while the time of the first cock's crowing draws near, and with it the time of death. No living being, not bird, animal, or insect, announces death like the cock does, but not in a single faith is the cock a symbol of death. One does not hear the sound of the cock crowing from anywhere, from any direction, in Sarajevo. Only the barking of the dogs, and later the creak of switches and the bell of the first morning trams, then the church bells, the taped voices of muezzins . . . But by then all those who had been destined to die are dead already, and those who will die tomorrow are certain of themselves.

Those twenty steps, from the old Drina to the Old Orthodox Church, were the last little piece of Sarajevo I would cross with a familiar sensation, even though I came to town because of her illness, and it was a happy thought that I'd never see Sarajevo again, never think of it as a living place, as when I was growing up in it, when Nona was still leading me by the hand and later, when I became conscious of my sexuality and imagined the moment when – as it was said at the time – the "scales would fall from my eyes" and I would lie with a woman, glide inside her, realize my masculinity, experience that greatest, most sung about physical pleasure, which, by the way, would never be as much as it had been when I imagined it, those twenty, or fifty, steps from the Drina entrance to the old church gate.

The Drina had not been an ordinary inn. I don't know when I realized this. It seems to me I understood from the time I was conscious of myself that the Drina was a whorehouse, that inside was Šuhra the prostitute, as old as Sarajevo itself, with whom nameless, invisible men would lie. They were invisible because everyone detested the Drina and the old whores, and because nobody would lie down in such a dirty bed. That was my first understanding of sex – the Drina and Šuhra. It seemed I'd been born with them, and everything else had come the way it does, from Sigmund Freud to today, to all the children of the world, as an annex atop what had started it all off. I was returning in my thoughts, from consciousness, life, and dream, not to the ailing person on the threshold of death but rather to Sarajevo, to those twenty steps between the Drina and the Old Orthodox Church, where my entire conscious and unconscious life marched forward.

I never saw Šuhra. Not in life or in a picture. I didn't even know what she looked like. I know how I imagine her today, but I don't remember how I imagined her twenty years ago, when the blockade began, or earlier, when I was in high school, or earlier still, when Nona would lead me by the hand past the Drina and the Old Orthodox Church.

I remember as a little boy, an eighth grader, and an adolescent, I was disgusted by the thought of enjoying being inside such an old, filthy woman. A man had to be hiding something despicable to want to lie with Šuhra. Later, sex transformed into a dark male fantasy of an old whore who smelled of urine, before which one finds pleasure when the illusion of paradise disappears.

They'd say: I saw Šuhra, ooh, Šuhra, she's so nasty, I heard it from Šuhra, my pops went with Šuhra, that's why he and mom got divorced – somebody told her, and: Šuhra came by a minute ago, wham, bam, thank you, ma'am, stood at the bar, knocked one down, and left without saying anything, and: ah, if only Šuhra were here to ease my troubles, oh, if only I were in Sarajevo to see Šuhra, ah, you know when Šuhra gave me the clap . . . And on and on like this from the start, from when I began school. All my friends, all my classmates knew her and saw her around, and later, in high school, some of them even lay with her. I was the only one who never saw Šuhra.

It wasn't a collective name for more than one woman, as one Slovene reporter wrote a few months before the war, in an article published in *Delo* that had the title "The City Where There Won't Be War Because Everyone Knows Each Other." That was a mistake, as was everything in his Sarajevo travelogue, though it was well intentioned and gentle. Šuhra was the only prostitute at the Drina. It was the only whorehouse in the Orient, or in Europe, where just one old prostitute worked. Everyone told stories about her from the moment they started school all the way to late in life, in retirement, at the chess club, the old folks' home on Trebević, on the bocce ball courts of retirees from Dubrovnik, on footstools in front of the vegetable vendors and shoe repair stands, or in front of the Sebilj, while feeding the pigeons bread crumbs and corn kernels, Sarajevo's old men would talk about Šuhra. About no one else but maybe Comrade Tito were such conversations carried on in Sarajevo, by both one group and the other, by both Young Pioneers and old pensioners.

Every time I passed by the Drina, I would look, without turning my head, toward the door, which was often open, especially on hot days, and I always saw the same thing: the dark interior of the inn, with several tables where no one was sitting, a floor of dirty ceramic tiles, like in a public bathroom, and immediately to the left outside the door, a bar counter and a white window with some hard-boiled eggs displayed. Maybe there was something else, but I missed it because I never dared to stop and look, instead increasing my pace until the

Drina disappeared from view, precisely and unforgetably inscribed. In this city that has grown into the most distant of foreign lands for me, and in which every dead thing strives to remind me that I am not from here, the only thing that has remained as my own privileged fragment of it, was the space of these twenty, or fifty, paces from the Drina to the Old Orthodox Church that I was crossing now.

The Drina's doors have been nailed shut, the display windows empty and covered with dust, and up above, an ad for a comics store stretches from one end of the building to the other. Perhaps Šuhra, the one prostitute in the only socialist whorehouse in Sarajevo, never existed and was, like Grozdana in Hamza Humo's poetic novel *Grozdana's Giggle*, only a comic book figure.

And so there I was before the Old Orthodox Church, passing by the cedar courtyard fence worn away by time and rain, and stinking of urine, passing it as I had always passed it, with the same feeling of shame because of Šuhra the whore and my thoughts about her. Even when my Nona had been leading me by the hand alongside that wooden gate with its eternal stench of urine, beneath the tiny, narrow-arched doorways, the onion domes above the heads of the passersby, the same guilt had taken hold of me. The Old Orthodox Church had been my first and last temple, if a guilty conscience is a measure of Christian faith, for it was there that I experienced a discomfort before God's power to know my sin and my thoughts. And who knows what my life might have been like and what sort of relation to God I might have had if by chance some other building had been there just below the Drina: a bank, a library, or a convenience store. Would my conscience have weighed on me at all? If it had, perhaps then my guilt would have lasted longer, expanding inside me across town everywhere I went. But as it is, that piece of Sarajevo remained just there, those twenty, or fifty, paces, and the last little bit of the city that remained to me was walled off.

I stood in front of the courtyard gate and seemed to hear voices within. Perhaps it was some Orthodox holy man or some early-morning prayer for which the monks – the two or three of them left in this city – had gathered, or perhaps it was just an illusion.

If I were to start banging hard two or three times right now on the door, would they be afraid I was some violent nonbeliever, or would they believe I was one of theirs and open the door for me to enter? Probably the former. There are barely any of them left in the city. This was why they were so dear to me. I was alone too. We were almost kin.

If I banged three times on the door and they opened, that would be a good sign, I thought. If that happened, that was a miracle and my mother would be cured. This thought was not enough for me to bang on the door.

I was always giving up on things. What would happen if one time I didn't?

The former Tito Street was empty and quiet. Nothing could be heard but, in the distance, the sounds of dogs barking. One dog let out a plaintive whine and was answered by two comrades with short barks, then a wail came from the other side of the Miljacka, somewhere near Bistrik, and then a response came from Vratnik or Kovači. Then it started again from the top: a quiet whine from far off, as if from having been poisoned, then the two others, furious and without commiseration or understanding, answered with barking, then from across the Miljacka, from Obilaznica or Soukbunar came a wailing, to which someone from Bjelave or Mejtaš responded, beneath my mother's windows as she slept, dreaming fitfully.

Did dying usually begin when the sick person could no longer get to the toilet? Or when she no longer had the strength to wipe herself? Or when she was no longer conscious of needing to go to the toilet? When did dying begin?

I crossed Tito Street and turned onto a little street called Prote Bakovića, and ten paces farther down on the right was a little courtyard that led to a restaurant I had once visited in September 1999 with a Sarajevo writer whose name I've been trying to forget for years who had claimed it was the best place to eat in Sarajevo. I recalled the cramped dive, whose walls pressed in on my shoulders like a tight graduation day jacket, and the thick odor of browned flour and oil in which Vienna steaks had been sizzling for days on end. I remembered the owner, a fat woman in a dirty white apron who addressed everyone as if they were her children. She cooked and brought the food out herself for three or four people at a time, to tables that had barely enough space. She would collect the money with her greasy fingers as people left. Little pieces of raw meat, burnt breadcrumbs, and palm oil would stick to the bank notes. Laughing and talking, they would press the banknotes with the faces of Bosnian-Herzegovinian poets on them into their pockets. The surprised faces, captured when they had had their identity pictures taken, and then employed in a deception for the purposes of eternity, folded up and smeared, would be mixed together with bits of pocket garbage. Bosnian-Herzegovinian poetry thus arrived in the pockets of the postwar poor gorging itself at the end of 1999.

The establishment was called "Auntie's Place," and all the customers had to call the proprietress Auntie. She didn't have another name, so no one knew what her faith was. But as the dive was located on Prote Bakovića Street, and *prota* was a term for an Orthodox priest, I believed Auntie was Orthodox. If not, she most likely would have said what her name was.

As she brought the food out, she reminded people: In this house you must finish your food and at the end wipe up the plate with your bread!

She had told us the same thing, after she put two plates filled to the brim with beans ("homegrown beans with pork sausage, Auntie's original," it said on the menu): In this house you must finish your food and at the end wipe up the plate with your bread!

To which my friend the Sarajevo writer smiled sweetly. It seemed that such was the custom. Whenever Auntie dropped a plate onto a table and delivered her magic phrase, the guests at the table would smile in the same way. Even if they came to Auntie's Place every working day and every time she delivered the same phrase in the same way in the same strict voice, the customers smiled as if it were happening for the first time. And probably the same shtick had been playing out for months and years, in the midst of the shifting political and historical conditions. God willing, given health and good fortune, everything would continue on in the same way in this city and this little establishment.

There are few things that can so unsettle a person and force him to face his natural limitations, even his own mortality, than a plate overflowing with a shiny brown sea of beans. Faced with such a trial, I was no longer hungry, though I hadn't yet dipped the spoon into the plate and was already imagining how to get out of all this, how to withstand the wave of Sarajevo humor that would follow the moment I got up from the table in a desperate attempt to escape.

My literary compatriot, whose name I try to forget in vain, because something always reminds me of him, did not take any notice of my faintness and incapacity before all such difficult instances of Sarajevo hospitality, but instead was heroically devouring the bean soup as if he were on the Western Front in 1915 somewhere near Caporetto and had sat down in the mess hall to gorge himself with utter abandon.

He clutched his spoon and worked with the bread, which crumbled between his fingers, but after every mouthful he managed to utter a new compliment to Auntie's cooking and even add a question for me:

How did I like the beans? Had I had better beans since the army?

Had *Sarajevo Marlboro* been translated into English? Really, that's too bad!

What was it like in Zagreb? Did they have concerts?

How long would I be staying in Sarajevo?

Why so little?

I remember answering him in short sentences, distracted, and felt how, in accord with my answers, his emotional state quickly changed. Maybe I could have got more into the spirit of it if I hadn't been so occupied by what I saw in front of me.

My friend, the clever author of a good novel about the siege and a few weaker novels about the dissolution of his marriage, had already eaten half his plate of beans before I got up the courage to take my first spoonful.

The soup was still hot. Thickened as it was with the flour, it cooled slowly, and I blew on the spoon for a long time. Every time I stopped to inhale, I would smell the dark, thick scent of the browned flour fried in oil, which covered all the other scents, along with the rather sweet and good-natured odor of precooked scarlet runner beans, that most valuable of Balkan leguminous plants.

My stomach would then turn as I inhaled the smell of the browned flour, which was that smell of a homely Austro-Hungarian childhood, inscribed into personal memory, the smell of the Stubler kitchen in all its difficult times, when sons died and it was necessary to cook an entire cauldron of beans for all those relatives, the rail workers, miners, manual laborers and their wives, who would come from their small industrial towns for the funeral and the long mourning. I wasn't conscious that I was thinking about the Stublers, for browned flour had been their signature and identity. Browned flour which spread through one's bowels and bloodstream, made its way to the heart, lungs, and brain, in the end spreading through one's entire person in the form of an afternoon melancholy that was especially pronounced on Sundays. And all the Stublers, men and woman alike, carried around in their heads lists of foods that harmed them. These dishes differed, and they would happily refer to their lists of harmful foods in conversations with guests, in the waiting rooms of the local clinic or at the bus stop, even with people they didn't know at all. To those strangers or to those they found odious or hateful, those they suspected or knew for certain were spying for the police, working for the Gestapo or the Yugoslav Secret Police, searching for enemies of the people or concealed Jews, to them they would talk about how bread dumplings did not agree with them, or egg drop soup, or string beans if they had a lot of tough veins, or that unfortunate, heavy, upsetting type of bean. In the same way that other people, in their small talk and concealment, were obsessed with meteorological conditions and the influence they had over achy bones, so the Stublers made small talk about dishes that did not agree with them. And it was as if it never occurred to them that it wasn't the dumplings or the meat that was bad for them, it was the browned flour that bothered their stomachs, that insufferable Austrian addition to every stew and broth, the baneful nature of which, perhaps, caused the empire's fall. Those who needed to be defending it had suffered terrible stomachaches after their lunch.

I swallowed the first spoonful, after that a second, and after that who knows how many more before the liquid level in the bowl had dropped enough for me to leave the place as quickly as possible and forget, as soon as I could, that I'd ever been there. First I had to resolve the problem with the writer and then with Auntie, who would use the occasion to work her maxim – in this house you must finish your food and at the end wipe up the plate with your bread! – into a short drama.

This is what happened. Auntie had a scene prepared for everyone present.

First she pretended to be strict, saying I wouldn't be allowed to leave until I had eaten everything. And it wasn't just me who couldn't leave but all these other people too, who had to go to work or get home to their wives and children, and she took her keys from her apron and went toward the door, pretending she was going to lock it.

Of course, as appropriate to the joke, everyone present joined in.

And everyone suddenly recognized me, in a very intimate manner.

I would never be a foreigner in this city, even once I had turned into the worst sort of tourist and Sarajevo belonged less to me than to any old American or Iranian, whom Sarajevans greeted with open hearts.

After that first onslaught, which was filled with scolding, she said, You're going to wipe your plate, or I'm not Auntie. You will, by God, or we're not getting out of here!

Zagreb has spoiled you. You've lost the taste for homemade food. You just eat crackers, caviar, and steaks there! The final three words she pronounced in a fidgety voice, tilting her head to one side, and blinking, which provoked the loud laughter of those present, including my friend the writer. He seemed to be brimming with pride that he had brought me to this place. Later he said something to me about writers who write about Sarajevo but who don't really even know the place. It seemed to me he had in mind all those who had never been to Auntie's Place.

Besides laughing, they continued to heckle me – God, I thought, am I going to get out of here alive? – and all my efforts to get out of it were futile. I answered some of them with jokes of my own, insulted Zagreb and the people I now lived with. I changed my accent and intonation, spoke as I never would have, in the manner of a Sarajevo lug, the worst actor in the most trivial TV serial, a Sarajevan trying to charm a Zagreb audience, but all of it was futile.

I was not theirs. They were demonstrating their hospitality to me. And they were doing it much more sincerely and resolutely than they would have with a real Zagreb native.

In the end she grew sad, so horrible was the insult to her that I had not eaten more than ten spoonsfuls of her famous beans. The chorus took this up with zeal, laughing and trying to persuade me to eat my beans, not deliver this slap to Auntie's face, at least finish half my plate, which she then took away, insulted, taking hold of my spoon in front of me and, in a single hysterical swoop, spraying me with drops of the undevoured bean soup. This too ended up provoking loud laughter from the others. My friend laughed too. Let her bathe me in her greasy, pork soup, then bake me in her moussaka, then plaster me with puree and spread feathers all over me, just get me out of here as soon as possible.

For years after I avoided that little street. Then once I had to go by it because I was with friends who had come to Sarajevo for the film festival, the editor Goran Rušinović and his wife Olga, and it would have been hard for me to explain why I never took that particular street, but all my fears turned out to be groundless. Auntie's Place no longer existed. No other establishment had opened in its place. The dusty door was padlocked shut, one of its two windows broken, and a light rectangular space appeared on the facade where the old business's name had once been displayed.

But all these were just Sarajevo travel notes, mementos, and memorabilia whose only purpose was to warm me up a bit, for it was getting colder as the morning came closer, and to shorten the time of my loitering around town, since I couldn't go back to the hotel room. It was hot as hell there and ugly thoughts kept catching me up, the fears of what would happen in the coming days and months as my mother began to die taking hold, and I wouldn't have been able to stop thinking them, so I walked and thought of other things, waiting for the morning, when I would visit her once more before getting into my car and heading for Zagreb.

Zagreb was so distant and beautiful, pleasantly foreign, as I thought about it on that little Prote Bakovića Street, just before morning on November 9th, 2012. And it seemed to me I'd never get back there. This scared me but still more filled me with grief. I was trapped in this city, this place within the narrow valley, which wrapped itself tight around my shoulders, and I'd never be able to escape.

I cried out but no one could hear me. I called out again, but no one was there, as though I were screaming in a dream and couldn't manage to wake up.

I'd been wrong to let Jahja go as I had. And to allow them to steal his photograph of Kranjčević being lowered into the grave from me. If he turned up, I wouldn't be able to show it to him. He'd think I had thrown it away. He might get angry. And now it seemed to me – suddenly I had an awful headache – that he was the only one who could help. If I had listened to him, maybe if I'd written down all he had wanted to tell me about the poet's life, perhaps he could have helped me get out of this town somehow, save myself if salvation was still possible.

I was going to cry out again.

As I cried out, calling Jahja, Jah-jaaaaa, Jah-jaaaaa, Jah-jaaaaa, like some sort of Turkish astronomer keeping vigil in the dead of night as word spread among the shops, mutely carried from one ear to the next, that the sultan had poisoned his own two sons so he could remain on the throne, and again I shouted Jah-jaaaaaa, Jah-jaaaaaa, Jah-jaaaaaaa, suddenly, from Sarači, on the little Prote Bakavića Street, two police officers showed up. As if I'd been calling them. The first people I had met on the street all night.

Fear took hold of me, and the moment they identified the source of the shouting, they increased their speed, the one on the left, the stockier one, automatically reaching for his baton. This was a warning, or a vocational bias: the moment you catch sight of a living creature in the middle of the night, roaring his head off no less, you go for your baton to get him to understand who and what you are.

"Your documents, sir!" says the fat one.

I take my Croatian passport from my inside jacket pocket. I could show my Bosnian identity card, but this is better.

"Miljenko, father's name!"

"Dobroslav."

"Mr. Miljenko, do you know what time it is?"

My watch has stopped. I look for my phone in my pockets . . .

"It's past three o'clock, and you, sir, are yelling. People are sleeping, Mr. Miljenko, while you're shouting. That is not right."

"I know. It isn't!"

"Then why are you doing it? Why aren't you in your bed sleeping like all respectable people?"

Confused, I don't know what to answer. Whatever I put together is likely to be more believable than the truth. But I can't call to mind a single lie.

I'm silent for a little bit.

He looks me right in the eyes. This is probably something they taught him. It's in the eyes one can detect a lie the quickest. And it's not easy to come up with something when somebody's staring at you like that.

"It's hot in my room."

"Pardon?"

"I said it's hot in my room, so I can't sleep."

"So it wouldn't be bad to open a window then!" says the other one, who's older and skinnier, upon which his colleague shoots him a look.

"What is all this stupidity?"

"The heater can't be shut off, and it's cold when the window's open."

"You're sleeping at a hotel!" asks the fat one in sincere bewilderment. "But why aren't you at home? Aren't you that writer from Sarajevo?"

"Yes. My mother's dying. There's no space in her house."

"Ah, I'm sorry," says the policeman sadly. "How old is she?"

"Seventy."

"Not that old. God I'm really sorry. So you're staying at a hotel tonight?"

"Yes."

"But why? You should be staying with a friend so you won't be alone."

I shrug. Again I don't know what to come up with. Even if I wanted to tell the truth to this stranger, I have no idea what the truth would sound like. Here I am imagining myself in an apartment on the sixth floor of a building on Alipašino polje. I'm lying in a child's bedroom, in the upper bunk; I can't reach the floor, but it's okay because I'm with friends. Men's checkered slippers on the linoleum flooring, with the design of a small town on it with streets for toy cars. The slippers smell of feet. The feet of someone no longer alive or who's off in North America – still on the other side of the grave – and the only thing left behind is that sickly indelible foot odor.

The silence was going on for too long, or the policeman had felt ashamed of his sentimentality. He turned quickly serious, handed me my passport, and said:

"Fine, sir. This is life. We all know it. A living torment. But you can't go around shouting and waking people up, sir. That, sir, is not right!"

He touched his cap with his index finger in saying goodbye. Prewar school, I thought.

"Good night," I said.

"Good night," said the skinny one.

"And quietly, sir!"

He had used the word *sir*, repeating it as children do when they're learning something new. I wanted to say something more to him but felt embarrassed. I wanted to apologize but didn't. At the same time, with another part of my consciousness, I kept trying to remember whose sixth-floor apartment it could have been on Alipašino polje in whose bunk bed I was trying to get to sleep.

I continued down Sarači toward Slatki Ćošet. The fountain by the harem wall of the Gazi Husrev-beg Mosque gurgled, the water was alive, flowing. It wasn't cold enough yet for them to shut it off. Though I couldn't remember ever passing by the fountain when it wasn't flowing. I remembered it flowing freely even in the middle of winter, when strips of ice would form around the drain. They probably turned it off unobtrusively when the temperature dropped to ten below or less. They trusted that people would not notice such things. For them the water flowed endlessly, even when it didn't. Their ears were used to the sound and heard it even when there was no water. Their eyes saw what wasn't there: a lively, free-flowing spurt that never stopped. And no one noticed that the people who took care of the mosque turned off the water so the pipes wouldn't crack beneath the mosque around which Sarajevo had grown and spread over the centuries.

The only ones who might be able to remark the day and hour when the water went off at the mosque's fountain were the former Sarajevans who had moved away across the ocean and didn't come here anymore or only came when they needed an overhaul on their mouths since dentists in Sarajevo were much cheaper than in America, but even they came mostly in the summer. They'd have to come in winter, in December or January, when Bosnia's at its coldest, and mist and smog presses in on the valley, but no one comes to Sarajevo then without great distress, much greater than cavities or porcelain crowns. You go to Sarajevo in winter only for a funeral of somebody you want to see for the last time. Then, maybe, you'll be that individual who sees and hears that they've shut off the water in front of the Begova Mosque.

I was standing in front of the display windows of a store that sold women's silk slippers and loafers decorated with fake silver and plastic jewelry. The slippers had acquired their own name over the years: *aladinke*. They'd been fashionable over the last fifteen years, so the hungover filmmakers would buy them the day before their departure to take back to their wives and girlfriends in Zagreb, Ljubljana, and Belgrade. Later the foreigners copied this custom, thinking as usual that there were some deeper reasons and roots behind it, like maybe that these slippers had been sewn in Sarajevo ever since the Ottomans adopted Bosnia, and that it was precisely there that the roots of the town had taken hold. This belief was securely held even by the owner of the store, a squat sixty-year-old with a shaved head and the characteristic eastern need to chat up the foreigners until he could find some fatal similarity between Sarajevo and the countries and cities from which they had come. This was probably something that had existed forever, but I only started to notice it once I had become a foreigner to these people. Before they'd been taciturn and ill-tempered: if they said anything at all, it was some story about Želja's ćevapi, *burek*, or yogurt, while today they'd probably use the same tone to discuss the genocide and Republika Srpska or peaceful Islam and the Israeli aggressors, such that I wouldn't ever learn a thing, and it would forever remain a secret to me, had I never moved away from Sarajevo, that the master slipper maker knew and loved Zagreb, that he practically had the whole map of the city in his head, along with all the details one can only learn from tourist guides since more often than not they're not even known by Zagreb natives. For instance, he knew in what year the Stone Gate had been built and that Ilica Street had once been the longest in Yugoslavia. He knew the habits of Zagreb's inhabitants as well as their antipathies, and he praised both even when they involved questions of outlook on the world and customs that were in complete opposition to his beliefs. Of course any foreigner, a Zagreb native for instance, might appear in the shop. The man was prepared to relate wonders merely in order to sell, for the price of twenty-five convertible marks, his silk-upholstered slippers, which reminded me of candies wrapped in tissue paper of the sort that had been sold in the Yugoslav provinces forty years earlier.

There was an ad in the display window: *aladinke* of all sizes and colors.

In the half-light of the shop, on the wall above the little table where the master worked, hung a *levha* panel with Arabic calligraphy. A framed photograph hung on the opposite wall: the master shaking hands with President Clinton there in the workshop during his visit to Sarajevo.

Some people looked at one wall when they entered, others looked at the other. He sold them slippers, telling each of them what he thought that person wanted to hear.

I remembered him with his bronzed forehead and obsequious smile, grasping my hand and looking into my eyes as he said what he thought I wanted to hear. After that I would hurry by his shop so he wouldn't see me and invite me in.

At Slatki Ćošet, there were two sweetshops across the way from each other: Ramisa's always had the shapeliest cakes, in modern showcases and refrigerators. That was where the tourists came and those in the know. On the other side of the alley crisscrossing Sarači was an older, skimpier sweetshop. Its name changed whenever the owner changed, or whenever the owner wanted to alter the signpost indicating the name of the business. For the longest time it was simply called Sweet Ćoše, from the Turkish word meaning "nook." It was there at the beginning of the seventies that I'd drunk my first boza.

Between the two confectionaries, at the very end of the Oriental market, before Sarači emptied into the Vaso Miskin Street, which today is called Ferhadija, hung the balance of a civilization, which was not conscious of itself or its own existence. I looked through the display windows of the Ramisa sweetshop: little stainless steel and fake marble tables, clean glass cabinet windows in which by early morning there would be cakes with bright artificial colors, cream, and candied fruit. The back wall was covered in mirrors to make the interior seem larger, and in them, the competing store from across the street was visible. While it was still night and the street light was barely flickering, it was possible to make out the worn café tables and chairs in the mirror, the opaque glass kolach case, which had probably survived the war, and two glass gallon containers on top of it, one for boza and one for lemonade. Even though there was always a bigger crowd at Ramisa, the people in the shop across the way never tried to make adjustments and compete in the way handbooks on capitalist business recommend. They had fewer clients, but their boza was better. And everyone knew the boza across the street was better. Maybe the kolach too? This was impossible to say, since no one but tourists went to Sweet Ćoše for the kolach. One went to Sweet Ćoše because such was the custom. And for the boza, which had always been better across the way. Maybe it really was better – maybe one drank the boza in the sweetshop across the way because it inspired faith in the poverty of its creation. Boza was something from the past, from an old, rundown sweetshop on the verge of being closed forever. One was always drinking it for the last time.

When either of the two sweetshops disappeared, or when the poorer one was remodeled into one that would compete against the other, richer one, all this would fall apart and the balance on which this Oriental city had always managed to rest would disappear, leaving it as gloomy as the town of Kars in Pamuk's *Snow*, as picturesque as a kitschy nineteenth-century veduta by a French traveler to Bosnia.

Ganimed Troyanovsky came to Bosnia on the invitation of Omar Pasha Latas. It was the spring of 1851. The trip from Paris to Sarajevo had taken him thirty-seven days. On the road he had contracted a fever that had long tormented him, rendering him weak in both body and spirit. And his character had not been particularly strong to begin with. He easily changed his mind and was never sure whether he had set off on the right path, so even when Paris was still in view as he turned around to look, he was bitterly regretting his acceptance of the invitation by this Bosnian serasker. But he could not go back, for Latas had sent two very well-educated Venetians to accompany him, one a bridge builder and storyteller named Sarchione, the other a certain Botta, about whom he knew nothing except that he very kindly watched over him. They had come with twelve helpers – porters, riders, coachmen, gendarmes – hand-picked men of the sort that were sent in those times through insecure lands and regions to convey cargo that was valuable to the vizier or the Sublime Porte.

On this occasion there was no valuable cargo but Ganimed Troyanovsky, who had just turned twenty-three, and it would remain a mystery how and through whom Omar Pasha had heard about him and why he had decided to bring him to Sarajevo for such a delicate and serious job, which was of the sort that only proven builders and artists were typically selected for, people at the height of their calling, or at its end, when they needed to put a finishing touch on a great career and secure the gratitude of the empire. He was inclined toward the Western taste and measure of Paris and Vienna, but instead of bringing a forty-year-old from one of those cities, he had invited someone who was practically a child. But the fact that Omar Pasha knew everything about him – namely that he was of an unstable nature, melancholic, and scatter-brained – is attested to by his having sent such an experienced group of men, led by Sarchione, who would entertain and encourage him and with whom, should he feel the urge, he might shorten the journey through conversations on art, poetry, and architecture, and by Botta, who would take care not to let the youngster lose his way.

The moment he sat down in the coach and a servant covered his legs with a wool blanket and offered him some chamomile tea, which he said would cure his ailment, Ganimed understood that things had begun to unfold beyond his will. This thought upset him, and it became cramped for him first inside the carriage and then inside his own skin, and soon he began to emit almost constant sighs.

He drank the tea. It was actually the first time in his life he had drunk chamomile, and he imagined it was some sort of Turkish narcotic plant that broke a prisoner's will to flee, lowered his spirits, and made him fearful. And so for days on end Ganimed cried – which first alarmed his escorts, then frightened them, and eventually entertained them – and was not up for conversations about bridges in the East or bridges in the West, or about Giovanni Battista Tiepolo, the Venetian painter and renegade, with his enigmatic Scherzi etchings, or about the Vienna theater project, or about the enormous expanses of Russia, whose imperial mission to Paris had brought Ganimed's father Ivan Vasilievich into contact with Ganimed's mother Elise and caused him never to return to Petersburg . . .

Ganimed didn't feel like talking. He wasn't interested in anything but going back home, and he bitterly regretted having answered the invitation of this unknown Turkish pasha. He had felt honored and, more than that, soothed in his limitless vanity in knowing that word about him had reached Istanbul, and he had felt he had no choice but to agree. Who would not have done so in his place? When he had answered in the affirmative to the pasha's invitation, six months had remained before the journey to Sarajevo. A full half year in which Ganimed could enjoy the honor being bestowed on him. But the time had passed quickly, and as the journey grew near he began to regret his decision and to consider how to put it off. And then he had come down with that strange fever – in the morning he would be fine, but by evening he would be gripped in turn by fever and trembling. This could have been a good reason for postponing the expedition, but even if Ganimed Troyanovsky had written a letter, or if he'd sent a messenger to Sarajevo, neither would have made it to Omar Pasha Latas. One could simply not get to the serasker. The pasha was the one to choose when he made contact with the world.

After Ganimed had a good cry, the state of his fever only got worse. They traveled slowly and uncertainly, for the sick man was constantly demanding things, and then they would wait for him to recover at some wayside Belgian inn.

This drove even the sedate Botta to despair, then to fury, which he would appease by having wrestling matches with Mula, the escort commander, a huge Turk with a shaved head and a Tatar braid. They would strip to the waist, rub oil on their torsos and hands, and go at it in the middle of a field. Remnants of winter were still visible in places – if the diaries, chronicles and notes of the day are to be believed, the winter of 1850–51 was one of the snowiest of the century, and it was somewhat unusual that Latas did not postpone Ganimed Troyanovsky's journey to Bosnia on this account – and there were Botta and Mula wrestling in the icy snow, which poked and tore at their backs. But they didn't feel anything in the heat of battle, going at it for two hours at a time, until eventually Mula would win.

Botta had studied wrestling along with a few other arts: throwing knives, handling Damascus swords, strangling a man with a silk scarf, remaining without air for a long time under water, slowing the heart, using poisons, setting traps along the road, in the forest, and in the desert – but also more refined skills like how to influence the masses through powerful words, how to offer conviction by means of a glance, such that he was preeminent among the whole group of them, that he wished them all well and was their leader, and among these finer skills was that of talking about books he had not read, as well as the most ordinary trick of all, that of convincing people they were hearing the most beautiful of all singing voices when he had merely opened his mouth. In journeying to the

East the Venetian had learned all these skills, among others. From Salonika to Istanbul and on to Samarkand, Bukhara, and Baghdad, he had studied the arts of self-control and dispassionate behavior, which rendered him one of the cruelest and most dedicated killers of his time, whose unerring nature is witnessed by the fact that he remained completely outside of history. Even Omar Pasha Latas, who prized him more than any other man in his surroundings, didn't know his full name. He knew him only, as did others, as Botta from Venice.

But still he could not overpower Mula and throw him onto the ice. Although he was physically stronger and better prepared than the Turk, and although he was more agile and unquestionably craftier – craftiness was something one learned from life, but also from books, and Mula was illiterate – and although according to everything he was pre-destined to be able to throw the weaker, slower Mula onto his back on the ice, he couldn't manage to do it. Wrestling, one of the fundamental skills of the Ottoman empire, was not something Mula had ever studied. He had been born into it, had wrestled from the time he started walking, and wrestled in the same way that he walked, without thinking about it, and never thought about wrestling as something one used to defeat another or humiliate another. Botta quickly understood: wrestling for Mula was a game he could not do without, as one cannot do without breathing.

This was what made Mula unbeatable. In order to beat him, Botta understood, he would have to eliminate in himself beforehand any inkling of superiority and wrestle with him as if with his own child. There weren't any boys in the caravan, so he went dancing around looking to see whether there wasn't some young Belgian or maybe a Gypsy he could convince to wrestle with him. The Belgians ran from the crazy Turk, hiding their children in the sheds and animal stalls. They thought Botta was a Turk, which in a certain sense he was. Actually, Botta was a Turk in almost everything – for he never thought about what he actually was or about what sort of clothing the God he believed in had put on him – except in the fact that he had gained all his knowledge through hard experience and there was more of it than in any Turkish killer or wise man, though they had acquired their knowledge and skills naturally. A true Turk would have had mastery over one or two of Botta's skills, rather than his thirty or forty, and would not have needed to learn more than that.

Mula, for instance, knew how to wrestle, could cut off the head of a live ox with a single blow of his sword, and could crack a whip in the air above his head. These were essentially all his skills.

The Belgians hid their children because they thought the Turk was strange when he proposed wrestling with the seven-year-olds. Rumor also had it that Orientals had a preference for boys. They would cut off the heads of men but they instinctively loved boys, believing that by the force of their love these boys could grow up into the most beautiful girls. Such was the belief in Belgium in the middle of the nineteenth century, during Ganimed Troyanovsky's journey to Bosnia.

The Gypsies didn't hide their children: they offered them to Botta for sale, in pairs or individually. He could take the children with him to Turkey so they would grow up with the pashas and great viziers. It was futile of him to offer them money just to wrestle with one and then return him. This made them terribly sad, and there wasn't a single Belgian Gypsy who would agree to let his boy wrestle with the Turk for any amount of money. When Botta asked one of the fathers why, the man said it wasn't humane to offer the child hope and then take it away. Let him either buy the boys or stay away from them altogether.

Botta stopped trying.

The story of Botta's wrestling with Mula would have remained unimportant and unrecounted if not for the fact that on the eleventh day of the journey, somewhere in the wide German plains, Ganimed Troyanovsky disappeared.

It was early afternoon, the caravan had stopped for lunch, and the two of them had gone off to wrestle. As always in such circumstances, Botta instructed two youths from the escort to keep an eye on the young man. But it seems they were not aware of what could happen – for why would the young lord run off anywhere? – or perhaps they'd been befuddled by the young wine they had drunk in big pots with the roast mutton, such that by the end of lunch Ganimed was nowhere to be found.

His porcelain plate, silver cutlery, and Murano glass cup were all that remained.

(Thus had it been ordered: all the others ate from tin mess kits, with their fingers, and with wooden spoons, while only Sarchione used the same sort of plate as Ganimed and drank from a Murano glass cup. It's true there was one more set of the lord's cutlery – for Botta – but he never used it.)

The search for the young man didn't last long. They found him in tears as he lay in a hay shed on the nearest village estate. But the fact that he'd run away was a great setback for Botta. His own vanity had made him careless.

The journey's continuation was difficult and slow for some time longer. Ganimed's fever did not abate. Every evening some serious ailment seemed to take hold of him, eventually causing him to collapse into his bed, and the entire caravan would worry – who would go before the lord to tell him the youth had died? – and then in the morning, after he'd had a good cry and slept, he would again seem to be healthy. And so they would travel for a day, camp for two, waiting for Ganimed to get better or, perish the thought, fall seriously ill.

The garrison slept inside or underneath the coaches – Mula the wrestler, always slept in the middle of a field and without any covering, so by morning the frost had accumulated on him and two or three times he was covered over with snow and almost suffocated – while Ganimed Troyanovsky, as the occasion dictated, slept in wayside inns, city hotels, or, most often, in a coach himself, since the inns across the Bavarian wastelands were rare and suspicious, and it was easy to get oneself killed since plunderers lurked, waiting for solitary travelers, who were often outlaws themselves. Carrying off the plunder from someone they had killed a night or two earlier, the thieves themselves would be run through or have their throats slit at an inn, and then, maybe fifty kilometers or so farther on, at the next inn, the same fate would befall those murderers. This was how gold coins, Turkish pocket watches, saffron, cinnamon, and nutmeg were transported from the east to the west of Europe, while all around such goods heads rolled, and very soon it was no longer clear where the gold coins had come from and who that first explorer and wretch had been who, in the distant Orient, in some Indian village, had bought the saffron, cinnamon, and nutmeg from a native for a pittance. This is why history does not even make note of such journeys and has barely an idea of the routes taken by such caravans, where death traveled from east to west, bringing gold and spices, progress, and a better life to Europe.

Eustachio Millas Sarchione was a man gifted in everything that made for adornment, accumulation, and zest in this world, especially in the realm of government and governing. A musician, a quack, and a fine portraitist, he had begun his career as a jester in the court of some now nameless Venetian grandee. He was – according to the documents – from a poor family that had lived at the edge of the lagoon and been ravaged by a cholera epidemic. Of the twenty members of the family of Lazarus Sarchione, only the youngest male child had survived, Eustachio. They had found him in a pile of garbage and his own excrement. He had survived for days by gnawing on the bones of his dead relatives. This prodigious story was passed from person to person among men and women, from one end of Venice to another, doing away with people's need to criticize the powerful, which was where the idea of revolt had always emerged. Venice's powerful, like those throughout the world, kept track of what eliminated people's need to speak ill of them, or redirected it from political figures to something else, something to one side, to men and women, the Church, or even God, as long as they were not saying anything about those in power. Natural disasters and epidemics were of great help to them in this, for they distracted the people from dangerous ideas. From the time that the empire had grown weak and shrunk down to one stinky lagoon and its immediate vicinity, and there were no more wars or threats of war, the only thing that could save them was cholera, small pox, malaria, or the plague, when their sailors and merchants happened to bring such things from distant lands.

The epidemic from Sarchione's childhood had been one of the largest. Or it had become such in his imagination, especially during times of travel, when he would gather around himself a group of listeners and narrate the story of his life from the very beginning. Everyone would listen, for in these stories Sarchione was an unrivaled artist.

He had been adopted by a rich widower, a patrician without children. The man had done this because of his gentle heart, or perhaps he had been drawn to him by the nearness of his own death. The old man, whom Sarchione sometimes called Muscha, sometimes Master Pio, Elder Silvester, Kanibal, Dužd, Elijah, or, most often, "my dear papa," was a terribly sad person, never laughed, and thought often of suicide. He had a collection of daggers and ordered that poisons be brought to him from all over the world, which he kept in hundreds of little bottles in the wine cellar. After a certain Dubrovnik sailor brought him the poisons of some New Zealand aboriginals, whose homeland had been reached just twenty years before by Captain Robert Cook, the first European to do so, the old man, without even knowing it, had brought together in his collection of four hundred bottles (here we cease estimating: there were 429 jars of various colors and sizes) all six continents of the future world, not counting the one eternally under ice, in a unique atlas of the world, probably the first such created in Venice, and maybe the first in Europe. Thus did our modern history, without the gray stains of a map or unexplored seas, begin with an atlas of poisons. Unless Sarchione had invented it to make his story more exciting.

The old man had procured the poisons, paying very little for them, by combining his two passions, one for collecting, the other for suicide. The first was typical of the Venice of his time: everyone was collecting something while the state was crumbling. The priests too started collecting treasure once they had stopped believing in God.

Meanwhile, recognizing his benefactor's other passion for what it was, the boy set out to entertain him and make him laugh. Though he was not aware of what he was doing and did not know he was engaged in one of the oldest occupations of our civilization, from as early as five years old he had been a small court jester. This was how he dressed and appeared before the old man every morning. Not once did his papa, Muscha, Master Pio, Dužd, or Elijah laugh, but the boy succeeded in distracting him. When the time came, he sent him to school with the Dominican friars, then with the Armenian monks, who would be the first to acquaint him with the enchantments of the East. And while the West was shallow, and one could quickly drown in the Atlantic Ocean, the East was deep and spread out to the farthest edges of the human mind and human understanding. The East, as the Armenian scholars explained, was more profound than even the universe with all its stars, so profound that no one had ever found its bottom. They had even directed him, after his papa had died, to set out on the road to the East. It turned out that he would never make it to Ararat or Yerevan, for in wondrous Istanbul all his talents would be realized: he would tell stories and compose Western sonnets and Eastern ghazals in competitions. Though the poets would never meet, for years between Istanbul and Samarkand heralds on camelback would carry scrolls with the latest ghazals and short inquiries about each other's health and whether enemies were trailing.

In Istanbul Sarchione would study calligraphy and painting, the goblet drum, and violin and piano. Thanks to the piano, he would become acquainted with the charming Lika Serb. Omar – elegant, educated, and witty – had just one fault: he was ashamed of his own imagination. And he was known to take pleasure in Sarchione's fantasies and invented stories for hours and days on end, especially the variations on his own biography. These had been known to mesmerize Omar.

Once in a while, in rare moments of weakness, Omar Latas would sigh:

Oh, if only such things came to me!

But the moment the Venetian began to improvise, assuring him it was in everyone's power to create new versions of his own life, Omar would turn sad, scowling and shrinking into his shell, and then quickly disappear. For weeks there would be no sign of him, and when he did appear he had only one thing to say to his friend:

We shall not speak of it!

Sarchione knew what Omar meant. It was simply not the case that everyone was able to embellish other people's lives, let alone his own. Some had no gift for it. Others were ashamed of such creation, as if of their own nakedness. As a rule, they were unhappy people. Then they made others unhappy.

In this alone lay the explanation for Omar Pasha Latas's unusual character and militant cruelty. He would kill and order others to kill, calmly and without an afterthought, without allowing his imagination to ruin his reason or inflame his emotions. At the same time, he was quite sensitive and interested in every form of art. It was as a young soldier in Vidin that he had been hired by the fortress commander to teach drawing to his children. The commander had recommended him to Istanbul, where Omar had become acquainted with Western literature and Arab poetry, studying the piano a little bit as well.

He believed in art more than in war. Like Sarchione he was sadly aware that his empire was declining, but this merely strengthened his belief that he had done the right thing in converting, changing from Mića to Omar. On one side he held Sarchione – a friend he admired – and on the other Botta – a killer whom he valued as much as his friend, for if Sarchione had a gift for the beautiful and the extraordinary and knew how to lie in such a way that his lie was recognizable as such but was still more beautiful, more humane, and more necessary to a person than was the truth, Botta had the unerring gift of being correct and just.

Eustachio Millas Sarchione and Omar Latas had met in the middle of the thirties, in Istanbul, where the future pasha was working as the drawing tutor for the future sultan Abdulmedjid. Omar was not yet twenty-seven, when a man's maturity begins, Sarchione was several years older. They were both foreigners in the great city, but this was not what brought them together. Rather it was their attraction to the arts and their fascination with the city of Caesar Constantine and its magnificence.

Before long Latas broke with the young prince or had nothing more to teach him and, fleeing from his own shame and the vices of the big city, returned to his fundamental military calling. As a young boy, Mićo from Jana Gora, near Plaški in the Kordun region, had graduated from a good cadets school in Gospić, and this would be quite useful to him in Constantinople. Strong of spirit and voice – his whisper alone could be heard from one hill to another if he wanted – and friendly with Abdulmedjid, he was quickly promoted to the rank of colonel in 1838. Soon thereafter, when Abdulmedjid became sultan, Latas was named pasha, upon which his great military career was immediately launched. The empire was tearing and falling apart like an old overcoat, and while he did not believe in its ultimate salvation, Omar sewed it back together and spared it with lightning speed. He quashed rebellions in Syria and Albania, then in the southeastern borderlands, in Kurdistan, dealing savagely with the national and political elites of those regions, where, in accordance with the prevailing European fashion, new nations had begun to be born. Constantinople was far away, the empire growing more outmoded and decrepit the more literate they became, and nothing awakens the need for freedom in a person more than that strange impression of a kingdom's outmodedness. Plus they counted on their apostasy to turn them into the fathers of nations. Latas soullessly cut them all down, and one might have said that there was even some private passion of his own in this. He was insulted by the suspicion that people were merely rats fleeing a sinking ship. If this were true, if people were rats, art would have no meaning.

The two would go for years without seeing each other. News would reach Sarchione of his friend's heroic exploits, his madly courageous attacks on enemy camps and fortresses, all of which confirmed that Omar was a man whose fierceness was so great it did not even allow him to perish. He would later ask him why this was. Because, Latas responded reasonably, one cannot do it otherwise. It would be too expensive, and maybe even impossible, to keep the borders of the kingdom if the enemy did not live in the belief that the keepers are insane and bloodthirsty and that they wouldn't stop once they had started. What about the fear? he asked. Every man fears in the same way. It's just that the majority of people fear in such a way that the world sees it, and a few bury their fear deep within. It's to those few that the keeping of the kingdom should be given.

When Omar was sent in 1850 to put down the uprising of the Bosnian begs, he invited Sarchione to join him so he would be near at hand. This was not convenient. While Omar had been building his career in the military, Sarchione had been occupied with the design and construction of bridges – that ancient passion of Istanbul artists and architects that, in the meantime, everyone had abandoned, and there was no longer so much need for bridges since, rather than conquering the other shores, they had long since lost them – and here was Latas inviting him to go to Bosnia. Sarchione knew if he stopped now, it would be for his whole life and he would not design or build the bridge he had been dreaming of, narrower than the one in Mostar, so narrow as to be invisible to anyone who didn't know how to look, but he also knew he would lose his friend if he didn't go with him.

Latas would have preferred not to go to Bosnia. At first he was afraid, but this fear of his was not ordinary. He was afraid of the sudden clarity that had lit up inside him when the grand vizier had announced this campaign. Before his eyes he could clearly see the thick, dark woods cut through with powerful mountain streams. He could smell the heavy scent of just-ploughed soil and see its color, a color he could distinguish from all the other colors and lands of the earth . . . He was afraid of the fact that he knew all this and could imagine it all beforehand, but there was something more that was much worse: he thought about the insurgent begs with a kind of joy that was sudden and demonic, those people he knew in his head, and he recognized in himself each of their motives. By contrast to every other commander or lieutenant in the Ottoman kingdom Omar Pasha Latas knew the people who were standing up against the sultan for some sense of their own rights and for an old-fashioned, primitive understanding of God and custom.

And he thought: How can they not be ashamed of themselves!

And whenever he thought this, the blood would rush to his head and he'd be ready to slaughter them all.

They were doing what he would have done if he, God forbid, had been in their place, if things had worked out that way, and if God had so willed it, the God in whom Omar did not even believe, and if instead of a Kordun and Lika Serb he'd been made a Bosnian beg and had managed to see how something that had been built to last for all time was eroding and crumbling in Istanbul, and how the kingdom was crumbling into little pieces at the edges. Yes, he would have behaved the same way if he'd had the misfortune to be a Bosnian beg. And then something occurred to him that would provoke a fury that was even more bitter: as a Serb on the Austrian frontier, a worthy and talented student of the Gospić school for lower officers, he had had the opportunity to see Istanbul, become Turkish, attain the rank of marshal in the Ottoman kingdom, but it would have never been possible for him, a boy from Janja Gora, near Plaški, to wake up one morning as a Bosnian beg.

They were, it so happened, above him.

This did not bother him.

They were, it so happened, above him and did not feel any sense of shame about what they were doing and what they planned to do.

This did bother Omar, and at that moment he turned his eyes from them, those Bosnian begs, with the eyes of a Turkish pasha. He saw in them what he had seen when he was Mićo.

And this frightened him. At that moment, he was no longer a pasha. He was a cut-throat and an arsonist, one who killed in a fit of passion. He was afraid he might really become that. This was why he had asked Sarchione to come with him to Bosnia.

The Venetian was not impressed by the poor, primitive country, not before he had seen it and not after he had been in Bosnia for several months. If there was anything that stirred him in connection with Bosnia, it was the fact that such an intelligent man could be put into such a state by the place as to lose his mind and peace. And he was not alone in this: in Istanbul, as they were preparing for the journey and later on the road and in Sarajevo, he had met many wise, composed, and gifted foreigners, people of diverse faiths and heritage who, like Omar, could be induced by the place to put all their bets on a single throw of the dice. He wasn't swayed by the understanding that it was a poor, backward land that wasn't worth his attention, where one could not find a single truly beautiful building or hear anything at all that was intelligent or great from the locals, except how great was their sadness that they didn't live in some other part of the world, and he understood that there was something in Bosnia that clouded foreigners' minds. Something like henbane or opium, which an infected spirit could only clean out with difficulty and which after a time turned fatal.

He went with Omar to keep him safe in Bosnia, and more than that, to watch out for the health of his mind and the purity of his soul.

Whatever anyone might have thought, Omar Pasha Latas was for Eustachio Millas Sarchione a man with a child's purity of soul. This was why he abandoned his life's dream of a perfect, invisible bridge, and went with the pasha to Sarajevo.

Omar Pasha Latas accomplished his work coldly and with lightning speed. He quelled the uprising quickly and easily, much more easily than in Syria because it became clear there was no great reason to have an uprising. The begs were not imagining Bosnia as some sort of France, or Prussia, or Venice, or Hungary. The begs were not even thinking about Bosnia really. What was on their minds had always been their own lands and status. And the moment they bumped up against this reality, they closed themselves up in their courtyards and paid no more attention to what was happening with the country or the people. But this was not enough for Omar, and he selected the most highly regarded from among them and humiliated them in the worst possible ways, setting out with his soldiers to confiscate and destroy their estates, beat and kill them like dogs. He counted on the fact that this too would enter into folk legend and national storytelling, in an epic song that would be sung for centuries. This people would lament its leaders, and this sadness.

Sarchione was amazed at this fury and wondered where it had come from and what was happening to Latas. Had this come with age? He had turned forty-two, his beard was going gray, his shoulders drooped, and he seemed to have somehow grown smaller – Sarchione was practically a head taller than him now while two years before they had seemed to be the same height. Perhaps this rage grew out of premature aging?

Everything in a person needs to be in balance, the Ancient Greek and Eastern sages taught, in order for him to be fulfilled and happy. But in Latas, in contrast, everything was out of balance. He had strong poetic and artistic gifts, but still stronger shame with regard to dreaming and imagining what was not actual or true. He was the marshal of a grand army, admired in both Istanbul and Vienna – too bad for the Swabians that they had lost such a man! – but at home and in his heart: desolation! The unhappy Latas had neither a kitten nor a pup. Actually, Sarchione had never married either, but that was different. Neither women, nor family life, nor children had ever attracted him. If things had been different, he would have become a monk in Venice, and he would not have broken the vow of celibacy. He would have violated all the other religious and secular rules and restrictions at least once, but in terms of celibacy he would have remained innocent and pure. But what was for him torment and revulsion with regard to female inclination and the body, for Latas was a great, unfulfilled hunger. Yet another imbalance of the soul. This made most people unhappy, but him it made wrathful.

While Eustachio Millas Sarchione's name is largely omitted from Omar Pasha Latas's biographies, probably for extraordinary and clandestine reasons, this was how his closest friend and secret confidant explained to himself Latas's deep Bosnian fall. When the biographies do mention him, they mostly note that it was he who, during Latas's military campaign across Bosnia, transported the first concert piano to Sarajevo.

While we were spending a great deal of time describing the story of Sarchione and Latas, during the caravan's trip across Bavaria nothing happened. Ganimed continued slowing down the journey, less with his capricious behavior and tears than with his consistent evening fever.

And he showed no interest whatsoever in Sarchione's stories. He seemed indifferent to music, and to poetry, and to the wonders of Arab calligraphy. In vain did the Venetian narrate his life's story to the people of the caravan in such a way that Ganimed could hear. In vain did he weave such fantastic details into the story that had been unnecessary in Istanbul, when he told it to the beauties of the harem and to women of the court, intelligent and educated women saturated with great love stories and passionate human destinies, for that was all they had heard their whole lives, and he would more easily pull them into his tale than he could the handsome Ganimed Troyanovsky, who would either be weeping or trembling with fever, and showed not the slightest interest in the vision of little Sarchione gnawing on the bones of his dead brothers and sisters.

It is no shame to invent! Sarchione said, somewhat insulted, in the middle of one of his tales that had fallen upon the deaf ears of the young man. Ganimed had been looking out the coach window at the clear day and the snow-capped peaks in the distance, sighing.

The shame is when a man has to invent in order not to be burned at the stake or impaled!

The youth had suddenly turned and for the first time looked him in the eyes: Do you think so?

Yes, I do.

From all that you told us, what was true and what was invented?

How would I know that? asked Sarchione in surprise. I've been telling stories for thirty years, and for twenty-three I've been writing down what I tell, first in Latin, then in Arabic. If I once knew what the truth was, or what really happened, by now it's been lost or mixed up together with what I invented.

Have you entangled them, sir?

I have not. What I want to say rather is that we invent our memories. Even the honorable serasker invents things and the shame torments him afterwards.

What really happened?

Nothing.

And this, this isn't happening? We're not traveling?

Sarchione shrugged and laughed:

It's not my place to tell you this. It would be improper.

The next day they came upon the trading posts of the last little town in the valley. After that the road entered the mountains, and there began the most difficult, most unknown part of the journey, which they could have avoided if they'd traveled across Hungary. But this would have extended the journey, and neither Botta nor Sarchione wanted that. Besides, neither of them feared the mountains. (And if either of them did, he would not have shown it before the other.)

Ganimed was in an unexpectedly good mood.

He took Sarchione by the arm and babbled constantly, jumping from one subject to another, the violin makers of Cremona, the differences between maple wood and walnut, Goethe, Dante, and Shakespeare, how in the future all distinction between a king and his subjects would disappear, the medicinal characteristics of melancholy and how somewhere in the middle of the Carpathian mountains, a Romanian would be born to an Orthodox priest, and he would write the following sentence: "If it weren't for melancholy, we would roast nightingales on a grill; it was just a shame we would not experience that moment since we would have all long since been dead by then." Then he babbled about daguerreotypes, the newest Parisian invention, which stopped time and put all the reality taken in by the eye into a silver-copper plate, about how in the future people's thoughts and then their persons would be imprinted on such plates whenever anyone grew tired of life and wanted to live in some other, distant future time, and also about how Russians were a bloodthirsty, sentimental lot, and they were more so in both domains than any other people, especially than those feather-brained Frenchmen obsessed with the pleasures of the flesh, and this was the main reason that the Russians, more precisely Grand Prince Vladimir, when selecting between Catholicism and Orthodoxy had chosen Orthodoxy, the most aesthetic and melodious variety of Christianity, to which he would add his own mystical Russian bloodthirstiness, and then he talked about a certain Jean Marais, who had murdered twenty-seven women in Lyons before he'd been caught, and then they had taken him to Paris to have his head chopped off with the Parisian guillotine, and Jean Marais had said he was satisfied because he had killed all those unfortunate women, then had seen Paris and died . . .

Nearby, the scent of medicinal herbs wafted from the wooden tables, goat's and cow's milk was being poured out from buckets, the children, out of boredom, were wrapping their arms around the enormous rounds of cheese: in this little town within reach of the end of the world, a person who could wrap his arms around the cheese such that the tips of his middle fingers touched was considered a grown-up man.

Old men with alpine caps followed the collection of unusual strangers with curious glances. The women wiped their palms on their aprons, their cheeks red as they tried to attract their attention, to get them to lower their glances to their wares. It was obvious that strangers were rare in these parts, that travelers and merchant caravans went around the Alps, most roads to the east cutting through Moravia and Slovakia, along the endless Hungarian lowlands. But these strangers, mustachioed Turks with long Turkish flintlocks and turbans, had been seen only in the illustrations of adventure novels. The least they could do was have a look at their cheeses, it wouldn't cost them anything, and it would mean a lot to the local housewives.

In a place no one visits, time moves slowly and life seems to last much longer. Every glance is important there, for a glance can be enough for the beginning of a folk legend.

Botta stood next to a counter in the market, following the youth with his gaze. Regardless of the fact that he no longer left Sarchione's side and Sarchione had taken him in hand, Botta kept to his job. After having been unobservant for an instant, he felt defeated and humiliated. He was trying, without success, to correct things and make up for his loss through an exaggerated zeal. He was doing what all bad spies always do, and it would take another day on the road for Botta to return to being what he'd been in this story and what he was in the biography of Omar Pasha Latas: the greatest clandestine killer of the waning empire.

This was why Sarchione had insisted on this apparently senseless walk. He was parading Ganimed by the arm in front of Botta's eyes, and he was prepared to do so until evening or until the market closed, when the baffled old men and women ran back to their homes, considering whether it would be better if Turks came by every week or, perhaps, much better and safer if they never appeared again. To them, and to the greater part of the caravan, it was unclear what purpose this ceremony served. Why was Sarchione walking around with the youth, who was suddenly babbling as if he'd lost his mind after days of being closed up and self-centered? Why was Botta standing in one place all this time, not speaking to anyone, staring at the two of them, as if he were verifying his eyesight, checking whether he could make out three or all seven buttonholes on Ganimed's shirt, or how many wrinkles were on Sarchione's cheeks, those tiny wrinkles that came from worry and others that came from joy?

It was a ceremony to cleanse the soul.

First that of one person: the killer Botta, who did not take his eyes from the person he was supposed to be watching.

Then that of another: the young Ganimed Troyanovsky, who had begun to speak about everything after weeks of melancholy, and for whom even the desire to return to Paris would soon evaporate, the pull to run back home rather than go to Bosnia, where he was drawn by the sweet, albeit quite masculine, compliments of a certain Turkish general.

And then this stroll along the edge of the market was healing a third soul: Sarchione's. He could at last be silent. He did not have to invent anything or tell any stories, for everything was now unfolding on its own.

After a full two hours of going round and round the little market and squeezing by the little wooden tables, Ganimed ran out of topics or lost his breath from all the babbling.

Shall we go? Botta asked.

They did not answer, just headed obediently toward the coaches.

The youth fell asleep the moment he dropped into his seat. Sarchione watched him for a little while longer, then pulled a little book from his coat pocket and plunged into an exciting novel titled Robinson Crusoe, a work by the English author Daniel Defoe. Usually on the road he carried philosophical books, Montaigne, or Dante, or Goethe, but now he was looking for something to entertain and rejuvenate him. And for some reason it seemed to him that a novel about a man who was the sole survivor of a shipwreck and lived by himself on an empty island and hunted and fished like people in the Stone Age was one that could return him to the years Ganimed was now experiencing.

As the column was starting up the first rise, Sarchione had just got to the moment when the dark man Friday makes his appearance.

At that point it stopped being a novel for children. In an instant the reader was doused with Latas's shame. He remembered the reason Robinson Crusoe had set out on his journey. He looked at Ganimed, at that face of a young ephebe, and quickly shut the book. He heard the deep, warm smack of two, firmly bound sheets of printed paper, like a collision of known and unknown worlds.

He had shut the book in such a way that he would not know his place, never intending to open it again.

The journey across the Alps was riskier and harder than anyone could have imagined. The roads were frozen and snow swept, the wide royal byways turned into narrow paths, then into mountain trails, and then the trails disappeared and all around was a wilderness that frightened both the horses and the people. The former whinnied, the latter prayed to God or, if they did not believe in God, examined topographic maps. But cartography in this place and at this time of the year was less help to them than prayers.

Ganimed, meanwhile, was calm. Surprisingly calm. To one of the porters, Jusuf from Anatolia, who spoke only Turkish, he explained that he shouldn't worry about a thing because he had come upon a book in an antiquities shop in Paris, in which it was written how and when he would die. He wouldn't tell him the date, for that was too intimate a thing to relate, but the place of his death was exactly 543 kilometers away from here, on a road that had not yet been constructed. So if Jusuf was afraid of dying, he should stay near Ganimed and he would be safe.

He asked Botta to translate all this for the frightened porter. And also to emphasize that the store was called Minerva, that it was located on such and such a street in Montparnasse, and the book was located on the shelves to the right of the door as one entered, in the seventh row up from the floor. It was high, but the bookseller, whose name was Joseph Levy, would fetch a ladder so that he could verify for himself that on the seventy-eighth page on the twelfth line from the bottom was written the time and place of Ganimed Troyanovsky's death, exactly as he had just said.

Jusuf was illiterate, but he believed everything the young man said, and did not leave his side after that, until, with God's help, through miracle and chance, they had broken through to the southern side of the Alps and begun to descend toward a valley.

If it wasn't surprising enough that Jusuf from Anatolia believed the unusual gentleman – how would the poor wretch not believe him when the glorious serasker believed him and had invited him to Sarajevo? – it seemed that even Botta believed the half-crazy story about the book in the Minerva antiquities store, despite the fact that he was professionally trained not to believe anything.

Why did you return the book? Why didn't you buy it since it contained something so important to you?

Why should I buy it? Ganimed asked, surprised. It was easy to remember something as simple as the time and place of my death. Nothing else in the book was of interest to me. It would have just collected dust in my library.

In the end he ordered Botta to write on a piece of paper for Jusuf:

"Right shelf, seventh row up, book bound in red leather, without any writing on the spine, on the title page in Latin script the words Sarajevo Dogs, seventy-eighth page, twelfth line from the bottom."

When you're in Paris the next time, and you surely will be on some errand of the state or your pasha, you can check to see whether the gentleman isn't telling the truth. It does not bother Ganimed in the least that Jusuf might know the time and place of his death. No evil can come from knowledge. Perhaps the knowledge will make them like brothers.

Jusuf held the little paper in his hand as if it contained a countercharm. It was the greatest valuable he had been given in his entire life. Though Ganimed's spell was saving him from harm, Jusuf was actually of much greater use to Ganimed. He helped him, carried him on his back, used his shoulders to lift the coach out of the snow, warmed him from the snow and ice, finding nothing difficult. He believed in the gentleman's immortality – or rather that his death was unfailingly intended for a distant future – but he was of constant help, as if it was the natural order that the strong should be of constant help to those who were more intelligent, especially if the more intelligent one was a lord.

It was not just this untutored youth who believed in the existence of the book Sarajevo Dogs, in the seventh row from the floor on the right-hand shelf, in which was written the place and time of Ganimed Troyanovsky's death. Botta did too. He went out to the coach and, from memory, which he had exercised in the spy schools of Venice and Istanbul, wrote down on the last page of Cervantes's Don Quixote – a book he took with him on journeys for he believed it would bring him good fortune, though he never read it to the end – he wrote the words down:

"Right shelf, seventh row up from the floor, book bound in red leather, without any writing on the spine, on the title page in Latin script the words Sarajevo Dogs, seventy-eighth page, twelfth line from the bottom."

Then he stopped and added:

"Perhaps made up? If so, to what purpose?"

By contrast to Latas, who never realized his artistic talents – never wrote his novel of the Lika Krajina, his bildungsroman about the son of the Vidin captain and the young Abdulmedjid, to whom he had taught drawing – because he was ashamed of every kind of invention, more so than his own nakedness, Botta did not understand why people invented things. What for the lord was a source of creativity and a reason why he himself could not be an artist, for Botta was merely a possible means of enemy espionage or a symptom of a dangerous mental disturbance. Either Ganimed was a French spy or he had lost his marbles.

From that moment he began to watch him even more attentively.

And the young man, now buoyant, his fevers dissipating as the caravan descended lower in the Alps, as if he had forgotten about them, dreamed up new lies all the time. It was clear to everyone, even his faithful Jusuf, why he was doing this: he was not able to be of any help to them, he was physically weak and bungled every task, and what he could have done they wouldn't let him, lest he injure himself, so he tried to be of use at least by entertaining them with his stories. Even Sarchione, the greatest master of storytelling, enjoyed them, for Ganimed's tales fascinated him in that they contained not the slightest bit of truth. Everything was invented, and everything was actually impossible. This was something new for Sarchione. For every one of his own stories, even the greatest of fabrications, began from something that had actually happened. But in these tales everything was filled with ships that disappeared in the midst of a storm only to reappear with all their sailors on the Danube or the Caspian Sea. Libraries overflowed with various secrets, improbable details about what had yet to happen and impossible explanations about what had just occurred. And there was Ganimed's tale of Jesus Christ, whose right hand had not been nailed well, the nail had loosened and fallen away, leaving the young man from Judea hanging by just one hand. He had screamed from the pain, called on his father to help him, deathly afraid, for as he was both man and God, he knew everything beforehand, and he clearly saw centuries and millennia into the future and the crosses on the walls of churches where a wooden figure that looked like him was attached, a mirror of his suffering. What happened? asked the horrified Christ. Why had one of his hands come free from the nail? What would happen to him next? Would he even be resurrected, and was he even the God-man, or was all this some sort of irreparable mistake? Perhaps his suffering was in vain.

As he listened to him, Botta was again suspicious. The Turks in the escort were laughing because the youth was narrating in a very funny way, waving his arms about like a woman tossing pita dough into the air, and Sarchione was watching him with enthusiasm, his mouth open in surprise while tears were rolling down his cheeks turning to ice halfway down and ringing onto his shoulders like tiny crystals.

Botta thought it must all be true. The young man looked crazy but wasn't making anything up. Who could have invented such a story about Christ screaming on the cross because his right hand had come free and he was using it to call to his heavenly father?

He took the paper out of his pocket and secretly read it again:

"Right shelf, seventh row up from the floor, book bound in red leather, without any writing on the spine, on the title page in Latin script the words Sarajevo Dogs, seventy-eighth page, twelfth line from the bottom."

It was nighttime on Golgotha, Ganimed continued, and the caretakers were trying to get some sleep. But how could they fall asleep when the wretch kept screaming? Well, if there were a ladder, somebody could climb up and nail the young man's right hand to the cross again. But where were they going to find a ladder at that time of night?

Botta was sweating in discomfort, though the temperature was twenty degrees below zero and a cold north wind blew against his back as they made their way down the mountains. The Turks kept laughing like imbeciles. They were enjoying the story and saw in it the crucifixion of an infidel, who had suffered and to whom something horrible had happened, something that would certainly change the history of European civilization and would of course be good for Islam too, the one just and true faith, and for Istanbul, and for the glorious empire, and the infidel's god would no longer be God. Bad luck, friend, it was bad luck for sure, but he could not be God. Bad luck was humanity's wont and fate, *at least for those who were sincere, profound unbelievers in the one true God, Allah the Almighty . . .*

What was just a comedy to the Turks in the escort, to the two Venetians was a wonder.

The difference was not a matter of faith, place of birth, or outlook on life. The difference was simply that the Turks were illiterate. Or they just barely managed to scratch out the serpentine lines of Arabic symbols, which under their harsh pens turned into the gnarled roots of olive trees. They found it all funny because they remained at the gates of Ganimed's stories. They understood Sarchione, but the young man not at all.

And so, in the stories and amid their wonder, they descended toward the Slovene river valleys. Their crossing of the Alps had been aided by Ganimed's fantastic stories, making it easier and more enjoyable than it would have been. All told, the frost had taken twelve toes from the escort. Mula the wrestler had expertly chopped off each one, applying a single blow with his heavy Gibraltar knife. The man would moan, the blackened toe would fly off into the weeds, the wound would be cauterized with a hot iron, and it would be over.

The view was magnificent.

Hillocks lit up by the spring sunshine – it was so warm that they cast off their peasant coats and shirts and made their way half-naked beside the coaches – and at the top of each hill a humble little church rose up, or a military outpost from some distant time. Everything was filled with light, the bustle, babble, and squeak of carts burst from every direction. It was a trading day. Some were rushing toward the market while others were returning home with their goods.

The column, which had provoked curiosity and fear wherever it had appeared from Paris through Belgium and the German lands, here went almost unnoticed. The local population, which communicated among themselves in a variety of Slavic, Germanic, and Romance languages, seemed accustomed to Turkish caravans.

Sarchione would ask people questions, buy a rooster, a basket of mushrooms, a sack of shriveled apples that had spent the winter in someone's potato cellar, a round of cheese, or he would just loudly compliment someone on his horse or ox in the local Slavic tongue, which he used quite well.

Sarchione was trying to free himself from some of his own fears, but he wasn't able to attract the attention of the locals either through his aggressive friendliness or his somewhat crackbrained need to purchase something from everyone. They weren't even surprised by him. They would laugh rather absentmindedly, their rosy faces and hair the color of corn stubble giving them the appearance of heroes from a Russian fairy tale. He'd seen them before, having had contact with Slovenes in Venice and having traded with them in Trieste, and even in Istanbul he'd met a tanner who was originally from Maribor, but after the long, difficult passage across the Alps he was now seeing them in a different light.

But for Ganimed Troyanovsky they were a completely new people. Turks and Arabs he knew, having met them in Paris or seen them in book illustrations or pictures and drawings displayed in the city's museums, but Slovenes or Southern Slavs in general he had never encountered.

He thought they were some sort of distant relations and went to his chest to take out his drawing pad, ink bottles of ten different shades, and brushes. What he sketched on the road from Maribor to Varaždin and Zagreb, five urban and pastoral vedutas, which he composed during stops at beer halls, inns, and basement shelters, as well as seven undulating virtuoso sketches in various hues of Indian ink, composed as the coach was moving, are today part of the collection of graphic arts in Zagreb's university library. They turned up completely by accident at the end of August 1992 on a heap of rotting furniture and assorted garbage before the removal of a load of waste. They were found in an old gray portfolio, ninety by seventy-five centimeters, which had been placed inside on an old Obodin washing machine from which someone had removed the drum. The portfolio appeared to have belonged to Anastas Popović, an eighty-five year old retired graphic artist, for on the cover were several sketches of the Arslanagića Bridge in Trebinje. Himself from Trebinje, Popović recognized one of the symbols of his native city and took the portfolio.

Popović took the drawings to be inspected by the poet and art historian Y. R., a close associate of President Tuđman and an advisor to him on Croatian cultural matters. Y. R. first offered to buy all twelve sketches for the sum of three hundred German marks, only to then withdraw his offer. When Antastas Popović asked for the drawings back, Y. R., according to the story in the weekly Globus, told him the drawings were a Croatian national treasure and as a Serb he might have problems were it to become known that they were in his care. In any case, he would have to explain to the police how they had come into his possession and who had given them to him.

"I found them in the garbage!" the old man supposedly wailed.

"No one will believe you," Y. R. answered calmly.

The gray portfolio with the sketches of Trebinje's Arslanagića Bridge remained with Popović. He was apparently ashamed of the ugly sketches on the outside. Until the old man's death, in January 1994, the portfolio stood in his living room, by the Gorenje television set.

The exhibit Twelve Sketches by Ganimed Troyanovsky *was held in the Arts Pavilion in October 1993, while Popović was still alive. At the opening, which was attended by the president of the country, Y. R. delivered a talk in which he revealed to the Croatian public these heretofore unknown works of the famous Parisian architect. The story resembled a scintillating spy thriller worthy of a Croatian Le Carré, which featured, besides Y. R., a beautiful young woman, a colonel in the Croatian navy who had once worked for the security services of the Yugoslav armed forces, an art professor in Belgrade, and an Orthodox bishop. In the story, which today in Croatia is considered the official version of the events in question, Y. R. actually traded for the drawings, yielding to the enemy side three less valuable Orthodox icons of the Greek seventeenth-century school, which they maintained had been stolen from the Nikolajevska Church in Zemun during the Second World War.*

After the Zagreb exhibit, Ganimed's twelve drawings were displayed in Vienna, Berlin, during the Croatian Culture Days in Germany, and Y. R. wrote a book about them entitled The View from the Carriage: A European's Meditations in Ink, *in which, as one inspired Vjesnik art critic put it, "he deconstructed each drawing, pulling apart the lines that had been assembled by the hand of the brilliant Parisian, analyzed each sketch, and then put the entire painting back together again, as if he were reassembling a perfect Swiss watch, which ran much better now that it had passed before the expert's eye."*

They stayed in Zagreb for more than a day.

The group arrived in the late afternoon on Saturday and settled at the "Blind Marica" inn, which was located at the base of the Gornji Grad, near today's Tkalčićeva Street. They were intending to continue their journey first thing in the morning but changed their minds when Sarchione was taken with a sudden ill humor or an attack of weakness and listlessness. He said he had shooting pains in his fingers, which was of course reason enough not to go on, but he was suffering from something else, worse than a heart attack – what happened to you when a marble slab sat on your chest, as he explained to them

– he just did not feel like going on. But it wasn't as if he did not feel like traveling that day or the next or on Monday, it was some misgiving that had taken hold of him about any movement at all. The best would be to stay here at Blind Marica's with its rotten straw mattresses rather than ever have to go anywhere again. He did not know anyone in Zagreb, though he had passed through this town, this German island surrounded by Slavic tribes on the edge of Pannonia, at least twenty times, nor did he have any desire to meet anyone here. He would just be here and not go anywhere else, his flight having been stopped at last.

Life is just one long flight! he said with a sigh.

Botta glanced at him in alarm but said nothing. He left his room and went out of the building into the night air. From far off came the stench of the sewer that flowed like an open stream. The smell of a western trading post on the way to becoming a city. At one point, when all the great kingdoms had fallen, and they would, when Vienna and Rome and Istanbul were no more, then these trading towns would rise up, transformed into metropolises, but before their greatness could be known there would be this smell of open sewers, by which one could tell the difference between western and eastern capitals. In the East it stank differently. The cities stank differently there. Of burnt oil and human sweat, of the sulfur of millions of rotten eggs, of gunpowder, of sheep's fat and the decaying innards of dead animals, of rotten onions and potatoes, of scalded milk, of meat roasted on countless fires, of human and animal shit, and of the sewers of course, but all these stenches mixed at every moment, competing and outdoing each other, changing places as the winds changed direction or as the pedestrian moved from one to another part of town. This was how it was in the East. In the West it was just the monotonous stench of sewage. It was as if the entire Western world boiled down to shit and was transformed into a single, collective, all-penetrating stench, into which all the individual stenches had been united until they could no longer be distinguished, those of all the city's inhabitants, believers and nonbelievers, victims and their killers, the fishermen of human souls, church pastors, bishops, and drunken family men, and all the nameless, invisible creators of God, chance passersby, wanderers, the poverty stricken, escapees from who knew what or whose law and who had eased their troubles in the Roman sewers and taken on that great, invincible, unifying stench of the Western world.

This was why the West would triumph one day, thought Botta restlessly, this most skilled cutthroat of the disappearing Eastern kingdom, invisible to all his opponents and to history, absent even to the most famous Bosnian storyteller Ivo Andrić, who in the last ten years of his life, nostalgic for olden times, would write his great novel of Omar Pasha Latas. However much the great writer searched, the executioner remained invisible and nameless to him. Andrić sensed an emptiness in his place, which tormented him and which he tried to fill with other figures, but it was all in vain. This was why Ivo Andrić never finished his novel about Sarajevo.

Then it occurred to Botta: so what was it Sarchione was thinking of when he said life was one long flight? What was he fleeing from? And the moment he began turning this over in his mind, Botta again felt well.

The next morning, as Sarchione wanted to be left in bed because the heavy stone tablet was lying across his chest, the rest of the caravan set off to wander about Zagreb.

The Turks from the escort, wearing turbans, which they otherwise did not put on, and with antique pistols and curved knives in their colorful belts, which they also never wore, set out into the surroundings of the small town. Perhaps they didn't want to disappoint the round housewives who peeked out from behind heavy curtains, sheltering their children's eyes, or their proud husbands, small and swaggering, with the mustachios of hussars, everywhere prepared for a fight, or maybe it pleased them every once in a while to look exactly like these people imagined they looked, like merciless Turks, ready for every evil. In Paris, and down through the Germanic lands, this had long since lost all meaning: they'd had their fill of seeing Turks, more in pictures than in real life, and their turbans and yataghans were no longer wonders for them, but here in Zagreb, the people did not cease to marvel. It was as if every morning they saw the world for the first time.

Ganimed Troyanovsky carried his sketch block under his arm while behind him, three steps back, followed the faithful Jusuf with the little case containing his ink bottles in all the different colors and his gold and silver brushes.

The youth sketched the whole day long, from the moment the people entered church during Sunday mass until the hour of taps' sounding, when the little town without street lights slipped into darkness. According to Sarchione's journal and according to the estimates of those experts who have tried to calculate how much time Ganimed would have needed for each sketch, he spent between six and twenty hours on every Zagreb drawing and veduta. Not one has been preserved. Either they were destroyed or they were lost amid the clutter of the Parisian archives and libraries from which for more than a century the sketches of the ballet dancer and architect Ganimed Troyanovsky's eastern travels, which extended all the way to Baghdad and Samarkand, had emerged with an almost regular temporal rhythm. It is possible that some of the sketches had been among the holdings of the National and University Library in Sarajevo, which was burned down during the Serbian bombardment in August 1992, the small but quite valuable graphics collection going with it. According to the testimonial of the last prewar director, Borivoje Pištalo, two lesser Ganimed sketches had been contained in the collection, a rough draft of the Kovači neighborhood and a very careful, detailed drawing of the interior of a Sarajevo bakery, but Pištalo noted that he personally had never been responsible for the graphics collection or its inventory, so it was entirely possible that there had been many more Ganimed pieces in the collection. The curator who had been in charge of the collection and who had performed this work for twenty-five years, since 1967, escaped to Belgrade in the first days of the war, where he died in a home for the elderly and indigent at the beginning of 1994, before it had become possible to interview him and attempt to reconstruct the contents of the destroyed graphic arts collection. Today one can only speculate about its contents, and in Bosnia and the Balkans, we know, from speculation arise myths that grow to improbable dimensions, such that the time is not far away when an entire burned down Bosnian Louvre might emerge from the memory of the little graphic arts collection. It is better therefore not to mention the possibility that the lost Zagreb works of Ganimed Troyanovsky had been located here.

Sarchione would not leave his bed for the whole day.

They took him his lunch and dinner in bed. He would eat a few spoonfuls of the barley porridge, that hard-to-digest dish which Miroslav Krleža would turn seventy years later into a metaphor for Serbo-Croatian relations. The state in which Sarchione found himself would one day be called acute depression. It had come upon him quickly, the result of long years of having no particular home, of rootlessness and constant movement from one town to another, the pain of which he had tried to hide even from himself, the pain of not belonging anywhere, of being no one's and, actually, no one. To everyone he knew and with whom he had easily become friends, and to the serasker himself, Sarchione was a story. He wasn't even a storyteller, for that would have at least been a trade and a calling. He was a story whose ultimate meaning was to intoxicate and bedazzle his listeners but behind which there was nothing. Sarchione lasted for as long as his story did, and once his story ended, he was a layabout, an idler, a bum. No one needed him, no one expected anything good (or even bad) from him. He was tolerated, given food and drink only because people figured he might come around and start another story. He grew silent, like Jusuf and Mula, who were incapable of recounting even the shortest of tales they had heard in childhood, or of uttering the simplest of things about themselves: how they felt, what hurt, what they wanted, what they dreamed of. Or did they not dream?

It suddenly seemed to him that he too could no longer dream. All he wanted was to stay at Blind Marica's, to have barley porridge brought to him every day, and to let that porridge finally become his name, heritage, and homeland. And then to die and be buried in this town at the edge of the eastern tip of the West. His whole life had been flight – one long flight – and he couldn't even remember what he was fleeing from, how all this began, why he had left Venice or why he had fled all the way to Istanbul.

Later, that Sunday, Botta would appear and look at him without uttering a word. Sarchione would recognize the man's professional doubt in that glance of his, because he had received an answer to the important question of why Sarchione had said life was one long flight, and at that moment everything would become easier for him, everything would again begin to make sense.

Morose and cold, Botta left the room, and the old woman who kept order in the life of the inn, who was perhaps blind Marica, was waiting for him:

"Is the lord going to die? Shall we call the reverend to confess him?"

"No," he answered abruptly. "He's a Turk!"

She went back into the kitchen, swinging her head left and right as if her neck was dislocated or she just couldn't figure out what it was about being a Turk that meant the reverend should be turned away when the reverend could help him, however much of a Turk he might be. Then she remembered and ran back:

"Shall we make him some chicken soup?"

Ganimed slept like a slaughtered man, in a deep, rich feather bed prepared just for him. The rest, including Botta and Sarchione, slept on ordinary army straw, but for him, as a special guest, the feather bed had been prepared that was kept, cleaned, and aired out in case one day, God willing, some Viennese prince or Pest count might stop at Blind Marica's. As it had been decades since any prince had been to Zagreb, let alone to their inn, they made use of the occasion to offer the feather bed to a guest worthy of such attention. And Ganimed appeared to be just such a personage: handsome and slender, with a lofty bearing like some Russian princeling. The truth was that the old woman and her young valet, with a mustache like that of the most refined postman, had not accorded this honor because of Ganimed but more for themselves and the story that they would tell for a long time thereafter, and which they would continue to live off until an actual prince might come, about the youth who was so handsome one could not look away.

He really did sleep "like a slaughtered man." The valet, who had learned this strange local expression, told him he would sleep precisely so in their bed of goose down. Botta translated his words calmly. Ganimed was shocked, but this served as the inspiration for his self-portrait, surely the best known of Ganimed Troyanovsky's drawings that have been preserved and about which we should say several words here, for later there will not be time.

The painting Self-Portrait with a Slit Throat was kept in the permanent exhibit of the Art Gallery of Bosnia and Herzegovina until the war. For financial reasons, or as a consequence of the lack of public interest in art, the permanent exhibit was never shown in its entirety again after the war, and the gallery closed for good in 2012. Self-Portrait with a Slit Throat was kept all this time in a gallery storeroom and only displayed on two occasions to the public over the last twenty years. The first time was immediately after the war, in 1996, at the exhibit The Free-hand Sketch – Drawn and Painted Works of Well-Known Architects, which was held in Paris's Museum of Architecture, and the second was when it was included in a small 2005 display of Ganimed Troyanovsky's works in the foyer of the Vienna Opera House on the occasion of the building's construction.

Self-Portrait with a Slit Throat is one of Ganimed's most elaborate paintings, with a multitude of details amid the five colors of the brush strokes and a slight watercolor overlay. The setting is a hotel room interior where a roughhewn wooden bed stands with a rich coverlet and a slightly oversized pillow. Under the bed is a ceramic chamber pot with a floral motif, and on the wall above the bed hangs a holy picture of the God Mother with her child. A spider's web sits in the corner of the room, with a spider spinning a new strand. The door looks to be rotting and has a heavy rusted handle and lock. The wooden floor is also brilliantly depicted, with recesses and exposed portions in the middle of the room.

Architects sometimes have difficulty with painterly perspective but Ganimed Troyanovsky was a complete exception in this regard. In his Self-Portrait with a Slit Throat, the space of the room, the distance of the objects from one another, the depth of perspective, are rendered with almost hyperrealistic imagination and classical drawing skill. It is truly the sort of "freehand sketch" the French curators had in mind when they selected it for their exhibit, despite the difficulty of getting access to it, for the preparations for the exhibit were undertaken during the siege of Sarajevo, when it was impossible to know with certainty whether the Self-Portrait with a Slit Throat even still existed. Ganimed's piece, however, ended up on the official poster for the exhibit.

On the bed lies a figure in striped silk pajamas with a quilt covering him to halfway across his chest. The expression on the face is gentle, slightly smiling, as if he might be dreaming of something, and the man's neck is slit open. This is Ganimed. His face is sketched very carefully and precisely, if slightly egotistically. If we compare this portrait with the two preserved daguerreotype images of Ganimed Troyanovsky, we see the same face, sketched with almost virtuoso accuracy but with one rather astounding defect. It is as if the sketch artist saw himself with a woman's face. It is known to happen that particularly attractive men, especially in their youth, have girlish faces. But such was not the case here: in the daguerreotypes Ganimed is exceptionally attractive but in a quite masculine manner. He seems, however, to have seen himself differently.

The neck has been cut as in anatomical manuals or crime dramas of today, in a very scholarly manner and without imagining anything that might be unknown to the painter. Quite simply he must have known in actuality what a slit throat looked like in order to sketch it the way he had. Somewhere he must have seen this.

And the most mysterious thing about the picture is that it's simultaneously ghastly and attractive, almost erotic: there is not a single drop of blood in the picture. Everything is perfectly clean. The viewer is at first bewildered, wondering where all that blood could have ended up, and then understanding what the Belgrade painter and art critic Marko Čelibonović so brilliantly explained when, writing about the Self-Portrait with a Slit Throat, he put forth the storyteller's hypothesis that it was actually "a satirical illustration of a certain Serbian or Serbo-Croatian expression: to sleep like a slaughtered man."

Ganimed Troyanovsky must have heard it on his way to Sarajevo and been so pleased that he had decided to construct a self-portrait from it. When this Čelibonović wrote his piece, it was the dark and difficult year of 1948 in Yugoslavia, and no one really took it seriously, but because he was a Jew and a true-believing revolutionary, it had been allowed.

This is the only self-portrait in Ganimed Troyanovsky's oeuvre. It is known he had it in his portfolio when he arrived in Sarajevo. They had hidden it away from Omar Pasha Latas before Ganimed showed him the pictures from his journey. They couldn't even imagine what the pasha might say about this drawing, and Sarchione had decided it should not be shown to Latas. Botta supported his decision. He already thought the Self-Portrait with a Slit Throat was a bizarre work, living proof that Ganimed Troyanovsky needed to be shut away in a madhouse before he killed someone. Most likely himself.

When the caravan set out from Zagreb, Sarchione's dark thoughts and listlessness began to pass, and when the city had disappeared completely, and the tops of Medvednica – the small mountain range on the other side of Zagreb to which the people had given such a big-sounding, serious name, as if to frighten themselves with – could no longer be seen, Sarchione was reborn, he told stories about everyone and everything.

Soon they had crossed the Sava by ferry near Gradiška, the buds were emerging all around, the nights were no longer cold, and there was no more morning frost. Nature was coming alive again in anticipation of the guests from the West, charming little towns with white minarets in the center alternated with Christian, Catholic, and Orthodox villages, low and compact, and a third kind of place, the strangest of all, villages and towns where it was impossible to know whether they were Muslim or Christian for they had both a minaret and a church, and the population mixed along the streets and alleys as if they were not even each other's enemies. Nowhere were there visible traces of the rebellions for which Omar Pasha Latas had come to Bosnia. It was as if war had not touched them. Instead all was gentle, naïve, lovely, exactly as a European traveler might have desired as he set off into the Orient.

While they were obviously distrustful by nature, the local people seemed eager to convince the traveler of their meekness. The Turks, local Muslims with blond hair and blue eyes just like those of the Christians, wanted of course to show their hospitality and understanding of Western customs and manners. Someone had clearly told them this was necessary.

The Christians, especially the Orthodox ones, who called themselves Serbs and people of the Krajina, were equally sincere about wishing to show the foreigner that this land was not so meek at all. There was no freedom here, they said, clenching their fists. But when you asked them what freedom was, what they understood by freedom, they either didn't know what to say or told you freedom was when there weren't any Turks. They were clearly prepared to die for this freedom, but the uprising that had begun in Bosnia had by-passed them. A good portion of them disagreed, however, for the authorities in Constantinople, under the pressure of modernization and reform inside the kingdom, were offering the Christians of Bosnia rights they had not had before . . .

Ganimed Troyanovsky listened to Sarchione as he spoke about this, meeting and shaking hands with the local Muslims and Christians wherever he had the opportunity, and he quickly forgot about his homesickness and the torments this journey had long presented to him, and all traces of the fever from which he had suffered and almost died were long gone.

In the course of just a few days, he had fallen in love with this land. But perhaps this is not something that should be mentioned. This sort of thing had happened to other travelers in Bosnia too, or such were the inventions of weak writers and loud traders who believed in the sentiment that somehow it became a commonplace that anyone who stepped foot across the Sava fell in love with Bosnia and its people. But this is not true. More numerous were those who ran away and never wanted to be reminded of this land again. Ganimed was not one of those.

Whether because of Sarchione's lessons and stories about Bosnian history and the character of the local inhabitants, or because of the conversations with people and the imbibing of šljivovica, the smoking of good Macedonian opium, and sprees in roadside Krajina inns and taverns, Ganimed painted only two pictures between there and Sarajevo. These are the prized Vrbas River Triptych, in which depictions of the Banja Luka market on a fair day, the Plitva waterfall in Jajce, and the little church in Podmilačje come together, and which is the property of the Albertina Museum in Vienna. Italo Svevo wrote about the Vrbas River Triptych, a little before his death, in the essay "What the Young Man Saw When He Looked in the Water," which some literary theorists consider the introduction to an unwritten novel that had to have been a sort of continuation of The Confessions of Zeno. Svevo describes Ganimed's sketches in great detail, examining them as a narrative whole, a peculiar form of comic, but as he not once mentions the *artist's name or hints at whose works are in question or where he saw them, it was long supposed that he had a fictional text in mind, which is to say that the author invented both the drawings and the artist, "a youth with an irresistible appearance, fragile and lithe, like a forest animal whose beauty belonged to the sex from which the eyes looked out." Besides the fact that the painterly depictions rather precisely correspond to what is found in Ganimed's work, Svevo writes of the artistic discovery of the journey through Bosnia, "a primitive Oriental land in which human passions heave, nothing is known of its true character or heritage, and human eccentricity, every corporeally expressed love, is paid for by death, inquisitional burnings at the stake, or wooden Ottoman stakes greased with animal fat." On this journey, writes Svevo, the artist discovers that "woman's beauty is like an empty walnut husk" and that he is more drawn to the "young ephebe, Roman, or Turkish, a dirt-streaked little boy." Svevo's invectives against Ganimed's homosexuality, prompted in all probability by the author's psychoanalytic obsessions, are actually not borne out by other sources and must be taken in the framework of a literary reinterpretation, especially if it is true that the prose work "What the Young Man Saw When He Looked in the Water" was to be a continuation of the psychoanalytic duology begun in* The Confessions of Zeno.

Ganimed Troyanovsky arrived in Sarajevo at the end of April 1851. Omar Pasha Latas was not in the city, having gone on one of his disciplinary trips through Bosnia, so he probably first met the young architect on the first or second day of May.

Sarchione accompanied Ganimed to Latas, then, after a short, formal exchange, withdrew from the pasha's chambers under the pretext of having some important work that could not be delayed. It was important for the two of them to get a feel for each other.

In this first meeting between Omar Pasha Latas and the architect who would design the Sarajevo opera house there was one additional mystery. They met, according to Sarchione's account, "at the noon hour," during a short official ceremony, which was supposed to show the young artist that he was being welcomed according to the state and kingdom's honors delegated from the Sublime Porte. All the pasha's military and civilian aides took part in the ceremony, lined up and ordered according to the strict hierarchies of the regime.

If Ganimed Troyanovsky met Latas on the first of May around noon, the event would not lie outside the normal framework for procedures of the Ottoman empire of the mid-nineteenth century. Besides being a hardened soldier, a fierce Krajina Serb, a convert repulsed by the backwardness and inconstancy of the Bosnian begs, Latas had artistic ambitions. He wanted to appear before Paris and also be remembered in Istanbul and in Bosnia as the person who had brought the first piano to Sarajevo. He had convinced Sultan Abdulmedjid to construct the first opera house of the Ottoman empire in Sarajevo, as a symbol of modernization and transformation, but also the acceptance of Western culture and manners, which the kingdom would adopt to the character of the Orient without holding back its own importance and presence in Europe. Centuries later they would speak of Istanbul's desperate attempt to halt the Habsburg incursion into the East and its occupation of Bosnia and Herzegovina by means of the opera, but there is some question about how much this was due to desperation and how much to Latas's brilliance.

If this meeting took place on Thursday, May 1, 1851, there would be no great surprise or possible scandal.

But if Latas hosted Ganimed on Friday, May 2, "at the noon hour," then something happened that was at the very least unusual: the state ceremony was ordered to take place during prayer time, when all Muslims would have been at the weekly public worship, except those with a reasonable excuse. And the arrival in town of a French architect was on its own not a reasonable excuse for not going to mosque. Not only would Latas not have gone to prayer – it is unknown whether the serasker did this under normal circumstances or whether he justified his absence because of his military duties – none of the others in his administration would have gone either.

At first glance, it seems likely that the meeting took place on Thursday, May 1. But why is there doubt only concerning this date when all the others during Latas's stay in Bosnia are securely documented in books and in the registries? How is it possible that already by the end of 1851, in the chronicles, court documents, memoranda, and Istanbul fiscal records, Omar Pasha Latas is noted to have met the Parisian architect Ganimed Troyanovsky on either the first or second of May of the year just ending? Because it was truly unclear which date it was, or because the intention was to conceal the fact that Latas had arranged for the ceremony to take place during prayers?

In all probability, therefore, Omar Pasha Latas and Ganimed Troyanovsky met on Friday, May 2, 1851, just after noon. Neither the chroniclers nor the other record keepers desired to pass over this circumstance in silence. They formulated it so that no religious or secular censure, basic human consideration, or sense of decorum could do anything more than sidestep and conceal it.

No one knows what they spoke about after the short ceremony, when they were left alone. Ganimed was silent on this score. He wrote nothing about it in his journals or reminiscences of Bosnia, nor do we find any testimonials of his friendship with the Turkish pasha in the rich correspondence he carried on, in old age, with the American architect Frank Lloyd Wright, at the turn of the century.

Sarchione asked both of them, but in vain. What they spoke about is unknown. They could have spoken of anything, but the most likely thing was drawing, for that was the art Latas was most familiar with. After all, it was through drawing that he had come to Istanbul, a military career, and a marshal's honor, but it was skill in drawing, said Sarchione, that forever remained his one unrealized desire. He had not wanted to be a soldier or politician. It had not been his wish to drive the Bosnian begs into the darkness, to save the kingdom, to be remembered as the man who never laughed, the dreamer who was ashamed of his imagination and wanted instead to be a calligrapher and sketch artist even if it meant living humbly and anonymously. But if it was possible for a Christian peasant from the kingdom's border to become a marshal in the Ottoman empire, one of the last great military leaders of a foregone age, there was no way for such a person to become a humble Parisian painter, a Constantinople calligrapher, or even a sign painter.

Ganimed Troyanovsky remained in Sarajevo for half a year. He left the city and Bosnia behind in the middle of October. The caravan for Paris had fewer people in it, and Sarchione was not part of it. But for the youth's security, Botta was the route commander. The return journey took nearly half as long. This was a rule: return, as a rule, took less time. No one knows, meanwhile, whether Botta visited the Minerva antiquities shop in Montparnasse to seek out the book bound in red leather, where it must have been written whether Ganimed was a fraud. If he did go there, he didn't tell anyone. Today it is impossible to verify anything since Botta left no evidence that he had ever existed.

In the course of six Sarajevo months Ganimed worked daily from dawn to dusk. He no longer laughed, babbled, drank, or smoked opium. He only worked with a group of designers and laborers, the best in Bosnia, assigned to him by Latas, to measure the land in Bistrik, perform excavation tests in order to verify, on both dry and rain-saturated days, whether the ground was stable enough, whether there would be danger of mud slides, *whether underground water would be a threat, and how deep it would be necessary to dig so that the structure would be sound and solid.*

Ganimed was not present for the construction of the Sarajevo Opera, and at its opening in May 1870 neither he nor Latas would be there. The pasha's life was nearing its end. He was ill in Istanbul after returning from Paris on his military mission, during which he had seen Ganimed Troyanovsky in public places – at the theater and in cafés – in Turkish garb, but the architect did not travel to Sarajevo for the opening of his first great building, curtly explaining that there was nothing familiar to him in the city anymore, and he would feel insecure among strangers.

The Sarajevo Opera opened with a performance of Mozart's Così fan tutte *by a traveling troupe from Vienna. There is little record of the production, except that it was adapted for Turkish mores so as not to incite temptation. For Sarajevo society and Bosnia as a whole, opera alone must have been quite a wonder. All three hundred forty seats, as many places as there were in the parterre, the balcony, and the royal box – the so-called Sultan's Box – were filled.*

It was the first and last opera performance in Ottoman Sarajevo. Ten years would pass before the next one. In that time, the kingdom would collapse, the Turks would prepare to withdraw from Bosnia, and Ganimed Troyanovsky's grand construction would begin to decay. The local people, mostly Muslims, who called themselves native Turks, were proud of the opera building, trusting in its grandeur and symbolism, hoping somehow that in its greatness lay a guarantee that the kingdom would not fall, but at the same time they really didn't know what that place was for and wondered whether the Swabians from Vienna would again be invited to bring those men who were as round as their sauerkraut vats and their enormously large ladies to squeak and squawk with their horns, violins, and drums after evening prayers.

Sarajevo would have to wait until May 27, 1880, for the next opera performance. The production of Johann Strauss II's Die Fledermaus *was covered in all the newspapers of the monarchy, which reported on this wondrous occurrence, "Strauss in the city of a hundred mosques." The news reached even Paris and London. New York's* Manhattan Tribune *ran a short, unsigned story – probably adapted from a larger article from the Vienna press – under the headline "Mohammed at the Opera."*

This production, it seemed, was more acclaimed in the foreign press and more important in the European perception of the Bosnian Orient than it was for the Orient itself, and it would not be going too far to say that in Sarajevo Die Fledermaus came and went in silence. The city was still under the influence of the events of summer 1878, when Baron Filipović's troops occupied Bosnia and took Sarajevo. The locals had not settled down with the new times. The Austrians were thought of as godless occupiers and interlopers, and it would be some time before Sarajevo accepted their ceremonies, manners, and operas.

Die Fledermaus was also experienced as a terrible insult because the Swabians had come to the Sarajevo Opera as if they'd built it themselves and seemed to be enjoying themselves at the Turks' expense.

Die Fledermaus had three performances, on May 27, 28, and 30, 1880. Each time the Opera was full, and the Vienna law student Vjekoslav Sunarić, a future Belgrade lawyer, was among the few locals present at the event. In his Memoirs of People and Events, there is only this regarding Die Fledermaus: "That evening was a sorry sight for the Austrian officers and their ladies, where one applauded, laughed, and danced as if at some provincial wedding. The orchestra was hopeless, the musicians fatigued from their journey, and Madam Rosie Felbingerova, in the role of Rosalinde von Eisenstein, and Master Markus Spitz von Marburg, in the role of Gabriel, sang as if they were battling terrible colds. Madam Felbingerova seemed to be sneezing in the pauses between the arias. A catastrophe, horror, and wasted evening during my brief visit to my hometown."

Only once more, just after the annexation of 1908, would the Austrian authorities try to infuse Sarajevo with the spirit of opera and thereby convey to the building Ganimed Troyanovsky's imagined intention. First, through the tour of the Milan Opera company, which would perform Verdi's Aida five times (in the second week of October 1908, just a few days after the announced annexation decree), and then, in the spring of the following year, through the attempt to form its own Sarajevo Opera Ensemble, which was supposed to hold its first performances during the 1909–10 season.

The Milan Opera tour and the formation of the ensemble are most fully explored by the Sarajevo historian Risto Besarović, to whom we owe gratitude for the extraordinary care with which he researched the topic and the collection of artifacts such as the entrance tickets to Aida, the posters, official invitations, the folding fan used by Madam Elisabeta

Marinelli, who sang the role of Aida, which she gave as a gift to an unknown woman who worked in wardrobe, and the menu for the official reception after the performance . . .

The Sarajevo Opera was founded according to the order signed by the regional governor, Anton von Winzor, before his departure from Sarajevo on February 14, 1909. Its first – and last – manager arrived soon from Zagreb, the one-time Vienna Opera baritone Emil Albori, along with three members of the voice company: the soprano Madam Nadica Štefan, and two tenors, Messrs. Dimitrij Pop Nikolić and Ferdinand Šupfa. The latter two had occasionally performed on the stages of Vienna, Pest, and Zagreb. While they were not retained long and, obviously, did not become wildly popular, the two tenors were not completely anonymous, while the name of Nadica Štefan is impossible to discover in the operatic or theater chronicles of the monarchy. No one knew who she was. She simply did not exist.

Old Sarajevo natives, however, remember the woman – there are still living witnesses to the time of Besarović's research – whom they would see with Mr. Albori walking arm in arm along the banks of Miljacka. He had just turned fifty. She was probably twenty years his junior.

At the beginning of summer, Milica Lukacz Bogdan, soprano, and Svetolik Sveta Bogdan, baritone, came to town from Belgrade. Albori had invited them and hired them for an engagement. They stayed in Sarajevo for several months, actually up until the idea of the Sarajevo Opera Ensemble collapsed. They returned to Belgrade, from which they fled to Paris at the beginning of the war and then on to the United States. There, as is known, Milica Lukacz Bogdan had a magnificent career as one of the greatest interpreters of Wagner's work outside of Germany, while Svetolik Sveta Bogdan went on to teach music at Princeton, where he wrote A Short History of Music in One Hundred Measures.

The Belgrade journalist Miroslav Radojčić, a native-born Sarajevan, met Milica Lukacz Bogdan in London in 1977. She was nearly ninety years old, "a well-preserved lady of the old order," quite eloquent, conversant on all the topics of the century that she would soon leave behind, but when Radojčić asked about her and her husband's Sarajevo episode, she said she didn't remember anything, except that it was cold and all night long the dogs barked in that city. It was so cold, she said, that they'd had to return to Belgrade at the beginning of October 1909.

"Did she ever return to Sarajevo after that?" Radojčić asked.

"No, she never did. Does Sarajevo even still exist?" the old woman asked, laughing.

Two years later, Milica Lukacz Bogdan died in Santa Monica, California. She is buried in a vault constructed of Brač marble, beside her Sveta and their only daughter, Svetlana, who died in 1941, not having reached the age of twenty.

The project of founding a Sarajevo Opera Ensemble experienced a breakdown on October 29, 1909, with the sudden death of Emil Albori, who was found dead in a hotel room. He was lying unconscious on one side of a twin bed. The other side was empty. He rented the room as a bachelor, but a pair of women's silk stockings had been found under the bed and on the nightstand a small bottle of Bulgarian rose oil. When they needed to send a telegram to Zagreb, informing someone of the sudden, tragic passing of the famous singer, no appropriate address could be found. Emil Albori no longer had any relations there. No one knew him in Vienna and Trieste either. In the end they did not send a telegram, and Emil Albori was buried in Sarajevo's Catholic cemetery in Koševo. A beautiful memorial was built using state funds, with inscribed verses by Petar Preradović, who proposed that Emil Albori loved his homeland and his Croatian kinsmen most of all.

It is unknown whether Madam Nadica Štefan attended the funeral, or whether anyone returned her silk stockings or Bulgarian rose oil, a gift from her dear Emil, who had brought it back after one of his short excursions to Vienna. Nothing more is known about Nadica Štefan. She disappears from our history the same summer morning when Emil Albori suddenly died of a burst vein in his brain, the first and last manager of the Sarajevo Opera from Habsburg times.

Ganimed Troyanovsky was invited several times to Sarajevo to see his creation but each time excused himself because of age and poor health, until he died in Paris at the beginning of the new year in 1920, leaving behind the most marvelous of all Sarajevo's buildings, which would never serve the intention for which it had been designed and constructed.

The day was still far off, light lay beyond the dark hills that surrounded the city on three sides. People had begun to leave their houses. Their faces gray and bloated, morose and distrustful, they came out onto the street, looked to see if any danger threatened or if rain might be on the way, and then set off, lighting up their first cigarette as they walked, then gasped and coughed, spitting out onto the sidewalk what had collected in their bronchial passages during the night, and slowly, without hurry, continued in the direction they had started out. They walked bent forward, looking just ahead of their feet so as not to fall into a crack in the sidewalk or an open manhole. They would cough again, stop, spit – this was the early-morning music of the city. Coughing was the bark of the people.

I approached the embankment that had once been called Obala Vojvode Stepe (the Embankment of the Warrior Stepa). I couldn't remember what it was called now. It had been tormenting me for three days. I kept forgetting to look, and I felt ashamed to ask. The former times were ugly and foreign, those were names of the enemy, the new names were the true ones, our own. It had always been this way. There were the ugly names of the past and the good names of today's warriors and heroes.

In the morning I would go to my mother's on Sepetarevac so we could see each other once more, so she could tell me stories about her childhood and youth, stories she believed I would put to use in literature, and then I'd return to the hotel parking lot for my car and set out toward Zagreb. How would I drive without having slept for nearly two nights? And how would I remember after all this that coughing was the people's bark?

I crossed the Careva Bridge, walking toward Bistrik.

The little river was dark and quiet, shallow still because there had been no heavy rains in September or October. I tried to make out its scent, but there was nothing in the air but bad, burnt heating oil and the thick damp stench that recalled the smell of the city morgue. On the other side of the bridge were the remains of a park, large rotten trees planted during Austrian times, piles of garbage, wet cardboard that perhaps a homeless person had been using for shelter.

A slight incline beside the old City Command and the Konak, not far from where Omar Pasha Latas's residence had been, beside the monastery and church of Saint Ante, and then farther on, next to the stone steps and water ravines, alleys whose asphalt had long since washed away and which I knew well from the time I used to come out for walks here with Nona. Back then I would still hear the whistle of the engine from the station at the top of Bristrik, where it set off on the narrow-gauge line for Višegrad, and Nona would always say the same thing when it sounded:

They couldn't put the opera here, for how would it have been to hear a train whistle in the middle of *Turandot*?

She would say this in a sort of victorious tone, like a great discovery as to why Sarajevo had for a hundred twenty years had a structure with Latin and Arabic letters on its front that read opera but the only real opera house, the one where people sang, was stashed in the small, boring, gray building of the National Theater founded more than a half century after Omar Pasha Latas began constructing that wonder in Bistrik. She would guide me as we looked at that unusual house, larger than all the other great, old Sarajevo houses, a building that looked like a cake from afar, especially when they opened its wide doors, wider in their time than the wooden doors of the Kingdom of Yugoslavia. When we were there making fun of the Opera, we would laugh together. Otherwise she didn't like it at all if I laughed at things she said.

In time I learned to say things that would make her laugh too. I don't know if she laughed because she really thought they were funny or just to encourage my inventive powers. But she must have known that I liked when she laughed at something I'd said about the Sarajevo Opera.

Then I began to invent things. These were my first metaphors, though I didn't know what they were called, my first hyperboles, parables, metonymies, and stories. This was how it started, in Bistrik, on sunny days in spring, summer, and fall. Mama would be at work, Nono would be engaged in something somewhere, studying a new language, reading articles on beekeeping (though he no longer had his hives), or sitting at the card table with his friends, and Nona would take me out to Bistrik, to the Opera. To make fun of it, and make things up. For her, after all that had happened in her life, it was necessary to be able to say:

They couldn't put the Opera here, for how would it have been to hear a train whistle in the middle of *Turandot*?

I know it was then that I actually began to engage in literature. My first literary work was to imagine something that would make Nona laugh while the two of us, twisting our necks, would stand in front of the Sarajevo Opera. This would make us both so hungry that on the way back we would surely have to stop by the Egipat confectioner's for a piece of cake, Nona's with white cream, mine with chocolate.

We'd stop at the Egipat every time, and then once, on a Sunday, the Egipat wasn't open, so we went to a different sweetshop. There I ate a piece of cake that forever made chocolate sickening to me. The next day I got up for school at eight. I had to memorize a poem by Dobriša Cesarić about the drops of a waterfall. The poem was short and easy, but it wouldn't stay in my head. I was sleepy and couldn't stop yawning, and when I yawned, my eyes would begin to tear up. Even with the tears in my eyes, I stubbornly repeated my mantra about the waterfall until it was at last carved into my frontal lobe. The first class was math, then again math, the third was art – the nauseating smell of the watercolors – and at four was Serbo-Croatian. One by one by last name in the roll call we recited the poem about the waterfall. I was number seventeen. With each recitation I felt the torment grow. I thought it was because of the poem. Even if I hadn't studied it, I would have remembered it from the monotonous, cyclical recitations of the class's excellent students. My head was spinning from their voices. When the turn came to Adnan Jakubović, number fifteen in the roll call, and when he tentatively started repeating the poem's words, I threw up uncontrollably.

I didn't know what was happening. I was on fire. They called Nona to come get me. They wanted to take me to the emergency room. She said it wasn't necessary. I had a temperature of forty degrees Celsius. I lay in bed, the covers wet and cold, tears streaming out my eyes. I didn't know what was wrong with me. I threw up again. Nona gave me water. I threw up the water too. Papa came with a nurse, and she gave me an injection. I lay there with a high temperature for three days, neither alive nor dead, Nona would later say, and then suddenly it all went away.

And since then, I have forever been repulsed by chocolate. Because it had been Sunday, the Egipat was closed, and we'd gone to a different sweetshop, and Nona had eaten a cake with white cream, while mine was with chocolate, and that had been that. Afterward we continued to go to Bistrik to walk along the crimson gravel in front of the Sarajevo Opera and think up ways of making fun of it and carry on serious conversations about life and death, but we never went for cakes again.

One approaches the Sarajevo Opera by the same route, narrow streets and alleys with potholed stone steps across mud and masonry boards. Back then with Nona I could get to the Opera with my eyes shut. Now I can't anymore. It's dark. My eyes no longer know the ground I'm walking on, don't feel the width of the stairs that, in the meantime, have shifted and been torn up by the spring and fall torrents. I tried hard to forget this place, to forget Sarajevo, but really I hadn't forgotten a thing. It was just that my feet no longer remembered its steps, my hands no longer knew the height of the doorknobs; the width of the tram tracks, much wider than in Zagreb, surprised me, as did the height of the tobacco stands and the depth of the holes that opened up beneath my feet. Zagreb was an alien land, shallow and light, tortured, an echoless place. Zagreb was the dust on the surface of a mirror.

I rambled on, hurling ideas into the wind to make it easier to walk up. My back was sweaty. This was the worst in Sarajevo. The town was so steep that a person would sweat and freeze at the same time, climbing up the monstrous, knotty inclines of its streets. There was only one way to avoid the sweating: by obsessively thinking about something else. I was climbing up through Bistrik again, where I had been so many times, but now I was an outsider, going to pay homage to Ganimed Troyanovsky and his dear friend and patron Omar Pasha Latas.

I was suddenly happy that something – at least for a minute – existed that was bigger than the fact that my mother was sick. For a moment I could think about it without it swallowing me, and it was almost as if I was prepared for the certainty of her death, for I was no longer me, as if this city was my friend and, when she died, it would bury her in hundreds of hearts and arrange her in as many graves, as if she would not fall upon my heart, for it was to me that she had given birth and I stood at the edge of the long, unhappy chain, the one who would close the doors forever on the empty rooms, in which light traces remained on the walls where pictures had once hung. But it was easy for me to think about all this now, jubilant as in a musical, for I was on my way up through Bistrik to the Opera.

I don't remember ever being there with my mother. I probably was. Probably at least once all four of us were there together: Nona, Nono, mother, and I. We were surely there, but I can't place it. My mother wouldn't have made fun of this structure, laughing until the tears ran down her cheeks. I don't remember her ever laughing at anything I said.

Nona had laughed until the tears ran down her cheeks – at that strange and senseless building, where operas weren't performed anymore, though it was said the hall had perfect acoustics, and at me, who knew how to dream things up that would make tears run down her cheeks. Nona would laugh so hard her heart throbbed. She grabbed her chest and shook, and it was lucky no one was close by, lucky no one was in front of the Opera when we came up, for the news that Mrs. Rejc had lost her mind would have spread all over Sarajevo.

There was no gravel on the little square in front of the Opera anymore, just packed earth atop which snow would soon fall, and perhaps not melt before the spring. The building was illuminated by some twenty floodlights so all its splendor could be seen at night. Ever since 1998, when the French government had renovated it in the name of the pacified city, the lighting design having been personally overseen and implemented by the famous Hector de Silva Jimenez, the building itself looked like an opera set. The French had remade it into a concert hall, which they gave the name Hall of Understanding and Friendship. Perhaps the bronze plaque with that name still hangs in the foyer, but the name was never used and no concerts were ever held there. At its official opening, at the end of August 1998, the violinist Gidon Kremer and the Kremerata Baltica had performed, and that had been the first and last concert held in the Sarajevo Opera. In the last fourteen years there have been several commemorative events in honor of worthy Sarajevans, deceased multiculturals, and in 2007, a three-day gathering devoted to Susan Sontag. Other than these occasions, the Opera has been empty. The French take care of conservation, protecting the metal door handles from rust, preserving the seats under white covers, covering the stage with plastic, heating the space in the winter . . . To make sure everything is cared for and kept in order there is one cleaning woman – Mrs. Fatima – and the building superintendent Ljupko Huterer, a prewar civil engineer who lived through the war as a refugee in Paris, from which he was brought back and put to work taking care of the Opera. A film about Fatima and Ljupko attracted great interest in Europe several years ago and was even screened in America. It provided a sensitive depiction of Sarajevo fifteen years after the war, viewed once and immediately forgotten. The one result of the film *Silent Opera, or The Story of Fatima and Ljupko* was that afterwards journalists and TV crews started coming, and there ended up being more work for the two of them, for every so often they needed to wipe off the door handles, open up the hall, take the plastic from the stage, and, after the journalists had gone and the cameras had been turned off, put everything back in place, and seal everything shut again.

The lights come on and soon Fatima is at work. At least this is how it's shown in the film. Ljupko arrives a little before noon, after seeing his friends on Baščaršija, drinking a cup of coffee and talking about the good old days, when people respected and valued one another, and Sarajevans would visit each other's homes for Christmas and Bajram. What were the Sarajevans doing during the other 355 days of the year when they weren't celebrating any religious holidays? According to the documentary and the stories of people, it seems that in the Sarajevo of that time every day was either Christmas or Bajram.

I made my way around the building, just as Nona and I used to, but it wasn't possible to go all the way around the Opera anymore. In back, about halfway around, a thick metal fence, rusted already, had been built.

I went back to stand in front of the Opera for a bit. I stepped backwards, checking to see how far I needed to back up before I could take in the whole building and hold it all between my two fingers when I spread out my arms, as I would do as a kid.

On the day after the attack in Sarajevo, the bodies of Prince Franz Ferdinand and Baroness Sophie were laid out on the stage of the opera house. The doors and gates had been opened wide. The day was sunny and quite beautiful, and a fresh, cool breeze came down from the mountains, as Sarajevo trembled, the windows of the Serbian shops were smashed in the marketplaces, and neighbor attacked neighbor.

Oh this self-pity!

I moved back, step by step, and came to the edge of the dirt square, but I wasn't able take in the whole Opera with my arms out. I could not hug the Opera as I had once so easily done.

The square was the same width. They hadn't made it narrower or shorter. It was strange that I couldn't take in the whole building between my hands anymore. I had brought the girl I was with here in 2000 to show her this great Sarajevo marvel, but she remained cold to it. She had seen greater marvels in her life. Afterward, disappointed, I hugged the Opera. I had not told her what I was doing or why I was spreading out my arms. We broke up soon after, upon returning to Zagreb.

A parade had first been planned for the crown prince and his wife, but the plan had suddenly been changed. In the canonical work on the assassination, *The Road to Sarajevo*, Vladimir Dedijer proposes that the absence of official funereal ceremonies was due to the chaos in the center of town, the lynchings, the destruction of Serbian shops. But anyone who comes all the way up here can imagine what the real reason was. Neither in 1914 nor today was it easy to get to the Opera: along the narrow winding side streets and alleyways the smell of urine and tubercular expulsions mixed with cabbage cooked in vegetable oil, across courtyards and kitchens, outside of the strict urban sense upon which the Habsburg monarchy insisted, with the grand, beautiful structure before one's eyes – you could see it but couldn't get to it – it was not possible to hold an honor procession for the man who had been destined to become the Austro-Hungarian sovereign but who instead became the victim of one reckless Sarajevo youth.

No approach route to the Opera had been envisioned that would accord with the grandeur and significance of the structure. Actually no approach route had been envisioned at all, and one had to make one's way along the same little back streets that had been used to travel to the old Kevrin plum grove.

Twice they made plans to create a wide road that would lead from the brewery and the monastery of Saint Ante to the Opera. The first was after the annexation in 1908, the second, during the time of the Kingdom of Yugoslavia in 1934. They came to old Mati Karivan from the city authorities with a letter and a sealed offer of purchase, for his house was located on the route. He accepted the offer and began talking with his wife about moving to Zagreb, for with the sum offered for the house in Bistrik they would be able to buy the nicest house in Tuškanac. Just as on the first occasion, political events delayed construction for a while, the first coming with the annexation crisis as the country was threatened by war, and the second arriving with the king's assassination in France, and everyone lost interest in the Bistrik road. Thanks to the painter and social activist Đoko Mazalić, by the start of the fifties the Opera had become a protected cultural monument.

Eventually, on that spectral Monday, June 29, 1914, on the morning after the assassination of Franz Ferdinand while a train was being prepared at the other end of town to take the deceased to Vienna, climbing up toward the Sarajevo Opera were only the most select members of Sarajevo's political and social life, assorted high-ranking royal and imperial officers and out-of-breath civil servants, to bow before the sovereign couple, who would have been able to see all Sarajevo with their dead eyes had they had pillows beneath their heads.

I knew that this would be one of the last times I would stand before Sarajevo's opera house. I would surely return to Sarajevo, but that visit would be still more painful than this one. Every subsequent visit to the city would be still more painful, and it was unclear whether the day would ever come when there would be no reason for me to visit Sarajevo. When that happened, I knew, I would not go anymore, nothing would draw me to my native city. I would not come to ask forgiveness of anyone.

I did not turn around again.

I would have liked to not look at the Opera for the rest of the time I was in Sarajevo. But "this white, rather ghostly structure, this spirit with a certain beauty of Paris, with which Latas fell in love during his six-month military delegation," as Ivo Andrić describes it, was visible from every point in town. "Ganimed's building long served as a reminder to Sarajevans, young and old, rich and poor, of every faith, of what they might have become but never would. It was a monument to dissatisfaction, to the misery of not living in some other place, closer to the sea or to the center of things. Looking at it evoked melancholy, the sort of soul sickness and thirst that marked the Bosnian soul. If they had understood how thoroughly their operaless Opera had saturated their lives with baseless chagrin, the Sarajevans would have set out for the building with picks and hammers to raze it to the ground. But fortunately for beauty's sake, they would never fully grasp this. Nor would they have heard it if someone had told them."

I still had at least three hours to kill. I couldn't go to my mother's before nine thirty. If she were sleeping, the woman would serve me coffee and juice, sitting me down on Nona's couch in the living room to wait for her to wake up. That would be unbearable. But by ten she should be awake. She'd be having her daily treatment then, the miraculous medicines for her illness, which would have cost fifty thousand dollars a month even if the treatment were not experimental. It was lucky, I told her, so lucky that a Sarajevo hospital had made an agreement with the German pharmaceutical company. If that hadn't been the case, she would not have had those miracle drugs.

I wouldn't go back to the hotel. I didn't know what I would have done there now, in the overheated room among the empty white walls – it seemed that in Bosnia there wasn't a law, as there was in Croatia, regarding how many pictures needed to be hung on the walls of hotel rooms. Could I write down the story that the news vendor Jahja had told me earlier about Silvije Strahimir Kranjčević? Not much time remained. No, it wouldn't be possible to write a story in three hours.

I went into the newly remodeled Vienna Café at the Hotel Europa.

Two cleaning women with heavy vacuum cleaners were collecting mud and dust from the red carpets with the routine movements of Buddhist monks. They were stroking the tubes back and forth, back and forth – it was impolite to look at them for too long – as if bringing two chubby hotel clerks to the pinnacles of pleasure.

The waiters stood morosely next to the bar. Leaning on their elbows in their starched white shirts, dazed from the previous night's drinking, they prepared themselves for another workday, their long commutes from the outskirts of town behind them. This was the way waiters in Sarajevo had looked since time immemorial. Elsewhere you would go to a café out of friendship or to spend an idle hour, but here one appeared before waiters as before the ancient ferryman who transported the dead to the other shore. And this had entered into their bearing: they looked at café patrons as if they were already a little bit dead.

I sat down at a table by the window. All four of them looked in my direction, evaluating me for several seconds. Without a word, a thick, strong man, the oldest among them, lifted his elbow from the bar and headed toward my table.

He walked for a long time, his pace slow.

Yes?

A short double espresso and a mineral water.

Short coffee with soda, he repeated, as if trying to remember.

He had recognized me and was correcting what I'd said. He thought: I was born here, in Sarajevo, but I said *kava* and *mineralna*, which wasn't right. I should have said *kafa* and *kisela*, for that was the way they talked in Mejtaš. In my home neighborhood, the waiter thought, as did others who recognized me here, they had always said *kafa* and *kisela*, and it was affected and pretentious, maybe even nationalistic, to say *kava* and *mineralna*. This was why Bosnia was now dead and broken, because people who'd been born with *kava* and *mineralna* now came here to *kafa* and *kisela*. Everyone had somewhere to go away to, thought the waiter, the Croats to Croatia, the Serbs to Serbia, and there they'd say: *kava* and *mineralna*. Only the Bosnian Muslims had nowhere to go and had to say it in the only proper way there was: *kafa* and *kisela*. The waiter thought this. Those who recognized me thought it, as did the Bosnian Muslims who had lived for twenty years in Rome, Vienna, and Berlin whom I met there and who recognized me to my horror, and all said the same: everyone had somewhere to go, the Croats to Croatia, the Serbs to Serbia, and only they, the Bosnian Muslims had nowhere to go. And these people, who even today so uncompromisingly said *kafa* and *kisela* and who around Rome, Vienna, and Berlin talked about how they had nowhere to go, failed to notice that they'd left twenty some years or more before.

I frowned and looked down, read something from my cell phone screen, took my notebook from my pack, opened it to the first page, which was dated

November 8, 2012, the day before, and at the cut-off story about Silvije Strahi-mir Kranjčević. I would never write the rest. A poet should never try to settle accounts with his hometown.

I started to read and edit what I'd written, just so I wouldn't have to look over at the bar:

He'd been sick for a long time. Ella had hoped to the very end that he would recover, but then she went to Don Serafim Urlić, the old Orthodox priest from Makarska who had been living by then for several years in Pale, near Sarajevo. There he confessed the believers and walked around Mount Romanija, certain that the mountain air would prolong his life . . .

At that point the waiter approached the table, coming up somewhat from behind me, saw me writing with a trembling hand, and placed the coffee, a glass, and a small bottle of mineral water in front of me. The demitasse was filled to the brim, though I had ordered a short espresso. This was his revenge on me for not taking up the game. My face darkened like the sky above Sarajevo, I drew myself in and tightened like the artillery ring around the city, and it didn't enter my head to debate linguistic quandaries with him or take it all as one big joke, part of the famous Bosnian sense of humor, the *kava* and the *kafa* and the *mineralna* and the *kisela*. A few months before, or a year or two, I would have been prepared to accept this joke, acceding to his arguments and doing all I could to win him over and gain his goodwill. For Sarajevo was, to use the language of waiters, my town and I was a Sarajevan wherever I might go. I'd carry my city on my back, dragging it with me wherever I turned. I was bent and hunched over from Sarajevo and its weight during all the years I had lived in Zagreb, and I was sorry not to have the strength for it. I wasn't strong and powerful like Saint Blaise, who carried Dubrovnik on his palm lightly and without exertion. If it were like this for me with Sarajevo, I thought regretfully, if I could carry it on my palm and not on my back, it would have been easier. But then something had happened, I had lost the will for these Sarajevo chats with waiters. I would not be staying in this city any longer than I had to, not a single hour more.

I had freed myself of Sarajevo the summer before last, at the end of May 2011. It was late afternoon, a storm had rolled into the city, where we'd come for the film festival. It was coming down on us as if God were emptying out the sky.

Three of us were making our way under two umbrellas across Čobanija Bridge, and just as we had turned in front of the Dva Ribara restaurant, on the Otokar Keršovani Embankment, and were heading toward Skenderija, from inside the covered courtyard of that ancient Sarajevo intellectual and artistic dive, a drunken voice pierced the air:

"Jergović, what are you doing here? Fuck your Ustaše mother in the mouth."

The young poet, a war veteran from somewhere in the interior of the country, who had moved to town after the war, repeated his choice words several times. He was obviously drunk, but the words had been composed during the long Sarajevo nights, which I had spent far from the city; they had turned into a poem-slogan, a programmatic verse for this Sarajevan Mayakovsky:

"Jergović, what are you doing here? Fuck your Ustaše mother in the mouth."

Delivered in this manner, with poetic variations, several times, in case it might provoke me into returning and coming over to him, drunk as he was.

I turned and saw that at the table with him was another local poet, whose verse I had once included in the anthology of young Bosnian lyric poetry *Conan Lives Here*. He said nothing. His face had the air of a flustered fool, and I could already hear him saying he had nothing to do with this ditty.

In fact, the next morning the story had spread around Sarajevo, eventually reaching the ears of my mother, that a certain young poet had been as drunk as the earth and had shouted in my direction:

Jergović, what are you doing here? Fuck your Chetnik mother in the mouth.

That small turning point, a caesura in a line of verse, where my mother changed from being an Ustaša to being a Chetnik, thus losing thereby a potential nationalist connotation in the utterance, reminded me just then of how happy I was that I did not live in Sarajevo and was far away from the new Sarajevo poetry.

We left town early the following morning. I dragged our red suitcase through the front hall, my backpack across my shoulders, a book bag in my hand. Loaded down like that, I barely managed to make it through the door. We trudged down the steps. My mother stayed up above, seeing us off from the entrance. I can imagine what I must have looked like in her eyes then, in the early morning light. That was the last time I saw her healthy. I didn't come back to Sarajevo for months.

I didn't fault the waiter or ask him to make me another coffee, instead of this caffeinated piddle – this was what Nona used to say when they made her weak coffee. He watched me from the bar, expecting something, at least that I might raise my eyes, but I kept my nose down and continued to revise the story that I would never complete:

Last year in May, when I was visiting Vienna for the last time and was at the hospital, I dreamed I was going back to Zagreb. Doctor Jelovšek had mentioned to me that somewhere on Pantovčak a splendid villa with an orchard was for sale for six thousand florins. It had been on the market for a long time, he said, the price was suitable, but there were no buyers. Far from Gornji Grad, far from the throng of the city, and on a hillside. If it were in the center, it would sell immediately for three times the price. And from the moment he mentioned it, from one night to the next I started thinking how nice it would be to collect the money, take out a loan, and buy that house. I'd get better immediately, it seemed to me. And the more I thought about it, the more it all seemed not so much an empty dream but something to accomplish. And the longer my sleeplessness and fantasies continued, the more attractive Zagreb became. I see now that after my death there might be debts worth more than the cost of the villa on Pantovčak. Illness is expensive – it shames a person in every manner, morally and physically.

I crossed out the last sentence and rewrote it:

Illness is expensive – it shames a person in every manner, morally and physically.

I did this out of caution so it would look like I was doing something. In some higher, metaphorical sense, my mother's illness had no meaning. Everyone has to die. But one could die in a different, easier, more humane manner. Her illness and her dying – was she dying already? – were utterly inhumane. It was as if she were somehow being punished by God, in whom she did not believe. Or as if the Stubler exile from Dubrovnik to Bosnia were part of her illness, with which our family's history in Sarajevo would come to a close. The punishment for supporting the railroad union's strike would be completed by her death. The Stublers would have left no trace behind them, no documents, buildings, or services rendered in the new history of the city.

I reached my left hand into my pocket, pulled out a fistful of coins, and from the kunas and euros picked out three and a half marks, exactly the amount of the check. I put it on the table so that it made a loud enough noise to be heard at the bar. I put on my coat and headed toward the exit.

"And the bill?" he shouted behind me.

I half-turned, without looking at him, and pointed toward the table.

Making my way out of the Vienna Café, I could hear him mumbling something behind me. The clang of the words that I no longer understood, though they were pronounced in my own language, reminded me of my childhood fantasy: that a person could consciously forget a language he knew. As a young boy I'd sit under a table where adults were talking and try not to understand them anymore, to make their words and sentences into a cascade of unconnected sounds that didn't mean anything. It seems to me in my memory that sometimes I succeeded in this: they spoke but I didn't understand. It might be nice to no longer understand the language others spoke and remain alone.

The air was heavy and fetid, stinking of a Sarajevo November morning, of coal smoke, and rot, a fog in which, like bed linen that has not been aired out for a long while, all the odors in the air have settled. The fog contained the memory of this city, all the odors of the last six hundred years. It was a memorial and grave marker of everyone who had lived here. I too was in the fog's odor, my walking to school thirty or forty years before, or being taken to the clinic on Skerlićeva Street to get vaccinated against small pox. When I was able to make out my own scent among the others, the temporal streams would separate, and I might happen to encounter on the street the self whose scent I had discerned.

When we looked into each other's eyes, the two of us would disappear. One would swallow the other, one time disappearing into the other, and the picture would multiply into infinity, like the mirrors in the big barbershop across from the Hotel Europa, in which I would examine the back of my head in the mirror, in which I could see the back of my head, until the mirrors within mirrors swallowed up everything that could be seen in them.

I tried to slow down time before heading to Sepetarevac. I was afraid of what I would see there. And of the leave taking. It was probably the last time I would see her alive.

I went to the *burek* shop at Sahat kuli.

The cramped little *buregžinica* had been there on Čurčiluk Mali for at least thirty years. Actually it had been thirty years since the first time I'd gone to Sahat kuli for *burek*. This place was by far the best for the type of *burek* known as *buredžike*. I haven't eaten these little pies, which are filled with meat and topped with cream into which white onion has been chopped, anywhere but in Sarajevo. Several years ago, when my mother was completely healthy and saying she planned to live to ninety-seven, she did a favor for one of her acquaintances, a woman from Sandžak, who had moved to Sarajevo after the war, and lived somewhere in the upper reaches of town. I don't remember what sort of favor it was, maybe she had lent her a little money, or it could have been something even less important, but this woman had wanted to pay her back. And little things that were paid back in Sarajevo usually turned into some big story or made their way into a person's destiny.

Bajram came around, and the woman took to the streets across town, from one hilltop to the next, with gifts for the season. It so happened that I'd come to Sarajevo just then, and among all these little holiday food gifts she brought around to those toward whom she felt indebted, I found some of the meat pies, mini *burek* – but they weren't actually mini *burek*. They were different, and there was something in the difference that could create in a person the sudden impression of having moved from one place to another, of having replaced one time with another.

When one reads great novels – something that happens only a few times in a life, for there are not that many great novels, and the time needed to read them does not often open up – or in the duration of some longer pieces of great music, Mahler's symphonies, the *Goldberg Variations* as performed by Glenn Gould, or in the face of the empty, frigid hall in which the paintings of Boris Bućan are displayed, a person suddenly feels that he is moving, one civilization is replacing another, a transfer to a thousand kilometers away, and he is certain at that instant that he will never again feel nostalgia for what he has left behind. The departure is easy when the Fifth Symphony thunders, for from where it is thundering everything is better and more beautiful, but it is not just that it's more beautiful. It feels more native to a person, belongs to him more, is his. And so for a short time worlds and convictions change places, a person is freed from the excesses that his homeland puts before him and what he wakes up with every morning. Filled with the music and what it contains, its history and the culture of another world, he easily becomes another. By means of the music, an entire life with a childhood included replaces his own emotions, memories, and youth, along with the mementos of his youth, without ever being lamented.

So this was what I experienced the first time I ate *mantije*. My mother said this was what they were called: *mantije* from Sandžak. She too had never heard the name or eaten that type of *burek*.

Ever since then, the woman I never met continued to repay her little debt. Whenever I was coming back to Sarajevo, my mother would call her up to make *mantije*. Before my arrival she'd bring over a big panful. I don't like meeting people. I don't like thanking them out loud for things that they've done for me. There always seems to be kernel of falsehood in such thanks. It would be nice if all the good we needed to express to others were understood and we didn't have to say anything, and it was seen and understood from the silence. Some people know how to do this: they are invisible and offer no occasions for ceremonial words to be spoken to them.

Now it had become clear: I would never meet that woman, nor would she ever bake *mantije* for me. Never again. My mother was dying.

Later she would offer money to the woman for the meat she used to make me the pies. The woman tried to refuse, insisting, but then my mother said it could be no other way, that her *mantije* meant much more to me than the flour, oil, and meat they were made from. This pleased her, perhaps filled her with pride, drawing her into a sort of mystic or metaphysical state, which certainly was not far from Mahler's Fifth Symphony or Bach's *Goldberg Variations*, and afterward she did not refuse money for her material expenditures, as if she were taking it for brushes, canvas, and paints. There was no shame when it was about art.

I sat down in Sahat kuli to eat my spinach pie. It was still early, not even eight yet, the *buredžike* would be ready around ten, said the young woman at the counter. She was uncertain about me, looked at me askance. She obviously knew me from somewhere but couldn't remember where. I didn't want to help her, instead I pushed my face into the metal plate and ate the yogurt-topped spinach pie with my fingers, knowing that if I ate it my face would be reflected in the mirror of the plate bottom.

I imagined the story of a man stopping at a burek shop early one morning before visiting his dying mother. He never ate breakfast and did not get hungry that early, feeling instead a thick morning nausea from when he'd been a smoker. But he forced himself to eat a spinach pie and, when he'd finished, was shocked to find someone else looking at him from the finely polished mirror of the metal dish. It was no longer him, a well-preserved forty-five-year-old who went to the pool and the sauna every day. What he saw was a sixty-five year old, ashen and gray in the face, who didn't even look like him.

His heart thumped, he tasted adrenaline, and his brain seemed to have leaped out of his cranium. He couldn't think of everything that would have to change in his life if he was no longer the person he'd thought but was this other one instead. So he thought about his mother, surely awake by now, waiting for him.

Actually he'd remained the same, only found himself in a different body. This had happened because he'd broken his rule and eaten breakfast. He'd eaten the spinach pie, and the spinach pie had eaten him.

There could have been some interesting parts – making his way around Sarajevo in search of someone to forge him a passport, meeting all sorts of people in a Kafkaesque atmosphere reminiscent of Paul Auster, while no one recognizes him, nor does he know anyone, but at the same time, he fears that someone might recognize the face of the man whose physiognomy he has assumed, if that man was even from there and not an alcoholic Pole, Finn, or Icelander, which was what he looked like. Then there was the mother, to whom the stranger would come and swear he was her son. There were his children and his wife, a rich Belgian he'd married many years before.

I thought of how he'd beg his mother to listen. He'd remind her of something to prove he was her son: how in 1971, in her Dubrovnik living room, Aunt Lola had taken off all her clothes in front of him, for in the book *You and Your Children*, a Vuk Karadžić edition from Belgrade, she'd read this was necessary for warding off a dangerous taboo in male children, concerning their own mothers. This he would tell his ailing mother, and she'd know it was him. And feel wretched.

I thought of how he'd beg his wife to listen. She'd try to slam the door in his face the moment he claimed to be her husband and the father of her children. Prepared for this, he'd stick his foot in the door-jamb and quickly start talking, for he wouldn't have much time since she'd be screaming about calling the police.

He'd remind her of her old Aunt Josephine, long since dead, whom they took to the seaside in 1996, just after the war in Croatia. She was eighty-five and wanted to see Dalmatia again, where she used to travel with her deceased husband Frank in the fifties and early sixties. But you don't remember your uncle Frank, he'd tell her, for he died the same winter you came into the world. This he would tell his rich Belgian wife, and she'd know it was him. And feel wretched.

That would be the end, I think, after they had agreed to separate and protect the children from the trauma – for surely *You and Your Children* has been translated into French – of learning what had happened to their father's face when he broke his own rule and ate breakfast.

Only outlines were visible in the turbid dish: the pallid, empty surface area of a face framed by hair and a beard. Without a face and invisible, as if everything that had happened over the past two days, and past ten months, would immediately be forgotten. It would be good if in the next instant, as things came to their end, I remembered nothing.

"I'd like to pay . . ." I said without looking at her.

"Three and half marks," she answered, her voice hoarse, sore.

It was nine o'clock, and though it was quite cold, people were out, bumping into one another along Vaso Miskin Street, embracing and greeting each other, religious greetings, some with irony, others out of faith and certitude. They uttered the word *Allah* in a very particular manner on this frozen morning, as if the word were a sigh and as if God were a sigh, and as if with the remembrance of God's name one might cast off some heavy burden from one's back. Some people said their *allahimanet* quite loudly, so it would be heard, and suddenly it seemed as if the entire Vaso Miskin Street was sighing. But the burden still rested on their shoulders, just as heavy as before, despite the sighs.

I rushed, squeezing through the people as if I had a clear goal and was already late – I was going to her on Sepetarevac. Only that, again, wasn't the reason for my rush: I didn't want anyone to notice or recognize me. I didn't want to hear my name called out from behind. I wanted to disappear. And for everything to materialize somewhere very far away.

I go inside. The door has been left unlocked, without fear of thieves. The hall smells of cooked cabbage.

Six steps to the room. Then right. The door is open. There she lies, groaning softly, her head on a low-pitched pillow. How are you? I ask, but the question means nothing. Shitty, she's been answering for months on the phone. Shitty, she says now. It's better when she says she's shitty than just bad. She turned seventy on May 10. Her head is clear, completely collected, circling around its own axis, just as she's been for as long as I've known her. For a long time her voice, too, remained as it had always been, that of a young person. It started to change in the last several weeks, thinning out and pulling back into her lungs. Only when she shouts, when the pain is terrible, does her voice again become young. She'd always been very musical. She could have become a singer. She'd had a clear, melodic, crisp voice, a slightly dark soprano. She used to scream hysterically when she fought with Nona, and, years later, after Nona's death, when she fought with me. This was how I'd once broken the glass in the door of the living room with my fist. You see now, I'd yelled, blood running down my arm. She wasn't impressed. She screamed. Today I have a scar in the shape of the letter *V* on my right wrist. I've had it for more than half my life. The scar reminds me of her. For a long time, years on end, I would look at it with anger and sorrow, despairing that we weren't like others: an ordinary mother and her son. Later, after my departure for Zagreb, I turned to the scar with a sort of love. When the war was still going on in Sarajevo, I would look at it wondering if she was alive or had been killed by a shell. She was alive. I felt joy in this, though more and more she was living only for herself. The heliocentric pattern of my mother: she was like a sun illuminating her own self. I am not angry when I say this. I am never angry. Perhaps I was when I was sixteen, when I still thought things could be different. They couldn't. She could have become a singer, I say. She screamed so much that the walls would come apart in the corners and the ceiling opened up to the sky. As my mother screamed our house had sky for a ceiling. And when she was in a good mood and wasn't fighting with me or Nona, she would sing as she washed the clothes in the bathtub: "U tem Somboru" and "Sejdefu majka buđaše," "Zagorje zelene," and "Tamo daleko," and oh, if the Croatian literary vermin knew that in the seventies, while she was doing the wash, my mother sang there far away, far from the sea, there is my village, there is my Serbia, they would curse my Chetnik mother at their gatherings, along with those minor Muslim poets and war veterans, but it's too late for that, as she lies on her back and will not be getting up again, and I search for some way to get her to shout, get angry, scream in her youthful singer's voice. My mother was musical, I say.

"Does anything hurt?"

"Everything!"

"It'll stop."

"No, it won't!"

"Well, it seems that way now. I've told you again and again you have to be patient. It's from the treatment."

She looked at me gratefully, and I knew she was feeling okay. When she was feeling well, she was grateful if I spelled out all her pains and torments, the skin that was turning into that of a dead person before her eyes, the bones that ached at every touch, all of it was the result of the miracle drugs. She believed me then as she never had before, living off this as if she were living off prayers asking God to have mercy on her.

"This morning, at sunrise, I was in Bistrik, in front of the Opera," I tell her, checking to see if she remembered.

"Where?" she asked, scowling.

"You know, in front of the Sarajevo Opera, in Bistrik, where I used to go with Nona."

She looked at me, not knowing what to say. What Opera? There wasn't any Sarajevo Opera! She was sad, wanted to cry, for she knew I was testing to see if she remembered, testing how present she was. She knew I was testing to see how near her death was too, which meant that I didn't believe she would survive. And that I was, according to my filial duty, merely seeing her off to the next world, just as she had seen off Nona and Nono according to hers. Lying if need be, if the state of the sick person demanded it.

She lay on her right side, closer to the wall end of the marriage bed that Nona and Nono had received as a wedding gift when they married in Doboj in 1922. Besides the bed, the room consisted of two dressers, two nightstands, and a three-piece portable mirror. The mirror in the middle had been struck by a shell fragment in the last war. It had a crack that radiated outward, as in a child's drawing of the sun. Ninety years before, in the autumn, the marriage gift had traveled in a freight car from Zagreb. At first the furniture had been placed in the bedroom of an apartment set aside for the train dispatcher. Nono would be promoted to become the station chief. The room would travel across Bosnia, accompanying him in his transfers. But as a railway official, he had the right to a gratis ticket, and could use a whole freight car for free. While it might not seem so, one could place an entire family history in a single freight car, together with its furniture and books. Nona's and Nono's bedroom set withstood five moves before they arrived in Sarajevo, where Nono landed in the highest position of the railroad hierarchy: he became a chief railway inspector. The room would move once more: when in 1969, from the building of Madam Emilija Heim, on Yugoslav National Army Street, just beside the theater, we moved to Sepetarevac Street. This was when my mother decided to rid herself of the whole lot. Old fashioned and out of date, it was unworthy of modern life. But she had already taken out two loans and didn't have the money for a new bedroom set. She didn't like that marital bed, for it reminded her of the distraught marriage of her parents and of their two instances of marital guilt. And perhaps it also reminded her of the fact that she had two broken marriages behind her by then, though she'd only just turned twenty-seven. The bedroom set was arranged in the northern room, in which she would sleep for the first several years. It was in the southern room, with the new socialist furniture, which has long since disappeared – chopped up, burned as kindling, recycled – that Nono lingered and died in the fall of 1972. Thirty-eight years later, in summer 2010, when she was renovating the apartment, she moved her parents' bedroom set from the northern to the southern room. She even called upon a furniture restorer – as carpenters were called in those days – to examine the bed and dressers, protect them against wormholes, and refinish them. The restorer told her the furniture had been made from high-quality ash. She felt proud and refused to remember that she had for forty years wanted to jettison the bed and dressers from the house.

Now she was ailing in the room in which her father had died, on his side of the marriage bed.

"I didn't sleep all night!" I was trying to distract her.

"Why not?" she asked and I felt she wasn't interested.

"The room was hot."

"You needed to open the window."

"It wouldn't open," I said, lying.

"What sort of a window can't be opened?" she said.

Her left leg, the one in which the sickness had begun, was enormous, distended. Lesions had started opening up on it over the last couple of days. There was some plastered-on gauze on the lower part. A little below her knee, on her pajamas, spots of bright blood had appeared, growing as we spoke.

She could not move her left arm. This had been the case since she got sick. When I touched it, she would cry out:

"Ay, ay, ay . . ."

Even when I touched her other arm, as if by some newly established habit, she would cry out, "Ay, ay, ay," somewhat more quietly.

It was as if there weren't a single part of her body that did not hurt. There was one fortunate thing about this. She had always been sensitive to pain, though she claimed the opposite, speaking of her superhuman birth pangs or migraines when her eyes were popping out of her skull as if she were someone condemned to the electric chair. But even when there wasn't anything that hurt, she would find a reason to complain. And so I consoled myself, convincing myself that it didn't hurt now and my mother was only pretending. I don't know how I would have endured it otherwise. For at least a half hour at a time, every day, in the morning or the afternoon, I heard how it hurt. The pain was quite authentic, and I grew accustomed to it. It fell next to me, crashing down like books during an earthquake, and somehow became my fault. This was how I felt my mother's pain. The moment I believed she was just pretending, I would no longer be to blame.

"Are you going to Zagreb today?" she asked, though she knew.

"Yes, I have to go to work. It's piled up."

She didn't ask me what had piled up. She probably knew I was lying, just as I knew she was. This was how our two modes of selfishness were supported. When she'd been asked several weeks before, compassionately, in the Sarajevo manner, why her Miljenko was not there, why he hadn't come from Zagreb, she had answered quite calmly: "He has to make some money – this illness is expensive!"

I don't know whether she was defending me or defending her own illusion that she had a son, something to hold onto while in this pitiful life's finale, with the smell of cooked cabbage and the metal taste of drugs. Whichever it was, she had known how to defend herself. And she still did, even transformed as she was into pain and patience, for everything she was able to defend herself against verbally was bigger and more important than what she needed in order to accomplish something. This was how it had always been. Although she had only written one poem in her life, my mother had always grasped onto words more than reality and actual life. She had been able to let all of it wash away: her family heirlooms, failed loves, money and the means of acquiring it, and friendships too, but words she could never allow to be unspoken or silenced. If someone said something ugly to her, insulted her, he would not have to wait long before it cost him dearly. Nothing was too dear if it was about words. If it was about words it was worth it to spoil one's nerves and health, for everything that was important in her life would come down to two or three words anyway. To having told somebody off, preserving herself and her reputation. What was my mother's reputation made of? Only words, what could be spoken. Other things were not important. Not money, or apartments, or cars, or any sort of material security; nothing was as important as words. And nothing in her life had offended her as what had been said to her.

When she talked she didn't think of her illness. Or rather: when she talked she wasn't sick at all. If she could have just talked, if I were there, or if we could speak on the phone twenty-four hours a day, my mother would be outside her illness twenty-four hours a day. She'd be healthy. She'd defeat her disease by telling stories, or leave her body behind, something she wouldn't have any need for anymore anyway, as she would have turned completely into story.

I know she's sorry I'm leaving. I think she knows she won't see me again. But that isn't what's hard for her, it's that she won't be talking to me. Even this morning she has things to say. She tells me this and I say again, as if I haven't heard her – I have to go to Zagreb, to work, it's piled up on me! Every instant I'm aware that I won't see her again – the next time I come she'll be lying dead in the city mortuary – and she won't ever tell me what she has to say this morning.

"Will you give me a kiss?" she asks.

And I kiss her on that remote right cheek.

There's no pathos or sentimentality in this. She has always insisted I give her a kiss as I go away. Sometimes I avoid it. This is her attempt, even if only in that brief ritual, to transform our relationship into a normal relationship of a mother and son. That kiss isn't for us but for some hidden camera that would record and preserve everything.

Once more, with a glance from the door to the room, I wave to her. An automatic gesture. Her face remains expressionless. My face too seems to remain blank. As her caretakers escort me out, I again excuse myself, saying that I'm pressed for time, that I have a lot of work to do. I have to fill up all those empty newsprint pages. It's a large, important job. One day, when completely empty newspapers, bound-up white pages, arrive at the news kiosks, it will be clear the world is dead and no one is left on earth.

I went into the hotel. When she saw me, the young woman behind the counter closed her book. Instead of a bookmark, a yellow pencil marked the spot where she had reached. I said I was leaving, paid the bill, packed my things. At the top of my bag was the fat book by Péter Nádas, *Parallel Stories*.

Making my way toward the parking area, I wondered whether someone might have again broken my window and stolen something from inside. I passed the taxi stand and overheard the unhappy conversation of two cabbies:

"They slit his throat for the Rolex!" said the older of the two. "Fuck God and this fucking life!"

On the ledge of a closed-up news kiosk there was a black-and-white photo with someone in mourning crape. Beside it stood a vase with some wilted funeral flowers. A green obituary notice was Scotch-taped above the little window through which the tobacconist had once looked out. The person's face looked familiar.

As I got into my car, I heard someone call my name. I sat down, turned the key, shifted into gear. The car moved along the uneven, unpaved driveway. The gravel grinding beneath the tires. A soothing sound. I could listen to it for a long time.

History, Photographs

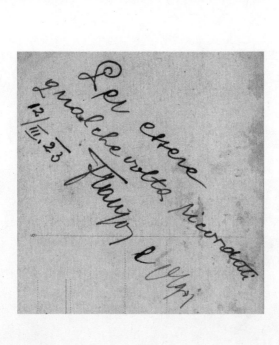

Their first picture together, taken in a studio on the day of their marriage. Franjo in a dark suit, a kerchief in his jacket lapel, and a bow tie. Her blouse has short sleeves and an open neck, although it is still winter. The picture was produced by a local photographer who, contrary to custom, did not sign his work or put a company stamp on it, and one would have to do some research to discover the name of the photographer working in Doboj at the time. Or, as it often happened in Bosnian backwater towns, the two studios had two master photographers who could not stand one another. This photograph was a gift to Olga's parents. They both signed it, but the message was composed by Franjo. Why did he write it in Italian rather than German? Perhaps he wanted to address them in the language of the sea? A little earlier, Franjo had returned to Bosnia after his imprisonment in an Italian war camp.

It is the summer of 1929, and Olga is twenty-four years old.

Olga, Franjo, Dragan, Mladen. This picture was taken in 1933, the last summer before the move to Sarajevo, in a meadow near Kakanj. "Photo: Kohn, Zenica" is stamped on the back.

Sarajevo, 1938. At the time it was unusual to have the parents in the middle with the sons on the edges. The father and mother appear not to notice them. Olga is wearing an expensive blue lace blouse, purchased in Vienna in a French boutique owned by a Russian émigré designer who was famous for having dressed the Romanov princesses. The designer barely spoke German, but his Italian was impeccable. She said that he spoke to her as if she were a dying child, which was why she was swayed to buy the blouse, the most expensive piece of clothing she ever purchased. Fifty years later, in the summer of 1986, the lace blouse was among the things that were carted off to the Red Cross, after they died.

The picture was taken by Ivica Lisac, the famous Sarajevo photographer and Franjo's friend. His stamp is imprinted on the back.

This is the only photo of Karlo Stubler without his beard. The year is 1938 or 1939. The photo is for an official document, perhaps for the purpose of travel. He was planning at least one more trip to Bosowicz, but the war broke out soon after. After 1945 he did not talk anymore about his birthplace or about his brother, sister, and relatives. Nor did he make any inquiries about them. He got some sort of serious infection on his facial skin, which required that every morning he pull each individual hair from his beard with a pair of tweezers. As soon as he woke up, while everyone else was asleep, Opapa would sit on the veranda. He'd pluck his beard in front of a little mirror on a stand, and tears would run down his cheeks. Around the mirror were pots with cactuses of various sizes. He had started breeding them after settling in Bosnia. Twenty years after his death there were still cactuses on the veranda table. At five years old, it seemed to me that my great-grandfather's ghost lived among those cactuses. I was afraid of ghosts so I never went out onto the veranda.

This picture was taken in Timişoara or Budapest. It was sent as a gift to Karlo Stubler in Bosnia. In those days, photographs were given as intimate heirlooms. We saw each other rarely, so stills served as memorabilia. Regina was a doctor, married to a Bulgarian, and until the war Karlo's children corresponded with her. She disappeared. No one knew what became of her after the liberation. Rudi made inquiries, wrote to Sofia, searched for her with the help of the Red Cross. Her name was spoken over the radio in various languages, Bulgarian, Serbo-Croatian, German, Romanian. Have you seen Regina Dragnev? They had not. The snapshot remained, and along with it a certain awe for the art of photography that had already reached an age where a face could exist without a single living eye ever seeing it.

Johanna Stubler did not like having her picture taken. The heart defect that the doctors discovered after the birth of her fourth child made her always anticipate death. Every spring was the last for Omama, and then every summer and every fall. Ultimately she outlived her husband and lived to a ripe old age. She never liked having her picture taken because she dreaded the idea that it would be used in her obituary. She avoided every family photo, ducking out quietly at the last moment, only to reappear after the photographer had left. Perhaps this is what extended her life. Death regularly leafed through the family albums and couldn't find her photo anywhere. Johanna's daughter Olga insisted: "When I die, please do not put my picture in the obituary." A wish she had inherited from her mother.

Johanna and Karlo's children: Olga, Regina (Rika), Karla (Lola), Rudolf (Nano).
The photo was probably taken in Dubrovnik, a little before Karlo's exile. The
sisters had not yet reached maidenhood or started going to the hair salon, and
the time of crazy extravagant hairdos had been ended by the Great War and the
Spanish flu that had ravaged Europe. A new era had begun. The Stubler sisters
were the children of art deco. Their youth would not last long. Rudi began to go
bald at the age of twenty-one, but instead of letting a little coronet form around
his pate, he shaved his head until the end of his life. He covered it with a hat: gray
in winter, rabbit hair, white in summer, Panama.

Marijaa Brana and Vasilj Nikolaevich in their Sarajevo home. The wall coverings or "wallrugs" they brought with them from Russia are visible behind them. Vasilj Nikolaevich was a high-ranking imperial officer. Karlo Stubler got along well with Vasilj Nikolaevich. Mostly they sat together without speaking. For years after Karlo's death, Vasilj Nikolaevich would visit them on Kasindol Street and sit without saying a word.

Ovako smo izgledali prvi dan rata, tako da je i fotograf našao za vrijedno da nas snimi

Photographers used to circulate around Dubrovnik's fish market, harbor, and beach at Porporela until the early eighties. They would photograph people as they walked by, fathers with children, foreigners and tourists. They would then approach the prospective customer, offering to develop it for a very attractive price. Were there people who refused to see what had been captured in the dark ventricles of the photographic chamber? Sunday, April 6, 1941, was a rainy day in Dubrovnik. The southerly was turning into a northerly. Lola was heading toward the fish market with Mina Jelavić. At that moment Mina became aware of Mr. Luja Berner and his camera. He took the shot. Croatian state radio had just announced that Belgrade had been bombed.

The wartime devastation is visible on the face of Home Army First Lieutenant Rudolf Stubler. Polytechnics student in Graz and Vienna, gifted violinist, lover of music, poetry, and mathematics, skilled beekeeper. Women loved him. A delicate soul, sweet and smart, when this picture was taken at the Winterfield Photography Studio, he was twenty-four years old and had not worked a day in his life. He sent the photo to his family in Kasindol. He had grown thin from fear, as he lay down every evening with Taps, turning his back to the sleeping Home Guardsmen.

The faces of those who would later come to grief in the war are smiling, cheerful, filled with optimism. Proud sons wearing wartime uniforms at a time when it was not known which would be the uniform of the liberators. The horrors of Europe's war can be seen on his face. He is not smiling or looking toward victory.

Brauwer
Zagreb 925

Svojoj baki i djedu prilikom prvog rodjendana
poklanja
Željko

Aunt Lola met Uncle Andrija after she had definitively refused to accompany her family in her father's exile. She remained alone in Dubrovnik, a twenty-year-old girl with a trade school education. He was twenty years older, a well-situated bachelor, a secretary in the trade office. Uncle Andrija loved Lola, but she married him from pure necessity. The moment he met her, he knew why he had waited so many years. And he understood his love would consist of humiliation, patience, and submission, and that, for the most part, it would not be returned. Željko was born in 1924; Branka six years later. Željko is the pilot in the novel *Gloria in excelsis*. In reality, as a heroic pilot of the Royal Air Force loaned out to the Partisans and then returned to Yugoslavia's wartime aviation enterprise, Željko wanted to study medicine. They would not let him. He was worth more to the homeland as a pilot than as a doctor. He could not get over this. He got drunk and took off from the Borongaj airfield, then plunged his plane into the ground. Branka studied medicine in Zagreb. She moved to Germany, where she worked as an anesthesiologist. She died from an aneurysm in her sleep in the fall of 1979. She was not yet fifty.

Uncle Andrija outlived his son by four years. He died in late summer 1955. Željko had perished in September 1951. Karlo Stubler died in April. Johanna ten years later. And Lola died in her sleep in the summer of 1974.

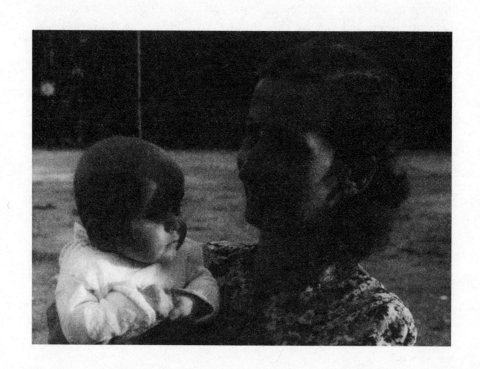

The birth went easily. The little girl lit into the world, in her mother's words, like a cork from a champagne bottle. At first she did not cry, and they thought she might be dead. The fat midwife picked her up and animated her with several expert movements. As if she were dancing, directing marionettes in a puppeteer's performance, kneading dough for a pie. They forgot the name of the midwife. They only knew she was a Serb. Once she got home from the night shift, she found her house empty. The Ustaše had taken away her husband and three sons. She hanged herself from an attic beam before the Ustaše let the four of them go, for someone had intervened. Were they really going to slaughter the husband and children of the best midwife in the hospital? They discovered her hanging there, a half meter above the Independent State of Croatia. The midwife who brought my mother into the world. Per custom, the photographer was waiting in ambush at the entrance to the maternity ward. When the mother left with her child, it was offered as an immortalized scene. Olga did not stay long in the hospital. She only spent the night. It was May 12, 1942. The photographer's imprint says "Šeher, Sarajevo."

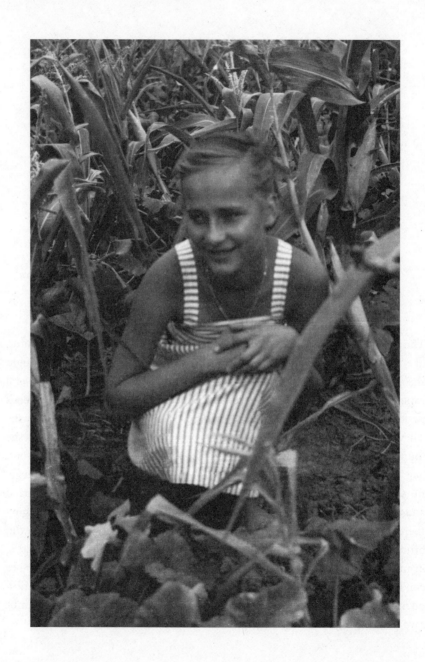

It is her twelfth year, at Ilidža, in the Stublers' model garden. It is August 1954 and Opapa has been dead for three years, but according to his plan, corn has been planted in one part of the garden. After ten harvests, when the earth is worn out, the corn will be given over to something else. Opapa read about this in some East German magazine devoted to advanced agriculture. Although he was near the end, he talked enthusiastically about what he was going to plant after the corn's decade had ended. Javorka is hiding amid the weedy stubble. The unknown photographer told her to hide so he could take her picture. She has the face of a grown woman already, a smile that would survive until her late forties but grow cruel with her life's experiences, her scattered marriages, anxiety, and dissatisfaction.

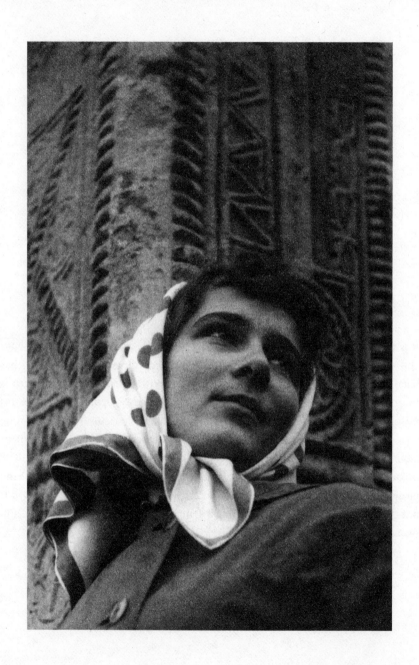

Javorka's final year of gymnasium. The house is filled with suffering and muffled fury. Olga and Franjo do not cease to blame each other for Mladen's death. Javorka has come into her own as a woman, which infuriates her mother. She is also infuriated by the girl's ambitions: she goes away to workers' actions, is a member of the Yugoslav Communist League, the municipal youth committee. She wants to study medicine . . . Olga likes none of this. She would prefer her daughter sit in the corner and be quiet. Her ambitious dreams remind her of Mladen, and the girl is not worthy of him. She was seventeen when Olga first called her a whore. Did that happen before or after this picture? It's impossible to know. It was taken during the months when Javorka posed for an art photographer in front of the stone engravings at the Natural History Museum.

The first car the Stublers owned was a secondhand 1953 Opel Olympia that Dragan drove back from a business trip he'd taken to Germany. A young metallurgical engineer, he was married and had two children by the time he bought the car in 1959. He used it for a short time, two Bosnian winters, and in 1960 they took it to travel to Serbia to visit Javorka, who was at a youth action for the construction of the Brotherhood and Unity Highway. Dragan took the picture, with Olga, Javorka, and Viola. Olga is holding a cigarette in her right hand. The Olympia's license plate has the letters *BH* in Cyrillic and the numbers 10640. They were still putting the republic initials on them then. Families used to take pictures of themselves around their cars. Pleated skirts were in fashion. These were important details in the family journey to the village of Džep in southern Serbia to visit the female team leader. One must imagine what she might be holding in the packet and reconstruct the most likely route they took. As an accompaniment to the story there should be a map with a meandering line in red pencil that crosses the Drina River at the town of Foča.

My father has my head and face, my expression, my way of thinking, and my slightly awkward smile. Her hand is on his knee. I look at this picture, which was taken by a passerby – Dobro gave him the camera and showed him how to shoot – and I feel her hand on the inside of my own right knee. The hand of my dead mother, young and pretty, on the knee of my dead father. And from the beach, someone else's eyes look at them.

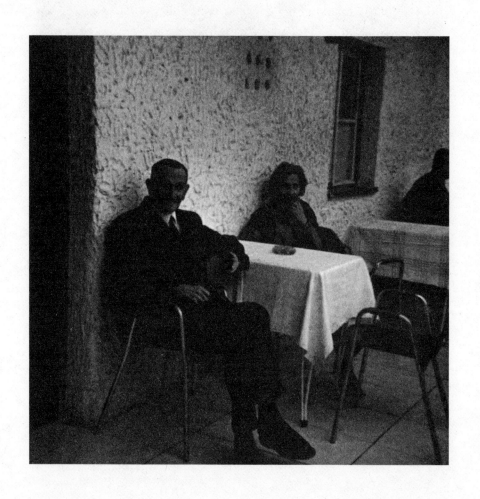

At the end of summer Olga would go away to Drvenik with her grandson, while Franjo stayed in the hospital. The boy was starting first grade – in the middle of June his grandma and grandpa had taken him for tests, without his parents' knowledge – and Nona needed to be there with him. They thought he was gifted and sent him to school a year early. Two weeks later, around the twentieth of September, Nona went back to Sarajevo. Nono was in the hospital, but they let him go home, and then he went back to the hospital. The lifeline on the EKG was almost inverted, dropping so low that every beat of his heart seemed the last. He was fine otherwise, clearheaded and calm. He just breathed with a bit of difficulty. No one wanted to acknowledge it, neither the doctors nor Dobro, but his dying had been underway for some time already. The muscle of his heart had been weakening for years. For the last twenty it had not been strong enough to push the blood into his lungs, though as late as the previous spring it had been good enough to let him walk the several kilometers from Drvenik to Donja vala or Zaostrog. In June he had taken the boy for tests before the start of school. And afterward he had ordered a rakija at a seafront bar to celebrate the boy's mind. He was proud like a man who still had big plans in life. The child would start school, the world would be dazzled by his gift, and then he would enter high school and college and become an architect. The boy spent days on end on the balcony or, when it rained, in the room that opened onto the balcony, making houses out of Lego blocks. Very imaginative, colorful houses with lots of windows. Or without a single window. He would build a whole city there on the balcony, as long as he had enough blocks. What else could he be but an architect? The grandfather could not know about the boy's sloppiness and lack of talent for drawing, and his stupidity – bordering on a mental defect – when it came to even the simplest mathematical operation. This would become clear only after the first months of school, but by then the grandfather was no more. Franjo Rejc would spend eternity in the belief that his grandson became a famous architect.

What happened after the shot of rakija with which he toasted his grandson's success?

Dobro sent Franjo to the home for the disabled in Trebević in September. It was one of those socialist healthcare hotels one could go to for a summertime tourist stay, but mostly people went there on a doctor's referral. The airy bathhouse above Sarajevo, where the air was sharp as a razor with the scent of pine sap, like verdant grass, and the sky was close, must have helped to enrich his blood with hemoglobin. It was easier for his heart to drive the rich, healthy blood, blood as thin as hospital soup. This was the doctor's gentle way of revealing the truth to his patient. At the end, when there was no other help, doctors often prescribed eccentric remedies. They didn't believe in miracles but rather were humoring the families of their patients who only believed in miracles. In this case Dobro was both doctor and family. He sent Franjo to the home for the disabled as a last resort.

He was placed in a single room with a wooden-frame bed – most of the beds were metal – and a thin mattress. The room had a sink with a mirror above it. It also had a night tray for the spittle for when he coughed at night. Nono took three books with him to the home: *A Dictionary and Grammar of English*; the *Schedule of Trains for the Yugoslav Railway* for 1972; and a novel by Dmitry Merezhkovsky entitled *Antichrist*, which was based on a biography of Peter the Great. He dragged around that book with him for a long time but never read it to the end. He had his brown suit, several white shirts, and two ties. As well as sweats, pajamas, and slippers. His pocket watch, a Pelikan fountain pen, a planner in which he noted down phone calls and when he received letters, New Year's congratulations, and postcards. He wrote down the names of the medicines he was talking, noted the visits of tourists to the view site near the home, the changes of seasons, the morning temperature . . . What use were all these notes to him? Was he delaying death by trying to remember every waking instant of the previous day?

Olga and Dragan came to visit him on the eighth day of his stay at Trebević. It was a Saturday. Dragan had come from Moscow to see him. He said he had some business in Zenica: a special order for a large quantity of steel for Siberia. There must be a notebook for recording all the lies told to sick people. In Nono's case the lies were not for his sake but for those who lied to him. He was happy to see Dragan but did not believe a word of what he said.

Dragan had brought a new camera with him, a Yashica that he had purchased for a lot of money in Germany. He used it for the first time at Trebević. He didn't know how to control the aperture, so the pictures came out dark. It was cold, as it often was in early fall in the mountains around Sarajevo. Olga covered her face with the shawl she had bought two years before in Russia, where she'd gone to visit her son and daughter-in-law. He waited for his wife and son in his suit, with a white shirt and tie. He would live for three weeks more. He smiles at the lens and at Dragan who is making a mistake with the aperture setting. Although the shot is dark, the colors are unusually natural. As if it had been taken at sunset. It is their last photograph.

Their visit did not last more than two hours before he went back to Sarajevo. On Tuesday Dobro came, listened to his heart, and looked at the latest EKG results. His blood might have been filled with hemoglobin, but that was not important anymore. The hospital van took them down to Sarajevo. He did not take Franjo home. He had Franjo admitted to his ward without any hope of making him better.

Five days before Franjo's death Dobro asked to have him taken home. Franjo lay opposite the window through which, from his pillow, he could see Trebević, the hamlets at the base of the mountain, and parts of the old town, when the light fell at the end of the day. He listened to the puffing of the steam engines when a train would come around heading for Višegrad. He was clearheaded until the very end. On the last night, Olga was overcome by fatigue and had to sleep. Javorka was watching over him. He said to her: It's just the two of us here. The rest are thieves. He died before first light. When Olga went into the room from which he had been removed, she felt as if there was someone there. This was what she said, but I never believed her. These were old wives' tales and superstitions. She opened the window and heard the flutter of pigeon wings but did not see any birds anywhere. There was no one.

There was one other episode so improbable that it was recalled reluctantly even when superstitious people were talking. Nor have I ever made use of it, for it seemed to me literarily implausible. Almost everything fantastical in reality is implausible in literature. The plausible are merely the normal things. Everyday minutiae turn into miracles. But let us tell it here, to accompany this photo. As Franjo was leaving us, Dragan was on a business trip to Leningrad. When he learned that his father had died, he changed his ticket and instead of flying to Moscow took off for Belgrade. The Tupolev jet flying from Leningrad to Moscow crashed after takeoff, and all the passengers and crew members were killed. If Franjo had lived another twenty-four hours, his son would have been on that flight.

The façade of the building that once belonged to Madam Emilija Heim taken on November 2, 2012. Several hours later would be the last time I saw my mother. I captured the building in passing, the picture serving as a memento for what I was feeling at the moment. After taking the picture, I went into the store and bought some Plavi Radion detergent because it was the only thing in the store that looked like it was from when we lived there. Then I walked around inside the aisles a little, trying to imagine where the apartment had been, the living room, the anteroom, our neighbors, the abandoned old Jewish woman, whose cries and prayers echoed in the stairwell when they took her away in 1941. Making my way around the store, I would have run into her several times, for somewhere here had been her anteroom, where she had once opened the door for the last time. So as not to seem suspicious to the cashier, I bought the Plavi Radion. I took it to Sepetarevac and left it quietly in the bathroom. Preoccupied with dying, she never noticed it.

Translator's note

The image of the translator sitting with a dictionary in a room by himself is perhaps nowhere more inaccurate than in translating a long, complex work like this one. It is a collective effort in many ways, and I could not have accomplished it without the help and support of many individuals and institutions. The process begins and ends with a publisher, and from the moment Jill Schoolman asked if I might be interested in translating this big book, she and her team at Archipelago Books have been supportive, generous, and professional.

I benefited greatly from the financial and professional encouragement provided by a PEN/Heim Translation grant and a National Endowment for the Arts Literature Fellowship, both in 2016. My thanks go out to the readers, staff, and selection committees. Also helpful were my colleagues in the Translation Seminar at Indiana University, where I discussed aspects of the translation and received helpful comments and suggestions in early 2018. The excerpt "Kakania" appeared in the summer 2020 issue of *The Massachusetts Review*, along with a short Q&A (https://www.massreview.org/node/9103). Readers will note that the excerpt announces that it was translated "from the Bosnian," while the book *Kin* claims to be translated "from the Croatian." Both are correct. Readers of the book will understand why.

Realizing early that I might easily forget some of the choices I had made in the first pages when I got to later ones, I kept a blog dedicated to "Reflections on Kin" at russellv.com, and the many comments and suggestions I received helped keep me consistent and critical vis-à-vis the strategies and principles I employed. Somewhere around page 100, an email arrived from an unfamiliar address. Its sender had been reading about my travails and graciously offered to help "should the author's services ever be needed." Miljenko Jergović's services were thenceforth prompt and forthcoming, and I thank him sincerely. Given that I address many of the technical and strategic issues that might normally be discussed in a translator's note there, readers should feel free to delve into those entries and send questions via the blog portal should they be interested in knowing more.

Several Indiana University colleagues provided help at crucial stages of my work. Larry Singell, Executive Dean of the College of Arts and Sciences at Indiana University, allowed me to take a much needed semester of administrative leave to finish draft number one in fall 2017. My colleagues Carolyn Lantz, Katie Kammer, and Jez McMillen helped to fill in the gap of my absence all while expressing enthusiasm and support for the book that would eventually result.

I also wish to express special thanks to my friend, colleague, and fellow translator Tomislav Kuzmanović, of the University of Zadar, for responding with patience and good humor to the many, sometimes arcane questions that arose during my several years of trying to find the right English words. In a number of cases those words were suggested by him.

Finally, translators often say that context is everything. This is true not only for translating. My family knows this well, and it is to Yasuko, Peter, and Dante that I owe the greatest thanks – for the rich and enduring context of our lives together.

archipelago books
is a not-for-profit literary press devoted to
promoting cross-cultural exchange through innovative
classic and contemporary international literature
www.archipelagobooks.org